the
assassin's
destiny

PRISON FOR SUPERNATURAL OFFENDERS BOOK FOUR

MEGAN LINSKI & ALICIA RADES

We the authors acknowledge that the United States of America is a country formed on stolen land. We respect and honor the indigenous peoples who have lived here for centuries, and we recognize there is still much work to do to make reparations and heal the damage caused to the many indigenous nations who were first here, both in the past and today.

May we remember the atrocities once committed, create a better world in the present, and look forward together for our future.

This book features characters with the following medical conditions. The information included is meant to educate readers on disabilities featured within the *Prison for Supernatural Offenders* series.

PARAPLEGIA

Paraplegia is a pattern of paralysis that affects the functioning of an individual's legs or lower extremities. Common markers include loss of sensation, loss of certain motor functions, and loss of sensory skills. Paraplegia usually affects individuals with nervous system injuries and conditions, including those with spinal injuries or neurological conditions. Over five million people in the United States live with paralysis each year.

In memory of James, the blind gay dwarf who inspired Alistair, loved Eddie, and brought a light to the Hidden Legends fandom. We hope you're laughing at us from the spiritual plane.

charlie
ONE

If all the beauty in the world could be condensed into a single fragment of time, I experienced its entirety the moment my wife woke from her coma. Every laugh, every smile, every caress of a loved one's skin seemed to burst through and slam into my chest. I became so overwhelmed that I turned to a statue. I couldn't think, couldn't *breathe* as I took in the miraculous moment.

A week ago, Ava-Marie had died. The compound beneath the Institute's graveyard— where the Warden had been running his sick experiments on inmates— had come crashing down on her. She'd created an explosion to save us all and stop the Infernal Underground. But through her phoenix form, Oberi had brought Ava back to life, though it'd been Ava's choice for her soul to return or not.

My friends and I had come to the hospital to say our final goodbyes, but we didn't have to say goodbye after all. Ava-Marie was *awake*. She'd returned from the Ancestral Lands. I'd thought for certain she'd chosen to stay in the afterlife... but she'd come back to me.

"Gods, Ava! You're back," Kallie cried out before I had a chance to say anything.

The hospital room erupted into a chorus of thrilled voices, our friends' glee overlapping one another.

"Welcome back to the land of the living," Marcus said cheerfully, though his voice cracked with emotion.

"By Atlantis, it's a miracle!" Ivy cried. He shoved me aside and threw himself past me. I couldn't see what was happening, but I assumed he was hugging Ava. I stumbled to the side a step, though I didn't let go of her hand.

"We're so glad you're awake." Opal sobbed.

Ezekiel spoke quickly through tears. "Sis, I'm *so* sorry about what I said to you. I never should've treated you that way."

Chancey and Alistair spoke over one another. I couldn't process what anyone else said. The sounds were overwhelming, swelling over me like white noise. All I could do was stand there in shock. I didn't know what to say. A moment ago, I'd made the decision to take my wife off life support. The doctors were certain she wouldn't make it. Now, her soft voice and lively energy filled the room.

Thank the ancestors, she's here! Oberi's relieved tone cut through my mind. He sounded so happy.

"Guys," Ava pleaded in a hoarse but confident tone. She must've pushed at Ivy, because he finally peeled himself off of her and stepped back. "I'm awake. It's not that big of a deal."

The room went dead silent as we all took in her words. Ava had *no* idea what a miracle this was.

Ava struggled to speak. "Can I have a moment with Charlie?"

No one moved for a beat, until Kallie answered. "Yes. Of course."

Everyone shuffled out of the room, until Ava and I were alone with Oberi. I squeezed her hand tightly, and tears of relief sprang from my eyes.

"Pidge," I said breathlessly. I couldn't express myself in words. All I could do was lean down and squeeze her into a gentle hug.

Ava stilled in my arms. "Charlie, what's going on? You're acting like we haven't spoken in forever."

I choked back a sob as I drew away. Ava may be awake, but she wasn't fully healed yet. I had to be extra careful with her. She was so fragile.

"We... haven't," I spoke in a broken voice.

The weight of the situation must've hit Ava. Her fingers brushed the sheets. "Charlie, lay next to me."

Immediate hesitation overwhelmed me. I was terribly concerned I'd do something to set her back... make her fall into that coma again. "I can't. You're still hooked up to the machines, and I could hurt you, and—"

"You'll be careful. I need to feel you next to me. Please."

She tugged lightly on my arm. I pulled the covers back so I could crawl into the bed beside her. I made sure to feel where the medical tubes were so I didn't tear them out as I carefully maneuvered into the bed.

I was extremely careful with her as I looped my arm around her shoulders. She hadn't left this bed in over a week, and she'd just undergone serious surgery. I needed to be gentle. Ava rested her head on my chest, and when she did that, I felt the weight of the world lift from my shoulders.

I heard Oberi's nails click as he padded to the other side of the bed. I felt his fur as he laid his head next to Ava's hand. *Ava. I missed you, my dear love.*

Ava gave a tired sigh. "You're all acting like I've been out of it for an eternity."

Sure felt like it. Oberi jumped onto the end of the bed and lay over our feet. I tried not to tremble, but I failed.

My wife was okay. This wasn't an illusion or a dream. The weight of her body in my arms was more real than anything I'd ever experienced.

Ancestors, it was exactly what I'd been praying to have for days. I thought I'd never get to experience a moment like this ever again. The gods had delivered just what I'd asked for.

I pressed my nose into her hair and inhaled her raspberry scent. I never wanted to let this woman go. She was *alive.* I thought I'd had bad luck my whole life from all the shit I'd been through, but I realized that I'd been saving all my lucky moments for her, so we could pull through this.

Ava sucked a breath, and I stilled. "Did I hurt you?" I asked.

"No," she assured me. "But I'm sore everywhere."

"I'm so sorry, pidge."

"It's not that bad, honest."

She was lying because she didn't want to upset me, but I knew what kind of pain she had to be in. She had blocked off her half of our bond, so I couldn't register her pain. She was trying to protect me in a moment where she was the breakable one. It was unfathomable.

"I love you." My trembling fingers delicately traced her face. "I thought I'd never get to have you again."

"I'm not going anywhere. Don't cry, Charlie." Ava wiped away tears from my eyes.

"I never wanted to let you go, but I thought it was the only choice—"

"I told you I'd never leave. Heaven and hell can't keep us apart," Ava said. "Death doesn't mean anything when you have a love like this."

That was the kind of thing people said in books and fairytales, but that was our reality. We had that once-in-a-lifetime kind of connection that couldn't be transgressed by any force. "I've been falling apart without you."

"You always had me. Even on the other side, I could feel you close."

"I couldn't feel you at *all*." I nearly suffocated on the words. "It broke me. You know you're my whole world, pidge. I didn't see the point in anything if you weren't here."

"It's all right now. We're together again, like it should be. It's going to stay that way."

Ancestors, I hoped so. I couldn't endure this a second time. It had nearly killed me the first time around.

Ava shifted against me. "Charlie... what happened?"

A lump rose to my throat. How could I begin to describe it all? The last week of my life had been like walking through ten layers of hell all at once.

But Ava had been the one to truly walk the afterlife. I had to be strong for her right now, because she needed me.

I swallowed. "You don't remember?"

She thought about it for a moment. "The details are fuzzy. I remember we found the Infernal Underground, and then... I remember Coyote Spirit. Charlie, I think I went to the Ancestral Lands."

I drew her closer. "You did," I told her. "I could feel it through our bond. Your spirit left."

"But I'm back now," Ava said simply. "Like I promised. I missed you."

"I thought I'd lost you for good," I admitted. "The doctors had lost hope. I thought you chose to stay in the Ancestral Lands."

"Never," Ava said. "I'd always come back to you, Charlie."

"I know you've promised me that before, but there are bigger things at stake here than us," I reminded her. "I thought I was honoring your decision to die."

"Honoring me how?" Ava sounded confused.

Ancestors, how could I have thought what I was doing was justified? Minutes ago, I thought I was doing the right thing. I'd been at peace with the decision. But now that I knew Ava had chosen to come back to me, it'd have been a terrible mistake. Guilt twisted in my gut.

"Ava, they... asked me to pull the plug," I spat out. I hoped she didn't hate me.

Ava snickered, though the sound turned to a whimper of pain. "*Pull the plug*? Ancestors, it's not like I was in a coma."

The air around me seemed to grow heavy. "Actually, Ava..."

She sucked in a breath, and my heart nearly shattered. "I was barely gone a day! It felt like..."

She trailed off as she tried calculating time in her mind. I wasn't sure how much she remembered.

"It might've felt that way in the Ancestral Lands, but here, it's been a week," I told her. "They've been treating you with healing magic, and you weren't improving. Pidge, I don't know if you realize this, but you died. Twice, actually. Once in the Underground, and again on the operating table. Oberi used her power to bring you back."

Ava sagged against me as she pondered what I'd told her. She sounded thoughtful. "I remember the gods... Coyote Spirit and Whale Spirit... they said something about Oberi having a gift."

"She's a phoenix," I said, a hint of pride in my tone. "We found her Anichi form— her Spirit form. Part of her power is one shot at regeneration."

Ava's voice wavered. "And she... used it on me?"

Of course I did, Oberi replied. He nudged his nose between our legs affectionately. *I'd do anything for you, Ava.*

"Oberi, that's so sweet."

"It was your choice to come back, though," I explained. "We weren't sure it would work."

Ava brushed hair away from my eyes. "I'll always come back to you."

Her promise meant everything. I couldn't help it when tears began streaming from my face. I hugged her close, and she snuggled into me.

"Thank you, pidge," I whispered. "I don't know what I'd do without you."

"You don't have to worry about that, because I'm not going anywhere," she promised.

Her lips connected with mine, and all the anxiety twisting in my gut melted away. My heart surged, until it felt like I was floating on a cloud with her. Having her back meant the world, and nothing could ruin this moment.

Ava slid her hand beneath the covers, and her fingers grazed my waistband.

I drew away. "Uh... what are you doing?"

She giggled. "I'm horny."

She slid her hand inside my pants and wrapped her fingers around me. I didn't mind when she took initiative, but I wasn't comfortable doing this here.

I grabbed her hands to stop her. "We can't right now."

"Why not?" she asked.

"You're hurt. You've just been through major surgery, for one, and you're hooked up to all these machines," I said.

"So? You'll be gentle."

"Pidge," I sighed. I didn't think she truly understood how fragile she still was.

"Come *on*. I'm alive and all. We should celebrate! With sex," Ava pleaded.

"Maybe when we get out of here," I told her reluctantly. I was honestly too afraid to touch her at the moment. We could be intimate again when I wasn't worried about setting her health back.

"Ugh, fine. Cockblock," Ava complained, and she drew her hand out of my pants.

The door burst open then, and a pair of footsteps rushed into the room. "Ancestors, she's awake!" Ava's mother cried.

Good thing Ava had decided *not* to mess around, because her mom had almost caught us with Ava's hand down my pants. I permitted myself a small laugh. Humor felt weird after such a dark week, but I could laugh again, because Ava was going to be all right.

"Mama! You're okay!" Ava sounded so happy to see her. "And you're still at the Institute."

"I never left," Sophia said. "You needed treatments. I just called your father and told him— oh."

Her voice fell flat. I knew exactly what they'd talked about. She'd told him we'd decided to end life support. Liam had to be in utter agony.

"You better call him back," I said firmly.

"I won't be long," Sophia said in a rush.

She fled from the room to call her husband and tell him the good news. She must've left the door open behind her, because several pairs of footsteps approached. Slowly, our friends came back in, and the door clicked shut behind them.

I forced myself to climb off the bed. I didn't want to— felt like cutting myself in half, honestly— but I wanted to give Ava some space, just in case she wasn't being honest about wanting me next to her.

"How are you feeling?" Ez asked timidly.

"Uh... good?" Ava said, though it sounded like a question. I could only imagine the pain she was in. "What happened, exactly? I remember bits and pieces, but not all of it."

Your memories should return in time, Oberi told her. *Your spirit's just a bit shocked right now.*

"We found the Underground," Kallie said.

"Right, beneath the cemetery," Ava recalled. "And the Elves?"

"They weren't there," Marcus said sadly. "We found records that showed the Warden had already moved them to some camp on the island. But Jaymin showed up with guards, and you exploded the compound to save us all."

"That's when Coyote Spirit showed up and took me to the Ancestral Lands," Ava said, like she was starting to remember.

"What was it like?" Opal asked curiously.

"It was... amazing," Ava answered in a way that made me wonder why she'd ever want to leave. "It was so beautiful. I saw a supernova explode, and this underground water tunnel— ancestors, I met so many wonderful people. You'll never believe what they have there. *A mall!*"

Ez chuckled to lighten the mood. "I bet that made the decision to come back hard."

"Not at all, actually," Ava said, and my heart warmed. "Did I miss anything? Ancestors, how did the Darke Games go?"

"We didn't compete, thankfully," Alistair said. "You sort of saved us from that, too. They were canceled due to the *sinkhole.*"

"That's the story the Warden's going with, at least," Chancey added.

"I'm glad I brought that place to the ground," Ava said. "The Warden will have nowhere to host his experiments for now, and his inferichite crystal supply will be low, now that I buried the devil's finger that he gets them from."

She sounded so proud of herself, but we hadn't even gotten to the worst of the story. But no one spoke up to tell her about the mounting war, or how the Hawkei tribe bombed the angel city. It was too much information to drop on her right now, and we didn't want to set back her recovery.

"Wait a dick..." Ava said, like she just realized something. "You said it's been a week. What day is it, exactly?"

"The twenty-first," I said.

A long, dramatic silence stretched through the room as she absorbed what I'd said. Ava surprised me by breaking into sobs. "Ancestors, Charlie! It's your *birthday.*"

"Uh... yeah," I stated. I didn't get why she was so upset.

"This is horrible! We had a surprise party planned, and we *missed it!*" she cried. "I *ruined your birthday* with my surgery!"

"Pidge, don't say that," I insisted. I knelt by her bedside and took her hand. "Having you back is the best birthday present in all the world."

"But we... I got you a gift, and I wanted to bake a cake and *everything,*" she sobbed.

Ancestors, she was more worried about my birthday than the fact that she'd *died.* I couldn't give a flying fuck that my birthday was here. All I gave a damn about was my wife's well-being, and she was okay. That was the only celebration I needed.

"I don't mind. It will be all right," I promised.

"Not until you get your present," she demanded. "We can do that, at least. Marcus, do you still have it?"

"Yeah, of course." Marcus must've conjured something, because I heard a bag rustle.

Ava pulled her hand out of mine to wipe her tears. "Thank the Great Spirit. We all pitched in."

I reluctantly took the bag from Marcus, but I hesitated. My birthday was nothing special. We should be celebrating Ava right now.

Everyone's watching, Oberi told me. *Go ahead and open it.*

I opened the bag and dug through the tissue paper, until my fingers curled around a small square item. I ran my hand over it and found several buttons. It reminded me of the voice recorder I used for recording lectures in class.

"What is it?" I asked.

"It's a music player," Ava said. "I got one to match the headphones I got you last semester. We've already downloaded a playlist for you, and a bunch of true crime podcasts."

"It only took a month with the Institute's shitty Internet," Alistair added playfully.

"I know you want to be a supernatural bounty hunter, so I thought you'd like to practice solving crimes by listening to the podcasts and trying to piece cases together," Ava rasped.

I choked up, and nearly broke down for the millionth time that day. Goddamn, it was such a thoughtful gift. Ava was the one person who actually supported my dreams and thought I could do whatever I wanted. Even lying all busted up in a hospital bed, she did her best to make things as amazing as she could for me. I didn't deserve this woman. "Thanks, guys. I really don't know what to say."

The door opened again, and I heard a barrage of voices coming down the hall. "I told the doctors she's awake," Sophia said as she entered the room. "They're coming to check on her."

Suddenly, the room became so crowded I could barely move.

"How is this possible?" a nurse asked.

"It isn't," one of the doctors answered.

"Everyone out!" someone barked. "She needs space."

Sophia placed a gentle hand on my shoulder. "They might need my healing powers. I've got this, Charlie. You can relax now. She's not going anywhere."

"Thanks," I said. In my heart, I knew Sophia was telling the truth. In my brain, I feared I might lose Ava again.

But if I wanted her to stay, I had to let the doctors fix her.

"It'll be okay, Charlie," Ava said, before she let out a short gasp, and she let her true feelings slip across our bond. I winced as I felt a small sting of agony ripple over my middle. I knew it had to be a hundred times worse from her point of view. I didn't want to leave, but her comfort was more important than mine, and she needed some pain relief.

"I'll be right outside the room," I told my wife before leaving. Oberi remained behind on the bed.

My friends went to the waiting room, while I sank into a chair right outside Ava's hospital room. I could hear the doctors unhooking Ava from the machines, but otherwise, the hall had gone silent. My head spun as I caught up with reality. Everything had happened so quickly.

I must've been sitting there a long time, because Marcus stopped by to ask if I wanted to go get food. I didn't, and I told my friends to go without me. Doctors came and went from Ava's room, until I was left in complete silence.

Footsteps sounded down the hall, though I didn't pay attention until someone said my name. "Charlie. I thought I'd find you here."

I stood, suddenly alert. "Uh..."

He reached out and shook my hand with a kind but firm grip. I hadn't been sure of his voice before, but his handshake was unmistakable.

"Professor Takahashi?" I asked.

"Yes. I have something for you. It can't wait."

Takahashi placed a hand on my shoulder. Something hard and flat touched my arm, and I realized he was holding a book. He guided me into the empty patient room across the hall. I went quickly, because whatever he had to say sounded important.

The door shut behind us. "What's going on? I thought you weren't supposed to return to the Institute yet. If the Warden sees you—"

"All is well," he promised. "I'm back on staff and preparing for the upcoming semester. I don't believe the Warden suspects me of anything, and I intend to keep it that way. The Demigod Guardians have run across information that you and your friends should know."

"If it's in that book, we need to hide it from the Warden," I insisted.

"The Warden should not suspect anything," Takashi assured me. "It's been right in front of us all along. This is a book of poetry— nursery rhymes and stories that are thought to be fables, all originating from supernatural societies. The book is widely available in the school's library. But there are some stories in here that have proven to hold truths, such as the Nivita legend from your own culture. The story told of a woman who died and became a tree."

"What does this have to do with demigods?" I asked.

"If that story is true, the others could be, too," Takahashi said. "We think we found a clue to the merfolk key that you and your friends will need to open the Elven Gate and fulfill your prophecy."

My heart surged with hope. "What's the story?"

"It's an old Atlantean story the sailors used to tell while at sea. It's called *The Assassin's Destiny*," Takahashi said. "It speaks of a woman assassin who stole *a treasure of the sea*. We believe that to be the merfolk key."

Takahashi began to narrate a verse aloud. It sounded like a poem.

"Into the dark she ran, with her treasure of the sea.
The key to her riches lies with the assassin's destiny."

Pages rustled as Takahashi closed the book. "We think this story is a treasure map that will lead us to where she hid it."

"This is great!" I cried. We already had four keys— after we stole the angel key from the Warden's safe— and already, we had a clue leading to another.

I pondered the words for a moment. "The assassin's destiny... what is that? Is this another prophecy?"

"It's likely," Takahashi said. "Which means—"

"It's about Kallie," I said simply. "She was an assassin in Malovia, before she was sentenced to the Institute. She's one of the demigods searching for the keys. So it must be her destiny to find it."

"We believe so," Takahashi agreed. "Which means that Kallie must be the one to decipher this. It is *her* prophecy, *her* destiny. She must connect with her origins and discover who this assassin was, in order to find where this mysterious woman hid the key."

"Maybe she already knows without realizing it," I said thoughtfully. "I'll tell her right away."

"Take the book," Takahashi offered, placing it into my hands. "Give it to Marcus. He can keep it in his stash."

"I will. Thank you so much."

"I know you're excited, but remember to keep your guard up," Takahashi told me. "I will see you in a few weeks' time, once our counseling sessions start up again. In the meantime, make sure to stay out of trouble."

That was always my prerogative, but with the people I hung around with, Takahashi was asking for the impossible.

I left the room buzzing with excitement. Ava-Marie was making a recovery, and we had a lead on the next key. All seemed right in the world.

When I entered Ava's hospital room, the doctors had cleared out.

"I found something about the keys," I said in a rush. "Well, Takahashi found it."

"We can talk about it when Kallie and Marcus get back," Ava said. "My mom just left to update my dad, and I don't have much time."

"Time for what?" I asked.

The bed creaked as Ava tried pushing herself upright. She groaned, and concern swelled over me. I tossed the book onto a chair and hurried to her bedside.

"The doctors unhooked me, but Mama won't let me get out of bed," Ava said. "She's *very* insistent I stay put so the doctors can observe me. They need to run more tests, and they don't know how long I'll be here. But I *need* a shower. I feel so gross. Can you help me quick while Mama's gone?"

"Yeah, of course," I said. I'd do anything she wanted. I helped her sit up, then tossed the covers off her feet and guided them onto the floor.

Ava sagged against me. She was still so tired.

I frowned. "Pidge, you can hardly stand. Maybe this wasn't a good—"

Ava went to take a step, but she let go of me. My heart lurched as I felt her going down. I grabbed her tightly and caught her before she crashed to the floor. Ava clutched my shirt, and her body trembled. Oberi whimpered loudly.

"I'm okay. I can stand," Ava said, but something in her tone worried me.

"We need to get you back into bed. You're not well enough to be moving around," I argued.

"No, I've got this." She sounded frustrated as she put an arm around my neck. "Just support me, okay?"

I wished to carry her, but that's not what she wanted. So instead, I steadied her as she tried to take a step... only she didn't go anywhere.

My heart slammed against my rib cage. This wasn't right. "Pidge, what's wrong? What hurts?"

Ava's tone wavered. "It... it doesn't. That's the problem. I... I can't feel my legs."

The world seemed to stop spinning. I couldn't have heard her right. "You can't...?" *Fuck!* My words trailed off.

Ava's panic ripped through the bond. I teetered on the verge of freak-out, but I didn't want to worry her further, so I shoved my emotions downward.

The door opened, and Sophia gasped when she saw me clutching Ava. "What are you doing?!" she cried. "Ava, I explicitly told you to stay in bed!"

I scooped Ava in my arms and set her on the bed. I'd gone numb all over, and my thoughts were completely blank. What was going on? We'd already been through so much... there couldn't be possibly more we had to endure, could there?

Oberi let out a low whine beside us, as if he knew this had been coming and wanted to protect us from it, but knew nothing he could do or say would help.

Ava's hands trembled, and her voice shook. "I just wanted a shower... Charlie, I don't understand. Wh— why can't I feel anything?"

I didn't have an answer to give her, and it tore me to fucking shreds. Sophia must've said something to Ava, but I didn't hear it. The whole infirmary seemed to turn upside down. I couldn't make sense of space or time.

A hand landed on my shoulder, and Sophia whispered softly, "Charlie... I need to talk with you privately."

Ancestors, I hoped she had an idea of what we could do to help Ava. I couldn't muster the strength to say anything as she pulled me into the hall. I raked my fingers through my hair. "Is she...?"

"While I was healing her, I discovered that some of the nerves in her spine were severely damaged at the base," Sophia said, her voice cracking. She sounded as if she was barely holding herself together. "The doctors and I did what we could to repair them, but even with my healing magic, we couldn't mend the worst of the damage."

My thoughts spun faster than a whirlwind. Most of the explosion had been concentrated around Ava's middle, as that's where her magic had blasted outward. But I didn't realize her spine had been injured, too. The doctors had never told me.

Then I realized why— because they didn't think Ava would ever recover enough for it to be important to mention.

"I'd seen the damage to her body, and I truly thought she wasn't going to make it. I didn't want to tell you and cause you more pain." Sophia sounded regretful. "But then she woke up. I was going to tell you both as soon as I came back to the room, but you already had her out of bed."

"So what do we need to do?" I asked. "Will she heal in time, or...?"

Sophia sighed heavily. "I'm sorry to tell you this, Charlie. But Ava-Marie is never going to walk again."

ava-marie
TWO

Ow.

Every part of me hurt. There wasn't a bit of my body that wasn't aching and wanting— and not at all in a sexy way. Each time I moved, I found new bruises. My flesh was soft and tender, and I struggled to take every breath. My lungs might as well have been pierced with a million knives and turned inside out.

My middle was particularly agonizing. They'd scrambled my organs and rearranged them.

Ancestors, I couldn't believe I'd survived all that.

Even my bones felt like elastic. They'd been mended back together and weren't sure how to function properly. The doctors repaired the worst of me with potions, magic, and modern medicine, but I could tell not every bit of me was fixed. From beyond the closed door, I could hear my mother and husband speaking in hushed voices.

I told my beating heart to calm down. I was scared right now. Scared as hell. I'd tried to put weight on my feet, and for the first time in my life, they'd failed to hold me up.

I did my best to concentrate on my legs, and found I had a very faint sensation in my thighs. I could barely tell the scratchy Institute sheets were rubbing against them, so much so that I wondered if it was my imagination and not an actual feeling. I tried to move my legs, but all feeling stopped at the knees.

Something was *definitely* wrong. I attempted to lift my left foot, even just a little, and it failed to move.

I swallowed down the lump in my throat and blinked away the tears. No more crying today. I'd been crying, and everyone else had been crying, for ancestors knew how long. I hadn't gone to the Ancestral Lands, come back again and survived every hell the Infernal Underground had put me through to lie in this bed and weep. No, sir. I was getting up and out of here.

Even if it only meant using some fucking shampoo. I bet my legs were hairy after laying around for a week.

It crossed my mind how absolutely ridiculous that was. Trust me to worry about something as silly as shaving when I didn't know if I could fucking walk.

But maybe that's how it was. My mind couldn't process what was happening to me, so it chose to fixate on something else. Something benign, something I knew I could fix.

I mean... I didn't even feel upset about it. Or... *worried.* My legs failing to work was just... a thing.

Was I in shock?

Charlie raised his voice, and Mama shushed him. I strained to hear their hushed words through the door.

"There has to be more you can do," Charlie insisted.

"But there's not." Mama sounded completely broken. "I've done my best, and I can't heal her. I don't know why my magic isn't working. My powers should've helped, if not outright fixed her spine completely. The doctors performed surgery to put everything back in place, then, once they finished, I tried to heal her, to help her recovery. But my magic couldn't fix it."

"The surgeons didn't allow you in the room?" Charlie asked.

"No, not until after, because the surgeons needed to set her spine and organs properly before my healing magic could fix the rest. She should be able to *walk*, Charlie. My Anichi magic is the strongest in our tribe... she should be completely well by now. But it did nothing."

What the hell did that mean? I'd never seen someone hurt so badly my mother's magic couldn't make it right again. She couldn't heal chronic illnesses, but my injury had resulted from an accident, and they'd gotten to me quickly. Why couldn't Mama reverse this?

"Do you have any theories?" Charlie asked.

"Perhaps my healing magic didn't work when her spirit was in the Ancestral Lands, because her body was alive on the operating table, but her soul was somewhere else. Anichi magic is Spirit magic, so if her soul wasn't in her body at the time, maybe the healing couldn't take place."

"But shouldn't you be able to heal her now?"

"I've tried, again and again. Something isn't right."

I attempted to break into Charlie's thoughts, but he firmly shut me out. I couldn't get past the iron barricade he'd put up, and I heard the sound of their footsteps as they walked away from the door.

I wasn't sure what the hell they were talking about out there, but I was damn well determined to get out of this bed somehow and fix my fucking hair. The matter that I'd died hardly had bearing on the fact that I needed to look good.

And right now, I bet I looked like shit.

Oberi lay at the foot of my bed. He gave a couple of thumps on the mattress with his tail and said, *I'm so pleased you're here, beloved. I feared for a moment you'd ditch me with Mister Sunshine over there.*

I would have laughed if I knew it wouldn't hurt, so I merely smiled. "I'm just happy to be alive. I guess I can't complain about the rest."

I groaned as a sharp sensation shattered apart my organs before fading to a dull ache. "Though I gotta say, the Ancestral Lands weren't easy to pass up."

Isn't it wonderful? Oberi gave a dreamy sigh and laid his head on my ankle. *My own memories of the Ancestral Lands are... muddled... but I recall enough to know that it is a very special place.*

"This is a very special place, too," I said. "Even the Institute."

Oberi gave a short laugh. *That it is.*

The door opened. In marched my husband, along with my mother, and they weren't alone.

A short woman followed behind them. I knew her— Doctor Marsh. She'd managed some of my treatments for my bipolar in the past and got me on the medication that was currently keeping my mood stable. She wasn't a bitch, and I trusted her, as far as Institute employees went.

"Mrs. Wahkin. I'm glad to see you're awake," Doctor Marsh started cheerfully. "We had to portal in a special surgeon from Celestial City just in time. You get very lucky."

She gave me a plastic smile, but I didn't return it. I knew she hadn't come in here to deliver good news. I was disgusted that the Warden had assigned an *angel doctor* to perform my surgery. The surgeon was probably working for him and reporting back.

But I guarantee he wouldn't have allowed any other supernatural doctor to work on me. Otherwise, he'd have let me die.

"When can I expect the feeling in my legs to come back?" I asked, and immediately regretted it. Charlie paled, and Mama had that crumpled face she got whenever she was about to cry, and damn, I hated it.

Doctor Marsh paused. "I have to admit, in your particular case... I haven't seen a patient come back from such an extensive injury. The chances of you walking, Mrs. Wahkin, are... quite low. To speak frankly, that you even awoke from your coma was a miracle."

Now it was starting to hit me. That inevitable black pool dragged me under as I comprehended the reality of it all. It felt so similar to the drowning feeling I'd had when Mama had explained my bipolar diagnosis, but even worse. I kept spiraling and spiraling, and I didn't see a way up.

Doctor Marsh began laying pictures on my lap— x-rays of my spine. "You have a fairly severe spinal cord injury, which has resulted in partial paralysis. The most damage was sustained to your lumbar and sacral vertebrae, which, as you can see from your x-rays..."

Blah, blah, blah. I couldn't give a fuck less about what this lady was saying, although I was aware Charlie was keenly taking in every word. He could listen for me, because I just couldn't. I had the facts delivered to me loud and clear. Everything else was white noise.

She'd been talking for nearly a half-hour before I found the courage to speak. "So I'll never walk again." I spoke the words plainly, cutting Doctor Marsh off mid-sentence. Everything else beyond that point was meaningless.

Mama teared up as Doctor Marsh replied, "That is indeed the case."

I experienced a brief moment without any physical pain, because at that second, I couldn't feel anything. I was hovering outside my body, disassociating from myself as I attempted to comprehend the inevitability of what she'd just told me, and failed.

Doctor Marsh shifted on her heels as she looked for an exit. "I should let you rest. You've been through an ordeal, and your recovery at this point is our top priority."

I snapped myself out of it, though dragging myself down to Earth had the equivalent feeling of being dropped like a brick onto a concrete floor from a thousand stories up. I couldn't walk, and never would again. That was the truth. And if there was nothing else I could do about it, I might as well get on with it.

I couldn't allow myself to fall apart because of this. If I did, I'd never get up. And there were people out there who needed me.

"When can I go back to school?" I asked. Classes weren't on right now, but I had to get back to my dorm, because I had shit to do.

Doctor Marsh frowned. "If you cooperate with your treatment— don't give me that look, Mrs. Wahkin. We've had struggles with you in the past, and you haven't always agreed to be compliant with your medical care."

"I'll be a good girl," I sneered. "Just give it to me straight."

"As I was saying, *if* you do everything you can to help us help *you,* we may be able to get you discharged in ten weeks."

"*Ten weeks?!*" I all but yelled. This was ridiculous! I couldn't sit in here until March!

"You need extensive physical therapy, as well as help learning how to use a wheelchair. Your whole life has changed. You need time and care to adjust to it," Doctor Marsh said firmly. "If there are more complications, you may have to undergo further procedures for your spinal injury. None of this can happen unless you're being monitored twenty-four seven by medical staff. This is non-negotiable."

"If I don't pass the semester I'll flunk out, and the Warden will send me straight to the adult penitentiary!" I protested.

"The Warden has given you an exemption," Doctor Marsh replied coolly. "You will receive no penalties toward your degree if you finish up the last few weeks of the semester once you've been released."

Of course he gave me an exemption, because he wanted me under his fucking control for as long as possible.

But I wasn't willing to sit here and have these doctors poke and prod at me for days on end while the world was at stake. "I refuse treatment. Give me a wheelchair and get me out of here!"

"Please, pidge, just do what the doctors tell you," Charlie pleaded. "You need to get better."

I deflated instantly. No argument any doctor could give would equal Charlie's begging. I couldn't fight back against it. I'd do anything he asked me to. Even if I hated it.

Oberi nudged my hand, and I said, "Fine. I better be able to do a cartwheel in this damn wheelchair by the time you let me out."

"It'll feel like no time at all, I promise," Marsh replied. "Merry Christmas."

Well, that sounded like a lie. Doctor Marsh hurried out of the room like her ass was on fire. After she shut the door behind her, Charlie asked, "What can we do to help Ava recover faster?"

Mama appeared contemplative, which was never a good sign. It always meant she was trying to hide the truth. "From what I've learned from my training as a healer, *some* paralysis can be reversed. The spinal cord has the ability to reorganize itself and adapt, due to the brain's neuroplasticity."

"Sure, because we know my brain is firing on all cylinders as it is," I said sarcastically.

Charlie frowned, and Mama hastily added, "The nervous system can rewire itself and make changes based on an individual's ability to practice and hone skills. Your spinal injury is incomplete, which means these neural pathways exist, but..."

Mama trailed off. Charlie was taking this as a sign of hope, but I knew Mama better than that. She thought I'd fucked myself up to the point there was no recovery.

"I understand," I said, as to not piss Charlie off and to give Mama the signal I got what she was saying. "We'll just have to adjust."

Mama leaned over and gave me a kiss on the forehead. "Whatever happens, sweetheart, we all love you no matter what. Our family's been dealing with health issues for a long time, and we're equipped to make this change."

I felt terribly guilty— which was more than messed up, considering this was happening to me and not anyone else. We had enough to deal with, if you included my dad's disease, my brother's illness, and my bipolar. Adding this on top of it was enough to make the entire pyramid fall apart.

Mama sighed. "I should talk to your father. He's doing his best to get here as quick as he can."

I couldn't imagine a universe where my father didn't tear the world down to get to me, so something really bad must've happened. Mama rushed out of the room— I'd rarely see her move so fast.

I rode through another bout of pain that shot through my middle, and I managed to ask through gritted teeth, "What's going on?"

"It's probably chieftain stuff," Charlie admitted reluctantly. "The news hasn't been... encouraging."

I could only imagine. I didn't know what was going on out there, and I wanted to hold on to that ignorance a little longer, because I knew eventually I'd have to face it.

"You're uncomfortable." Charlie moved closer. "Is there anything I can do?"

I shook my head, before I realized he couldn't see it, and forced out, "There's nothing anyone can do at this point but give me time to heal."

Charlie's mouth was flat. He didn't like that answer. He wanted to do something about it. "Oberi, can I give up another part of myself so Ava can walk?"

"Fucking hell, Charlie!" I yelled, giving a cough as a harsh pain flared over my sides. Raising my voice was difficult. I'd just *known* he was going to ask that question the minute we were alone.

Oberi narrowed his eyes. *I accredit the audacity of the male species that you have the gall to ask such a question to my face.*

"Why not? I gave up my sight so Ava could live. She was supposed to die the night she was born, but she didn't, because I gave her my eyes," Charlie argued. "Why can't we do the same here?"

It doesn't work that way. When you gave up your sight to save Ava's life as a young child, that was with the help of Eagle Spirit, who, may I remind you, is a god, Oberi said dryly. *The power I had to use to call Ava's soul back from the Ancestral Lands wasn't even as strong as that.*

"You're strong, too. Your magic is powerful. I have no doubt that if we put our magic together, it would work," Charlie insisted.

Even if we could, I wouldn't allow it. If you two keep giving up pieces of yourselves to save the other, then by the end we'll have nothing left, Oberi replied in a stale voice. *I'm not going to patchwork the two of you back together after this one, because let me make this clear, this can* never *happen again. We managed to keep our bond hanging on by a thread. Be grateful we saved that much.*

Charlie gave an aggravated sigh. "Ava deserves to live a full life."

I was annoyed at what he was implying, because honestly, he knew better. "I can still live a full life! It's not like my life is worth any less because I can no longer walk. I didn't throw you in the bin because you don't have your sight."

Charlie pinched the bridge of his nose. "I *know* that, but this isn't something you should have to deal with!"

"I get that it presents complications. We'll have to work our way around them." Not like I'd ever let obstacles stop me before. Though this felt like climbing a mountain.

In space.

Which was on fire.

His jaw worked. "I still think—"

"Charlie, the bigger deal you make out of this, the harder it's going to be. Just support me, and we'll get through it together. There's a lot I have to learn from this point, and it'll be easier if you let me figure it out."

Charlie huffed, then plopped into the chair at my bedside. "Okay."

He wasn't going to give up, but he'd let me win. For now.

"What about you?" Charlie asked, directing his attention to Oberi. "You have a phoenix form now. Don't you have other healing powers you can access?"

I would love to, but unfortunately, I've done all I can here, Oberi replied snidely. *Do you honestly think I'd let Ava be in pain if there was something my magic could do about it?*

"Yes," Charlie replied bluntly, and Oberi lifted his upper lip to growl.

What had transpired between them when I'd been gone? They both seemed bitter.

"Anyway," I persisted, wanting to break the tension between them. "I still want that shower."

"Let me ask the doctor." Charlie walked out. It was about fifteen minutes before he came back, followed by a nurse.

"The doctor says it'll be fine. The stitches will hold up in the water," Charlie said.

"Let's get you out of bed," the nurse offered.

Finally. I was tired of lying around. Charlie turned the water on in the attached bathroom. As he was doing so, the nurse used some sort of machine to pick me up out of the bed and set me onto a wheelchair. She pushed me into the bathroom, beside the stream of water that was coming from the shower head, and went to remove my hospital gown.

I cringed as she started undoing the ties, and Charlie sensed it. He stepped forward to say, "I'll do it."

There was a mirror in here, one of those fake, plastic ones with a phony surface that spanned the length of the wall. Still, it showed everything. My cheekbones were elevated on my gaunt face, and two swollen black eyes peered back at me. I'd dropped a scary amount of weight from being in a coma for so long, so much that the bones were poking through the skin.

Shit, no wonder everyone thought I was going to die. I really did look like a corpse.

As the gown fell away, I held in a sharp breath. My skin had blossomed with a variety of bruises. The tone had practically turned purple.

If I shut off my half of our bond completely it would alert Charlie I was upset, so I slowly closed the connection, bit by bit so he wouldn't notice. Charlie couldn't see the damage, and I wanted to conceal as much of it from him as I possibly could.

I hadn't come out of the Underground the same. Part of me had never left there at all.

More carnage caught my attention. A large bandage was wrapped around my middle, and it was matted with dried blood.

That had to come off if I was getting clean. The cloth had stuck to the wound and was painful to pull away. I hunched my shoulders as the nurse tried to peel the bandage off.

"I think it's best if you help," the nurse stated to Charlie. She clearly picked up that I didn't want her near me. Tears dotted my eyelids as Charlie unraveled the bandage, though he apologized profusely.

As the wrappings fell away, my insides withered inward with a simple look at my reflection. Worse than all of it was the scar. From the top of my left shoulder all the way down to my right hip bone was a raised, knotted line, threaded with black stitches and fiery red.

My eyes began to water. I'd had the *perfect* body before, and I'd gone and ruined it. I couldn't let anyone see me like this. They'd get scared and run away, afraid of the Frankenstein monster.

"Is something wrong?" Charlie asked, voice full of concern.

I cleared my throat and said, "Nothing. Is the water warm?"

"Yeah. It's nice."

We heard shouting coming from the corridor outside the room, from two different people. It sounded like one student had hurt himself badly. The other was mentally deranged, and looking to make it worse.

"Martha, we need you out here! It's a code black!" Lady Helga's voice echoed as she quickly ducked her head inside my hospital room.

The nurse appeared frantic. She glanced toward the door as she said, "I'm sorry— we've been overrun with patients this morning, and we're out of beds. Is it okay if you finish up here, Mister Wahkin? I'll try not to be long."

Without waiting for him to say if it was, the nurse ran off. We hadn't even started my shower.

Charlie's mouth was flat. "I get this is a prison school, but you need more help than anyone here."

"They're understaffed. The Institute doesn't have the employees or the supplies to take care of an injury like this," I said tiredly.

"You should be their first priority," Charlie growled.

"I don't care. I'd rather you help me, anyway." I didn't like strangers touching me, not even if they were women. And unfortunately, I was about to get a whole hell of a lot of that for the next ten weeks.

Charlie reached out to close and lock the bathroom door, so we could get some privacy. The wheelchair kept me propped up, because I didn't have much strength in my hips and none at all in my core or back. Doctor Marsh had mentioned that I needed a back brace, but I didn't have one on me now. I kept sliding down the chair, and Charlie had to pull me up. My arms were too weak to lift my own weight.

"I'm trying to be gentle," he apologized.

"It's okay," I pressed, because it really was. He wasn't trying to hurt me, and there wasn't any movement I could do that wouldn't be uncomfortable right now.

Charlie got undressed, and I watched him put his clothes neatly to the side. Damn, he looked delicious. I was kind of bummed out that he'd refused my offer to get it on earlier, although I really didn't think I could, at the moment.

Desire washed through me, and it felt blissful, until I noticed that it stopped just below my belly.

The sensation of a hand wrapping around my throat and squeezing slammed into me. I couldn't feel much past my hips. What if…?

A terrible thought leveled my soul. Ancestors, I loved sex. I wasn't being dramatic when I said I didn't think I could live without it. It was important for married people to be intimate; at least, it was important to Charlie and me. What if I'd lost that? What if I couldn't feel any kind of pleasure at all, and could no longer enjoy what we had?

I refused to go there. The thought was nearly worse to me than not being able to walk again. Even if I couldn't experience that kind of pleasure, we'd figure out a way to still make it enjoyable.

We *had* to.

Charlie reached up to grab the handheld showerhead, then began spraying my body down. Dried blood and some residual dirt began rolling off of me and down the drain. The feeling was similar to peeling off a new skin. The water slipping down the drain was brown, mixed with rusty red.

I was too sore to lift my arms, so Charlie had to wash my hair for me. I tried to close my eyes and enjoy the sensations of the suds streaming through my locks, although my neck was too tender to tip my head back. Charlie was careful, protecting my face from the wayward water and being extra careful with the soap as he rinsed me down.

I wanted to stay in the water forever, but Charlie said the doctors insisted I could only have a quick wash. He applied a healing cream to my scar, then wrapped me up again. I was honestly kind of impressed with how well he did.

"You're being so sweet," I said as he dotted off excess water on my arms with a towel.

"I want to get you better as soon as you can. I'll do anything to help."

Right now, all I was looking forward to was another nap. This tiny bit of activity had me very tired. Charlie helped me into a new hospital gown before he carried me back to bed. As he set me down, I beamed as I saw a fresh pot of tulips growing on my bedside table.

Are you pleased? Oberi wagged his tail. *I used my Earth powers to grow them from seeds I found on the windowsill.*

"They're beautiful, Oberi." It sure brightened up this dreary-ass room.

Charlie grabbed my hairbrush from the bedside table, which I figured Mama must've dropped off while I was in the shower. He brushed my wet hair, and it was the one bit of relaxation that I'd felt all day.

"I'm sorry, I don't know how to braid it," he apologized.

"It's okay, Mama will." I closed my eyes, and slipped off into another nap without having the ability to protest against it.

Nurses started coming in an hour later, poking me and testing me. I felt smothered and vastly uncomfortable. Charlie nearly punched out the dude who stuck me three times trying to find a vein for an IV. Lady Helga finally dismissed him and did it herself, after she had to apply some new bandages.

I didn't think the Institute was equipped to handle situations like this, and it fucking showed. They were used to healing inmates who got the crap beat out of them, or kids who needed to detox after overdosing, not major surgery cases.

I couldn't have anything solid, so this hospital gave me a strawberry smoothie to eat. My sensitive throat ached while I sipped the cold drink. It was pretty good going down, but I puked it back up.

Ancestors, it was awful. I held a pillow to my stomach as I retched, to keep my muscles tight and try to suppress the pain. I didn't have any core strength left since my surgery, so it felt like my guts were going to come squishing out my stitches as I heaved.

Charlie winced as he held a plastic bucket underneath me to vomit into. "When can she start eating?"

"It's going to be a struggle. Her digestive system has to get readjusted," Lady Helga said apologetically. "It'll be some time before she's able to consume anything that's not a liquid."

I trembled as I finally stopped heaving. I'd just gotten over my issues with food, and now I had to start all over again. This really sucked.

The staff didn't leave me alone for what felt like forever. By that point, I was even more wiped out than I had been before. I wanted to see my friends, and my family, but I just didn't have the strength. From the other side of the door, I heard Doctor Marsh tell a few people— Kallie, Marcus, Ezekiel, probably— that I needed some rest and they could visit in the morning.

I begged Charlie to lie beside me again as he dimmed the lights in the room. My eyes were nearly drooping shut. Just being in a hospital was exhausting.

"Things will get better, pidge. It's only the first day," Charlie told me as he crawled into the bed.

I didn't have the capacity to respond. He snuggled up beside me, and Oberi lay at my feet.

I spent the short moments I had before sleep contemplating my recent predicament. I wasn't sure how I was going to move forward or where I was going from here.

"I don't want you to push yourself, okay?" Charlie asked. "Just take it easy. We've got time for you to recover."

I didn't know if that was true, with whatever the Warden was planning. But honestly, that creep was the farthest thing from my mind.

"I want to get back to a regular life."

Charlie didn't say anything for a moment, before he added, "That's over now, pidge. It's gonna be a whole new world from now on."

"You accepted your blindness. I can accept this, too," I said.

"I went blind when I was three. I barely remember life with sight. Being blind is all I've ever known," Charlie said quietly. "You have to change your whole approach to life at twenty-one. It's not really the same, pidge."

My throat got tight, and tears welled in my eyes, but I refused to accept defeat as an option. This was hard— so much harder than I could imagine it being— but it didn't mean I had to roll over and submit. Whatever lay ahead of me, I couldn't face it like I had before.

I'd have to find a new way.

THE MOONLIGHT WAS COMING through the bars of the window when I woke up. It was dark, really dark— had to be around three in the morning.

Charlie and Oberi were still curled up against me, still as statues.

Someone was sitting in a chair beside my bed. I didn't think they allowed visitors this late at night, but there was nobody who was stopping my father from getting to me when I needed him. He must've just arrived.

He slowly sat up when he realized I was stirring. Even in the soft light, I saw the haggard look on his face and the deep bags under his eyes. This whole thing had aged him at least a decade overnight.

His voice was deep and brusque as he said, "Ava-Marie."

"Huh?" I was barely awake. I was already slipping off again.

He reached out softly to take my hand. His fingers trembled as he said, "*Never* do that to me again."

I squeezed his hand back, tightly as I could, although my grip was loose like water. I closed my eyes to drift back off to sleep. "Yes, Daddy."

I DIDN'T WAKE up again until nearly eleven. I'd slept, but people had been coming in and out all night to check on me and run more tests. It was exhausting, and I felt violated. I knew the doctors were trying to help me, yet my privacy and sense of self had been invaded. I really hoped I got out of here sooner than ten weeks.

Charlie's head was nestled on my shoulder, and one of his arms lay carefully across my hips. He was really tired. He had to be, if he was still sleeping. He was an earlier riser. I couldn't imagine he'd gotten much rest over the past few days.

Oberi's ears pricked as he stared at the closed door. Daddy's chair was empty, but I heard his voice outside, along with Mama's, speaking in hushed tones. I kept my eyes shut, to focus on the conversation outside.

"We have to get Ava out of here. Damn the consequences, damn the law. We'll hide her in *Hok'evale*. They'll never find her there."

"They're not like us, Liam. You can't rip these kids apart. It'll kill them."

"He'll do whatever he has to in order to keep Ava safe. We all saw how he acted that night. He's willing to be a true husband in every sense of the word. He'll stay behind until we can make a plan to get him out."

Daddy sounded like he had the utmost respect for Charlie now, which blew my mind. What exactly had gone down the night I'd died?

"She won't get better without him. A *minai* bond is a powerful thing. There's no stronger bond in Hawkei culture than the one between two people who share a soul. Ava has to draw energy from their spirit if she's going to recover, and that won't happen if they're separated. The only reason she's still here is *because* of him, and we don't have the resources to help both of them escape, not with how closely the Warden is watching. We're already under scrutiny from the Union because of the bombing."

Bombing? What the hell?

Mama went on. "Last week proved they can't live without each other. Neither of them can. Whatever happens, they have to stick together."

Daddy sighed. "I know you're right. I wish there was an easier way."

"It's not going to be easy for any of us from this point out."

Their footsteps roamed away. They must've left to get coffee.

Charlie finally stirred beside me. His hair was a mess as he sat up and gave a couple of bleary blinks.

I didn't give him time to wake up. "There was a bombing? Charlie, what are you hiding?"

His expression was blank. He didn't want to tell me what was going on.

Before he could answer, the door opened again. I caught a flash of red hair as my little sister walked into the room, along with Ezekiel. Alana looked painfully worried as she looked me over, although Ezekiel appeared nothing but relieved.

"Sis," Ez choked out. He stroked back my hair. "I really am sorry about what I said."

His words were distant to me— I vaguely recalled our argument, how he'd said he'd wanted me out of his life, but the memory was muddled. I had no emotion attached to it, though Ez was clearly harboring guilt. "It doesn't mean anything, Ez, I promise. Shit like that doesn't matter in these kinds of situations. I'm just glad we're all together."

Ez let out a choked noise and dropped his head. At my side, I watched Alana keenly observe Charlie. They had never been properly introduced.

"Alana, this is Charlie, my husband, and Charlie, this is my little sister, Alana. Sorry you weren't at the wedding. I know you would've wanted to be there," I apologized.

"Hi," Charlie said. He reached out to shake Alana's hand. She took it formally, grasping it lightly the way Grandmother Eleanor did. For seventeen years old, she moved with so much grace.

Alana smirked. "Ha. You sure are Ava's type. Tall, dark and broody."

Charlie's eyebrows furrowed. "What's that supposed to mean?"

"She likes them with dark hair and edgy pasts, and I'm sure you've got both," Alana joked.

"Okay, cut it out," I told her. "The interrogation's over."

Charlie smiled. "It's all right. I'm sure when you get a boyfriend your siblings won't stop teasing you about it, either."

I snorted, and Ez let out a chuckle. Alana smiled slightly as she replied, "I prefer women, actually."

Alana sat on the edge of my bed and scratched Oberi's ears. My heart ached as I took her in. I hadn't seen her in a year. She'd grown so much.

"I can't believe you're here," I said, grasping her arm. Charlie slid off the bed and sat in a chair on the right side of the bed.

"They don't allow anyone under eighteen to visit the Institute, but they made a special exception for Maverick and me, so we could see you," Alana explained. "Mav's with Mom and Dad. Are you feeling okay?"

"Is everyone safe back home?" I immediately asked, avoiding her question. We could discuss my health once I knew what was happening out there.

Ez frowned and dropped his gaze. Alana ran a hand through her hair, grabbing at the fiery locks. "It's... it was fucked, Ava. The whole thing is."

"What do you mean?" My heartbeat picked up. I was already expecting the worst.

"We don't need to excite her," Charlie insisted. "Ava needs to relax, so she can heal."

"She's gonna find out anyway. It's all anyone ever talks about," Ez stated.

"I can't lay here and not know what's going on. It'll shoot my anxiety through the roof," I told them. "I need to know what's happening."

Alana chewed on her lip for a moment, before she spat it out. "The day after you went to the Infernal Underground, I was at home with Mav. I was making dinner when I heard a sound like thousands of wings beating. We hurried outside... it was angels, hundreds of them, flying through the sky."

My mouth went dry. I imagined Maverick and Alana on the beach, her arm around him as she tried to keep them both calm, the shadows of angel wings scanning their faces from the forces above.

"I remember how the earth rumbled as they went on the attack. They used magical bombs, spells, whatever they could." Alana's voice was hoarse as she made the recollection. "Maverick and I rushed into the basement. The whole house shook all night. It was so loud we could barely hear each other speak. It was terrible. We didn't know if we were going to be dead or alive by morning."

My body grew cold with every word she spoke. My siblings were still *children*, and they'd had to endure the worst completely alone.

"Dad showed up the next day. It was such a relief," Alana said, letting out a sigh. "Luckily, the angels missed our house, but so much of Kinpago was damaged, or outright destroyed. They must've burned down half the city. The angels kept coming back, but the tribe fought them off until they finally went on the retreat. That's why it took us so long to get here. We couldn't leave until the area around Kinpago was fortified from other attacks."

Alana gave a heavy sigh. "Mav and I have spent the past week in a bomb shelter with hundreds of other Hawkei, praying we'd make it out alive. Kinpago's safe, for now, but we don't know how much longer it will be."

"But why? Why would the angels do that?" I pressed. "Did the Warden order them to do it?"

"It was a counter-attack," Ez replied. "Chieftess Vanessa couldn't get ahold of our parents once they'd gone to find you, because Jaymin had kidnapped them. Vanessa considered it an act of war and ordered Koigni bombers to lay siege to Celestial City."

My limbs were like stone, immobile on the bed. I refused to accept this. "No. Chieftess Vanessa wouldn't do that."

"She's a Koigni chieftess with Fire in her blood. She was looking for any excuse to get on the offensive and protect our tribe," Alana explained. "To be honest, I can't really blame her. The war was going to start any day. It was smart of her to do something about it before we became a target."

I had to see proof. "Turn the news on."

"But—" Charlie objected.

"I have to see it!" I insisted.

Before any of them could move, Oberi put his paw on the remote that sat on the bedside table. The small television mounted to the wall began flashing pictures.

It was already set to the news station. Disbelief gripped me as I observed the devastating images rolling across the screen.

Celestial City had been completely destroyed. Vanessa's dragons had laid waste to the entire city. There was nothing but the remnants of blackened buildings that were still smoking as residents picked through the rubble, searching for survivors.

The voice of the broadcaster played over the violent display. "As of this moment, five thousand Celestial residents have been confirmed dead, with thousands more injured. Over a thousand Celestials are missing, and the majority of the city's residents have been displaced, fleeing as refugees to other cities."

The screen switched to live footage of a subway station. Hundreds of angels were clustered inside, using the place as a makeshift bomb shelter. Everyone looked confused and upset. They carried backpacks, blankets, whatever food they had. Some held on to pets, clutching their cats and dogs like they were all they had left. Nobody seemed to know what to do or where to go.

A reporter began asking questions to a haggard-looking woman whose eyes were completely dark with grief, face marred with tears.

"Why are they doing this?" the woman wailed. "We've done nothing to them. My sister has children... I don't know where they are. We have no home. We have nowhere to go. Everything I had was demolished. My entire street is gone. What have we done to deserve this? Why can't the world work together! Please, we need to coexist in peace!"

The broadcast switched, showing footage from last evening. People pulled victims out from the buried rubble, some alive, but most dead, their bodies limp like dolls.

I watched as four angels carried out a pregnant woman on a

stretcher. She clutched her belly, which had been ripped open, her limbs twisted and her eyes far away. Her entire form was covered with blood as she begged the paramedics to kill her in order to save the baby.

"This woman was in the maternity ward of Celestial City's hospital when Koigni bombers began shelling the building," the newscaster announced. "We've just confirmed that she died from her injuries. The child was delivered via c-section, but unfortunately, showed no signs of life."

Pain grew in my aching middle as their words cut through me. It was easy to paint the angels as a judgmental society of religious radicals when you weren't faced with images like this. These weren't the power-hungry Deacons of the Celestial Church or the deranged Warden suffering. These were average people.

The broadcast switched back to the newsroom. The reporter straightened her papers as she stated, "Elementai citizens of Kinpago are suffering their own losses. Reports have come in of angel soldiers marching through villages inside tribal lines and committing acts of violence against tribal members in retaliation for the bombing of Celestial City, with victims spanning from the elderly to small children—"

"That's enough," Charlie said. "Turn it off."

Oberi put his paw on the remote, and the television went dark. Alana sounded haunted as she said, "It's truly terrible. Mom and Dad are moving us to *Hok'evale* once we leave. They don't want us in Kinpago."

"Is *Hok'evale* safe?" I asked. I didn't think anywhere was.

"*Hok'evale's* a place of refuge for all supernatural races, even though it's an Elementai city. Chieftess Luana has already said that all refugees of war are welcome there, and that the Anichi tribe will help everyone heal. If the angels attack *Hok'evale*, they'll be killing their own," Ez said. "They wouldn't do that unless they were desperate."

Alana stood. "We should find Mom and Dad, tell them you're awake. Mav will want to see you."

Ezekiel followed her out. I swallowed down a lump in my sore throat as I said, "This is our fault, Charlie. This wouldn't be happening if we hadn't gone to the Underground."

"It was going to happen anyway, pidge. We just struck the match."

"And that means we're responsible."

"What were we supposed to do? Let Eddie and the other Elves be tortured and delivered to those concentration camps without trying to do something about it?"

I was wrecked with remorse for everything that had happened, but guilt was worthless. It wouldn't stop this. We had to find a way to change what was happening out there while we were still locked up in here.

Kallie and Marcus entered almost immediately after my siblings left. If anything could ease the sadness in me from what we'd done, it was seeing their faces.

Marcus knelt by my bedside, while Kallie immediately embraced me. It wasn't the tight hug I knew she would give, but a gentle touch, as if she was a mother wolf protecting me from the outside world.

"We're so glad to see you, Ava," Marcus said eagerly. "We really thought for a minute we'd be planning your funeral."

Charlie sucked in a sharp breath, and Kallie socked Marcus on the side of the arm. "Ow! That hurt," Marcus whined.

Kallie ignored him and said, "I'm *so* proud of you. You're one tough bitch."

"I guess the Great Spirit thought so too, because I came back," I agreed. "I'm grateful we all made it."

Rishi jumped up on the bed and lay beside me, purring loudly.

I stroked his fur. "Did you guys learn anything while I was out of it?"

"I did," Charlie said. "Professor Takahashi came and spoke with me yesterday."

"We shouldn't be talking about this where people can overhear," Marcus said nervously.

"I'll put a silencing ward on the room," Kallie said. "It won't hold for long, so we should be quick."

Kallie worked the spell. Once she was done, she said, "Okay, Charlie. What did you learn?"

"Takahashi has an idea of where we can start looking for the merfolk key," Charlie began. "He thinks the key was stolen by an assassin, and that Kallie might be the way to figure out where she hid it."

"Hold on," I said. "Start from the beginning."

Charlie went over everything Takahashi had told him, and Kallie was contemplative as he finished. "If this woman's story is a treasure map to the merfolk key, and my origins are the way to discover who she was, then I'll bet anything she had to be a fae. I can start researching fae assassins right away, so we can get on the right track. There has to be a legend among the Arcanea connecting one of our assassins to the Atlanteans."

Charlie handed over the book of children's tales to Marcus, who subconjured it immediately. Marcus conjured another book entirely, a small leather-bound journal with thick pages. "By the way, Ava, we stopped by your cell and grabbed your journal. We figured we should go over it again, since it's been a while since we looked at it."

Marcus laid the journal beside me and began turning pages for me to look at. "By the drawings and inscriptions your Aunt Maddie gave us, we can see that some of the events she predicted already occurred. The drawing of Forevermore symbolizes its downfall, which already happened, and the page of black ink *has* to symbolize the Infernal Underground."

Marcus turned to the middle of the journal. "Then there's this, which Kallie and I realized already took place."

"The drawing of the girl in the tunnel of light, and the phoenix on the following page," I mumbled. I re-read the words *Ancestral Lands*, and *destined meeting*. Things started becoming clearer.

"My aunt must've known I would die and come back," I said. "That's what one of the lines of my prophecy means. *She dances the line both dead and alive.*"

"This journal is scary accurate," Marcus said, and he shuddered.

"So what's left?" Charlie asked. "What hasn't happened yet?"

"Well, the Institute hasn't yet caught fire, and there's definitely confirmation in this journal that's coming," Kallie said. "What makes it scarier is, if this journal's laid out in chronological order, that's next."

"Then we have the drawing of the Elven ships, the page of blood, the sketch of the half-man, half-woman, the crystal cave, and the Institute symbol," Marcus said. "Along with a bunch of scribbles around all of them that don't make much sense."

My eyes narrowed as I contemplated the drawings. "Let me read my prophecy again."

Marcus went back to the front of the journal, to the page with the prophecy's wording. I read it aloud, looking for clues.

"The balance between the light and the dark
Will be brought together by the light of the new dawn

A discovery of the ancient ones on the island of shadow
Will change the course of our universe

A second war breaches the horizon
Mountains will fall and villains will stand

The heavens will crumble and hell will open wide
Unleashing the demons that fester within

The path she will walk determines our fate
She dances the line both dead and alive.

A new world formed from gods of old
One from ashes or one from light
The choice is hers alone."

I scowled. "Half of the prophecy's meaning seems obvious, in this light. But the rest of the lines are still unclear."

"My prophecy isn't any clearer, either," Charlie said. "We have more keys, but we're farther away from helping the Elves reach the Blessed Haven than we've ever been before."

"Did you guys try getting ahold of my aunt?" I questioned. "I know she said before that she can't interpret what her visions meant, and she gave us everything she knew, but maybe she's figured something out she didn't realize earlier."

"We tried— and so did your dad," Marcus confessed. "But, uh... here's the thing. Don't be mad... I mean, you have the *right* to be mad, but—"

"Spit it out, Marcus," I complained.

"Your aunt's gone," Kallie said. "We can't find her anywhere."

"What?" I coughed, struggling to get air into my lungs. Charlie reached for some water and helped me sip it before he guided me back onto the pillows.

"We don't think she's been kidnapped," Kallie clarified. "Your dad sent someone to their house, and it looks like she and her husband left of their own accord."

"Why wouldn't she come here to check on Ava?" Marcus asked.

"Because she knew I'd be fine," I said. "But I don't understand where she would go, or why."

"She knows the Warden will start looking for whoever made your prophecy eventually, and that he'd figure out it was her," Charlie said. "She went into hiding to protect you, so he can't torture her to get information."

"That makes sense. I just hope she's safe."

The faintest of memories broke into my thoughts. It didn't come from my mind, but rather, from my soul. "Lindsey and Miranda promised they'd help me with this," I murmured.

"Who are Lindsey and Miranda?" Kallie asked.

"They were my mother's friends. They died in the Hawkei Civil War, but before they did, they helped my Aunt Maddie write this journal. It's their handwriting that describes her visions," I said. "I met them in the Ancestral Lands, and they said they'd be there to help me interpret the journal, though I need a special tool to get in contact with them."

"And where the hell are we supposed to get this *special tool*?" Charlie asked, sounding irritated.

"My mother already has it," I said. "I just have to ask for it."

"Hmph." Charlie sat back in his chair, and I caught his thoughts as they raced by. He was tired of our lives being interfered with by gods and dead people. He wanted them to leave us alone.

Unlikely. We wouldn't be left alone until this prophecy was complete.

I glanced at Kallie and Marcus. "Has war broken out everywhere? What about your people?"

"The Miriamic Coven moved to mobilize the witches immediately in defense of the elementals," Marcus said. "Vampires and angels both have been attacking Octavia Falls for days, but our wards are strong, so they can't get in. My mom convinced the rest of the priestesses we had to fight back, so that alliance has already been made."

"And the rest of the races?" I asked warily.

"It's not looking good. We're already outnumbered," Marcus said.

"The Atlanteans decided to make an alliance with the Celestials. The seas are no longer safe."

"What? But the Atlanteans sided with us during the last Great Supernatural War!" I said.

"And were nearly wiped out because of it," Marcus said. "The merfolk don't want to risk losing more of their population in a war against angels and vampires. They've been at the bottom of the supernatural world's hierarchy for ages. They think if they can appease the angels by helping them win this war, that they'll become accepted by the other races and it'll raise their status."

"That's not going to work. The angels and vampires are going to dispose of the merfolk the second the war is over with," I said.

"As far as the merfolk see it, they don't want to become the next Elves," Kallie pointed out. "They think this is their only shot at survival."

"What about the fae?" I asked Kallie. "They have to be doing something."

The fae had fought with the angels and the vampires in the last war, but they could change sides in this one. Kallie shrugged. "I don't know. My brother hasn't decided who he's going to ally himself with."

"Certainly not the Celestial Church," I said scathingly.

"No, but the elementals *did* attack first," Kallie said. "If I know my brother, and I do, he's going to want to keep the fae out of it as long as possible, until he has no other choice. And trust me, he's not going to be able to hold out much longer. He's getting pressure from all sides to make an alliance."

Kallie sighed and slumped in her chair. "Not like he doesn't have enough to deal with. Our heads have already been spun sideways."

"What do you mean?" Charlie asked, and he leaned forward.

"Do you guys remember when I was crying on the bleachers the other day?" Kallie asked, as if she hated to bring it up.

"Yeah. You didn't want to talk about it," I said.

Kallie scowled, and Marcus reached out to put an arm around her shoulders. "I didn't, and still don't," she said. "But you guys deserve to know. My brother and I... we're adopted."

"What?" I gaped. "But— you look so much like your mom!"

"Because we're still blood related. My mom isn't really my mom.

She's my aunt," Kallie explained. "My biological father was my mom's twin brother. And my biological mother was his mate."

"Ancestors," I said. "Are they—?"

"I'll never get to meet them. Both of them died in the Malovian Revolution, shortly after I was born," Kallie said sourly.

"Kallie, I'm really sorry," I said gently.

She didn't acknowledge my apology. "I don't really care that I'm adopted. I love both of my parents. They'll always be my mother and father, no matter what. I'm more pissed that they lied to me and my brother about it."

Kallie clasped her hands. "But there's more. My biological mother... she was a goddess incarnate."

Charlie and I both gasped aloud, but Marcus failed to have any reaction to this news. She must've told him everything right away when she found out.

"It must be shocking to you guys, but to me, it wasn't unbelievable," she said. "I just *knew* there was something different about me. I'm actually the daughter of Neva, the Phantom Doe of Shadow and the fae goddess of time."

"So that's where you get your time powers from," Charlie confirmed.

"Yes. I'm actually a *sidhe* fae, a descendent of one of the goddesses of the Arcanean pantheon. That's why my parents forged my birth certificate, and told everyone we were their children. My birthday isn't even my real birthday. They had to fabricate it all."

"Does your brother show any special abilities?" I asked.

"No. I think my biological mother's time powers only passed down to me, because I'm her female offspring, and her heir. My brother couldn't inherit them, because he's male," Kallie said.

"It still has to be a shock," Charlie replied.

Kallie nodded. "I was pretty pissed about it all, at first, but Ava's surgery and coma put everything into perspective. I hate to admit it, but I think my parents did the right thing. The fae world is so cruel, and if anyone knew I was the daughter of a goddess, things would've turned out bad. There's no telling if me or my brother would've survived."

"You still have the right to be mad at them," I pointed out.

"Maybe. I'm not sure." Kallie shrugged again. "The worst part is that

I'm not actually related to my dad. We're really close. Finding out I wasn't his biological daughter was crushing."

"I can't imagine." I'd go nuts if I realized Daddy had been lying to me my whole life about being his child.

"And I have no idea who these people are, these people that gave life to me," Kallie continued. "My parents talked about them every now and then, but not enough to know who they truly were. I think it hurt my mother too much to bring them up, because she and her brother were attached at the hip. She never got over his death. But I really want to know more about them. I'm just too afraid to ask."

"Will your brother remain king if the public finds out?" Charlie questioned.

Kallie bit her lip. "I don't know. Adoption is fully accepted in the fae world, because our illusion magic is our intention. Blood doesn't matter much, because once you *proclaim* a child to be yours, they are, no matter if you're blood-related or not. That's how adoption is seen, in the eyes of the fae."

Kallie crossed her arms. "But my parents lied about our origins to keep us safe, and worse than that, they fabricated legal documents and gave false royal decrees in order to do so. That would *definitely* call the crown into question. The governing body in Malovia would want to do an investigation, and that could potentially kick my brother off the throne."

"So we need to keep this a secret, so your brother stays in power. We don't want anyone governing Malovia that we don't know and can't trust," Charlie said.

"Exactly." Kallie let out a short breath. "But that's not all. My mother told me that during the Malovian Revolution, when I was just a few months old, I accidentally created some sort of time portal and transported her, myself and my brother forward nine months in time."

"Ancestors. I can't believe it," I breathed.

"Neither could I, but my dad told me they had proof— the three of us vanished for nearly a year without a trace, and no one knew where we went until my mother reappeared at the same spot she'd vanished in. To her, it'd been like seconds had passed, but for the others, months had gone by." Kallie shook her head.

"If you've got that kind of power, we need to utilize it," Charlie said firmly. "There's no telling how we could change things if you can go forward and backward months, or even years in time."

"I don't know. I didn't think it was possible before, because time magic is so difficult. I can't understand why I was able to transport myself and two other people through time effortlessly as an infant, and I struggle to make time stop for even a few seconds now." Kallie's voice was thick with frustration.

"You must've been triggered by something as a child, and it threw the magic into overdrive," Marcus theorized.

"That's what my dad thinks, but we have no way to confirm it." Kallie shook her head. "I wish there was a way to talk to my biological mother. I've tried performing ceremonies and meditations to speak with Neva, and it's like she doesn't hear me, because she never responds. She's a goddess— why is she ignoring me? I'm her daughter. I just want to understand who I am."

Marcus squeezed her shoulder. "I'm sure that your mom would talk to you if she could. There must be something going on in the spiritual realm that's stopping her from contacting you."

Kallie glanced at Marcus. "I just hope that by investigating my biological mother, I can learn how to control my own time powers. I almost wish my brother had demigod magic, too, so we could figure it out together. We've combined our magic to make spells before. But I don't think he'd be capable of helping me pull off time manipulation spells."

"Maybe he could. Twin magic is weird," Marcus said. "Rishi and I showed that down in the Underground."

"Uh... Rishi's a cat," I said. Rishi let out a loud meow.

"He is, but in Miriamic culture, we believe that the souls of our loved ones come back to us in the form of cats after they die," Marcus said. "I've had Rishi for a long time. He's more than just a cat. He's actually my identical twin brother, Dean."

I was stunned, but tried to keep the shocked look off my face for Marcus' sake. I wanted to ask how his brother died, but that would be way too invasive.

Kallie, though, was an obnoxious fae, and failed to tone down her reaction. "You had a *twin brother*? What the fuck, Marcus? Why didn't you tell anyone?"

"It's not exactly something that's easy to talk about," he snapped back, and he pulled his arm away from her.

"You could've told *me*," she insisted.

"He did tell someone," Charlie added. "I knew about it."

Kallie huffed. "Wow. You'll tell Charlie, but not me. I thought we were closer than that. What other secrets are you keeping?"

I resisted rolling my eyes at this fated mate bullshit. Kallie needed to tone it down and stop being a bitch.

"I wanted to tell you, but how could I have the words?" Marcus asked. "My brother *died*, Kallie. I didn't know if you'd understand how that felt."

"I know perfectly well how devastating it would be to lose your twin," Kallie said. "I wish you would've trusted me, Marcus."

He stared at her. "My choice to tell you things is exactly that. *My choice*, Kallie. I'm not obligated to do anything. The rules that apply to your culture don't apply to witches. You've always had my trust, even when I didn't want friends. But sometimes, I need your support more than I need your judgment on how little you think I care about you."

Kallie's expression softened. "Of course. I'm sorry, Marcus."

There was an awkward pause, one I didn't want to get any worse with how strained things were between them, so I asked, "Does that mean Dean would've been a demigod, too?"

"Well, identical twins in the Miriamic Coven are rumored to share a soul, so I think so. But I also believe Dean maintained some of his demigod powers even though his soul transformed into this new body," Marcus stated. "Rishi was able to fuse himself with my magic down in the Infernal Underground and use spells of his own."

Oberi crawled over to where Rishi lay and began licking his ears. Rishi's eyes scrunched up as his chubby face was squashed by Oberi's tongue.

"I knew there was something off about that cat," Kallie commented. "He's just as weird as Marcus."

"I'm not weird, I'm eccentric," Marcus objected. "Don't act like you don't think it's hot."

Kallie let out a— too loud— laugh. "You, hot? Those are two words that shouldn't go together in the same sentence."

"Aw, your flirty banter is so cute," I said.

"Huh?" Marcus gaped. "What do you mean?"

"Look, if you guys want to kiss or something, we're not going to care, so you might as well do it," Charlie teased.

Kallie wrinkled her nose, and Marcus blushed a deep red. "Huh? Why would we k— kiss?" Marcus stammered.

"You two like each other. It's time to get it over with," I insisted.

"Ugh. I'm not going to kiss *Marcus*," Kallie grumbled.

"Yeah, guys, quit being weird," Marcus said. "I mean, we only did it *one time*, and that barely counts with the situation that we were in."

"Oh, yeah." I wiggled my eyebrows. "That was after you gave Kallie CPR when you pulled her out of the siren lake when you two tried to break out during our first semester, right?"

"What?" Marcus blinked. "That wasn't how it went."

"Marcus, shut up," Kallie growled.

"Uh, *no*. It was the other way around. *You* gave *me* CPR, after you pulled *me* out of the lake after I threw myself in to save you from the sirens, then *you* started kissing *me*," Marcus accused. "That's why you owe me a fae life debt. Because I made myself bleed to distract the sirens and stop them from eating you. And pulling me from the lake when I was going to drown doesn't count, because you put me in danger in the first place."

I found it funny Kallie would lie about that. She liked Marcus more than she would admit to anyone. Kallie mumbled something indiscreet, and Marcus opened his mouth again to argue about it, but they were cut short when my parents and Alana walked into the room.

They were followed by Maverick. His eyes got wide as he surveyed me on the bed, looking me up and down. He was utterly quiet, remaining glued to my dad's side at the head of the room. He looked like he wanted nothing more than to turn around and go back the way he came.

"Hey, Mav. I'm so happy to see you," I rasped.

He didn't say anything back. Mama gave Daddy a worried look.

"Go say hello to your sister," Mama said, and she gently gave Maverick a push, but he refused to take a step forward.

"I... I don't want to," Maverick said, and he stared at the floor.

I felt like I was falling inward as he stood at a distance. He was clearly so uncomfortable.

Charlie stood from his chair and stuck a hand out. "You're Maverick, right?"

Maverick glanced at him, then crossed the room to carefully shake his hand. "Yeah."

"I'm Charlie. I'm married to your sister. I guess that makes us brothers now, right?"

"Kind of." Maverick took in Charlie's tall stance. "Mom sometimes reads Ava's letters to us. You and Ez had a fight."

"Yeah, me and Ez threw a couple of punches last semester," Charlie joked.

"Ez annoys me, too." Maverick nodded eagerly. "You look like you'd be good at fighting."

"I am. Want me to show you some moves?"

"Would I!" A huge grin spread across Maverick's face. Charlie beckoned for him to follow, and they left the room. I could hear Maverick laughing as he and Charlie horseplayed out in the hallway.

Tears dotted my eyes, and I said, "He's afraid of me."

"He's really young. He needs time to get adjusted. He was really scared when he found out what had happened," Alana told me. "He still loves you."

I wiped away a couple of stray tears. "Mama, I need something from you. Lindsey and Miranda told me it was important."

Mama's expression fell into shock. "Lindsey and Miranda! How do you—?"

"I saw a lot of people in the Ancestral Lands. Grandpa Liwanu, Aunt Stevie, even Uncle Ezra," I rambled on.

"You met my father and brother?" Daddy gasped.

"Oh, yeah. Grandpa Liwanu was a little grumpy, and Uncle Ezra was so lazy and lovable." I grinned. "I can tell he and Aunt Stevie are really happy up there. I know this is dark, but Stevie had a way of making death funny, you know?"

Daddy gave a wry smile. "Yeah... that sounds just like them."

"They were all so great. Lindsey and Miranda said they could help me with my prophecy, but that I needed something from Mama to help me decipher what messages they were trying to send from the Ancestral Lands."

"Your mother's compass," Daddy said. Mama glanced at him. He nodded, and Mama fished in her coat pocket.

She laid a small object on my lap. The compass was lacking the traditional cardinal markings, and had a small, spinning needle. It looked ancient, as if it had been passed down for centuries through the Toaqua tribe.

"Your Grandma Haloke gave this to me during my Hawkei wife training, before I married your father," Mama said. "It's a very special gift blessed by the ancestors, and it has power. The compass will always point you in the right direction, to what you need most. I don't know if I would've fulfilled my prophecy without it. I always carry it with me, just as a reminder of the Hawkei Civil War and what happened. It belongs to you now."

I knew this was exactly what I needed. "Thank you so much, Mama. I'll use it well."

I visited with my family for the rest of the day, until it was evening and they had to leave. Maverick eventually warmed up, although I could tell by the crinkle near his eyes that he was still upset. My parents promised me they'd stay as long as they could, though they didn't think it'd be for more than a few days. Both of them were needed back home, and they had to do their best to defend the tribe. I insisted I was all right, that they could leave.

I was strong, and I had my friends. My parents had to get my youngest siblings to safety and fight back against the angels, because I knew the Celestial Church wasn't going to let the bombing of their city go without severe repercussions.

On Christmas morning, I woke up to a large box on the edge of the bed, wrapped in Christmas paper with a big green bow. A bunch of people were already stuffed in the room— Charlie, Kallie, Marcus, Chancey, and Ivy. They'd been waiting eagerly for me to wake up.

"Happy Birthday, Ava!" Ivy sang, throwing his hands up. He wore a *very* revealing red fur dress, complete with a Santa hat and matching boots. "Mrs. Claus has made her delivery!"

Oberi barked, shaking his head. Ivy had put a Santa hat on him, too, complete with a jingle bell.

"We all pitched in," Charlie said as he passed out hot chocolate from Commissary.

"But it was Charlie's idea," Kallie added. "We've been collecting things since November."

A huge smile spread across my face. I *loved* getting gifts. I started ripping apart the paper, and opened the box. Inside was an incredible collection. Unicorns flooded out of the box as I turned each item over. There was a unicorn blanket, unicorn slippers, a unicorn coin purse, a unicorn sweater, and so much more. Everything in the box was pink and sparkly and had a unicorn on it.

I'd never seen such a display of treasures. I gave a squeal of delight. "This is amazing!" I sang. "Thanks so much, you guys!"

"Well, we all know how obsessed you are with unicorns," Kallie joked.

"Yeah, there's unicorn suckers, unicorn stickers, unicorn folders, unicorn erasers..." Marcus rambled.

"And a unicorn nightlight," Charlie finished.

I gave a tiny smile. Charlie was the only one who knew that I was afraid of the dark.

"Are you happy you're finally twenty-one?" Chancey asked.

"I don't think I'll be going on any crazy bar hops any time soon," I said as Charlie helped slip the unicorn sweater over my head.

My Christmas joy was interrupted when three guards carrying noxite guns entered the room. My stomach churned. The guards usually stayed out of the infirmary. Something was wrong.

"Can we help you?" Kallie asked scathingly, and Oberi growled. Both of them were looking to pick a fight.

One of the guards rummaged in his pocket. "Warden's orders," he began. "The four of you are to start wearing noxite cuffs immediately."

"Excuse me?" Marcus yelped, while Charlie immediately stiffened.

"Kalina Nowak, Marcus Taylor, Ava-Marie and Charlie Wahkin are all to receive noxite cuffs," the guard rattled off. "You've proven to be disruptive to the prison system, and therefore, have to be more carefully monitored. You're required to wear these noxite tracking devices until further notice, to observe your movements and put a restraint on your magic."

"I don't think so," Ivy hissed. "You ain't doing a damn thing."

"Yeah, we ain't gonna take this lying down," Chancey threatened.

"You want to interfere, and you're next," the guard snarled.

Chancey backed off, though Ivy didn't look like he was going to. Chancey's hand on his arm was the only thing stopping Ivy from pouncing on the guard and draining him of his blood on the spot.

"My wife can't wear a noxite cuff! It'll hinder her recovery!" Charlie argued.

"You looking for a ticket to Cellblock 9?" the guard snarled. "Because I have orders to take you down there for non-compliance if you refuse to put them on, and rest assured, the Warden will send *both* of you down there, whether your wife is stable or not."

Charlie fumed, but there was nothing any of us could do. I wasn't strong enough to be out of the hospital, let alone be thrown into Cellblock 9 with the rest of the thugs and murderers.

The guards slapped the cuffs on our wrists. My stomach churned once the cuff was on me, and I immediately knew that whatever was in this bracelet, it wasn't noxite. From what I observed once the bracelets were on, there was no way to get them off, no gap in the metal that we could use to break it. I didn't think the metal could be cut, either, due to the magical qualities.

Once the guards left the room, Charlie scowled. "These cuffs aren't noxite. They're filled with inferichite."

"The Warden must've used the last of what he had to make these cuffs for us," I mumbled. I couldn't really tell there was inferichite in the cuffs, because I felt pretty shitty already, but I knew the others had to be experiencing side effects.

"I already feel nauseous," Kallie moaned, putting a hand to her mouth. Marcus looked similarly green.

"That's bullshit. Inferichite is poisonous to you guys! He's killing you slowly!" Ivy protested.

I closed my eyes, because I felt dizzy. "I think he put enough in the cuffs to keep us sick, but not enough to kill us. He needs to keep us around, so he can siphon our magic for himself."

Kallie cast a small illusion spell, one where a miniature carousel horse floated around the room. It faded quickly, and Kallie snapped her fingers twice. She shook her head and added, "I can still cast regular fae spells, but I can't stop time."

"So it blocks our demigod powers, but not standard magic anyone can do," Marcus said in a choked voice.

"That doesn't help. This is going to make us weak. If we can't use our demigod magic, we can't defend ourselves, and we can't find a way out of here once Ava gets better," Charlie moaned.

"Yeah, and since these are tracking cuffs, the Demigod Guardians won't be able to break us out even if they wanted to," I said hoarsely. "The Warden would just follow us wherever we went unless we can get these off, and as far as I can see, they're impenetrable."

"Do you think we can find a way to overpower the inferichite, like we did with the noxite?" Marcus asked, before he gagged.

"That's going to take time," Kallie said. "For right now, we aren't going anywhere."

The rest of Christmas was kind of ruined, with how crappy everyone felt due to the inferichite cuffs. My family didn't visit for long, because they could tell I needed even more rest than usual.

Charlie had been lying on the floor of the bathroom for nearly an hour before I finally convinced him to go to the nurses and ask for some medication. He didn't want to leave me, but clearly, he was suffering. Oberi went with him, guiding Charlie to the nurse's station and leaving me completely alone for the first time since before we'd gone to the Underground.

I wasn't alone for long. I'd been wanting to drift off to sleep, but my eyes shot open as an intimidating figure strode into the room and shut the door. The dim lights illuminated the Warden's pallid face. He straightened his suit jacket as he loomed overhead.

He wasn't the only one who'd arrived. A canine with red lines running through his blue fur sat silently in the corner of the room, observing. The Warden couldn't see him, but I sure could.

Coyote Spirit was here with me. He wouldn't let the Warden hurt me.

The Warden's tone was cool as he said, "So here we are again, Mrs. Wahkin."

"Here we are." I raised an eyebrow. "Come to deliver more empty threats?"

"I'm not sure you could do anything about them, in your condition. You're more vulnerable than you ever have been."

"You're wrong. I'm more dangerous." My words were flat and

pointed. "I've been to the other side and back. I've witnessed things you can't even imagine."

I could see the greed in the Warden's eyes. He wanted that information and what I knew. To die and come back again with all that knowledge... he saw that as a rare gift, no matter what I'd given up to get it.

"I'm sorry to say we nearly lost you. What a waste that would've been," the Warden purred. "I wanted you alive more than the others."

"You don't get it. You kill one of us, you kill *all* of us," I stated firmly. "My friends and I will do anything to stick together, so we can take you down."

"Your sentiments are charming, but I have no doubt you'll all turn on each other when the time is right. Criminals always do," the Warden replied in a bored way. "One day, the four of you will have a disagreement, a difference of opinion that'll lead to division. Then it'll be simple to pick you apart, like picking the wings off a fly."

"You want to drive a wedge between me and my friends, you're going to have to do better than this." I jangled the cuff on my wrist.

"Oh, my dear, I already have. The inferichite cuff is only the beginning of your troubles."

"You think this little bracelet is going to stop me? You're wrong," I seethed. "Though I have to thank you for the Christmas present. I always did like jewelry."

"You're entertaining. I'll give you that."

The Warden paused. He glanced over his shoulder, as if listening to something. Then he said, "You've no doubt reasoned that it is I who has been sending dark spirits into your cell in order to demoralize and degrade you. I can assure you that is the least I can do, and I get stronger every day. I have eyes everywhere, my child. You may have outwitted me once, and in doing so, have caused a war that I wasn't ready to fight. But I am ready now, and I won't make such a misstep again as to underestimate just how foolish you're willing to be. You got lucky this time, Mrs. Wahkin. It'll only be so long before your luck runs out."

The Warden swept out of the room. Coyote approached me, walking toward the bed with small steps. *The words he speaks are true. He knows Charlie is the Elven heir. He has access to hell and all of its power. And he is working on learning how to use the inferichite crystals to siphon your power for himself. You must be careful, for you're in more danger than you ever have been before.*

"I'm not afraid. The ancestors and the gods are on my side," I replied.

There's only so much I and the other gods can do to protect you from this moment forward. The dark gods are stirring, and soon, they will be unleashed from the Eternal Torment. Then there will be war in the spiritual realm as there is war here on the mortal plane, and we won't be able to defend you anymore.

"I understand," I told him. "I won't let you down."

You mustn't, Coyote said urgently. *Whale Spirit and I put everything on the line to advocate for your return to this life. If you fail, we all do.*

Flames began licking away at Coyote's form as he vanished into darkness. *You'll have to be braver than you ever were before. We're counting on you... all of you.*

THREE

I was done with this place. I'd rather go back to the streets than be locked in the Warden's prison any longer. At least out there, I could take care of my family. I knew how to hustle for money and find a place to stay. No matter how shitty our lives would be on the street, at least I could keep Ava away from the Warden.

Here, this man was God. *I step away for one minute, and the man comes in here like he owns the fucking place,* threating *my wife!*

How dare he even stand in the same room as her! If I knew how to kill an angel, that man would be buried as deep into the earth as my magic could reach.

On second thought... maybe that wasn't such a bad idea. But it's not like burying an angel alive would kill him. The other angels would just dig him up, and he'd be even more pissed and come after us.

Fuck! How did you fight a man who was practically immortal? I clenched my hands from where I sat in the chair beside Ava's bed.

"Stop trying to hide how you feel," Ava insisted. "I know you're worried, but what the Warden did wasn't permanent."

"Not *permanent*? Pidge, you can't walk!" Hell, I didn't want to take my anger out on Ava, but she was acting like this wasn't a big deal.

"But I got to keep my life," she said. "That's what matters."

"Only because you fought for it. The Warden's playing dangerous games, pidge. He's already gotten you killed once. I need to make sure that *never* happens again."

"That's not your job," she said gently. She was trying to reassure me, but I was so worked up I couldn't see a damn thing past my rage.

I took her hand in mine. My fingers grazed against her inferichite bracelet. My stomach twisted— and not just because the damn stuff made me nauseous. "I can't help it after everything he's put you through. He took your life once— now he has to take your recovery with this damn bracelet."

Ava laid her free hand atop mine. "You're wrong, Charlie. The Warden and the Underground might be the reason I died, but he never took my life. I continued into the Ancestral Lands by choice, and my spirit would've lived on there if I chose to. I did what I had to in order to save the people I love. You know that I don't do a damn thing against my own will. I came back for a reason, and nothing can stop me— not the Warden, not my broken body. He can't break our spirits unless we let him. Screw the damn bracelets. Screw my diagnosis. It doesn't change what we came here to do— and we're going to do it together, no matter what."

Pidge was right. No matter what the Warden put us through, we always pulled through. I had to believe we could manage this time, too.

Ava and I didn't talk about the Warden after that. It didn't change how I felt, though. If anything, I felt worse. If I wasn't blaming the Warden for what happened here... I was blaming *myself*. I was the one who'd brought her back to a broken body in a broken world.

Each day, I was forced to listen to nurses and doctors come and go, with nothing more than uncertainty in their tone each time they spoke. I helped Ava to the bathroom, carrying her because she couldn't walk, and helping her with tasks she was used to doing by herself. After every meal, I listened to her heave, since she couldn't keep anything down. The hospital staff was pumping her full of morphine and pills to try and keep her pain at bay, and still, I heard her muffle the sobs at night when she thought I was sleeping.

The worst of it all was what was inside her head. I caught stray thoughts of hers that she tried to hide from me... how she was so independent, but had been forced into a situation where she felt like she was dependent on everyone. She had no idea if she'd gain any sort of autonomy again over her life and body, and that, to her, was terrifying.

My wife was in so much agony. I had to wonder if I'd made the right decision bringing her back. Ava had promised me this was her choice to return to this life, but I felt like my selfish actions had *forced* her into being with me, stealing away the one thing that meant the most to her... her freedom to live her life on her terms.

Sometimes, I felt I was as bad as John, and that sickened me. I was worse than a monster. I was no good for her.

The only solace I had was in knowing my pidge had defied the odds before. The doctors said she was going to die, and she didn't. Now they said she'd never have a normal life because she was bound to a wheel-chair, but they were wrong again. They had to be, because Ava-Marie wasn't like other people. The rules of physics— hell, the rules of *magic*— didn't apply to a soul as special as hers.

Once classes started up again, I was forced to leave Ava's side daily. The nurses wouldn't let me sleep in the hospital anymore, and the Warden had ordered me back to my factory shift. It was absolutely maddening being forced to stay in our cell alone, and go through the motions every day, knowing Ava was enduring some sort of treatment by herself. Her discomfort, both physical and emotional, came through often, and it made it hard to pay attention to what the professors were saying, even though I could tell she was trying to block it from me. I'd made Oberi stay with Ava, because she needed our Familiar more, but damn if I didn't feel lonely every second I wasn't visiting her.

I didn't want to be away from Ava, but if I didn't play along and do as the Warden wanted, he'd take me away from her for good.

I wasn't going to let that happen. So, naturally, I began scheming on how to solve this problem permanently. Ava couldn't be moved out of the hospital just yet, but once I knew she was stable, nothing could stop me from protecting my girl.

I met with Takahashi for required counseling the first week of the semester. He'd asked us to meet in Professor Hemlock's classroom. Ava was asleep in the hospital, so Oberi was with me in her unicorn form. Kallie and Marcus were already there when I arrived.

"Thank you for meeting me here," Takahashi said calmly. "It's safest if we meet here from now on. Follow me."

Takahashi led us across the room. I wasn't sure where we were going, until I felt a shift in the air when he led us through a doorway. A tingle spread over my skin, like we'd just passed through a magical barrier.

"Professor Hemlock's illusion room is the perfect place to meet," Marcus said. "The Warden won't be able to hear us here."

"Yes," Takahashi agreed. "That detail is critical, due to the topics we'll be covering in our meetings."

"Which is what, exactly?" I asked.

"Demigod lessons, of course," Takahashi said. "Please, have a seat. We have much to discuss."

Oberi guided me forward, until my hands felt the smooth wood of a chair. I sat next to Marcus.

"I trust that the keys you've obtained are safe," Takahashi started.

We'd hidden the keys in the Lair, inside a magical chest Kallie created with her illusion magic. Even if the Warden found the Lair, he wouldn't be able to get inside the chest. She'd enchanted it so only one of the four of us could open it.

"No one will find them," I confirmed. "Perhaps it's best you don't know, so the Warden can't torture you for information."

"That's a wise decision, Mister Wahkin, as the keys are meant for the demigods alone," Takahashi said. "For the time being, the Warden doesn't know I'm on your side. I suspect he believes me to be a neutral party, and more or less assumes I don't know what's going on here at the Institute. That's good, because he thinks I'm easily manipulated. We can use that to our advantage. The Warden has permitted me to return as your counselor, under strict orders that I report everything covered in our sessions. Of course, I have no intention of doing that, and I will be forging my notes to lead him astray. But I must be careful. People on his side have already died, and I intend to assist you as long as possible."

"Who's died?" Kallie asked, taking on a diplomatic tone.

"Professor Cusak has passed," Takahashi said. "The official word is that he's left the school to pursue other employment."

"It's obviously a cover-up," I said. "The Warden threatened to kill Cusak if our parents found out what was happening in the Underground."

"The Demigod Guardians are aware," Takahashi replied. "Our spies have confirmed his death. His body was found along the rocky shoreline on the other side of the island. All his feathers had been stripped from his wings, and evidence shows the trauma occurred before his death. We believe the Warden stripped him of his feathers so he could not fly, then pushed him off a cliff, so that he would drown in the frigid waters below."

My stomach twisted. The waves along the rocky shoreline had to be brutal. I couldn't imagine that Professor Cusak had died quickly.

"And now you want to give us demigod lessons?" Marcus asked, sounding skeptical. "How exactly is that going to work? These inferichite bracelets are blocking our demigod powers."

"In our first lessons, I will train you to resist them," Takahashi said, yet he didn't sound entirely confident.

"But you don't know if that's possible," I accused rather harshly.

Takahashi shifted in his chair. "The Demigod Guardians haven't had a chance to test the theory, but from what we know about inferichite, it is stronger in large volumes. You won't be able to resist significant amounts of inferichite, like the remnants around the Institute, but I believe you can learn to resist the bracelets."

"No," Kallie said firmly. "I couldn't stop time when inferichite was in the room with Jaymin during our counseling session, and then I sped it up too fast in the Underground. It's clear my time powers are unreliable when inferichite is around. I won't risk it."

"You must learn how," Takahashi pressed. "Need I remind you what is at stake? All magic is at risk if the Elves are killed off. They were the first supernaturals, and without them, our magic doesn't stand a chance of survival. I'm asking for your help not just to save the Elves, but to save us all. Now is the best time to begin training. The Warden lost the majority of his inferichite when the Underground collapsed. He will keep you imprisoned here until he can grow more."

"How's he going to do that?" Marcus cut in. "We destroyed the devil's finger he was using to grow the inferichite."

"The Demigod Guardians believe he has alternative stores of devil's finger, though we suspect the fungus is not yet mature," Takahashi said. "It will take him time to rebuild his arsenal, and once he does, he won't hesitate to use it against you."

That was why he hadn't touched us yet, why he'd merely threatened us in the hospital. He truly had us right where he wanted us.

"Right now, we've bought ourselves some time to grow your powers so you can get out of here and to safety," Takahashi said.

"How exactly will we get out?" I asked.

"The Demigod Guardians are working on a plan as we speak," Takahashi said.

Great. They still had no fucking clue.

I frowned. "That's not good enough. We're not doing anything until you can assure us the Guardians have a plan. Where will they take us once we escape? How do they plan to fight the Warden once we're out? It's too uncertain that they can get us out at all."

"They will," Takahashi promised. "It's going to take time and resources."

I trusted the Demigod Guardians to have our best interests at heart, but I didn't trust a damn person to get us out of here before it was too late. They wanted to be careful and take every precaution, but we were far past that by now. If life had taught me anything, it was that if I wanted something done, I had to do it myself.

"We'll attend your lessons, but I'm taking precautions," Kallie said. "I won't use my time powers until I'm confident I can resist this bracelet."

"Very well," Takahashi agreed. "I want you all to feel comfortable with your abilities."

Marcus scoffed. "I'm not comfortable with my powers as it is. I doubt I can resist inferichite."

"Marcus, you're a goddamn demigod," Kallie said. "If anyone can resist inferichite, it's you. The least you can do is *try*."

"I didn't say I wasn't going to *try*," he replied.

"In the meantime, we shall meet weekly," Takahashi cut in. "I will assist you in learning demigod lore and pushing the limits of your powers. We can't meet as often as I'd like, as that would raise suspicion, so I suggest you each continue your training in private. However, you must keep doing as you were before. Dropping your extracurriculars would look suspicious, and we want the Warden to believe he has defeated you. Marcus must keep painting, Kallie must keep playing on the football team. Ava and Charlie can continue their music."

I didn't know why Takahashi insisted we keep going like nothing had changed, because it was a lie. *Everything* had changed. We may still be locked in this prison, and I may still be married to Ava-Marie, but nothing else would ever be the same.

Takahashi stood. "Let's begin. You should each have access to your basic magic, as inferichite blocks only your demigod powers, and you have built an immunity to noxite. Charlie should still be able to cast Earth and Air powers. Kallie can still perform illusions, and Marcus can continue to receive visions."

Marcus scoffed and mumbled, "It'd be great if my visions were actually *useful.*"

I didn't think Takahashi heard him, because he continued. "Our goal, then, is to use the magic you already possess to overpower the inferichite. If your magic is strong enough, you'll be able to break the crystal inside, and it will no longer hold you back."

"And the Warden will have no idea," Kallie said, sounding hopeful. "He'll think we're still bound by them as long as we're wearing them."

"Precisely," Takahashi said. "Our strength in opposing the Warden will be in deceiving him long enough that he can't launch a counterattack."

"Okay, let's try it." Marcus' chair squeaked as he stood. "Maybe a battle orb will fry this motherfucker."

I heard the crackle of magic, then a high-pitched squeak. Kallie cried out the same time something heavy hit the floor. Marcus must've knocked himself out with his own battle orb.

"Marcus, you dumbass!" Kallie screamed. Her chair knocked over as she leapt out of it to check on him.

"Wow, um, okay, that didn't work," I said.

Oberi snickered from beside me. *It was entertaining to watch, though.*

I elbowed her hard. *That's our friend, jackass.*

"Is he going to be all right?" I asked.

"Mister Taylor!" Takahashi shouted as he slapped Marcus a few times.

"Ugh," Marcus groaned as he came to.

"Inferichite is not something you can destroy with brute force,"

Takahashi explained. "Believe me, the Demigod Guardians have tried. Inferichite breaks only from the inside out through strong emotion."

"Like it did in the Underground," I realized. "When Jaymin started torturing me, Ava got so angry that the crystals in her cuffs exploded."

"The crystals were absorbing her power," Takahashi explained. "But they couldn't contain the magic she produced through her anger."

"So all we have to do is get really angry," I stated. "That should be easy."

"Not as easy as you might think," Takahashi replied. "My understanding is that Ava was able to break the crystals in the Underground because your life was in danger. Summoning intense emotions outside the Underground will not be so simple. However, I believe you will be able to chip away at the inferichite's powers bit by bit. To begin, you must surrender your power to the inferichite."

"Surrender?" Kallie balked. "No way."

"Your resistance is what's making you sick in the first place," Takahashi said. "The inferichite is warring with you, trying to absorb your power, and you are fighting against it."

I shook my head. "Jaymin tortured Ava by trying to siphon her powers. Why would we surrender to this evil thing?"

"Because it's the only way to infiltrate it," Takahashi said. "You don't break a water balloon by pouring water on it from the outside. You must fill it from the inside, until it bursts."

"If we let it absorb our power, what's to stop the Warden from taking our bracelets off and using the crystal inside to harness demigod powers?" Kallie asked.

"The crystals are not nearly big enough to contain the power he seeks," Takahashi assured us. "I said this would not be simple, but I believe it will be easier than you think."

Honestly, I didn't really care how we did it. I wanted these bracelets off. I wanted to end these pounding headaches and get Ava back on the track to a speedy recovery.

Do you think it's safe to try? I asked Oberi.

She sounded uncertain. *I don't have complete knowledge on inferichite, but I believe it's worth a try. If anything is going to help you resist these bracelets, it's as Takahashi said.*

"I'll give it a shot," I offered. I rested my wrist on the table and placed my other hand over the bracelet. My stomach lurched, and I nearly gagged as the inferichite worked its magic on me. I let my walls down and relaxed my shoulders.

Relaxed was a relative term. As soon as I surrendered to the power of the bracelet, the world began spinning. I couldn't make sense of up and down, and I thought I laid my head on the table to steady myself, but I couldn't be sure.

"Charlie!" Marcus's voice sounded distant. I thought I felt him shake my shoulder. I couldn't tell, because my whole body was trembling. A sheen of sweat broke out across my skin, but I didn't hold back. If breaking these things helped Ava recover, then I'd keep pushing until I couldn't push any longer.

"Good," Takahashi said. "You're infiltrating the crystal. Now cast a spell. The more power you use, the more you can chip away at the inferichite's powers."

I wasn't sure I processed everything he said. All I really heard was to use magic. I cast my Air magic without thinking about it, and a powerful wind swept through the room. I felt my magic twist into a vortex, and something heavy got caught up in it.

Rishi yowled, and I realized what I'd done. I pulled back on my magic immediately, thinking I'd let Rishi down gently, but he continued to cry out from somewhere above us. He had to be stuck in the rafters— the same ones we'd hidden in when we eavesdropped on Hemlock's secret meeting.

"Hold on, Rishi!" Marcus cried.

"I've got this," Kallie said. She must've used her wolven telekinesis to help him down, because I heard his paws lightly land on the table. He scurried away to hide.

I was too nauseous to say anything, so I continued my experiment with the inferichite. This time, I cast Earth magic. The ground began to shake beneath us. My whole body convulsed in tremors, and I didn't know what was me and what was the earth. I heard a chair smash to the ground.

"Charlie!" Kallie screamed.

I had to keep going. I had to break this damn bracelet— for *Ava.*

"Charlie, cut it out!" Marcus cried. He smacked my arm, but it didn't feel like much.

Charlie, you need to stop! Oberi snapped in my mind.

Oberi poked me with her horn, yet I didn't pull back. She grabbed my ear in her teeth and chomped down.

"Ow! Fuck!" I screamed. My hand slapped to my ear, and I felt blood trickling down the side of my face. The ground stopped shaking, but the inferichite's power didn't stop pulsing through me. I doubled over and began heaving beneath the table. Everything I'd eaten in the last twenty-four hours spewed over the floor, and I kept gagging until there wasn't even bile left.

Everyone remained silent, and I could sense their concern from me.

"What the hell?" I finally asked Oberi.

You were going to bring this whole place down and expose us, Oberi said. *I did what I had to do.*

"Are you all right, Charlie?" Marcus asked.

I wiped my mouth. "I'll be fine. Someone has to do something to figure this out, though. How are we going to overpower the bracelets? Using enough power to break them could bring down the whole school."

"Maybe we just need a different kind of magic," Kallie suggested. "One that isn't so destructive."

"Like illusion magic," Marcus suggested.

I scoffed. "Kallie's taking the reins on that one."

"But Elves can cast illusions, too," Marcus pointed out.

"Except we can't make them solid like fae can," I reminded him. "Elven illusions are completely visual, and I don't understand that. It'd take a miracle for me to cast an illusion I can't feel."

I opened my palm as if to demonstrate. And I tried... I really tried. But judging by the silence in the room, nothing happened.

Takahashi cleared his throat. "I think we have a good start. We'll continue working with the inferichite. I'm confident that with practice you will learn to overpower it."

I damn well hoped so, because if we didn't break through the inferichite and learn our demigod powers soon, we would never escape the Warden.

Takahashi excused us. Through our bond, I felt Ava wake shortly after dinner. I hurried to the infirmary before my late factory shift. Oberi followed, and Ava seemed happy to see us.

"How are you feeling today?" I asked as I sat beside her bed.

"I'm fine."

She was lying. I could feel it through our bond. She was frustrated and in a lot of pain.

I reached for her hand and squeezed it. "Pidge, please, let me help you."

"I don't need any help right now," Ava said. "Honest."

Ava couldn't walk and had six-inch rods placed in the base of her spine, and she still didn't think that was enough to ask for help. It broke my heart.

I sighed. "I know you're capable of anything, pidge. I don't doubt that. But it's not always about what you *need*. I want to make things easier for you."

"There's not much you *can* do," she replied. "Most days, I just have to focus on not throwing up. My meds make me puke. I don't want to move too much as it is, because I don't want to injure myself more. You're giving me everything I need by being here with me."

"Just let me take care of you. It'll give me some peace of mind."

"If you want to help, you could rub my legs," Ava offered. "I keep getting phantom pains. The doctor says it's because my nerves fire in a weird way that makes me think I feel something, but there's nothing actually there."

Finally, I could be fucking useful. I grabbed lotion from the nightstand and gently pulled the covers off. I ran the lotion up and down Ava's legs. I found a knot in her calf muscle and focused on massaging that.

"Is this helping with the phantom pains?" I asked.

"It's so weird." Ava spoke curiously. "I can't feel you massaging my leg, but my thigh seems to be relaxing where I have a little more sensation."

I was glad it was helping. I hummed a tune while I moved my hands over her legs. I knew music always made her feel better.

"Is that my song you're humming?" she asked.

"Is it?" I feigned. "I've had the melody stuck in my head all day. I can't think of the lyrics, though."

"Yeah. It's my song *Summer Skies*." She softly began singing along.

Clouds above my head; it's freezing rain

I'm tired of these dark nights
The sun will come; the clouds will stray
I'll be ready for summer skies.

I smiled as I listened to the soft sound of her voice. I didn't think Ava realized what she was doing. This was the first time she'd sung since she'd been in the hospital. She didn't stop, either. She kept singing, moving from one song straight into the next while I gently massaged her. I rubbed her feet, then moved up her legs, until my hands caressed past her knees and were on her thighs.

Ava giggled, interrupting her own song.

"Can you feel that?" I asked.

"A little," she admitted. "It's different than it was before. It feels good."

"I'll massage you as long as you want," I offered.

Ava chuckled. "Charlie, it's not *that* kind of massage I like. Your hands are so close to... other places."

"Oh." I drew back. *Oh.*

"I want you to make me come," she said. The comment was so direct and blunt it almost made me laugh.

"We can wait." I didn't know how I felt about all this. She was still so fragile.

"Maybe *you* can," she teased. "I'm feeling pretty good right now."

"I don't want to hurt you," I admitted.

"I'll let you know if anything hurts," she promised. "We'll both go easy."

I smirked. "And if a nurse walks in?"

Ava snickered. "That's the fun of it, isn't it? The thrill of potentially getting caught?"

"You and your sexual escapades." Our time messing around in the closet was a good memory... but it was the last good memory we'd had before we'd gone down into the Underground, and we hadn't had any moments together since.

"Secret hospital sex sounds like fun!" Ava exclaimed.

"Not if you tell everyone about it before it happens." She was loud enough someone would hear her if they walked past.

"Look, I'm horny. If you don't play with my clit, then I will. Make your wife happy, why don't you?"

Hell, I wanted to; that was for sure.

Oberi thumped his tail against the ground. *You two fuck more than anyone I know.*

"I'm sorry, are you in the room when other people are fucking?" Ava asked. "If you don't like it, go keep watch."

You two owe me for this one. Oberi's paws padded across the floor, and he pulled the door open and left the room. He wouldn't go far, and he'd warn us if anyone was coming.

Ava took my face in her hands and yanked me toward her. I carefully climbed over her as our lips connected, falling beside her as she shoved her hand in my pants and immediately grabbed my dick. Hell, she wasn't playing around.

Ancestors, I missed being close to her. I lay on my side next to her, then tossed the blanket over her legs. I slipped my fingers under the blanket while I kissed her, lifting her hospital gown.

She didn't like to wear panties in the hospital. She'd told me once that when she sat all day, they dug into her skin, and she got uncomfortable. A bonus, because it gave me easy access.

I felt the scars across her skin, and a sense of sadness overwhelmed me. I didn't care that Ava's body was different, but I knew she cared... *a lot.* I wanted to make this feel great for her. I wanted her to feel sexy, because she'd always be the sexiest girl in the world to me.

My fingers slid downward.

"Mm..." she moaned. "That's more like it."

"Keep moaning like that and the nurses *will* walk in to check on you," I joked.

Just then, we heard footsteps out in the hall. "Who's a good boy?" a nurse said. Oberi's tail smacked against the wall so loudly we could hear it. The nurse must've pet him, because he sounded really happy.

Ava let out a moan for fun, just to tease me. I silenced her with a kiss.

"How does this feel?" I gently massaged her clit, then slipped one finger inside of her. Her smooth silkiness made my head spin. I was expecting her to gasp, or at least hitch a breath, but she didn't make a sound.

Something was different. I knew it was.

"Pidge?" I asked, and I kissed her neck.

"I can still feel you," she said, though she sounded unsure. "How does *this* feel?"

Ava slid her hand down my pants and grasped my dick firmly. My body jolted in surprise. It'd been weeks since she touched me there, and I didn't realize how desperate I was for her touch until now.

"Better than ever," I told her, though I had a faraway thought that she was redirecting.

"Good," she said dreamily, before kissing me again.

I couldn't help it when I moaned, and Ava bit down on my lip to silence me. I held my breath, trying to hold back so the nurses wouldn't hear. We were trying to be sneaky, but we weren't very good at hiding our passion.

Ava's tongue slid inside my mouth, and I kept massaging her. Passion welled in my chest. I loved her so damn much, and I wanted to pour my love into her. Once or twice, I had the urge to climb on top of her, before I realized I could really hurt her by doing that.

I was enjoying myself, but we'd been at this for a while. My hand started to ache, and Ava's kisses became softer, until she seemed almost withdrawn.

I drew away from her. "If you want to stop, we can."

"I don't *want* to." Ava sounded concerned. "This is all wrong. I should've come by now."

The last thing I wanted was for her to feel bad about this.

"It's not wrong, pidge," I whispered. "It's just... different."

That's how things were going to be from now on, I realized.

"Just... don't give up on me, okay?"

She wasn't talking about the sex. I grasped both of her hands and promised, "Never."

I knew things weren't going to be like they had been ever again. And I was fine with that.

I didn't know if she would be.

aVa-marie

FOUR

This couldn't be happening to us.

Charlie and I had the perfect sex life. As far as romance went, there wasn't any room for improvement. Neither of us had ever been left unsatisfied, and most of the time, we were forced to stop because we got too tired after endless rounds of sex... and *never* because we couldn't finish at all.

It was absolutely my worst nightmare. Nothing could be worse.

I didn't care if it was dramatic. I craved sex more than I craved food, or water. I didn't need it to survive, but I needed it to be *happy*. Those times spent with Charlie silenced the voices and made my crazy go away. Sex made me feel normal, and made me want to fly all at once, instead of reminding me of what a monster I was... like everything else in life did. It was more than fun. It was an escape, a promise that I was the only one he wanted and the only one who could make him feel this way. It was a secret world for us tucked away from the Institute and the bull-shit of the world. It was a piece of him I didn't have to share with anyone, and I greedily wanted that all for myself. If I couldn't sustain that, how would this still work?

"What do you want to do?" he whispered.

I damn well wasn't ready to give up. "Fuck me. Right here, right now."

"We should wait a few more weeks. At least until you're out of the back brace."

"Come *on*. You want it as bad as I do."

"Not when you're still healing."

I was going to be healing for the rest of my life, but I wasn't going to argue with him about it and kill what little was left of the mood. "Just... let me touch you for a while."

Maybe if I took a break and came back to it, it would quiet my wild thoughts enough so I could concentrate. I began stroking him, all while trying to figure out what the problem was. Usually, when Charlie and I messed around all I could think about was him, but in the back of my mind was the nagging worry that this might never get better. And I couldn't live with that.

Charlie kissed my neck and gave soft moans as my fingers roamed up and down his dick. I wish he could've kissed my breasts, because I was sure that would get something going on my end, but the back brace made access difficult, and maneuvering around enough to do this in one was hard enough already.

Charlie started massaging me again of his own accord, spurred on by my movements over him. He seemed to have no control over himself as he sank into some kind of bliss. I wanted to be swept up again in that magic, because I missed it terribly, but my thoughts were just racing toward worry.

At his touch, I felt tingles running from the core of me through my veins. I could feel *something*, so that was a huge plus; although, the sensations weren't as powerful as they had been before. At the very least, I was excited that he was managing to stimulate me at all... but it wasn't enough to get me off.

I noticed I had more feeling left on the left side than the right, which was slightly distressing. I tried to keep my focus on what continued to work instead. I wanted to enjoy what I still had, not worry about the nerves that I'd lost. But as more time went on, the enjoyment faded away, leading to nothing but frustration.

I felt it in my head before it happened. Charlie gave a quick, loud gasp, and his body tightened beside mine. An orgasm exploded across our bond, and the familiarity of it, and the stark remembrance of what had been, nearly pinned me to the bed.

Charlie froze. I drew slowly away, wiping my hand on the sheets.

His voice was embarrassed. "Oh... oh, hell. I'm so sorry."

"Don't be. It's fine."

"I really didn't—"

"It's okay."

What did I expect him to do, hold on forever? It was cruel to ask that of him. Just because one of us couldn't get a release didn't mean the other one had to suffer.

He sheepishly buttoned his pants. "You want to keep going, or..."

"I'm really tired. We should probably stop."

And I was. This whole escapade had worn me out. I was actually glad he'd managed to get off, because I didn't want to take that pleasure away from him, no matter what I was unable to experience. And despite how much I wanted to continue, I couldn't keep going even if I tried.

Charlie shifted as he moved closer to me. "It feels wrong."

"You don't need to feel guilty." I parted a lock of his hair back. "Your pleasure gives me pleasure."

"But when you're lacking that, it's like something is missing."

My thoughts turned a little darker, and I immediately shut off the connection between us. I didn't need to hurt him like that. He already did a lot for me. There wasn't any reason for him to carry this burden, too.

"Don't go blocking me out," he begged. "I hate it when you do that."

"Sometimes it's better that way."

"Just tell me what's on your mind," Charlie said. "We should be open and honest."

"I don't want to hurt you."

"That's marriage. Sometimes, it's uncomfortable."

"I know you. You'll just... think it's your fault I'm like this, when that couldn't be further from the truth."

"I won't blame myself. I know there are extenuating circumstances now." He lay on his back and asked again, "So what are you thinking?"

I let out a frustrated breath. "How can this be right? We're never going to have wild sex again. You know how I love rolling around under the sheets. We can never do that now. *Ever*."

"We can adapt," Charlie said gently. "There's going to be a long learning curve, but we'll get there."

"It's not you. You're perfect," I assured him. "But I'm... not. I came with broken parts already, and now there's even more to fix."

"You're not broken. You're Ava, and you're more perfect than I could ever be."

Perfectly fucked up, maybe, I thought, but I didn't dare say it aloud.

"I'm going to look at this as an opportunity, and so should you," Charlie said. "Maybe this could open up new doors for us."

I scoffed. "You think exploration is going to save this?"

"Well... we *do* like being experimental. If regular sex isn't going to cut it, we'll have to find more interesting ways going forward. I'm willing to try anything."

I was intrigued by the idea, but felt too low to get excited about it. Those hours we'd spent having crazy sex in the closet felt so far away now.

I caressed his forehead and realized there was a small bruise there I hadn't noticed before. "Where'd you get this?" I asked in concern.

"I hit my head on the wall last night by accident," he explained. "Bad dream. I smacked it pretty hard."

I passed my hand over it, and the bruise healed immediately. I kissed where the mark had been, determined to keep him close to me until the nurses kicked him out.

I knew sex didn't define a marriage, and that a lot of couples didn't consider it a priority. But that wasn't the kind of marriage I wanted to have. Charlie and I could survive anything. We'd already proved that.

Although I worried how strong our connection could remain if I wasn't able to be intimate with him in the way I wanted. It changed how I viewed myself, and worse, damaged my confidence, which was cracking into pieces ever since I'd woken up in this hospital.

A long time ago, the Warden had told me personally that the inmates who weren't reformed by the time they graduated the Institute never left this place at all. He'd promised he'd do the same to me— break me, in order to change who I was at a fundamental level. Back then, I'd sworn to myself I'd stay true to who I was, and not lose myself, no matter what methods he used to make me crumble. Turning into the scared little girl he wanted me to be would mean I'd become the real monster.

I was terribly worried I was already there. Because if the Institute could take *this* from me... it could take anything.

"AGAIN."

Doctor Marsh made a face as she and a neuropathy specialist assessed the results of my most recent medical test, listening for sounds and looking at a graph of electrical signals. I lay on the examination table and wished they'd get this the hell over with.

An electrical current traveled through multiple needles that were inserted into my legs. These needles were hooked up to several electrical lines that were connected to a machine. I cringed, although I couldn't feel the slight pain the nurses warned me that I might experience. My muscles were supposed to contract, but so far, they'd failed to respond to the current.

The procedure was called an electromyography, or an EMG test. It was meant to measure my nerve-to-muscle signal transmission, and see if there were any neuromuscular abnormalities in the area that had been caused by my accident.

I thought this test was pretty fucking pointless, because the answer was obviously yes— there *were* abnormalities— but the doctors had insisted.

"Ava, can you try lifting your left leg again?" Doctor Marsh asked.

I didn't know why she bothered. She knew I couldn't. When it failed to move, as fucking expected, she gave a grim nod and stated, "I thought so. The muscle tissue isn't receiving any information from the nerves in the spine whatsoever."

Well no fucking shit, Sherlock. Did she expect me to tap-dance out of here or what?

The EMG test took an hour, which felt like an eternity. Doctor Marsh promised me that the results of the test would help them determine the extent of the nerve damage, and hopefully give them a path ahead to start treating it, although she wouldn't give me a straight answer on what she had in mind.

I wasn't convinced these asshats really knew what was going on with me, and if they did, I severely doubted they knew how to make it better.

I wished Mama and Daddy were still here. They'd been forced to return home after the first couple of weeks, but they'd been able to advocate for my care when I just didn't have the energy to. I missed them so much that it ached worse than my injuries. If there was anything worse than doing this, it was doing this alone, without my loved ones.

Charlie, Oberi and Ez were the only family I had in this place, and I didn't want to ask more of them than what they already generously provided. Because of that, I felt like I had to shoulder the brunt of my recovery by myself. By this time, it was the beginning of February, and although I was only halfway through my stay here, I'd never been more ready to leave.

I slept all day after the EMG test, before a couple of nurses woke me up the next morning and dragged my ass down to another room for physical therapy. Most of it involved stretching, improving my arm strength, and learning how to use a wheelchair. I was rough and in a hurry, so I banged the wheelchair on stuff a lot and kept knocking things over.

"Patience is a virtue, dear," the therapist kindly said.

"Patience is for people who don't have somewhere to be," I responded, before I rammed into a rubber ball that went bouncing across the room and knocked over an entire rack of equipment.

"Sorry," I mumbled as the therapist headed over to pick it all up. I went to help, and *slowly* reached out to pick up one of the exercise bands. The back brace I was wearing got in the way.

I looked around for an alternative, and saw there was an exercise pole leaning against the wall. I reached for it, trying to grab it so I could hook the exercise band on the end of it and help clean up the mess I'd made.

Before I could, the therapist picked up the exercise band for me, along with the rest of the things I'd spilled, and put them away.

I felt so helpless. I'd been problem solving, looking for a way to adapt, and someone else did the task for me.

It really would've made me feel better if she had just let me pick it up.

I was so used to *just doing* things. Before, I didn't have to think when I wanted a drink of water, or desired to move across the room to grab something. I just got up and did it, and the task was done in seconds... seamlessly.

Now I had to adapt to a brand-new way. Everything in my life was completely different. Small, tiny tasks that I'd done since I was a toddler were suddenly brand new.

I had to re-learn life. And honestly, life was enough of a bitch without her pegging me in the ass like this.

I had a smile on my face after physical therapy was over, because the rest of my day was supposed to be free and clear. I was looking forward to turning on the small TV in my room and letting the noise lull me to sleep, but the grin slid off my face as I saw another nurse waiting for me at the door to the physical therapy room.

"You need another MRI," the nurse said, with a near apologetic tone. "Doctor's orders."

I slumped in my chair. The constant tests were wearing on my mental health. The minute they got me out of the intensive care unit they'd wheel me into the psych ward, if this kept up.

By the time the MRI got done, it was only noon, yet I felt like I'd been without rest for days on end. Even so, I couldn't sleep. I remained awake in my hospital bed, staring at the walls.

Modern science wasn't the only thing the doctors had tried— they'd had angelic and Anichi healers come in to try and help me multiple times a week, to no avail. Magic or medicine, it seemed like nothing could reverse this.

I didn't trust other magical healers to perform magic that I knew I could cast better myself. In secret, I'd been casting Anichi magic on my body for weeks now, attempting to heal my spine, to no avail. No matter how much Spirit magic I used, I couldn't gain feeling back in my legs.

I tried once again, taking off my back brace and hovering my hand over my middle. A soft white glow appeared around the edges of my fingers, though I ceased to feel the magic's warmth penetrate my body. The scars I'd gained from my surgery had more or less healed over, but nothing, it seemed, could heal my spine.

I let out a frustrated huff. "Okay, this is getting ridiculous."

Not being able to walk again was one thing, but I was determined *not* to endure another one of these fucking tests. One more night in this hospital was too much. I wanted out, and I was leaving now, dammit!

My brain worked ceaselessly to come up with solutions. And since I was in the hospital, time was what I had boatloads of. Unfortunately, my mind wasn't exactly up to capacity. I forgot everything. I couldn't hold on to a thought for more than two seconds before it was gone, and I was left wondering just what I'd been thinking about. I'd blown away half my brain cells along with my spine.

I just wanted to find a way to walk again, before the answer slowly clicked. My legs couldn't move... but my magic was working. My Anichi powers couldn't heal my spinal injury, but that was a problem with my body, not the power itself. I'd healed Charlie's bruise the other day, so I knew my magic was still up to par.

I began to theorize. I could attempt to use my Water magic to walk... move the blood to my legs and force them to maneuver the extremities. I'd seen Marcus reanimate dead bodies. Why couldn't I do the same with my living vessel?

My heart began to race as I thought of the possibilities. Oberi was off with Charlie, and good riddance, because I didn't want a lecture for what I was about to try. Brilliant people didn't find solutions to huge problems without taking risks.

Maybe other people had tried this before, but I wasn't *other people*. I was Ava-Marie. I could do anything I wanted, and if I wanted to walk again, I'd find a way.

With a tremendous amount of effort, I used my hands to lift my legs to the side of the bed, propping myself upright at the same time. It was painful and took a while, but thankfully, no one came in to catch me.

I took a deep breath and focused on moving the water in my blood. I felt it begin to rush downward, toward my feet. My heartbeat pounded against my ribcage, and I dared to put some weight on my right foot.

It held! I couldn't believe it! Although my Water magic was protesting for me to stop, I forced the magic to keep doing my bidding, moving my left foot, then the right, until I was walking again!

"Ancestors, it's fucking working!" I yelped— but not before I became extremely lightheaded. The room began to spin, and my heartbeat became so quick I feared I was having a heart attack.

My legs buckled underneath me, and my Water magic refused to comply with my demands. The floor rushed up to meet me quicker than I expected it.

"Ava!" I heard someone cry my name, then footsteps came as they rushed forward to catch me. I let out a fresh cry of pain as someone grabbed my middle before I completely blacked out.

I MUST'VE ONLY BEEN out a few seconds, because I was slightly aware that my brother was carefully carrying me back toward the bed, my feet dragging behind me against the floor.

Shit, I hadn't even made it two steps. My experiment hadn't worked after all.

"What happened?" Ez asked, clearly in alarm. "I saw you walk!"

I forced out the words. "I tried using... Toaqua magic..."

That was all I had to say. I saw the flash of his anger through my dreary haze as Ez spat, "Should've known you would've tried to pull a stunt like that."

"I had to try. Please don't call for help," I begged weakly.

"You severely threw off your blood pressure," Ez worried as he carefully laid me back down. My body sank into the mattress, experiencing sweet relief as my heart rate returned to a normal state.

"Yeah, kinda worked that out as I was falling toward the floor."

"That was fucking stupid, Ava. I'm gonna tell Charlie," he threatened.

"Ancestors, no! I'll never hear the end of it," I begged. He'd worry himself to high hell, and putting my husband through more bullshit than I already had wasn't my idea of a fun time.

Ez was fuming, but he took the chair beside me as he said, "Promise me you won't do anything like that again, okay? That was scary."

"I won't. It's clear that's not an option."

Ez heard the heartbreak in my tone. He pulled the chair closer as he leaned his arms on the bed. "Don't get down on yourself. I know you're desperate. But the rest of us are desperate not to lose you again. So please be careful, okay?"

"Sure." I put a hand to my temple, because I had a raging headache. I closed my eyes to get the room to stop turning. "Ez, there's something I've been meaning to talk to you about. I need to apologize."

"Apologize?" he seemed baffled. "For what?"

"I took the attention away from you... again."

"What are you talking about?" Ez grabbed my hand. "You didn't do anything."

"Yeah, I did." I took the longest breath my aching sides would allow me to have. "You got the courage to stand up to Daddy and tell him how you really felt about being overlooked growing up. That moment was about *you*. And I took it away, because I got hurt, and now I'm in the hospital, stealing your spotlight when you really need our parents' attention."

"I'm not mad at you for any of that," he insisted. "I said what I needed to, and Dad gets it now."

"No. What you said, about being sick too... you are, Ez. And you deserve attention and love for it."

"And I'll get it. Dad and I spent a lot of time talking when he was here. Like, *really* talking, deep conversations. I feel like I can adjust to my illness now, instead of continuing to run from it. In a way, you being hurt has actually given us time to connect."

"Well, at least that's a positive." I shifted against the bed and groaned. "Seems like I'm always the one who needs help, aren't I?"

"We all need help, at different times," Ez said. "I used to think some of us needed more help than others, but I recently realized I'm just really good at shouldering other people's problems, because asking for help makes me feel—"

"Like a burden?"

"No. Like... if I ask people to take care of me, they won't want me anymore."

Ez grasped my hand tighter. "It's hard to describe this, Ava, but I take care of other people. Other people don't *really* take care of me. You're the oldest daughter, so you can understand what I'm getting at, but I'm the oldest son, so I felt like it was my responsibility to be a helper to everyone else, and asking for that help in return was selfish, because I was the selfless one who was supposed to keep giving and not ask for any of that in return. And I didn't understand why I did that until I talked to Dad. He told me that he has this problem, too. We're both caretakers at heart. We show people we love them by taking care of them, but then we forget that other people can actually enjoy taking care of us as well. I don't have to be strong all the time. So don't feel like you have to, either, because I know that you're in pain."

Tears welled in my eyes as I said, "It hurts so fucking bad, Ez."

I could be honest with him, because he was my brother. Telling Charlie wasn't the same— he'd get upset and blame himself.

Telling Ez was easy, because he had a chronic illness, and he dealt with pain every day. Though he wasn't in my position, he could identify with struggling to feel relief.

"I know it does, but it's not forever, because all pain ends, or changes somehow," Ez said gently. "Someday you won't feel this shitty. Even if the pain is still there, it'll be different, more manageable. When I got diagnosed, you told me I'd feel better, and I did. So hold on, because this is the worst of it."

I squeezed his hand. "Tell me what I have to look forward to."

"First thing. When we get out of here, we need to start a band," Ez joked.

"Why not? What did you say was a great band name? *Ava-Marie and the Fuck Around Gang?*" I smirked.

"Hell yeah, it'd be awesome! You on vocals, me on bass, Charlie on the keyboard, and I'm sure we can teach Kallie to play the drums. Opal's already learning guitar. And shit, Marcus can even wave a tambourine."

I laughed. "We'd kill each other on the tour bus."

"But it'd be one sick band, though."

"It definitely would." We'd make some amazing songs together.

Then my heart dropped as I considered the reality. Starting a band and touring the country seemed just as implausible as buying that cottage Charlie and I always talked about. Right now, the only thing that seemed like a sure thing in my life were keys, prophecies, and darkness. I couldn't imagine living a life that wasn't villainous and criminal. Even if I didn't want it anymore, that's just who we were. We couldn't avoid trouble and sadness... couldn't avoid an existence of pain. Not even if we wanted to.

And it sucked, because we were in our twenties. We should be out having fun and making mistakes. Not worrying about fixing the problems the generations before us had created... not considering giving up, because that seemed like a better solution than continuing to fight.

I shook myself out of it. I'd never been in a darker place than last semester, and I didn't want to go back there. I refused to go into that pit again.

Ez noticed I was spiraling, and changed the topic. "Grandpa and Grandmother wanted to see you, but the Warden wouldn't let them in. Not Auntie Imogen or Uncle Jonah, either. They all came here, but they were denied entry. Told that since the war was getting worse, they couldn't allow any visitors, for security purposes."

"I suppose Grandmother Eleanor was perfectly cordial about the denial." I snickered.

"Oh, ancestors, she nearly blew the place up. The entire perimeter around the Institute was on fire. Her Koigni magic just erupted. It was something to see," Ez said fondly. "The only reason Grandpa managed to convince her to leave the island was that they'd be detained and sent to the adult penitentiary themselves if she kept throwing fireballs at all the guards. You could hear her screaming all the way inside the walls. Everyone's talking about the hot grandma who called the Warden a rat bastard."

"I wish I would've been there." What a legend. If I could become half the woman my grandmother was, I'd be a sight to see.

I winced as I heard the door open again, my body curling in revulsion. *Please, not another test.*

I relaxed as I saw it was only Marcus. "Hey!" I said brightly. "I didn't know you were gonna stop by."

He paused. "Um... we all agreed to meet up after dinner, like we planned yesterday."

"Oh, yeah... that's right." I'd totally forgotten— like I forgot everything. I couldn't remember a second of that conversation yesterday, either, and that worried me more than a little.

He stopped at the edge of my bed and looked down. "It's just... weird, seeing you like this."

"Go on," I offered. "Say what you mean."

"I don't want to make it all about me."

"But you think about it."

Marcus sighed. "Yeah. I... I keep thinking that if I had tried to hold my magic back when I killed all those people before I came here, it would be me in a wheelchair instead of you. Or dead, more likely. But at least then, the witches and warlocks I killed would still be alive."

"We don't get to choose everything that happens to us," Ez encouraged.

"Yeah," I agreed weakly. "And sometimes, even the right choices end up being the wrong ones. So how are you to know?"

Marcus shrugged miserably. "I guess."

I sighed. "Ancestors, Marcus, you're such a little emo kid."

"And we love him for it." Kallie strode in, followed by Oberi, who was bouncing rather happily. Charlie followed, looking a little less peachy, though his lips uplifted into a rather slight smile when he heard my voice.

"What are you guys up to?" Kallie asked, plopping on the side of my bed. Oberi jumped onto the mattress, tumbled off, then jumped onto it again with an embarrassed sniff.

"Nothing, just hanging out," Ez said innocently.

I had to find a way to thank Ez somehow. He was a good brother.

Charlie closed the door behind him. "Has anybody made any progress in getting these stupid cuffs off?"

He scratched at the area where his inferichite bracelet sat, and I noticed his skin was red with a harsh rash. I'd tried to heal it several times, but it returned every time, worse than it'd been before.

"If we had, do you think we'd still be wearing them?" Kallie replied. "Never mind, I just wear it because I *enjoy* feeling like ass all day."

"We'll just have to find a way to escape regardless," Charlie stated.

Marcus and Kallie eyed each other, and Ez asked, "Uh... escape?"

"Yeah. We need to break the hell out," Charlie said bluntly. "The Demigod Guardians want to get us out, but I don't trust them to take the proper risks. We have to leave by ourselves."

"Hold on," I started. "I'm in a wheelchair. Clearly, I'm not going anywhere fast."

"It's *because* you're in a wheelchair that we need to get out, before you or the rest of us get hurt worse than we already are," Charlie replied.

"Sorry to break it to you, pal, but we aren't going anywhere until these inferichite bracelets are off," Kallie protested, and she jangled the one on her wrist.

"We'll just find a way out of here with them on, and then get them off later," Charlie said roughly.

"Because *that* won't be impossible," Marcus muttered. "They've got trackers in them."

"If we wait for things to be perfect, we'll never try. I'm so tired of running into a brick wall every time we attempt to do something," Charlie argued. "There has to be a way to move things in our favor. We still have access to our normal magic, which means if we can get off Institute grounds and away from the wards, Kallie can cast a portal to get us off Darke Island. We can use magic to disable the trackers."

"That's a great plan, except we have to get past the fence first," Marcus said sarcastically. "We've already tried, and we can't get past the inferichite perimeter."

"We're demigods," Charlie growled. "I'm sure once we break these inferichite bracelets, we can come up with some creative solution the Warden hasn't thought of yet."

"What about waiting until next Christmas?" Kallie theorized. "The Warden let you go home for Winter Break your first semester, Ava. What if we just ask our parents to take us out of here during the holidays, then we elude the officers who are meant to guard us, and get out that way?"

It seemed ridiculous we hadn't thought of it before, but Charlie scoffed and said, "Doubt that would work. The Warden let that happen once, but there was no reason for Ava not to come back. Now that the war's started, he's not going to give the four of us a chance to escape. We can't wait that long, anyhow. Ava's journal says the Institute burning is next on the timeline. Frankly, we should be out of here before that happens."

"Charlie's right," Marcus said. "A new mandate was just announced this morning that inmates aren't allowed to leave Institute grounds for any reason during their sentence, no exceptions, save for if a student is under a court order. A couple of the rich kids' parents are up in arms about it, but the United Supernatural Union backed him up."

"I'm guessing no more field trips into Shade Hills, either," I stated.

"Nope." Marcus shook his head. "Those were canceled after our second semester here. I think the Warden was using those field trips to have students look for clues to Forevermore, and we sure led him right to it."

"I wish you had gotten out of here, Ava." Charlie rubbed his eyes. "If you had run away when your parents had taken you back to Kinpago for Christmas after the Darke Games, none of this would've happened."

"I knew I had to come back to the Institute, because there were still keys here," I argued. "Not to mention I wasn't going to leave you. The Warden knew that. It's probably the only reason he let me go home the first time."

"Yes, but if you hadn't come back..."

"I knew the risks of staying at the Institute, but I returned anyway, because here had what I needed," I said firmly. "In more ways than one."

"You mean the keys," Charlie stated bluntly. "Why not forget about them? We don't have to fulfill any of these prophecies."

"Yes, we do!" I argued. "We can't just give up on a world full of people."

"It'd be better than giving up on you. On us."

He had to let this go. This... guilt that was eating him alive because of what had happened to me wasn't just hurting him.

"Caring about people and trying to save them is what got us here in the first place," Charlie said. "Everything we've done in pursuit of the prophecy has only made things worse. The Warden found Forevermore because of us. We went after Eddie and the Elves in the Underground, but we were too late. And look what happened to you."

"We're not abandoning the prophecy," I stated firmly. "I'm not compromising on that."

"Then we'll fulfill it somewhere else, where we'll be safe in the meantime," Charlie offered. "Once you're stable enough to leave, we'll get out of here and portal somewhere safe."

"Where is safe?" Kallie threw her hands up. "The war is everywhere."

"We need to leave the magical community," Charlie insisted. "We can go to the human world. I know people in Detroit. The Warden isn't going to find us there."

Kallie scoffed. "Sure, Charlie. That's an option."

"We'll all go," Charlie offered. "We'll work together to survive— we can break out the others, too. Ivy's street smart, and Chancey knows how to run a long-con. We can make some good money together."

"And what's your definition of that? Because a couple thousand dollars a month isn't going to be enough to get us all by, let alone pay for Ava's care without insurance!" Kallie snapped.

"It's better than what's going on at the Institute!" Charlie argued.

Kallie's knuckles cracked as she bunched her hands into fists. "Charlie, you couldn't support *yourself* when you were living on the streets. How are you going to take care of Ava?"

"How *dare* you imply I can't provide for my wife," Charlie snarled.

"I'm not going to let you put Ava in a situation where she's not getting what she needs, because you don't think you can protect her here!" Kallie yelled.

The wind picked up in the room, and Charlie's body stiffened. I saw a yellow sheen pass over Kallie's eyes, and I knew the two of them were getting ready to fight.

Marcus stepped between them. I knew I had to say something to calm them both down.

"*Either way*, we still need to find those keys," I said, interrupting the argument. "Charlie, you and Marcus did that Miriamic locating spell last semester. You figured there were three keys on the island. We already found one in the Warden's safe. We assume there are two left on Darke Island. The Warden knows that what we're looking for is here. If we leave the island, he's going to have an army patrolling Darke Island's shores, waiting for the moment where we inevitably have to come back and obtain what we're after. Then we'll head right into a trap."

"If we're strong enough to break out using demigod powers, we'll be strong enough to come back," Charlie insisted.

I sighed. "It's not that simple, even as demigods. We haven't mastered our powers yet. We're bound by inferichite, and even if we can break these bracelets, we still have clues to find. If we're leaving, we're leaving for good. We need to find those clues before we make a break for it, because if we leave the Institute, I am *never* coming back. We already have a lead on the merfolk key. Promise me we'll stay until we find it, Charlie."

"That's a big promise to make, pidge."

Oberi reached forward to nudge Charlie's hand gently with his nose. *I know you desire to be free of this place. But our exit must come at the proper time.*

Charlie turned away from him. "Seems like that day will never come."

It will, Oberi insisted. *Trust me. Once that day arrives, there will be nothing that can hold you back anymore. It is my vow.*

Charlie's shoulders slackened at Oberi's words, but within me, they only caused terror to rise. It didn't feel like we were safe anywhere.

But at the same time, if we really wanted to fulfill these prophecies and set things right, we had to make the choice between remaining here and searching for the keys, or taking our chances somewhere else, where it could be even more dangerous.

Charlie squeezed my hand. "I'll go wherever you want me to. As long as you promise me we're getting out of here soon."

A lump formed in my throat, because I didn't know if that was a promise that I could keep. Leaving the Institute wasn't an option. Neither was staying.

Unlike Charlie, I didn't think we had a choice. Fate would put us in the right place.

We just had to survive wherever it took us.

FIVE

I was done with the prophecies. I was done being a prisoner. I was ready to leave.

Ava wasn't, though, and I'd made a vow to my wife that I intended to keep. I just had to be ready to move the second we found the merfolk key. Kallie was still working on uncovering clues, but it was my job to get us out once she found them.

And I intended to make Ava keep her promise once we had the merfolk key in hand. Once we got that key, we were out of here. I wasn't sticking around anymore.

I sat on the bleachers in the prison yard, listening to the sounds of Kallie and Marcus tossing a ball for Oberi and Rishi to chase. Ava was sleeping, so Oberi had come down to see me for a few hours. Chancey stretched his wings above us, flying as high as the noxite fences would allow, which wasn't more than a few feet off the ground. It was the end of February now and the air was chilly, but not too cold. We had some free time after class, and we were waiting until Ava awoke before we could go see her.

"I think we should assassinate the Warden," I stated simply.

My friends went silent, as if my suggestion had come out of nowhere. Even the pad of Oberi's paws on the ground had stopped.

I didn't know why they were so shocked. I'd been thinking about this for a while now.

Marcus was the first to speak. "How do you think you're going to get away with that?"

I shrugged. "I'm sure we can come up with something."

"We've already discussed this," Kallie said. "Angels are immortal, and nearly impossible to kill."

"There's got to be *some* way to kill them," I argued. "Getting rid of the Warden would solve a lot of our problems."

Chancey flapped his wings, then landed beside me. "We'd never pull it off. My kind doesn't cork over easily."

"Tons of angels died in the bombings of Celestial City," I argued.

"Yeah, because they were torn apart so badly they couldn't heal quickly enough," Chancey said. "You ain't gonna get a bomb where you're at, buddy."

"Ava did it," Marcus said nervously. "She blew apart the Underground."

"She barely came back in one piece," Kallie shot at him. "We can't try that again without killing ourselves. That kind of magical prowess is impossible to control."

"If you wanna survive an attempt on an angel's life, you're gonna need magic, and a lot of it," Chancey insisted.

"And we're demigods, so we've got access," I sneered. "Professor Cusak was found dead just a while ago, drowned in the ocean after someone plucked all the feathers from his wings and tossed him off a cliff. He was an angel, so if he can die, so can the Warden."

"It ain't the same. Number one, Cusak died because angels can't survive prolonged damage. His body couldn't rapidly heal fast enough after his wings were plucked, so it gave up, and he drowned. To kill an angel, you've gotta torture them longer than their body can heal," Chancey replied. "Number two, Cusak was nothing more than a glorified grunt for the Warden. Angels got a hierarchy, levels, kinda, with more access to power the higher you go. There's a big difference between some ordinary angel and the Deacons of the Celestial Church, who are basically untouchable, and the Warden's the strongest Deacon the Church has."

"Where do you land on the scale?" Kallie asked curiously.

"I got the wings and I can throw a harder punch than most supes, but that's about it," Chancey said.

I took an irritated breath. "I don't care if he's the Pope—"

"Deacon," Chancey corrected.

"— of his stupid church. He needs to die."

"You're barking up the wrong tree," Chancey pressed. "The Warden can't be killed. He's too strong."

"How do we know if we've never tried?" I challenged.

Chancey scoffed. "If you're gonna kill him, you only get one shot at it, pal."

"So we'll make it a good one," I insisted.

Fabric rustled as Chancey crossed his arms. He sounded curious as he said, "All right, smart guy. Let's hear your ideas."

"We cut his heart out," I offered. "How's he going to get around without a heart? He may be immortal, but angels still need blood to function."

I got excited at the thought of doing it myself. It'd give me some damn satisfaction to rip it out of his chest and squeeze it in my hand as I listened to his demise.

Chancey gave a cold laugh. "You think *that's* going to stop him? Angels heal at an incredible rate. That's not enough."

"He's not just going to grow a second heart," I said.

"Oh, he's not?" Chancey replied sarcastically.

"I'm sick of sitting around doing nothing," I growled. "If you don't want to help, fine."

"Charlie, you can't go after the Warden alone," Kallie argued. "Even if you could kill him, his allies will go after you. The only reason we're still alive is because the Warden knows what we are and wants to use us. But his friends? They won't hesitate to kill you. Even without your inferichite bracelet inhibiting your powers, a demigod would have a hell of a time standing up to an angel army."

"So we just bend over? Is that it?" I asked.

Chancey sighed. "Let me show you something, Charlie. Oberi, if you would."

I felt through the bond as Oberi shifted into a Fire unicorn. I nervously got to my feet. "What are you doing?"

Relax, buttercup. He'll be fine, Oberi said.

"Buttercup?" I balked.

I heard the sound of hooves clattering against the ground, then a hard impact. A squelching sound came, like a noise like flesh being forcefully sliced open.

"Gah!" Chancey let out a pained cry. Kallie gasped, and Marcus gagged.

"What the hell!" I ran over to Chancey and Oberi, and my hands landed on them both. Oberi had her head bent.

My stomach clenched when I ran my hand up her horn. It was sticking straight into Chancey's chest! Oberi had *impaled* him. Warm, sticky blood coated my hands as it gushed out of Chancey's chest.

"What have you done!?" I yelled.

Chancey sucked a breath as he took a step away from Oberi. I felt her horn pull out of his chest, and I heard the sickly squish of his flesh. Chancey grabbed my hand and placed it on the bloody gap inside of him. Something soft pulsed underneath my fingers. I realized that I had placed my hand into a hole in *Chancey's heart*.

"See?" Chancey asked in a strained voice. "The wound's already healing."

He sounded like he was in a lot of pain, but he was right. My fingers entered the hole in his chest, and it felt like the threads of a torn t-shirt knitting itself back together.

"Do you believe me now?" Chancey asked. "The Warden's stronger than me— way fucking stronger— so it'd be even *harder* to kill him. If I'm practically invincible, what are you gonna do to him?"

I scowled as I ripped my hand away. "You didn't have to do that."

"Yeah," Marcus agreed. "That was... intense."

"You weren't gonna listen any other way," Chancey said. "I just saved your life."

"Chancey's right," Kallie added. "We'd never get close enough to the Warden to do it— let alone have the tools or power to pull it off. At least not at the Institute."

I sighed as I wiped the blood on my pants. I wasn't giving up on my plan, but I was putting it aside... for now. "All right. Killing him is out of the question. Where are you at with the key?"

Kallie sighed. "I've analyzed *The Assassin's Destiny* wording, and I'm trying to find what I can elsewhere, but if we really want to uncover clues, we need to talk to Ava."

"She's still recovering." I didn't want to bother her with talk of war. She had to focus on her rehabilitation.

"She's going to be recovering for a long time," Kallie said gently. "You need to trust her to handle the situation. Her body may be broken, but she's still your Ava-Marie."

"I *do* trust her," I replied.

"Then let her be a part of this," Kallie insisted. "You can shield her from this war forever. She's Ava. She'll find out."

I sighed. "You're right about that."

"You'll have to go without me," Chancey said. "I have a paper to write that's due tomorrow."

I was pretty sure he was lying, because Chancey had never turned in a paper in his entire life on time. He was in more pain than he was letting on, which was fair, considering he was healing a hole in his heart. We walked with him all the way back to his dorm room, to make sure he got there safely.

I washed up in the bathroom before we went to the hospital. Oberi shifted back into a husky, and he barked loudly when we entered Ava's room.

"Aw, Oberi," she said in a sing-song voice. "You brought me more flowers?"

Grew them myself, he said proudly.

The hospital bed groaned as Oberi jumped onto it to snuggle against Ava. I reached out for her and found that she was propped up in a sitting position. I leaned down and placed a kiss on her lips, but they were all wet.

"Ew!" I wiped my lips. "Oberi, is that your slobber?"

You bet your ass it is, he replied.

Ava chuckled. "Oberi likes to show affection."

I shook my head and sat on the bed beside Ava. I placed my hand in her lap, and my fingers met something long and wet. I realized it was the flowers Oberi had brought Ava in his mouth. I twisted the stem of the flower around Oberi's ear, then placed the rest on the nightstand. I turned back to Ava. I wanted to ask how she was feeling today, but I didn't want to discuss it in front of our friends. I wanted her to feel normal.

Instead, I said, "Ez and I tuned the piano in the music room."

"Oh, I can't wait to hear it!" Ava gushed. "You corrected that b-flat that was out of tune?"

"Yeah, she sings really well now," I replied. "Except the A and G that are damaged on the highest octave. Ez is getting some parts from Professor Warbright, so it should be fixed soon."

"That's great," Ava said. "Kallie, how'd your first football scrimmage go?"

"My team won," Kallie said proudly.

Marcus stepped forward. "You'd be proud of me, Ava. I got a B+ on my necromancer essay!"

Ava shifted, and I heard the slap as she gave Marcus a high-five. "That's awesome! I knew you'd do well."

"I couldn't have done it without your feedback," Marcus said.

"I'm glad you're all *doing* something," Ava added. "This hospital room is getting really boring."

"Maybe there's something you can help us with," Kallie suggested. "We've been researching as much as we can about the assassin story that Takahashi gave us, but I haven't been able to draw any connections. Our library resources are limited, and we have to be really careful on the phone lines, so I haven't contacted my parents yet. Do you have any other ideas on where to start?"

"I've obviously had a lot of time on my hands, so I've been doing my own research." Ava sounded excited— like she was glad to have something to focus on other than her recovery. "I've read over the story dozens of times, but it's written like a riddle. It's hard to understand without context, but I'm thinking if we can just uncover one clue, we can unravel the story and make sense of it."

Something rattled, and Ava continued. "My mother's compass is supposed to help, so I was thinking you guys could take it and..."

She trailed off, sounding confused.

"What is it?" I asked.

"The compass..." Ava whispered. "It always spins around in a circle, like it can't figure out which way to point, but it actually stopped this time. On Kallie."

"Me?" Kallie took a few steps back.

"It's still on you. Go over there," Ava instructed.

Kallie walked to the other side of the room, and Ava hitched a breath. "It's following you."

"We already know that the story's connected to Kallie in some way," Marcus mused. "But the compass has never pointed to her before."

"Maybe the compass isn't pointing at me." Kallie's coat rustled. "It could be pointing to *this*. It's a family grimoire my mom gave me when she and my dad visited a few months ago, written by my grandfather. It was lost during the Malovian Revolution, but when the royal palace was rebuilt after the fae war was over, it was found in the rubble. I'm the third generation to own it. I guess the grimoire helped my mother establish her place on the throne. It's very powerful."

"Can I see?" Marcus asked. His footsteps sounded as he walked around the room.

"The needle's following the book," Ava said.

"That must mean our first clue is in my grimoire!" Kallie exclaimed.

Kallie and Marcus gathered closely around the bed. Pages rustled as they flipped through the book.

"There must be a spell in here that can help us..." Kallie theorized. "Wait, go back!"

Kallie must've taken the book from Marcus, because I heard the sound of pages flipping in her hands. "It's got to be one of these," she stated confidently. "The compass is pointing to this section of locator spells."

"Marcus and I tried a locator spell," I reminded her. "We only got vague visions. Even Ava's compass can't point to the keys."

"We haven't tried a fae spell yet," Kallie said. "A strong spell might be able to lead us directly to the merfolk key."

"Then why hasn't the Warden used a fae spell?" I wondered.

"For one, he doesn't have access to the right ones," Kallie said. "The spells in this book belong to my family. My grandfather invented most of them. Two, the Warden's not a demigod. That's the only reason Marcus' locator spell worked in the first place."

"Your demigod powers are blocked by inferichite, though," I pointed out.

"But the compass wants us to try it, so I say we forge onward," Kallie suggested. "But... not here. We can't get caught, and we *definitely* can't let the Warden find out I have this grimoire. If we can locate a key with this spell, so can he."

"You guys should go to one of the abandoned cell blocks," Ava said. "No one ever goes down there."

"We're not just going to pursue this without you," I stated.

Ava sighed. "You're going to have to. I'm not getting out of here for a few more days, and we're not waiting that long. A nurse could come in at any moment. You have to go somewhere private to perform the spell. Kallie shouldn't even have that grimoire out right now."

Kallie quickly shoved it back into her coat. "We'll let you know what we find."

I reluctantly left Ava's side. Part of me didn't want to pursue any of this without her. Another part of me wanted to leave her out of this as much as possible, for her own safety.

We left the hospital and snuck toward the abandoned Cellblock 7. The hall was supposed to be locked down so students couldn't get in here, but the locks had been broken a long time ago. We found an empty dorm room and ducked inside. Oberi kept close to my side as we gathered around Kallie's grimoire.

"There are a few different spells here," Kallie said, sounding thoughtful. "An Unseelie spell is going to be difficult, but I can definitely pull off this illusion spell. I'll create a glowing arrow that should point us toward the key, similar to Ava's compass. It says here in my mother's notes that one of her friends created it, so we can trust it."

I heard a strange sound, a distinctive hum that rose and fell in pitch as it moved through the air. I felt the magical arrow spinning with my Air magic, trying to hone in on something nearby. Something swished through the air, and I noticed the heat of the glowing arrow from where I stood.

"Kallie..." Marcus said, warning her. "It's getting too hot. You should call off the spell."

"The key is nearby, it has to be!" Kallie exclaimed in excitement. "The arrow is getting excited. I bet it's—"

"Kallie!" Marcus shouted, but his voice was cut off as the arrow gave a high-pitched squeal.

An explosion blasted us backward as the arrow shattered. I landed flat on my back, squashing Rishi's tail beneath me. He yowled loudly, and I rolled over to free him.

That was not fun, Oberi complained as he clambered off of me. *Thanks for being my pillow!*

He stepped on my face as he got up. I grumbled and pushed him away.

Kallie coughed as she righted herself. "I don't know what happened! The spell was working fine."

Marcus groaned as he got to his feet. "Clearly, the easiest spell isn't going to work, because the keys are too strong. We need the heaviest spell we can get."

"Definitely," Kallie agreed. "The spell must've backfired because it couldn't overpower the magic inside the key."

"How do we perform the other spell?" I asked.

"It's an Unseelie spell," Kallie said. "There are two different types of fae magic— Seelie magic, which is known as light magic, and is pulled from inside of you; and Unseelie magic, which is known as dark magic and pulls from objects around you. Unseelie magic was banned in my country until my mother came into power. She's a powerful Unseelie fae, and so was her brother. I know some of that power was passed on to me... though I've hardly dabbled in Unseelie magic."

"Why?" Marcus asked, and I agreed. It wasn't like Kallie to avoid something that gave her power.

"Because it's very dangerous," Kallie admitted. "I'm... afraid of it."

Kallie never admitted to being afraid of anything. That told me Unseelie magic wasn't anything to mess around with. But that must be why the compass wanted us to try it, because it was the closest to demigod magic we had right now.

"My mother insists that I'm strong enough, that I've got talent," Kallie continued, seemingly speaking her own thoughts aloud. "Most fae can't perform Unseelie magic, because you've got to have it in your blood and be descended from ancient dark fae."

Her voice became soft as she turned away from us. "My brother's a natural at it. He can cast Unseelie spells without breaking a sweat. But it's not so easy for me. I'm different— people have considered me a monster and a freak since I was a child. I don't want to make that reputation worse. I'm worried about the dark magic taking over me and turning me into something I'm not. Something I can't control."

"That sounds like what happened when you tried to kill your brother," Marcus mused. "Did you use Unseelie magic against him?"

"I believe so, but I can't remember," Kallie confessed. "I think I must've cast an Unseelie spell to gain revenge, and it took control of me. That's why I lost my memory of that night. It's the only thing that makes sense to me. I haven't touched Unseelie magic since, because I don't want to lose myself."

"If we want to find the keys, we're going to have to make some tough choices, Kallie," I reminded her.

Kallie sighed. "I know. If Ava can do what she did for all of us, I can do this for her. Just... promise to bring me out of it if I lose control, okay?"

"We won't let you lose yourself. Not ever," Marcus promised.

"Then let's do this. Hold this, Charlie." Kallie handed me the grimoire.

"How does it work?" I asked.

"I need to prick my finger and read the incantation as I bleed onto the petals of a flower."

I reached into Oberi's fur and pulled the flower off his ear. "Here's a flower."

"Thank you," Kallie said. "I can create a solid pin with my illusion magic no problem. Let's get started."

We sat on the floor, and Kallie placed the flower between us. She drew a sharp breath as she pricked herself. *"Fae ancestors of the briar, lead me to my heart's desire."*

Something happened. Wind picked up and began spinning around us in a vortex around the room. I tried to manipulate it with my Air magic and failed.

"It must be working," Marcus whispered to me. "Kallie's gone into some sort of trance—"

Marcus didn't finish his sentence before I heard the *thud* of Kallie's body dropping to the floor. Marcus and I rushed forward at the same time. I reached out to find her body stiff and cold as ice. I could feel her magic rolling off of her with my Elf powers, but it was like she'd turned from a living, breathing person into a corpse in seconds. She was still alive, but we didn't know for how long.

Hell, she hadn't been kidding about Unseelie magic. It wasn't something to fuck with if you didn't know what you were doing, and of course, we had no fucking clue.

"Kallie!" Marcus yelled, but she didn't respond. She remained immobile and silent, like a statue.

Her worst fear had already happened. She'd lost control of the spell, and her mind had gone with it.

"Marcus, do something!" I screamed.

"I'm not a doctor!" he snapped.

"You're a warlock *and* her bonded mate," I reminded him. "Can't you get inside her head, pull her out of this?"

"Uh... m— maybe," he stammered.

I grabbed his shoulder tightly to help bring him back to the moment. We couldn't lose Kallie because Marcus was panicking. "Then do it! She needs you!"

Marcus gulped, then positioned himself over Kallie. He laid his hands on her, and his whole body jolted.

"Marcus?" I shook him, but he didn't answer. "Oberi, what's happening!?"

He's gone into her subconscious, Oberi said. *He looks like he's having a vision.*

I sat back on my heels... waiting. Nothing changed.

"How long is it going to take?" I demanded. The seconds ticked by, and Kallie was still unresponsive.

Magic like this takes time.

"Not this much time," I retorted. "They're trapped!"

Well, gods, they're not ordering a pizza! Oberi snapped.

I touched Kallie's arm. If Kallie got any colder, her body would freeze. I could already feel frost creeping across her skin. This spell was strong enough to kill her.

I reached out to shake Marcus and pull him out of the trance, but Rishi swiped his claws out and cut my hand. At the same time, Oberi grabbed the back of my shirt in his teeth and yanked me away. I landed on my back.

"Oberi, what the hell!? I'm trying to help them!" I yelled. I scrambled to my feet, but Oberi planted himself in front of me.

Charlie, you can't! Oberi barked.

"Their bodies can't handle this!"

You have to trust your friends, Oberi insisted. *The kind of work you're doing to find these keys involves risk, and if you want to do it all by yourself, you might as well turn back now, or else we're done for!*

I was about to argue further, until Marcus coughed. It sounded like he was gasping for air after holding his breath for too long.

"Marcus, you with me?" I held my breath, awaiting a response.

Finally, he rasped, "I'm okay."

Relief flooded through me. I reached for Kallie's hand and found warmth returning to her skin. A small noise escaped her throat.

"Kallie, thank the Goddess," Marcus said breathlessly. "You're safe. I've got you."

Marcus must've curled her in his arms, because I heard the muffled sound of her gasps, like she was burying her face in his chest for comfort. Kallie's voice broke as she said, "It didn't work."

"What happened?" I asked.

Kallie steadied her breath, though she still sounded shook. "I tried to locate the merfolk key, but the magic is too strong. My visions shifted, and I saw... I don't even *know* what I saw, really. It must've been the merfolk key, but it was like I was looking into the past. I saw a woman steal the key from a vault somewhere in Atlantis. It was almost like I was looking *through* her eyes. Then Marcus appeared... but he wasn't supposed to be there."

"You were trapped inside the vision," Marcus whispered. "I got you out."

"Could this woman have been the assassin in the story?" I asked.

"I think so, but the spell wasn't supposed to take me to the past," Kallie said. "I was supposed to be able to find the key as it is today."

I pressed my lips together. "We know the keys are protected by magic, so maybe the spell had to change, because that's all it could give you."

"Then I have to figure out who this woman was, and how to access her memories again," Kalie decided.

Marcus wasn't on board with that idea. "You're not doing that spell again. It's too dangerous."

Kallie staggered out of his arms and picked up her grimoire. "There might be other spells I can use. I'm going to keep looking for clues. If I can see into her memory once, then I can do it again. If we're lucky... we just might find out where she hid the merfolk key."

"We should rest before you try again," Marcus suggested.

Marcus and I helped Kallie to her feet, and she swayed. "You're probably right," she admitted. "But we're starting back up at it tomorrow."

She could be just as stubborn as Ava. Our lack of progress made me feel worse that she wasn't here with us right now.

Ava was the heart and soul of this team. She always managed to piece things together quicker than the rest of us could. She saw patterns and clues we didn't. I was convinced the three of us weren't getting anywhere close to the merfolk key without Ava's help.

No matter how badly I wanted to escape the Institute, it was clear we weren't going anywhere.

ava-marie

SIX

It felt like a fucking eternity before I was finally—*finally*—released from the infirmary. My ten weeks were up, but I'd had to spend a couple extra days there beyond what we'd planned, because the damn inferichite bracelet was slowing down my recovery.

I wasn't completely in the clear. I still had to go back for physical therapy several times per week— ugh— and I was on a constant rotation of painkillers, yet at least now I had some breathing room.

But I was out of that damn bed, and that was all that mattered.

I couldn't wait to get back to my life. I knew Charlie had missed going to class with me and meeting up with me in the cafeteria for lunch. Sleeping apart from each other for over two months without end was absolutely grueling.

It was over now, so I told myself that I never needed to stay in that hospital again. For any reason.

"About damn time," I grumbled as Charlie wheeled me out of the hospital. I drew a deep breath. "Fresh fucking air."

"Now that you're free, where do you want to go?" he asked.

Psh. I wasn't free. Not really. We were still prisoners, as the Warden liked to remind us every fucking day.

But at least in the Elementai greenhouse or the Atlantean pool, we could pretend things weren't so bad.

"Anywhere, as long as it's far away from this place," I stated, flinging out an arm. "Lead the way!"

Oberi walked by my side as Charlie pushed my wheelchair through the school. It was such a different dynamic... I'd always been the one leading *him* around. Now *he* had to navigate for *me*.

It wasn't easy. I told him where to go, but I was terrible at giving directions, and him pushing me around was kind of equal to Charlie driving a car. He bumped my wheelchair into two corners, and rolled over a cat's tail. He nearly ran Oberi over, who barked and shouted a few obscenities at us.

Fucking all, Charlie, who can't walk, Ava or you? Oberi snapped at him.

"Just go forward," I instructed.

"I don't know where *forward* is," Charlie grumbled.

I huffed. I knew I wasn't communicating well, but my brain was still foggy, and it was hard for the thoughts in my head to travel down to my mouth.

"It's okay," I said. "My arms work. I can do it."

"I'll get it," he told me. "I'm just getting used to it."

If I was being honest, I didn't have the strength to push myself around the prison at all hours of the day, at least not yet. I depended on Charlie to help me get around now.

Conversation buzzed through the halls, most of it vulgar slurs aimed at other magical races. We tried to avoid the crowds as much as possible, but we could still hear shouts coming from the cafeteria when we passed.

A crowd had formed at the entry. Two students circled each other, an Elementai and an angel. The angel had his wings out, and the Elementai had a ball of Fire in his hand, ready to strike.

Fights weren't exactly uncommon at the Institute, but this one seemed different. "Stop for a minute," I told Charlie.

"We don't need to get involved," he said immediately.

Before we could move on, the angel said, "I'm sick of looking at your kind, hanging around here like some sort of fucking disease. The world would be better if monsters like you didn't exist!"

This wasn't your daily Institute trash-talk. This fight meant something.

The Elementai laughed, but it wasn't funny at all... it sounded dark. "I'm not afraid of you. Your people were ripped apart by *our* Firebombs."

That really pissed the angel off. His face went red as he screamed, "My mother's *dead*, and it's your fault, you savage!"

"Your mom deserved it!" the Elementai shouted back. "My sister was assaulted by your people!"

"Your sister's a dyke," the angel growled. "She deserved far worse than what she got."

The angel's words made me sick. A loud growl came from the crowd. A man stormed into the center of the circle, erupting into a griffin. A shifter had taken on their animal form to defend the Elementai.

"Take that back," the griffin threatened. *"Or you'll live to regret it."*

"And what are you gonna do about it, traitor? You gonna switch sides in order to win, since we lost the first war?" A vampire girl stepped out of the crowd. She stood tall beside the angel, like she was certain that he was right.

The crowd around the area was quickly beginning to take sides. Students paired up with either the Elementai or the angel, ready to partake in something that was much bigger than a prison brawl. These people were angry about the attacks and battles that were happening in the world out there, and they wanted blood.

This is what we'd done. We'd caused this division amongst so many people.

Screams erupted throughout the room and into the hallway as the Elementai pulled out a knife. Who knew where he got it. When I looked closer, I saw it was some sort of homemade shiv, one the inmate must've put together from stuff he'd cobbled around the prison.

Charlie knew when to get the hell out of situations before they got bad, so he wheeled me away before chaos erupted. Oberi guided him down the hall as the group behind us erupted into a vicious free-for-all. A couple of girls screamed that someone had been stabbed, and my stomach dropped. I heard the click of noxite guns as the guards scrambled to end the fight.

"Don't pay attention, pidge," Charlie told me. "This happens a lot lately."

My stomach dropped. The inmates were all worked up over the war, and they couldn't stop arguing about who should win.

"We should do something. Break it up," I suggested.

Charlie paused, like he was thinking about it. Then he shook his head and stated, "I'm never leaving your side again."

Oberi nudged my hand with his nose. *Let's get out of here, before they bring the fight to us.*

I didn't say anything more about the fight. Usually, I'd rant about how unfair it was that the rest of the supernatural world called us *savages*, and go on about the social injustices of the prison system. I'd want to get involved and find a solution that would bring everyone together, despite this war tearing us all apart.

But I let Charlie wheel me away without another protest. Something was very different about me now.

And I hated it.

I thought about the fight for the rest of the day and throughout the night. At five a.m. I'd hauled myself out of bed and into my wheelchair. It'd been difficult. I was still tired most of the time, and using what little strength I had to pull myself into my chair was excruciatingly painful. Our cell was dark, and for once, the prison was quiet.

Charlie had stirred, but I'd managed to get into my chair quietly enough that he didn't wake. He needed the sleep, and these days, it seemed it was only then he managed to find a semblance of peace.

Oberi watched me, ruffling her feathers. I stubbornly waved her off, insisting I didn't need help. I could still do things by myself. Just had to find a different way.

Thankfully, the doorways in our apartment were big enough for my chair to get through, but the place was still tiny, and maneuvering around it in my chair was aggravating. I kept running into things.

I was exhausted, but the ache in my stomach clearly told me I wasn't getting any sleep, so I went into the other room and rummaged through our stuff for two things; my mother's compass, and my journal. I sat with both in my lap, trying to decipher what was coming next.

The compass needle did nothing but spin relentlessly when it touched the journal, twirling in a mad circle like it was overcharged. I scowled. My mother had told me that if the compass was spinning, I already had the answer. Which was absolutely infuriating.

I didn't know how to work this thing, and I wasn't sure what clues anyone could send me with an object that seemed unpredictable at best.

I didn't get it. Lindsey and Miranda said they'd help me, but this compass wasn't working. I fiddled with it for another hour, but couldn't get the arrow to slow.

Around six, I heard a loud *thump* from the other room. I startled as I realized Charlie must've fallen out of bed. "Pidge! Where are you?"

"I'm fine!" I called out. "Just in the other room."

His voice had been frantic. His steps were quick and heavy as he came into the other room. "Don't scare me like that. I had no idea where you went."

"I'm right here," I said calmly. "Just didn't want to wake you."

My first day of class was today, so we'd be forced to separate. I could already tell the thought made him anxious.

Me too, honestly. I didn't feel safe spending a single moment away from my twin flame... not anymore.

"How'd you get out of bed by yourself? You shouldn't push it," Charlie worried.

"I just wanted to mess around with the compass," I explained.

He made a non-committal noise, but didn't say anything further. Oberi flew past me and settled on the back of my chair. *Let's get to it. We have a big day today.*

I was dreading the thought of getting through classes, but we had to start somewhere. I was able to take down a few bites of French toast, along with a protein shake, before Charlie wheeled me off to class.

He hesitated when he dropped me off at Ancient Magical Societies. He didn't want to leave, and I didn't want him to go.

My gaze scanned the room, until I caught Ivy's familiar white locks peeking out at the back of the class. My shoulders fell. Charlie wasn't in this class, but Ivy was, so I'd be okay. My vampire friend would tear anyone apart who dared to try and hurt me.

"Ava, come sit back here," Ivy called.

Charlie seemed less tense once he heard Ivy's voice. He squeezed my shoulder and asked, "Are you going to be okay?"

"I'll be fine," I said, though my tone wavered. "We'll meet up in an hour."

Oberi flew ahead of Charlie, flapping her wings. She seemed the least concerned out of any of us. Her faith in me was inspiring, but I couldn't feel it in myself yet.

Ivy's fashion choices today were glamorous. He wore glittering gold eyeshadow with flared yellow eyeliner, purple lipstick, and a million gaudy costume rings on his fingers. None of this stuff was *allowed* at the Institute, but he'd wear it for as long as he could get away with it.

Ivy leaned against his desk. "How them legs working for you?"

My voice got quiet as I said, "They're not."

He frowned. "Well, what do doctors know, anyway?"

I shook a steadying breath. "I can learn to live with this. I can get around it, but I can't handle this affecting the relationships with the people I love."

Ivy's expression slackened. "What do you mean?"

I teared up. "Ivy... I can't..."

"It'll be okay, precious, I promise." He reached out to squeeze my hand. He understood what I meant without me having to allude to it.

"It's important," I insisted. "We tried messing around, and nothing happened. I could barely feel anything. I can't be intimate with my husband, and it's killing me."

"Don't be afraid. Charlie loves you, no matter what," Ivy said. "I know it's hard to hear, but your silver lining's coming, you got me? You just gotta be brave enough to look for it."

I nodded, but didn't get to add anything, because Hemlock walked into the room. Her expression didn't change as she recognized me. She merely gave me a short nod before she came to the head of the room.

At least Hemlock wasn't treating me any differently. She still had faith I was more than this broken... thing.

"Good morning, everyone," Hemlock began. "Today, I'd like to move on to a new module discussing..."

She didn't finish her sentence before a guard walked in. He stood at the back of the classroom, holding a noxite gun and remaining silent.

Hemlock's tone was flat. "May I help you?"

"Just here to observe, ma'am," the guard replied. "Act like I'm not even here."

Hemlock's eye twitched. They were dictating what she could teach in her classes. "Very well. Everyone keep up. We've no time to dally."

Hemlock diverted her lecture to speak loudly about overbearing tyrants who had damaged magical history by going mad with power. I really thought she was pushing it, but the clueless guard didn't appear like he made any connections. She didn't assign any homework before dismissing us, slamming papers down on her desk before the guard walked out.

Ivy snickered as he pushed me out of the classroom. "Ooh, Hemlock is *pissed*. I bet she's coming up with a plan of revenge against the Warden as we speak. I can't *wait* to see it."

A guard grabbed Ivy's sleeve as we roamed by. "Hey, you! Your old man's come to see you."

I hated how the guards treated Ivy like he was a thing and not a person. They always refused to use his name. The inferichite bracelet warmed against my skin as my Fire magic came to the surface.

Ivy's gleeful mood instantly evaporated. "Right now?"

"He's not a patient vampire," the guard replied shortly.

Ivy gulped. "Just... give me a couple minutes." Ivy took off in the other direction without a goodbye, racing to his cell block. The guard followed.

Well, fuck. I didn't like how he'd left me in the middle of the hall like this. I decided I'd wait for Charlie, and rolled myself to the wall so I wouldn't be blocking traffic.

I saw Chancey come down the hallway, making his way over to me. He carried a small brown box. Somebody knocked into him, but he shoved them aside, and they flopped onto the floor.

"Hey, Ava. I was down at the mailroom, and they had a package for you. I, uh, picked it up," Chancey said, handing it out to me.

"And who said you aren't a sweetheart," I teased. There was a letter attached to the outside of the package. I opened it, recognizing my youngest brother's handwriting.

Hi, Ava!

I hope you're okay, wheeling around a bunch of tough guys. I know you can handle it, because you're scarier than the rest of them.

Charlie was so awesome. He's the best bro-in-law ever. Mom said the prison can be mean about helping him with his classes. These should help. I made them! They're glasses that will analyze and read any text on a screen or piece of paper out loud. And don't worry. I crafted them so they'll resist the magic around the prison, so they'll work right. That should make things easier.

Can you send me some stories about what goes on at the prison? I want to know all the gnarly details. It sounds way more interesting than middle school.

Also, tell Ez I'm taking his surfboard, because he's not using it.

Your awesome brother, Maverick

I laughed. Maverick was the only one I knew who'd think going to prison was cool, but I guess he *was* a little boy, and anything extreme interested him.

Maverick was extremely smart when he tinkered with things. He had a talent for rigging up all kinds of mechanical objects, but it was incredible that he'd managed to invent a piece of technology that was able to resist magic, something the best magical engineers of our time hadn't figured out how to do. The kid was practically a genius.

I observed the glasses in awe and slipped them on. When I put the letter in front of my face, it read the words out loud to me in a robotic voice.

These were wonderful! They'd really help Charlie. I was so grateful to Maverick. I intended to get started on a plethora of prison stories right away for him— *embellished*, so he'd think they were even cooler.

I slipped the glasses into my bag before Chancey asked, "Have you seen Ives?"

"We were just in class. He got called down to visit his dad," I said.

Chancey's face became hollow.

"Oh, fuck. That was *today*?" Chancey's eyes nearly bugged out of his head. "He wasn't supposed to show his scummy ass up until tomorrow."

"Um..." I didn't know much about Ivy's dad. I knew he hadn't particularly wanted Ivy, and that he was the leader of some vampire gang in

Chicago, but Ivy had avoided giving any other details. Apparently, he wasn't Chancey's favorite guy.

An announcement came over the intercom. *"All students are to report to the Hall of Mirrors for an assembly immediately, by order of the Warden."*

That was it. Both of us looked around nervously for our significant others, but didn't see them.

"We should go," I said as a crowd began forming in the direction of the Hall of Mirrors. "Can you push me that way?"

"Yeah." Chancey put his hands on the back of my chair. "Maybe Ives will already be there."

We didn't find Ivy, but Charlie, Marcus and Kallie were at the front of the Hall. Oberi flew above them in circles, while Rishi batted at the feathers she dropped.

"Thanks for getting her here," Charlie said, clasping Chancey's hand and slapping him on the back.

"No problem." Chancey turned in a circle. "What's this meeting supposed to be about, anyway?"

Nobody had an answer, and apparently, the Warden wasn't in a big hurry to get on with the show. We waited for over an hour for everyone on campus to show up, and the crowd was getting restless, shoving each other and trying to pick fights.

"Where the hell is Ivy?" I asked, looking around. "The visit with his dad shouldn't have taken this long."

"Dunno." Chancey seemed worried. "He'll get an infraction if any of the guards realize he's missing. We gotta come up with a cover story for him."

I opened my mouth to start making suggestions, when the sound of the Warden clearing his throat echoed through the room. The area went dead silent. Two figures stood on the balcony wrapping around the edge of the room. One was the Warden, the other, a spindly-looking girl I'd never seen before. She had to be at least seventeen, but couldn't be older than that. It was almost like she was too young to come here.

"Welcome, students. I'd like everyone to get to know my niece, Miss Esther Taurus," the Warden said as he made a sweeping gesture toward the girl. "She's new here at the Institute, and will be a valuable asset to our school, as no doubt you all are."

Esther gave a huge, white-toothed smile. "I'm absolutely thrilled to be accepted into the Institute! I'm *so* excited to meet you all, and can't wait to attend the academically-challenging courses I've heard so much about!"

Murmurs went up around the room, like everyone thought she was kidding. Nobody was *ever* excited to come to the Institute. People had to be dragged here against their will. As for academically challenging, it was hardly fucking Harvard. This girl was faker than press-on nails.

"What's her charges?" Jeffrey Johnson shouted out from the crowd. It was meant to be a joke. A few people laughed, but the laughter instantly died when the Warden turned his beady eyes on them. He fixed his gaze on Jeffrey, who paled under the Warden's cold stare.

"My niece is the first student in the history of Darke Institute to attend *willingly*," the Warden hissed. "She has chosen to do so in order to raise the prestige of this school, and as a full-honors student, we are lucky to have her."

Jeffrey gulped, and I felt bad for him. The Warden was going to make him pay for his comment eventually. The kid had a ticket to Cell-block 9 now.

Esther cleared her throat and gave a little *tee-hee* noise, before she tapped her shoes and said, "Darke Institute is a wonderful place to be. When I first heard about this incredible school, I knew it was my calling to attend this establishment and serve the poor, unfortunate souls who've found themselves within its doors. I truly believe that anyone can be redeemed, and that any sin can be cleansed. It is my mission to minister to the students here and bring them into the holy light, so that my lord's will be done, and not my own."

She was talking about doing *her lord's* work, and by the proud look on the Warden's face, I was pretty sure it had nothing to do with the god of the Celestial Church. Esther threw her arms out wide, posing like some virtuous saint, and a couple inmates nervously clapped.

If anyone looked out of place at the Institute, it was Esther. With her blonde ringlet curls and dimpled cheeks, she appeared more like an ornament you'd put on top of a Christmas tree than a juvenile offender.

Then I looked again. Her eyes didn't have anything in them. They were as dead as anything, void of any emotion except the desire to cause pain. I didn't know this girl, but I immediately sensed that we must've despised each other in a past life, because something about her rubbed me entirely the wrong way.

She looked down at me, and the sides of her lips curled upward in delight. The gloating smile was eerily similar to the Warden's. I got the firm sense she enjoyed seeing others in pain.

Oh, yeah. Make no mistake about it. She *definitely* belonged here.

Esther moved forward on the balcony, putting her in closer proximity to us. When she did that, my entire body vibrated with some kind of frequency. It was a subtle shift, similar to the feeling we all got when Kallie stopped time.

A pit formed in my aching stomach and sat there. Esther was a demigod. She *had* to be.

Charlie put his hand over mine, to tell me he felt it, too. I didn't know why he didn't just speak to me telepathically, until I realized we didn't know what this girl's power was. If she was like us, she could read minds, or something even worse. We had to be careful.

Marcus and Kallie automatically moved closer to me, and though the movement was small, the Warden noticed. He gave a smirk as he said, "We're happy to have you, Esther. I'm sure once you get settled in, this place will feel just like home."

I sneered. The Institute would *never* be home to people like Esther. This place belonged to us. The Warden had control here, but *we* owned this school. This bitch was going to learn that sooner rather than later.

"I'm delighted, truly," Esther replied in a bubbly tone. "It's an honor to be one of your students, Uncle."

"The pleasure is all mine, my dear. I know every student at the Institute will offer you a warm welcome."

He didn't add, *or suffer the consequences,* but it was clearly implied.

The Warden turned away, and the assembly began to disperse. As he turned to leave, Esther reached out to touch him, grazing her fingers along the small of his back.

I blinked. Did she just...?

I shook my head. No. I was imagining things.

Chancey tugged on Charlie's arm. "We gotta get out of here." A sweat had broken across the top of his forehead— he was pretty serious.

We followed Chancey to an empty staircase. It wasn't the greatest place to hold a conversation, but we couldn't be sure our cells were completely safe, and there were few other places in the prison where we wouldn't be overheard... save for the Lair, which we were doing our best to keep concealed.

"What the hell was that?" Kallie asked once we were alone. "He didn't call up the entire prison to introduce them to his niece."

"He wanted to show her to *us*," Charlie said. "She's his new weapon, like Jaymin was."

"Why do that, though?" Marcus asked. "Isn't it a better move to conceal her identity, get us to trust her so she can infiltrate the group and ferry back information?"

"He wants us to feel intimidated," Charlie said flatly. "Getting us to comply is more important than finding out whatever we know, because if we manage to get out of here, there's no controlling us from that point."

"Yeah, but why'd it have to be *her*?" Chancey complained, giving a sigh.

"You know her?" I asked.

"Oh, yeah, Esther's one of a kind," Chancey said darkly. "We used to run rackets together back in the day."

"She looks more likely to sing in a church choir than run a gambling scam," Kallie said.

"She's got a dark side, and tough as it is to believe, it's blacker than ours," Chancey assured us. "But I never knew her to be one to get caught. She knew how to slip out of trouble, and with all the connections her family has, no way she would've been sent here unless the Warden called her in to fulfill a purpose."

"He wants her to spy on us," Kallie said.

"Or something worse," Marcus added with a shiver.

"What's she like?" I asked curiously.

"She's nobody you want to get involved with, that's for sure. She helped me set up that little gambling den of ours, but she sure left me to take the heat when the fuzz came pounding on our door." Chancey scowled.

"There's something else..." Charlie said reluctantly. Kallie and Marcus nodded, and we all knew.

"She's a demigod," I told Chancey. "She has to be. Something about her set the four of us off. She gave off some kind of… signal or something."

"I'd say it was more like a resonance," Charlie said. "Our powers are getting stronger, so we're able to seek out those of our kind that much more easily."

"If she's like you guys, that ain't good." Chancey shoved his hands in his pockets.

"Her powers must've recently awakened, otherwise, she would've been here sooner," Marcus theorized. "But why wouldn't the Warden experiment on her, instead of going after all of us? He cares more about his plans than he does his family."

"Because she's useful to him," Charlie said. "Her loyalty is more valuable to him than her power, for now. She's a tool he can use against us. He's using one demigod to get four. It's a better deal for him."

"Yeah, but why is she here now?" Kallie pressed. "It's the middle of the semester. If the Warden's telling the truth—"

"Which he never does," I grumbled.

"— And she chose to be here, she shouldn't have arrived until the start of fall," Kallie pressed.

"Then the Warden must've been impatient to get her here," I suggested. "He doesn't want to wait until the fall to put her up to whatever she's got planned."

"Or Warden already gave her a job, and she completed the mission he gave her early," Marcus worried.

"That's absolutely terrifying," Charlie stated. "We have no idea what kind of task he asked her to do."

"Is there any possible way we can get her on our side?" I pressed.

Chancey shook his head. "Doubt it. She'll do what it takes to be at the top, and she ain't gonna help you outta the kindness of her heart. You're not gonna be able to beat whatever the Warden's offering her."

"Maybe we could trick her," Charlie said.

"I wouldn't try," Chancey warned. "She's a master manipulator and will see right through it."

I gave a cold laugh. "She hasn't met me yet."

"I know it don't make much sense, but she's *very* religious, and she doesn't mind whipping out any verse our holy book has as a weapon against people. That makes her more dangerous than most of the prisoners in here," Chancey insisted.

"She probably thinks serving the Warden is her duty to the Celestial Church," Kallie mumbled.

I gave a scoff. "I'm not worried about some choir girl attempting to convert inmates with her fire and brimstone sermon."

"You should be," Chancey warned me. "Religious texts in the hands of bad people can be used to start a lot of chaos, especially when it's being preached to some angry individuals. And there's a lot of angels in this prison who are really angry about what happened to Celestial City."

"You sound like you know," Marcus asked curiously.

"My parents left Celestial City for New York before I was born, and I never would've gone back to Celestial City if the Church hadn't forced me to return," Chancey said. "Let's just say before I got sentenced... what was being preached in the halls of the Church was enough to make my blood run cold. And I ain't an easy guy to scare. All I'm saying is, you guys better be careful. Real careful."

Marcus ducked his head out of the entrance to the staircase. "We better get back to class. Don't want anyone to notice we're missing."

We went to the main entry hall. Chancey stopped dead in his tracks, causing Charlie to push me into him. Chancey stumbled forward, catching the attention of two people standing before the fireplace.

I had to look twice, because I didn't recognize him. He'd taken a potion to dye his hair black, and his makeup and rings were gone. The skirt he'd been wearing this morning was replaced by plain slacks and male dress shoes. That mischievous spark in his eye had been snuffed out.

It was Ivy. But he looked less *Ivy* than he ever had before. It was one of the saddest things I'd ever witnessed, and I'd seen some sad shit.

What's going on? Charlie asked.

Ivy's dad showed up, I told him. *Our friend doesn't look like himself.*

Looming in the shadow of the firelight was a tall, lithe man, with slicked back hair and a tailored suit that was completely out of place amongst the filth of the prison. A pointed nose, high cheekbones and heavy eyebrows accentuated his masculine features. Everything about the man was staunchly vampire. Dude could call Dracula a poser and get away with it.

Ivy for sure looked like his mother. Ivy's father hardly shared anything in common with his son.

Ivy saw us coming. He faced us warily and gave a nod toward his father.

The movement was so out of place. Ivy flowed like a dancer, but this gesture was firm and stiff. "Hey, guys. This is my dad, Salvatore Bianchi."

Salvatore didn't say anything, merely looked us up and down. He was surveying us like we were merchandise.

Oh, goodie. I met *two* new people I instantly hated today. I gave Salvatore a heavy glare, though Ivy was pleading with me not to.

Salvatore must've thought he couldn't make a profit off any of us, because he pulled his eyes away almost abruptly, quickly becoming bored.

His gaze leveled Chancey, though. "Who's this?"

Salvatore could pick out the one person in the whole group he knew Ivy liked, though I'm certain Ivy didn't tell him. Everything got really tense.

"He's my... friend." Ivy's tone was instantly defeated. All he could do was give Chancey a pleading glance.

"Yeah, uh... we're good pals," Chancey took the hint instantly.

"Hm. Angels are good company," Salvatore commented. "Walk with me, son."

Salvatore didn't even give us so much as a goodbye before he walked off. Ivy hurried after him, casting an apologetic look at Chancey behind him.

"Wow," Kallie said. "Ivy's dad is a dick."

"You okay?" Charlie asked, reaching out to nudge Chancey.

"It's fine," Chancey insisted. "Whatever he needs."

"That couldn't have been easy," Marcus stated.

"It don't mean nothing," Chancey insisted, before giving a huff. "I'm sure Ives can't tell his dad he's screwing a man."

"Chancey, come on," Charlie moaned, but Chancey had already stormed off. I frowned, feeling awful for both of them. It was terrible that Ivy had to deny himself the authenticity of who he was, not even for acceptance, but for safety.

I made sure to add Salvatore Bianchi to my list of individuals I'd like to make suffer.

When it was time for lunch, we decided to take our food out to the bleachers to eat, as it was a fairly warm day for March. Ez was out on the basketball court with Opal, shooting some hoops.

Charlie fed me a couple of blueberries— my favorite fruit— out of a fruit salad we'd picked up from the cafeteria. As we ate, an annoying giggle wafted over the prison yard. Esther sat on a bench between Naya and Mad Dog, laughing loudly at something one of them had said.

"Looks like Esther found some friends," Kallie said sourly.

Esther caught us staring at her and gave a big smile. She stood from the bench and approached us, her grin more deranged than welcoming.

"Oh, dammit. She's coming this way," Marcus said. He hastily tried to hide himself behind his sketchbook, and fumbled with the papers so they went flying everywhere. Esther bent down to pick them up, handing them back to him.

"Do be more careful," she said sweetly. "It's not nice to litter."

"Thanks," Marcus said, but he cringed as he took the papers from her.

Ugh, Oberi complained. *She smells like soup, and not a good kind.*

Apparently, she didn't care if Esther could overhear her. But Esther didn't react, so I checked mind-reading powers off the list.

"I just wanted to see how you're doing. I've heard a lot about you, so no introductions are needed," Esther gushed.

"We're sure you have," Kallie growled.

"I came over to see if you guys had any suggestions for the Institute. I'm sure I can pass them along to the Warden, since I'm his niece *and he gives me whatever I want.*"

Esther silently mouthed the last part of the sentence— which I thought was stupid, considering Charlie had no idea what she was doing.

He got the concept, though, because my husband instantly launched into a complaint. "I mean, if you really want to know, he could make it accessible for people to get around. There are no elevators, and my wife's wheelchair doesn't fit through half these doors. Not to mention he didn't exactly make it easy for a blind guy like me to pass classes."

"Well, *actually*," Esther began. "The proper term is *a person with visual impairments.* You shouldn't call yourself blind, Charlie. It's offensive."

Charlie's mouth fell open. Kallie and Marcus appeared similarly nonplussed. I had a shorter fuse now than I had before I went into the Underground, and Esther lit it immediately.

"What the fuck is offensive about him determining what he wants to call himself?" I burst.

"Ew, language," Esther said, and she wrinkled her nose. "There's no need to use vulgarity. It's a sin."

"What's wrong with being disabled?" Charlie asked.

"You're still using the wrong language. *Disabled* is a really negative and outdated term," Esther purred.

"I identify with that term, and I don't have a problem with it," Charlie said slowly.

"But the world doesn't revolve around you," Esther replied. "We should be using words *everyone's* comfortable with."

I was gonna jump out of this wheelchair and pound this cow into the ground. My fists still worked, and she was about to catch these hands, even though I was only strong enough to get one good smack in.

But Charlie already had his hands on my shoulders, and I couldn't budge his firm grip on me.

I took a breath. "Look. It's perfectly fine to use the term *people-with-disabilities.* But the word *disabled* itself isn't a bad word, and shouldn't have a negative connotation associated with it. And it's especially ableist to tell a *disabled person* how they're allowed to refer to themselves."

Esther sniffed. "I'm on your side. I want to be a good advocate."

Oh, she was a social justice warrior, just like I was. But she was the worst kind— the type of person who liked using big words and talking points to act like she was smarter than other people. She had no real interest in being an ally to marginalized people. She just wanted to look smarter than everyone else.

Chancey was right. This bitch *was* dangerous. She was intelligent enough to twist someone's advocacy for themselves against their own self-interest. All she had to do was plant the wrong idea in someone's head, then let it run wild.

"If you want to be a good advocate, you'll listen to what disabled people have to say," I pressed. "Everyone with a disability deserves validation, no matter if they're chronically ill, need mobility aids, or have to take medication for mental illness."

Esther gave a little laugh. "We all know mental illnesses don't count."

"Bitch, I swear to the ancestors, I'm gonna hit you," I snarled.

"Ava," Charlie warned.

"No! She's an able-bodied person, and she's dictating to us how we're allowed to identify. That pisses me off!" I shouted.

"Excuse me, *Ava*, but you don't know my life or what I've been through. I know what it's like to have a disability, *actually*, because I have loved ones who are differently abled, so I get what you feel *completely*. And it's *so* offensive you would think otherwise," Esther sneered.

"Every disability is different," Charlie said calmly, trying to level the situation. "I don't expect Ava to understand what it's like being blind because she's in a wheelchair, and vice versa."

Esther puffed out a breath. She went to say something back, but I heard a low growl from behind me.

Kallie looked ready to shift into her wolf form. She hadn't yet, but her eyes had taken on a yellow sheen, like she wanted to. Charlie could hold me down, but Kallie was a shifter, and he couldn't hold her back unless he used his Elf powers to siphon her magic, which the inferichite bracelet made difficult.

If I didn't start a fight with her, Kallie sure would.

A brawl on her first day would ruin her honor-student image, so Esther shook out her curls and said, "I was just trying to help, but as Uncle tells me, you can't save people who don't want to save themselves. If any of you want a listening ear, trust me; I'm here for you."

I hardly waited for her to be out of earshot before I mumbled, "If she really gave a shit about your blindness, she would've made sure you could understand what she was communicating when she was mouthing words like a moron."

"She just came over here to pick on us," Marcus said.

"She's trying to get into our heads," Kallie agreed. "The Warden probably filled her in on all our weak spots."

Charlie shook his head. "She's a distraction. We have to focus on what's important, which is meeting with Takahashi tonight. We can't afford to let Esther get under our skin, because that's what the Warden wants. If she can keep us busy with drama, we won't be able to work on what matters."

"She's already out of my mind," I grumbled as I turned my wheel-chair around, so I didn't have to face her.

The prison yard began to clear out as people went back to their classes. Eventually, the yard was nearly empty. We were going to move, too, until a loud noise boomed through the air. It was a deep bray, like the sound of a deer in pain.

"What's that?" Kallie asked. I made a gesture for Oberi to check it out.

Oberi flew upward. Her wings beat in a panic as she said, *There's a Familiar tied up in the fence line!*

My throat tightened. That barbed wire was sharp. Anything that tried to get through the fence would be cut to ribbons.

Ez and Opal had been finishing up their basketball game when the bray echoed through the yard again. Ez had been standing completely still the first time the animal cried out, but when it screamed again, he began to *move.*

I'd never seen my brother run so fast. Opal tore after him in the direction of the noise. Marcus and Kallie hurtled after them, but Charlie had to push my wheelchair through the grass, so that took forever.

Hurry, hurry, Oberi said nervously. Rishi kept dancing around my wheels, and we almost ran over him, so Oberi flew down to pick him up in her claws. The cat yowled loudly as Oberi carried him through the sky.

The trees eventually broke. I caught sight of my brother, looking upward at a gorgeous creature that was dangling twenty feet up from the top of the fence line. It was a massive male peryton, with white fur and curling golden lines running through his coat. He had giant antlers which glowed with a golden light, though that light was pulsing, as if it was beginning to fade. The peryton's pink nose quivered as he continued to cry out for help, and blood ran from his blue eyes. The winged deer had an arrow shot through one of its wings, and could no longer fly.

Barbed wire tangled in its antlers. The peryton hung from it, twitching as he attempted to twist his neck to escape. It looked like the peryton had attempted to fly over the prison, then fallen from the air after someone had shot through his wing.

The knotted metal around the peryton's antlers created a deadly barrier. The more it struggled to break free, the harsher the wire cut around its face, and the deeper the creature bled.

We couldn't get close to the fence line. With the inferichite lining the property's edge, and the bracelets on our wrists, the closest any of us could get to the fence without passing out was ten feet. The four of us were forced to watch as Ez and Opal took action.

"We need to help him." My brother's tone was full of panic as he reached up, seemingly wanting to touch the deer with a trembling hand. "He's struggling to breathe!"

"Ez, we can't get any closer!" Charlie called out. He was holding a hand to his head, pushing off what I knew was a splitting headache, like I had.

"You don't understand! He's *dying*!" Ez shouted.

He wouldn't know that unless he was connected to this deer. The peryton's appearance only meant one thing. Ez was bonded to this creature, and if we didn't get him free, Ez would die just as soon as the peryton bled out.

Without warning, the barbed wire holding the peryton captive suddenly snapped. The peryton let out a bray as it tumbled through the air, landing harshly against the ground. Ez immediately ran forward and began untangling the barbed wire from around the peryton's antlers and neck. My brother cut open his palms trying to set the peryton free. It was tedious work, untangling each line of wire away from the peryton, but the animal stopped moving once Ez's fingers skimmed his coat, like he knew he was trying to help.

Once the peryton was free of the line, Ez struggled to help the deer up. He wasn't strong enough to lift the creature, but at his pleading, the peryton staggered onto his hooves and walked a few feet. The peryton managed to fall in a heap before us, but he couldn't move any farther.

My Anichi magic could feel the life draining away from this creature. Ez had freed the peryton, but it didn't matter. The poor thing had lost so much blood.

"We're far enough away from the fence line that you should be able to use magic," Ez pleaded. He panted with the effort of freeing the deer. "Ava, you've gotta heal him."

I steeled my resolve. Marcus and Kallie helped me out of the wheelchair and onto the ground, so I could put my hand over the peryton's body.

Careful, Ava, Oberi warned, like she worried I wasn't well enough to do this.

I tried. I attempted to draw power from her and Charlie, but I immediately felt some kind of pushback, and I nearly threw up.

"I'm sorry. I'm too weak," I said frailly. "Oberi, please."

Oberi flew above the peryton. She landed at his head, but before she made a move to lay a feather upon the creature, she spoke softly. *If I attempt to heal this creature while you are so fragile, we could lose you all over again. I draw my strength from our bond, and therefore, work best when you and Charlie are at your greatest strength. This is a high risk.*

I was about to tell her to go ahead and do it anyway, but Charlie cut that off immediately.

"No," Charlie said sharply. "We aren't doing that."

"What's going on? Why isn't Oberi helping?" Ez asked weakly. Tears welled out of him at the overwhelming experience of bonding with and potentially losing his Familiar all at once.

I told Ez what Oberi had said, and he shook his head. "I won't accept this. He's my Familiar. If he dies, I die, too."

Ez knelt beside me, barely containing his sobs. "Whatever happens, I'm going with him."

Ez spread both of his hands across the animal's pelt, to bury his hands inside the bloody fur. When he touched the peryton, his body ignited with a golden light that matched the halo coming off the peryton's antlers. I was awe-inspired, as I'd never seen anything like it. I watched as the smaller cuts on the deer's coat stopped bleeding and started to fade away.

"Ancestors, Ez. You're a dual caster," I gasped. "You can heal."

Ez's expression went wide with surprise, but there was no time to sit and marvel. "What do I need to do?"

"Healing wounds and broken blood vessels is easier than curing an illness. You just have to knit what's cut back together," I told him. "You're doing just fine now, but try to speed it up. You can encourage the body to regenerate the blood he lost by giving your Familiar some of your magic. You share a connection, so the transfer should be easy."

Ez nodded firmly, then put all his concentration into healing his Familiar. I observed as the harsh wounds and deep gashes that the barbed wire had delivered vanished completely at the touch of Ez's light. The rattled breaths the peryton gave became healthy and strong. Ez broke off the shaft of the arrow and carefully removed it from the animal's wing. I watched as Ez's Anichi magic knitted the hole the arrow had made back together, sinew and bone regrowing until it was as good as new.

I never thought my brother was a gifted caster. He was always behind in our elemental class, and he'd never been very good at any spells I'd seen.

But he was able to use Anichi magic effortlessly, despite all the struggles he had casting Toaqua magic. No, better than effortlessly... he was *talented*. Healing had to be his primary gift, while Water was just a secondary trait. It just hadn't shown up until his Familiar arrived.

Eventually, the peryton was able to get back up. He stood tall, tossing his antlered head and letting out a bray. Ez scratched the peryton behind the ears, and the deer gave an affectionate snort.

"Stop touching my merchandise!" The snarly voice of an ugly old man beckoned from the other side of the fence line. Through the metal and barbed wire, I saw that he was carrying a crossbow.

I snarled. He had to be the one who'd shot the peryton. What was more, this was the guy who ran the magical creatures shop in Shade Hills— *Precarious Pets*. I knew he had to be, because I'd seen him on our field trip into town during our second semester. The peryton must've been trying to escape, and this despicable jackass had shot him down.

"He's not merchandise, he's a living creature, one that breathes just like we do," Ez replied cruelly. "And he's staying with me."

The shopkeeper's lip twisted. "The hell he is, boy. That deer is my property, bought and paid for!"

"Yeah, and I just bonded with him," Ez snapped. "Get lost, loser."

"I don't care if he's your long-lost lover. I paid good money for that peryton, and I spent my morning chasing after him once he broke out of the shop. Busted up half my stock, too. I'm going to turn him for a profit, whether that be by selling him on the black market or to a meat factory," the shopkeeper sneered.

"I'll pay you for him. Just leave us alone," Ez said.

The shopkeeper snorted. "You inmates don't have any money."

"I'm the eldest son of the Toaqua chieftain. Contact him, he'll give you whatever you ask for," Ez said firmly. "But you're not walking back to town with my Familiar."

Daddy was going to be broke by the time all us kids got done asking for money, with the kind of trouble we got into. The shopkeeper narrowed his eyes, but he ceased to throw out a comeback as he saw a group of ten guards approaching, carrying noxite guns.

Clearly, he didn't want to deal with the Warden any more than the rest of us did, because he said, "Your father better pay up, boy. Or I'll be looking for you the second you set foot outside this hellhole. If you ever do."

The shopkeeper hustled back into the woods. Immediately, the guards set on making the entire situation our fault.

"What are you kids doing?" a guard barked. "Trying to escape?"

"No," Ez replied harshly. "I was rescuing my Familiar."

"Quit lying, Mitoh, you don't have a Familiar on record," the guard snapped.

"I just bonded! And if I hadn't gotten here in time..." Ez rubbed the peryton's head, and the deer gave a snuffling noise.

"We'll see," the guard replied. "We're taking you and this animal in for a bond evaluation, to make sure you aren't lying. The rest of you are going down to Cellblock 9 for trying to break out!"

"We weren't trying to break out, dipshit. The only part of the fence that's broken is the barbed wire at the top," Kallie replied dryly. "And if you haven't noticed, none of us can get close enough to get over it."

"We'll be the judge of that," a guard replied. "You'd better check your attitude, missy, before I decide I don't like your tone."

Kallie wrinkled her nose at him, which didn't help. Three guards escorted Ez and his peryton back to the prison, while the rest of the guards forced us to go in another direction. I had the thought that we should fight them off and try to make a break for it, but there was no way we were getting past that inferichite without possibly blowing a hole in our heads.

Charlie helped me back into my wheelchair. The guards took us to an evaluation room, where they grilled us with a bunch of pointless questions. When it was clear they didn't have anything on us and they couldn't prove we were trying to break out, they let us go— but not without a bunch of pointless threats. We hurried along to the Villain's Den as fast as we could, to get some relative privacy from these assholes.

Once the guards left us alone, Opal began fretting.

"Oh, I do hope Ez will be all right," Opal worried. "I'm not sure what a bond evaluation is, but it doesn't sound good."

"Marcus and I had one, ordered by the Warden," Kallie said dully.

"Yeah," Marcus agreed. "It wasn't pleasant. It was a while ago, right after the Darke Games. He was already watching us at that point."

I didn't ask why they hadn't told us. It definitely wasn't something I wanted to go through.

"Did it... hurt?" Opal asked, and she hiccupped.

"No." Kallie shook her head. "But it was... very invasive. They have a fae cast a spell to take your bond out from your spirit and look at it, magically. It doesn't do anything, but it feels a bit like being naked for the whole world to see."

"But Ez will pass," Marcus assured me. "They have a true bond. It just makes you feel really vulnerable."

I never wanted that to happen to Charlie and me, and I hoped the Warden wouldn't bother. Nobody needed to go prying into the connection we had.

Our next class was Elemental Magic, so we parted from Kallie and Marcus so we could practice under the instruction of Professor Summers. We cast small spells to keep Professor Summers happy, though she mostly ignored us. She knew we were talented spellcasters, so she devoted most of her time to helping others in the class.

Though we could use our normal powers under the influence of inferichite, the magic was dull and unimpressive. We had to get these cuffs off somehow.

Ez didn't show up. The bond evaluation must be taking a long time. I wasn't sure why, as it was clear he shared one with the peryton. The prison board had to be arguing if they were going to allow Ez to keep him at the prison. I assumed they were fighting about Ez using the peryton to escape, but if the peryton couldn't fly over the fence due to the noxite surrounding the school, there was no reason to not let him keep his Familiar.

Charlie was quiet most of the class period. I couldn't read his thoughts, though I was more or less scared to try. "What's on your mind?"

Charlie waited for a moment before he replied. "Did it seem like Ez secured his bond with his Familiar right away?"

The question was gutting. "I don't know. Maybe he did."

I'd observed Ez carefully as the guards had led him and the peryton off. They'd practically been breathing in sync, their attention diverted toward the same place, even looking ahead at the same spot. When Ez moved, so did the deer, to mirror him. It was uncanny, something I'd only seen in bonded partners that had been together for a long time.

Though Charlie couldn't witness any of this, he'd sensed it. Magically, something very strong resonated between Ez and the peryton. And it was unmatchable to what we had with Oberi.

"How is that possible? I thought you had to build a relationship with your Familiar before that happened," Charlie stated.

Some bonds can be secured almost instantly, upon meeting, Oberi commented. *And the situation the two of them found themselves in certainly pushed them together.*

Charlie's emotions flooded into me, and he didn't bother to block them this time. He was jealous.

I felt a little envious, too. The three of us had been through a lot in the past two years, and our soul still hadn't found complete unification.

Elementai who had secured their bond with their Familiar could perform stronger magic. They had a deeper connection with their magical creature that other Elementai did not, which enabled them to protect and serve each other better. It was more like the feeling of being one soul in two different bodies, rather than being two separate entities living apart. The sensation, as it had been described to me, was fluid and seamless.

The three of us weren't even close to that. Sure, we could communicate telepathically, and our magic was strong, but it was difficult getting all three of us on the same page at the same time. We argued and had disagreements constantly, and I knew Oberi always felt like she was pulled between Charlie and me.

That wouldn't happen when our bond was secured. She wouldn't have to make decisions to pick and choose who to side with, because Charlie and I would truly be one soul. Despite all the work we'd put into our relationship, there was a constant tug-of-war we experienced that left Oberi confused, feeling like she wasn't doing her job to unite us.

The disagreement about breaking out of the Institute was a prime example. Charlie and I both wanted to save the world, but we couldn't agree on how to do it. That wouldn't happen when our bond was finally secured, because whenever we made a decision, it would be a unified one.

Considering how different the three of us were, I worried we'd never get there.

Charlie frowned. "Why does it work for everyone else but not for us?"

It's going to be harder. There are *three of us,* Oberi pointed out. *That means three different pieces of our soul to reunite as one. And each of us have quite strong personalities that can make that difficult.*

"I figured our bond would secure when we got married," I said. "I felt something happen when we took our vows."

We definitely came closer, Oberi said. *But we're just not there yet.*

"So what can we do to make it happen?" Charlie asked. "If we secure our bond, we'll be able to perform stronger magic. Maybe we'll be able to get these cuffs off."

Bonds are unified through strong emotion. The Elementai tribe once attempted to force the unification through the Elemental Cup, Oberi mused. *It worked, for a time. Life-or-death situations have a way of bringing souls together*

I nodded. The Elemental Cup had been a deadly competition where past Elders forced newly bonded college Elementai and their Familiars to survive against a trial of elements. My parents had participated in it when they were young, and a lot of kids had died over the years. After the Hawkei Civil War, my parents and others had changed the competition. The Cup still took place, but it wasn't deadly anymore, and was more of a coming-of-age ceremony than an actual trial.

"We did that in the Darke Games, and it wasn't enough," Charlie objected.

Oberi ruffled her feathers. *Clearly, it's going to take something stronger.*

"Being scared isn't the answer. Fear won't help us unify," I noted.

To secure our bond takes more than feeling. It takes alignment, Oberi insisted. *There are different pieces inside all of us that are at war. Until we learn to bring them together, our bond will never be whole.*

I felt discouraged. This was going nowhere. If we hadn't managed to secure our bond by now, I wasn't sure what else it was going to take to get there.

Or what else we'd have to go through to make it happen. And that terrified me.

We dicked around in our classes for the rest of the day, and waited until after dinner to meet Takahashi in the secret illusion room. We got there before he did, so while we were waiting, Charlie tried out his new glasses. He was super excited about them, turning pages of books that were spread out on the round table.

"I've never gotten to *read* before. I can read braille now, but the glasses will give me access to things that haven't been converted," he said.

He talked about reading like it was a marvel. Something so simple, that so many people could do, was a rare gift for him. It was wrong that the world had robbed him of that experience for so long.

"It'll definitely make research easier," Marcus said. He kept having to yank books out from under Rishi, who lay on every tome Charlie opened.

I'd been feeling a little down, so Charlie had gotten me a caramel macchiato from Commissary. It helped a little. Apparently, I wasn't the only one, because Kallie didn't look happy. She was off in the corner by herself, turning pages listlessly. She didn't appear bored, rather... upset.

Oberi fluttered her feathers from the back of the chair she was sitting on. I jerked my head at her, and she nodded in understanding.

Hey, Charlie, since we're waiting, why don't you and Marcus go dig up those books on Elves that you so ridiculously hid while you were trying to conceal information about Forevermore, hm? Oberi asked. *They could prove useful now.*

"That was forever ago, back during our second semester. I'm not even sure I know where they are," he objected.

Well, you're the one who buried them, so perhaps you boys can put a brain cell or two together and figure it out, Oberi said brightly.

"Fuck you, Oberi." Charlie sighed. "But you're right. Come on, Marcus. Oberi thinks we need to find those Elf books I buried, and she's not wrong. There might be something in there we could use."

"Why do I have to be the one to go with you?" Marcus complained.

"Because no one else wants to. Hurry up."

Rishi padded behind them with a flick of his tail. Once the boys left the room, I rolled my chair over to Kallie, while Oberi observed us keenly from a distance. "What's up? You seem bummed."

She startled. "Oh, I'm not. Just... thinking."

"About what?"

"I really don't want to talk about it," she said.

"I didn't have Oberi come up with a bullshit excuse to get the guys out of here just so you could refuse to tell me what's wrong. Something's on your mind," I insisted.

"Just trying to keep my dirty thoughts to myself," she mumbled.

Fireworks of excitement immediately erupted within me. "Ooh, I want to hear everything!"

"Better you than Marcus," she replied. "He's been working on his mind-reading powers, but it's still dirty thoughts he can hear the clearest, and mine are filthy."

"Tell me!" I leaned in closer, and she dropped her voice.

"I've been thinking... what if Marcus' twin brother had survived?" Kallie asked. "Twins in the Miriamic Coven share a soul, and I'm bonded to Marcus... so wouldn't that mean I would've bonded with Dean, too?"

"Is that possible?" I asked.

"Sorceresses can bond to two mates at once. It happened with my grandmother," Kallie explained. "And I was just thinking... why choose? I'm sure Marcus would share."

I was absolutely giddy. "Ancestors, you're totally into the thought of having a threesome with Marcus and his twin brother!" I put my hand over my mouth, thrilled with how juicy this was.

"Yeah, and I haven't been able to *stop* thinking about it since. It's hot!" Kallie insisted. "I'm sure you could imagine how fun two Charlies would be."

"I think I would die of happiness," I said, but left it at that. Kallie didn't know about my struggles with our sex life, because honestly, I felt embarrassed to tell her. Sharing what little I had with Ivy had been painful, and besides, this conversation was about her. I didn't need to go rambling about myself.

She sighed. "It's never going to happen, though. Since Dean is dead."

"But are you bonded to Rishi, too? Obviously in a non-sexy way," I stated.

"I think so. I share a connection with both of them."

Her shoulders dropped. "I guess daydreams are all I'm going to get, though. Marcus has zero interest in dating me. And the longer we ignore our bond, the weaker my magic gets. He either needs to reject me or admit what we have, because I can't do this for much longer."

"Aren't there Arcanean ceremonies you can perform to break your bond with him?" I asked.

"I could... I've *tried*... but I won't. I don't have the heart," she said sadly. "He's gotta be the one to do it. Otherwise, we're just stuck in limbo."

I thought about suggesting Charlie's help. He could use his Elf powers to break their bond, and neither one of them would have to go through the pain of doing so, but my intuition flat out rejected that idea immediately.

I had an inward knowing these two were going to end up together. Just how long it was going to take, I didn't know.

"I mean, it'd be easier to break it off sooner than later, since you guys haven't done anything," I pointed out.

Kallie got *super* quiet, and I gave a loud, obnoxious gasp. "Wait. *No.* Oh, Kallie, you liar!"

She blushed deeply before she exclaimed, "I wanted to tell you, but I don't even know what's happening myself!"

"Do you? Because the last thing I knew, you and Marcus weren't a thing. Now you're sexing up the place!"

"We didn't have *sex*, gods." She rolled her eyes. "We just... did other things."

"I *cannot* believe this. Kallie, when did this happen?" I asked.

"The first time... you were in the hospital." She dropped her gaze away from mine. "We didn't know if you were going to make it."

"Of course, the good stuff happens when I'm not around to hear about it," I grumped.

"Nobody did! I'm just telling you about it now because I can't hold it in any longer!" Kallie shouted.

"Okay, so go on. What steamy encounters did two of my best friends have when poor, broken little me was fighting for her life in a hospital bed?"

Kallie's look turned sheepish as I reached for my coffee. "We... Marcus ate me out in a stairwell."

I spat out my drink. *"What the hell?!"*

"You're telling me!" She shook her head. "One minute, I'm sobbing my eyes out, and the next, my skirt's hiked halfway up my stomach and he's making me feel things with his mouth I never have before."

"Excuse me— back up." I held up my hands. "That's a hell of a transition. What's the whole story?"

"I told you... when we came back from the Underground, I didn't know if you were going to be okay... I was pretty sure you were going to die, actually. I'd run off to be alone," Kallie said. She reached out to grasp my hand and squeezed it tight. "I was just falling apart, and I didn't know what to do."

"Kallie, I'm so sorry." I clutched her fingers back. "You know I'd do anything to get back to my friends. I didn't just come back for Charlie. I fought to come back to you, too."

"I know that." Kallie wiped her misty eyes with the palm of her free hand. "But it was rough, Ava, and really scary. For the first time in a really long one, I was so scared, because I was terrified I was going to lose my best friend."

I immediately started crying. I leaned forward to hug her. "Oh, Kallie! I didn't know you felt that way about me."

"Of course I do! It's rare for me to have a female friend." Kallie squeezed me back, before she pulled away. "The girls in Malovia hated me. They were either jealous of me because I was the princess, or we didn't get along because I'm just too... me."

I knew what she was saying. Too aggressive, too blunt, too loud, too straightforward.

Too much.

People had treated me like that too, back home. They'd tolerated me, because I was the chieftain's daughter, but it was rare for anyone outside of my family to actually *like me*. There was a reason I'd suffered so badly when Monica died. I didn't have anyone else.

"You'll *never* be more than I can handle, Kallie. I like you just the way you are," I promised.

"I know, and I didn't want to lose that!" She sniffed, then laughed lightly. "I didn't know what I was going to do with myself if you were gone. You say you're an asshole, but you care about and love everybody, Ava, no matter who they are. After we became friends, you accepted me without a second thought, and that's something I've *never* had in the fae world. You're a really special person. The world would suffer if you were away. I know I would."

I reached forward to wipe the tears off her cheeks. "Well, I'm not going anywhere, so you don't have to worry about being alone."

"I don't know what I'd do without you." She smiled as she gave a sniff. "I don't think you realize how much you mean to me."

"I love you too, Kallie. I wouldn't want heaven without you, anyway." I gave a watery chuckle. "Enough with the sappy stuff. I want the sexy details! So you were in the stairwell, and...?"

"And Marcus came in, and there wasn't any hiding it from him," Kallie confessed. "When he saw me sobbing, he just... held me, and before either of us knew what was happening, we got carried away. *He's* the one who went to take my panties off, by the way, not me. It wasn't my idea."

"And I'm guessing once it started, you didn't want it to stop."

"Oh, gods no. I'm telling you, he kissed me down there, and it was game over." She let out a dreamy sigh. "Then... he finished me off, and it was so awkward after that neither one of us said or did anything. He didn't leave my side, though. Not for one moment, until you woke up."

Poor Marcus, sitting there in a stairwell with blue balls.

"And it hasn't stopped since?" I asked.

"It's not like it's all the time," she protested.

"How often is this a thing?"

"Honestly?" She ran a hand through her hair and tugged on the ends. "We don't get together unless one of us is... triggered. He gets upset, or I do, and we try to comfort each other, and that comforting leads to... something else."

"Oh, that sounds so healthy!" My voice dripped with sarcasm.

"It's not my fault!" she insisted. "I'm not the one making the moves!"

"I can't believe that. There's no way Marcus is taking the lead on all this."

"I thought so too, until he had me on my back."

"Just how far have you two gotten?"

Kallie blushed. "Well... we were naked on top of the Witch Tower yesterday."

"What the hell!"

"We've never gone all the way," Kallie assured me. "But we've pretty much done... everything else. Please, don't tell Charlie."

"I keep no secrets from my husband," I said coyly. "Not to mention this puts the team in jeopardy, what with you two having secret rendezvous all over the fucking prison. We need to know where you guys stand with each other."

"Fine. Just don't go spreading it around," Kallie growled. "I don't need Ivy trying to give me tips."

"At least tell me it's good."

"He worships the ground I walk on," Kallie said gleefully. "It's amazing he's such a rockstar at it, seeing as how he's never done any of it before."

"He never messed around with Anya?" My eyebrows shot up.

Kallie shrugged. "He said it was just kissing. Nothing more than that."

And he'd gotten that attached...

I cleared my throat. "Is it different than it was with Scarlet?"

She gave an obnoxious scoff. "Scarlet was fun and all, but that was hollow compared to how Marcus makes me feel. There's nothing like being together with the person you're destined for."

I absolutely agreed. I'd experienced as much with Charlie.

But her choice of words had me worried. "Kallie... this is dangerous."

"Why?" She immediately got defensive. "You and Charlie did the *friends-with-benefits* thing."

"And it turned out horribly."

"Until it didn't!"

"You guys need to have a commitment in place, so it's safe for both of you," I said firmly. "Messing around... especially having sex with your bonded partner... if you're not on solid ground, you're testing that soul connection. I'm not saying you need to rush to the altar, but ancestors, at the bare minimum you should be his girlfriend. You deserve that much."

"Like Marcus would ever go for that. The man's more afraid of his feelings than he is his own shadow."

"You can't keep stringing each other along because *feelings are scary.*"

Kallie scowled. "Look, Ava, you haven't even been married for a year. You can't sit here and say you're some maven of nuptials because Charlie put a ring on your finger."

"But it takes a lot to make a wife, Kallie. I haven't been married long, but I know that much. This isn't some fling. You and Marcus love each other."

"Yeah, easy to convince him," Kallie replied. "Whenever I bring it up, he just goes all *troubled bad boy*, and complains about his dark past or whatever."

She did a simpering impression of Marcus, with the trembling lip and everything. It was quite good.

"This is small stuff," I argued. "There's something else holding you back."

Kallie took a breath. When she finally began speaking, her voice trembled. "Because... because at the end of the day, he's still in love with Anya. I know he is. And until he can let her go, we can never be a thing. She might be dead, but it's not over between them, Ava. Not by a long shot. I can't compete with his feelings for a dead girl."

I didn't believe her. She might think Marcus was still in love with Anya, but I knew where his true feelings were.

"You can," I reassured her. "Because Marcus loves you more. He's confessed that to Charlie, and I know he's not lying."

She sighed and dropped her head. "Maybe."

"Look, you've gotta give this mating thing a shot. Marcus just needs a little *push*. Hell, maybe things aren't as bad as you think!"

"You sure are saying *hell* a lot." Kallie smirked.

I shrugged. "Charlie's rubbing off on me."

"Is that the only thing he's rubbing?"

"I could ask Marcus the same thing about you."

I knew by the spark in her eye she was about to come back with some smart-mouthed answer, before the door to the room opened and cut off what she was about to say.

"We're back!" Marcus' triumphant voice echoed through the room. "We got the books!"

He and Charlie had returned. The books that had been buried were in their arms, covered in dirt but presumably unharmed.

"Yeah, and they're still readable," Charlie said in what seemed like relief. He put one of the filthy books in front of his glasses, and they robotically read a few lines. "We can still gain some information from these."

The books were cool and all, but I was more wrapped up in the Marcus-and-Kallie drama. Fuck, I couldn't look at him now without picturing what Kallie had told me. Our Marcus, a true stud. I wanted to shake his hand and congratulate him myself, but if I did, he'd melt into a puddle on the floor.

Marcus glanced at me, and the second he saw the expression on my face, he turned red.

Oh, shit, I was bad at hiding at. He totally knew what Kallie had told me.

His gaze landed on Kallie, and she stiffened beside me. They didn't say a damn word, but I knew they didn't have to, because their eyes had a whole conversation.

Charlie noticed the tense silence and went to speak to me privately.

Did something happen? Charlie asked me telepathically.

You are not going to believe what Kallie just told me, I gushed, but our mental conversation was interrupted when Hemlock strolled into the room, followed by Takahashi.

She made no effort for a greeting as she stated, "Professor Takahashi has told me you four are having trouble resisting the inferichite cuffs, and we simply can't have that. We're making progress in breaking the hold these cuffs have on you today, one way or another."

Okay. It was clear she wasn't letting us out of this room until we figured this out.

"We've determined that the key to destroying inferichite is using strong emotion," Hemlock began. "I'm sure with enough determination, coupled with practice, the four of you will be able to harness enough energy to shatter the inferichite binding you. Let's begin."

Hours passed. We worked tirelessly at attempting to damage the inferichite, but our efforts didn't put a crack in the stones. Kallie, Marcus, and Charlie got more frustrated with every minute that passed, attempting different spells and theories, but the inferichite resisted whatever strategy they came up with.

At least the others were doing something. As far as strong emotion, I just couldn't harness any.

I tried... I really did. I thought about how angry I was that we were in this situation, how desperately I wanted to protect Charlie, and how much I hated the Warden.

Usually, when I thought of the Warden, heavy feelings came up. That man could get an inferno of rage stoked up in me quicker than gasoline thrown over a bonfire.

Not since the Underground, though. I was still mad at him, don't get me wrong, but I felt my anger was being blocked somehow. I just couldn't be bothered to care. It sucked.

"I can't do this, Oberi," I said tiredly. "There's nothing left in me."

Don't worry, I think Cheerful Charlie over here's got it handled, Oberi grumbled.

Charlie was losing his fucking mind. He tried everything to break the bracelet's hold. He attempted to rip it off with roots he grew from the ground, smashed bricks onto it, even borrowed some magic from me so he could attempt to freeze the bracelet off using Water, or melt it off using Fire. The room was a mess, and the bracelet didn't look damaged in the slightest. I was starting to get worried he'd try sawing off his arm next.

"Charlie, I think it's time to calm down," Takahashi said steadily.

"*Calm down?* How can I calm down when the entire world's going to shit?" Charlie screamed.

"We're not going to get anywhere when you're acting like a psychopath," Kallie snapped, and she dropped the illusion blade she'd been bashing over the bracelet. "Get it together."

Marcus hurried to defend Charlie. "Who are you calling a psychopath? You're the sociopath. You went around assassinating whoever you felt like back in Malovia. At least Charlie's only killed people who've tried to kill him."

Kallie slammed her hands against the table. "I'm *not* a sociopath! Contrary to popular opinion, I have fucking feelings, and I can feel sympathy for people!"

"You sure aren't feeling sorry for me," Marcus spat.

The subcontext in this argument was huge. Marcus knew exactly what we'd discussed and was pissed at Kallie for telling me what was going on, and because of it, he was going to take out his feelings on her about something else.

But she needed support. How could he expect her to keep hiding what was between them, and be satisfied with what he was giving her? It was wrong.

"Because I'm not going to chime in on your pity party!" Kallie said. "You've done your share of bad things, so don't go there."

"What I did was an accident. You're a serial killer by choice!" Marcus shouted.

"I kill monsters who fucking deserve it, to *protect* innocent people," Kallie growled.

"You're a menace to society. That's why you're locked up in here," Marcus spat.

"Well, look in the fucking mirror, because so are you." Kallie shoved Marcus.

"Enough of this," Hemlock snapped, coming between them. "Clearly we need to reassess at another time."

"I think we should take a moment to rest," Takahashi said soothingly. "We'll retire for the night. Things will look better in the morning."

Kallie punched the door on the way out and left a hole, so she clearly didn't think so. Marcus sat in a chair and pouted, though Rishi yowled at him to go after her.

I didn't think they'd argue like that unless both of them were feeling entirely helpless. This was my fault. My friends wouldn't be wearing these bracelets if I hadn't destroyed the Underground.

After our practice, Charlie had a late-night factory shift, and didn't get back until it was close to curfew. He was still fuming as he helped me into bed. I had wanted a shower, but I couldn't get one, because I still needed help washing up and Charlie wasn't allowed in the girls' bathrooms. We'd have to wait to go back to the infirmary tomorrow and use one of the private showers there.

I knew he was frustrated about all the obstacles we had to get around now, because I couldn't walk. The weight of responsibility fell even heavier on me.

I pulled one of Charlie's shirts over my head to sleep in before I lay back. It was huge on me, more like a dress, and was really soft from years of use. I loved it, because it smelled like him and was comfortable, but he hardly had anything new.

I was getting this boy some damn clothes the next chance I had. No husband of mine was going to walk around looking raggedy.

"What are you thinking about?" Charlie asked as he lay beside me. Oberi had changed into a husky and jumped up to spread out on the foot of the bed.

"What colors go best with your skin tone," I replied. "Do you prefer wool, or cashmere?"

His tone was full of disbelief. "You're worried about clothes at a time like this."

"Well... yeah. Is that wrong?"

He appeared perplexed. "I don't know how you're not overwhelmed with everything that's going on."

"What can we do about it? We're working on finding a solution, but one isn't available right now. I'm not going to beat myself up when we're doing the best we can."

The answer sounded very Oberi. I wonder if more of him had bled into me since I'd returned from the Ancestral Lands.

"We could do more." His voice ached.

"More to make ourselves feel bad, probably. But we can't blame ourselves for information we don't know."

"There has to be a way to get these inferichite bracelets off," Charlie insisted.

"I'm not just talking about the inferichite," I said. "Charlie... I know you still feel horrible about everything that happened in the Underground."

His words were thick. "I can't stop thinking that I could've prevented this, and I didn't. You didn't have to lose your ability to walk, but you did, because I didn't do my best to protect you— not even close."

"What would we have done differently? We didn't know going down there was going to kill me. I didn't know when I cast that spell it would take away my ability to walk. How do you expect us to be angry at ourselves for knowledge we didn't have at the time?"

I sighed. "And even if I had known... I don't think my decision would've been any different. I gave up something to save all of you, but that sacrifice was worth it, because we all got out. So be happy we all survived, and stop getting upset because you have to help me."

"I'm not upset that I have to help you. But I didn't want this for you." Charlie stroked back my hair.

"You being sad because I'm in a wheelchair makes me feel less-than. I don't want pity. I just want to get back to living, whether I'm walking or not. I understand it's something to grieve, because losing the ability to walk is a huge loss. But being in a wheelchair isn't the part that bothers me. It's all the struggles I have to face, because the Institute isn't accommodating, and it sucks how people... *look* at me now. It's not like I'm any different, inside, but *you* treat me differently. And I hate it. I want to be your equal again, not some fragile fucking flower you have to dance around."

He sniffed. "I didn't want to make you feel like that. I've been doing the best I can. I don't regret the position we're in."

"Stop lying. I know what you're thinking. Sometimes you wonder if it would've been better to let me go."

He started to tear up. "I'm glad that you're here. But I hate to see you in so much pain."

"You made the right choice. You're not a monster for wanting me to stay with you, and you shouldn't feel guilty for bringing my soul back," I insisted. "If I didn't agree, I would've stayed in the Ancestral Lands. I figured coming back here to party on Earth was the better option."

"Wish it was under better circumstances," Charlie mumbled.

"I want to get to a place of acceptance, at the very least. Yeah, this is traumatic and new, but it doesn't mean my life is over. It's scary because I have to learn how to ask for help for the first time, and that's terrifying, because I'm so independent."

I looked toward the ceiling. "I'm determined to help myself. I've grown up around people with disabilities, so I know I can still do everything I want to. I'm not angry that I'm in a wheelchair. I'm angry I have to relearn everything in my life. I'm angry at how people treat me. So don't be one of those people. Just be Charlie. That's all I ever wanted from you. A sense of normalcy."

Charlie gave a skeptical noise. "We're anything but normal."

"Normal for us. And I mean, look at the positives," I said. "I get to do wheelies whenever I want, I get to cut in line, my upper body strength is going to be *amazing*, and I can accidentally roll over people I hate. Those are all huge benefits."

He laughed through the tears. "Those are pretty good points."

He swallowed. "I'm just... I'm sorry I put you through this. The surgery, struggling to learn how to live again... all of it. I know how difficult it is to learn how to navigate the world when you don't have the same tools as everyone else, and I didn't want that for you."

"Well, in my mind, there's nothing to say sorry for. But I forgive you anyway. And I think you should forgive yourself, too."

Charlie drew a deep breath and promised, "I'll try."

He laced his fingers through mine. I called Fire to my skin, just enough to warm his fingers and show him I cared. A light breeze made my hair flutter in front of my face. Charlie was thanking me without having to say a thing.

A cracking sound met my ears, and the bracelets on our wrists shook. I gasped. I lifted the cuff up to my eye level, observing the inferichite trapped within. The stone had several cracks running through it.

"What just happened?" Charlie asked.

"The inferichite broke," I said in wonder, grabbing his wrist to check his bracelet as well. The crystal within his cuff had turned to powder, leaving an empty slot where it had been.

You severed both, Oberi said in awe, gazing at me. *It was your magic.*

"I feel so much better," Charlie said. "How'd we do it?"

"It must've been our power of forgiveness," I explained. "I think we're always looking for negative feelings to fix things. Rage, desperation... but there are stronger emotions than that, more powerful ones. I realize now that I didn't break the inferichite in the Underground because I was angry. I broke it because... I loved you. And all that love, the inferichite couldn't hold."

Aw. How sentimental, Oberi purred.

"You're incredible, pidge." Charlie swung his legs out of bed. "We still have some time before curfew. Let's sneak out to the fence line and see if we can break that inferichite, too."

He went to grab my wheelchair, but I grabbed his arm. "We'll get harassed by the guards if we take the chair. It's too slow, and we can't avoid them as easily. Let me ride on Oberi, and you can ride behind me. Then you can make sure I won't fall off."

He frowned. "You could get hurt."

"Please, Charlie. I miss riding."

His shoulder slackened. "It's a good compromise. I guess it's okay."

Oberi changed into a unicorn. Charlie lifted me onto her back once we were out of our cell and into the hallway. Charlie rode behind me. He wrapped his arms around my middle, because my legs weren't capable of gripping her sides to keep me on. Once outside, we stuck to the shadows and the trees, avoiding the sight of the guards.

"They're going to know we snuck out here. The trackers in the cuffs are still active," I told Charlie.

"It doesn't mean anything, not as long as we get back to our room before ten. We're not breaking the rules," Charlie said.

We approached the fence line. The guards had already fixed the barbed wire that Ez's Familiar had torn, making it seem like it'd never been disturbed at all.

Ten feet out, a nauseous pit formed in my stomach.

"Stop," I said, and Oberi halted in her tracks. "I can't get any closer without getting sick."

"Can you affect the inferichite from here?" Charlie asked.

I cast out my magic, but now that I was actively *trying* to mess with the inferichite, performing spells was harder. I already knew I wasn't going to be able to break what was underneath that fence line with the energy I had.

"You try. I can't do it," I said tiredly.

A couple of moments passed. There was a sharp noise that was muffled by the ground, like a minor explosion had gone off underneath the earth.

"I heard something break," I noted.

"You heard something *shift*. I was able to disturb the crystal, but I couldn't shatter it like the ones inside the cuffs," Charlie said. "Those crystals are a lot bigger than the ones inside our cuffs."

I frowned. "Looks like we only have enough magic to break minimal amounts of inferichite. What's buried under the fence is still too over-powering. The Warden must've put whole inferichite bricks under the property and lined the entire fence."

"It doesn't matter. We've proven we can do it," Charlie insisted. "This is a huge breakthrough. If we can learn how to break small amounts of inferichite, eventually, we can become strong enough to get through the fence line."

"Then we're home free," I whispered.

Charlie drew me closer to him as he kissed my head. "I love you, pidge."

"I love you too, Charlie." I let my head fall back on his chest. "Someday we'll get out of here."

That someday was soon. Hopefully the Warden didn't have any plans for us before then.

Though I knew whatever he wanted to do with us would come when we were least expecting it. When it did, we had to be ready.

SEVEN

We'd broken our inferichite bracelets. It was progress.

But breaking the inferichite was just the first step. We still had to learn our demigod powers if we had any hope of getting out of here. We knew Ava had healing magic and Kallie could manipulate time. But me? I didn't even know where to start. And Marcus? Well, he had to break his inferichite first if we wanted to learn what his demigod powers were.

At the very least, Ava was with us again, and she'd only been back for a short while before making a huge breakthrough. Ava was such a vital part of our team, and that became increasingly apparent during her time in the hospital. We were already halfway through the semester, and we hadn't gotten anywhere investigating the keys on our own. I had the thought that if Ava *had* died in the Underground, we'd all be totally fucked, because we weren't finding those keys and saving the Blessed Haven without her.

The bed beside me was empty when I woke on Saturday. My heart gave a start, until I heard Ava humming from the next room. Oberi clacked her beak. I didn't know what was going on, but they both sounded content.

I rolled out of bed and walked over to the dresser to pick out clothes for the day. It was the weekend, so I could wear whatever I wanted, thank the ancestors. That scratchy uniform had been nice at first, but nothing could compare to the soft t-shirts Ava's mom had brought me over winter break.

My knee slammed into something hard. I tripped and toppled over.

"Everything all right in there?" Ava called.

I felt for what I'd run into and realized it was the middle drawer of our dresser. Ava must've left it open when she was looking for clothes this morning.

"You forgot to shut the dresser drawer," I told her.

"Oh, sorry. Whoops," she said.

I frowned as I shoved the drawer back into place. As I got up, the top of my head slammed into something hard. I cursed and felt outward. The top drawer was open, too. As I felt around, I realized all our clothes were tangled in a big heap.

My stomach lurched, because I was always careful to arrange my clothes perfectly. *Ava...*

This was one of the big struggles about living together, because I was a neat freak, and— there was really no nice way to say this— Ava was a slob. She threw stuff everywhere, and wherever it landed, that's where it stayed. Which was annoying, because that made it difficult for me to find things. It'd gotten a little better, because we'd worked on it a lot, but sometimes I still tripped on random shit she left lying around.

Not to mention she had a bad habit of wearing my shirts to bed— which was fine, I didn't care— except that she never quite put them back.

I pulled the clothes out of the drawer and spread them out on the bed, folding them into neat piles and placing them back into the drawer. Once I felt better that things were back in order, I slipped on a t-shirt and jeans. I wiped the blood on my knee away— there wasn't much— and put on my socks and shoes. I reached for my comb in my shower caddy... but it was gone. I frantically ran my fingers over the top of the dresser, but there was nothing.

"Uh, pidge?" I asked.

Ava stopped humming. "Yeah?"

"Where's my shower caddy?"

"I'm using it."

I counted my footsteps as I left the bedroom and emerged into the main room of our apartment. "Using it for what?"

"I'm dyeing one of your old t-shirts. You don't mind, do you?"

Ava-Marie was the only person who I let touch my things, but I didn't like my stuff being moved. Order was the most effective way to navigate my environment, and without it, I'd have no idea where my possessions were.

"It's an old t-shirt," she assured me. "That one with the hole in the side? I'm going to sew up and make it look better, though."

"All right, but how are you dyeing it?" I asked. "We're not allowed to take supplies out of the crafts room."

"Oh, simple!" she said chipperly. "Oberi took me down to Commissary."

I furrowed my brow. "And...?"

"And we got a smoothie! You know, fruit makes a really good natural fabric dye."

"You used your Commissary points to buy a smoothie so you could soak a t-shirt in my shower caddy?" It didn't make sense to me, but this was Ava. I'd learned to roll with it.

"I'm done dyeing it. I'm just soaking it in cold water now. It should help the color set."

I yawned. "You've done all that this morning? What time is it?"

"Past ten," she said. Holy crap, I hadn't realized I'd slept in that long. Though it'd been a hard factory shift last night. I'd come back really tired.

"I really like how the shirt's turning out," she said. "It's a very pretty pink."

I went over to the counter, where we kept bottled water. I reached for one, but my hands met nothing but air. Everything was out of place. I tried to keep my voice steady as I turned back to her. "Where's the water?"

"I'm using it," she said innocently. "Don't worry. We can get more."

"That's not what I'm worried about," I snapped. I didn't mean to, and I felt bad the instant I said it. I pushed my fingers through my hair. "It's just... this is the one place I have control over my environment, and nothing's together this morning. You should've asked me before digging through my drawers and dyeing one of my shirts."

"I thought it'd look nice," she said.

"It's not about the t-shirt, pidge," I insisted. "I know how much you love fashion. I'll let you cut up one of my t-shirts if it makes you happy. I'm bothered you didn't put stuff back. I *need* organization in my space."

A beat passed before Ava said, "I was just trying to help."

Her voice was so small. I hadn't realized she'd been trying to help me. I thought this was one of her fashion pieces she was experimenting with.

I realized then that her parents couldn't send us more clothes right now, because the Warden probably wasn't allowing them to come through. She was trying to repair the shirts I had, because she knew I didn't have much, and what I did have was worn and years old, if not falling apart. This was her way of trying to help me feel better about what I wore.

Oberi ruffled her feathers, and it suddenly occurred to me that maybe Ava *couldn't* put things back in order. Organizing the top drawer of the dresser from her chair couldn't be easy, and she must've had trouble bending over to close the other drawer, because it put pressure on her surgery scars.

Now I felt like an asshole.

"If it's too much trouble, you have to tell me," I pleaded with her.

"No, you're right," she said. "I should've accommodated you."

I hesitated. Ava never gave in so quickly. Usually, she'd fight— *tell me* I was being an asshole for not considering *her* limitations. But today, she just let me win the argument. This was so unlike her.

Ava hadn't had a problem fighting with Esther. I had felt through our bond she was ready to smash that bitch's face in. But with me? She didn't even try to put up a fight.

Something drastic had changed between the two of us, and that worried me to the very core. I should've apologized and told her I understood, but I had to be sure of what was really going on. Was she backing down because she couldn't admit she needed help, or were things really different between us?

I cleared my throat and leaned against the counter. "I could get an infraction for manipulating my wardrobe, like you did last year."

Ava sloshed the t-shirt around in the water. I expected her to argue, but instead she said, "You're probably right."

Um... What. The. Hell?

She wasn't even going to mention that it didn't matter since it wasn't a uniform?

I wanted to ask Oberi what was wrong with her, but I worried she'd hear me. Instead, I said, "Chancey wanted to get the guys together today to work out."

I held my breath, awaiting her response. I expected her to mention fight club. I knew that was a sore spot for her. I thought I'd have to explain that this was nothing like fight club— just some friends getting together to keep our strength up.

But all Ava said was, "Sounds good."

"You... don't have a problem with that?" I asked curiously. "Because if you want me here, I'll stay."

"No, it sounds fun," she said. "I have homework to work on, anyway. You should hang out with the guys."

It almost felt like Ava *wanted* me out of the room. It made me really sad that she didn't need me around, but if she needed her space, I'd honor that.

"I'll see you this afternoon?" I asked.

"Yeah. Sure," Ava said in a tone that was difficult to read.

I hesitated. It didn't seem right to leave her here, but it didn't seem right to stick around, either. My stomach sank as I left the room. I didn't know what was going on between us, but something wasn't right.

I was a nervous ball of energy when I met up with Chancey outside the cafeteria.

"Charlie, good to see ya," Chancey said. "Ready to hit the weights?"

Was I ever. I had to do *something* to process the weird encounter I'd just had with Ava. "Where's everyone else?"

"They went on ahead," he said. "They're waiting for us."

Chancey led me down the hall, while he spoke in soft whispers. "Now don't go snitchin' on me, ya hear? If Captain finds out I snuck a few weights out of the gym, I'm dead meat. He's already got it out for me now that his best bookie is gone."

The mention of Captain left a bad taste in my mouth. "Well, he's just going to have to live with it. We made a deal with him."

"And a fine one at that," Chancey said proudly.

We wove through a maze of hallways, until I couldn't tell where we were anymore. "Where exactly are we headed? I thought if you'd built a secret training room, it'd be in The Devil's Playground."

"Nah, Ives doesn't want to give the wrong impression, you know? I've got a better place. Even the guards don't know I'm there."

"Oh?" I asked curiously.

Chancey opened a door and guided me through. It sounded like a heavy metal door, like the ones at the end of each cell block. I ran my hands along the wall as we walked and realized we were in a long hallway. Up ahead, I could hear the muffled sounds of a conversation going on, but that was it. It didn't seem like there was hardly anyone down here.

"Cellblock 7," Chancey said proudly. "Snagged us an old dorm room no one's using anymore. What do you think?"

Chancey opened another doorway, and the muffled conversation I'd heard earlier became clearer.

"I'll shove a battle orb up that man's ass," Alistair said.

Marcus quickly chimed in, "Look, I'm not shoving anything up *anyone's* ass, but he'll take a battle orb to the face from me."

I heard someone grunt, like they were lifting too many weights. "I'll... send... Tahoma after him," Ez said. His Familiar puffed a heavy breath, like he agreed. "He'll get an antler up the ass, that's for sure."

"Who's getting one up the ass?" Chancey asked nonchalantly— like we talked about assholes all day.

Come to think of it, the topic came up more than I cared to admit.

"Ivy's father," Alistair practically spat. His cat Pig hissed, like just the thought of Ivy's dad made her uncomfortable. "I heard he came around the other day."

"Thanks for the offers, but you don't have to worry about it," Ivy assured us. "Things are different around my dad, but it's fine."

Chancey scoffed. "*Fine?* Ives, he dead-named you every chance he got."

"Yeah, well..." Ivy didn't quite sound like themselves. "It's easier to be that dead person around him. I can raise my old self from the grave every now and then."

"You could get away with joking about that if you were a necromancer, but you're not," Marcus said, sounding concerned. "This isn't funny, Ivy. Your dad's a real piece of work."

"You think I don't *know* that?" Ivy demanded. They stood from whatever piece of furniture they'd been sitting on— I couldn't be quite certain of the layout of the room yet— and started pacing back and forth. Ivy fidgeted so loudly I could hear it. "You guys don't know my dad. You think the vampires in *this* prison are bad? You have no fucking idea what's out there, and what kind of power my dad has."

Something wasn't right with Ivy, and it wasn't just nerves. They held it together when their father was around. I'd heard how Ivy spoke around him. This was different.

"Everyone calm down," I insisted. "If Ivy doesn't want to talk about their father, then let's respect their wishes."

Ivy immediately stopped pacing, and an awkward silence ensued.

"What?" I asked innocently.

"You... called me *they*," Ivy said timidly.

"You said you wanted to try out different pronouns. If you don't like it—"

I was caught completely off guard when Ivy slammed into me, squeezing me into such a tight hug I couldn't breathe. I didn't know Ivy had that kind of strength— they were a lot smaller than me. But then again, they were part vampire, part merfolk.

"Thank you!" Ivy gushed. "You don't know how much that means. Chance and I try different pronouns in private, but to hear it in casual conversation! Oh, it's a delight."

Ivy's choice of words sounded odd, even for them. They drew away, and that's when I caught it— a sickly sweet scent that didn't seem to have a place inside these four walls. It was reminiscent of an alchemy room. Whatever was on Ivy's breath had magical properties to it, and I suspected it wasn't the kind of potion an inmate could find in their classes.

A dark heaviness shrouded me, instantly bringing me down to a dark reality. I had suspected Ivy was using for a while now— ever since my wedding, really. It explained Ivy's odd behavior and the smell on their breath. I wondered if Chancey knew.

"You smell... nice today," I remarked, testing their reaction.

"Ivy loves perfume," Chancey said.

"Yeah, it's my favorite," Ivy added.

"I think it smells awful. It's gotta smell different to a vamp-merfolk nose," Chancey said.

Chancey didn't have a clue Ivy was using. That, or he was actively denying it. He had to be, because he knew what addiction looked like.

Ivy was being unfair. Using drugs didn't just affect them— it affected Chancey and all the people who cared about them. The least they could do was tell someone, so they could get the help they needed. I wanted to rush back and tell Ava immediately, but it would crush her. I didn't know where she was at mentally right now, and I couldn't risk hurting her like that.

And telling Chancey? Well, that wasn't my place. I needed to talk to Ivy before I told anyone.

Ivy turned back to the others. "Anyway, we're not here to rag on my dad. We're here because Marcus is a string bean and needs to bulk up."

"Hey!" Marcus whined.

"If I can do it, so can you," Ez said. I heard a light *thwack* as he playfully punched Marcus.

"Ow!" Marcus complained.

"All right," Chancey called. "We're not here to spar. We're here to keep up our strength."

"Give me some weights," Alistair said. "I'll show you what a real man can do."

"You think you can outlift me?" Marcus challenged. "Let's go."

As the others competed with each other to see who was the strongest, Chancey walked me around the room to give me the layout. "We've got a few dumbbells we stole from fight club, a bench we found in a classroom, and a bar above the window we've been using for pull-ups. And if you're really ambitious, Ez and I dug this boulder out of the yard. It was one hell of a time getting it back here, but we managed."

Chancey groaned as he lifted the rock, then dropped it into my arms. It was heavier than I expected and practically the size of my chest, but once I got over the initial shock of its weight, it felt as light as a feather.

"You think *I'll* have trouble lifting *rocks*?" I asked. "Brother, you're forgetting who you're talking to."

Just to play with him, I let go of the rock and used my Earth magic to hover in mid-air.

"Wow, I'm impressed," Ez said, taking his attention off Marcus. "I thought you'd struggle now that you've got those cuffs on."

I shrugged. "Noxite doesn't affect demigod powers, and Ava and I broke the inferichite inside it. I'm stronger than ever."

Sort of. Cuff or not, I still didn't know how the hell to utilize my demigod powers.

"Then why's string bean over here still struggling with a ten-pound weight?" Alistair cracked. "You'd think as a demigod, he'd have super strength."

"First of all, that's not how demigod powers work," Marcus said diplomatically. "Second... I haven't broken the inferichite yet."

His voice got really quiet at the end.

"You'll figure it out," I encouraged.

"How'd Charlie and Ava do it?" Alistair asked. "Just do that."

"It kind of... just happened," I admitted. "Inferichite can't handle big emotions. We were talking about our feelings, and it just broke."

"All right, I'll just *talk about my feelings*," Marcus said sarcastically. "It's worked out *so great* in the past."

"Yeah, fuck feelings," Alistair agreed. "That shit ain't gonna save the world."

"Or maybe it *is*, and that's why we haven't saved the world yet," I snapped. "I'll say it. I'm not ashamed. I talk about my feelings with my wife, and we've made progress. Fuck anyone who thinks it makes me less of a man."

The room went dead silent.

"All right. Wow. I was just making a joke," Alistair said.

"It was a bad joke," I replied. "I know you want to lighten the mood, but now's the time to get serious about this shit. Ava and I found a way that works, and until Marcus and Kallie talk it out, we're sitting on our potential without doing something useful with it. Hell, Kallie's time powers could get us *all* out of here, but she can't access it until she figures stuff out with her mate— with Marcus."

"You think I want this for us?" Marcus demanded. "The last thing I want is to hurt Kallie. I have my reasons for not being with her!"

"And all of your reasons point to avoiding the inevitable!" I growled. "You think putting it off will make things *better*? Dammit, Marcus. It's only going to make the moment worse once this all comes to a head. You don't want to hurt her like you hurt Anya? Then make an effort to fix it before it's too late!"

If I thought the room went silent before, it was nothing compared to now. Nobody *breathed.*

Finally, I heard the rustle of fabric as Marcus crossed his arms. "Perhaps we should talk about this in private."

"All right," I said, taking him up on his bluff. He wanted to act like a tough guy, I sure as hell could play.

"I— I..." Marcus fumbled with his words for a second, and when he couldn't find them, he grabbed me by the arm and dragged me toward the door. I nearly tripped over Rishi, and I ran into the bench on my way out. It should've hurt like hell, but I was too worked up to care. I heard the door slam behind us as we entered the hall.

"You're being a real ass, you know that?" Marcus snapped once we were alone.

I gritted my teeth. "I'm aware."

I didn't give excuses, but I had a hundred on my tongue. I was worried about Ava. Oberi was no help. Ivy was on drugs, and I didn't know if I could tell anyone. We were running out of time to figure out our magic. This whole charade with the Warden was nothing more than a shit show.

I pressed my fingers to the corners of my eyes. "I'm sorry. There's a lot going on right now. I just don't want to see you get hurt."

Marcus took a long breath. "That's the last thing any of us want."

"Look. Kallie's a fae, and we can't get around that," I said. "She'll never be able to access the full height of her abilities if she's not mated, and we need her to do that if we're going to do everything we've been planning on. You share a bond with her. You either need to fulfill it, or break it and have it over with."

"I don't want to do that, either," Marcus whined.

"You can't keep leaving her in limbo! It's selfish, and it puts the team at risk!" I insisted. "Her magic keeps getting weaker the longer this drags on, and if she can't use her powers... dude, we're fucked. If you can't be her partner, you need to let her be with someone else who's willing to step up to the plate."

Marcus made a strange sound, like the thought of her being with someone else was unfathomable. His jealous behavior when Kallie had dated Scarlet last semester made everything so obvious.

"You don't want to be with her, but you don't want to let her go," I stated. "Have you given one single thought to consider what *she* wants? This isn't fair to her."

"Who are you to talk? You and Ava put everyone through so much drama last semester because you two couldn't figure out how to get back together until you were forced to," Marcus accused.

"Yeah, and it was fucking stupid dragging it on for as long as I did," I insisted. "I should've put in an effort to work things out with her before the wedding happened. I caused both of us so much unnecessary pain because I thought it was easier keeping us apart, but it *wasn't*. Instead, I gave up, and that's exactly what you're doing now. You're too afraid to make a decision, so you've decided not to try. And that *is* a decision, Marcus, no matter how far you run from it."

Rishi meowed, and Marcus mumbled, "I don't know what to do."

"Secure your bond, Marcus," I demanded. "I know you and Kallie have been screwing around. You love her, no matter how much you try to deny it."

"Yeah, and that's the problem!" Marcus yelled, so loud his voice echoed down the empty hall. "I loved Anya, too, but what I feel for Kallie is *so* much deeper. Losing Anya nearly did me in, and I can't go through that with Kallie. Worse, I can't put *her* through that. If she has a mate, she can lose a mate, which is worse than hell for a fae. With everything we're facing, we're bound to lose each other. It's better to stop loving her altogether than to lose her!"

I crossed my arms. "I don't believe that for a second. If you truly thought that, you'd have broken your bond."

"I can't!" Marcus insisted. "Believe me, I've done everything I can to fall out of love with her, but my feelings for her aren't going anywhere. If Kallie's going to lose me, then she'll lose an unbonded mate. It will be easier that way. I saw how fucked up you were when Ava died. I'm not putting her through that."

"So you're just going to keep your mating bond hanging in limbo?" I demanded. "Eventually, you and Kallie aren't going to be able to resist it any longer. You've already acted on your bond with Kallie. You're going to have a hell of a time coming back from that, *if* you even can at this point."

Marcus huffed. "You don't know anything about what's happened between Kallie and me. Whatever details Kallie spilled to Ava doesn't cover what's really happening."

"So tell me," I pleaded. "Let me help."

"So you can guilt trip me into making a decision about my own life?" Marcus snapped.

I sighed. "That's not what I'm trying to do, Marcus. I'm trying to help you see the situation for what it is."

"What makes you think I don't know what's happening?" he growled.

"Because you've started something with Kallie that you can't stop, even though you want to leave that door open. Push any further, and that door's gonna come slamming straight shut behind you. Your mating bond will secure before you're ready for it, and then there *won't* be any going back."

"You think I've done this all on a whim, without thinking about the consequences?" Marcus demanded. "I overthink every damn move I make. The moves I made on Kallie? *I could not stop.* Don't treat me like an idiot."

My stomach sank, and my tone became lighter. "You're not an idiot."

"Then why do I feel like it sometimes?" Marcus' voice cracked.

"Love makes you feel crazy shit," I told him. "I'll tell you one crazy truth, Marcus. If I had to choose between losing Ava all over again or never loving her in the first place, I'd lose her a million times, because the time I got to love her meant everything."

Marcus swallowed. "Do you really mean that?"

I nodded. "With my entire soul. I think you and Kallie deserve a shot together. Ava and I can be there with you. We'll go on a double date. That'll make it easy."

"I'm not sure..." Marcus started.

"I'm not asking you for results," I said. "I'm just asking you to try."

He gave a defeated sigh. "I guess we could give it a try."

"So we're good?" I asked.

Marcus groaned. "Aw, man. Don't make me talk about my feelings."

"You'll get used to it," I told him.

We returned to the workout room. Ez groaned on the bench while he lifted dumbbells above his head, and Alistair grunted as he tried to lift the boulder. I could feel with my magic that he got it a few inches off the ground. Air swirled around Chancey's ankles as he did chin-ups on the bar.

Ivy didn't work out— just sat there observing.

"If I keep this up... those vampires won't know... what hit 'em," Alistair said as he struggled with the boulder. "Eddie's gonna think... I'm so hot... when he sees me next."

Guilt rattled around in my gut, because despite our best efforts, we still had no idea where the Warden's concentration camp was— and even if we did, we'd have to get out of this place first to rescue Eddie and the other Elves. Hell, we didn't even know if they were still alive. My magical connection to Eddie grew weaker by the day. Since he was my sworn guard, I should be able to tell if he was still out there or not. I really had no fucking clue, and that terrified me.

This was why we had to expedite our demigod training. The Elves didn't have time to sit around and wait for us. Their time could already be up.

Alistair's comment must've made Marcus really uncomfortable, because he suggested, "Maybe it's time to call it a day."

Nobody argued. We'd barely gotten here, and I was already over it. We all were.

"Yeah, I'm starving," Ivy agreed.

I didn't believe them. Ivy just wanted to ditch. Everyone began filing out of the room. I planted myself between Ivy and the exit. Someone hesitated in the doorway. It must've been Chancey.

"Can I get your opinion on a gift for Ava?" I asked.

"Absolutely!" Ivy said. "What are you thinking?"

"Well, uh... she likes dresses," I said slowly.

That was enough to get Chancey out of the room, because the door clicked shut, leaving Ivy and me alone.

"Ava would look sexy in a red—"

"Cut the crap, Ivy," I snarled.

Ivy snapped their mouth shut.

"I know whatever I smelled on you wasn't perfume," I accused. "You haven't told Chancey."

"I don't know what you're talking about." Ivy sounded so confident. They'd denied this so many times that they were a master at it, but they couldn't fool me.

"Yes, you do," I said. "Let me help."

"I don't need *help*," Ivy insisted. "For fuck's sake, Charlie, I'm not some low-life vagrant who can't get clean."

I was screwing this up again. "I'm not here to judge you. I just want to help you get better."

Ivy's voice was flat. "I appreciate that, but I'm fine, really. It's only a little every now and then. It's not like it's dangerous. There's nothing you can do."

"I *can*," I insisted. "I've been around this stuff before. Hell, there was a time *I* needed help—"

"And what *exactly* are you going to do?" Ivy challenged. "Report me to my counselor? Send me to rehab for the millionth time? There's no way out of the Institute, and there's no way out of this. Let me deal with my life the only way I know how."

"So let's deal with it together," I offered.

Ivy scoffed. "You're fooling yourself. I'm sorry you had a hard life, but we're nothing alike."

"Then help me understand," I pleaded.

"You never can, and you never will."

"This is going to kill you if you don't stop," I hissed. "What are you on? Nightshade?" I knew that's what it had to be.

Ivy huffed. "Of course you'd assume that. You have *such* a low opinion of me."

Ivy's deflection wasn't going to deter me. "At the very least, go to the infirmary for a detox, or talk about it in group therapy. That's what it's for," I suggested.

"They're just going to sell me the same bullshit they always do, tell me the same shit they tell every addict. They don't really care about me," Ivy sneered.

"Well guess what, your friends do. How's Ava going to feel when she finds out?"

"Don't tell Ava." For the first time, Ivy actually sounded scared. "She doesn't need to know about this. She's got enough to deal with."

"Everyone's going to find out if you keep using, and you can't stop on your own. Then what are you gonna do?"

Ivy gave a teary laugh. "Well, everyone always leaves me eventually, so why do I care?"

My mouth got dry. "We're not like your parents. We're not going anywhere. If you don't care about yourself, think about Chancey. What's this going to do to him?"

Ivy didn't have anything to say to that, and maybe that's because the question was unfair. I really *was* being an asshole today. I didn't get a chance to add anything else before Ivy pushed past me, slamming their shoulder into mine. They hurried out of the room, and I sighed as I followed behind them. I barely made it out the door before I slammed into something. It moved, and I realized it was Ivy.

"I thought you were walking away," I said.

"I *was*. But then I thought..." Ivy trailed off.

"You thought what?" I asked. *That I was right?*

"I thought I saw someone down the hall."

I instantly became more alert. "Who'd you see?"

"I don't know," Ivy admitted. "I'm sure it was nothing. I mean, what would a girl with blonde curls have business doing down in an abandoned cell block? We're the only ones who know about the workout room."

My veins turned to blocks of ice. Blonde curls could only mean one thing.

Esther.

The Warden had her spying on us. Surely she couldn't have heard anything inside the room. But what had Marcus and I said out in the hall?

We had to be more careful.

THE WEEK AFTER, I wheeled Ava into Rehabilitation Skills. It was more or less an advanced Home Economics class to teach us how to assimilate back into society once we left this hell hole. Most students didn't pass.

"You need a haircut," Kallie said from the table next to us.

"I like my hair long!" Marcus countered. "I can almost fit it into a ponytail."

"Imagine if you slicked it back, though," Kallie suggested. "It'd look hot."

They were talking like nothing had changed. Obviously, Marcus hadn't asked her on that date yet.

"Girl, you don't know what you're talking about," Alistair piped up from the table behind them. "Marcus is already one hot piece of ass. He doesn't have to change *anything*."

"Uh... thanks?" Marcus said.

"Are you hitting on *my*— on Marcus?" Kallie demanded. Very possessively, I might add.

"Look, I'm taken," Alistair said. "Doesn't mean I don't recognize a good slab of meat when I see it. You agree, don't you, Thaddeus?"

Thaddeus laughed from beside Alistair. "I'm not really the right person to ask."

"You hear that, Kallie?" Marcus said proudly. "I'm a *good slab of meat*."

"You know what wolvens like myself do with meat?" Kallie asked. "We eat it."

"Ooh," Alistair and Thaddeus sang in unison.

"I *bet* you'd like to eat Marcus' meat," Ava mumbled. It was the first time she spoken since we arrived.

It made me feel better to hear her joking around. Oberi's feathers fluttered from the back of Ava's chair as she added, *I'm sure she already has.*

"What was that?" Kallie demanded.

Ava raised her voice. "I said, I bet you'd like to taste Marcus'—"

"Students, please, let's quiet down," a female voice came from the front of the room. I hadn't realized our professor had entered.

"Aw, fuck, *she's* here?" Alistair hissed. "Thaddeus, hide me!"

"What are you—?" Thaddeus cut off. "Get out from underneath the table."

Pig meowed loudly. Alistair must've stepped on her tail or something.

"You don't understand," Alistair insisted. "She pulled me aside after class last week and... let's just say our professor hates me."

"I'm sure she doesn't—" Thaddeus started, but the click of heels cut him off.

Our professor strolled straight up to Alistair's table and stopped there. She must've had the harshest look in her eyes, because all the chatter in the room died.

"Is something the matter, Mister Martin?" she asked Alistair sharply.

"Uh, n–no, Professor Ziva," Alistair squeaked. "Everything's fine here. Just, uh... dusting off my cat."

Pig gave a loud meow in protest.

"I expect you to sit quietly in your seat and pay attention to the lesson, Mister Martin," she sneered. "You wouldn't want to *fail*."

It sounded like a threat if I ever heard one.

Alistair shuffled back to his seat and didn't say another word. I didn't know what it was about this woman that could possibly scare Alistair. Nothing made the kid go quiet. *Nothing.* But something about this woman seemed to strike the fear of god into him.

Once satisfied, Professor Ziva returned to the front of the room. "Today we'll be learning proper etiquette, which will help you secure job interviews and schedule doctor's appointments, should you graduate."

Someone at the front of the room scoffed, causing Professor Ziva to get very stern with them. "Don't you roll your eyes at me," she snarled. "In Astromancer society, if a woman doesn't know how to properly place a phone call, she'll be hung up on. Good luck scheduling your husband's appointments."

"Astromancer? I thought you were a witch," someone said.

"Half-witch, half-Astromancer," Ziva clarified. "I grew up in Octavia Falls, free to practice my magic. Once I graduated, I spent some time with the Astromancers, learning of my heritage and how my magic connected with the stars. In Astromancer society, women are not allowed to practice magic, let alone hold down a job. An Astromancer woman's greatest asset is her ability to manage the household and serve her husband. Consider yourself lucky if you think these skills are beneath you."

"There's no way I'm staying home to iron your shirts, let's get that established right now," Ava mumbled to me.

Half-witch, half-Astromancer. Why did that sound so...?

It hit me then. Alistair had been sent to the Institute for poisoning a visiting Astromancer professor. But she wasn't just visiting Octavia Falls... she'd returned there, perhaps to apply for a position at the school. But Ziva had ended up in the hospital after Alistair slipped her the potion. She must've lost the job. She couldn't teach in Astromancer society, so the Institute was her last resort.

No wonder Professor Ziva hated Alistair. He was definitely screwed.

"I've prepared a script for you to practice," Professor Ziva said. "I've assigned you to random pairs, so that you don't get *too comfortable* practicing with your friends. Names are on the board. Let's get started."

Papers rustled, and chairs squeaked as people began to move about and pair up.

"You're with Thaddeus," Ava said. "I'm with... ugh. *Danielle.*"

Danielle was one of Naya's minions. I hated the thought of leaving Ava here with her, even if I was just one table away.

"Excuse me," a female voice sneered at me. "You're in my seat."

I didn't move right away, but Ava placed a gentle hand on my arm. "I'll be all right."

I didn't like Danielle, but Professor Ziva was barking at the front of the room to hurry it up. "I'll be right here if you need me," I told Ava.

Don't worry, Oberi assured me. *If this bitch comes anywhere near Ava, I'll peck her eyes out.*

Damn right, you will, I replied.

"See you later, Charlie," Danielle cooed to me. I kept my expression flat, and it was difficult, because I wanted to sneer. Danielle was awful to Ava, but she was always nice to me...

Too nice, if you got my meaning. I was married, but even if I wasn't, I'd have absolutely no interest in Danielle, so she needed to leave me alone.

I got out of my seat and found my way next to Thaddeus. My fingers brushed against the feathers of his hawk Familiar as I passed his chair. I knew him pretty well by now, since we'd worked the mines together and had been paired up in Elementai Magic more than once.

"How do you want to do this?" Thaddeus asked.

"I've got it," I said, pulling my reading glasses out of my pocket. I held my script in front of me, and the glasses began reading the words out to me.

"Wow!" Thaddeus raved. "Those are epic."

"Aren't they? Ava's brother Mav really knew what he was doing when he developed these."

"Maverick?" Thaddeus asked. "I remember him. He was my reading buddy back in high school. They'd pair us up with the kids from the elementary school and we'd read to them every Thursday. He's really come a long way, hasn't he?"

"Yeah, he's a great kid," I said.

Thaddeus sounded really excited for Maverick, which was so different from all the other inmates. I suddenly realized I never knew why Thaddeus had been sentenced. He was young— barely nineteen— and had a kind heart. Even the Institute hadn't managed to fuck him up yet.

I set my script aside. "Can I ask you something?"

"Sure," he said in a bubbly tone.

"Why are you here?" I asked gently.

"Uh, it's in my schedule."

"Not this class. I mean... why are you at the Institute? I never heard the story."

"Oh." He became very quiet. "Maybe we should get to our project."

I felt a little sad that he didn't trust me. Everyone had a story to tell, whether it was the whole truth or not. I barely knew a thing about Thaddeus.

"If you don't want to talk about it, that's all right," I offered.

Thaddeus hesitated. "I don't want you to think I did anything bad, because I didn't. Well, maybe that's not true."

He took a deep breath, like talking about it was hard. "The truth is, my parents died a few years back in a boating accident. The tribe did what they could to help, but there's only so much you can do for... whatever it was I had. PTSD, depression, I'm not sure. I got involved with the wrong people and was caught trading magical goods with some witches."

"Magical goods?" I asked warily. "You were dealing drugs?"

"More or less," Thaddeus admitted.

My stomach sank as I suddenly saw myself in Thaddeus— the lone, orphaned kid trying to find his place in the world, only for a gang of drug dealers to take advantage of him. I didn't blame him. It wasn't his fault. Thaddeus was just trying to cope— to *survive*. I suddenly hated that I hadn't been there, that I hadn't found the Elementai sooner. I could have mentored him, taught him how to survive on his own.

Maybe I still could...

"I'm sorry you went through that," I told him.

"Sorry for me?" Thaddeus balked. "After everything you've been through— finding Forevermore and Ava almost *dying*— my problems look like a walk in the park."

"Just because I had it worse doesn't render your problems obsolete," I said.

Thaddeus scoffed. "It does in this prison. Seems like everyone's competing on who's got it worse. And, well... I don't want to enter the Darke Games, so I keep quiet. No one pays me any attention."

"Consider it a blessing," I said. "There are people in this prison whose attention is the *last* thing you want."

"Like the Warden?" Thaddeus whispered.

I nodded. "Like the Warden."

Thaddeus shifted in his seat and lowered his voice even further. "You're going up against him, aren't you?"

"I'm going to try."

"Let me help," he offered. "Like I said, no one notices me. I can be an asset— a spy."

I shook my head firmly. "No. You could get hurt."

"So?" he challenged. "I may not *seem* tough, but I've been in this prison long enough to learn a thing or two."

"You're going to have to know a lot more than that to stand a chance against the Warden." I couldn't be responsible for this kid if he got hurt.

"All right, maybe I know more than a couple of things. You wouldn't want me snooping around on my own, would you?"

"Ugh, fine," I caved. He wasn't going to back down, and at least if we were working together, I could keep an eye on him. "I'll let you know as soon as I have a job for you."

"That's not good enough," Thaddeus argued. "I want a job now. Otherwise, you'll just blow me off and stall."

I groaned. "Fine. What are your skills?"

"I blend in very well," Thaddeus said. "I can follow people and eavesdrop. They wouldn't suspect a thing."

I hesitated. The last thing I wanted was to get this kid involved, but it sounded like he was going to go after the Warden one way or another. He'd get himself killed unless I kept him distracted.

"Keep an eye on our angel professors," I instructed. "They know something, and I'm not sure what. Report back to me what you hear, okay?"

"Yes, sir," Thaddeus said, sounding happy to be on board.

I was sure the angel professors knew *something*, but I wouldn't be at all surprised if the Warden was keeping them in the dark. At least if I gave Thaddeus something to focus on, he'd stay away from the Warden.

"Thank you, Charlie," Thaddeus raved. "You won't regret it."

I heard the click of heels, then Professor Ziva sneered, "Stick to the script!"

Thaddeus' Familiar bristled his feathers, and Thaddeus laughed under his breath. His Familiar must have a sense of humor. We didn't get a chance to talk any more after that. We read off the script until the end of class.

I wheeled Ava out of the room, and my friends followed behind us. I heard a commotion down the hall, and someone ran into me as they passed.

"Watch it!" a deep voice growled. Sounded like a guard. Another brawl must've broken out up ahead.

Thaddeus walked at my side. "So, does this make me part of the Villain's Club?"

"What's he talking about?" Ava asked.

"That's what you guys called yourselves during the Darke Games, isn't it?" Thaddeus said.

I sighed. "Thaddeus is going to help us gather intel."

"Hold up," Alistair said. "If Thaddeus is helping, I want in. You *know* I'm good at gathering intel!"

"Let's not get ahead of ourselves," Marcus said. "You guys *do* know who you're dealing with right? The Warden is ruthless."

"Hey! He's got Eddie," Alistair snapped. "I'm not letting my man rot without doing something about it. So if you're letting people into the group, I want in."

I slowed as we turned the corner. "You two can work together," I offered. It was the best I could do to get them out of trouble. "How does that sound?"

"Works for me," Alistair said.

"I guess we could use more eyes and ears," Kallie admitted.

"Ava?" I asked, to see what she thought of it.

"Ava-Marie." Someone clicked their tongue as they passed us in the hall. Footsteps slowed— several pairs, by the sound of it. "Now that's a name you don't want to hear while wandering these halls."

"What do you want, Deuce?" Ava demanded.

Aw, fuck. Not this asshole. We'd fought this vampire in the Darke Games, and he'd only gotten worse since then. I absolutely despised him — he'd beaten me in fight club once, and though I'd never admit it, I hadn't gotten over it. Secretly, I was still looking for my chance to get a rematch, so I could put him in the ground.

"Your head would be a good start." Deuce chuckled, and his cronies laughed along with him. By the sounds of it, there were four of them total.

Someone cracked their knuckles and spoke in a raspy voice. "I'll take Charlie. Still can't speak right after what he did to me in the Games."

It was Kyle, the merman whose windpipe I'd nearly crushed. A shoe squeaked, and Thaddeus crouched behind me as someone approached.

"Take one step closer, and I'll finish the job," I threatened.

Deuce scoffed. "Like we're scared of you? Two blind guys and these two bodybuilders? Looks like they've never seen a weight room in their life."

"Yeah, well, I wouldn't test them," Ava sneered.

Deuce chuckled. "Oh, the invalid talks. Like she matters. Maybe I'll take your *legs* first. You're not using them anyhow."

It all happened at once. I heard the squeak of Ava's wheels, then Oberi's squawk the same time Ava gave an agonized scream. I felt the pain in her spine ripple through our bond, and the *thud* of her body as it hit the floor.

Fucking hell! Ava's thoughts slipped through the bond, and I knew she was in more pain than she'd ever admit to.

Deuce had pushed her out of her chair! Ancestors have mercy, because I sure as hell wouldn't give any to this bastard.

"Kallie, Oberi, get Ava out of here *now!*" I screamed.

Kallie could use her telekinesis to lift Ava back into her chair. I didn't have a moment to think beyond that before magic burst out of me. Air magic blasted Deuce back so hard I heard the stone wall crack as he landed against it. This bastard was going to pay for laying a hand on my wife.

Deuce let out a primal roar. Air swirled past me as he closed the distance between us in an instant. My friends screamed as Deuce's gang descended upon them. I heard Ava's distant protests as Kallie wheeled her away from the danger.

Rage ignited in my bones so quickly that once it lit, there was no putting it out. Air swept down the hall in a whirlwind so powerful that it swooped Deuce and his gang up and tossed them a dozen yards away. The stone walls around us began to shake, and I realized it wasn't just me controlling them. Thaddeus was *pissed*, and he was losing control of his Earth magic. Battle orbs crackled as Alistair and Marcus conjured them in unison. Rishi and Pig squealed, and a hawk's cry echoed down the hall.

Deuce was strong, and my magic barely fazed him. The gang closed in on us so fast, I could barely make sense of it. I heard a snap, followed by Alistair's pained scream. Somebody grabbed me by the throat and shoved me against the wall. It was probably Kyle, judging by the strength. I gasped for breath that didn't come, then resorted to stealing the merman's strength with my Elf powers. My friends cried out as the other two assholes delivered blows. A mere second must've passed before I was powered up enough to shove the merman off of me. By then, it was too late.

"Hold him down!" Deuce growled. He jumped me, and I felt the sharp stab of his fangs against my neck. He didn't release any venom, but that didn't mean it didn't hurt like hell.

This dick obviously didn't know who I was or what the fuck I was capable of. Magic exploded out of me— a mix of Air, superstrength I'd siphoned, or something. I wasn't sure. What I *did* know was that it was enough to blast both Deuce and Kyle off of me. I heard the crack of their bodies as they slammed against the ceiling, then the *thud* as they landed against the ground. Deuce groaned on the floor and didn't get back up.

Good. I hoped I killed him.

Kyle, on the other hand, lunged for me again, but Marcus body-checked him and tackled him to the ground. All right, so I underestimated Marcus. I didn't know he had it in him to drop a merman.

"Get away from him, you jerk!" Alistair shot out another battle orb that crackled so powerfully my hair stood up.

"C— Charlie!" Thaddeus rasped.

Someone had Thaddeus against the wall. My rage instantly turned to something darker, *much* more sinister. I didn't even have a word for it. Thaddeus was tangled up in this mess because of me. I wouldn't let him go out like this.

I grabbed the guy and yanked him off of Thaddeus. My super strength was multiplied by my rage, and the guy landed on the floor next to Deuce. I held my hands up and forced the air around him to contract. I did as I'd done in the Games to Kyle— pulled the air tighter and tighter around him until I felt his windpipe crush. This time, I made no mistakes. I sealed that fucker off tighter than the Warden sealed us into this prison. He struggled and tried wheezing for air, but no sound came out.

"Charlie!" I heard Ava's cry somewhere in the distance. She mustn't have let Kallie take her far. I couldn't make sense of her voice, though. Even Ava couldn't stop me now.

Charlie, the guards are coming, Oberi warned. She broke through enough that I dropped my magic and took a step back. The click of noxite darts filled the hall a moment later.

"Let's get out of here!" Kyle shouted to his friend, and they scurried away.

"Wait for me..." Deuce groaned, but his voice trailed off.

Okay, not dead. On the edge of consciousness for sure, though. And his buddy? Didn't even try to breathe. He was gone for certain.

Thaddeus grabbed my arm as I backed away from the two men lying slumped in the middle of the hall. "Charlie, what did you *do?*" he hissed.

"What he had to," Marcus said simply.

"Everyone on the ground!" a guard shouted. They'd been preoccupied with another fight, but they were back now and hungry for blood.

"All right, all right!" Alistair yelled as Pig hissed. "You can get the barrel out of my back now. I'm getting on the ground."

I lifted my hands in surrender and lowered myself to the floor.

"Speak up," a guard snarled. "What happened here?"

Fabric rustled as a guard knelt beside Deuce and his buddy. "Dead, sir."

I should've felt guilty. I had, after all, just taken a life.

But these guys had gone after my friends. I didn't feel a goddamn thing but victory.

"It was the vamp," I said coldly. "He jumped us while we were heading to class."

I exposed my neck to show evidence of the blood trickling down my collarbone. "He bit me, then choked the other guy out."

"Is this true?" a guard asked.

"Y— yes," Thaddeus stammered.

"Every word," Marcus lied in an even tone. He didn't seem fazed by the whole thing, either. I couldn't say the same about Thaddeus, though. I couldn't be sure he hadn't pissed his pants.

"Cuff him," a guard said. "Take the vamp down to Cellblock 9. The rest of you, get to class!"

Deuce must've slipped off into unconsciousness, because there were no arguments, no protests. I heard the sound of metal clink, and then... we just walked out of there.

It was so easy.

"Good thing I can't see, because my eye will be swollen for a month," Alistair said. "Not sure about my arm, though. Think it's broken?"

"*Think?*" Thaddeus balked. "Alistair, your arm is folded in half! I'm taking you to the infirmary immediately."

"Come to think of it, it does hurt a bit..." Alistair trailed off. A *thud* sounded as he slumped to the ground.

"Fuck," Marcus grumbled.

"Guards!" Thaddeus cried, but no one paid us any attention. They didn't give a flying fuck.

"He's gone into shock," Marcus said frantically.

This was how I knew I felt zero remorse for what I'd done. Those fuckers deserved everything they got for hurting my friends.

"Oh, for the gods' sake," Kallie sighed. She'd been pushing Ava's wheelchair, but she abandoned Ava to kneel beside Alistair. "Grab his cane and Pig. I'll help him to the infirmary."

Let me help first, Oberi offered. She flew off her perch on Ava's chair and fluttered down beside Alistair. I felt the warmth of her magic in my chest as she worked her healing on him. *It's not perfect, but it will speed up his healing. Get the doctors to set the break immediately.*

I quickly translated, then our friends took off, leaving Ava and me alone with our Familiar.

She reached out for my hand. "Charlie, are you okay?"

Her voice was full of pain, and I knew she had to be crying. Deuce had really hurt her.

"It's just a little blood," I said. "I'll be fine. But you need to get some help. We have to go to the infirmary."

"No," she rasped, her tone pleading. "Don't make me go back there."

My heart dropped. "Ava, we need to make sure you're okay."

"Oberi can help me," she insisted. "I don't need another doctor telling me they can't help, like they always fucking do."

Oberi's wings fluttered as she hovered before Ava. I felt magic leave her, like I had when she'd healed Alistair's arm, and she said, *My magic doesn't detect any injury, just irritation and pain from aggravating the wound. She'll be all right, but she needs rest.*

"Good." Ava gave a light cough. "Let's get out of here."

I hitched a breath. "I'm not sure—"

She is fine, Charlie. I would not tell you she is if she was not, Oberi noted gently.

Her reassurance was welcome, but barely enough to satisfy me. At the same time, I wasn't going to drag Ava down to the infirmary kicking and screaming. I knew she'd had a horrible time there.

"If your pain gets worse, we're going in," I said.

"Whatever," Ava breathed. "Just take me somewhere I can forget about it."

I wheeled her to the Arboretum, because her mood always seemed to brighten whenever we were there. We stopped by the small pond inside, and I took a seat on the ground while Ava gulped steadying breaths beside me.

"I'm sorry Deuce pushed you out of your chair," I said quietly.

"It was horrible," she said bluntly. I heard a splashing sound as she threw something into the pond— probably a rock. "Just another reminder I'm fucking helpless now."

"You're not helpless. Deuce is just an asshole. I'll teach you how to defend yourself, just in case magic isn't quick enough," I promised.

There was a heavy silence, before I added, "I tried to make it right."

"You can't kill people for me."

"Well, why not?"

"Because it's going to change who you are."

It took a moment for her meaning to hit. "Pidge, those guys broke Alistair's arm and tried to kill Thaddeus. If we're going to save the Elves, we're going to have to do a lot worse."

"You didn't have to take that warlock's life. You chose to," Ava said. "There's a big difference."

I shrugged. The gesture would seem cold to someone on the outside, but I couldn't help it if I felt detached from it all. This world couldn't keep pushing me to my limit and expect me not to fight back.

"I know we've killed people to protect ourselves. I killed a lot of people down in the Underground when I caused that explosion. But look at the cost," Ava stated firmly. "I paid the price for what I did, and if you keep going down this path you're on, you're going to have your own consequences to face."

"You aren't in that chair because you killed Jaymin and all the bastards who were trying to kill us. You're there because I failed to protect you. That situation never should've happened."

"But you're trying to change the past by resorting to violence now. No matter how many lives you take, it's not going to make me walk again."

I brought my legs to my chest and draped my arms over my knees as I said, "I can't change the past, but I can stop things from getting worse. No one's gonna touch you, pidge. Not ever again."

She didn't say anything more, but I let my thoughts flow freely to her across our bond so she'd understand. If we were in danger, we had to do everything we could to teach the people around us we wouldn't be threatened without delivering the ultimate price. What had happened in the Underground couldn't happen again. We wouldn't survive it next time. So if other people had to die in order to prevent that fate, so be it.

At least Ava would be safe.

ava-marie

EIGHT

"Charlie, this isn't right."

I dug through my bag before we left for class. A pill bottle sat on the dresser, nearly empty. My throat got tighter and tighter as I rummaged through the backpack, yet didn't find what I needed.

"What's wrong?" Charlie asked as he tugged his sweater over his head.

"Some of my pills are missing," I said. "I had three yesterday, but there's only one left."

"That's not enough to get you through today," Charlie said. "We need to get a refill."

"We can't tell Doctor Marsh I lost them," I moaned. "I'll get into trouble."

Inmates were required to obtain pills from the nursing station every morning, and weren't allowed access to them otherwise. The infirmary had made a once-in-a-lifetime exception for me, because there were so many different pain medications I had to take now, on such a frequent basis, that it was easier for both the medical staff and for me to keep them on hand at all times, instead of making multiple trips to the nursing station every day.

Except I'd been told that if I got caught selling or otherwise distributing the pills, it'd be an instant trip to Cellblock 9. They wouldn't believe me if I said I lost them.

"I'll have to suck it up until they give me another refill tomorrow," I said tiredly. "There's no other way. I'll take half instead of the full dose."

Charlie frowned, and I rubbed my eyes. "I must've misplaced them. I hate that I'm so careless."

"You've been through a lot. It's okay to forget things," Charlie said. "We'll just have to keep better track of them next time."

"Okay." It helped that he was so understanding. Charlie was always patient with me.

Oberi lay on the bed as a husky. His voice was flat as he said, *Perhaps you didn't misplace them. Someone might've taken a few out of your bag.*

"I wouldn't put it past the assholes at this place," Charlie grumbled.

I shook my head. "No. It's probably just me being brainless again, like always."

I'd been in a weird place mentally. I wasn't exactly depressed, or sad, but it was hard for me to focus like I could before. I was in a fog all the time.

Oberi let out a huff. *Charlie, I need to speak with you—*

"We're already running late. There's no time," I said. "You guys can talk later."

The compass sat on the bedside table following another failed attempt to get it to work last night. After a long struggle with my intuition, I received the feeling I wasn't supposed to use the compass until I was spiritually *prompted* by the device. Trying to force it to work wouldn't lead anywhere. Until I had a sense of inspiration driving me to the compass, I wasn't meant to use it to help us.

It went against all logic and my determination to get out of here. But I'd found that my intuition had grown even stronger since my return from the afterlife, and it wasn't like the Ancestral Lands made any sense, anyhow. I'd have to go against logic and follow my heart if I wanted this compass to work right, and for the moment, Lindsey and Miranda didn't have any messages for me.

We passed Kyle in the hallway. He saw us coming and quickly hurried out of the way, having no desire to provoke Charlie further. He'd seen what Charlie could do in the heat of anger, and Deuce had paid the price for it by ending up in Cellblock 9.

I should've been concerned about Charlie's lack of empathy... how casually he'd lied and said it was Deuce who had ended the warlock's life, and not him. I should've been more bothered that I hadn't flinched as I'd watched my husband take the life of another inmate.

But I wasn't. I hardly cared at all. We'd tried saving people's lives, but the world kept attacking us. We couldn't be responsible if there were morons out there who were stupid enough to get in our way.

The only thing I cared about was if these murders had the potential to change Charlie into someone I didn't recognize. *That's* what I was worried about. I was terrified his impulsivity would one day cause him to make a split-second decision that he'd regret... one that would have unfathomable consequences for both of us.

"Do you regret it?" I asked Charlie quietly.

He instantly got my meaning. The emotion that came across our bond was cold. "No."

Oberi padded beside my wheelchair, giving a slight nod. *You two must understand that anyone that attempts to harm you is no longer a person, but something that must be eliminated in order to protect your own lives and save the world. Nothing can get in the way of what you're destined to achieve.*

I thought about all the guards I'd killed in the Underground, how I'd ripped Jaymin to pieces with my magic. I felt nothing but a grim mark of satisfaction. That was the mark of a villain— to put their own goals and ambitions above the lives of others.

We wouldn't kill for pleasure or vengeance. But we damn sure would take a life if it meant defending each other. That much I knew with a bitter resignation.

I'd accepted I was a villain a long time ago. To know that I was truly turning into one, and taking the label with pride, was like accepting myself to the highest degree... without judgment.

I'd never admit this to anyone, but honestly, it felt like a relief to look in the mirror and finally be okay with what I saw.

We got a quick breakfast, then headed down to the music room near the chapel. As we passed by a window, I glanced out of it, then told Charlie to stop. "Wait," I said. I peered closer, not sure if I was seeing things. I saw a couple of guards jump into the lake and transform, their legs morphing into fish tails before their fins slapped the top of the water to go downward.

"What's going on?" Charlie asked.

I waited to make sure, and when I was certain I wasn't hallucinating, I said, "The guards are searching the lake."

"Really." His eyebrows shot up.

"Yes. They've got stunning rods to keep the sirens away. A couple of merfolk guards keep diving in. There's a whole mess of them."

"What do you think they're looking for?"

I thought the answer was obvious. There was something in the lake the Warden didn't want us to find.

Music class with Professor Warbright was my favorite time of the week. All my friends were in that class, and it was the one time we could let loose and allow our creativity to truly take flight. I hadn't released any new vlog posts since I'd gone down into the Underground, and I was worried about explaining my new condition to fans. I hoped to make up for it by making some incredible new songs in the meantime. With Warbright's help, I was sure whatever I posted next was going to really impress my base. For as bumbling and inept as the man was at magic, he was a master at the musical arts.

I grimaced as I shifted in my chair. I'd only been able to take half a pain pill this morning, because I needed the other half for this afternoon. A bundle of aching nerves sat right above the base of my spine, and my middle felt seared with red-hot pain. I'd burst out into tears if I wasn't so accustomed to it.

Charlie sensed my pain through our bond. "I can take you back if you want. I'm sure Warbright will let you out if you tell him you need a medical exception."

"No. I want to be here," I said, though tears beaded my eyelids. "Let me stick it out, just for a bit."

Charlie didn't like when I pushed myself, but he knew how much I loved this class, so he remained silent. Kallie kept glancing at me, ready to lend a hand if I needed it.

"I'm very glad you're all excited," Warbright said as he passed around sheet music. "I hope you've been working hard, because I know how important this class is to all of you."

What we did in music class varied every day, though there were some consistencies. Charlie was always on piano, and I was usually head soprano. Most of the time, we acted like a choir class and sang different songs, or spent our time learning the different intervals in music theory. It was the one fucking class at the Institute that actually felt like a college course instead of a reform program, and it always put me in a good mood. The class had about twenty people in it, and besides our friends, it was filled with a variety of people who weren't cruel— people like Velma and Melody. They were normal students who you didn't have to watch your back with, like you did with Mad Dog and Naya. It made things more comfortable.

Charlie played a couple notes. Oberi started to howl, and a couple of girls giggled. Warbright bent over Oberi and said, "Now, now, little chap, you'll get your turn. On my ready, one, two, three, four!"

My voice shook a little as we began the opening melodies, but I tried focusing on the sound of Charlie playing the piano and Marcus singing baritone beside me instead of how uncomfortable I felt. As time went on, I found that the music took my focus off of my pain and onto the notes. Music could always dull the ache, no matter how bad I felt. I didn't even care that the Warden had required us to learn a hymnal from the angel holy book. No matter what the song was, music never failed to lift my spirits.

By the end of class, I found I wasn't experiencing much pain at all. As I put the sheet music into my folder, Marcus and Charlie remained at the back of the class, speaking in quiet voices. I was curious, so I rolled myself over to listen in.

"Just hurry up and ask her," Charlie said, and he nudged Marcus. He looked momentarily frozen, as if he was terrified at what my husband was suggesting. Charlie had told me Marcus planned to ask Kallie out on a date, but hadn't done it as of yet.

"I can't," Marcus insisted. "I'm too scared."

"For fuck's sake, we're not in eighth grade," Charlie grumbled. "You want to ask me how to hold her hand next?"

"I'm supposed to hold her hand?" Marcus yelped.

"I hate to bring this up, but you *did* have a girlfriend before," Charlie said. "Did you completely forget?"

"Anya asked *me* out, and she didn't really give me a choice about it, either," Marcus hushed back. "She just told me we were dating, and I went along with it."

Clearly his type is dominant women, Oberi mumbled.

I leaned in and whispered to Marcus, "Hey, I had to ask Charlie to *marry me,* and that was way harder. It's just one little date!"

"You're braver than I am," Marcus whimpered. "What if she says no?"

"What are you guys talking about?" Kallie stood before us, clutching her books to her chest. She raised an eyebrow, appearing completely unimpressed with whatever meltdown Marcus was having.

Marcus took a deep breath. He held it so long I thought he was going to pass out. Then, like a withering balloon, he asked, "W— would... would you like to go on a d— date with me?"

Kallie's mouth fell slightly open in a visage of surprise. She glanced at me, as if to make sure this wasn't some kind of joke. I made a gesture for her to hurry up and say something.

"Uh... yes." She gave a soft smile, which was *very unusual* for Kallie, and yet somehow, it suited her. "I think that'd be nice."

"Really?" Marcus squeaked, and his cheeks tinted pink.

"Sure. I think it'd be fun," Kallie said. "What are we doing?"

Marcus paled, as if he didn't think he'd get this far. I could see he needed some help, so I quickly subbed in.

"It's a double date, with all of us, tonight," I said. "And it's a surprise."

"I enjoy surprises," Kallie said. "I'm very excited. Can't wait to see what you have planned!"

Kallie walked out, swaying her hips as she did. I got a very contented feeling watching her leave like that. It was nice to see her... in love.

Meanwhile, Marcus sank down against the back of the chair, like he'd just received some kind of death sentence. "Great. Now I need to come up with something that'll impress her. What the hell can a guy like me do to impress a *princess?* She probably had lords and princes all around her, throwing diamonds at her beautiful feet."

"You can't tell me you haven't been thinking about it," Charlie pressed.

Marcus got a thoughtful look. "Well... I *did* consider singing her a set of show tunes from my favorite musical, but I don't have time to make the costume. Do you think that's too much?"

I cringed. That was thoughtful, but a little over the top for a first date. "How about we start with dinner?"

"Dinner. Yes, that's brilliant." Marcus gave a resolute nod. "I already know her favorite meal. It can't be that hard to make. I'll get supplies from the Arts and Crafts room. I'll make everything look perfect in the Arboretum, like a stage set. She'll walk in and be starstruck."

"You should make it simple," Charlie suggested.

"No way. It has to be *perfect*," Marcus emphasized. "This isn't some last-minute production like your wedding."

"Hey asshole—" I started.

"Do what you think is going to make her happy," Charlie said. "I'm sure she'll love whatever you come up with."

Marcus let out a tiny peep, and Rishi meowed in his lap.

When we left music class, I saw the guards were no longer at the lake, which meant they'd either given up... or found what they were looking for. Either possibility was unsettling.

The rest of the day was pretty boring. I was somewhat uncomfortable, but I didn't feel pain like I had before music class, though I didn't have much medication left. By six o'clock, it was time for our double date.

Charlie helped me into a dress, but I was too tired to fix my hair. I didn't often have the energy to doll myself up like I used to. It definitely was a huge blow to my self-confidence.

My husband must've read my thoughts, because he ducked down and kissed my cheek. "I know you look beautiful."

I smiled. Charlie pushed me into the Arboretum, and we made sure to stick to the curved concrete paths within the greenhouse. Flat surfaces were easiest for me to maneuver, as uneven ground, like grass, gravel, or woodland, was a pain to navigate. It certainly upset me, because being in nature was very important to me, though I could no longer enjoy it unless I had Oberi or Charlie physically take me there.

I struggled to gain access to one of the main things that made me what I was... an Elementai, who should have a connection to the elements. I could no longer run through the forests like I used to, and that thought was more crippling than my condition ever could be.

"Oh, wow," I said as we came to the display, peering upward at the spectacular sight.

"What did Marcus do?" Charlie asked warily.

"He used his Mentalist powers to levitate the table and chairs ten feet off the ground, and there's black candles floating alongside them," I noted. "The entire space has been decorated with Gothic designs and skulls. There are a bunch of animal skeletons from the witch lab running around in the air that he reanimated, and it looks like they're carrying food to serve the table. There's a huge vase of black roses in the middle, and a violin playing itself."

"He really went all-out," Charlie noted.

As we came close to the table, we found that Marcus' Mentalist magic levitated us upward without Charlie having to use his Air power. Charlie sat in a chair, while I pulled myself up to the table. Oberi did somersaults nearby, poking Rishi. The cat let out a yowl as he tumbled through space.

Marcus nervously poured some sort of drink into wine glasses set around the table, shaking in his chair. A bit splashed onto his jeans, and he let out a curse. He'd put so much gel into his hair to slick it back that it looked stiff. A reanimated mouse skeleton skittered around the table, straightening silverware.

I facepalmed as I realized Marcus was wearing his suit jacket from the Villain's Ball... and nothing else under it.

"Marcus, where the fuck is your shirt?" I hissed.

"I thought fae girls liked that kind of thing," he mumbled back. "Werewolf dudes are always walking around with their shirts off."

I was almost certain he'd gotten that from a movie, because male shifters were some of the most stuck-up people I knew, who wouldn't be caught dead in anything but a silk button-up.

"In certain situations, I'm sure she'd appreciate it, but this is hardly the time," I jabbed back.

"I don't think I have time to run back and change..." Marcus whimpered, until his words cut off and he straightened.

Kallie approached, holding up the edge of her black dress. It had a slit in the side, which ran up her leg, and her blonde hair was unbound. Alette fluttered on her shoulder, giving cooing noises. I thought she was absolutely glowing.

Kallie stopped below the table and looked up. She took in the sight of Marcus' bare chest before she giggled and said, "Good evening."

Her wings appeared as she flew up to the table. Marcus scrambled to help her into her chair. He lost control of his levitation abilities, tumbling out of the sky and landing face-first on the ground.

He brushed off his coat, embarrassed, before he levitated back up and gave a hasty bow to her. "M— my lady."

"Someone's been researching Malovian customs..." I mumbled to Charlie. Marcus floundered again as he fumbled for his floating chair, landing into it with a *thump*.

Kallie let out a small giggle. Alette waved her tiny wings in a greeting to him.

"Uh... hi," Marcus stuttered. "I'm glad you came."

"There's no place I'd rather be," Kallie replied, and she honestly wasn't being sarcastic. She picked up the wine glass before her, sloshing it in a circle. "What is this? It smells divine."

"It's called matus tea. It has a calming effect. I brewed it myself," Marcus said.

"Nervous?" Kallie noted.

"Of course not!" Marcus squeaked. "I just thought you'd like it. And I added mugwort, because I thought it'd be a good aphrodisiac—"

Marcus stopped babbling immediately. Kallie lifted an eyebrow and said, "I didn't know it was that kind of evening."

Marcus took on the color of a tomato, and I said, "I'm starving. What's for dinner?"

"I— I made you a lemon alfredo," Marcus said, locking eyes with Kallie. "I know you miss it from home."

"You *have* been paying attention," Kallie said. "I'm impressed."

Marcus' shoulders rounded, and four floating monkey skeletons placed trays onto the table. They pulled the silver covers off the plates. I nearly gagged as an awful smell hit my nose.

For the love of the ancestors, he'd charred it *black*. Nothing resembling pasta was on my plate. It appeared like a heated mess.

Kallie's expression quickly took on a note of surprise, but she rearranged her features to be polite as she said, "Oh, this looks... delightful!"

"Thank you." Marcus gave a nervous laugh. "I worked on it all afternoon."

Is that how long you left it in the oven? Oberi commented. I offered him a bit of blackened chicken, but he turned his nose up at it.

I did my best to swallow. The noodles were *crunchy,* like they'd come straight from the package. How he'd managed to undercook and overcook the food at the same exact time was an act of Mother Miriam herself.

Silence resonated around the dinner table as each of us took a bite. The sounds emitting from our mouths resembled the chomping of bones.

This is really bad. Charlie's thoughts slipped into my mind. *I've dug food out of dumpsters that was tastier than this.*

We can't let him down. Just eat it, I pressed. I still had trouble eating a lot, anyway, but even if I could, I didn't think I wanted the rest of my meal.

Kallie liked Marcus more than she was letting on, because somehow, she managed to eat her whole plate. She drank the rest of her matus tea in two gulps before she leaned over the table in a feminine way and said, "This is actually really nice." She looked around at the skeleton birds that were flitting from tree to tree. "It's cool that you put all this together."

"I've been practicing a lot with my powers," Marcus admitted. "Since I'm a demigod, and I've got powers from all five Casts, I can do anything any witch can do. I've been experimenting a lot, too, seeing what kinds of different spells I can make."

"Your magic is exceptional." Kallie put out her hand, and Alette crawled to the end of her fingertips, batting her wings as a skeleton bird landed beside her. "I had no doubt you could create such wonderful things."

"It was easy to make them... once I thought of you," Marcus confessed bashfully.

"I enjoy the dark aesthetic," Kallie said. "You know me well."

Charlie and I were more or less here to be a buffer, but I honestly thought this was going really well. They barely knew we were around.

"I made you a gift," Marcus started abruptly, and he dug in his jacket pocket. He placed a small crystal ball in her hand, one that swirled with purple magic. "I used my Seer powers to put my memories inside this crystal ball. It replays the day we met, and all my favorite moments of... time we've spent together."

"Oh, my." Kallie raised the crystal ball up to her eyes. I couldn't see what was inside the smoke, but apparently she could, because I watched her tear up. "This is lovely."

"I just thought... you should have the right to know," Marcus said quietly, almost to the point I couldn't hear him. "To see yourself like I do. Through my eyes."

A true romantic, Oberi commented dryly.

He's got some smooth lines right now. Think he rehearsed it? Charlie added telepathically.

Well, he is the dramatic type, I thought. Shakespeare himself couldn't be more amorous.

"I'll treasure it, truly," Kallie said. She clutched the crystal ball like it was her lifeline.

She was acting so different, but not in a way that felt fake. Rather, her responses were genuine. I had the firm notion that *this* was the real Kallie. Soft and sweet, with that regal fae elegance sorceresses always had. That tough girl persona she put on was just that— an act to protect herself. When Marcus stepped up, she had the ability to relax and be who she truly was... a gentle girl from a noble family. I never thought I'd seen Kallie be more authentic to who she was than right now.

Kallie hadn't acted this way before around me, but I knew she must've let her guard down around Marcus more than a time or two, because he was looking at her in a way that was utterly familiar. This is who they really were. I was proud of them for letting their walls down long enough to appreciate each other.

"Do you like roses?" Marcus asked. "I enchanted these ones for you, so they'll never die."

Kallie inclined her head. "I have a reserved fondness for them."

Marcus plucked a flower from the vase, then leaned over to place it in her hair. The black rose stood out against her blonde locks, and Alette fussed over the petals.

"Thank you," Kallie replied lightly. "It smells blissful."

"I dyed the petals by hand, painted each one," Marcus said with pride. "Got a bit distracted with it, actually."

Is that why you ruined dinner? Oberi wondered.

Kallie was absolutely glowing. "That's incredibly thoughtful. I always thought I'd like to craft a potion to make black rose hybrids. It'd be nice to have a garden of them outside my home someday."

Marcus gave a huge smile. "Yeah. I'm sure our kids would love them."

"Slow down..." Charlie murmured under his breath, and I winced. Ancestors, Charlie and I hadn't even talked about kids yet, and we were *married.* Marcus was moving way too fast.

I watched Kallie bristle. "What do you mean by that?"

Marcus definitely realized he made a mistake. "I only— I just think our kids would be cute, is all."

Fucking hell, Marcus. One good date did *not* mean a lifetime of commitment. I braced myself for the worst.

Kallie barely managed to hold her composure as she said, "Cute. I'm sure they would be. All mutts are."

Marcus' face darkened. I heard a bit of resentment come into his tone as he said, "Right. Our kids would be *mutts.* I'm sorry I'm not a snobby fae, hooked on bloodlines and good breeding. But I should know my background isn't good enough for a princess."

Something shifted in Kallie. Her voice changed, and her eyes were different. I visibly watched her morph from that refined, tender girl into a blighted and fractured Institute kid as she snapped, "How do you expect us to raise them? We grew up in completely different societies."

"Neither one of our societies want us anyway," Marcus shot back.

"You're right, they don't. So where are we going to live, huh, Marcus?" Kallie sneered. "Malovia won't take you, and the Miriamic Coven sure as fuck won't accept me, so what do you want to tell these kids when they start asking why no one wants to accept them?"

"*We'll* love them. That's all they could ask for!" Marcus said.

"That's not a good enough life for a child!" she yelled back. "Community is important!"

"What's important is loving yourself more than depending on other people for your identity!" Marcus cried.

"Guys," Charlie started, trying to break up the fight. But they were on a roll now, and there was no stopping it. I was certain this was an argument they'd had before, because the responses were just too quick to be anything other.

Kallie huffed as she sat back and rolled her eyes, adding snidely, "Oh yeah, I forgot. You're a *warlock*. You put yourselves and what *you* want over everyone else. It's not like your kind needs anybody. You can get along just fine all by your lonesome."

"That's not how it goes," Marcus growled.

"It's selfish!" Kallie shot back.

"No! What's *really* selfish is continuing to give and give to other people until there's nothing left of you, because you don't know who you are unless you're connected to somebody else," Marcus screamed.

"I'm sorry that I'm a fae, and my culture and heritage mean something to me!" Kallie shouted. "Marcus, this is who I am! I identify myself on what I mean to others, and it might be the wrong way, but it's the way *I* was taught and the way my people live. You can't force that out of me!"

"You can heal yourself *to* heal your community!" Marcus snapped. "That's why you have to put yourself first!"

I really thought they were arguing about the same damn thing, and you couldn't have one without the other. I opened my mouth to say something, but Kallie shouted over me.

"And how would *you* know, Marcus?" Kallie asked. "You haven't done a damn thing to recover from what you did, because if you had, we'd be together by now, and I wouldn't be dragged along on your ridiculous redemption parade to nowhere!"

"You can choose to be with me or not! It's not like you're forced," Marcus replied. "The gods give us free will to choose."

"There's no such thing as free will. Our lives are predestined. The gods have our lives planned out, and all we have to do is walk the path of destiny," Kallie insisted. "I'm stuck with you, whether I want to be or not."

"That sounds really stupid," Marcus said condescendingly. "Some gods you have, forcing you to take a journey you don't want."

Insulting her religion was clearly one of the worst moves he could make, because Kallie erupted. "I don't know why you even bothered to ask me on this date if you're so godsdamn independent. Let's face it, I'm a shifter, which means I need you a hell of a lot more than you need me. It must be nice to only care about yourself."

"*I need you too!*" Marcus screamed. I watched as his Seer magic welled out of control, bursting the inferichite that was embedded in the cuffs on both of their wrists.

But the inferichite crystals weren't the only things that broke. Cracks formed up the sides of the crystal ball that Kallie still held, threatening to erupt.

"Marcus!" I yelped, crying out a warning. He saw the crystal beginning to shatter, and panicked, but it was already too late.

The crystal ball exploded. Kallie's palm was sliced to pieces as the crystal ball broke. A large piece flung off of it, cutting underneath her eyes and across her nose. I heard Alette give a high-pitched scream of pain, and things started falling out of the air. Charlie kept me, himself and Oberi levitating, but everyone and everything else, including the table and chairs, dropped to the ground.

Marcus and Kallie both fell hard onto the ground, and Rishi landed on a pile of dishes. The reanimated skeleton animals became dead once more, their corpses lying in a degraded heap.

"Kallie!" I shouted. Charlie let me down, and my arms ached as I forced my wheelchair through the grass to get to her. She was on her knees, clutching her face as blood ran down her cheeks.

I reached out my hands to heal her. My Anichi magic worked quickly as I mended the cut on her face, then stitched the cuts on her hand. As I worked, Marcus stared at Kallie with a vacant look, like he was horrified at what he'd done...

And yet, not surprised, like he'd been expecting this.

"It's okay," I said in a rush, and Charlie and Oberi landed behind me. "I mended everything. You're no longer bleeding."

"Alette!" Kallie whimpered. She held up the little moth in both hands. Alette limply fluttered in Kallie's bloody fingers, one of her wings hanging on by a thread. The glass from the crystal ball had nearly severed it off.

"I can fix it," I offered quickly. "Give her to me."

Kallie cried as she placed Alette into my outstretched fingers. I felt the moth begin to die as my healing magic connected to her body. I wasn't going to let that happen, so I forced Anichi magic into her. Her wing started to mend, and life flooded back into the little moth as she lifted her antennae to feel the air. In a few moments, Alette was as good as new, hopping around my hands like nothing had happened at all.

"She's okay," I said, and I gave her back to Kallie. "No harm done."

Kallie didn't respond, but I knew she was thankful. She clutched Alette to her chest as she ran off sobbing, blood drying across her tear-stained cheeks. Rishi yowled at her to stay, but Kallie didn't even look back.

Marcus stared after her and cringed as the door to the Arboretum slammed shut. "I cut her face— I could've *blinded* her— and I almost killed her faekin."

"It was an accident," Charlie insisted.

"People end up dead when I start having *accidents*," Marcus shot back. "I lost my temper for two seconds, and she got hurt. If I had *really* lost control, she might've died!"

"Marcus, the one thing I know about Charlie and me is that we can take anything we throw at each other. We're strong enough to survive each other's storms. You and Kallie are the same way," I pleaded. "She's a demigod just like you. She can take it."

"She shouldn't have to!" Marcus bellowed. "I never should've let you guys push me into this. It was a mistake."

Marcus turned his back to us. I was going to ask if he needed help cleaning up this giant mess, but clearly, he wanted to be left alone.

Charlie pushed me back to the sidewalk. I was exhausted from healing both Kallie and Alette, and I couldn't maneuver myself around. I sagged in my chair, feeling a new bout of soreness rising from my middle.

Well, that escalated rather drastically, Oberi stated, shaking his fur. *And it was all going so well.*

"They have more problems than I thought," I said softly.

The guilt resonating from Charlie was palpable. "I shouldn't have pushed Marcus to do this. But I really thought they were ready, whether they knew it or not."

"They can't be ready until they decide they are. We had to figure that out ourselves, too," I said, and I reached back to touch his hand. "Don't blame yourself. Maybe they need to fight to get through it."

Charlie went silent, but I was there to meet his regret with hope. Sometimes, when you loved someone, you had to go through the worst of shit in order to come out on the other side and be happy. Perhaps it was going to take something big to bring these two together.

The thing was, I worried just how terrible things would have to get before they accepted that they loved each other. And if, by that time, it would be too late.

THE NEXT DAY was my first physical therapy appointment since being out of the hospital. I felt nauseous the moment I woke up. My stomach churned just thinking about going back to that infirmary again.

If I never returned to that place, it'd be too soon. But I had to. The impending dread I felt the further I got into the infirmary was a crushing weight, overwhelming all my senses and making it hard to think about anything but how much I wanted to get out of there.

We were able to refill my prescription just fine, but the moment I was pushed into a room by Charlie to wait for the physical therapist on staff, I got a sensation like I was about to be drowned. My heartbeat swelled in my chest, blood rushing through my ears so I couldn't hear anything but my own panicked breathing. The walls of the hospital closed in around me. It was hard to breathe. I felt suffocated by the white paint and the smells of antiseptic.

The sight of the medical machines stored in the corner caused my lungs to cease up. I recalled how pinned down those machines made me feel when I was hooked up to them, and although I'd been out for it, I vaguely recalled the discomfort I'd felt when they'd removed my breathing tube.

Though I hadn't been conscious for so many of these things, my body remembered, and it was rebelling at the idea of being here at all.

Charlie, she's not doing okay, Oberi said. He placed a paw on my knee, giving a low whine.

"Pidge, what's wrong?" Charlie knelt by my side, but he was speaking to me through a fog. I opened my mouth to try and talk, but no sound came out. I ran my tongue over the roof of my mouth to try and comfort myself, a habit I'd acquired whenever I felt uneasy, but the absence of cool metal made me even worse. They'd taken my tongue ring out when they'd put the tube down my throat, and I didn't know where it had gone, because nobody had ever told me.

"Change of plans," Doctor Marsh announced as she came into the room, followed by a nurse. "Her latest x-rays from last week show severe inflammation. A lumbar steroid injection should cut back on some of the pain."

"What, in her spine?" Charlie asked.

"Yes. It will help the rehabilitation process," Doctor Marsh said. She was already preparing for it, taking long needles and syringes out of drawers, not bothering to ask if I was okay with this. "It won't take long."

"You're not going to knock her out for it?" Charlie asked.

"We can't put her under complete anesthesia. It's unsafe. She needs to be partially awake for the process," Marsh stated. "I can give her a numbing agent. She won't feel much. Once the steroid is administered, we can continue with physical therapy in our next session."

I couldn't take being prodded with one more needle or examined by one more doctor. I didn't care so much about the pain. But I couldn't stand being touched and tampered with anymore. I'd sworn years ago I wouldn't allow anyone to do something to my body again without my consent, not even if it was for my own good. I couldn't stomach any more of this.

The nurse approached me, to lift me onto the bed. I practically clawed up Charlie's side trying to get away from her. Tears ran down my face, and my whole body shook with tremors.

"You need to hold her down," the nurse growled, and she came closer.

"No!" I managed to get that much out. My arms locked around Charlie's torso and refused to let go.

Doctor Marsh let out an impatient sigh, like she had better things to do. "Mrs. Wahkin, if you don't cooperate, I'm afraid we can no longer continue with your treatment."

"Pidge," Charlie begged.

I had to speak; otherwise, they were going to do whatever they wanted to me, whether I wanted it to happen or not.

"I want to go," I choked out. "I can't do this."

Doctor Marsh scowled. "I'm sure with some coaxing—"

"She doesn't consent to this," Charlie snapped, and he began wheeling me away.

"You have to understand if she doesn't comply with her treatment plan, the chances of her recovering fully are slimmer than they already are," Doctor Marsh said firmly.

"I'm going to take her outside," Charlie said.

Charlie wheeled me out of the infirmary. Oberi laid his head on my lap, and I stroked his ears as I waited.

Inside, I felt a small sense of failure. On the other side of the door, my husband argued with Doctor Marsh.

"You can't just throw her out," he said harshly. "She needs physical therapy."

"She clearly has medical trauma from her time spent here," Marsh replied. "Which is understandable, but the Institute isn't equipped to handle the kind of care she needs. Our budget and resources are already stretched thin."

They didn't care about me. The staff didn't want me to come back at all, because they'd never had to deal with a patient in a wheelchair and didn't know how, so it made them uncomfortable. They just saw me as another inmate... one who'd already thrown her life away.

"Nobody in this prison needs your help more than her," Charlie demanded.

"Mister Wahkin, I'm sorry to restate the obvious, but your wife is never going to walk again," Doctor Marsh said shortly. "The physical therapy will help with her pain, but it won't make her mobile, and continuing to act like it will is giving her false hope."

I wasn't shocked at how Doctor Marsh was acting. I'd watched my father struggle to make doctors take him seriously about his condition, and Ez often told me when he came to the infirmary for his weekly treatments, the doctors thought he was making stuff up when it came to his symptoms. If doctors couldn't fix things easily with a pill, they'd give up and act like you were a burden who was wasting their time.

I'd experienced similar treatment with my plethora of rotating therapists who'd been unable to help me manage my bipolar. The months I'd spent in the infirmary had only made me feel more invalidated. I understood these people had helped me and had saved my life. At the same time, I recognized I was just a number to them, and they figured they'd done all they could. To them, I was being overdramatic about things I couldn't change.

"You can't give up on her like this," Charlie hissed.

"I'm sorry. We have other students we need to help."

"Give me her exercises," Charlie said bluntly. "We'll do them ourselves."

Papers rustled, and Doctor Marsh said, "Good luck."

Charlie must've snatched the papers out of her hands, because I heard a sharp sound. Heavy footsteps approached, and I watched as he punched the door open.

All the anger flooded out of him as he came near. Charlie knelt down and hugged me. "I'm sorry."

I embraced him back, the sense of panic finally lifting from my shoulders. "Charlie, promise me you'll never take me back to this hospital. Even if I'm dying, let me die. Just don't make me come back here."

Charlie stiffened, but he finally said, "I promise."

Oberi blinked at us with big black eyes. I wrapped my arms around my middle as I asked quietly, "Now what do we do?"

"We don't need anyone. We'll get by without them," Charlie said crossly.

"You don't have any medical training, and I don't know anything about healing spinal injuries," I said in defeat.

"It doesn't matter. I can help you a hell of a lot more than they can," Charlie said firmly. "Let's take some down time before class. We'll start fresh tomorrow."

I was pretty bummed out the rest of the day. I didn't pay attention at all in class and half-assed my homework. I was all but ready to crawl into bed and avoid the world as we sat in the Villain's Den that evening. Charlie had his reading glasses on and was working on a presentation, while I watched the news. Oberi lay over my feet and nibbled on a chew toy.

"Breaking news! A small boy with a curable illness who was taking refuge in the bunkers of Celestial City has died, due to being unable to access treatment," the broadcaster proclaimed. "His death contributes to the thousands of lives lost in the previous weeks, with assaults on Kinpago and Celestial City continuing through the month. This morning, Octavia Falls was targeted by a Celestial air raid, which caught fire to half the town."

The broadcaster went on to say that it didn't look like a ceasefire was going to happen anytime soon. I frowned and turned away from the television. None of this helped to make me feel better.

Kallie came rushing into the Villain's Den— in a much brighter mood than yesterday, I saw. Marcus wasn't with her. She ignored the carnage playing across the television, which felt heartless... and yet, wasn't. There was so much bad news playing across the screen day after day now we'd already grown desensitized to it. I don't know if any of us listened anymore.

"You seem rather cheery," I noted.

"Ivy's having a powder paint party at The Devil's Playground tonight," Kallie said. "The dancers are going to toss a bunch of colors into the crowd. It's going to be amazing."

My heart lifted. It was the best thing I'd heard all day. "Ancestors, that sounds like so much fun!" I said in excitement. "Charlie, can we go?"

Charlie leaned back in his chair. "I'm sorry, pidge, but I have to get this project done for Criminal Justice before my shift. It's due tomorrow. I would if I could."

"I'll take her," Kallie volunteered. "We'll have a great time."

Charlie hesitated, and I started to beg. "Please? I really want to."

He finally relented. "Sure. You'll be fine if Kallie's around."

I want to go, too! Oberi said in excitement. *It's been ages since I've been to a rave.*

"We should get ready now," Kallie said. "Before tickets are sold out."

An hour later, Kallie and I had donned neon shorts and white t-shirts. She wheeled me down as fast as she could to The Devil's Playground. Oberi followed behind, shaking all the ribbons we'd tied into his fur.

A world of wonder opened up to me as we entered the club. The club was mostly dark, with blacklights glowing against the stage and vibrant powder paint splattered everywhere. The paint was in round pouches that were stacked on barrels placed around the room. Inmates were everywhere, dancing through the strobe lights and tossing the powder paint at each other.

I heard Ivy's voice resonate throughout the club as he sang a popular song. A couple of guys had lifted Ivy onto their shoulders and were carrying him around the room. He wore a cut-off shirt and silver panties with a mesh green skirt overtop. He was covered in all kinds of powder paint, and had bangles running up and down his arms. He threw his head back to the music, running his hands over his body in a sexy pose. Above him on the stage catwalks, Chancey was wearing an army helmet and throwing dollar bills down to the crowd below, making it rain money.

"Looks like Ivy's having the time of his life!" I shouted to Kallie.

"So are we!" Kallie yelled back. "Come on, let's get on the dance floor!"

Oberi gave a hearty woof, and we navigated our way to the middle of the club. We grabbed powder pouches off the barrels and tossed them at each other. The powder got all over our clothes and hair, and best of all, it was filled with *glitter*. I laughed as I tossed an orange powder pouch over our heads. It exploded, covering us with an array of paint and sparkles. Oberi looked like a multicolored rainbow, running in circles with his tongue hanging out.

I couldn't dance like I used to, but I still had some moves. A smile spread across my face for the first time that day. This was so much fun! I was really glad Kallie had brought me here. It felt like old times.

We stayed on the dance floor for an hour, acting silly, dancing song after song as we smashed powder paint all over each other. Eventually, we needed a drink and headed off to order at the bar. I rolled myself over — and stopped dead.

A singular stair led up to the bar where you had to place orders. I'd never noticed it before... because I'd never considered it an obstacle. Now, it was a big one.

Kallie came to a halt. "Hold on. I'll give you a boost."

"Sure." I gripped the armrests as Kallie used her telekinetic magic to levitate me and the chair up onto the platform. I was aware everyone at the bar was watching, and nobody gave me the courtesy of pulling away their stare. People at the Institute could be real dicks.

I was truly thankful that my friends were willing to help me. At the same time, it was a little embarrassing that everyone had to help me with so many things that I used to take for granted.

I rolled up to the bar, but it was taller than I was sitting down, so the bartender didn't see me. Kallie had to order for me.

A horse-like laugh filled the room, and I wrinkled my nose as I looked around the end of the bar. Fucking Danielle. I didn't know how she'd gotten in here, since anyone who hung out with Naya was forbidden to set foot in Ivy's club. She must've snuck in here. She had a full fifth of vodka in front of her, and was drinking it straight from the bottle.

Even worse, she'd brought Esther. Of course, Esther, good girl she was, sipped at plain sparkling water.

Whatever. I just wanted a drink. But before the bartender could process our order, Danielle's pruny eyes settled on me.

She gave a disgusted noise. "Do you and your stupid wheelchair always have to be the center of attention? Nobody wants you here."

"It's Ivy's club, Danielle. If anything, you're the one who needs to leave," I shot back.

"You should be *resting*," Danielle said in a placating voice. "Unless your condition isn't as bad as your stupid husband says. Where is he, anyhow?"

"Cut the shit, Danielle. I'm sorry you're jealous he's fucking me and not you," I said bluntly.

Danielle's face flushed, and she took a hasty sip of vodka, but Esther added quaintly, "*Can* you still do that? Be intimate with your husband, I mean."

She did not, Oberi gasped.

I was momentarily speechless— something that had never happened before when I was in the middle of an argument. *Well done, Esther, for being a shittier person than I thought.*

Kallie came back holding two drinks for the both of us. She'd overheard what Esther had said and shouted, "Wow, takes talent to be that much of a dick!"

"Come now. What Danielle says has to be true. Ava must not be *that* sick, if she can go to a club," Esther said. "She can probably walk. She's just faking it."

Kallie turned toward us. "Ava, I'm sorry if you're thirsty, but this has to be done."

She stomped toward Esther and dumped both of the drinks onto her head. A margarita and virgin cocktail trickled down her blonde curls and all over her face. Esther shuddered, her lips opening to form a quivering look of rage.

Danielle stood drunkenly from her seat and went to storm toward Kallie, but Oberi placed himself in front of her. She tripped over Oberi and fell on her ass, spilling vodka all over her dress.

Esther let out a shriek that was louder than the noise in the club. We took that as our cue to leave. Kallie had to help me down the step, and Oberi let out loud barks as Kallie wheeled me away from the bar. Esther began running after us, but she stumbled into Danielle, and the two of them lost us in the crowd.

"That was fucking amazing," I told her, giving a laugh.

"I wish we'd ordered more," Kallie said. "Gods, what a bitch."

"Fuck her! Let's get out and dance again," I suggested.

We immediately went to the middle of the crowd. The music changed, and I was about to ask Kallie if she had any more paint, before I was roughly jolted forward.

"Ow! Hey!" I exclaimed. I did my best to turn around. Someone had accidentally run into my chair.

No big deal. At least, it wouldn't be, if the dick who'd done it didn't look like he was set on ruining my day. Worse, it was Edwin— one of Charlie's enemies that I couldn't fucking stand— as well as Brianna. By the way she was hanging on him, I had to assume they were dating.

"You must be lost. The infirmary's that way," Edwin sneered, jerking his thumb toward the door. His girlfriend laughed.

"Excuse me?" Kallie belted, while I felt myself melt into my seat.

"You need to get off the dance floor. You're taking up space," Brianna whined.

"She has just as much a right to be here as you!" Kallie snapped, placing her hands on her hips.

"Yeah, right. This is a bar," Edwin growled at me. "It's not a place for sick people who need to rest."

"I use a wheelchair, I don't hate fun," I snapped. Beside me, Oberi gave a wicked growl.

"Well, you're inconveniencing other people, so get lost," Edwin snapped.

I opened my mouth to say something else, but before I could, Edwin put his hands on the back of my chair and *moved me out of the way*.

I was shocked, and scared. There wasn't like I could do anything to stop it, either. I was totally helpless.

Back off, baldy! Oberi flashed his teeth, then sank his fangs into Edwin's leg. He didn't let go, either. Edwin tried shaking Oberi off, but he wouldn't let go.

"Oberi, down!" I grabbed his scruff and yanked him back. He came away with some of Edwin's pant leg.

Kallie looked positively murderous. "Fuck you, asshole! You asked for it!"

Kallie pulled her fist back to deck Edwin in the face, but I caught her arm.

"Kallie, don't. It's not worth it," I said quietly.

Her eyebrows furrowed in confusion. Edwin took his chance to limp off, clutching his bleeding leg. Brianna sent me a glare as she helped him hobble out of the club.

I shook as I remembered how casually he'd moved me out of the way. I *hated* it. My wheelchair was a tool I used to get around, but it was also an extension of my body, and that jerk had touched it without permission.

"What's wrong with you? Did you get a personality transplant while they were sewing you back up?" Kallie questioned. "I was expecting you to rip Edwin a new asshole."

My mouth ran dry. Yeah, that was me. The *old* me.

I wasn't that person anymore.

I convinced Kallie to let it go, though she shot the loser and his girl-friend the finger as we moved off the dance floor.

My thoughts were dark as the bass thrummed around me. People thought that I had to be in pain all the time because I used a wheelchair. And yeah, I was in pain a lot, because I was recovering from surgery. But that pain was getting better every day, and soon, I'd feel better. Why couldn't I have fun at a party like everyone else could?

"Are you okay?" Kallie asked, looking concerned.

I tried to keep my voice steady as I said, "I just want to go home."

Kallie's face fell, but she nodded and wheeled me off the dance floor. "Okay. I was getting bored, anyway. Do you need to use the bathroom?"

I shook my head, and Kallie said, "Well, I have to go. I'll be right back."

Kallie ducked into the club's restroom. The second she was gone, I sniffed and wiped my nose with the back of my hand. The Devil's Playground used to be one of my favorite places, but I no longer felt like I belonged here. At this point, I just wanted to go back to my cell. Oberi laid his head on my lap, licking my fingers to try and cheer me up.

"Ava!" Ivy came storming out of the crowd, a neon pink purse dangling off his shoulder. He stopped before me and grabbed my hands. "I heard what those dickwads did to you. My security team is handling it, don't you worry."

I couldn't help it. My lip started to tremble. "I can't do anything I used to, Ivy."

"Sure you can! I saw you. You were having a blast before those pricks opened their fat mouths," Ivy protested. "Why didn't you tell them off? That's the Ava I know and love."

"You don't understand. I've... *changed* since I've come back." I put my head in my hands. "I don't want to *be* that ugly girl I was, who was mean and cruel. I just want to be a good person."

"You ain't a good person. You don't wanna be! Trying to save other people is what got you put in that chair!" Ivy insisted. "You keep giving up parts of yourself to other people, there's gonna be nothing left! You gotta give what you have to *yourself*."

"I don't know if I can do that anymore, Ivy."

Ivy shook my shoulders. "You listen to me. Don't ever let nobody stop you from doing what you wanna do, you hear? Not Charlie, or Oberi, or even me! You be the biggest scumbag that's ever walked this Earth, because that's what's gonna keep you alive out there. I'm not losing you again, Ava. None of us are. As for the rest of the world... fuck 'em. Fuck 'em all."

Ivy began digging in his bag. "And *speaking* of fucking, I have a little toy you and your husband may want to share."

He smirked as he pulled a plastic package out of his bag and set it on my lap. I inspected it with a bewildered look. "A vibrator? What the hell, where did you get this?"

"Don't worry. It's brand-new, still in the package," Ivy told me.

"One of the guards was able to order it and sneak it to me, after I gave him some cash. He didn't think much of it, given my former occupation."

"How's this supposed to help?" I asked.

"It's called a rabbit. I did some research on the sexuality of women who have spinal injuries, and that particular device has been known to work wonders," Ivy said. "The stimulation vibration can give has been known to overpower damaged nerves. That one in particular is made for women with spinal injuries, to cause a kind-of... reflex arousal? I think that's the term they used."

"Do you really think this will help me?"

"From my research, it seems different for everybody. You'll have to try it out and see if you get a response. I can't make any promises, but it just might help."

At this point, I was willing to try anything. "Thanks, Ivy. You're a lifesaver."

"I've got to get back to entertaining my public," Ivy said with a dramatic sigh. "And you... give your man a show."

Ivy scampered back into the crowd. Oberi eyed the device in my lap and said, *I ain't helping you with that.*

"Ancestors willing, you won't have to." I was scared, excited, worried and thrilled all at once. If this didn't work...

But if it *did*... ancestors, I wanted to jump into bed right now.

Kallie came out of the bathroom, then looked down. "Uh, where'd you get a dildo?"

"A little sex fairy stopped by," I told her. "Esther has the balls to ask if I can still fuck my husband? I guess we're gonna find out."

"You get your man, girl," Kallie sang joyously.

Once we walked through the doorway of The Devil's Playground, the powdered paint vanished magically from our clothes and skin, leaving no trace of the party. When Kallie dropped me off at my cell, she gave me a wink and went cackling all the way down the hall.

I'm staying firmly on the couch, Oberi said as he jumped onto the cushions. *I pray all goes well for you two. Oh, if only dogs could wear earplugs!*

Then he lay on his back and promptly went to sleep. I always envied how he could drop off in just a few seconds.

Charlie walked in from the bedroom and asked, "What's he talking about?"

"Oberi's just being Oberi," I said, trying to keep the nerves out of my voice.

"Makes sense. How was the party?"

"It was... fun," I said. I didn't tell him about all the bullshit that happened. It'd piss him off, and I wanted his mind to be on nothing but me tonight. "Can you help me into bed?"

"Sure."

I kept hold of the vibrator and put it on the bedside table before Charlie lifted me onto the mattress. I started taking off clothes the minute I sat down. Charlie didn't notice until I rolled next to him and started kissing him, taking his hand and placing it on my breast.

"Uh, hi." He pulled away. "What's all this?"

"I want to get back to... us."

Charlie paused. He kissed me again, before he said quietly, "I don't want you to be disappointed."

We hadn't messed around since that awkward night in the hospital, and I knew he had to be dying for some kind of connection. I was. He just didn't want to ask, because he was scared about how it would go. Charlie had always been super cautious about sex.

But I didn't want us to turn into roommates. Even if I turned out to be disappointed, I wasn't going to stop until we found a way around this.

"We have to try. And Ivy might've gotten us something that might make it easier, batteries included."

His head tilted as I began opening the plastic package. I placed the rabbit in his hand, and he said, "Interesting. Never used one of these."

"It might help me regain some sort of feeling," I said. "Never know until we try, right?"

I put the batteries in, then set it aside. Charlie took off his clothes so we could be skin-to-skin. He started on my breasts, kissing my soft skin and sucking on my nipples.

I could orgasm from stimulation there alone— at least, I was able to before. I felt my form growing hot and my pulse increasing as he ran his lips along my neck and skimmed his tongue across my sensitive areas. Arousal rose within me and radiated outward as his lips caressed my breasts, and I had hope that maybe this was going somewhere.

He left a trail of kisses across my stomach, before he moved my legs open and started sucking tenderly on what waited between them. He nibbled and made love to my apex the same way he did to my mouth, and I savored the feelings, eager to see what would come up.

Charlie kissed my hip bone and asked, "Does it feel good?"

"Yes," I whispered. In the past, I would've already came, but it was obviously going to take more time than it usually did. I didn't feel impatient like I had before, though. After all, we had all night.

"Let's try that thing," Charlie said eagerly. "I want to see what it does."

I handed him the rabbit, and he turned it on. I was pretty wet already, from being turned on and from his mouth, so he put the tip of it against my clit.

I jumped a little. "It tickles."

"Is it too much?"

"No, I just wasn't expecting it. Do it again."

Charlie drifted the top of the vibrator back and forth along my clit. I was able to feel the device easier than his fingers or tongue. At last, I had some sort of sensation. My back arched off the bed a little as Charlie asked, "Do you like that?"

"I love it," I breathed. "Put it inside me."

The rabbit was built so it had a shaft that went inside, and an external simulator for massaging my clit. As Charlie gently nestled it in, I found that the feelings working through me were like waves, drifting me up and down with the speed of the vibrator. There were so many sensations— the delicate brushing of my clit, Charlie's intentful contemplation as he figured what worked best. On his side of our bond, I could feel his excitement growing, his longing to make love to me equal to his desire to make me feel like he once had.

I would've loved this thing before I got injured, but even so, it was magical. Inside of me, the vibrator thrusted, and I felt my eyes roll back a little as the movements continued to build. I practiced different movements, shifting my hips so that it sat in me differently. I could move everything up until my knees, and I found a better angle.

I couldn't feel Charlie sitting between my legs, and he had to move them for me in order to spread them apart. There was a lot of maneuvering we had to do to get it right. Finally, I felt it. An orgasm pulsed through me, starting at my clit and blossoming outward to engulf the rest of me with it. I let out a couple of moans of relief, and my head hit the pillows as I gasped for breath. It took longer than it usually did, and the feeling itself was different than it had been before. But I could definitely still get off. The relief I felt was almost as good as the orgasm.

But not quite.

"I want you in me," I said. I couldn't wait any longer— I had to know. I reached for him, grasped him by the back of the neck, kissing him again.

"I'm more than willing. How?"

I wasn't sure. I wanted to retain the sensations the vibrator gave me, and have him inside of me at the same time. Being on top could be a challenge, as I didn't have anything to pull myself up with, and my legs couldn't boost me up and down. Not to mention other positions meant moving my legs around, and I didn't have great control of that.

Charlie sensed I didn't know, and said, "Come here, baby girl. I got you."

He lay down on the bed and pulled me to him, so my back was against his chest. He slid into me from behind, and I let out a tiny sound of delight. He put the vibrator against my clit from the front as he started thrusting, and I started to be carried off by bliss.

I was aware that his dick was moving inside me, though again, I had more sensation on the left side than the right. It wasn't quite as satisfying as it once had been, but it was still pretty damn good.

His arms curled around me, laying across my surgery scars. I had the fleeting idea that I was ugly— gross— but Charlie's thoughts invaded my mind and pushed that aside. I'd never be ugly to him. Always, I'd be the most beautiful woman in the world, and nothing I or anyone else could do would change that.

Sex seemed to go on forever. I was completely aware that Charlie was doing everything he could to make it last, and not go before I was ready, taking long, slow thrusts instead of fast ones. Heat and passion exploded out of me when I realized that, and ancestors, it made me love him even more.

With the combination of the rabbit massaging my clit and Charlie moving in and out of me, I finally got there once again. I gave a loud moan, my hands fisting in the sheets as I gave a cry of ecstasy.

When I came, so did Charlie. The combined orgasm was almost too much for both of us. I scratched at his arms with my long nails, and he clutched my torso tighter. We rode it out together, until both of our bodies had stopped trembling and the dizziness in our heads had faded, leaving us to float back down again.

I couldn't help the contented smile that spread across my face. Sex was definitely different for us now. But it was *so* worth it. We could still share that part of life with each other. There was nothing to worry about.

Yet there never was, with Charlie and me. We always managed to find a way, in the end.

"Did you enjoy that, pidge?" Charlie questioned, kissing the back of my head.

"I think you know," I said playfully. "But, yes. I can't feel as much as I used to, yet it's still enjoyable, and that's what counts."

"I'm glad. It's good that we tried."

We were quiet for several long minutes. At first, I figured he was just enjoying the moment, relieved that this hadn't been ruined for us, as I was.

But I could sense there was something else weighing on his mind as the seconds ticked by. Curiosity demanded that I know. I did my best to roll myself over, so I could face him. "What are you thinking about?"

He swallowed, as if he was nervous. "This is a weird thing to bring up, but... I feel guilty about lying to you."

My chest tightened with all kinds of horrible possibilities. "About what? Did you not like it—?"

"It's nothing like that," he said immediately. "I loved what we did, really. Just... please don't be mad."

I was starting to panic, but I kept my voice even as I asked, "What's going on?"

"Do you remember when I told you that I slept with twelve women when I was trying to get off the streets?"

"Yeah," I said, vaguely remembering. "That was so long ago."

"I wasn't really being truthful. It actually... there were so many women it got to the point I stopped counting. I don't know how many women I've been with."

He sounded embarrassed. I reached out to grasp his fingers. "I don't care about that. It's all in the past. You're with me now, so that's all that matters."

"I should've just been with *you*." He sounded frustrated. "I wish it would've been possible for that to happen. I didn't just put myself at risk. I gambled with your health, too."

"I mean, you *could've* given me something, but you didn't, so it's not a big deal."

"I didn't take that chance. I got tested before I even touched you."

"When did you do that?"

"Over winter break, right after the Darke Games."

I blinked. "That's news to me."

"I really liked you. I thought if there was a possibility we'd hook up once you got back, I wanted to make sure I was safe for you to mess around with."

He sighed and fisted a hand in his hair. "I tried to lie and come up with a number that I thought was low, and then I felt even worse once I said it, because twelve was the lowest number I could come up with."

"It's no good to shame yourself for decisions you made in the past."

"I used to hate sex. It was never fun," he said. "I couldn't understand why everyone acted like it was so enjoyable. Then you came along, and you just... you make me so happy."

His voice was choked, like he hadn't been able to understand what happiness was before, because he'd been so sad all his life. Now that it was here, it was almost overwhelming to him.

I understood. Something had always been missing for me, too, until he showed up.

"We make each other happy," I said, and I snuggled into his front. "I don't care what you did before. As long as I have you now, that's all I'll ever need."

MY MOOD WAS MUCH UPLIFTED as we headed to our demigod lesson the next evening. We'd woken up that morning and had gotten right back to what we'd been doing last night.

Bliss couldn't describe it; it was paradise, an escape from everything that had gone wrong. Being together felt like righting our wrongs and getting things back to how they should be.

Charlie definitely had a brighter spring in his step as we wandered toward Hemlock's secret room, and I had a permanent smile on my face that couldn't be misplaced. The world would right itself again, so long as everything was well between Charlie and me.

On our way, we heard a bit of discontented mewling. Kallie was pushing Rishi in a baby carriage she'd conjured with illusion magic. The cat was wearing a big blue ribbon around his neck and a baby bonnet. He appeared quite surly as she cheerfully wheeled him beside us. Oberi flew around the carriage in a tizzy, ruffling her phoenix feathers and chuckling.

"How was *your* evening?" Kallie asked, nudging me playfully.

"Pleasant," Charlie responded. "Whatever you're doing to Marcus' cat probably isn't fair."

"Of course not. He loves it," Kallie insisted. Rishi gave a yowl.

"Rishi!" Marcus called throughout the hall, somewhere up ahead of us. "Where'd he go...? Has anyone seen my cat?"

Marcus came out of the crowd. He halted when he saw Rishi in the baby carriage and Kallie pushing it around.

"Why are you torturing him?" Marcus asked. He reached out to lift Rishi from the carriage.

Kallie yanked it back. "Well, since Rishi is technically your twin brother, and I'm bonded to both of you, I think he's half mine. Which means you have to share custody."

"What? That's ridiculous. He's *mine*," Marcus said, and he tried to snatch Rishi away. Kallie snagged him from the carriage and held him tight.

"You should let Rishi choose," I offered.

"How does Oberi decide who to be with?" Marcus demanded.

Whichever one of you is annoying me the least that day, Oberi said dryly, and she landed on the back of my chair.

"She goes back and forth depending on how she feels," I said.

Marcus reached for Rishi again, but he clung to Kallie, swishing his tail and purring loudly.

"Traitor," Marcus grumbled as we entered Hemlock's classroom, sulking as we passed through the secret door.

We gathered around the round table with Takahashi, who was already waiting for us. Our professor wore a bright smile as he said, "It shows exceptional progress that the four of you managed to break the inferichite cuffs. Now that your powers are no longer bound, we should hone in on growing your demigod powers. I thought we should start with an assessment of what those could possibly be. We know Kallie has special abilities relating to time. If she can harness her powers to be able to go back in time, or even forward, we'll have a better chance of beating the Warden."

Kallie shifted in her seat and hugged Rishi closer. "I don't know how. I only have so much access to my time powers. I can stop time, speed it up, and go forward, but the control I have over the whole thing is very limited. It seems to change day by day."

"Perhaps you can only influence time on a minor scale, at the present moment you're in," Charlie suggested.

"No. I think I *can* go back in time," Kallie said. "I've already done it once."

"What? When?" Marcus nearly fell out of his chair.

Kallie stroked Rishi as she spoke. "Before the Darke Games, I told Ava about a strange vision I had as a child. I was playing with my brother at the palace, in the middle of the day, but during the vision, I was transported into some nighttime scene. I saw a woman with silver-blonde hair and blue wings. She was smiling at me, until the vision ended, and I was transported back to the parlor room with my brother. Up until now, the vision didn't make any sense. But now I realize that I must've traveled back in time. I saw my birth mother... when she was alive."

"That's incredible," I breathed.

"Yeah." Kallie slouched in her chair. "Too bad I can't figure out how to do it again. I don't recall if anything prompted it, but I don't think it took any energy out of me back then to time travel. Which is so weird, because I get exhausted when I experiment with my time abilities now."

"There is a missing link to your time abilities that we aren't yet aware of," Takahashi said. "Once we discover it, it could mean access to a world of possibilities. In the meantime, we must contemplate what magic the rest of you may have."

"How do we figure out what our powers are?" I asked.

"I think we *may* have an idea," Takahashi stated. "From our research as the Demigod Guardians, we know that a demigod's special magic is often linked to their more banal powers. If I were to theorize correctly, Charlie's demigod abilities would most likely lie somewhere within the higher realms of Elf magic, while Marcus, as he has the mark of all five Casts of his coven, will be able to push the abilities of witch magic to its fullest."

"I've been practicing," Marcus said proudly. "I think I made a break-through with my Seer powers. I've been trying to read the Warden's mind, but he's somehow protected. I realized, what's to stop *him* from using other Seers to spy on us through visions or mind reading? If he hasn't been trying to read our minds already, then he's surely searching for a Seer who can do it. I figure I can combine Seer magic with ward magic to protect our minds from other witches with mind-reading abilities."

"Is it safe?" Charlie asked.

Marcus shrugged. "I guess we'll find out. You're my first test subject."

Charlie hesitated, but he didn't protest as Marcus approached him. It was important we blocked our minds from any magic that could be used against us, as long as we had the means. Marcus splayed his palm over Charlie's forehead, and sparkling purple magic emitted from his hand.

Charlie tensed for a moment, before relaxing. "Did it work?"

"Think something dirty," Marcus said. "It's still the only thoughts I can read."

"Uh..." Charlie hesitated, before his thoughts came through our bond. *I fucked Ava to the high heavens last night.*

A thrill traveled through my chest as I replayed the memories. I waited for Marcus to say something, but he didn't catch Charlie's thoughts.

"I got nothing," Marcus said.

Kallie sighed in relief. "Thank the gods. Do me next."

Marcus placed the mind-reading ward on each of us in turn. The magic tingled through my head, before settling. Charlie, Oberi, and I could still communicate through our bond, but Marcus couldn't read our thoughts anymore, which meant the Warden couldn't get inside our heads either.

I didn't want to cut off communication with Marcus, in case we needed to use it, but he could only read our dirty thoughts for now, which wasn't any use to us. It was better if we cut off everyone to protect ourselves from the Warden.

"That brings us to Ava's powers," Takahashi said.

"My demigod power lies in exceptional healing," I stated.

It is as I said. Your healing ability is not that of other Anichi, for Anichi can only speed up the body's natural process, and mend what nature already would with time, Oberi stated. *Ava, dear, you have the ability to surpass what is possible, and heal what no others on this Earth can.*

I translated what Oberi said to the rest of the group, and Charlie breathed, "Ava, you healed your dad when he was sick with pneumonia. There was no other way he could survive. The other Anichi healers did all they could, but you were able to regrow his lungs, which is basically impossible."

"That must be it," Takahashi said victoriously. "Ava has the ability to cure ailments beyond what's possible by normal magic. Ava shouldn't have been able to heal her brother from sepsis last semester, but her healing abilities are such that she is able to *replace* what's already been too damaged to repair. That is why her father survived his illness."

I chewed my lip. "But what were those blue eyes staring at me in my father's hospital room? I thought they were the ones doing the healing."

"A teacher, perhaps, from the Ancestral Lands, guiding your magic before you knew you had it," Takahashi commented. "You should take note to see if this teacher appears to you again."

"But if I could heal my father and restore his lungs, why can't I heal my own spine?" I asked.

"Exactly. Ava should be able to heal anything," Kallie argued. "Ez should've been cured of his disease when she healed his sepsis."

Not without proper training, Oberi objected. *And even then, there are conditions, ailments and ways of being, that we agreed to undergo in order to gain knowledge and experience before we came to Earth, as is what's stated in our soul contract. Ava would not be able to cure such conditions without a revision of such a contract, and a statement of free will.*

"I can't just call up my healing magic on a whim, though," I argued, after I'd explained what Oberi had said. "I've been able to heal beyond what any Anichi should, yes, but I struggle to heal a paper cut when I'm not under pressure. It's hardly easy for me. I know my demigod power is strong, but I don't know how to grow it, or how to use it properly."

Maybe there's a way to practice your healing powers without so much resistance, Oberi hinted. *There has been a time when it was easy.*

Something came to me, and I was shocked by the thought. "I... I was singing in music class the other day. When we came in, I was in so much pain, because I didn't have any medication. But by the end of it, I almost felt nothing at all."

"Do you think your healing abilities are connected to your music?" Kallie asked.

"Yes! I think that's the way to access it without having to force myself," I said in excitement.

"We need to try out this theory," Charlie said. "Does anybody need healing? Something simple."

"I hurt myself during football practice earlier," Kallie said, and she raised her sweater to show a large, mottled bruise running all along her side. "Usually, my shifter blood would've healed it by now, but I got tackled by a dragon, and this one really hurt. I had busted ribs by the end of it. It's still not completely better."

"It's a good place to start," I said. Kallie set Rishi on the table, who immediately took off his bonnet with a grumpy wave of his paw. She walked over to me, and I gently placed a few fingers on the bruise. She hissed at the contact, and I pulled my hand away.

"Do I just start singing, or what?" I looked to Oberi for guidance.

What song comes to mind? There's always one, Oberi said. *Don't try to force the magic. See what comes up.*

I looked at Kallie's bruise. A couple of notes rose to my thoughts, one of my favorite songs.

As I started humming the opening medley, I watched as the purple welts on Kallie's side faded away. I sang a couple of the words softly, and the bruise vanished, until all that was left was brand new, pink skin.

I sat back in my chair with a gasp of disbelief. I didn't feel tired, either. Accessing my healing abilities through song didn't make me exhausted. It gave me *energy*.

"Oh my gods, it's all better!" Kallie said, touching the new skin.

"It's like a phoenix song," Charlie said in amazement. "Oberi's Spirit form fits perfectly."

"This is wonderful news," Takahashi said as he stood. "I say we go around the room and see how far we can extend these abilities of yours. Experimentation is paramount."

Charlie was giddy as he rose from his seat. "I can't believe it! If you can heal yourself... pidge, you might be able to walk again!"

I didn't know how I felt about that. I was thrilled at the idea of being able to get out of this chair, but at the same time, I didn't know if it was truly possible. I'd been able to heal other people from terrible things, but I wasn't sure if this was something I could fix.

It wasn't like I didn't know if I *could*. It was more like... I was too afraid to believe it was possible, because the disappointment I'd experience if it wasn't would be worse than being unable to walk again.

Charlie, mind your own magic, Oberi said calmly. *Ava needs to concentrate on hers.*

Charlie paused, before he nodded. Marcus led him to the other side of the room, where they began discussing methods they could attempt to draw out special abilities.

"He's excited. Don't damper his enthusiasm," I told Oberi.

Pressuring you at a time like this is far from helpful, Oberi noted. *I am here to guide you.*

I busied myself with singing songs the rest of the hour, attempting to heal myself with music. I found the magic worked best when I didn't try to force it, and when I sang songs that were consistent with my mood, rather than forcing me to be in one state or another.

By the end of the lesson, I'd managed to ease the pain in my back. But I was far from being able to get out of this chair.

"Why can't I heal myself?" I asked Oberi. "My mother told me stories of the Elementai Civil War. She healed herself from terrible things— beams getting rammed through her, nearly bleeding to death. If our theory is true and my ability surpasses even what she could do, I should be able to repair my spine easily."

Indeed. It is a puzzle, Oberi agreed. *As I told you before, you must find the source of your healing. A conduit, as you would say, for your demigod powers.*

"But demigods don't need to draw their magic from an outside source. They can create energy from nothing."

What I'm saying is you must find the source inside yourself, Oberi explained. *Until you find the motivation that is driving your magic, it will remain inaccessible to you at its greatest power. These things take time. There is certainly no rush.*

It sure felt like it, what with the war going on and the Warden looking to cleanse the Earth in his tirade of insanity. But Oberi was an immortal being who was beyond the binds of time and space. I was certain she was never in a hurry for anything— save for dinner.

It's taco night, Oberi complained, and she flapped her wings impatiently. *Can we wrap this up?*

Oberi was wonderfully helpful about ten percent of the time. The other ninety percent, she was little more than a nearly-omniscient nuisance.

Kallie sat in a chair, wiped out. She hadn't found any success in experimenting with her time magic, though she'd stopped and sped up time at several moments throughout the hour. She was clearly beat by the end of it. Whatever her access point— her *conduit* was— she was far from enabling it to make this easier.

Marcus seemed like he'd made some progress. Takahashi had brought a chest of items for us to practice with, and he'd gone through it, pulling out potion bottles, wands and crystals. He'd been stuck on reanimating a skeleton, which he'd even enabled to talk— something I'd never seen a necromancer do before, because there weren't any vocal chords left to enable.

"My necromancy abilities are the strongest," Marcus noted as he allowed the skeleton to drop. "I think I need to start there. Death magic is the way to go."

Charlie shook his head in frustration as he attempted to cast an Elven illusion and nothing happened. "Something's not right. I just don't understand illusions. And if my demigod power is connected to my Elf magic, my illusion magic, which I can't understand, how am I supposed to access it with any kind of success?"

"You've gotta have a key to access, like Ava and Kallie do," Marcus said. "Just have to figure out what that is."

"You boys are on the right path," Takahashi praised. "Let's call it a night. We don't want to push ourselves too hard, and this is good progress."

Despite not making headway with his Elf magic, Charlie was exceptionally cheery during dinner. I knew he was excited about my healing magic and the possibilities it had for us.

I tried not to feel pushed, but I kind of did. We knew the potential to heal me was there. But what if I couldn't do it? Would he be mad at me?

Oberi changed into a husky and ate his tacos— all twelve of them. Kallie and Marcus had a painting for their art class they needed to finish, so they split off from us to head to the Arts and Crafts room.

There was supposed to be a movie night going on in the Villain's Den, so we decided to head there. Usually, the TV just had the news on, but the Warden was coming up with excuses not to play it. I didn't think he wanted us to know what was going on out there. Thus, the guards put on whatever family-friendly film they could get their hands on during weeknights, and *approved, uplifting* media the rest of the time.

Whatever. So long as I didn't have to listen to one more horrible headline without being able to do something about it.

"Do you even like movies?" I asked Charlie, looking behind me. "You can't really watch them."

"I can listen to them," Charlie said with a shrug. "But there are special captions for blind people that they make for movies— it's like listening to an audiobook. Sometimes, when you go to the theater, they'll give out audio assisted headphones for the blind, to give narration to what's on screen. It's actually really exciting."

There was so much to learn about Charlie's blindness. I was learning more every day.

"When we get out of here, I want to try it," I said.

Loud voices came from the angel cell block up ahead. Charlie's eyebrows knitted together. "That's Chancey."

"And that's definitely Ivy," I added. "Ancestors, half the Institute can hear them."

After the disastrous date between Kallie and Marcus, neither one of us had any desire to get involved with our friends' relationships. We tried to go the other way, but the voices got closer. It sounded like Ivy was trying to get away from Chancey, and he was chasing after. We were forced to halt in place as the two of them came tearing around the corner.

"Just leave me alone, Chance," Ivy snapped. "I'm sick of you."

"*Me?* You're sick of me." Chancey gave a cruel laugh. "That's real rich, after the shit you've put me through."

"You ain't no saint. You got a lot of promises, but you sure as hell can't keep them," Ivy said. "What comes out of your mouth is pillow talk, nothing more."

"It meant more than that! I told you I was gonna set us up real good once we got outta here—" Chancey started.

"I'm having a hard time believing you can keep *your ass out of jail!*" Ivy screeched. He whirled around to face Chancey and put a hand on his chest, shoving him backward.

"Oh yeah, and you can't put down the drugs, can ya?" Chancey flung at him.

"Take your righteous act and shove it. I fucking saw you snort coke in the bathroom," Ivy said nastily.

"Back when we first met! I dumped all the blow I had down the drain when we started dating, you know that?" Chancey snarled. "I haven't touched anything since, but I sure as fuck can't say the same about you."

Ivy made a scoffing sound. "Like you could give two shits. You make one thing *very* clear, all this is between us is *you* wanting to fuck *me*. And I used to be that for you, but not anymore."

"You gonna say that to me, after everything we've had?" Chancey demanded.

"I caught you sleeping with her!" Ivy screeched.

"That was a mistake. I didn't care about Scarlet. I was pissed!" Chancey pleaded.

"So you get back at me for doing drugs by fucking around with someone else. That's a class act, Chance. You're just like every other bum that comes crawling into my life looking for a piece of ass. I'm done with it; I really am."

"You go ahead and accuse me of that, but you know I've always loved you. I'm sorry I didn't know how to end it any other way," Chancey said.

"Bullshit. You did what you did because you wanted to punish me," Ivy spat. "You're a coward, Chance. You always have been. And no matter what you say, nobody who truly loves me could do this to me."

Chancey caught my gaze and froze. Ivy spun around. Both of them became deadly silent. Neither of them had realized we were there until just then.

"Ava," Ivy whispered. "I..."

Chancey shoved his hands in his pockets. "You gonna tell her, Ives? Or should I?"

"What's going on?" I asked, innately realizing I didn't want to know.

"Ivy's been using," Charlie said bluntly. "He has been for months. I'm sorry, Ava. We didn't want to upset you."

Chancey looked down at the ground, and reality hit me like a brick to the face. That night at The Devil's Playground last semester, when I'd performed my song... a guard had asked Ivy about a shipment. I assumed it was alcohol, but I knew now what it had to be.

Ivy was ferrying drugs through the club. Worse than that, he was using them.

Ivy's eyes started to water. "Yeah, so it's all out in the open now, huh? Everyone knows I'm back on nightshade." Ivy started to shake. "My business can't be my business, I guess."

"You need to stop," Charlie said firmly. "Your life's never going to get better until you quit using."

"Your judgment of me is real rich, considering I ain't the only one who's sold myself to get what I needed," Ivy sneered. "I'm not the only slut here."

Charlie's face was stricken, and for the first time, I was really pissed at Ivy. *No one* should bring up what happened back then. I went to say something, but my husband beat me to it.

"I did what I had to in order to get by," Charlie shot back at him. "You sleeping around isn't the problem. You're going around hurting people without giving a shit if you do."

"And *he* hasn't fucking broken *my* heart?" Ivy yelled, tossing a hand at Chancey.

"This is about more than us," Chancey said, a note of disappointment in his tone. "You're missing pills, aren't you, Ava?"

I thought my heart went flatline all over again as I stared at Ivy. Tears welled in my eyes as I whispered, "You stole them."

I saw the truth when I looked deeper. He was higher than a fucking kite. Even now.

Ivy fiddled with his hands. "I... I didn't *mean* to, Ava. I just needed a quick fix, you know? Something to take the edge off. I wouldn't if I could've gotten a hit somewhere else. You believe me, don't cha?"

A coldness ran through my veins. Oberi had known. That's what he wanted to speak with Charlie about yesterday. Our Familiar just hadn't found the words.

Charlie grabbed Ivy around the neck with both hands and slammed him against the wall. His fingers began tightening around Ivy's throat. Ivy didn't fight back, just went limp, as if he wanted Charlie to end it all.

"Charlie, stop!" Chancey yanked Charlie away. Charlie had enough sense to let go, and he stumbled back a few feet. I could feel through our bond it took all of Charlie's self-control to hold himself back from attacking Ivy again. Oberi changed into a unicorn and planted herself in the way, acting as a barrier.

Chancey immediately moved to face Charlie, his hands already formed into fists.

"What Ives did was wrong, but don't go there," Chancey warned. "You don't wanna fight me, Charlie. Not when I'm willing to fight back."

I looked between the both of them, feeling completely lost. Chancey might've cheated on Ivy out of spite, but it was so fucking obvious how in love with Ivy he still was. He'd put himself on the line if it meant defending the person he cherished... even against his friends.

Charlie took a step forward, like he didn't care. I grabbed his wrist. "Don't," I pleaded.

His arm trembled in my hold, but he remained at my side. Didn't stop him from blowing up.

"What the fuck is wrong with you?" he spat at Ivy, completely livid. "Ava's in *pain*. If you had gotten caught with her pills, she would've taken the fall for it. You know that. But you didn't give a fuck, did you? All you cared about was yourself. We can't trust you anymore, Ivy.

You're no friend of ours. You never have been. What you did is unforgivable."

Ivy coughed and rubbed his throat. His gaze was weak as he rasped, "Ava..."

What could I say? There was nothing. I knew I should've felt betrayed and furious that Ivy had done this to me.

But I didn't feel that way. All that was in me was sadness. And confusion about how it'd ended up this way.

"I need to rest," I said finally. "Take me home, Charlie."

At that moment, all I could think of was dissolving the situation. More words and threats wouldn't do anything to fix this.

Charlie wheeled me off, hurrying in the direction of our cell. The movie we'd been planning to see didn't even register in my mind. Chancey didn't add anything, but I heard the sound of Ivy's sobs echoing down the hall for what felt like miles.

As Oberi trotted after us, I asked quietly, "Did Chancey really do cocaine?"

Charlie paused for a moment. "He used to, before fights. It would get him amped up for the ring. But he doesn't anymore. He stopped after he met Ivy."

"You didn't do any drugs in fight club, did you?"

"Hell, no. You know better."

I nodded solemnly. Those days were far behind Charlie, long before he met me.

Oberi squeezed through the door to our cell, then changed into a husky to rummage through our stash of Commissary snacks. He liked to eat when he was stressed.

Charlie carried me into the bedroom, then sat me on the bed. "What do you need?"

I'd had a long day, filled with a lot of triumphs and some pretty dark lows. The contrast between the two was stark and confusing. "I just want you to hold me."

"I think that'll both do us some good." Charlie lifted me onto his lap, and I curled desperately into his warm body.

We didn't talk about what had happened, but it was just as well. I didn't want him going off the deep end again.

Charlie fell asleep, but I lay against his chest and counted his heartbeats long into the night, delving deep into my thoughts. I wasn't willing to give up my friendship with Ivy, not even now. He'd rescued me from myself when I was at the lowest points of my existence. If I was being completely honest, without him, I might've done something permanent to end it all, because I didn't know how to get through life unless I had my friends by my side.

Ivy had helped me through my dark times, so I wasn't turning my back on him through this. I knew Ivy was hurting. He was an addict and mentally ill. I didn't blame him for the actions that he took as a result of his illness. I just wanted him to get help.

At the same time, I didn't know if it was healthy for me to keep associating with him. Or Chancey, for that matter.

I didn't get much sleep. I woke up around six the next morning, before Charlie did. I knew he wouldn't be asleep much longer, so I managed to pull myself into my chair and wheel out of the room as quietly as possible.

We'd previously made an agreement that I wouldn't get out of bed without his help, and I hated going back on that. But if he knew my plan, he'd stop me from where I was going, and I couldn't have that.

Oberi wrinkled his nose when he saw me roll toward the door. *And what do you expect me to tell Sir Rages A Lot when he wakes up?*

"Just keep him busy. I won't be long."

I hated lying to my husband. Getting mixed up in all of this could potentially drive a wedge between Charlie and me. I had to be careful.

But I also had to at least try to save a friend.

I found Opal first. She was in Commissary, sipping on coffee and doing her homework. My brother was sitting next to her, while Tahoma lay across the rug. The peryton let out a soft bugle as I approached, and his antlers glowed a soft white in greeting.

I patted Tahoma's head softly, before I said, "Hey."

"I already know what you're going to ask," Opal began. "It's wrong, Ava, any way you spin it. You shouldn't even care about getting involved after what Ivy did to you."

Ez nodded darkly. "Yeah. Pretty fucking pissed about it, myself."

"We have to do something," I insisted.

"I'm tired of helping him, but at the same time, it's aggravating to cut my relationship off with my cousin for the millionth time." Opal rubbed her face. "This is a vicious cycle. It's been going on for years."

"He can get help," I insisted.

"Sure, but it never lasts. He's in rehab for a while, he does okay for a month or two, then something will trigger him, and he'll be back out there with a new fix to chase after," Opal lamented.

"I know this can change," I insisted.

"Loving someone with an addiction is one of the hardest things I will ever do," Opal said flatly. "I can't forgive him for stealing pills from you, Ava. Not this time. I need to protect myself and think about what I need to do so I can provide a good life for my daughter once I'm out. That means getting her away from our family."

She sighed, then bent back over her homework. "Ivy's just as bad as the rest of them."

Clearly, she was done with it, and probably done with Ivy, too. I couldn't blame her for not wanting to ride the rollercoaster any longer.

Yet Ivy had gotten me through some of the worst times of my life. I wouldn't abandon him now, not even if he'd done something as terrible as all this. "Do you know where he is?"

Opal gave a disgusted noise. "Probably at the club, feeling sorry for himself."

"I can't get there all on my own. It's too far." I sagged in my chair, my energy already spent for the day.

Ez's face twisted, but he said, "I'll take you to The Devil's Play-ground, but don't ask me to get involved, sis."

"It won't be but a moment. I just need to talk to him alone."

Ez and Opal shared a glance, before my brother got to his feet. "I'm probably gonna regret this, but... sure. Five minutes, Ava."

"I'm not coming," Opal said bluntly. "I can't even look at Ivy right now. It's horrible, but sometimes I think that if he overdosed again, and no one came to save him this time... at least it would be..."

She put a hand to her mouth to hold back the tears, and I knew. For as much as Opal loved Ivy— and it was a lot— she wanted this to be over.

Ez laid a hand on her shoulder, and I straightened. "I won't let that happen. Come on, Ez, let's go."

It didn't take long to get down to The Devil's Playground. I saw Ivy sitting on the floor at the base of the bar. He had wine in a plastic cup, and his hand shook as he lifted it to his lips, the red spilling over onto his fingers. He looked like absolute shit.

Ez didn't leave, just stood at a distance with Tahoma. He wouldn't let me be alone with Ivy, not even for this.

Couldn't say I blamed him. I rolled closer to Ivy and whispered, "I know it takes a lot to make you cry."

Ivy's lips slightly lifted. It was the same thing he'd said to me when he'd found me sobbing over Charlie last semester. No matter how fucked up on drugs and alcohol he was right now, he remembered that much. "It hasn't been the best day."

"How do we make it better?" I asked. I reached out so he could grasp my hand, but he didn't take it.

"You need to leave me alone. I'm no good for you."

I coiled my hand back into my lap. "How are you and Chancey?"

"We're on a break." Ivy's voice cracked.

My insides became hollow. "Oh, Ivy. I'm sorry."

Ivy sniffed. "He doesn't wanna be with an addict like me. I don't blame him."

"He'll give you another chance. You can beat this. I know you can."

"You can't forgive me for this. I stole *pills* from you."

"So stop."

"Not that simple."

"I know you've tried this so many times before, but try one more time," I said. "Go back to rehab. Get treatment. I'm not giving up on you."

Ivy looked away. "I'll think about it."

My throat got tight, but I swallowed the knot that was forming. "Okay."

It was pretty clear the conversation was done. Ez moved to wheel me away, and I did my best not to feel like shit for leaving Ivy in his drunken stupor. I'd done all I could. There wasn't anything more I could offer.

Charlie and Oberi were waiting for me outside the dining hall. My husband did *not* look happy. Ez left me by Charlie's side without a good-bye, more than pleased to get out of there as soon as he could.

Charlie scowled. "You sneaking off is *not* cute."

"I'm sorry. I had to."

"I don't want you around Ivy anymore."

I looked down. "Probably best to stay away."

Charlie gave an aggravated sigh, but he didn't berate me further. "We need to get some breakfast. Kallie wants to meet us in the fae illusion room as soon as we can get there."

I nodded, doing my best to put the whole situation out of my mind. I couldn't think about Ivy right now. He'd made his choices. I had to do what I could to make the decisions that were best for me.

I'd never been to the fae illusion room on campus. Naturally, it had to be on the highest fucking floor of the prison. Oberi carried me up the steps as a unicorn, while Charlie dragged my chair behind.

When we opened up the door to the fae illusion room, I was struck with awe. It was a beautiful space full of sunlight that poured from a glass ceiling. There were bookshelves lining the tower all around, with spiraling gold staircases. Growing from the bookshelves were an assortment of climbing flowers, with hundreds of butterflies flitting throughout the room. They were in every color— some smaller than a tiny gem, others as large as my head. I laughed as a massive group of butterflies landed on Oberi's horn, and she sneezed. The room smelled like honey, and harp music came from somewhere unknown, along with birdsong.

I was sure the elaborate array was just a bunch of illusions. It was probably some ugly Institute room like any other. But what the fae had done with the place was incredible.

What was underneath our feet wasn't really carpet, but moss. In the center of the room were a variety of tables and chairs for fae students to study at. This time of morning, none of the other fae were here. Kallie was the only one sitting at one of the massive square desks, picking books off stacks that floated in mid-air. Alette hovered above her, giving chase after monarch butterflies.

After I described the room to Charlie, he said, "Sounds very elaborate."

"Definitely the prettiest room on-campus," I agreed.

Marcus was already here, sitting on a levitating armchair while Rishi batted at butterflies. He read Kallie's grimoire, which appeared to be upside down— but maybe that was just the cover, and the contents inside were right-side up. Fae were funny like that.

Charlie helped me down from Oberi and into my chair. I resolved to stay put. It wouldn't be easy rolling through all this moss.

"You must've found something if you called for us this early," I said, scanning the books beside her. They were written in Malovian, which was one language I couldn't yet read.

"I've been researching fae assassins, as we planned, to find the girl in my previous vision," Kallie noted. "There've been so many in history it's been complicated going through them all. I attempted the tracking spells from my grimoire again since I broke the inferichite cuff, and nothing much came of it, but the Unseelie spell at least gave me a direction to start looking."

"So you found something?" Charlie asked.

"A bit," she admitted, and she waved her current read in the air. "The merfolk key has been lost for centuries. But from what I can conclude from history, something like it resurfaced again a few hundred years ago. I dug into ancient conflicts, stuff from before the Great Supernatural War. In one of Malovia's history books, I discovered that the merfolk began a conflict with the fae over something the fae had stolen from them during the time of King Minos' reign. Specifically, something the sister of King Minos took."

"Does it mention a key?" I asked.

"No, but it sure does talk a lot about the king's sister, Duchess Amalie," Kallie said. "She was quite popular with the people, but she had a secret. I believe this is the same woman I saw in my vision."

"Let me guess, she liked killing people," Charlie suggested.

"Correct. She was an exceptional assassin, hired on behalf of the crown to take out enemies to the royal family," Kallie said. "They sent her to Atlantis to eliminate a political opponent, but while she was there, she found something extraordinary. The book doesn't mention what it is, as the royal family wanted to keep it secret, but historians have guessed it was an object of great magical prowess."

"So she was successful in stealing the key from Atlantis," I said. "Where'd it end up after that?"

"The merfolk went through a lot of trouble to get it back," Kallie admitted. "But I don't think they ever did. And get this— once she stole it, she refused to hand it over, or tell anyone where she'd taken it. Whatever Amalie took from the merfolk was lost, and she couldn't give it to the crown, as they'd asked. Eventually, the king was forced to behead her on grounds of treason."

"She must've realized what she had and sacrificed herself to keep it safe," I said quietly.

"That's what I figure," Kallie said with a nod. "Unfortunately, all clues end there. If we're going to find out where the key is, we have to learn more about Duchess Amalie, and where she might've hidden it."

"What else do you know about her?" I asked.

"Not much. Besides her assassinations, there wasn't much written about her, because she was ruled a traitor. Therefore, most of her historical documents are stricken from record." Kallie let out a huff. "Stupid royal decrees."

She shuffled through a bunch of papers. "*But,* I've been investigating her lineage, and she *did* have a son before she died. Who had another son, and so on and so forth, until eventually I came to a common ancestor we both share— Arthur Cedrick."

I couldn't believe the similarities. "Arthur Cedrick is one of my ancestors, too, on my father's side," I noted. "He's an immigrant who came to California and built Orenda Academy after he befriended the Hawkei tribe."

"That's amazing! You guys are related," Marcus said in awe.

"Very distantly, but yes. My grandfather told me so," Kallie said. "And although Ava and I have the same ancestor, she doesn't have enough fae blood in her line to have any illusion abilities. But Arthur Cedrick's family has a direct line to me, with very strong Unseelie influences."

"And that's where my research comes in." Marcus shut the grimoire and hopped off the floating armchair. "We can use Kallie's bloodline to find out where her ancestor Amalie took the merfolk key."

"Can we do that?" Charlie asked skeptically.

"Absolutely," Marcus said eagerly. He waved the book in the air. "And *this* tells us how."

"My grandfather's grimoire has all kinds of Unseelie spells," Kallie said.

"Including an ancestry-recession spell," Marcus said. "Memories can be passed down through the centuries, from parent to child. This stuff isn't easy to access, not once you get past the next few descendants of offspring. But with Kallie's demigod abilities, she should be able to dig through her ancestry and find them. And the best part is, we don't have to go through a complicated ceremony to do it. We just have to put Kallie into a trance, and see where the vision takes us. Maybe Amalie can tell us where she put the key."

"Kallie, you sure about this?" I eyed her warily. "The last Unseelie spell you used to locate the key didn't work."

"Because I didn't believe in my ability to perform it, which you must do if you're going to cast fae magic," Kallie stated. "But I trust that I can pull off *this* spell, because the answers are already in my blood. We just have to unlock the memories. It's the only way to learn where Amalie took the key."

She was already climbing onto the table. "Let's get this over with."

Kallie sprawled across the table on her back. Marcus opened the book he'd been reading and began to recite a verse. *"Phantom Doe of Shadow, Neva, Goddess of Time, take us back through distant past, make clear through path divine. Answers found in ancestors, hidden soon be known, through graves of ancient ones we dig, blood to blood, bone to bone."*

Kallie's eyelids fluttered closed, and she went very still. At first, the vision seemed fairly peaceful. Kallie's chest rose and fell evenly, and Alette rested gently on her nose.

Minutes passed. I wasn't sure what Kallie was seeing, but she didn't seem to be in any distress. We waited for her to awaken, hoping she'd see something that would help us.

Then, the room darkened. The sunlight filtered out from the windows, ending all the illusions in the room and leaving us in shadow. I lit a ball of Fire in my hand, so Marcus and I could see. Several things in the room crashed and broke, though I couldn't tell from where. Books started flying off the shelves, and Alette gave a cry of alarm as she fluttered upward. The room shrank as it returned to its normal size.

Kallie started to convulse. Her body shook as her head slammed back against the table, like she was having a seizure, and a deep laughter infected the room. I didn't know where it was coming from, and it scared the shit out of me.

Marcus immediately started to panic. "Fuck. Fuck, fuck, this isn't supposed to happen!"

"What went wrong?" Charlie bellowed. He had to yell over the noise.

Marcus clutched the grimoire. "The meditation is *supposed* to be performed by an Unseelie sorceress, but since I'm a Seer and the magic is similar, we thought I'd do just fine—"

"Goddammit!" Charlie smacked his face. "Should've known you two would try to cut corners!"

Kallie's body began to levitate off the table, shaking in tremors. "Marcus, make it stop!" I yelled.

"I... I don't know how!" he yelped, flipping frantically through pages. "Oh, good Goddess, help!"

I frantically searched the room for clues. Above Kallie, a translucent force zoomed back and forth. It was nearly invisible, but not quite. I recognized it, because I knew the terrible feeling I got whenever these entities were in my presence. The insane laughter suddenly made sense.

"It's the dark spirits," I said, catching on. "They're interfering with the ceremony."

"Finally, something I can handle," Marcus said frantically, throwing the grimoire down. He dug in his pockets for cedar oil and salt, and immediately started screaming at the spirits. "Get the hell out of here! Leave her alone!"

I heard their wicked cries as the dark spirits resisted Marcus' orders to leave, and failed. Light came back into the room, and all the illusions returned as the area went back to the magical state it had been.

As Marcus chased the spirits off, Charlie reached out and grabbed Kallie, yanking her back down to the table. She slammed down onto it, and several books toppled off.

Kallie's eyes shot open. She sat up on the table, and Alette landed on her head as Marcus ran the remainder of the spirits out of the hall.

Marcus panted as he came back to the table. "Kallie, are you all right?"

She blinked. She seemed to have no recollection of the dark spirits, or the scary shit that had just happened.

"The vision was so... *vivid*," Kallie said. "I was acting as Amalie, through her eyes. I *watched* as I stole the key from Atlantis. She was the girl from my first vision."

"What else did you learn from the vision?" Marcus pressed.

Kallie paused for a short moment, as if recollecting everything she'd seen. "From what I saw and heard, the year was 1867. Amalie was in Atlantis, and she knew about the merfolk key. She'd been contacted by Neva, the goddess of time, who told her the merfolk key needed to be kept safe until the proper individuals could take ownership of it."

"Demigods," I murmured.

Kallie nodded. "She stole the key... she had help, but I couldn't see who— some Atlantean diplomat, I think. The memory was murky. She and her ally planned to go to Darke Island... that's all I could gather from what I saw."

"Did you see where Amalie hid the key?" Charlie asked.

"I didn't get that far," Kallie complained. "The vision broke before I had a chance to see where she concealed it."

"But you think she hid it on Darke Island?" he pressed.

"I believe so. It's here. Amalie brought it to the island, before she was captured and sent back to Malovia to be executed."

Kallie's face brightened up. "Still, I did find a clue... something Amalie left behind for her own reference before she was beheaded by King Minos. She burned it, but I can copy it. I need some paper, something to write with."

Oberi hastily moved to give her the items she requested. Marcus and I clustered around the table as we watched Kallie draw, growing curious. She designed a set of lines, some strange depictions of monuments, and a curving path.

"What is it?" I asked, completely lost as she finished the work.

"It's a treasure map," Kallie said eagerly. "And it's going to lead us right to the merfolk key."

charlie

NINE

I couldn't believe this. This was the biggest clue we'd received in weeks! This map could actually bring us straight to what we were looking for.

"What's on it?" I asked curiously.

"It's a map of the entire island," Kallie described. "There are three clues to the merfolk key, and all of them are located on campus. The first spot on the map points to the siren lake."

"Which the Warden is already searching," Ava said glumly. She'd mentioned the guards were scanning the lake earlier this week. I couldn't believe we were this far behind the Warden. "He has to know about that clue, at least."

"What about the others?" I asked.

"The second location is somewhere in the middle of the school, but it's hard to tell which hall. It could be one of the abandoned cell blocks," Kallie stated. "The third is somewhere in the forest, on campus grounds. A line connects each dot, starting at the siren lake."

"That probably means we have to go in chronological order," Marcus noted. "Otherwise, the clues won't make sense, and we'll get confused on what they mean."

"Which will slow us up," Ava confirmed. "One piece leads to the next, and you can't put together the mystery without receiving the whole picture."

Marcus fidgeted beside me. "We've been gone awhile. We should go somewhere people can see us, so the Warden doesn't send guards to search for us."

"If he hasn't already," Kallie grumbled.

"Let's check the lake," Ava suggested. "We need to dive down there as quickly as we can."

We hurried outside and to the campus grounds, but stopped dead in our tracks when we heard the sound of guards near the lake.

"The guards are still here," Ava sneered.

"Fuck," I growled, before I realized something. "Although, if he's still looking, that means he hasn't found whatever's down there."

"We better pray he doesn't," Marcus added. "Because until he gives up, we can't go into the lake. We'll be caught, and the Warden will take whatever we find."

"Our only choice is to wait until the guards abandon the search," Kallie said. "The last thing we want is to lead the Warden to the merfolk key. Sooner or later, he's bound to give up."

My guts twisted. "That's if he doesn't find it first."

We had no choice. The Warden had already laid claim to siren lake, and there were too many guards to get past to investigate on our own. Without the clue to whatever was in the lake, we couldn't be sure what we were looking for at the next two locations.

I was a bundle of nerves the rest of the day. I really wanted to pursue these clues and get the fuck out of here. I bet the asshole didn't even know what he was searching for. He heard *merfolk* and went to investigate the closest body of water he could find.

During our lunch break, I decided to head to Commissary for a drink to help calm my nerves. A group of inmates were discussing the war at a nearby table when I walked in.

"My parents said Midnighters swarmed a building in Chicago and were arrested by Union officials on-site," a girl said. "They called themselves anti-war protestors."

A guy scoffed. "Anti-war, my shiny dragon ass. They're going to expose us all, which will lead to war with the humans. We all know how disastrous that can be. How is our magic going to withstand nukes?"

"We could take on the nukes," another guy added. "The Union just wants us to be afraid so we don't protest. I saw the news clip. The way they shoved these vampires into those vans, we'll never hear from them again."

"*We?*" his friend asked. "Where do you think you're protesting? You're locked in a prison."

"I'm graduating at the end of the semester. When I get out, I'll—"

"You think they actually let anyone out of here? Clearly you're insane. They'll send you to the adult penitentiary if they hear you talking like that."

I ignored the argument, because I couldn't take the fuckers in this prison. I stepped forward as the line moved and ordered a Calming Cappuccino.

The girl at the counter rang up my total. A dog barked beside her, and I realized it must be Heather. She was an Elementai in some of my classes— Earth, like me, and she even had a husky Familiar. Last week we found out we shared a birthday, and she joked that I was trying to steal her identity.

"Oh, um... I'm going to have to cancel your order," Heather said.

I furrowed my brow. They must be running low on ingredients. "That's fine. Just give me something with caffeine in it."

"The problem is with your account. You're out of Commissary points."

I couldn't be *out*. I was careful about where I spent my points, never spending more than I earned. I refused to go back to being broke, so I budgeted meticulously.

I realized this had to be a mistake. "Check again," I insisted, quickly running through the balance in my head. I knew what had been in there yesterday, because I'd just checked. I wondered if someone could possibly hack the system and use my points.

"I did. I'm sorry, Charlie, but your balance is at zero," she said sadly.

No. This wasn't possible. I felt like melting into the floor as I realized I was, once again, completely out of fucking money. I had nothing— I'd been *robbed*!

Talk about fucking identity theft, only this time, it wasn't a joke.

I'd stolen plenty from loads of people in my life. I was getting a taste of my own medicine, that was for sure. Everything else I thought impossible apparently existed. Why not karma, too?

"Charlie, there you are!" Ava called out to me from far away. She must've pushed through the crowd, because her hand was suddenly on my wrist, and she yanked me out of line.

She couldn't wheel herself with one hand, so I helped her out of the room. Oberi ruffled her feathers from the back of Ava's chair.

I stopped in the hall, already losing my shit. "We're out of Commissary points. Someone robbed us! That's all we have to live on! When I find out who, I'm gonna beat their ass!"

I couldn't help freaking out as I paced in front of her. Our Commissary points were one of the few things that gave us freedom inside this prison, as well as the only ways we were able to buy things we needed. If our Commissary points could be taken away, anything else could, too.

"Charlie, calm down," Ava insisted. "It's not a big deal."

"Not a big deal...?" I trailed off. She sounded like she knew what happened. "Ava, what's going on?"

She didn't say anything right away. I tried to search her mind for the truth, but she wouldn't let me in. Her thoughts were locked down tight, and unless she gave me permission to hear her thoughts, or they slipped through on accident, I wasn't getting answers.

"Ava, did you have something to do with this?" I pressed.

Oberi hissed with what sounded like laughter. *Caught red-handed.*

"I didn't *mean* it, okay? I didn't realize our Commissary points had been combined when we got married," she said nonchalantly. "I just thought I had extra, so I thought, why not spread the love?"

My jaw dropped when I realized she'd spent them. *She fucking spent them!*

She must've seen the incredulous look on my face, because she groaned and mumbled, "Ancestors, this is worse than when I maxed out Daddy's credit card. Please don't be mad."

"Don't be—?" I gaped. "I know you didn't have to think about money growing up, but I never had access to resources. So forgive me if I'm a little angry that's been ripped out from under me."

She took an annoyed breath, about to launch into one of her long explanations. "Look, I wanted a macchiato, and Oberi wanted a cookie, so we went to get those things. But the line was *huge*, and I felt bad, because a couple of people ahead of me couldn't pay for their drinks, because their parents didn't load up their card. So I bought a coffee for them— or two. Then I thought, wouldn't it be so nice if I bought a coffee for *everyone*? I never got to do the thing where they say, drinks all around! So I thought that this was my chance. And I just started buying, and buying... and pretty soon, I spent the three hundred points we had. Which is like, three-hundred dollars. But to me, if people are happy, it's money well spent!"

I pinched the bridge of my nose. "You're manic again."

"What if I am? This morning, I'm the coffee queen!"

"A broke coffee queen," I said flatly.

"So what?" Ava asked. "I'll ask Daddy to reload our account."

I sighed. To Ava, this was a non-issue. To me, it felt like one breath away from living on the streets again.

"I don't *want* to ask your dad for money, pidge," I said. "I want to provide for you. I may only be making pennies per hour at the factory, but at least I'm providing *something*, even if that's just a few snacks a week and one bottle of shampoo a month. I didn't come from a place where money is limitless. It's a precious resource to me, and it scares me that it's all gone."

"Oh," Ava said quietly. "I see."

Why didn't you stop her? I demanded of Oberi.

I'm an enabler, she said. *It's not my job to prevent Ava from living her best life.*

I gritted my teeth. This wasn't okay, and it brought up all types of scary things for me.

Ava must've felt that, because her tone softened. "Charlie, I'm so sorry. Money has never been an issue for me, so I didn't think this would be a problem. If it really bothers you, we can make a budget. It's what married couples do, right?"

Her offer struck me, and I realized I was being too hard on her. She sounded genuinely sorry, and she wanted to work with me on this— as a team. If she said it was an honest mistake, then it was an honest mistake. Ava wanted to love and be friends with everyone, and she was just trying to be nice. She wasn't good with money, but I could help her with that. I could manage our finances so something like this never happened again.

I relaxed. "That sounds helpful. I like the idea of doing *married couple* things with you, even while we're locked up."

Ava snickered. "We've been doing married couple stuff all week."

I smirked. "*Besides* that."

"You can handle our finances," Ava offered. "I'm used to it anyway, since my parents had to regulate my spending. If someone's not telling me how much I can spend, I'll blow it all."

"Yeah, I've noticed," I said sarcastically. "But I think this will be good for both of us."

"Did you still want to help me with physical therapy today?" Ava asked.

"Yeah, of course." I placed my hands on the back of her wheelchair. "I have just the place."

Since the doctors didn't give a shit about Ava's treatment, it was up to me to help her with physical therapy. I wheeled her to Cellblock 7, to the room where Chancey had stashed his stolen work-out equipment. I placed my hands on her legs, and I helped bend her knee and stretch her ankles to keep blood flowing to her legs. Ava shivered as my hands traveled up and down her legs.

"Everything all right?" I asked.

"Just watching you do that... it reminds me of what it used to feel like," she said. "It's sexy."

I smirked. It was *definitely* sexy running my hands up and down her body. "Right now's not a great time, pidge."

She chuckled lightly. "Are you afraid we'll get caught?"

"You certainly wouldn't mind," I teased. "You'd fuck me in front of the Warden if you could get away with it."

"Hell yeah, I would," she said. "Don't tell me you haven't thought about it, too. I have this fantasy where you hang me upside down from the ceiling in the entry hall, and you fuck me in front of everyone."

I raised an eyebrow. "Upside down? I don't even know how that would work."

"Oh, we'd find a way. I want the Warden to know exactly how much I don't give a fuck about anything he says."

"By... giving a fuck in front of him?" I laughed.

Ava chuckled, and I was happy to hear she was having a good time. "Exactly. It was Ivy's suggestion, really."

I frowned. "I thought you and Ivy weren't talking."

"Not really, but I still want to help him," she said. "He'll get better. I know he will."

Ava couldn't see the reality of the situation. What Ivy had done was unforgivable. I had no interest in helping them after what they'd done to her.

Ava started rambling, talking so quickly it was hard to keep up. She really was on one of her high days. I really hoped she didn't crash later this week, because since she'd gotten in that wheelchair, her lows had been worse than ever. I'd been having trouble getting her out of them.

"I'm actually sure he'll be fine," Ava continued on without missing a beat. "You know, Monica and I had a fight once, and we didn't talk for months, but we worked it out, and everything got better, just like I knew it would. Ivy's just going through a hard time right now, like all of us."

She kept talking, but I didn't hear her. When Ava drew a parallel between Monica and Ivy, it was striking. I realized Ava was trying so hard to save Ivy because she was trying to make up for not being able to save Monica. Ivy was the troubled friend she was going to rescue this time around. It didn't matter that Ivy had betrayed her, because in Ava's eyes, they could still be saved.

And I admired that so much... but I feared she'd get hurt in the process.

"I want to believe you about Ivy getting better, but until they're recovered, I don't want you around them," I said. I didn't want to be the guy who told my wife what to do, but Ivy wasn't safe. It was my job to protect her.

"How can I help if I *abandon* Ivy?" Ava replied.

"You're not abandoning Ivy by taking care of yourself. I'm not trying to control you. That's the last thing I want. But Ivy hurt you, and that's a hard line for me. This is *not* a good situation, and I'm not letting you get in the middle of it. If Ivy starts treatment, then we revisit this. But until then, I need to know you're safe."

I hated this, but I wasn't going to budge on it. Ivy had stolen pills from Ava, and she couldn't be in a situation where she was vulnerable like that again... especially not from someone she considered a "friend."

"All right." Ava sounded defeated, but she let it drop. I think she understood more than she was willing to admit. "Hand me those weights, would you?"

Ava seemed to like working out, which was great for us, because it gave us a *thing* to do together. More couple time was always a plus.

Ava told stories about dance class back in Kinpago while she lifted weights, and I stretched out her legs. She didn't talk about home much. I wondered if she was trying to distract herself, too.

Ava and I went our separate ways for our majors. I told Oberi to stay with Ava, and I counted my steps as I made my way to Advanced Criminal Justice. I took my seat, and someone plopped into the seat next to me, tossing a bag onto the desk.

"Lucky you. I'm early enough to snag a seat by the man of the hour."

I furrowed my brow. "Chancey?"

"Of course. Who else smells this good?" He waved his hand through the air, fanning his scent toward me.

Ancestors, he must've put on a whole bottle of body spray this morning. It was gross. I started coughing. That shit was illegal at the prison.

"Where'd you *get* that stuff—?" I cut off, because I realized the answer before I finished. "You made a bet to get your hands on it, didn't you?"

"I won it in a card game. So sue me," Chancey said nonchalantly.

"Gambling's what got you in here in the first place," I hissed. "You said you stopped when you and Ivy got together."

"I did," Chancey replied. "That doesn't mean I can't start up again."

"You know it's not good for you. If you don't stop now, you're going to take it too far."

"Relax," Chancey said. "I know how to control myself. I don't have a reason to stop anymore."

Chancey was a filthy liar. If he could control his gambling, he wouldn't be at the Institute, and he wouldn't have ended up taking bets for fight club.

I hoped his addiction didn't send him back there. It'd been hell getting him out.

"I didn't put my ass on the line with Captain to get you out of fight club so you could blow what little progress you've made on cards," I growled.

"It's not a big deal," Chancey insisted. "I'm only taking good bets so I have something to show for when I get out of this place."

"What are you talking about?"

"You really inspired me, you know that, Charlie? You want to be a bounty hunter. At first, I figured it was kind of stupid, because I didn't think you'd ever have a chance of being one, what with your record and all."

"Thanks for that."

"Hear me out. Anyway, you didn't give up on it, and so... I kinda thought I could be one, too. You gave me the idea that I can have a good life once I graduate, and, well... I figured I could use the gambling money I've got to get our practice off the ground. That is, if you wanna be partners."

I choked up. I didn't think I'd ever *inspired* anyone. Most people in this major didn't really care about it. They'd joined more or less to learn how to avoid the criminal justice system once they got out of here. Chancey actually cared about making things better in the world. Better than that... he wanted to be a bounty hunter, too, be my partner and fight crime together.

"I'm honored. I'd love to start something like that with you. We'd be good partners," I said.

"Yeah. I had an idea that once you and me set up shop, I'd be able to put some money away for me and..." He trailed off.

"For Ivy?" I asked. "I thought you two broke up."

"We did."

"But...?" I asked.

"There is no but," Chancey insisted. "Ives and I are over."

"Then why are you still using their nickname?" I asked.

Chancey fell quiet for a few beats.

I sighed. "Look, if you want to have a future with Ivy, you're going to have to do some deep soul-searching, because what you did was really fucked up. You really hurt Ivy."

Ivy wasn't the only one on my shit list. Chancey was one of my best friends, but what he'd done was fucked, too.

"You're on Ivy's side then?" he accused.

"Hell no," I said. "I'm not taking sides."

"Then you've got to understand," Chancey pleaded. "You and me, we're cut from the same cloth. I grew up around that shit, drugs everywhere. I've seen more friends die from overdoses than killed on the streets. Too many of them corked off right in front of me. I sure thought I'd had enough of it, but clearly I didn't have my fill, because I got tied up with Ivy."

"You can't say it was nothing," I argued. "It's definitely messed up, but you still care. You've cared about Ivy since before you guys got together."

"Yeah, well, I knew better. That's what you get for falling in love with a prostitute."

"Don't be like that," I said scathingly. "How could you sleep with Scarlet? Seriously, what were you thinking?"

"I just lost it when I found out Ives was stealing pills," Chancey confessed. "The nightshade... yeah, I knew about it for a while, but I've had my fair share of it, too, and I figured I could get Ives off it eventually. But then I saw Ives take those pills, and I thought about Ava... how she was, all hooked up to those machines and dying... we had a real big argument, but Ives made it pretty clear that the pills were more important than us. Than me."

His hands shook beside me. "And I got so mad, thinking about Ivy stealing those pills from her. So I wanted to hurt Ivy like Ava had been hurt... like *I'd* been hurt. That was the only way I could figure how to do it. So I set it all up and made sure Ives walked in. I couldn't give a shit about Scarlet... she was just a tool. I *wanted* Ives to see."

"What the fuck is wrong with you?" I asked in disgust. Ava and I had our problems, but these two were completely insane. Toxic didn't even come close to describing how fucked up they were.

"I wasn't brave enough to break up to their face," Chancey admitted. "This was easier."

"You could've broken up without going the abusive route." Yeah, I knew what I said, but Chancey needed some tough love.

He sighed, like he knew he'd fucked up. "I didn't know how. I love them too much."

"That's not good enough," I growled. "In fact, that makes it worse."

"I can't watch them die, Charlie. I'll never get over it. So don't ask me to give Ives another chance, because you'd never get over Ava, either. I know— I saw it. And I don't *ever* wanna be in a situation like you were in. Because if that was Ivy, and I fucking found them..."

Chancey cut off. It sounded like he'd wiped his face on his sleeve. He cleared his throat and said, "Anyway. I ain't talking about this no more."

"I won't say anything else about it. But nothing's right unless Ava and I are okay. I think it's like that for you and Ivy, too."

I heard him sink in his chair. "No way. I'm done."

Professor Jobe cleared his throat at the front of the room, and it was obvious the conversation was done. I felt bad for Chancey, but I didn't bother talking to him about it further.

I could only help these people so much.

We listened to Jobe's lecture about the various high-profile criminals who had gone through the prison system on Darke Island. We discussed their criminal history, and how they'd been caught by criminal profilers. They had all died inside the adult penitentiary— most of them decapitated by other inmates. Like most of our Criminal Justice material, it was meant to scare us. Jobe never mentioned the ones who had been reformed, only those who had met horrible deaths.

Toward the end of the hour, our professor announced the details of our final paper. "Criminal profiling is a department of the United Supernatural Union that seeks to identify personality traits and personal history of specific criminals who don't leave enough evidence behind to prosecute. You will be required to write a criminal report on an active criminal within the supernatural community. In your report, you will detail the history of the crimes and present a profile outlining the suspect's personality and behavioral characteristics. In cases of exceptional research, these profiles have been sent directly to the Union, and they've been used to catch criminals in the real-world. You could prove to be a hero. I suggest you start thinking about the subject of your profile now. You'll be turning in your project proposal tomorrow."

That didn't leave us much time. Something about the project rubbed me the wrong way. *You could be a hero.* They didn't want us becoming heroes, so what was this about?

Cheap labor, I realized. The Union wanted us to help them catch criminals, even though we were criminals ourselves. They probably hoped we'd out our friends. Hell, they'd draw up criminal profiles for *us* based on our own analysis.

I didn't think I had much to worry about, considering I didn't personally know anyone in the supernatural community outside of the Institute. Now I just had to pick someone... but who?

I found my way to the Villain's Den after class. Cartoons played on the TV, and the sound of the air hockey table whirred. I hoped she was here…

"Charlie, over here!" Kallie called.

Bingo! I went over to her and sat down.

"You look bummed," she mentioned. I heard her scribbling something down, and I wasn't sure if it had to do with her map. She didn't offer any information.

"I was thinking you could help me," I said. "I have to write a criminal profile for my major, but I don't know anything about the criminals in supernatural society. You used to hunt criminals before you were arrested. Would any of them work for my paper?"

"Charlie Wahkin, you've come to the right place." Kallie sounded excited. She set her art supplies aside. "If you want to get an A on this paper, write about the Dollmaker."

"Why's that such a sure thing?" I asked.

"Because I know everything there is to know about that sick fuck," she said. "I could write this paper with my eyes closed."

"Do you know how to write a criminal profile, or even where to begin coming up with one?" I asked.

Kallie hesitated. "Not really. But I know his history— every victim, time of death, all of it. I've even kept up to date since I've been at the Institute."

"He's still killing?" My mouth became dry. To think I was behind bars for stealing a boat, and this guy was still out there… it made me want to upchuck my own intestines. "How many?"

"Ten girls since I've been here," Kallie said. "So that makes… twenty-two victims."

"Twenty-two…?" I nearly choked. "And they haven't found this guy yet? How's that possible?"

This man deserved the death penalty, and worse.

"He's *very* good at what he does," Kallie said. "I was dead set on catching him and putting him behind bars before I was sentenced here. He was the one criminal that managed to get away from me. Gods, how I'd love to take out that sack of shit."

"Between you and me, maybe we can piece this together," I said hopefully. Kallie knew his history, and I knew how to get into the mind of a criminal. I'd been around criminals all my life and had been studying them in class for months. After all, I was one myself, though I was nothing like this monster. "Maybe we can get this guy off the streets."

"Here's what I know," Kallie said. "He kills at night. Every time. All of his victims have been young women, fae sorceresses, between the ages of thirteen and twenty-two. He cuts their wings off and takes them as mementos. After he kills them, he dresses his victims up as dolls and poses them."

I almost second guessed my desire to write about this guy. He was a real sicko. But someone had to get him off the streets, and if my profile was of any use to the Union, maybe he *would* be found and executed.

"How do you know all this?" I asked.

"I broke into the Malovian records office when I was hunting him back home. I saw the crime scene photos," Kallie said. "And one more thing..."

She leaned in to whisper, so no one else would hear. "I followed him one night."

"Kallie, you could've been killed," I hissed.

"Look, he's good at what he does, but I'm better," she insisted. "Or, I would've been, if I hadn't been arrested before I could identify him. Anyway... I got to the body too late, but I *did* find evidence. I know how he kills his victims, which the police haven't released."

The suspense was killing me. I leaned in closer and asked, "How?"

"He kills by bloodletting."

Shivers traveled down my spine. A real sicko, indeed.

I hated asking this next question, but it was critical for my profile, and could give us some clues on how to catch him. "Does he sexually assault his victims?"

"No. There's no signs of rape. My guess is he gets sexual gratification from the act of killing itself."

I nearly gagged. I couldn't imagine how anyone could find sexual pleasure in murder. I was going to have to entertain the idea, though, because if we were going to catch this guy, I had to get inside his head one way or another.

Kallie sighed. "And he leaves no DNA behind, either, or any magical traces that can be helpful to the investigation, which is *very unusual*. Usually, these types of crimes are easy to trace, because the scenes he leaves behind are sloppy. But somehow, the police still have no idea who this guy is."

"It's a performance for him," I said confidently. "He likes to take his time and watch his victims die, but he dresses them up as if they're a part of the act— a participant."

Kallie sounded intrigued by my analysis. "It's not his way of posing them like a trophy, then?"

"No, that's what the wings are for," I said. "Dressing the victims up indicates he's creating a scene out of his fantasies. He's probably young himself, still identifying with the ages of his victims, but he's aging them down because he's fixated on a girl from his childhood. Something bad must've happened to him, and she was central to his trauma. His victims are made to be participants, and killing them is his way of fulfilling the fantasy he never got to play out with this other girl."

"Do you think the person committing these murders performed other crimes first?" Kallie asked. "I could never connect him to any other crimes. Perhaps I overlooked something."

"It's possible," I said. "There are groups of serial rapists who move on to becoming serial killers, because they no longer get the same emotional high from the domination aspect of the sexual assault, so they have to take it a step further and take the life away from the victim in order to receive that high. Then, as they keep killing, they make the murders riskier in order to get high from the gamble of potentially getting caught by police. He might've escalated to murder because he needs the thrill of humiliating his victim, like addicts need to retain the high from drugs. But maybe he's not one of these guys."

"That's still a lot of assumptions."

"Let me guess. When he dresses up the victims, it's always the same?"

"He always puts them in a navy-blue dress."

"It's the same girl, over and over."

"No, it's a doll," Kallie said. "I think you're looking too deep into this. He's a sicko, and there's no rhyme or reason to it. He probably got his kicks chopping off dolls' heads as a kid, and he escalated to real people."

"You don't do that without some serious issues," I pointed out. "This guy was severely traumatized."

Kallie got quiet for a moment, then said, "So, he wants to kill *her*—the girl who hurt him."

"No, actually. He wants to *impress* her," I realized. "He's not that helpless little kid anymore. He wants to show her he's powerful."

"That doesn't make any sense," Kallie said. "He's exercising power *over* her. If it's a fantasy about killing her, she must be the one who hurt him."

I shrugged. "It's my first time creating a profile. I'm not saying it's perfect, but I'd wager a bet that I'm on to something. And when the Union finally finds him... I hope he's young enough to be sentenced to the Institute. I'll gladly blood let him like he did his victims."

"Charlie," Kallie said harshly.

"Don't lecture me," I replied. "You were an assassin. You just admitted you've thought about killing this guy countless times."

"Of course I have," she hissed. "But what good does it do? It feels good taking out monsters who do nothing but hurt people. You think you're doing the right thing and protecting everyone. But once you start, it's hard to stop. I've already done it before. I can do it again. And if the Dollmaker ends up here, I won't hesitate. That asshole is *mine*. But you, Charlie?"

She breathed a heavy sigh. "I can't watch you become what I was."

"I've killed people before," I said bluntly.

"And that's what terrifies me," she whispered harshly. "Killing in a time of war is an entirely different feeling than hunting people down, okay? I got addicted to acting as judge, jury and executioner to the people I assassinated. I started assassinating people when I was *fourteen*, Charlie. Did those predators deserve it? Probably, but why was that my call? I hope to the gods that warlock you killed in the hallway will be your last, because I can't see you lose yourself in this."

Kallie was always pretty serious, but this was on a whole other level. Forget Cellblock 9. Forget hell. This was deeper and darker than anything I could ever imagine.

"All right," I told her. "I won't go there."

"You better not. I'll be holding you to that promise," Kallie said darkly.

Problem was, I wasn't sure if I could keep it.

KALLIE DIDN'T MENTION our conversation after that. I thought she might say something in our demigod lesson the following week, but she didn't. I couldn't tell if she knew I was lying about my promise not to kill people.

It wasn't that I *wanted to*— but I would. If it meant protecting the people I loved and putting some dirtbags in the ground, I wouldn't hesitate anymore, because I was *done* putting myself and my friends in danger trying to keep my morals intact. This was prison. You had to do what you had to in order to survive. And sometimes, that meant becoming something you didn't want to be, and choosing to kill, or be killed.

I put it out of my mind and focused on the lesson. We gathered in Hemlock's secret illusion room, honing in on our demigod powers. Battle magic sparked in my fingers, and I felt the heat ripple up my arms. It was an Elf power I had yet to tap into, and it made me feel powerful.

"This has got to be it," I said. "I've always been good at fighting. This must be my demigod power."

"I'm not sure," Takahashi said thoughtfully. "We should keep our possibilities open."

He walked around me, while Kallie and Marcus levitated themselves around the room with their telekinesis. It was no surprise those two were meant for each other— their powers could be so similar at times.

They were supposed to be practicing simultension. They'd been trying to combine Kallie's time powers with Marcus's Seer powers to look into the future and influence future events. It wasn't working, and they'd gotten bored. I wasn't sure that was something we were capable of, even as demigods, but Takahashi insisted we try everything.

Ava sat near me. She was humming, so I knew she was deep in thought. She and Takahashi were both inspecting me, trying to figure out what the hell my demigod power could be.

Perhaps it's best if we don't force this, Oberi said.

"Easy for you to say," I told her. "You're not the one destined to save the world."

She ruffled her feathers. *Technically, since I share a soul with the two of you, and the prophecy is about you, it's my duty to help.*

"Then perhaps you can give us a hint," I suggested. "You knew Ava's power before the rest of us."

That's because she had already used it, Oberi said. *I was able to sense the difference in her magic. I've told you before— I don't know everything.*

"Well, that's helpful," I said sarcastically. I was getting frustrated. We'd been at these lessons for weeks, and even Marcus was further along than I was. I mean, he hadn't exactly figured out his *demigod* power, but his warlock magic was improving.

"This is good," Ava said. "If Oberi can feel our demigod powers once you use them, and she hasn't felt yours yet, it means it's something you haven't used before. We can narrow it down."

"So not battle magic, then," I said in disappointment. "What if it's not tied to my Elf powers or my Elementai powers?"

"Charlie," Ava said softly. "I think we already know."

I was drawing a blank. "I've tried everything. Earth. Air. Energy manipulation. Battle magic... wait. Strong Elves have unique powers. What if I have something like mind reading?"

"Maybe, but there's one other thing we haven't tried yet," Ava said. "Illusions."

My stomach dropped when she said it. *No way.* I couldn't create illusions. Never in a million years. Elf illusions weren't the same as fae illusions. They couldn't become solid, which meant the magic was all in the visuals.

Ava must've noticed my unease, because she quickly added, "I have some ideas."

"It's not going to work," I insisted. "Without being able to feel what I'm creating, I can't do it."

Those are strong words for a guy who's destined to save the world, Oberi said.

"You think it's so easy? Then *you* do it," I told Oberi. "You're part of my soul. You have access to my powers."

If I could, I would've already, just to stop your whining, Oberi said in a snarky tone.

"Ava-Marie is right," Takahashi said. "Elf illusions may not become solid, but there are other elements to the illusion— scent, for example."

I paused. Scent, I could work with. "I guess we could start there. I'm going to need some help from Kallie."

"Did I hear my name?" Kallie and Marcus landed, though Kallie was so quiet on her feet I barely heard her. Marcus practically shook the whole room when he fell onto the floor. Rishi let out a scared yowl as he scampered out of the way.

"Any tips on creating illusions?" I asked.

"It's all in your imagination," Kallie instructed. "The way it works with fae magic, you have to believe in the illusion you're creating. The stronger your belief, the stronger the illusion becomes in reality. That's why our illusions can become solid."

"But I can't do that, because I'm not a fae," I said.

"The concept is the same. Let's start by picking a scent."

"Roses?" Marcus suggested, almost too quickly. Did the guy have a thing for flowers or something?

"Uh, sure," I said. "I can try roses."

"All you have to do is imagine the scent in your mind," Kallie said. "Then believe it into existence."

It sounded easier said than done, but I closed my eyes and tried to imagine I was in a field of roses, inhaling their scent. A whole minute must've passed, and nothing changed.

"It's not working," I finally said.

"What's going on in your head?" Kallie wondered. "Maybe I can help."

"I'm imagining I'm standing in a field of roses," I said.

"You've got to go deeper than that," Kallie told me. "This isn't a daydream. You need to make it real. Don't put yourself in the field of roses. Bring the roses to you, into this room. Believe that it is already done, and it will be."

My eyebrows pinched together. I didn't know how I could believe in something that wasn't real, but Kallie knew more about illusions than I did, so I had to follow her lead.

I started by getting into my body, feeling the ground beneath my feet and listening to the sound of Ava's breathing to ground me in the moment. Then I imagined the room filling with roses, pictured their soft, silky petals and sharp thorns. I imagined what it would smell like if the room was full of roses, like a flower shop.

"I smell roses!" Kallie said in excitement.

It threw me off initially, because I didn't smell anything. Could I have actually done it?

"Yeah, I think I smell something, too," Marcus said. "It's definitely floral."

"Oh... they smell so sweet," Ava added.

So divine, Oberi said sarcastically, and I took a playful swipe at her. She fluttered out of the way.

"A job well done," Takahashi encouraged.

Tingles of magic spread through my body— so light I barely noticed it. It wasn't like the other magic I'd cast before. Slowly, the scent filled my nose. It was light at first, but as my friends began to show excitement, the smell became stronger.

"Holy shit, I actually did it," I said.

"You did!" Kallie cried in excitement. "Do you want to know the secret? We didn't actually smell anything at first."

"You were lying?" I asked.

"We were *demonstrating*," Kallie clarified. "I was trying to get you to believe you'd done it, because you can only create an illusion if you believe it's already complete. Once you thought you'd already cast it, it happened."

I wasn't mad that they'd lied to me. I'd actually accomplished progress, and that made me feel powerful.

"This is great! What else can I do?" I wondered.

"I said I had an idea," Ava announced. "I don't know if it'll work, but the least we can do is try. Charlie has powers the other Elves don't. I wonder if he can use simultension on himself to make his illusions solid, like how I used simultension on myself during the Darke Games to combine Fire and Water."

"That's a very good theory," Takahashi said. "Would you like to try it, Charlie?"

"How would it work?" I asked curiously. "Illusion mixed with Earth... you think I could make a tree solid— just create plants out of nothing?"

"I think that's exactly where we need to start," Ava said.

"Just remember, it is already done," Kallie encouraged.

I drew a deep breath, hoping to soak up some of her confidence. "All right. I've got this."

I pulled my Earth magic to the surface and held it there. A spruce tree sprang to mind immediately, since Christmas trees reminded me of Ava. I imagined the tree sprouting in the center of the room. I pictured its strong, piney scent and the brush of needles across my fingertips.

It is already here, I told myself. *Hemlock never took down her Christmas tree. She spent three hours decorating it, and she had to go into Shade Hills for extra ornaments.*

Tingles spread across my skin as I continued creating the story in my mind. I felt my Earth magic intermingle with my illusion magic, and my confidence soared.

Hemlock chose icicle ornaments with glitter on them, because they remind her of winter in Malovia. The fae can be over the top with things, so of course she used ten strings of lights—

"Oh, Charlie! It's beautiful!" Ava cried.

"I did it?" I asked, a little shocked. I shouldn't have been, considering I was actually starting to believe the story I was telling myself.

"I love Christmas— and not just because it's my birthday," Ava said. "Look how pretty it is!"

"Impressive indeed," Takahashi said genuinely.

"Wow. You got the lights and everything," Marcus said.

"The icicles are gorgeous," Kallie added. "Ice skating is a big deal in Malovia. This tree reminds me of home."

I didn't know if they were just trying to make me feel better, lying as they had before to make me believe it. But Kallie couldn't have known I was going for a Malovian aesthetic. I must've really nailed it.

"It's all white," Kallie said. "Did you do that on purpose, to make it look like snow?"

I shook my head. "I didn't really think about the colors, because that's not how I experience the world. I bet I can work on it, though."

Rishi must've liked it, because I heard an ornament clink to the ground, and he started meowing as he batted it around the room.

Ava wheeled herself forward and took my hand. "Come see it, Charlie."

I stepped to the center of the room, and a strong pine scent filled my nose. I reached out, my fingers grazing across the spruce needles. Amazed, I continued running my hands around the tree. I could feel the strings of lights, right down to the heat they emitted. My fingers trailed over the smooth ornaments, until they met the rough glitter swirling into beautiful shapes across the glass.

"How is this possible?" I wondered. "I mean, I should be able to make a tree with simultension, but the rest of this..."

You're a demigod, Oberi reminded me. *Your illusions must be stronger than the other Elves. It could be your special Elf power. I definitely felt something different when you cast this illusion. I think we may have found your demigod power.*

"That's wonderful!" Ava cried, before turning to the others. "Oberi thinks illusions are Charlie's power."

I got excited. "If I can feel what it's like to make things solid through simultension, I might be able to make any illusion solid."

"Your illusion is different than the fae's, though," Kallie observed as she paced around the tree. "I can't quite figure it out... this is more solid than my illusions. It's like I can't tell it's made of magic. Most fae could only conjure a visual and scent at most, or make it solid without the smell. This is impressive. It's actually... real."

"That must have something to do with combining my Earth powers into the illusion," I theorized.

"With illusion magic like this, we could escape the Institute!" Marcus exclaimed.

I shook my head. "Not with all the inferichite surrounding the property. I'd never get an illusion to hold near the fence."

"Then we'll have to find another way out," Ava suggested. "Charlie's illusion magic just might be our key to escape."

ava-marie

TEN

"**G**ET OUT OF MY WAY, I'M DISABLED!"

I pushed my way through the crowd, rolling over people's toes and shoving them aside in order to get to the front of the line. Charlie squeezed through the crowd behind me, while Oberi flew over the fray, looking for spots I could push my chair through.

This time of morning, Commissary was packed, and we had to fight through a wave of people just to get to the counter to place our order. We'd been able to load a few more points on our card so we could get a couple of necessities for the rest of the month. We were in a hurry, so I wanted to get our drinks so we could get out of here. I barged my way through, and a couple of people swore at me, though I flipped them off before continuing forward.

It was rude that everyone stayed rooted in their spot when they could literally just take two steps aside so I could get through. They saw me coming and were just being jerks.

I didn't expect the world to cater to me... but I'd always been a little princess, so yes I did!

"Do you have to be so obnoxious?" Charlie complained as I elbowed a girl aside.

"I will use this chair as a weapon," I threatened. "Don't tempt me. I've considered it more than once."

And I was actively planning to. Just looking for the right excuse.

Someone's in a mood, Oberi teased. She used her talons to grab at a guy's hair and yank him out of the way. He waved her off, but it'd made enough room so I could finally place my order.

"Yay, it's you," Naya sang in a hateful tone behind the counter. "What do you want this time, to blow all your points again?"

"I'll have a white chocolate mocha with oat milk," I said as I slammed my card on the counter. "Don't poison my coffee again, bitch."

Naya gave a sneer, though she went to make my order. I kept my eyes on her, to make sure she didn't slip anything else in it.

By the time we got our coffee, everyone knew to move, or face my wrath. We found a little spot by a window to enjoy our morning and split a chocolate croissant while Oberi morphed into a husky and horked down a breakfast sandwich.

"That's a lot of caffeine," I said as Charlie took a huge gulp of his drink. He'd ordered six espresso shots in his coffee.

"If I don't drink it, I'll fall asleep," he told me. "The job only asks that I use a fraction of my brain cells."

It was the weekend, and Charlie was required to work a double factory shift. I didn't like how he was being booked for extra hours.

They'd moved me from the laundry room to the secretary's office, as it was easier for me to do. I'd gotten excited, thinking I'd gain some access to files we needed, but they'd put me in a back room and had me doing nothing but transcribing old speeches that the Warden had given at past events. It was boring, and didn't give us any resources, although I was only required to work there a few hours each week due to my recovery.

"I'm sorry. I know you hate that job."

"If I have to label or pack one more box, I'm going to scream." Charlie rubbed his eyes. "I really wish they'd put me in a different department."

"You could ask to be moved."

"I've tried, and they won't. It doesn't help that I know I'm helping the Warden make weapons to use against the people we're fighting for."

He leaned against the wall. "It won't be for much longer. I'll never go back once we're out of here."

It really sucked when your husband had a job he hated. Charlie's mood was off whenever he had to go into work. It wasn't every day, but when he disliked what he was doing this much, even one hour was more than either of us wanted him to spend there.

"If you're going to be holed up in that stupid factory all day, I'm going to the library to see what I can find out about the lake," I told him. "We should know what we're getting into before we go down there."

The minute those guards withdrew from the lake, we were going in. And by the looks of things, they were close to giving up on the search. Fewer guards were out there every day, and they stayed for shorter periods of time.

After we'd finished our coffee, he gave me a kiss goodbye, and we went our separate ways. Oberi bobbed behind me, dancing to whatever music was inside his head.

I was on my way to the library when I spotted Ivy. It was the first time I'd seen him in forever, and he did not look good. His clothes were stained and torn. He hadn't stopped wearing the male uniform since his dad had shown up, and it just wasn't natural for me to see Ivy in anything but a skirt.

His hair... it was an absolute wreck, something resembling a matted disaster, still that shade of black that didn't suit him.

Charlie had told me to stay away from Ivy, and I had for weeks. He was right when he said that Ivy wasn't a safe person to be around right now. But when I was confronted with how he looked now, I just couldn't turn away. There was a hole inside of me where my close friend was, and the only one who could fill it was him.

Go to him, Oberi encouraged. *We know he did you wrong, and yet, you still care. Give it one more chance.*

Oberi's encouragement pushed me forward. Ivy saw me coming, and tried to run off. I called out, "Ivy, stop! I... I need help."

Ivy halted in his tracks, then reluctantly turned to face me. "What do you need help with, precious?"

"I need you to get better," I pleaded. "So I can get better, too."

Ivy's eyes got even sadder than they already were, and he said, "I don't know why you should care about me. I sure don't."

"Because... I can't possibly lose another friend again." I buried my head in my hands. "It's too much. I feel like I'll break. I couldn't stand saying goodbye to Monica. Don't ask me to say goodbye to you."

Ivy knelt down so we were eye level, and he reached out to brush my hair away from my eyes. "I'm too far gone, precious."

"Don't say that. I'll do anything to save you."

"You and I both know I gotta save myself, and I just don't wanna do that anymore. I'm ready to give up, so let the drugs take me."

"I can't let you go. If I had to keep fighting through all the pain of being in that hospital and coming back to all of you when it would've been so much easier to stay away, and stay dead, then I'm begging you to try, at least one more time."

Ivy stood tall and wiped his nose on his sleeve. "I look like shit."

"Come on. Let's go somewhere."

I had him take me back to The Devil's Playground. He sat on the floor in front of me, and I began working on combing out his hair. Oberi lay across Ivy's lap, ears perked and attentive.

I always had a comb on me, just in case my hair got out of place. But Ivy's locks were a ratted mess. There were huge tangles that had turned into knots, and spots where there were chunks missing. I didn't think he'd had a shower in days, if not weeks.

I did my best not to cry, because that would only make him feel worse. I got to work on detangling what I could. I couldn't stop Ivy from using, but I was a damn good cosmetologist, and I was at least determined to save his hair.

"I don't even like drugs," Ivy murmured, trying to give a helpless explanation. "I don't know if I ever did. But they helped."

I pulled out a snarl and set it aside. "How'd you even get started on them, anyway?"

His tone was despondent. "I didn't really wanna do 'em… wasn't interested, to tell you the truth. But life at home kept on getting harder and harder, and the jobs I took weren't getting any easier… I hated going home with those clients, so I'd just numb myself out to it, because I couldn't stand what they did to me. Every new guy that picked me up made it worse. So I just kept on getting higher and taking more drugs, so by the time they got done with me I hardly knew where the hell I was. It was the only way, you know?"

I didn't answer, because I didn't know if it was. But I wasn't Ivy, and I hadn't been in his place or had to deal with what he'd gone through, so there really was no way for me to know.

"I'm named after my dad," Ivy said quietly, and he wrapped his arms around his legs. "Just so you know."

My heart dropped into the pit of my stomach. No wonder he'd been so attached to his stage name as a dancer. "Your dad isn't you."

"Bullshit. I'm a scummy asshole, just like him. Nothing but bad choices all my life." He scoffed. "I named myself after my favorite *drug,* for crying out fucking loud."

"You wanna know what I like about ivy? People try to trim it, or cut it down, but it grows and grows until it overcomes everything in its path, and when that happens, everyone is forced to accept that it's beautiful." I brushed his hair back. "The drug isn't you. You've taken Ivy and made it your own. You got to choose your own name and share it with the world. That's pretty special."

"Easy for you to say, when you have a name as pretty as yours."

"Yeah, but I'm pretty picky about how people use it."

"How so?"

"It's okay when strangers call me Ava, but I don't like people calling me Ava-Marie. Not unless they're close to me. I know it's my name, but it's special. I want to save it for people who I really love."

A warm fondness took over me as I recalled my first kiss with Charlie. It'd been at the Elven gate outside of the Institute during the Darke Games. "I guess that's why I kinda lost it when Charlie called me Ava-Marie for the first time. Not Ava, or pidge, but who I really was. It was like he was seeing me for the first time."

"I've never felt seen like that. Not even by Chance," Ivy mumbled. "I suppose I can't, if I don't even know who I'm supposed to be."

"What do you want to be called, Ivy?"

"I don't know," he confessed. "I'm still experimenting with pronouns, and it's all so confusing... I feel happy when Charlie and Chance call me *they*, but I don't mind when you say *he*, either. I feel like both, and that's right *and* wrong at the same time."

"Only you get to decide."

He dropped his head. "I wish I didn't feel so lost."

Oberi reached up to lick at Ivy's chin, and Ivy gave him a couple of pats. The door creaked open. My eyes flashed upward as I saw Chancey stride into the room. Ivy stiffened, but I acted like I didn't see him there.

Chancey stared at Ivy, like he wasn't sure what— or who— he was looking at.

"Where's your stash?" Chancey didn't say anything else. He was asking if Ivy had any drugs left.

"Under the stage. It's all there is." Ivy sniffed.

Chancey strode toward it. I noticed him pocket away a square, wrapped package before he walked out.

When I was done combing out Ivy's hair, I had a pile of strands that looked more like a wig, or a rat's nest. Looking at it made my stomach churn. I couldn't believe Ivy had sunken this low, and we hadn't been able to do anything to stop it.

I rummaged around in my bag and pulled out a potion bottle. "I made this for you. It'll dye your hair white again."

"My dad hates it that way," Ivy mumbled. "He wants a strong Italian son."

"Fuck your dad. That's not you. Drink up."

I uncorked the bottle and handed it to him. Ivy took the bottle and drank it in two chugs. I watched as the potion made his hair clean, changing the black locks to stark white, with that streak of red on the side that he loved. Oberi got off his lap and barked, doing a couple of happy circles.

"There's the Ivy I know." I cupped his chin. "Don't you look so much better."

He gave a wry smile as he stood on shaky legs, and looked in the mirror behind the bar. "Yeah."

Ivy looked down at his stained sweater and torn pants. "I really need to change, huh? This definitely isn't me."

"Well, you always make an appearance, but not like that."

"I'm gonna clean up," Ivy said. "I'll meet up with you later."

"Can you take me to the library first?" I asked. "I've got something I need to get done."

"Anything for you, precious."

Ivy took me there, then left for the showers. I wheeled around the library, looking for books on merfolk lore, when I spotted my brother in the corner. He was at a table, papers sprawled out everywhere while Tahoma lay at his side.

I rolled over, and he gave me a wave. "Hey? What's all this?" I asked, shifting the papers around.

Ez blushed slightly. "Nothing. Just my... research."

"Research? For a class or something?"

Ez shook his head, before he added, "This is a personal project. Something that means a lot."

I waited for him to elaborate. Ez took a short breath and said, "Since I bonded with Tahoma, everything has become so much clearer. Before him, I was wandering around, not sure of what I wanted to do or where I wanted to go. I was happy, but I didn't feel fulfilled."

I nodded. I understood what he was getting at. The closer I became to Charlie and Oberi, the more life made sense.

"Then Tahoma came to me, and so did my healing power. Once I realized I could perform Spirit magic, everything clicked into place. I really am talented at it. And it feels like it gives me a purpose." Ez sat back in his seat.

"You *are* talented, Ez. You're barely a beginner, but your magic has so much potential."

"That's what Mom says. So anyway, what I'm trying to say is... I've declared my major. I want to become a doctor. After I graduate from the Institute, I'll go back to Orenda Academy and get my PhD, so I can find cures for illnesses, like the one that affects me and Dad. Tahoma and I promised each other we'd work our whole life to find a cure for Chronic Magical Suppression Syndrome."

Joy erupted out of me. "Ez, I can't believe it!" I leaned forward to give him a hug. "How exciting this must be for you!"

"It really is." Ez gently hugged me back, before giving me a broad smile. "I've told everyone I can think of. I can't stop talking about it, really."

"Daddy must've been so proud."

"Ancestors, Dad was bawling over the phone. I've never seen him like that." Ez's eyes got misty. He was getting a little choked up himself.

"He's excited for you, Ez. All of us are. This is great news!"

"We really worked things out between us. Dad's been so helpful since I've started this whole thing. I feel like we're really bonding. I mean, all of us in the family have always been close, but I never got to have that special connection with Dad like you do, until now."

"This is incredible. I'm thrilled this is the path you've decided to take."

"Yeah, and it'll be a good job, one that will be steady enough to support Opal," Ez said. "She and Marina are gonna need a fresh start once we're out of here."

I was hesitant to ask if Ez was ready to be a dad, but I figured we'd have that conversation later. "Are you worried about being able to keep up with a job?" I asked cautiously. Ez did his best, but his physical well-being wasn't optimal most of the time.

Ez shrugged. "Dad managed to make his job work for him, so I figure I can make my dreams work for me, too. I know people say that disabled people can't work in the medical field, because the job takes long hours and a lot of stamina. But I want to try and change that, too— make working in hospitals and other care facilities more accessible, so more disabled people can hold careers in places like that. Because I really think if we had disabled people treating *other* disabled people, the stigma and judgment in medical facilities could change."

I thought that was a great idea. Doctor Marsh had done all she could for me, and I was thankful for that, but she was able-bodied and extremely healthy. She couldn't relate to me or understand what I was going through, not to mention she didn't have the experience of being disabled, so she was less likely to believe me when I relayed my symptoms to her.

Ez would be a good doctor. He knew what it felt like to be ill, so he'd be inspired to come up with more creative and innovative solutions to the struggles of his patients. "I know you can change things, Ez. You'll do your best to help anyone who needs you."

"I do want to have patients and help people, but my main focus would be working at a research facility," Ez stated. "I really want to use my career to fix and reverse medical conditions, not just smother patients with pills or short-term solutions."

"That's fucking amazing. I really couldn't be happier that you're pursuing this." I looked down at all the papers. "Is that what you're working on now?"

"Well, a cure for CMSS isn't the only thing I'm investigating," Ez confessed. "I wanted to start with something that's a bit more of a mystery."

It dawned on me slowly. "You're trying to figure out how to mend my spine."

"Yes," Ez confirmed. "I want to help you walk again."

I began curling inward. Everyone wanted me to get better. At this point, I felt pressured to go back to my old life, instead of being supported to live a different existence on my own terms. I knew my brother meant well, but part of me wished he'd just leave it alone. He should be working on finding a cure for himself, not me.

"And what kind of information did you find out?" I crossed my arms.

Ez glanced away. "I... uh... might've snuck into the records office during one of my treatments and stole a couple of your files."

"What were you thinking?" I snapped. "If you had gotten caught—"

"Yeah, but I didn't get the stuff I really needed," he said in frustration. "What I stole only creates a partial picture of your injury and the treatments that failed to cure it. They have the rest hidden somewhere."

"Yay, that's not scary," I mumbled. I wondered where the rest of my medical files were.

"They're probably in the Warden's office. We all know how obsessed he is with you."

It made my skin crawl to think of the Warden going over documents about my body and what was going on with it. "We're not getting in there anytime soon."

"Exactly. So I've got to try and piece together the full story of your injury with incomplete information. Which is aggravating, to say the least."

"Ez, this has got to be taking up all your time. You've got classes and other things to focus on."

"It's actually very interesting." Ez's eyes sparked. "I've never realized how fascinating the body is. Don't worry, I'm still keeping up with everything. This is more of a free-time thing."

I let out a short, irritated gust of breath. "Just don't get caught, okay?"

"You're one to lecture me, after all you've done. I deserve a free pass."

"Yeah, yeah."

Ez looked toward the ceiling. "What concerns me is that Anichi magic should've helped you. Mom and I have spoken about it at-length, and she doesn't understand why she wasn't able to heal your spine, or why your own magic didn't heal you during your surgery."

"Don't ask me. It's a total mystery."

Just like my healing magic was. It was connected to my demigod magic, which meant it wasn't straightforward at all.

"Right. You healed me from sepsis last semester, when I was moments away from dying. If you could do that, fixing your spine shouldn't be an issue."

"We could try again," I offered. "I've had more time to recover since then, and you restored Tahoma's blood loss. Maybe you can fix it."

"Let me try."

My brother splayed his hand across my stomach. I felt Ez's healing magic working within me, and the warmth of its power as it flowed through my muscles and radiated throughout my veins. It was just as strong as my mother's magic was, if not stronger. I half expected to regain feeling in my legs and to stand up again, but the sensation of his magic stopped at my knees and didn't go any farther. The Anichi light hovered over my middle before fading out completely.

Nothing happened. My throat tightened, and I told myself how stupid it was to have hope. I was lying to myself if I thought this was getting any better.

Ez shook his head. "My magic isn't helping you. Something else is at play here."

My stomach tumbled as I said, "Wish we knew what it was."

"That's what I'm working on," Ez promised. "Don't give up hope, Ava. I'm going to figure this out."

I tapped my fingers on the desk. "I know your research is important, but there might be someone who needs your help even more than I do right now."

"Ivy." Ez leaned over the table, though he gave me a skeptical look. "What'd you have in mind?"

"I think he's ready to quit using," I told him. "He didn't tell me so, but there was something different about him. I just... knew. Is there something you've been researching that can help him?"

Ez stood and began gathering up papers. "I can try. You stay out of it for now, Ava. I'll do what I can."

Tahoma gave me a friendly nudge as they left, and I patted him between the antlers before the two of them wandered off. I turned my attention away from Ivy and toward what I'd come here for.

I pulled out a couple of books of merfolk mythology and spread them out across a table before I removed the books on Elvish lore from my bag. They'd been damaged pretty horribly by being underground for so long, but at least they were still legible. So far, I'd only gotten through one book. I wanted to compare the stories the Elves had with those of merfolk, to see if I could find any similarities between legends that might help us locate the next key.

I went through the Elven books, which cracked and dropped dirt on the table as I read them. From what I discovered, I read that merfolk were one of the eldest supernatural races, and had been allies with the Elves for centuries. What had changed?

As I turned a page, a thrill welled up inside of me as I witnessed a drawing of seven keys scrawled across the parchment. There was an inscription at the top of the page... *The Divinity Keys.*

I knew by the drawings the book referred to the keys we already had in our possession, because they looked just like them. I searched for more, but there was only one paragraph about the Divinity Keys, and all it said was they were made to bring the supernatural races together, which wasn't very helpful.

But at least now we had a name for the objects we were looking for. The rest of my research came up flat. I was really excited to tell the others what I'd found out, but I got tired around lunchtime, and I didn't have the energy to roll around the prison to find them, so I went back to my cell to take a nap. Oberi curled up beside me on the bed, and we got so nice and warm that I stayed there for hours.

I didn't feel well enough to get out of bed until it was dinnertime. Charlie wouldn't get off his shift until it was time for curfew, and I was hungry, so Oberi and I went off to get something. I looked for my friends in the cafeteria, but absolutely *no one* was around, which was really weird. I wasn't used to eating alone, so I ate my sandwich in silence as I listened to gossip traveling around the room.

"Where is everyone?" I asked Oberi once we'd left the cafeteria. I knew Kallie and Marcus were at their weekend jobs, same as Charlie, but by this point I should've run into someone I knew.

Chancey's up there, Oberi noted, pointing with his nose toward the foyer.

We locked eyes, and Chancey came over. He shoved his hands in his pocket as he said, "Ava."

"What happened to the nightshade?" I'd been meaning to ask the moment I ran into him.

"I got rid of it," Chancey said.

I didn't press, because it didn't matter. Whether he'd dumped it down the drain or given it to someone else, I didn't care. All I cared about was it was out of Ivy's hands.

"Where's Ivy?" My hands gripped the arms of my chair as I worried what the response would be.

Chancey jerked his head toward the angel cell block. "He's in my cell. You wanna see?"

"Yeah. Help me get there."

Chancey took me to his dorm. My breath caught as he opened the door. Ivy sat on Chancey's bed, a blanket draped around him as he clutched at a small waste bin. He was shaking, trembling with unstoppable convulsions. It hadn't even been twenty-four hours, but Ivy was already having withdrawals. Bad ones, it looked like.

I hadn't realized how many drugs he was on, but now that I saw it for myself, I realized that Ivy really couldn't stop.

Several people were gathered in the room. Opal sat beside Ivy on the bed, an arm wrapped around his shoulders, while Ez rifled through pill bottles, appearing puzzled.

Had Ez stolen medication from the hospital to help Ivy? My plea for him to help our friend came back to bite me. Whatever Ivy was going through, I didn't want to put my brother at risk.

But we were all friends. We were in this together now. Addiction didn't just hurt one person. It ruined everybody who was around.

Chancey stood in the corner of the room and observed it all. I didn't know if they were back together or not, but something had to be going on between them, because Ivy was here in Chancey's cell.

I dropped my voice to speak to Chancey privately. "This is dangerous. He should be in the infirmary, not detoxing in your room."

"Ives isn't gonna quit any other way. Gotta let them do it on their terms."

Ez held out a bottle of pills to Ivy. "Here, take these."

"Get that fucking shit away from me," Ivy sneered as he slapped the pill bottle away. "It makes me worse."

"Ives, you gotta. You could go into shock without 'em," Chancey begged.

"Dude, I'm not risking my neck— and my treatments— to sneak in and steal these for you for nothing," Ez warned. "If I get caught, my ass is grass, so you'd better take them."

"He's the only one with regular access to the hospital because he's always going for treatment, Ives. Just do as he says," Chancey said.

Ivy scowled, but he swallowed two massive pills without another complaint.

It was seriously a group effort to keep Ivy going, and if I was being honest, none of us were equipped to handle this. Just watching Chancey fall apart as he tried to pull Ivy together was breaking *me* in half.

"Get him away from me," Ivy mumbled, and he recoiled against the bed. "I don't want to see my father."

He was hallucinating. Fuck. Opal rubbed Ivy's shoulders as he vomited into the bucket.

"Let me try and heal him," I offered. Other Anichi healers had struggled to heal addiction before, and sometimes, it backfired onto the caster and caused them to feel the agony of the withdrawals. Sometimes, it even made the healer become addicted to the substance themselves. But I wasn't going to sit here and let Ivy suffer if I could do something about it. My mother had told me addiction was one of those things you couldn't mend with healing magic, and it was dangerous to try, but I was a demigod, so I was certain the rules wouldn't apply to me. Whether it hurt me or not, I was taking the risk.

"Ava, no," Opal protested. "You'll hurt yourself."

I was already doing it. I reached out for Ivy's hand, grasping it within my own and curling my fingers around his. My healing magic sank deep into his body, looking for the source of his addiction, so I could destroy it.

It was like drowning. Seriously. Ivy's body was searching for any sort of fix it could get right now, and without something to keep him high, it was going into full panic mode.

I could do this. I could heal the addiction, take Ivy's symptoms *away*.

The moment I found the source of the addiction, and tried to rip it out, it resisted immediately. It wrapped around Ivy and planted itself inside, refusing to let go.

But that wasn't all. Once the disease came close, the addiction wrapped itself around *me*, too. Cramps and aches enveloped my entire body as a vicious chill took me over, and a heavy nausea settled into my stomach. Sharp pain settled into my bones as I began experiencing tremors, so severe they made my chair shake. The pain in my middle grew, until it was ricocheting up my spine and aggravating my injury to the point I cried out in pain.

I attempted to pull my magic back, but it wouldn't let me go. I was too far deep in it now, stuck in the thick of it with Ivy.

I couldn't help my friend. I couldn't even help myself.

"Cut it out!" I felt Ez rip my hand out of Ivy's, grasping it with his own. The warmth of my brother's healing magic swelled over me, washing over me like a calming wave as it chased the effects of Ivy's withdrawal out.

My entire body ached as Ez pulled back his healing magic. I slumped in my chair. "That was harder than I thought."

"That was *stupid, Ava*. There's a reason Anichi healers are very careful when they heal addicts. The addiction doesn't just go away," Ez snapped.

"I'm not an average healer. I'm better— I can fix this!" There were tears in my voice as I pleaded with him. I couldn't let Ivy suffer.

"He's gotta fix himself," Opal said sadly. "There is no other way."

"Ava, get out of here," Ez said roughly. "Let me handle this."

My brother knelt in front of Ivy. He took it slow as he used his healing magic at a cautious pace, trying to find the source of the symptoms so he could mitigate them.

It was a better plan than I'd had. I'd tried going in there full force and removing them altogether. Ez was right. I put myself at risk, for something I didn't know I could change.

"You know, nobody's ever done something like this for me," Ivy slurred, his head rolling. "You guys are some true friends."

The rest of them didn't give me a choice but to leave. I barely held back a sob as Chancey escorted me out. He wheeled me across the prison and into my cell, then tossed a blanket over my chair before he took a spot on the couch.

"You can go to Ivy. I'm not going anywhere," I said sourly.

"Nuh-uh. I'm not leaving until your babysitter comes back."

I wrinkled my nose at him, but still shuddered. Ez had done his best, but the side effects of taking some of the withdrawals for Ivy hadn't worn off.

Here. Oberi reached out and touched her beak to my forehead. *This will help.*

Her healing magic washed over the symptoms, and I felt them lessen. My healing magic was strong, but Oberi's almost seemed... stronger.

As we waited for Charlie, Chancey rifled through his pockets, appearing scattered.

"Fuck, I gotta get more cigarettes for Ives," Chancey mumbled. "I don't know who I'm gonna find to bum another pack off of."

"Does he really need them?" I didn't approve, but I guess in this case, smoking cigarettes was better than taking a hit of nightshade.

"The nicotine helps take the edge off, and the caffeine makes the withdrawal easier, but fuck all, I wish they'd drink water." Chancey ran a hand through his hair.

"I knew withdrawal was bad, but I didn't think it'd be this awful," I admitted.

"Ives will pull through," Chancey said, but he almost sounded like he was reassuring himself.

I swallowed. "Doesn't the magic in his blood help him?"

"Supernaturals gotta take more street drugs than humans do to get high, unless the drugs are magical, and Ives has been on a diet of nothing more than nightshade since the club opened," Chancey told me. "Ives has been taking way more than the usual dose. It's gonna take a while to come down."

"But he's a vampire. Doesn't that give him more immunity?" I asked. Mad Dog liked to brag about how high his tolerance was.

"Ives is half-merfolk, too, and their blood is closer to water, so it's more susceptible to inebriation. It could take anywhere between a week and a month for the symptoms to stop showing up. We gotta find a way to get them through class."

Ivy could barely sit up in bed, let alone sit at a desk. Not getting caught during this process was going to take a miracle.

Chancey ran a hand through his hair. "Anyway. You shouldn't be dealing with this, Ava. You've done enough."

"He needs me."

"What Ives is going through, you can't do anything about. Believe me— I'd take the pain for them, if I could."

I attempted to argue further, but ended up dozing off in my chair. Trying to heal Ivy had taken all of my energy.

When I began rousing, I heard quiet male voices. My eyelids fluttered open, and I saw Charlie sitting across from me in the armchair. Chancey slipped out the door without a goodbye, closing it with a soft *click*.

Before he could even speak, I said, "Ivy's bad. I'm worried that..."

Anything could happen. A heart attack, a seizure... withdrawing from nightshade was no joke, and as much as Chancey swore Ivy would pull through, I still worried Ivy's situation could turn deadly before any of us could help him.

"Chancey told me you tried to heal Ivy," Charlie said abruptly. "Pidge, what were you thinking? You could've made yourself really sick."

"Who cares? It's not like I can get any worse," I mumbled.

"That's not true, and I care! So should you." Charlie's eyebrows furrowed. "Sometimes I don't know what's going on in your head."

"I figured if I could take it away, he wouldn't have to deal with it anymore, and it'd all be over."

"You know it doesn't work like that." Charlie leaned in closer. "You're addicted to getting involved in the lives of other people, and you refuse to admit they have choices. You can't save everybody."

Yeah, well, I can damn well try.

I crossed my arms. "I still want to be his friend."

"When Ivy is better. Then we'll see."

I knew Charlie thought I was delusional for wanting to make this right. He figured I was taking unnecessary risks and putting myself on the line to help someone I loved, like I always did, and it was going to lead to me getting hurt.

Maybe I was delusional, but I wouldn't admit it. I knew I could do anything, as long as I put my mind to it.

Even rectify the mistakes of my past. I wouldn't let Ivy become another statistic like Monica. He was staying with me, because even if hell came pounding at his door, I wasn't going to let his demons take him.

I DIDN'T HAVE time to consider visiting Ivy the next morning, because Charlie was up before I was and already making plans to meet up with Kallie and Marcus before I even had time to put my tits in a bra. He had a whole day planned of working on homework, taking walks around the prison yard and playing games in the Villain's Den, from breakfast all the way up until bed.

I knew he was just keeping me busy, but honestly, it was kind of a relief he was saving me from myself. I didn't know if I could stop interfering unless I was forced to.

We had omelets for breakfast— which were fucking gross today— and waited for Kallie and Marcus to show up in the grand entryway. We were supposed to go to the Arts & Crafts room early, so we could work on a group project for one of our classes together. I read a book and enjoyed people-watching all the stupid fucks who passed us by, while Oberi squeaked a chew-toy at my feet, but Charlie was impatient. He bounced in his chair, obviously annoyed we were being stood up.

"Hey." Kallie was nearly breathless. She hurriedly combed her messy locks as she and Marcus stormed in. "Thanks for waiting for us."

"You're late," Charlie said. "We've been here forever."

"Sorry," Marcus panted, and he straightened his button-up. "Just got a little... busy."

What a *word* for it. The guilt was all over their faces. And *shame.* Oh, this was juicy.

They were messing around again, Oberi noted. He chomped down on the chew toy, and it gave a withering squeak.

Charlie scowled. I went to say something— you know, because I *wasn't* the kind of person who could let the mention of sexy times pass her by without avidly pointing it out— but Charlie cut me off before I could give an enthusiastic gasp.

"Can we just go?" he asked.

Kallie cleared her throat and walked forward. Marcus dragged his feet as he dawdled behind her.

Damn, guess we should've taken our time this morning, too, I told Charlie telepathically.

Guess so. They sure weren't in a hurry, he complained. *We've nearly wasted an hour.*

It would've taken us that long to finish, anyhow. We'd already broken the vibrator, because we used it too much. It was hard for me to get off without it, so intimacy was still enjoyable, but not as fulfilling. We needed to figure out how to fix that thing and get back to business, stat.

"Guess what?" I stated. "I read the Elven books, and I actually discovered the real name of what we're looking for. The Divinity Keys."

"Is that what they're called?" Kallie questioned.

"Yes. Unfortunately, the book didn't say anything more about them. But at least it's something, right?" I asked.

As we moved toward our destination, I noticed Hemlock standing outside her classroom, surveying the students that walked by. When she spotted us, her shoulders relaxed on her statuesque frame.

"Ah, Mrs. Wahkin, there you are," Hemlock said, almost in relief. "Your father is on the phone, asking to speak with you."

"I can take Ava down to the phone room," Charlie offered, and he spun my chair the other way.

"Oh no, dear, he's not calling the main line. He contacted me directly," Hemlock informed us. "Less of a chance you'll be... overheard."

"Must be important." I tilted my head.

"It certainly can't wait," Hemlock confirmed.

Charlie hovered behind, but I said, "You guys should go to the Arts & Crafts room like we planned. I'll catch up with you once I'm done.'

"I can wait," Charlie offered.

"This will be a long conversation. Time to get on with it," Hemlock jabbed.

Charlie took the hint from her that I needed space, and Oberi guided him off after Marcus and Kallie. Hemlock opened the door for me, and I rolled inside, heading toward the antique rotary phone lying on her desk. Old technology was the only kind that worked on campus. I picked up the receiver and Hemlock shut the door behind me, standing outside to guard the entrance.

I put the phone to my ear. "Daddy! I'm so happy you called!"

"You sound much better," Daddy noted. His voice, which appeared heavy, lightened when he said the words. "Are you doing okay? Treatment going good?"

"Um, well, I got kicked out of physical therapy," I confessed. "But it's fine. Charlie and I are doing the exercises on our own. We don't need those doctors, anyway."

Daddy grumbled something I couldn't decipher, before he said, "How's your pain?"

"It's... manageable." I couldn't say anything more positive without telling an outright lie.

"Just take it day by day. We're all here for you."

I wasn't here to talk about my health. I wanted *details*, ones I wasn't getting anymore because the Warden didn't let us watch the news. "Have you made any peace talks?" *Or more declarations of war...*

"Don't worry about all of that. Your mother and siblings are in *Hok'evale*, safe and sound, and Kinpago is standing its ground, for now. Just focus on feeling better, and we'll handle everything back home."

"I'm really glad you're all safe."

"It's wonderful to hear from you. Though that's not the reason I called." Daddy didn't sound happy... rather, he sounded miserable. "I'm sorry, Ava-Marie. I wish I had happier news."

My throat seized up as I asked, "What's going on?"

"I called to tell you that John Smith has been arrested. Your Uncle Jonah caught him attacking another girl, a freshman at Orenda Academy."

Pieces of myself that I thought had been put back together began crumbling inside of me. I did my best to hold it together, but was only able to whisper, "Ancestors, no."

"Unfortunately, your uncle got there too late to stop it, though he did intercede before it went any further."

My mouth went completely dry. "Further?" I squeaked.

"I don't need to tell you the details, peanut."

What Daddy didn't say amplified my worst fears. John had escalated from rape to attempting to murder his victims.

That could've been *me*. For the first time, I was glad I was in a wheelchair, because if I had been standing and not sitting, I would've been unable to remain upright. "What did Uncle Jonah do?"

"He nearly killed him, to tell you the truth. The thought of refusing to traumatize that girl more than she already was held him back."

I swallowed the knot in my throat. It settled over my heart, invading my ribcage. "Well... at least he got caught, and people know what he is now."

"It's more than that, peanut. Since his arrest, four other Toaqua girls have come forward with accusations. The Elders are going to prosecute with some heavy charges. If convicted, he faces a number of years in the Hawkei prison."

"The Elders have to secure that conviction, though."

"You don't have to do anything, sweetheart."

"But if I come forward and testify, it'll increase the chances he'll receive a harsher sentence, and be put away for longer."

Daddy's tone was reluctant, but confirming. "Yes."

I had evidence, too. His DNA was all over me when I turned in the rape kit. This could actually put him away.

I steadied the phone in my shaking hands and said, "A trial could take years. There's an international crisis going on."

"Just because there's a war doesn't mean the justice system is put on hold. And it seems like the Elders want to move pretty quickly on this one."

The phone crackled against the silence, and I slumped in my chair. "I don't know, Daddy. I need to think about it."

"Take your time. This bastard isn't going anywhere."

"Okay. Love you, Daddy."

Even after I'd hung up the phone, I found myself stuck to the spot for long minutes, trying to comprehend what my father had told me.

It'd been nearly five years since I was assaulted. I didn't know if anyone would believe me, let alone secure a conviction on my behalf, even with DNA evidence.

Five other girls. The knowledge was enough to make me sick.

But it didn't have to happen again, not to anyone else. I could get justice for what he'd done to me, after I never thought I would. The Warden couldn't stop me from telling my story— if I had a court order, he'd be forced to let me leave Institute grounds so I could testify.

At the same time, a trial would humiliate me. I'd have to go on public record and tell the world what he'd done. People would never look at me the same.

I couldn't think about this right now. I just wanted to shut it away, compartmentalize it for a while so I could pretend this wasn't my life. I had to get my mind on other things and give myself time to process, because at the moment, the thought of facing John again was too much for me to handle.

Hemlock opened the door for me when I tapped on the other side. "I hope you're faring well."

"Peachy as can be," I grumbled. "I guess you know now too, huh?"

"Your father told me about what the accused has allegedly done, but your name didn't come up in the conversation at all," Hemlock said.

"You must've understood why he called."

"What I can infer has no bearing on what I think of you, child."

I sighed and dropped my gaze into my lap. "I don't know what I should do."

"The only thing you can do— what's best for yourself." Hemlock's eyes became steely, and I caught a glimpse of the younger, bolder woman she'd once been. "If it were me? I'd give him hell."

I gave her a short nod. She went back into her office without another word, and I continued onward.

As I moved toward the Arts & Crafts room, the people in the hallways began winding down, until I was pretty much alone. The sound of heels clicking on the floor caught my attention, and as I turned a corner, I halted my chair in place.

It was Lupe, along with her wolf Familiar. I hadn't seen her in a long time. Since she was an upperclassman, I didn't share a lot of classes with her.

She was carrying something... an emerald green gown, with a square cap.

"Oh, hi, Ava," Lupe said, and she stopped to talk to me. "Need some help?"

I didn't reply right away. At that moment, the sight of the cap and gown in her hand was the most magical thing I'd ever seen. "What... what's that?"

"Oh, this?" She raised it. "It's just my stuff for the ceremony. I had to pick it up this afternoon."

My lungs depleted of all air. "You're..."

"Graduating. Yeah, finally." She patted her Familiar on the head. "I can't wait, honestly. It's been a long four years."

And they were just letting her leave, as a free woman. It was the strangest feeling to see someone actually *leave here*, when so many didn't.

A question crossed my mind. "What are you in here for anyway, Lupe?"

She snorted. "A bunch of petty bullshit. Getting into too many fights and destroying public property. I hung around the wrong people, mostly. My record had one too many hits, so the Elders got tired of it and sent me here."

It wasn't so different from my own story. "You must've had it rough."

"It was okay. My mom did her best, and my stepdad was great, but I never got over growing up without my biological father. If he hadn't died, I never would've come here in the first place."

"Your dad passed away?" My heart dropped.

"Yeah. My dad died in the Hawkei Civil War. He used to be a professor at Orenda Academy, before everything went down back then. Mauricio Lopez was his name. And that's about all I know about him."

I vaguely recognized the moniker. My dad had told me he'd had him as a teacher, a long time ago for his Hawkei Legends class. "I'm sorry you lost him."

"Don't be. I never knew him— he'd had me the year before the war started, and died soon after." She scowled. "But it made me so angry he wasn't here, when he should be."

Lupe's shoulders relaxed, and she smiled... which was so strange to see, because she wasn't the kind of person that did so, hardly ever. "But it doesn't have to affect me anymore. Once I walk out those doors, I can finally put the past behind me."

"Do you think being here helped you?"

"Oh, yeah. I know everyone thinks this place is a shithole, and it is. But without the Institute, I'd be dead. I'm sure of that."

She looked toward the barred windows. "But at least now, I have a future."

I looked down at my lap. "That future seems so far away, for me."

"You want some advice? The time served here is long, but it's not as long as it seems. Nothing's more important than focusing on your life after you get out of here, and what *you* want to do. I know we all got friends here, and responsibilities we can't avoid. But your dreams are important, too, probably the most important thing. Don't let anybody take them."

Lupe walked off, cap and gown in hand. Her Familiar bounced beside her, and I watched them go with a sort of reverence. She'd gotten therapy, found friends who cared, and earned a degree. Now, she was free.

I knew a lot of programs for troubled kids were abusive and full of problems. Kids left more traumatized than they'd come in. At the same time, there was a need for rehabilitation programs for people who needed a little extra help to get on the right path.

I wished the Institute could be better, because everyone within its gates needed it to be. It really could be a wonderful school, if it wasn't darkened by the terror that went on behind closed doors by the guards, some of the teachers, and the Warden himself. It didn't have to be a place where bad kids went to be punished. It could be a space where hurting kids went to heal.

I craved to grace that graduation stage and feel proud of my accomplishments. I hadn't gotten to walk at my high school graduation, and I wanted to make up for that. I wanted my parents to cheer and cry as I received my diploma. I wanted to have a graduation party, and celebrate with my friends.

We could all do it. Charlie and I could graduate. We could get jobs, buy our cottage, maybe even have cute little babies. We could live a *normal life.* The Institute didn't have to be the end, as much as it felt like it was.

I was completely enraptured by this vision by the time I rolled into the Arts & Crafts room. Marcus gathered the supplies we needed for our group project with Kallie, while Charlie wrestled around on the floor with Oberi. Professor Celosia was busy teaching a group of girls in the corner how to make clay sculptures, so she wasn't paying attention to us.

Beside the table was a painting that Marcus had finished yesterday. It looked like his home, Octavia Falls, in wintertime. Snow dusted the streets and lined the limbs of barren trees. A soft light glowed from shopfronts, and cats were littered throughout the scene. It appeared so peaceful, and the lighting of the painting changed color when you looked at it from a different angle.

"You're so talented, Marcus." I sighed as I observed the painting. "It's like you're actually there."

"Thanks. It's a textured painting. I've never done one before," Marcus explained. "I actually heard about this exhibit where they have paintings that blind people can experience, so they can enjoy them just like sighted people can. You use a special kind of paint that gives depth and texture to the canvas, so when blind people touch them, they can actually make out the details of the scene."

"Really?" Charlie perked up.

"Yeah. I thought that it was really sad you couldn't enjoy art like the rest of us can, so I decided to make one for you," Marcus said. "Come and see."

Charlie got up from the floor, and Marcus placed his hand on the canvas. Charlie lit right up when he began to experience the painting. His fingers moved over the different textures, ridges and raised lines. "Wow. This is... I can't even describe it. It's... incredible."

"What's it like?" I asked in interest.

"It's... almost like using my Air magic to determine where things are, but on a smaller scale. It's some sort of town scene, isn't it?"

"That's right," I said in astonishment. I couldn't believe he could interpret the painting so clearly, despite not being able to physically see it.

"I'm glad I did it right." Marcus' shoulders slumped in relief. "Apparently, if you mess it up, it can be hard to get the translation across."

I could see on my husband's face how much this meant. He wasn't able to enjoy drawings or artwork the way the rest of us could, but Marcus had found a way to make it accessible for him.

Charlie stepped away from the painting and cleared his throat. "You did a great job. I can picture it so clearly."

"That's not all. Check out what Marcus and I can do!" Kallie said.

She pressed a hand to the painting, and I watched with amazement as the scene began moving. The cats in the painting started meowing and moving around, and the snow fell from the sky as the lights on the storefronts flickered. A bit of snow blew out of the painting, and a chilly wind drifted over our skin.

"Is it moving?" Charlie questioned.

"Yeah. We can make the paintings come to life by fusing our powers together and using simultension," Kallie said eagerly. "Pretty neat, huh?"

I thought that was awesome. What were we doing messing around with prophecies and getting ourselves mixed up in political bullshit, when we could create cool stuff like *this*? Our art, our music... they were all much better pursuits than trying to convince shitty people to stop doing shitty things.

"What did your dad want to talk about, Ava?" Marcus asked.

"Just... personal family stuff," I said.

I didn't tell them about the phone conversation I'd had with my father. I wasn't ready to consider my options. It was really hard for me to talk about this, even to Charlie. I'd rather sweep it under the rug and refuse to face it, rather than get help, because getting help made me feel too vulnerable. I knew that was one of my downfalls, but even so, the thought of bringing this up was overwhelming. I needed a few days to conjure up the courage to speak to Charlie about it privately, and to see what he thought. For now, I just wanted to keep it to myself.

We all had our own family issues, so nobody pressed me for answers. I hurried to change the topic. "Guys, guess what? Lupe's *graduating*. Isn't that magical?"

"Really? Good for her," Charlie said. "I'm glad she made it."

I dropped my voice, just in case Professor Celosia was listening in. "That's just the thing, though. Why are we talking about breaking out? We could just... wait until we graduate. Lay low, don't cause any trouble. Then, once we're done, the Warden has to let us go!"

"That's never going to happen. Graduation is two years away," Kallie objected.

"We've already survived two years here," I insisted.

"Yeah, and it's nearly killed all of us several times over," Marcus said.

"Because we keep poking our noses into things we shouldn't!" I replied. "If we just sat back, went to class and let things play out as they will, we could make it!"

"Do you know how many people in Lupe's class are graduating, compared to the amount of people that came in?" Kallie asked.

"No. Does it matter?" I sneered.

"One-fourth. The rest of the kids in her class either died here, or they're getting transferred to the adult penitentiary," Kallie said firmly. "That means if we try to stay low and play by the rules, statistically, *one* of us is graduating."

"And the Warden isn't going to let us leave. He knows what we are— he's never going to let us go," Charlie added. "Especially not you, Ava."

"If we meet the United Supernatural Union's requirements for graduation, he can't hold us back!" I protested. Oberi got up from the floor and laid his head on my lap. I brushed my fingers through his ears. This was a way out! Why could no one see that?

"The Union didn't stop him from kidnapping and murdering Alice, Wesley, and Despona when their team won the Darke Games, or all the other inmates who died in the Underground," Charlie argued.

My temper snapped when he spoke that awful name. I never wanted anyone— *anyone*— to mention that horrible place again. "The Underground is gone. I fucking died and came back to make sure I destroyed that place. And as much as I want to fulfill the prophecy and save everybody, I'm getting pretty tired of involving myself in things that end up making my life worse. What about *my* dreams?"

Lupe's advice had been ringing in my ears ever since I'd spoken to her. Since I'd come to the Institute, my mission was to fulfill the prophecy in order to stop terrible things from happening, but so far, all I'd done was manage to cause terrible things to happen to myself. I hadn't helped anybody— the Elves in Forevermore, Eddie, countless others were dead or missing because of me and my actions. If we weren't going to get a win here, what was the point of continuing to try and save other people, when I could just focus on all the life I had left to live? It was a miracle I was still alive, and I wanted to treasure that.

"You can't just... bury yourself in academia and pretend things aren't happening," Marcus said meekly. "You're not an average college girl, no matter how much you want to be. We're all demigods. We have responsibilities that go beyond ourselves and what we want."

I was so tired of having that conversation, so I decided to cut it short. I threw my bag on the table, and it landed with a *thud*. "Fine. Whatever."

Kallie and Marcus cringed, but Charlie was used to my tantrums, so he plunged forward. "We don't have to talk about it today. Let's just take a breath and—"

"Oh my gods!" Kallie yelped. "There's no one by the lake!"

"What?" I turned in my seat, which was difficult, due to the stiffness in my spine. I wheeled myself to the window. As I peered out of it, I saw that she was right. The lake was completely deserted for the first time in weeks. Not a guard in sight.

"Finally. Let's jump in that lake and see what we can find," I said, already turning my chair around.

"We should find Opal. It'll be helpful to have a mermaid," Charlie suggested.

"We'll go get her. You two meet us there," Marcus offered, and he hurried off with Kallie.

Charlie and I returned to our cell first, so I could change into a swimsuit underneath my clothes. When we got onto campus grounds, Oberi did a gallop around the lake, to see if it was truly deserted.

All clear, she said, and tossed her horn. *But that doesn't mean there isn't anyone watching us.*

"We have to take a chance," I said. "This could be the only shot we get to search that lake."

Hurried footsteps came from behind us. Charlie turned my chair so I could watch Opal, Kallie and Marcus run our way.

"Heard you guys need help," Opal said. "What are we looking for?"

"It's a key, something that'll resonate with strong supernatural power," I explained. "You might not be able to feel it, but the rest of us will."

"But the key might not be here," Charlie said. "So we're searching for any clue that could lead us to it."

Opal nodded. "All right. I'll see what I can find."

We moved toward the lake. Kallie waved her hand around as we walked. "From what I can tell, there aren't any wards or alarms around the lake. The area is clear."

"Why would the Warden give us free range of the lake?" Marcus asks.

"Because he can't find what he's looking for, so he hopes we do," I said.

"That's why the campus is so big," Charlie said, voice lightening with clarification. "The prison yard has acres and acres. It shouldn't be that huge if he's trying to keep inmates in."

"But he's taking that risk, because he knows there are keys here on the grounds, and he wants demigods to find them," Kallie said. "Brilliant, actually."

Marcus gave a shiver, and asked, "So how do we get around the sirens? The lake's overflowing with them."

Opal frowned. "There isn't really a way, since the pool inside the Institute is connected to the lake, so they can go back and forth. They're far from reasonable creatures."

"How do merfolk and sirens differ?" Charlie asked.

"Sirens are genetically different from merfolk. You have to be born a mermaid, but you can be *made* a siren, as long as you have merfolk blood," Opal explained.

"So they're like succubi, who used to be vampires," I said.

"Exactly. There's a change involved, but I'm not clear on the details. It's a bit of a murky subject."

Probably had to do something awful to become one, I bet.

"They're much stronger than regular merfolk, and their magic is better. But they're always beholden to their hunger. They can eat regular food, but what they really like to consume is people, because it makes them stronger, and once they consume the flesh of another supernatural being, they become addicted, and will never stop looking for more bodies to consume," Opal explained. "Tons of sirens end up at the Institute every time they bring a bus load of kids in, because they need to murder people in order to feed. Sirens prefer the flesh of other supernaturals than merfolk, though. They'll still eat us, but I've heard sirens say before that they don't like the taste."

"What are the similarities?" Kallie asked.

"They share siren screams with mermaids, but the worst part is that sirens can compel people to do what they say with their singing voice, unlike merfolk. They aren't safe to be around." Opal sighed as she stopped at the lake's edge. "Might as well try speaking with them first, see what they want."

She knelt by the surface and stuck her fingers into the water. I think her mermaid magic was calling to them, asking the sirens to come to the surface.

A head bobbled out of the water. I watched as the top half of a beautiful woman pulled herself onto shore, crossing her arms as she laid on the beach.

I'd seen her around in classes, but I didn't know her name. She was wearing a mesh top that resembled seaweed, and didn't seem bothered by the cold. I knew sirens, when underwater, were supposed to be hideous, but in the open air, this girl was enchanting.

She lounged casually as she said, "I figured you'd all come by eventually, seeing as the Warden has had his goons up our fins for the past month."

"You've been expecting us?" Charlie asked.

"I'm Arsinoe. You guys don't need to introduce yourselves. Everyone knows about the Villain's Club. You're practically celebrities around here," the siren replied.

We didn't associate with anyone outside of our friends, so her statement was weird.

"We try to keep to ourselves," I said.

"We know, but we're still watching. Everyone respects you, even the shitheads," she continued. "Your little group is the only one brave enough to consistently piss off the Warden. We don't need to like you to acknowledge you're infamous behind these bars. My question is, what are you here for?"

"The same thing the guards wanted," Kallie replied. "Did they say what it was?"

Arsinoe scoffed. "No, but they made it known that we were to stay out of their way. They had electric stun wands they used to make sure we kept our distance."

She lifted her sleeve, and I saw a welled-up bruise from where the stun gun had hit her. It spanned across her entire bicep and over her skin.

"I'm really sorry that happened to you," I apologized.

"Don't be. I got curious." Arsinoe leaned her head on her hand. "I should tell you right now there isn't anything down here. The lake's empty, save for us."

"You could be lying," Kallie accused.

Arsinoe smirked. "If you want to come in, be our guest. But you're not going to find anything. One of us would've stumbled upon it by now."

"I don't trust you!" Marcus protested. "I recognize you— you tried to eat me when Kallie and I fell in the lake!"

"That's before you were who you were," Arsinoe explained. "I won't bother you, but I can't promise nobody else will. The other girls get hungrier than I do."

A couple more heads popped out of the water, dazzling girls observing us. The sirens were more monsters than people. No matter how much they claimed to respect us, if they got hungry enough, they'd attack.

"We have to search the lake safely. It's not an option to have others do it for us," Charlie said.

"Then have the fae girl make us a deal. She'll have to honor her word, and we'll be bound to the contract. Everybody wins." Arsinoe looked at Kallie.

Kallie crossed her arms. "Fine. What do you want?"

"A body. We don't get fresh meat often around here, save for the kids who die in fight club, and their bodies are so mangled by the time the guards throw them in that they don't taste very good." Arsinoe shrugged.

"We aren't giving you a body," Charlie snarled.

"Take your chances, then. Unless you really don't want what's in the lake."

Arsinoe began to move away from shore, and Kallie said, "If you want a body, fine. We'll deliver it when we decide it's time."

"No fae tricks," Arsinoe complained. "You deliver a fresh body to us, for our consumption, before the semester's over, and no siren within this lake will do any of your party harm. Otherwise, you don't get to search the lake."

Kallie's eyebrow twitched. "Deal."

"Kallie! Where are we going to get a body?" I hissed.

"People die at the Institute all the time. We'll find a body to give them at one point or another," Kallie whispered back. "This is our only shot."

Kallie knelt by the lake and reached out her arm. Arsinoe shook her hand, sealing the contract together.

"It is done," Arsinoe said, and she began swimming away. "You may come in at any time. We won't attack, upon condition of the contract."

The sirens floated away, until they were a significant distance across the lake. Their eyes still watched us, waiting for us to come in.

I sure hoped Kallie's contract held up. Opal slipped off her clothes, revealing a bikini as she walked into the water. I watched as her legs morphed into a tail, and she flipped it upward to dive down. Oberi changed into a narwhal and dove in horn-first after her. I began pulling off my sweater, to reveal my bikini, while Charlie helped me take off my pants.

"Marcus and I can search around the edge of the lake, while Ava and Opal go in the water," Kallie said. "We'll be quicker that way."

"What should I do?" Charlie asked.

"Stay here in case something goes wrong, and keep alert for guards. We need to know if you hear someone coming, so you can alert me and get us out of the water quickly," I said.

"Are you sure you're going to be okay in the water by yourself?"

"I have Toaqua magic. I'll be fine."

Charlie carried me over to the water's edge. Once he put me down on the soft sand, I pulled myself toward the water, until I was able to slide into the lake smoothly. I used my Toaqua magic to propel me forward slowly, until my entire body was suspended in the lake. The temperature was freezing, but I called upon my Koigni magic to warm my skin, and I felt Fire seeping through my veins until I experienced the sensation of drifting in a warm, relaxing pool.

I experimented with my Water magic. I found my powers could move me any way I wanted to. I took a breath and sank downward, opening my eyes to observe the darkness of the lake.

I didn't need help to maneuver through water, didn't need someone to push me or a tool to move me around. Ancestors, for the first time since I'd been put in that chair, I was *free*. I felt in complete control of my body as I rocketed through the deep. I tilted myself in any direction I wanted to do, was able to perform loops and spin around in the water.

My magic was there to support me all the way, and I had autonomy over what I wanted to do and where I wanted to go. The water did all the work for me, so my body didn't have to strain itself as I zoomed around the lake.

Doing okay? Charlie asked from on shore.

It's wonderful, I told him. *It feels like... I'm running again.*

Like I'd taken a gasp of air for the first time since we'd gone into the Underground.

I was a talented Toaqua, so I could hold my breath underwater for up to ten minutes. I remained underwater as I continued to perform tricks and drift happily through the lake, before I told myself we had a job to do. As liberating as this was for me, I couldn't keep drawing out my enjoyment of the lake without remembering what we were here for. I surfaced again to take a breath, then dove downward.

I looked through the murky water and saw a flash of mermaid scales, as well as the point of Oberi's horn. Opal could breathe underwater, so she stayed down at the bottom, surveying what she could as Oberi trailed her path. I rushed down to join her, and we swam side by side, taking in the massive scope of the lake.

A couple sweeps of the lake didn't reveal much. I caught something swimming toward me, and jumped when I realized it was one of the sirens. I had the terrifying thought they were about to go back on our deal, but as I looked closer, I realized it was Arsinoe.

Arsinoe was absolutely beautiful out of the water, but submerged underneath it, she was hideous. Her sallow face resembled a corpse, and green, scaly skin stretched across her pointed cheekbones. Her stringy hair swarmed around her face as nails the length of talons curled out from her fingertips, and there were scales rotting off her tail. Her crooked teeth stuck out of her bottom lip as she turned to observe me.

Hey, I wasn't going to judge. We girls had the right to look fugly if we damn well pleased.

She waved a clawed hand, to tell me to follow her. My Toaqua magic pushed me forward, and Opal trailed behind us. Arsinoe led the way through the lake, and I observed her as she gestured to the rocks lining the lake floor, and the pipelines that led from the lake to the merfolk pool inside the Institute.

The whole area was desolate. I sent my Toaqua magic out, scanning the entirety of the lake. I found no disturbances, no objects that the water swelled around. The ripples I created moved clear through, from one side to the other.

Nothing. If there was something in here, my Water magic would've sought it out by now.

There was a low croon— an echo that resonated through the water, along with some kind of chirping sound. The spines on Arsinoe's tail bristled, and she immediately darted behind a nearby boulder to hide.

I went still as I saw a massive tentacle, hundreds of feet long, float by me. One suction cup was the size of my entire body. I caught the sight of a great orange eye, which blinked before drifting away.

Oberi was suddenly at my side. She swam circles around me, defending me from whatever monstrous thing was lurking in the depths. The chirping sound faded as the creature turned away and went further into the blackness of the lake.

Arsinoe came out from her hiding spot and pointed upward to the surface. I followed her, and as our heads broke the top of the water, her gorgeous features returned again.

"See?" Arsinoe said as I caught my breath. "Nothing."

I shook my head in what felt like defeat. "I guess you're right. This lake really is empty."

"I really wish we could be of more help," Arsinoe said. "We want to stick it to the Warden as badly as you do."

"What was that massive thing we saw in the water?" I asked. "It was huge."

"It's the giant squid. He's been here longer than we have," Arsinoe stated. "The rumor is that the squid was here before the Institute was."

"Yeah, but how did it get in the lake? Squids are saltwater fish. It should've died immediately when put in this freshwater lake. It could survive in the sea surrounding the island, but it shouldn't be able to live here."

"It is a magical creature. Perhaps it adapted," Arsinoe suggested.

"But what's it eating? There aren't enough fish in the lake to sustain it."

"I've watched it devour sirens who got too close," Arsinoe confessed with a shudder. "I don't suggest going anywhere near it."

Ew. Definitely didn't want to piss it off.

Kallie and Marcus were waving us over. I hesitated to join them.

I didn't want to get out of the water and lose my mobility. I wanted to stay.

Charlie had been listening to my thoughts, and hushed, *We'll go to the pool later. Promise.*

I couldn't let my friends freeze. My Water magic regrettably pushed me toward the shoreline, and Charlie pulled me out. Opal's tail transformed into legs as she walked onshore. I used my Toaqua magic to pull the water out of our swimsuits and hair, and called upon my Koigni magic to warm us up.

As we pulled our clothes back on, Oberi flopped onto shore, bursting into a Fire unicorn in an array of sparks that singed Marcus' eyebrows and made Rishi scamper up a tree.

"Is there any other way we can be of service?" Arsinoe asked.

"No," Kallie grumbled. She sounded pissed. "We did what we came for."

"Very well," Arsinoe replied. "Don't forget our deal."

"Don't worry. I can't," Kallie stated bluntly. Arsinoe did a backflip into the water. She and the other sirens swam off without another farewell.

"We should talk somewhere private," Opal said as she turned to me.

"Let's go to the Lair," I offered. "It's not far."

Charlie moved branches and rocks out of the way with his magic, and smoothed the path so I was able to move my chair more easily through the forest. I couldn't squeeze my chair through the Lair's entryway, so Oberi carried me inside, until we entered the comfort of the rock formation's center. A couple of our things were still here, along with all of Marcus' wall paintings.

Lonesomeness came over me as we entered. We used to hang out here all the time, and now, it was virtually abandoned. I really missed this place.

"So this is your guys' secret hideout," Opal said, looking around. "Pretty neat."

"Did you find anything?" Charlie asked desperately. Kallie conjured us couches to sit on, and the rest of them took a seat while I threw a fireball on the floor for warmth.

"No," Marcus said sourly, while Rishi meowed in his lap.

"We didn't, either," I said, and I stroked Oberi's mane. "There wasn't anything to see."

"I searched everywhere," Opal said tiredly. "The lake floor, the surface... I did *circles* around that lake, and the only things to see are the sirens and the giant squid."

"There's a giant squid in the lake? I thought that was just a story," Charlie said.

"It's definitely real. Oberi and I saw it, too," I confirmed. "It's fucking massive."

"A little strange that there's a monster living on campus," Charlie mused.

"There are monsters all over the island. It's not unusual one's living in the lake," Marcus pointed out. "After all, the Warden keeps opening up portals to hell for monsters to slip out of during the Darke Games. It wouldn't be weird if a couple of them managed to run off and make this their new habitat."

"Do you think the squid can lead us to what Amalie left behind?" Kallie wondered.

I was doubtful. "If the Warden thought the squid had something to do with the key, he would've killed it by now. And since it swims around the entire lake, I don't think it's protecting anything but its food source... which are the sirens, by the way. *Gross.*"

"There must've been something we missed. Amalie wouldn't mark this spot on the map for no reason," Kallie insisted.

"But if there's nothing in the lake, why is it important, and why is the Warden searching it?" Marcus asked.

"Maybe what Amalie put here was already moved," Charlie said.

"Or the Warden found it," I said darkly. "Whatever was in the lake is already gone. The Warden stopped sending guards down there to search, so he must've already found the first clue before we did, which puts him ahead of us."

"Probably." Kallie punched the rock wall, and a bit of granite shattered off. "Ugh! This is a waste of time. We should proceed to the next spot on the map and hope that the clue makes sense when we get to it."

I agreed, although I wish we had a better course of action. From the way things looked, I wasn't sure if Amalie's treasure map was anything but a road to nowhere.

charlie

ELEVEN

The Warden was already ahead of us. He'd found whatever Kallie's map was leading us to, and he was one step closer to finding the merfolk key.

That was our best assumption, at least. Based on Kallie's map, what we could tell was the points led to *clues* to the merfolk key, rather than the key itself. The Warden had the first clue. I prayed it wouldn't lead him to the second before we found it ourselves.

The map wasn't clear on what we were looking for, though. We knew the map pointed to a general area inside the prison next, but we didn't know what we were looking for once we got there. Kallie led us inside the school, until we came to a long hallway.

"There's nothing here," Marcus complained.

"Amalie must've hidden it, whatever it is," Ava insisted. "Keep looking."

We walked up and down the hall, searching for *anything* that could be considered a clue, but there was nothing. Either the Warden had already gotten to it, or we were missing something.

I ran my hands over cinder blocks, and Oberi sniffed the floor at my feet. Ava kept making little involuntary sounds, like she was uncomfortable. We must've been searching for over an hour, and her fatigue began to slip through our bond.

"Maybe we should call it a night," I suggested.

"No," Ava protested. "We have to keep looking. The Warden's already found one clue. We have to find the next one before he does."

There was nothing here. Perhaps he'd already found it, but I didn't voice my thoughts. I wanted Ava to be right, and I wanted to get to the clue first.

"Pidge, you're ready to fall asleep," I pointed out. "We need to rest. We can regroup in the morning and keep looking."

"What if the Warden finds the clue by then?" Ava pressed. "Please, Charlie. We can't stop."

"We'll have to stop at some point," Marcus said. "I've got janitorial duty before curfew. If you want, Ava, I can take you back to your room, and Charlie and Kallie can keep searching."

"That's a great idea," I agreed. "We'll stay until curfew. Go get some rest, pidge. We've got this."

Ava sighed and reluctantly agreed. Our friends left, along with Oberi and Rishi. Kallie and I searched the hall high and low until curfew approached, but we found nothing.

Finally, Kallie said, "We should probably head back, before we're locked out of our rooms for the night."

I gritted my teeth. I didn't want to leave here with nothing, but I wasn't sure there was anything here to find. "We'll come back another day, I guess."

Kallie and I left the abandoned hallway. We were on our way back to our dorms when we heard a sobbing voice around the corner. "Th— they're saying it was the Dollmaker. I can't believe Regina is gone."

A single beat passed before Kallie rounded the corner. "*What* did you say about the Dollmaker?"

"He's claimed another victim," a guy said solemnly. It sounded like Edwin, though his voice was softer than normal. Whatever happened must've rocked their world. These two had always been rude. To see them rattled was unusual.

"Who'd he kill?" Kallie demanded.

"It was Brianna's cousin, Regina," Edwin said.

My guts twinged. Normally, I wouldn't care what the fuck happened to Edwin, but this went beyond any animosity between the two of us. Sometimes I forgot the jerks in this prison still had families out there. Brianna was devastated, and Edwin sounded desperate to help, but didn't seem to know how.

Brianna hiccupped loudly. "She wasn't just my cousin. She was my best friend. My oldest memories are of Regina hiding in the tapestries at the castle. We used to visit with our parents and play hide and seek behind suits of armor and statues. I just can't believe she died in such a happy place."

Kallie's voice turned sad. "I remember her. She was a few years younger than us. She was murdered in the castle?"

Brianna sniffled, but she didn't answer. She must've been nodding her head.

"Tell us *everything*," I demanded.

Brianna's voice trembled. "Regina was a debutante, and this year, she was invited to attend the annual debutante ball."

"What's that?" I asked.

Kallie turned to me to explain. "It's an annual event in Malovia where noble daughters are revealed to the public. It's a right-of-passage for nobles to start dating, in order to find their mate."

"And now she'll never find one!" Brianna cried. "According to my aunt, Regina was there one minute, and then she was just... gone. There was a stage for the live band, and when the curtains opened... oh, gods."

"What happened?" Kallie growled. "I need to know. This is important!"

Brianna was near the point of hyperventilating. "The curtains opened... and Regina's bloody body was staked to the back of the stage with knives! It was like he put her on display for the whole ball—"

Brianna got so choked up she couldn't speak anymore.

"I think that's enough questions," Edwin said. "Come on, Bri. Let's get you back to your room."

He led Brianna away, but Kallie and I didn't move. We could hardly process what she'd just told us.

My hands curled into fists. "This sick fucker's still out there. We've got to get our hands on news reports if we're going to find anything to add to the criminal profile."

"We already have one clue," Kallie stated. "These debutante events are invite-only, and there's high security all around the castle. You're not getting in unless you're a servant or of the noble class."

I shook my head. "A servant doesn't fit the profile. They're too closely monitored to think they could get away with something like this."

"Except the Dollmaker is cocky," Kallie pointed out. "It could very well be a servant trying to impress the noble class. He *did* put his victim on display, in a place he knew they'd all see it at once. It's a show to him."

"No, not a show," I said. "A *game*. Servants would be the first suspects, but this guy knows he's not going to get caught. It amuses him watching people scramble to figure it out. He thinks he's smarter than everyone else, because they can't catch him."

"Who exactly is he trying to impress?" Kallie asked. "What person on this planet would find it appealing to assassinate people in such a brutal, cold manner?"

"I don't know, but he's got to be a noble. A servant wouldn't dare to be this bold. It's the only thing that fits."

"No," Kallie argued, her tone growing hollow. "If he *is* of noble class, that means I know him. I know all the lords and ladies, dukes and duchesses, and all their kids. I grew up with them."

"Then tell me... which of them could get away with this for so long?"

Kallie gulped audibly. "I don't know, Charlie. And that absolutely terrifies me."

Kallie and I didn't have much more information to go off of, but I was determined. Once we found the merfolk key and got out of here, we were going after this guy ourselves.

Two weeks passed, and we were no closer to answers. I paid close attention in my Advanced Criminal Justice classes, hoping for some information that would help me catch the Dollmaker for good, but so far I had nothing. I entered the classroom on Friday and took a seat beside Chancey. We didn't get to talk before Professor Jobe strode to the front of the class.

"We don't have much time today, class, so pay attention. Today, we will be discussing the history of Darke Island," he announced.

I suddenly became more alert. I didn't have any more information on the Dollmaker, but Amalie had left behind clues for us to uncover on the island about the merfolk key. Perhaps a history lesson would help us put the pieces together.

"Darke Island has historically played a significant role in the supernatural criminal justice system," Professor Jobe said. "You'll want to understand the role it plays in order to pass your upcoming exam."

He turned to the front of the room, as if addressing pictures on the board. "The history of Darke Island dates back to 1781, when it was discovered by a group of British explorers. Due to the size of the island and the resources available, these explorers settled on the island. They built the first church, which stands on Institute grounds, along with cabins and other buildings that came to be known as Shade Hills. Humans attempted to inhabit the island for twenty years, but they continuously ran into problems, due to all the dark supernatural activity that took place here. We know that is because... who can tell me? Yes, Cain?"

"Magical ley lines?" Cain questioned.

"Exactly," Professor Jobe said. "Darke Island is a site of magical activity. That is why we host the Darke Games every year, in order to eliminate magical threats that appear annually. The humans, however, grew scared of this magic, and were ready to abandon the island when supernaturals arrived in the early 1800s. We discovered the island lay upon one of these ley lines, and we took over the island for ourselves."

I knew all of this, but I leaned forward in my chair so I didn't miss any new information.

"Darke Island was intended to be a place of neutral territory, belonging to all supernatural races," Professor Jobe continued. "That is why when international treaties were broken, offenders were sentenced to Darke Island. At that time, the largest building on the island was the church, so prisoners were housed in the chapel and put to work building the surrounding community. By the 1850s, they had run out of room in the chapel, so the prisoners built a new holding center, which became the asylum."

I knew from previous history lessons that the asylum was built to house the worst criminals, but something about this lecture seemed off. I wasn't sure we were getting the whole story.

Professor Jobe continued. "The asylum is one of our oldest buildings on Institute grounds. By the 1860s, both buildings were becoming too crowded, so another building was constructed next door, which was the first cell block. This provided enough space for some time, but demand grew exponentially following the Great Supernatural War in the 1940s. The United Supernatural Union formed at the end of the war, and they had hosts of war criminals and prisoners of war to deal with. There was no room for these people on Institute property, so a new adult penitentiary was built on the other side of the island. The chapel, asylum, and first cell block were connected and converted into the Darke Institute for Supernatural Offenders facility, where it remains to this day."

I leaned back in my chair. Professor Jobe had no new information. It was the same story we'd been told over and over again. I didn't know why the Warden liked to tell it so often...

Unless there was something we were missing... something he wanted demigods to find for him. That was his whole purpose here, wasn't it? The Darke Games, the ridiculous size of the Institute's property— it was designed to find and use demigods. The Warden must think there was something in the island's history that would lead us to the keys.

I barely got a chance to consider any of it before the door opened and a woman cleared her throat.

"Ah, Professor Mazur, please come in," Professor Jobe said. "Everyone, please give Professor Mazur your undivided attention. She has an announcement to make."

I scowled. Professor Mazur was an angel professor working with the Warden, and she'd refused to provide me any accommodations in her classes. This lady was a real piece of work. I wasn't interested in anything she had to say.

Her heels clicked as she walked to the front of the room. "Students, I hope you'll pay attention, so as to not waste my time. It is my pleasure to introduce you to a new career placement program here at the Institute."

She sounded so fake. Mazur was a real bitch, but for the first time, she seemed happy about something. It couldn't be good.

"We want everyone here at the Institute to succeed, and we believe that begins by providing you security for your future," she continued. "This program is optional, but through it, students will receive guaranteed job placement upon graduation."

Cain scoffed. "That's *if* we graduate."

"That's the beauty of The Mission," Mazur said brightly. "Through this program, we anticipate record graduation numbers. Students will be trained right here at the Institute through a paid internship, and given a career once they've satisfied graduation requirements."

It sounded too good to be true, and I was instantly skeptical. Whatever they were training people for had to be useful to the Warden, or he wouldn't bother with the program.

"What exactly is this training *for*?" Chancey piped up.

"Missionary work, of course," Mazur said, like it was obvious. "With tensions high between the supernatural races, missionary work is a growing and thriving career field. Any students who are interested can sign up now."

Nobody moved. We weren't exactly rushing to sign up as one of the Warden's puppets.

Professor Mazur cleared her throat. "This internship comes with its perks, including fifty extra Commissary points loaded to your account per week— and that's just during training. Once you've passed training, you'll be eligible to attend mission trips on the mainland, outside of Institute walls."

"That sounds great, Professor," a girl said apprehensively. It sounded like Melody, one of the mermaid girls. "But we don't really know what's going on out there. Perhaps we'd be more willing to sign up if we had context on what we might be walking into. It could be dangerous."

"Mission work is not for the weak at heart, Miss Lowe," Mazur said. "The witches and elementals have launched attacks upon Celestial City, and the angels are struggling to find resources in the wake of this tragedy. I'm not going to lie— the death toll is only growing. That is why The Mission is so important. We must help these poor, misguided souls convert, so we can prevent such tragedies in the future. If you truly want to be reformed, The Mission is the way to do it. You could walk out of the Institute a hero."

Murmurs traveled around the room, and I knew she'd already sold it to several students. I wasn't so easily convinced. There had to be a catch; there always was. Why was Mazur admitting to the attacks now, when the Warden had cut off all war news weeks ago?

There were things they didn't want us to know, and the Warden made sure only *his* message got through. He'd been planning this for a while now, I bet.

"Is that all you can tell us?" Melody begged. "There's more going on. We can all feel it. My mom called this morning, but the phone line cut off before she could tell me anything. I'm worried my pod is under attack and my family won't survive."

"Then I suggest you pray about it," Mazur said.

Wow. So helpful.

"I don't think *praying* is going to stop this war," Melody replied, sounding offended. She'd been looking for real support, and Mazur was blowing her off.

"If you pray to the *right* deity, perhaps you'll have more success," Mazur said simply.

"Our gods aren't to blame," Melody argued. "They're not the ones bombing our cities!"

"Know your place, Miss Lowe," Mazur said harshly, sounding more like herself. "You all seem so eager to know what's happening out there. The truth is, this war began with the gods. Your gods have the power to protect their people, so why are so many dying? Because your gods *don't care*."

"How can you say that?" Melody demanded. "Our gods would never abandon—"

"Your gods have already abandoned you," Mazur interrupted. "Look around you. Every one of you has a story, and no one comes to the Institute with a good one. You've all seen death and abuse, and some of you have murdered people yourselves."

Just rub the salt in the wound, why don't you? She wasn't saying all this to show compassion. She was saying it to make a point.

"Do you really think any of you would be put through such pain if your gods cared?" Mazur continued. "Your gods pick and choose who they care about, and then throw the others to the wolves. I did nothing wrong, and my daughter was taken from me. She was a devout member of the Celestial Church, and her sentence was terminal cancer. If anyone is going to rule us, then it needs to be someone who cares about *all* his people. The angel god didn't cure my daughter, but if someone else were to take his place, others would be spared the same suffering."

As much as I despised Mazur, she made a good point. The Hawkei gods stood by and observed from the spirit world when I was taken from my parents as a baby. They watched me grow up on the streets and never stepped in to help. Hell, our gods watched Ava suffer. If they really loved us, they couldn't let something like that happen. I loved my wife so damn much, and sitting here watching her be in pain was the worst. I wouldn't be sitting around doing nothing about it if I had the power to stop it, yet our gods were doing just that.

At the back of the room, a guy scoffed. "And who's going to step up and fight the old gods? The Warden? What a *compassionate* fellow, taking us *rejects* in when our gods abandoned us."

"That's exactly what he did," Mazur said proudly. "The Warden has done nothing but protect you all and give you an education. You should all want revenge for what your gods have put you through. You should want to build a better world."

"Only the Almighty One can build a better world," a student said ahead of me. His feathers rustled, and I knew it had to be an angel.

"There can only be one god," Mazur said. "But gods have risen to power before, and a new god is rising. When multiple deities have a say, it throws off the balance. They must be eliminated so that a new god can rule— a god who *cares*. The world would be a better place with only one god in power."

There it was. There was always a catch with the angels, wasn't there?

"The Warden received a revelation to create The Mission, to guide you along this new path and into the light. Doctor Taurus is the prophet of The Mission, and he will bring us to a new god of peace," Professor Mazur pressed. "If we allow ourselves to open our minds and think in new ways, the world can be healed. Supernaturals have gone to war because their gods told them to. If we were all governed under one god, there'd be no reason for war. The Mission seeks to unite us as one, so that we can follow the rising god to salvation. The God of The Mission will reveal himself when the time is right, but only once his followers have proven themselves."

Murmurs traveled around the room. It sounded like several people were buying it.

"You've all come to the Institute to be reformed," Mazur said. "If there's any way for a student to better themselves, The Mission is it."

I leaned over to Chancey and whispered, "You're not actually considering this, are you?"

Chancey scoffed. "Nah, but the other angels are. Can't say I'm not intrigued, though, even if just for a better shot at graduating."

"You could offer me all the money in the world, and I still wouldn't work for the Warden—"

"What was that, Mister Wahkin?" Mazur demanded. Her heels clicked as she approached our table.

I cleared my throat. "Just discussing our options, ma'am."

"Surely you'll join," she stated. "After all, what other job prospects could someone like *you* have? I'm sure The Mission can find *something* for you to do."

"Someone like me? You mean because I'm blind?" That really pissed me off. I crossed my arms and leaned back in my chair. "Thanks for the offer, but I've already declared my major."

Mazur laughed. "Criminal Justice? You may want to think more realistically about your options before it's too late, Mister Wahkin."

"What's wrong with him majoring in Criminal Justice?" Chancey demanded.

"What role could *he* possibly serve in a criminal justice department?" Mazur sneered. "He certainly can't be solving crimes out in the field, and he won't be pushing papers behind a desk."

"You clearly didn't see his performance in the Darke Games," Chancey growled. "For your information, Charlie's going to be a supernatural bounty hunter, and a great one at that!"

I grabbed his arm to stop him, but he was royally pissed off.

Mazur laughed harder. "Is that so, Mister Wahkin? You're going to hunt down criminals like yourself? How... interesting."

My guts sank. It was such an innocent word, but the deepest of insults. I shouldn't have given a shit what Mazur said, so why did it bother me?

Mazur walked to the front of the room again. "I suggest you all think very carefully about your futures. Fever dreams have no place at the Institute. The Mission is taking sign-ups now."

People seemed eager to join, and a crowd formed around the sign-up sheet at the end of class. I had to push through them to get out the door.

"Where are you going?" Someone pushed me back.

"Keep your hands off him, Cain," Chancey growled.

I didn't know Cain well, other than he was in some of my classes. He was a warlock, and I could easily take him in a fight.

"You really think you're going to be a supernatural bounty hunter?" Cain scoffed. "So you're just going to turn against your own?"

"My own?" I asked. "Meaning, what? Criminals?"

"You're here for a reason," Cain snapped. "That makes you a criminal. But you're gonna betray your own kind, and hunt us down once you get out of here. What a stand-up guy, working for the fucking cops after running from them all his life. You think that makes you better than us, huh?"

"I never said that," I sneered. "Keep your record clean, and you won't have to deal with me. Or do you want to piss me off and see what happens?"

I'd had a reputation around here after my string of wins in fight club. Cain didn't want to mess with me.

He huffed and said, "You'll never amount to anything, Wahkin."

I really didn't give a shit what Cain thought. His words didn't even warrant a response. I pushed past Cain, and Chancey followed.

I lowered my voice to whisper to him. "The Mission is nothing but bad news. We need to get everyone together. Now."

Fifteen minutes later, my friends and I had gathered in our secret workout room, where we wouldn't be heard. Ivy was noticeably missing, but everyone else was here.

"I assume by now, everyone's heard about The Mission," I said.

"Yeah. Some asshole angel professors showed up in my Miriamic Magic class to deliver the news," Alistair said. "They want us working for the Warden? Hell, no."

"It's worse than that," I stated. "Mazur says The Mission is all about uniting us under one god— some new, rising god."

"Excuse me?" Alistair balked. "Mother Miriam is a better fit to lead us all."

"What's that supposed to mean?" Ez demanded. "You're just going to forget about *our* gods, or the entire Arcanean pantheon?"

"I meant nothing by it," Alistair said. "This whole thing is bogus. People should be free to worship who they choose."

"That's what started this war in the first place," Chancey replied. "People disagreeing about which god to worship."

"You're not on their side," Ava insisted. Oberi ruffled her feathers from the back of Ava's chair.

"Nah, but... they make a good point, right?" Chancey said. "Uniting the races *would* prevent war."

"I thought you left the Celestial Church," Marcus said. "How can you agree with The Mission?"

Chancey hesitated. "I guess... you can take a guy out of the Celestial Church, but you can't take the Celestial Church out of a guy. Look, I'm still deconstructing. They hammered that shit into my head, so it's really hard to get it out. So you gotta explain something to me. What makes choosing your own faith better if it's only going to get people hurt?"

"Because no one *has* to get hurt," Kallie said. "Not if we tolerate our differences. The Celestial Church takes every belief that isn't their own as an attack upon their god, but *they're* the ones attacking people."

"Mazur says the witches and elementals have been the ones launching attacks on Celestial City," Chancey argued.

"That's not true, and you know it," Marcus said. "The witches have been on the defense for months, trying to protect their city. The angels bombed *them*, and they had to retaliate. A lot of people died. My mom told me herself. It's really rough out there."

"The angels attacked because the witches aligned themselves with the Elementai, who *did* attack first," Chancey reminded him. "So yeah, it *is* true."

"How are we supposed to know what to believe?" Alistair growled. "The Warden controls what information comes into the Institute."

"All in the name of *converting* people to his *mission*," Opal sneered. "But why bother getting students to sign up?"

"He's creating an army," Ava said. "He's getting people to sign up so he has a host of followers that'll do whatever he tells them to, both inside the prison and in the outside world once these kids graduate. The bigger The Mission grows, the more people the Warden has to dispense to do his will."

"The question is, what do we do about it?" I asked.

"We can't stop The Mission," Kallie said. "But part of the Warden's plan involves finding those keys, so we've got to unite them first. I'm still working on the next clue."

I paced around the room. "I had a thought. We keep hearing about Darke Island history in our classes. Professor Jobe covered it in Criminal Justice today. What if the Warden's teaching it on *purpose*? If he wants to use us to find the keys, perhaps he thinks we'll find information in the island's history."

"It's definitely a good place to start," Kallie agreed. "What did Jobe cover?"

I went over the history lesson with my friends. There wasn't really much, so the conversation was short.

"That can't be all he said," Alistair insisted once I finished.

"That's all the information I was given," I replied.

"The Warden's twisting the history!" Alistair cried.

"It's... wrong?" I wondered.

"Not exactly," Alistair said. "But it's missing important details— namely, the *Elves*. Eddie taught me all about their history here on Darke Island, and it was super important."

My heart ached at the mention of Eddie, and Oberi gave a sad noise. My connection to Eddie had grown so weak, I wasn't sure he was still out there. I thought of all the times Eddie had tried to tell me about Forevermore, and Elvish history in general. He'd given me so many dates, I couldn't keep track of the information, and I hadn't retained any of it. I'd been fighting so much with Ava last semester, and been so depressed because of it, that I mostly blocked Eddie out whenever he tried to tell me something important. I mentally kicked myself for not paying closer attention.

"What do you know about the Elves' history?" Ava asked curiously.

Alistair cleared his throat. "Listen up, because this is going to be a full course on Darke Island history— the *real* history, this time."

Alistair wasn't the kind of guy to cut a lecture short, so I knew we'd be here for a while. I took a seat on the bench we used for weightlifting, settling in for a long lesson.

"Our story begins eight-hundred years ago," Alistair began. "As you know, the Elves and the fae once lived together in a magical realm called Edinmyre. As their numbers grew and resources dwindled, war broke out amongst the two races. In order to save the Elves, their goddesses, Idril and Caralyn, offered them a place of refuge and a purpose in a new land. The Elves were forced out of their city of Ithriel and retreated to Earth. The goddesses portaled them to Dark Island *through* the Elven gate here on the island, and made them protectors of the gate, giving them seven keys. The purpose of these keys were so the races could commune with the gods together to resolve conflict."

"Why seven keys, though?" Marcus wondered. "There weren't seven major supernatural races back then. Witches didn't exist until the 1400s."

"Seven is the most powerful magical number," Alistair said. "Back then, the Elves tried to create the first United Supernatural Union, in order to unite the existing races so they could use these keys together. Angels, merfolk, fae— they all came together. The Elves invited leaders from all races to come commune with the gods. For a time, the races *did* unite, and the Elves remained caretakers of the keys and the gate, which was the only way for supernaturals to maintain their connection with the divine."

"That couldn't have gone over well with the fae," Kallie theorized.

"Things went well for a while," Alistair said. "The Seelie and Unseelie fae were in a civil war, so they left the Elves alone, feeling like they'd already won by driving them out of Edinmyre. But tensions continued amongst the fae, and they were banishing their own people to Earth for hundreds of years. By the 1600s, the fae had been cast out of Edinmyre by their own gods to Earth, as punishment for all the infighting. Their portal opened in Europe, which is where they settled to form their country of Malovia. The Elves were barely an afterthought to the fae, because they were so focused on building up their own infrastructure."

"So where were the Elves at this time?" Chancey asked.

"On Darke Island," Alistair answered. "But they didn't call it that. It was Forevermore, their safe haven. If it was anything like Eddie described... oh, it sounded wonderful! The island was nothing like it is today— cast in shadow and darkness. This place was rumored to be beautiful, radiating sunshine and flowing with waterfalls. It was a paradise on Earth due to the Elves' magic."

"How did things go so wrong?" Marcus asked.

"Things changed in the supernatural community," Alistair continued. "For four hundred years, the races were on good terms. Then the fae came to Earth, all while the witches were gaining traction as a new magical race, and the Elementai were gifted their powers by their ancestors. The angels did *not* like new supernatural races coming in on their turf."

"They'd certainly see the Elementai as a threat," Ez said thoughtfully. "We weren't like the witches. We didn't start with one family and grow our numbers over time. The Elementai were a group of five Indigenous tribes who came together to form one singular tribe, in order to protect themselves from colonizers. The Anichi tribe was forced out of their home when the Spanish began colonizing Central America. They came together with the Toaqua, Nivita, Koigni, and Yapluma tribes, who were forced west from their homes and into Northern California. It was when they bound together that the ancestors gifted them powers of the elements to protect themselves, and made them caretakers of all magical creatures. They got their powers all at once, which means their numbers, along with their magical creatures, were suddenly a major threat to other supernatural societies."

"Exactly," Alistair agreed. "Things turned hostile when the witches and the Elementai petitioned to join the Union. The fae took this as a threat, because they knew witches were the only race who could counteract their own magic. The Elves suggested splitting up the keys amongst the races to show they were united. They believed no race should control them all, and that it was beneficial for everyone to share power. But the angels felt that they were a chosen community, and their race should hold their own key *and* a key for underrepresented supernatural communities. The Elves disagreed, and people began fighting, trying to steal the keys for themselves so they could have control over the Elven gateway and the afterlife. Legend says the Unseelie Fae got a hold of three keys, which were intended for the witches, fae, and Elementai."

"Which have been found," I said. "The races must've got them back from the Unseelie, because we have all three keys, passed down through the generations."

"That makes sense, since the Elementai had ties to the Unseelie Fae," Kallie said.

"What do you mean?" Ava asked.

"Arthur Cedrick," Kallie reminded her. "The Unseelie Fae who allied with the Elementai? Our shared ancestor?"

"Uh... right," Ava said, sounding a little flustered. "He must've returned the Elementai key to our people, but what about the witches? How'd they get theirs back, until Marcus got his hands on it?"

"Don't ask me," Marcus said. "My mom gave it to me. All I know is it's been in my family for years. Though my family has a history within the Imperium Council, our highest governing body. I've heard stories of my great-grandfather stealing artifacts from the Council when he was a priest, in order to protect them. He might've stolen the key."

"Does it matter?" Kallie asked. "We have it now."

"Kallie's right," Ava agreed. "We need to figure out what happened to the others, so we can find them."

"The merfolk, angels, and vampires all took possession of their own keys and hid them," Alistair explained. "You guys got the angel key from the Warden, so that's accounted for. It's possible the others are still with their respective races."

"What about the Astromancer key?" I asked.

"Eddie didn't know," Alistair replied. "He said the Unseelie might've taken it, but it's also possible the Astromancers had their key and lied about never receiving it, in order to keep anyone from coming after it."

"What happened after the keys were divided?" Marcus asked.

"The angels threatened war," Alistair continued. "The Elves were forced to leave Darke Island, in order to prevent the Elven Gate from destruction. Before they left, they built the Mirror of Ingress deep within the caves, so that they could move on and off Darke Island freely. They portaled from the mirror to the Mediterranean, far away from other magical races. That way, if the angels attacked the Elves, the gate would remain safe. The Elves left monsters behind and opened a magical leyline— a portal for dark energy— in order to deter people from coming for the gate. Forevermore was left abandoned, and Darke Island quickly deteriorated to what it is today, withered and ugly. The Elven Gate knew it had been left behind, and the island grew to reflect that."

"That's why these strange supernatural occurrences happen here," Chancey said thoughtfully. "The Elves designed it that way."

"That's how Eddie described it," Alistair confirmed. "Once they left, the Elves spread throughout the world, in order to search for the lost keys. Over time, people forgot what Darke Island once was."

"Forevermore had been forgotten by the time the British landed here," I realized. "They must've thought it abandoned, if there was even evidence left."

"I don't think anything but the gate survived," Alistair said. "But the British found the mines, and settled here to search for valuable resources."

"They were mining noxite?" Ava wondered.

"Noxite didn't exist yet," Alistair said. "Not until the Elven genocide."

"Oh. Yeah, you're right," Ava said, a little blankly.

"But the Elves had left by then." Kallie sounded confused.

"For a time," Alistair confirmed. "When the supernaturals found out humans had settled their island, they came to take it back. That's when they formed the prison, which quickly became infamous for torturing and killing its prisoners."

I scoffed. "The Warden certainly left that out of the history lessons."

"He wants the Institute to have a *good reputation*," Alistair said.

Yeah, that's going so well for him, Oberi said sarcastically.

Alistair cleared his throat. "Anyway, according to Eddie, the Great Supernatural War was a multi-faceted war— partially an argument about exposing the supernaturals and using magic to control humans, and partially due to the conflict over the keys. The fae, angels, and vampires were still hunting the keys and believed the Elves knew where they were. This is why the angels targeted the Elves so heavily. They began exterminating Elven colonies all over the world in a mad conquest to find the keys. With the majority of their race spread out so far around the globe, the Elves found it difficult to mobilize against their enemies effectively, and they couldn't fight back. That's what brought them back to Darke Island."

"They must've sought refuge here because it was neutral territory," Kallie said.

"That's exactly what Eddie told me," Alistair replied. "The Elves came to commune with the gods and stop the Great Supernatural War, but they were exterminated in a bloody battle. Noxite was a result of that battle. The Elves' blood seeped into the ground and infused the metal with magic."

"A few survived," I recalled. "My father and grandfather fled into the caves with their people."

"Yes," Alistair said. "They hid underground, and the other supernaturals declared the Elves extinct. The Great Supernatural War came to an end, and from it formed the United Supernatural Union, which was considered to be a protective measure to prevent another supernatural world war from happening again. They named themselves after the Elven Union, to honor their memory, although it was an empty promise. Within a decade, the United Supernatural Union became corrupt. The angel representative was assassinated in the 1950s, though the murderer was never caught."

"I remember this story," Chancey said. "They tell it in our church history. The angel assassinated was Masci Taurus."

I furrowed my brow. "Taurus. As in the Warden's ancestor?"

Chancey scoffed. "Not just any ancestor. *His father*, if I remember right."

"The Warden's dad was on the Union council?" I asked. "He must've known about the keys. That's why the Warden's so obsessed with them."

"I would think so," Chancey said. "The Warden is relatively young as far as angels go, but his father? That man was *ancient*— like, hundreds of years old. He might've been old enough to remember the Elven migration from Edinmyre."

My insides twisted. "The Warden's not just going off legends and map clues! He's going off a first-hand account from his father. He could be more than a step ahead of us— he could be miles ahead!"

"And yet he's been searching for these clues for what— a hundred years?" Kallie pointed out. "The Warden may have information, but he's missing huge pieces. He doesn't have the full picture from his dad, or he'd have found these keys by now."

"It's us," I pressed. "We're the full picture— demigods. He needs us to find the keys. Maybe it's best if we abandon our search, because clearly, he needs us to find them for him."

Ava reached for my hand. "We can't do that. There has to be a reason demigods must find the keys. It's part of our prophecy. We won't let them fall into the Warden's hands."

"What if he already has them?" I asked. "He had the angel key. Who's to say he's not hiding others?"

"If he is, we'll find them," Ava pressed. "Right now, the merfolk key is our priority. Once we find it, we'll have over half the keys."

I furrowed my brow. Ava was starting to worry me. First she'd forgotten Arthur Cedrick was Unseelie Fae. Then she forgot noxite was formed after the Elven Genocide. These were things we already knew. Now she'd miscounted the keys.

"We already have four out of seven keys," I said gently.

Ava hesitated. "Right. And the more we have, the less chance the Warden has of using them against us."

"Then we have to keep searching," I said. "Kallie, do you have any more information?"

"I'm working on it," she insisted. "I'm going to have to cross reference this history with what I know about Amalie. Let me get my notes together, and we'll meet up later to discuss, all right?"

We agreed, and went our separate ways. I guided Ava back to our room. I didn't have long before my factory shift, but as I closed the door to our cell, I couldn't help but admit I was concerned. Something was wrong with her memory, and that terrified me. Were there other things she was forgetting, and what could I do to help her remember?

I knew she'd deny anything was wrong if I asked her, so I felt around our bond to see if there was a way to get inside her head and help her out. I found an opening and nudged my way inside, but I didn't get a glimpse into her mind before the doorway slammed shut completely. The effect was so strong it made me stagger backward. Ava whirled around, and one of the big wheels of her chair rolled over my toes. *Ow!*

Oberi squawked loudly and clacked her beak at me. She wasn't pleased with me, either.

"*What exactly* do you think you're doing?" Ava demanded.

I took a step back. "I— I was just trying to help."

"I felt you poking around in my head!"

"I didn't mean to upset you," I said gently. "I just wanted to figure out what was wrong. Apparently, that wasn't the right way to approach this."

"No!" Ava cried. "What made you think it was better to invade my thoughts than to just *ask* me?"

"I noticed you're forgetting things, and I'm concerned about your cognitive function. I didn't know if you'd tell me."

"That's up to me," she insisted. "At least give me the choice."

"Pidge, please," I begged. "I don't want to fight."

"Then you shouldn't have gone poking around in my head! That's not okay. Just because you have the ability to do it doesn't mean you should. I love that we have this connection, but I still need my privacy."

My shoulders dropped. "Are you hiding something from me?"

"Ancestors, no!" Ava sounded even more upset now.

"Then why can't I look inside your head?" I honestly didn't understand. If she trusted me, why couldn't I help her?

Ava blew a breath. "Are you serious?"

"Yes. I'm trying to help, and you're overreacting."

"Oh, I'm sorry I asked to be *respected*," Ava sneered. Her wheels squeaked as she opened the door and started wheeling into the hall.

"Pidge." I sighed. "Where are you going?"

"Somewhere else," she said coolly. "Come on, Oberi."

I'm with you, girlfriend. Oberi huffed and hustled away.

I chased her down the hall. "Pidge, please don't! You can't just run away."

"You're right. I can't," Ava replied. "I'm *rolling* away."

In style, Oberi added.

I scrambled in front of her. "Let's not do that, either. Please."

"You're making it worse."

"Explain it to me," I begged. "I just want to understand."

"I'm not *overreacting*, Charlie. I feel disrespected. You tried to get inside my head without asking. That's like picking up my phone and going through it."

"Well, I wouldn't know what that's like."

"You're hurt because you think I'm hiding something from you?" Ava continued. "*I'm* hurt you would feel the need to poke inside my head, anyway!"

I took a step back. "You're right. I was out of line. I just wanted to help, so let me know how I can. Can we talk about this?"

"I wanted to talk about it when I was ready," Ava seethed. "I *know*

I've been forgetting things. I know my mind's not here half the time, and realize I can't remember stuff we've gone over a million times. It's fucking embarrassing!"

You two need to calm down, Oberi warned, as if she worried the situation was getting out of hand. She'd gone from snarky to serious in an instant.

"How could I know that?" I asked. "I wasn't even sure you knew it was happening."

"It's just so humiliating that I have to face up to it, after going through everything else. I wish you'd never brought it up. I don't bring up that you—"

Ava cut off. She sucked in a breath, refusing to say another word.

I furrowed my brow. "You don't bring up what?"

Ava hesitated. A hint of guilt slipped through our bond, and I could tell she felt bad— terrible even— about whatever she was about to say. "It's nothing. I'm sorry, I shouldn't have said anything."

I gritted my teeth. *Now* I was getting angry. "That's not fair. If there's something wrong with me, I should know about it."

"I don't want to upset you. Just let it—"

"Ava, *tell me.*"

Ava drew a deep breath. "I don't bring up that you can't see. So don't ask about my memory."

I gaped. "We talk about that all the time."

"Not how your eyes are losing the ability to track."

My stomach dropped. "I'm... what?"

Ava's voice got small. "I thought you knew and didn't want to talk about it. Your eyes don't move the way they used to. When I met you, I couldn't tell you were blind. You were good at making your eyes follow movement and noises, because you had to. Now, it's obvious. They just stay in one spot."

Terror twisted in my gut. It'd always been a strength of mine, hiding my blindness. People were less likely to take advantage of me. It horrified me to know I was losing my ability to track.

I swallowed the lump in my throat. "I was always in survival mode until I came here. I had to learn how to hide it. Now, I guess I don't need to."

"I'm sorry, Charlie—" Ava started, but I cut her off.

"It's not your fault."

Several long moments passed as I processed this new information. I didn't know what to do with it. If I couldn't hide that I was blind, how was I going to protect myself, or anyone else? It made me feel extremely vulnerable... like back when I'd had no one. I hated that feeling.

We all have things that hold us back, Oberi offered. *Let's work on them together.*

Ava's tone became soft. "The doctors said I'd experience memory loss."

"You don't have to tell me just because I feel bad. I want you to come to me at your own pace."

"And I want you to have context," she said. "My poor memory is a symptom of my spinal injury. I'm aware of it, but I'm still trying to figure out the extent of it. And it sucks so bad, because as shitty as my bipolar could get, I always held on to facts and information like a steel trap. It's helped me out of so many situations, and enabled me to figure out solutions to problems nobody else could answer. Now I'm losing that, too. And if I'm not as sharp as I used to be, I'm even more of a deadweight to the team."

"You're still wicked smart, pidge, and you're not dragging the team down. I just want to figure out a solution," I offered. "I'm worried that if you're confused, I need to be able to get inside your head to help. What happens if you experience a psychosis episode? We're connected, so maybe I can pull you out of it."

Ava hesitated, like she was scared of the idea. "I *do* want your help, but we need to trust each other. You can invade my thoughts if it's necessary, but be warned— it's not fun inside my head."

"Can we still share our thoughts with each other?"

"Yes, of course," Ava said. "I just want to maintain privacy, but we have to trust each other in that privacy, and respect each other. If there's an emergency, you can poke inside my head, but otherwise, we need to give each other permission."

I nodded. "All right. That sounds fair."

Even though we'd agreed to the boundaries, things still felt off when I left for my factory shift. Ava insisted Oberi come with me, like she thought I needed her right now.

I was fine. Really.

Ancestors, why couldn't we just communicate properly? We had this bond, and we still couldn't figure out how we felt.

Oberi shifted into a husky and padded alongside me. *It's okay that you can't track anymore.*

For once, he was trying to help, but it just made me feel worse.

It isn't, I argued.

Yes, it is, Oberi insisted. *You don't need to track, because you did it out of survival. You're safe now with us. You have a community that can help, and we'll all protect each other and keep each other safe. Ava and I are here for you.*

I drew a long breath, then patted him on the head. He had no idea what that meant to me. *Thanks, buddy.*

When I arrived at the factory, I went straight for my station, but someone stepped in front of me. I guessed it was a guard by the sound of his boots. "Wahkin, you've been reassigned. Come with me."

"Just when I was starting to love my job," I said flatly.

I didn't know what to expect, but if it got me out of labeling boxes, I was all for it. That work was boring as shit. At least stimulate my mind a little. This was supposed to be a reform school, after all.

The guard led me out of the factory with several other students. We entered a large room and were guided to join another group of students.

"Is this some kind of joke?" I heard a familiar voice say.

I walked over to Alistair. "What's going on?"

"They've reassigned us to a new factory," Alistair growled.

"Maybe it's not a bad thing," I suggested. "It's got to be better than labeling boxes. What are we making?"

"Braille books," Alistair said flatly.

I nearly choked. "They're making *us* manufacture braille books?"

Alistair huffed. "The irony isn't lost on me. Did you know they're one of the top products incarcerated people make every year?"

I scowled. "This sounds like *fun.*"

"Listen up!" a guard yelled. We were forced to remain quiet as we were led around the factory floor for training. It wasn't much help, and no one bothered to adapt their lesson for the blind.

After our tour, Alistair and I were led to an area where we were supposed to secure the bindings on the books. We both just stood there, not sure what to do.

"What's the hold up?" a guard growled.

"I'm not exactly a visual learner," I said.

"It's not that hard," the guard sneered. "You have the easiest job in the room. Now, get to work, or I'll report you to the Warden."

"Here, let me show you," a familiar voice said. Ivy stepped between Alistair and me.

I pulled away immediately. I didn't want to be around Ivy, not after what they did to Ava... but it wasn't like I had a choice.

"I've been working the binding table for months," Ivy said. "It's easy once you get the hang of it. What you're going to do is take one of the spines off the shelf in front of you."

I reached out and felt a stack of shelves, piled full of plastic spines. Each spine was made of flexible rings that would slip through holes in the pages of the book and secure them together. It wasn't high-tech or anything, but it worked.

"That goes right here on the binding table," Ivy instructed. I felt for the table and found a sloped device with a lever on it. Ivy helped me situate the spine correctly, but as they did so, I noticed their hands shaking. Their voice remained steady, but I could tell Ivy was still suffering withdrawals.

Hell, and they'd still been made to come to work. I'd feel bad for them if I wasn't still pissed.

Ivy instructed me to pull the lever. "That opens the spine so that you can insert the pages."

I felt around again, and I found that the plastic rings had opened up.

"Now we take the back cover and slip that through the rings first," Ivy said, directing us to the stack of covers. "Once that's on, you take your internal pages, slip them on and finish up with a cover. Voila! You have a finished book."

"Thanks, Ivy," I mumbled.

"No problem," Ivy said, before instructing me to try another one by myself.

Oberi helped by pulling the lever with his teeth, while I straightened the pages and slipped them on the spine.

Oberi hacked. *Bleh! That lever tastes awful.*

"Looks like you've got it," Ivy said. "If you need any more help, I'm one binding table away."

It was weird that Ivy was being so nice, after the way I treated them. Ivy went back to their station, and I got to work.

"You were right!" Alistair said brightly. "This *is* better than labeling boxes."

In a way, it was. I was actually helping blind people, which gave me far better purpose than packaging weapons for the Warden. But I was still part of his machine, earning him profit without a choice. It made me sick, really.

I shrugged. "Yeah, I guess."

"Hey, what's got you down?" Alistair asked.

"Maybe it's the cheap labor," I replied.

"Nah, it's more than that," Alistair insisted. "That's never bothered you."

I sighed. "Ava and I had a spat."

"A spat, or a fight?" Alistair asked.

"I'm not sure, really," I admitted. "She let something slip that bothers me."

"Ah, trouble in the bedroom," Alistair said.

"No," I insisted as I pulled the lever on my table. Oberi was licking his lips, trying to get the taste out of his mouth. "Ava said I'm losing my ability to track with my eyes. I just don't get it. How can I feel so safe here, of all places? I used to be in survival mode all the time. It's how I tracked so well. Now, it's like... like I'm *comfortable* here, and that really bothers me, because this isn't a good place for me or my wife. What if there's a part of me that doesn't want to leave the Institute?"

"That's bull," Alistair said. "You want to get out of here. I know you do. You'd never put Ava in a dangerous situation if you had a choice."

"Maybe I'm scared that it's more dangerous out there," I said. I didn't know if I believed anything I was saying. I *didn't* want to stay here, but maybe I was lying to myself, because as terrible as the Institute could be, there were good parts to it. It was home, pretty much the only real home I'd ever had. My body was revealing what my mind didn't want to admit.

"You think it'll be more dangerous when you get out of here because you can't track anymore?" Alistair asked.

"That worries me, yeah," I admitted.

"You're worried you've changed, but you haven't," Alistair said. "If anything, you're more resourceful since you came here. You can do anything, Charlie. Your ability to track doesn't change that."

"I guess," I agreed. "But if it doesn't change anything, why was Ava so reluctant to tell me?"

"Maybe she knew your self-confidence would take a hit," Alistair suggested. "She wanted you to believe you're as tough as always."

I sighed. "Wouldn't it be better if she told me and treated it like it wasn't a big deal, instead of making it this big secret she had to keep so she didn't hurt me? It feels worse this way. I don't know what to think."

I knew I'd made a mistake earlier, trying to get into her head. My overwhelming drive to protect Ava was starting to erode her consent, and though I wanted to keep her safe, she had to make those decisions. But how could I stand idly by and watch her deteriorate without doing something to help?

"You two are still adjusting to this new life," Alistair said reassuringly. "I watched my parents go through the same thing. My mom was paralyzed in a bad car accident shortly before I was born, then I came along with all these health issues. I know they struggled, especially because they had to learn how to take care of a disabled kid before they'd hardly learned how to care for my mom's disability. I feel for Ava, I really do, because seeing her in that chair reminds me so much of my mom. And goddess, that woman is a saint. Didn't matter what she was going through. She and my dad were always there for me."

Alistair got a bit choked up talking about his parents. He cleared his throat and continued. "As I grew up, there was always something new to deal with, because I was always in the hospital. And when I wasn't, it was my mom. We did all right financially, because my parents were both lawyers. Lydia and Quentin Martin were the best damn lawyers in the whole Miriamic Coven, and then they had a delinquent son like me come along to ruin their reputation. It wasn't fair to them, really. I took things out on them whenever some bully came along to make my life a living hell. But that's how it was in our family. We were constantly learning new ways to handle life because our health was never steady. But my family was there for each other. Didn't matter how many jerks picked on me, or how many doctors blew us off, we always had each other. It's like that with your family— you, Oberi, and Ava. You guys have each other, and all the rest is bullshit. I know you three will figure out anything life throws at you."

It was rare for Alistair to get sentimental, which made his words have all the more impact. I nearly teared up.

"You're right," I said. "Ava and I *can* get through anything. Thanks, Alistair."

"Can I offer some advice?" Ivy asked from their table.

I hesitated, though I was curious what they had to say. "I guess so."

"It sounds like Ava and you need to establish better communication. That starts with trust," Ivy said.

"I trust Ava," I insisted.

"*Do* you?" Ivy challenged.

It was a rhetorical question, but I felt the sting of the answer. I'd tried to prod into Ava's head without her permission. Would I do that if I trusted her?

It wasn't that I *didn't* trust Ava. I'd put my life in that woman's hands. But there was this gray area we were playing in that lacked the mutual trust we should have as husband and wife.

Trust wasn't just knowing someone was going to catch you when you fell. It was knowing they'd ask you to catch them when *they* fell, too.

I drew a deep breath. "How do we establish trust?"

"Trust, my friend, begins in the bedroom," Ivy practically sang.

They already hump like bunnies, Oberi joked. *What else do you expect of them?*

My shoulders dropped. "Look, I appreciate the help you gave us last time, but I don't need sex advice—"

"Sir, this is not *sex advice*," Ivy emphasized. "This is *therapy*. Ava's mind is all over the place. The woman runs on chaotic energy and always has, but it's to the point of her own detriment. She's suffering, and I hate to see my precious suffer. You've got to find a way to help her focus— on you, on her body. Help her find a set point, and it will ground her to the moment, and she'll be able to hold on to what's slipping through her head. You're very self-controlled, and now you need to teach her the same."

I nearly snorted. "Me? Self-controlled? I pinned you against a wall and nearly choked you out."

"You lost your temper, and I understand why. I forgive you for that,"

Ivy stated. "But in a lot of situations, I've seen you keep calm when the rest of us would've completely gone insane. Ava's floating around right now, not sure what to think or do. She has to be grounded, and it's your job to keep her there. This helped me, and I know it will help you guys."

Oberi ducked under the table and grumbled, *I don't think I'm going to want to hear this.*

I sighed. "All right. What's your idea?"

Ivy leaned in. "Pay attention. Here's what you're going to do…"

🔗

My head was still reeling with information Ivy had given me by the time I left the factory that night. I had a token we'd snuck from one of the stations in my pocket, and I listened intently for the sound of guards around me. I didn't want anyone catching me with it.

"Charlie!" someone called, and I jumped. "Do you have a few minutes?"

I relaxed when I realized it was Kallie. "I'm, uh… actually on my way to check on Ava."

"In that case, can I borrow Oberi?" she asked. "I might've found something, but I need Oberi's trusty nose to help me narrow things down."

You go on ahead, Oberi told me, giving me a playful nudge with his nose. *I don't want to be a part of what you have in mind. Have fun!*

Oberi was teasing me, and I scowled. "Yeah, he's delighted to help," I said flatly. "Just have him back by curfew. He gets ornery when he has to sleep on the floor."

"I will," Kallie promised, before walking off with Oberi.

I headed back toward my dorm, but my hands shook the whole way. I wasn't scared of what Ivy had suggested, but doing this with Ava felt so… new. I wanted to do it right.

When I entered the room, I heard a scratching sound. "Pidge?"

"I'm right here." Her voice came from somewhere near the couch.

"What are you doing?"

"Filing my nails," she said nonchalantly.

I frowned. "You stole another emery board from the craft room. You'll get in trouble if you're caught with it."

"That's why I won't get caught," she replied roughly.

I sighed and sat on the couch. "The last thing I want is to fight. I'm sorry about earlier. I want to make it up to you."

"Oh?" Ava sounded intrigued. "What did you have in mind?"

I reached into my pocket and pulled out the rope I'd snagged from the factory.

Ava gasped, and a gleeful snicker escaped her lips. "Are you serious?"

"If you're open to it," I offered.

"Yes," she answered, almost too quickly. Her mood had shifted quickly, which I figured meant I was on to something. She sounded really excited, and that made *me* excited. My heart fluttered, and my dick hardened.

"We're going to take it slow," I told her. "I want this to feel really good, so if at any time you feel uncomfortable, you let me know."

"We should have a safe word," Ava suggested. Hell, she was practically bouncing out of her chair already.

I smirked, "First, we've got to come up with something you don't normally yell during sex."

Ava laughed. "You mean, *oh god* and *Charlie, harder* aren't good safe words?"

I smiled. "How about we use colors? Green to keep going, yellow to slow down, and red to stop?"

"That's perfect. Now tie me up!"

Ava shoved her hands in my direction, and her enthusiasm enthralled me. My dick was rock hard before I had the rope secure around her wrists. I tied it in the way Ivy had taught me, tight enough to make it fun, but loose enough that she could slip out of it if she wanted.

"Tighter," Ava begged.

I shook my head. "I want you to be able to get out if you need to."

"What if I don't *want* to escape?" she teased.

My stomach flipped, enjoying her enthusiasm. "Then you're going to have to beg."

Ava paused for a beat, before she said, "Green light."

I pulled the rope tighter around her wrists, but I secured it in a loose knot, so that one tug of the rope would undo it completely. When I finished, I took her hands in mine, and I ran my fingers over her nails. The ends were smooth and rounded.

"Your nails turned out beautiful," I told her.

"Thanks. I tried," she said brightly. "But maybe you should check out the rest of me."

I ran my fingers over the backs of her hands. Her skin was really soft, which I loved. I moved up her arms, trailing my fingers across her skin lightly. She shivered under my touch, and I knew she liked it. I went to touch her shoulders, and my breath caught. I expected to feel fabric, but all I felt was skin.

Ava snickered, and I ran my fingers downward, until I felt the swell of her breasts. My fingers grazed her exposed nipples.

"Ava-Marie Wahkin. How long have you been naked?"

She gave a devious laugh. "Since you left for your factory shift. I was wondering how long it'd take you to notice. Was that bad?"

"Not at all," I told her while my hands moved over her bosom. "I rather like—"

"Charlie," she cut me off. "Was I a *bad girl?*"

Oh.

"Yes," I answered with a smirk. "Yes, Ava-Marie. You've been a bad, bad girl."

Ava laughed. "Then you should probably punish me for it."

I was ready and willing to do just that. I helped Ava out of her chair and tossed her over my shoulder, then smacked her ass lightly. She replied with a light moan. I took her to the bedroom and laid her gently on the bed, then guided her hands above her head.

"Don't move," I instructed.

Ava snickered, but she did as she was told. I left her on the bed while I went to our dresser and pulled out the vibrator we hid there. It'd taken some time, but I'd figured out how to fix it after it broke, and now it acted brand-new.

I placed it between her legs, but I didn't slip it inside of her or turn it on. Ava wiggled, anticipating the coming sensation, but I didn't provide it.

"Green light," she begged.

"Not yet. We're taking it slow."

Slow was good. I wanted to ground her in her body, to help her focus. I swirled my hands around, and a small gust of air swept through the room. Ava shivered, and I felt it through our bond. But it came with something else, too. I sensed a slight bit of fear, and I hesitated.

"Is this all right?" I asked.

"Green light," she told me, sounding confident.

I continued teasing her with Air magic, and that fear seemed to melt away. Ava made a small noise, and I asked, "How does that feel?"

"It tickles," she said.

I flicked my wrist, and the air shifted course, flowing through her hair. I could tell the ends of the strands were tickling her skin, because she laughed.

"Keep quiet, pidge," I whispered. "The guards will hear you."

It wasn't true. These walls were thick, and the guards had never bothered us before. But Ava liked it when I gave her orders. I could feel the thrill travel through our connection. Ava snapped her mouth shut, and she didn't make another sound.

This was a trick Ivy had suggested. The more trust we established, the more I'd be able to feel her thoughts through our bond. I didn't need to hear her moan to know how she felt. It was a test of our bond, for sure.

I continued tickling her with my Air magic, sending tiny sensations up and down her belly and over her breasts. Fabric rustled as Ava wiggled on the bed, but she didn't let a sound escape her lips.

I stripped my shirt off, then climbed onto the bed beside her. I hovered my hands over her skin, but I didn't touch her. Tiny whirlwinds of Air wisped out of the ends of my fingers, targeting sensitive areas of skin. I swirled my fingers around her nipple, and she moaned.

I stopped what I was doing and pressed an index finger to her lips. "Hush, pidgeon. Safe words only."

Ava pressed her lips together.

I was supposed to give her commands. That's what Ivy had said. I didn't know if I liked it yet. It was a weird dynamic, telling Ava what to do— and she actually *liked* it. That never happened.

Then, after I'd thought about it for a while, I'd figured it out. Ava actually preferred it when I gave her direction. Her thoughts were so chaotic and scattered that she had trouble maintaining control of them, and control of herself. She didn't have any sense of direction, and that chaos wore her out. It was easier for her, sometimes, for someone else to make decisions. This was supposed to help with that.

"Stay here," I told her, even though there was nowhere for her to go. It was all part of the game.

Ava nodded obediently, and I pulled my finger away from her mouth and got out of bed. I went to the other room, where we kept our water bottles, then returned to the bedroom.

I sat beside her and leaned down to kiss the side of her neck. "Every time you make a sound, I'm going to stop," I warned.

"Yes," Ava whispered, and I immediately pulled my lips away from her. I was teasing her— testing her. She didn't say anything again, and after a few beats, I kissed her again.

"I'm going to draw magic from you," I told her. "Offer me a piece of your magic, and I'll reward you."

I felt our bond open wider immediately. Ava was intrigued.

I uncapped the water bottle and poured a few drops into my hand. Using Ava's Toaqua magic, I turned the water to ice, then pressed the small cube between Ava's breasts. Her chest lifted, but she didn't make a sound. A thrill traveled through my heart, and I almost felt the cold sensation on my own chest. The bond was getting stronger.

I moved the ice cube over her skin, swirling it around her nipples, then dipping it down to her belly button. The cube melted on her warm skin, until it disappeared completely.

"Eyes on me," I told her as I created another ice cube, larger this time.

Ava didn't say anything, but I felt confusion cross the bond, like she was trying to ask a question.

"How can I tell?" I asked. "I know you— the way you close your eyes and tilt your head back when you're enjoying yourself. But I want you to focus. Don't look away for a second."

Okay, Ava agreed through the bond.

"Ava," I warned.

Hey, you said I couldn't make a sound. You said nothing about talking to you through our bond. Technically, not a sound.

"That's a tell-tale sign of a bad girl. You know your way around the rules."

And I pride myself in it, she replied.

"Not another word," I warned.

Ava didn't say a thing. She didn't want me to stop. I placed a large ice cube on her belly, then ran it over her skin, until she was trembling under my touch. I could feel the tingles of pleasure coming through our connection. When I was satisfied that she was grounded in the moment, I guided the ice cube downward, over her most sensitive areas. She must've been able to feel something, because my heart fluttered to mimic hers.

I placed the ice cube in my mouth for a few moments, and she shivered beneath me. Slowly, I lowered my mouth between her legs and slipped the ice cube inside of her with my tongue. She gasped. I drew away, because I'd told her I'd stop if she made a sound.

"How does that feel?" I asked Ava.

She sent a tiny jolt of energy through our bond. She was careful not to cry out. I figured that meant she could feel the ice cube and liked it. I was curious, so I slipped my fingers inside of her. She was warm and silky— warmer than she should have been, because of her Fire. I felt around for the ice cube, but it was already gone. She was really wet— and not just from the water. My fingers slid in and out of her effortlessly. It drove me mad, and I wanted to be deep inside of her already. I forced myself to resist.

Instead, I turned on the vibrator to its lowest setting and slid it inside of her. I felt her move on the bed.

"Keep your eyes on me, pidge," I reminded her.

A warm, happy sensation filled our bond. She was enjoying every second of this.

I turned up the vibrator. "Don't come until I tell you. Understand?"

Yes, she said through the bond.

I left the vibrator between her legs, then stood and undid my pants. I could *feel* her eyes on me as I undressed. She was practically catcalling me through the bond. At least, that's what it felt like. It made me feel wanted.

I climbed onto the bed and knelt between her legs. I began working the vibrator, slowly guiding it in and out of her. She seemed to melt into the bed, enjoying the slow, tender sensations. I didn't expect her peak to come so soon, and the moment I felt it growing through our bond, I pulled the vibrator out of her. The high settled, and she hadn't quite reached the edge.

Green light, she begged in my mind.

"Not until I tell you," I reminded her.

I ran my fingers over her clit, then slid my fingers inside of her again. I didn't need our bond to know how much she wanted me. Hell, I didn't know how much longer I could hold out. She was so damn sexy, and every moment I spent teasing her intensified our connection.

I gave her a few moments to recover from the high before slipping the vibrator back inside of her. It took a while for the sensations to build up again, but I could tell she was enjoying every second of it. As she built up to her peak a second time, I withdrew the vibrator again.

Green light! she cried through the bond.

I didn't satisfy her wanting need.

One more time, I turned up the speed, and I slid the vibrator inside of her. This time, she reached her peak much sooner. As her desire began to build, I could feel her holding back, waiting for my instructions.

Neither of us could hold out any longer. "Come," I ordered.

She reached her peak, and my eyes rolled back as a glorious sensation burst through our bond. Ava finally allowed sound to escape her lips, and she moaned loudly, unable to contain herself. I tossed the vibrator aside on the bed, then grabbed a pillow. In a swift motion, I turned her over and slipped the pillow beneath her hips. The pillow helped prop her hips up so I could slide my cock into her from behind. Our sweaty bodies collided as I bent over her, and her ass felt perfect against me. Passionately, I pinned her tied hands to the bed, then tangled my other hand in her hair and tugged. Ava gasped as I held her down and yanked on her hair with every thrust, and as my thoughts tangled around hers, her mind finally went blank, concentrating on nothing but how amazing this made her feel. I was caught up in it, too, centered around thoughts that this was my pidge and she needed the control I gave her. She contracted around me as I fucked her, and I met my peak moments later.

The floor might as well have fallen out from beneath us, because it felt like we were floating high above the Institute. Hell, I forgot we were at the Institute at all, because at that moment, all that seemed to exist was *her*.

I collapsed onto the bed beside her. It took several minutes before my head finally stopped spinning. Ava nudged me through our bond, bringing me back to the present moment. I'd nearly forgotten she was still tied up.

I propped myself up on my elbow and took her hands in mine. "Yes, you can talk now," I told her.

"I don't know if I have the words," she gasped. "That took my breath away."

I tugged at her rope, and it untied effortlessly. I set the rope aside, next to the vibrator. After cleaning up, I grabbed a bottle of lotion, then returned to the bed and began massaging it into her wrists, where she'd been tied up.

Damn, it felt good to be so close to her, and after what we'd just done... it was heaven.

"Mm..." Ava sighed deeply as she snuggled into me.

"Is that something you want to do again?" I asked.

Ava laughed. "Notice how I never told you to slow down."

I stiffened a little. "Why not?" I wondered. "I felt something there at the beginning. You seemed... scared."

"It wasn't you," she said. "It was an intrusive thought. But you helped me forget about it."

My shoulders relaxed. I wanted to ask what had scared her, but I didn't want to prod. I'd promised her I wouldn't, and I was going to keep that promise.

"I'm glad I could help," I whispered, before kissing her shoulder.

Ava seemed to melt into the mattress. After several long beats, she spoke up. "It was about John."

My stomach knotted, and rage ignited in my belly. I *never* wanted to hear that name. To think that he'd permeated her thoughts when *I* was making love to her made me want to tear down this prison and go after him. I hated that the memories of what he'd done to her would never go away, and that there was nothing I could do to make those nightmares stop.

"It's not what you're thinking," Ava said. "I know I'm safe with you. It's something else... John was caught. He's going on trial, and I want to testify."

Forget about tearing down the Institute. I'd bury this whole damn island to get to that motherfucker. I was going to be a supernatural bounty hunter one day, and I'd make damn sure he was the first person I hunted. If he went to prison, I'd never get to make him pay.

"I know you probably don't want me to, because I'd have to face him again," Ava started.

My first response was blinding rage, but the last thing I wanted to do was deprive Ava of the chance to stand up to him. This wasn't about me. I needed to calm down and ask what she wanted.

"I don't think that," I told her.

"You can be honest with me," she said softly. "I can feel your anger."

"I'm angry at *him*, not you," I assured her. "I want you to do whatever feels right. If that means staying here and never entering the courtroom, then I'm here for you, and I'll make sure you'll never have to face him again. If that means getting on that stand and telling your story, I'm here for that, too."

"I don't know what I want to do, Charlie," she whispered. "Both options terrify me. I felt so much shame when it happened that I never came forward. Now I feel guilty that I didn't turn him in, because he went after other girls."

"That's not your fault," I insisted. It broke my heart that she could feel guilty for what *he* did.

"I know," Ava said. "John's the only one to blame for his actions, but I can't help but think those girls would be in a better place if I'd come forward. Now I have the chance to put him behind bars, but to do that, I have to live through all that shame again. I have to face him. And I'm not sure I'm ready for it, or if I'll ever be."

I smoothed her hair down. "Whatever you decide will be the right decision. I know it. And I'll be here for you every step of the way."

She squeezed my hand. "Thanks. I don't know what my choice is going to be. But if I'm going to do this, I'm going to need to be really brave... braver than I ever have been."

"You're the bravest person I know. It's completely up to you if you want to pursue this or not."

I hesitated before I added, "I was surprised you were so ready to jump into this, after what happened."

I didn't say it out loud, but I figured Ava would *never* want to be tied up or held down, especially not in a situation that resembled anything sexual.

"It's not the same," she said immediately. "When you've got me bound and I can't move, it feels safe... like I'm being embraced instead of trapped. I know I'm in a place where someone else is considering what my needs are one hundred percent. That's nothing like what happened to me."

"I didn't know if this was going to be something you liked. You hate being told what to do."

"Yes and no. When you give me instructions like you just did, it shuts the voices out and makes them stop. I *have* to be in the moment, because there's no other choice. It makes my thoughts go still. My whole life, it's always felt like my brain doesn't belong to me. It's just some monster that runs rampant and ruins my life."

"Well, you did beautifully."

"I like being submissive. I don't have to be in control."

I wasn't sure I was getting her point. "Can you explain it a little better?"

She nestled in closer to me. "I know on the outside, it appears like I'm a hurricane, destroying everything in my path. But you have no idea how much work it takes to keep that hurricane a small storm, and not a total calamity. I have to be in control of my life *all the time*. My thoughts, feelings, actions, every second of my day has to be monitored to keep me from spinning out. It's gotten so much worse since I've been in a wheelchair, because now my body has to be monitored, too. I just can't take it anymore. Sometimes I want to turn it all off, like a switch, but it's always stuck to *on*. Then you came in here with that rope, and everything seemed to center into one moment. I didn't have to think about the rest of my life. It went away."

Ava squeezed my sides tighter. "Anyway, how'd you get the idea to do all that?"

"Ivy," I said simply.

"I thought you two weren't talking."

"We're... working it out," I said. "I don't know if I can forgive Ivy for what they did to you, but Ivy really does care about us, and our relationship. Not to mention their advice was completely on-point."

Ava giggled just as a frantic knock came at our door. I startled, and

Ava asked, "Is some stupid guard here to tell us there's rules against sex now?"

"Told you that you screamed too loud," I teased, and Ava snickered.

I scrambled out of bed to throw some pants on. I wasn't sure who was bothering us, but I wanted them to go away.

"What's going on?" I demanded when I opened the door.

"Gods above, Charlie, put a shirt on," Kallie sneered, and I heard Marcus laugh beside her. "I found a clue."

I frowned. Ava and I had been sharing a *moment*.

Your moment's over, Oberi said snidely. *Come look what we found!*

I sighed. "It's almost curfew. If we leave, we'll be locked out of our rooms overnight."

"Then I guess we're pulling an all-nighter," Kallie said. "You guys aren't going to want to wait to see this."

ava-marie

TWELVE

Excitement rushed through me as Kallie and Oberi led the way to what she'd described as a hidden cell block. My mind and body were still rushing with the delightful, delicious sensations of my rendezvous with Charlie moments before, but we had to put that aside for now, because we could be that much closer to the merfolk key, and that was thrilling all in itself.

It was past curfew, so we had to be quick. The darkened Institute halls loomed, and with every inch closer to our destination, they felt taller, as if the very walls were going to come crashing in on us. The wind howled outside, battering at the windows as a heavy rain began to fall. I glimpsed through the glass and saw that a gloomy mist was starting to spread over the island.

"Wait," Marcus whispered ahead of us, and Charlie brought my chair to a halt. He peered around the corner, then flattened himself to the stone wall as footsteps approached and light loomed from magic in the corridor beyond.

Guards. They were coming this way. Kallie let out an aggravated noise, but Rishi darted between her legs and ran forward. He turned the corner, padding down to where a couple of classrooms lay in waiting.

I heard a loud crashing noise as what sounded like a shelf of alchemy pots toppled to the floor. The guards immediately started running the opposite way to investigate the noise. Marcus checked again, then waved us forward as Rishi came scampering back.

We returned to the hallway we'd been investigating earlier. We seemed to walk forever, and the further we went, the darker it got. Eventually, the entire area turned cold. My hands tightened on the handles of my wheelchair as the blackness seemed to swallow us up. In this part of the prison, I could hear my heartbeat pounding in my ears. We had Marcus' witch light to illuminate the area, but the small light it gave off felt like dropping a pin into the ocean.

"I never realized just how big this place is." Charlie's words echoed off the walls, and I shivered.

"The Institute is massive," Kallie replied.

We came to a stone wall. Kallie tapped on it and said, "Solid as a rock... or so you think. There's an illusion here."

"How'd you find this, Oberi?" I asked, patting his head.

Illusions smell funny. They're not quite right, Oberi explained. *Once I pointed out the smell to Kallie, she caught on right away.*

"Oberi kept pawing at this one spot, so I changed into a wolf and started sniffing around. Once I did, I realized the Warden must've had someone put an illusion up," Kallie said. "It was strong enough it didn't leave any signatures behind, so my fae magic didn't recognize it. But now that I know it's there, I can bring it down."

Kallie ran her fingers over the stone, and as she did so, a rippling effect took place, and the wall wavered like water. I watched as the bricks dissolved, leaving a plain metal door in our way.

Marcus reached for the doorknob, and it opened easily. "It's unlocked."

We took a small, narrow passageway that was shaped like a U, one that was difficult for me to navigate. Once we'd shoved my chair through, Marcus opened another door. As I rolled through, an entirely new area of the prison opened up.

The room was large and square, with a variety of wooden benches attached firmly to long tables. The tables were chained to the floor, and a few feet away from the walls was a line of chain-link fencing, with the same fencing running above us about twelve feet from the ground in order to prevent inmates from reaching the low ceiling. Above the area were guard boxes with bulletproof glass, and broken windows along the double bars. It was a miniature cafeteria.

This definitely had more security than any part of the prison that I'd seen. I got the creepiest feeling... like we were being watched. And not just by one being, but a whole entourage, who were just waiting on the sidelines for an opportunity to strike.

Beyond the cafeteria was another door. We went through it and came to a massive cell block that was unlike any of the others I'd seen at the Institute. The area was four stories tall, and hundreds of cells lined each row. These cells weren't like our rooms— they had nothing but bars for doors, and two tiny metal bunks attached to the wall for people to sleep on. The cells were insanely small, only five-by-seven feet, and weren't humane to hold one prisoner, let alone multiple.

It was easy to hide this cell block within the interior of the Institute, because it was so narrow. The paint on the walls was peeling away, and I read obscene things the prisoners here had written on the walls. Some were pleas to escape; others, prayers for death, or promises of revenge once the author escaped. I rolled over a puddle on the floor that had accumulated from moisture dripping through the cracked ceiling, and I spotted blood stains mixed in with the fading concrete. I knew it wasn't that cold out today, but even so, I could see my breath in here.

"Kallie... where are we?" I asked.

"This is where they kept the worst of the inmates, when the Institute was still an adult penitentiary," she explained. "The people who came here never got out."

"You're saying this is death row?" Charlie stopped.

"It is," Kallie said. "The prisoners that were kept here were scheduled for execution."

I swallowed a lump in my throat and wrapped my arms around my torso. "Can you imagine how many ghosts must be in here? This place has gotta be haunted as fuck."

"Oh, they're watching us," Marcus promised. "I can feel it."

"Well, maybe we should leave." I frowned.

"Fuck that! I'm gonna go inside and punch those motherfucking ghosts out!" Marcus shook a fist, and from two rows up, I heard a cell door slam shut of its own accord.

Marcus let out a tiny whimper. "On second thought, maybe we should reconsider—"

"We can't leave until we find Amalie's clue," Kallie said. "Come on. We've got all night in here."

Don't fucking remind me. I lit a small fire in my hand, and Kallie cast a glowing illusion to provide her own light. We began poking our heads into the cells, looking around for anything we could find.

"We should stick together," Charlie said as he pushed my chair behind Kallie and Marcus. "If there are ghosts in here, they're the spirits of the prisoners who were executed on death row, and we can bet they weren't nice people."

Stay close to me, Ava, Oberi beckoned, and he put his nose to the floor. We moved slowly, cell by cell. Each cell was identical, save for whatever was written on the walls, and I couldn't help but wonder what Amalie wanted us to find down here.

I heard a wayward moan. "Do we know how these people died?"

"Some by hanging, a couple by electrocution," Kallie informed me. "Although these were supernatural criminals, so a lot of the executions were carried out in group fashion, a fatal blow dealt by every race."

"Professor Mazur told me something similar, a long time ago," Charlie noted.

"She probably made it sound a lot better than it actually was. If every supernatural race had to take part in your death, they'd purposely keep you alive and draw it out so everyone could get a hit in." Kallie shook her head. "I was looking into records... there was an inmate here who was scheduled for execution. Almost every race went to do their part to end the prisoner's life, but when they got to the last executioner, he didn't have the stomach to finish the job. So they threw the inmate back in a cell and left them there to suffer, fatal injuries and all, until they found someone who was willing to put a stop to it."

"That's just sick," I spat. "It's no way for anyone to die."

"Death might've been better than how they were living here. They shoved three people into a cell at a time and made one of them sleep on the floor," Kallie said. "Then the guards would shove food into the cell and make the inmates fight over it. You'd get an hour a day to shower and walk around in the highly guarded area of the prison yard meant for death row inmates—"

"Which is where the basketball court is now," Marcus added.

"After that, you'd get shoved back in your cell with no room to move or breathe for the rest of the time. It was a brutal way to live," Kallie informed us.

"Honestly, if you made it to your execution day, you were considered the baddest of the bad," Marcus said. "A lot of the criminals that ended up on death row were stabbed to death or strangled by the other inmates in their own cell. Of course, that was with the weaker supernaturals. Stronger ones would just tear you apart, and let the guards take out your dismembered limbs."

"How do you know all this?" Charlie asked.

"Kallie and I have been doing research on old areas of the prison since we started looking for the Infernal Underground," Marcus replied. "There's a lot of history to the Institute they don't tell you about, but it's all in the library, if you bother to look. Back then, we figured death row didn't exist anymore, and why wouldn't we assume that? The wards guarding the place kept it hidden well."

"I can't believe they caged people like this," I said. "It's way worse than they treat us."

"It's one of the reasons the prison was shut down and turned into a juvenile detention center." Kallie stopped before a cell block and peered in. "I thought the Warden wanted to hide death row because he wanted to bury the history that's concealed here, but truth be told, I think he knows there might be a key here and he doesn't want anyone else to know."

"Well, he already has the first clue to the merfolk key, so we have to beat him to this one," I grumbled.

We continued searching cell after cell. I wasn't able to navigate the balcony on the cell rows above us, because they were too small for my wheelchair, so Charlie, Oberi and I remained on the ground floor while Kallie and Marcus continued poking around above us.

"You can feel the bad energy in this place," Charlie said, shaking his shoulders. "The whole atmosphere is just so... heavy."

I agreed. The memories of the inmates who had suffered here permeated every pore and surface of the cell block. I just wanted to find our next clue, so we could shake it off and be rid of it.

"Can your Earth magic feel anything in the metal or stone?" I asked, glancing at Charlie.

He knelt to the floor and spread his hand across the concrete. There was a slight quake underneath me as the ground shifted at his power, and a bit of dust fell from the ceiling. Oberi sneezed when it fell on his head.

"I don't think there's anything in these cells. But there's another room, straight across from where we are, at the end of the cell block," Charlie said.

I looked down that way, but it was too dark to see a door, or anything that was at the end of the hall. "We should search that next."

Out of the corner of my eye, I saw a tall, lone figure standing at the end of the cell block. I couldn't make out any details, just a black shape resembling the figure of a man. I shot a fireball at the ghostly specter, and the figure darted into a cell and out of view.

"What's going on?" Charlie's voice was on edge as he heard my Fire rush by.

"Oh, nothing, just a creepy shadow man that ran away once I turned a fireball on him."

"That's comforting." Charlie turned his face upward. "Hey, you two, hurry up!"

"We're coming down now!" Kallie's voice echoed from four flights up. I heard their heavy footsteps on the metal stairs, until Kallie gave a loud scream, and Marcus gasped. I looked up sharply, and my stomach plummeted as I saw Marcus tumble off the edge of the railing on the third floor and toward the ground. I didn't know where Kallie had gone.

"Charlie—" I yelped, but he'd already sensed something was wrong. He lifted his hands to cast his Air magic, and he was able to catch Marcus in a gust of wind just before our friend hit the ground. Marcus was thrown slightly into the wall, but not hard. He rolled a few feet as Kallie rushed down the stairs, Rishi giving loud mewls behind her.

"Marcus, are you okay?" Kallie asked. Her words stuttered as she helped Marcus to his feet.

"I'm all right," Marcus panted, though he coughed a few times. "Shit, that was scary."

"Why didn't you levitate yourself using telepathy?" I asked. "From that height, you could've died."

"I panicked. I didn't realize I was falling until I'd almost hit the ground." Marcus' face was stark white as he said, "Something shoved me off. I felt someone's hands on my back before I went over."

"Good thing we managed to catch you," Kallie said, rubbing his back. "I would've saved you myself if I hadn't been thrown into a cell."

"Thrown?" I raised an eyebrow.

"Something tossed me. That's when I screamed. I felt someone pick me up and throw me, but when I landed on the ground, nobody was there," Kallie replied.

"It was somebody, all right. You just couldn't see them," Marcus said darkly.

Fear froze my senses. I felt pinpricks of terror creeping over my skin, making my pulse race. Every instinct I had told me I needed to get the hell out of here as fast as I could. This was *not* a place where we should be fucking around.

"We need to get a move on," Charlie said, and he put his hands on the back of my chair. "The activity's picking up, and the spirits are getting more malevolent. Ava thinks we found another room we can search."

"Let's hope it gives us more info than this place did. The whole cell block is a bust," Kallie grumbled, casting wary glances over her shoulder.

I dared to look behind myself, and I wished I hadn't. The shadow man was following us. He remained at a distance, and though I couldn't make out any facial features, I was certain he was staring at us. Whoever he was— or whoever he had *been*— he wanted us to know that this was his area and that he wanted us to *leave*. Immediately.

Once we went through the next door, I gained a noted sense of relief, and my shoulders felt lighter. I didn't think the shadow man had followed us here.

We took another U-shaped hallway, one that led to a smaller area that looked like an office space. There were a variety of desks in here, along with plenty of file cabinets. When I checked the dates of the papers pinned to billboards on the walls, I noted that the earliest was December 31, 1949. This room had been frozen in time since that day, untouched for decades. The employees had literally gathered their things and walked out, abandoning the rest to time.

I noticed there wasn't a way out through here. The only doorway to this office was connected to the death row cell block. Which meant we'd have to go back through it to leave.

"This was definitely used for the staff," Kallie noted as she looked around. "Probably the people who set execution dates."

"It's a records room," I said.

"Yeah, but what are we looking for? Amalie never came to the adult penitentiary. I know from my vision that once she was captured, she was taken back to Malovia and executed," Kallie stated.

"Maybe someone she knew was here," I said. "She had an ally who helped her steal the merfolk key, a diplomat from Atlantis. What if they ended up behind these walls?"

"It's possible," Kallie said with a shrug. "Amalie was beheaded for treason in Malovia, but her ally could've been sentenced here."

"We don't even know this person's name," Marcus objected.

"Doesn't matter. If her ally was executed here, the crime will be listed in the records, and something will stick out," Charlie said. "We might as well start looking through them."

This was an area of expertise I was good at. I opened a cabinet and started pulling out files, searching through the information. Kallie and Marcus helped me, starting in on different sides of the room. Charlie had brought his glasses, and used them to read some of the shorter files aloud.

Charlie remained close as I went through the files, though he kept jumping, as if he was hearing things. Oberi pulled files out and laid them on my lap for me to look at, but I tossed each one on the floor after scanning them quickly. Out of all the gruesome deaths and horrible crimes noted, none of these prisoners fit the bill.

"Where'd they put all these people?" Marcus asked. "They killed a lot of prisoners on this property. Did they just throw them in the lake or what?"

"By these files, the guards buried them everywhere in unmarked graves," Kallie replied. "There wasn't a set cemetery or burial ground to put them in, so wherever they landed is where they were buried."

"Makes sense. The guards take the kids who die in fight club and toss them in the woods in shallow graves, or into the siren lake if they're feeling particularly gruesome," Charlie said. "I'm not surprised they didn't care about these inmates, either."

A couple of hours passed in relative silence, with nothing but the robotic sound of Charlie's glasses reading files. It was nearly five-thirty in the morning when Kallie let out an irritated huff and kicked over an empty file cabinet with her boot. A shiver raced from the top of my head and over my shoulders as I heard loud, chilling laughter echo from the cell block beside the office.

"Would you quiet down? You're gonna piss them off," Marcus hissed at her.

"Where's big, bad Marcus, looking to *punch out these motherfucking ghosts?*" she snapped. "You sure lost your courage quick."

"Kallie, we have to focus," I told her. "We'll never find what we're looking for if you're too busy throwing a tantrum."

"There are thousands of records here. It could take us another night to come back and look through them all!" Kallie yelled.

"If that's what we have to do, then so be it," Charlie said. "We can't let the Warden get farther ahead of us than he already is."

I was *not* coming back here another night. We were getting this information now, even if it took until morning.

What about this one? Oberi pawed at the bottom of a cabinet, trying to get at a file that was underneath it. Someone must've dropped it and kicked it underneath the cabinet by accident.

Kallie noticed Oberi whacking the cabinet, and she moved to pick it up. Oberi grabbed the dusty file, then plopped it in my lap before giving a cough. *It's pretty heavy.*

I opened the folder and read the name on the first page aloud. "Dante Winselt. Race, merfolk. Sentenced August 18, 1869 for high treason. Execution, April 3, 1873."

"August 1869 was the same timeframe that Amalie was arrested," Kallie noted.

I eyed a picture clipped to the page, an aged, black and white photograph that was nearly two-hundred years old by this point. It showed the mugshot of a merman with a mess of wild curls and a scrawny frame.

He looked... absolutely terrified. I felt awful for this individual, though I wasn't quite sure what he'd done.

"Is there more?" Charlie asked.

I scanned the next few paragraphs. "It says he was sentenced for stealing an item of importance from the Atlantean government with an accomplice, and fled with the object to an unknown location. He was apprehended after a long chase across the ocean. The accomplice isn't listed."

"That could be Amalie," Marcus reasoned.

"Maybe. There's nothing else that describes the crime," I said as I began flipping through pages. "Just records of his time spent here at the prison, and... oh. Graphic details of his execution."

"What happened to him?" Kallie rasped.

"It was a supernatural execution," I said grimly. "Each race took a turn... the last person to torture him was a witch. They used telepathy magic to hover him in the air, before dropping him from four stories high. The first drop didn't finish him off, so they had to do it again."

"That's barbaric," Marcus croaked as his face turned green.

Kallie walked over to me. As she looked over my shoulder at the photograph, her eyes narrowed. Then they glossed over completely and took on a pearly sheen. Her body began to shake, like it had when she'd experienced the ancestral memory meditation. She quivered so hard that she slammed into one of the cabinets and knocked it over, though she didn't wake from whatever vision was holding her now.

"What's wrong?" Charlie demanded.

"Kallie's gone into some sort of trance." I was starting to panic, wondering if one of the ghosts around here had possessed her body.

"Kallie?" Marcus hastily crossed the room and shook her shoulders. "Come on, snap out of it!"

At his touch, her tremors ended, and she began to stir. As Kallie came out of the trance, she shook her head slowly.

"You okay?" I asked.

"I remember this face..." Kallie murmured as she clutched the photo-graph. "It was in a memory."

"What, one of Amalie's?" Charlie asked.

"No," Kallie said, and her features lightened with clarification. "From *mine*. I was Amalie. It's all so clear now... she was one of my past lives."

The revelation was huge. A weight dropped into my stomach as I asked, "Are you sure?"

"Yes. I can't believe it. But I'm certain that I was her. No wonder I was able to access her memories so easily... she's me."

Kallie put a hand on the wall to steady herself. "It's flowing through me now... I remember being an assassin and working for the crown. And I remember aligning myself with Dante in order to get the key out of Atlantis."

She shook her head, appearing sorrowful. "He put so much on the line. His whole life was at risk. His title, his position on the council... but he wanted to help me, because... he loved me. And he paid the ultimate price for it."

"Let me see that photograph," Marcus asked, and he reached out for it. Kallie placed it into his hands, and he looked at the photo of Dante.

Once his eyes connected with the photograph, Marcus let out a strangled gasp. His eyes gave that pearly sheen Kallie's had, and he launched into a worse set of seizures. He toppled backwards onto the floor, rolling around as his body launched into convulsions.

"Marcus!" Kallie screamed. She dropped to her knees to shake him, but he didn't come out of whatever trance held him captive.

Rishi hissed loudly and bit his leg. Marcus gave a strangled yell as he sat upright, glancing around like he'd been suddenly woken from a bad dream. When his eyes landed on the photograph again, he let out a shrill scream. Outside, the menacing laughter of the ghosts grew louder.

"Fucking hell, Marcus, it's not going to bite you," I said crossly.

"It's not that!" he yelped. "That Dante guy... I was him!"

"What?" Charlie asked. He sounded both astounded and skeptical.

"I know it sounds like I'm making it up, and usually, I would think I did, because I don't trust my powers. But that vision was so intense," Marcus blurted.

"Of course," Kallie breathed. She tilted her head and moved toward Marcus slowly, as if seeing him in a new light. "It *is* you. I recognize it now. You both look so different, but I'm sure you were once Dante."

"And I *know* you were Amalie," Marcus stuttered. "The resemblance... it's uncanny."

"This is crazy," Charlie stated. "You can't *both* be Amalie and Dante. It's too ridiculous."

"It isn't that unbelievable," I argued. "Hemlock told us about past lives, how they're all connected. What if the four of us have been going through the centuries, searching for keys and attempting to put them in the right places for our future selves to find right now?"

"Oh, gods, Marcus, *that's* why the one ghost tried pushing you off the balcony earlier," Kallie exclaimed. "They knew who you were, and were trying to recreate your death for some laughs."

"These are some sick fucks around here," Charlie mumbled.

"You can't talk me out of it. I know that I was Dante, because I remember dying here," Marcus said, and he shuddered. "My death was *so* painful. But I considered it a relief, in the end. I couldn't really protect myself. The other inmates picked on me constantly. Now it makes sense why I beat up one of Mad Dog's guys on my first day here. It was so unlike me, but somehow I just *knew* what prison life was like. I knew I had to win my first fight so they wouldn't mess with me. I told Charlie to do the same thing the day he got here. It must've been some sort of residual memory from my past life."

"Do you guys know where you hid the merfolk key?" I pressed.

"I remember that we got the key, but the time between us leaving Atlantis with it and us getting caught is foggy," Kallie said.

"I don't remember how we fled Atlantis, either, or how we got arrested. That part's still a blank," Marcus noted.

Kallie wound a lock of hair around her finger as she thought. "I think that I gave the key to Dante. They were looking for me primarily, not him, and I figured if we didn't manage to escape, he'd have a better shot of keeping it safe."

"I had the key on me. I was the last person to have contact with it," Marcus said, and he bent down to pick up the file.

"Do you think the authorities who apprehended you took the key after you were caught?" I asked.

"No." Marcus shook his head furiously. "I'm certain that key is safe. The recollections are... sporadic... but I... I remember walking to my execution knowing the only comfort I had was that no one was ever going to be able to find that key."

"Dante must've kept the key on him. He hid it somehow while he was living on death row, and took it with him to his grave," I said in excitement. "It could be buried with Dante's body!"

"And if Dante's remains are in an unmarked grave on Institute property, the key is still here," Kallie added. "If we find his grave, we'll find the key!"

"Finally, we're making some progress," Marcus said in satisfaction. He subconjured Dante's file for us to look at later.

"We should get out of here, so we can start searching the grounds for the grave." I spun my chair around, looking forward to leaving.

"We have to return to death row if we're going to get to the exit. There's no way out through here," Marcus said.

I would rather bathe myself in acid than roam back through those cells again, but there was no other method of escape. We left the office behind and entered back into death row. This time, the feeling permeating the air was even worse. Dread settled into my bones and grew more intense the further we got into the cell block.

Oberi's fur stood on end as he stopped once we got to the middle of the room. He lifted his lips in a snarl and began to emit a harsh growl.

Get back, he told us, planting himself in front of Charlie and me.

I grabbed Charlie's arm as something materialized twelve feet away. The shadow man. He stood completely still, waiting for us to approach. He knew we'd have to walk past him if we wanted to get to the door.

"He wants us to talk to him," Marcus said. "He asked me to use my magic to make it so you guys could hear him, too."

"Fuck him. Let's just go," I hissed.

"*What are you here for?*" a rasping, chilling voice asked. The shadow man hadn't moved an inch, but I knew that voice came from him.

"I didn't do that," Marcus said, and his words held an edge of terror.

I gripped Charlie's arm tighter and tried not to scream. For this ghost to be able to vocalize what he wanted without the aid of Marcus' magic meant that he was one strong motherfucker.

"*It's been so long since someone's been down here,*" the shadow man said. "*Why not stay awhile?*"

"We don't belong here. We have to leave, and you can't come with us," Marcus replied.

"*You do belong here. I know who you are. You killed eleven people. I did the same, once. Though I picked them off one by one.*"

"It was an accident. I didn't mean to do it," Marcus said. His voice dropped low, to give the ghost a warning.

"*Doesn't matter. They're still dead. You must feel so much regret for what you've done.*"

Marcus swallowed as he asked, "Do you regret what you did?"

"I only regret getting caught."

The shadow man proceeded toward us, one step at a time. My skin began to crawl, and I tried to tell him to leave us alone, but my words didn't come out of my throat.

Marcus immediately conjured cedar and a lighter. He lit the cedar and took a breath to recite the incantation to scare the ghost off, but the shadow man only laughed.

"That won't help you now."

Marcus gave a gasp as the cedar and lighter flew out of his hand in different directions. The cedar went spinning down the hall toward the office, landing in a puddle and fizzling out. The lighter traveled toward the shadow man, who caught it in his palm, where it instantly exploded.

All the cell doors in the block— hundreds of them— came slamming shut all at once. The sound rattled my ears and caused panic to race through my blood. At the same time, the temperature in the room turned from freezing cold to boiling hot in seconds. Sweat began rolling down my skin, and Marcus cried, "Run!"

We went to bolt forward past the shadow man, but he raised his hands, and two cell doors opened beside us. Kallie and Marcus were thrown into the cells, and the doors came crashing shut. They wrenched at the bars, but couldn't get free.

"Get out of here!" Marcus yelled as the shadow man approached their cells. "We'll deal with this!"

"It's a straight shot, just run!" I told Charlie as he grabbed the handles of my wheelchair. He pushed me at a dead sprint as we raced to the other side of the cell block. Oberi remained beside me, snapping at the heels of the shadow man, while Rishi darted ahead of my chair. I heard battle orbs explode behind us as Kallie and Marcus attempted to escape the cells.

Moans erupted throughout the cell block as hundreds of ghosts came flooding out of the cells ahead of us, spirits wearing jumpsuits with cruel, hateful grins. They filtered into the hall and surrounded Charlie and me, so we couldn't get to the doors.

"Stop!" I yelped, and Charlie wrenched the chair to a halt. I gasped, putting a hand to my middle as a fresh bout of pain ripped through my abdomen at the abrupt halt.

Once we stopped, the ghosts swarmed in like locusts. They soared over us with devilish cackles, ripping at our clothes and hair. Oberi snarled as the ghosts bit into his pelt and tossed him around the room. Rishi remained in the corner, hissing and swiping at the ghosts, while Charlie cast harsh gusts of wind to throw the floating spirits off course. I summoned a barrage of icicles from the puddles lying around the room, but the icy daggers merely floated through the spirits, not doing any harm.

Charlie let out a cry of pain as a spirit with insanely long claws cut into his back. The claws sliced through his sweater, making him bleed.

That pissed me right off, so I forced my brain to come up with a solution. I'd destroyed the lichen during the Darke Games with my blue Fire, and that monster certainly had more power than the ghostly fucks here.

I gritted my teeth as I used simultension to combine my Fire and Water magic to create the blue flame, then shot it out in an arc around me. The ghosts squealed as the blue fire touched their forms, then raced upward to escape it. A couple more approached, but I shot blue fireballs at their forms, which left holes burning in their sides. They wailed as they drew away, hovering above us in a search for an opening to attack.

Dust billowed throughout the room as an explosion shuddered throughout the cell block. Kallie emerged from the smoke, in her shifter form with Marcus on her back. The shadow man faced him, crouching downward as it gave a horrid noise of rage.

Marcus' whole body shook as he held on tightly to Kallie's fur. He looked *pissed*.

"I order you to be gone. You must go back to the darkness, where you belong," Marcus raged.

"*You cannot leave this place! You will stay with us forever!*" the shadow man bellowed.

"No one stays here forever. Not even you," Marcus seethed. He pointed to the hundreds of ghosts waiting in the rafters above, then to the shadow man, as he uttered, "Destroy him."

Screeching noise, like nails on glass, emitted from the ghosts as they swept downward in a circular, torrential vortex. They went right for the shadow man, using their long nails and broken teeth to rip into his spiritual form. The shadow man gave a wicked bellow and threw off a couple of the ghosts, but was soon smothered by the hundreds of beings that rushed in to hold him down. The shadow man gave one final scream of anguish, before he and all the other ghosts vanished in a spectacular flash of green. All that was left was Marcus, who was still panting, and Kallie, wagging her tail.

Holy shit, Oberi muttered, and I lifted an eyebrow. Holy shit, indeed.

"What'd you do to him?" Charlie asked as Kallie padded toward us.

"I made the other ghosts drag him off to the Abyss, because he refused to go," Marcus said darkly. "Death row should be a lot less haunted, after tonight."

"I've never seen someone who was able to control ghosts like that," Kallie said. *"I didn't even think it was possible."*

"That's right. Marcus, you *commanded* those ghosts to do what you told them to," I marveled. "They didn't have a choice but to listen."

"I don't know how I did that. I just felt like I should, and I didn't question it this time, like I have in the past," Marcus stated.

"Well, you should try practicing that during our next demigod lesson, because it'd be helpful if you could do it whenever you like," Charlie noted.

"If I'm a demigod, I have to start using my power," Marcus said. "I'm sick of being scared and pushed around. I remembered him— that shadow guy— from my time here as Dante. He tormented me until the day he died, then he came back as a ghost to torment me until the day that I did. After all these years, I figured it was time to repay the fucking favor."

Charlie let out a noise of discomfort, and I patted his side. "Turn around. Let me see your back."

He pulled off his soaked sweater, and the movement made a slick sound echo throughout the chamber. He knelt beside me, and I winced as I surveyed the damage. Three large, bloody gashes stretched across his back, several inches deep. He'd need stitches if I didn't fix them right away.

I moved my fingers over the gashes, whispering a song. I watched as the cuts healed up, good as new, and Charlie rolled his shoulders as the blood dried on his skin. "Feels much better, thank you. Are the rest of you okay?"

"The ghosts didn't hurt us," Kallie said as Rishi gave a meow, then jumped to land in Marcus' arms. *"Just gave us a fright."*

"Those were much stronger than your average ghosts," I noted.

"They've had a lot of time to grow in power here, feeding off the misery of the other inmates," Marcus said. "But they won't be a problem anymore."

"And we got what we came here for," Kallie sang. *"Let's go looking for Dante's grave right now!"*

"We should start later," I said. "I know we're close, but we need time to rest, after all of that."

"But it's six o'clock. Curfew is over!" Kallie objected.

"We'll go on ahead," Marcus said, touching Kallie's shoulder. "Ava needs some time to rest."

Kallie nodded firmly, and she went off with Marcus to start scanning the grounds. I really wanted to help, but I was exhausted. My middle still hurt, and having multiple heart attacks due to the freaky ghosts on death row had been far from a trip to the spa. I needed to lie down, at least for a moment.

"You should rest as much as you can," Charlie said as he helped me into bed. "It's Saturday, so if you need to, just sleep all day."

"Oberi already is," I mumbled. He was at the foot of our bed with his legs up in the air, snoring away.

I don't think Charlie got any rest, the way he kept tossing and turning beside me, but sleep was never hard for me to achieve these days. My bipolar had made it difficult to fall asleep before, even kept me up for days at a time, but now, if I didn't get a solid ten hours with a nap in between, I was pretty much dead in my chair.

I laid on my back and closed my eyes. I thought I heard the chirping of a bird before I began to slowly drift away.

THE AREA *around me was stark, the earth underneath me made of nothing but salt. The ground was white, tinted with a hint of red, bloody mountains looming in the distance. A smell like sulfur, rotting and dense, suffocated my senses so I longed for fresh air.*

I was on my feet— I could walk again. This should've been revolu-

tionary, but I failed to react as I turned in place, surveying the situation around me.

I saw two groups of people, separated by the gleaming rays of a white light, a large orb shining in the sky above us. On one side were students who belonged to The Mission— they wore white robes and sang some sort of low song that had no words. They lifted their hands to the white orb in the sky, facing away from the opposite group.

All around me were my friends. Charlie, Kallie, Marcus, and others. Ivy stood beside me, as did Chancey, my brother, and Opal. We stood underneath a bare tree, one that appeared like it was withered and dying, watching The Mission silently as they continued their song, moving in a circle underneath the orb.

I realized that I was a part of this secondary group. I went to turn away from The Mission, but as I did, burning embers began falling from the sky. They struck my friends, who gave tortured screams as the burning embers ate at their flesh and dissolved their bodies into ashes that were carried away on the wind. As the embers struck the members of The Mission, they didn't burn, but instead, grew wings, and were lifted toward the sky to join the white orb above. It was a scene out of some kind of apocalypse, until all that was left was Charlie and me, and The Mission being raised up into the sky.

I reached out to touch Charlie, but as I reached for his face, an ember struck his cheek, and he began dissolving. His ashen remains swept across my face, and I blinked as the rest of his body faded through my hands.

Above me, I saw an olive cardinal land on the branch of the withered tree, before that caught fire, too, crumbling into a pile of nothingness. The olive cardinal flew off toward the light and joined the ranks of The Mission, becoming encompassed in the safety of its warmth as the world around me became only dust, and I was left behind.

⛓

I WOKE UP IN A HAZE, feeling like there was ash in my mouth. I relaxed when I saw Charlie next to me, and I ran a hand through his hair. He didn't turn to dust, so I knew what I was experiencing was real.

His eyes opened straight away. By the haggard look on his face, I knew he hadn't gotten much sleep. I glanced at my watch, and saw that it was twelve o'clock in the afternoon.

Ugh, it is too early, Oberi complained as he gave a yawn. *I could sleep for about a thousand more years.*

"Have you done that?" I asked curiously.

A few times. There were points from when the world was first formed to now where it got terribly boring, and there's no beauty treatment like a nine-hundred-year nap.

Charlie started rifling through our clothes. I took an outfit from him without comment. I felt him approach the edge of my consciousness, where my thoughts were faded and cloudy. He wasn't invading, just observing.

"You all right, pidge? You seem a little off."

"Just... really weird dreams." I rubbed my arms, then said, "It's probably nothing. Let's go search the yard."

When we got to the prison yard, Charlie knelt to the earth and spread both hands over the dirt. There wasn't anyone out here but us, but still, I looked around, because anyone could be watching. There were a couple of guards at the door, glaring at us, but we weren't doing anything that unusual. It wasn't a crime to sit on the ground.

"Can you locate Dante's grave?" I asked curiously.

Charlie waited to respond, as if double checking, before he said, "It's a big campus, pidge. There are hundreds of people buried here, graves that are new and old. I can sense where some people have been buried, but that doesn't mean it's the right grave, and we shouldn't be digging up any bodies unless it's the one we're looking for."

Sounds like a good way to get ghosts. Or maggots. Neither are fun problems to have, Oberi commented.

"Looks like we're going to have to resort to other methods. I hope Kallie and Marcus figured out something."

We hoped to find them at lunch but they weren't in the cafeteria. We picked up some food to share before I spotted Chancey and Ivy, sitting at the end of a nearby bench.

I was relieved. Finding a place to eat in this cafeteria was a pain in the ass. Before, I could sit anywhere, but now, I had to sit at the end of the table, because it was the only place that could fit my chair without the stupid bench getting in the way, and people always loved to sit at the end, so I ended up with my food tray in my lap more often than I would like. Sometimes Charlie scared people off, but that didn't help us stay out of trouble, so I did my best to get him to stop. When my friends were able to snag a spot at the end, it really helped us out.

I hadn't seen Ivy in the cafeteria in a while. He appeared a little brighter, though the bags under his eyes were still prominent. I didn't think the effects of the withdrawal had quite ended, although he appeared to be through the worst of it. Now the hard part of staying clean began.

I really hoped he could do it. He—- all of us— had worked too hard for him to start backsliding again.

Ivy gave me a slight smile and said, "You two look like you've had a long night."

"We did... but not just for the reason you're thinking," Charlie stated.

Ivy chuckled and took a sip of synthetic blood. "Glad I could be of service."

"We had happy married fun times," I informed him. "Then *after* that, we snuck out."

"Where'd you go?" Chancey asked.

"We finally found where Amalie was hiding the next clue. It was on death row. We had to fight a hell of a lot of ghosts to get out," Charlie said.

We gave them the run down of what had happened, and I finished by saying, "I think the after-effects of the ghosts are still wearing on me. I had the strangest dream last night."

"Weird dreams, huh?" Chancey asked, appearing intrigued. "What'd you see?"

He seemed genuinely curious, so I told them about the dream. When I was done, Chancey frowned and said, "That doesn't sound like ghosts. That's angelic interference, for sure."

"Angelic interference? Like, what, angels can influence your dreams?"

"Yep. Angels can influence your dreams, and do it all the time," Chancey stated as he scarfed down a sausage. "It's one of our abilities."

"Why do they do that?" I questioned. "Seems like a weird magical practice to have."

"It's supposed to be a gift to help deliver spiritual messages, from our god and the like," Chancey explained. "Except we angels realized pretty quick that fucking around with somebody's dreams can be an efficient way to trick them into doing as they're told. Dreams from angels leave traces... signatures, if you will. And what you're telling me sure sounds like an angel dream."

My lip curled as I thought of who would want to mess around with my head. "That bastard. The Warden couldn't read my mind after Marcus put that ward over my thoughts, so now he's got to go in through a backdoor. Is there any way to keep the Warden out of my dreams?"

"Well, we don't know that it's him yet," Chancey stated before he grabbed a sausage off of my plate and started eating that, too. He wasn't the most tactful person around. "There are a lot of angels in this prison. Can you run it by me again?"

I retold the dream, and made sure to include smaller details that I'd forgotten about before. Once I'd gotten to the end, Chancey nodded and said, "Ah, that's it. The olive cardinal. That's Esther."

"Are you certain?" Charlie asked.

"Oh, yeah. We used to play a game when we were kids where we'd try to get into each other's dreams. When I had a particularly bad nightmare, I knew it was her, cause I'd always see an olive cardinal."

"What's *your* signature?" Ivy asked curiously, putting his chin in his hand.

Chancey's face soured. "I ain't talking about it."

"Come on, you can't play me like that," Ivy teased. "What is it?"

Chancey scowled. "A striped weasel."

"Oh, Atlantis, if that doesn't fit you!" Ivy howled, and Chancey wrinkled his nose.

"What's the purpose of Esther sending Ava these dreams?" Charlie asked.

"Yeah, and the religious symbolism is weird, too," I argued. "It would be obvious to another angel, but I'm an Elementai. None of this shit means anything to me."

"She's trying to convince ya that joining The Mission is the only way to save supernatural kind. She thinks if she sends you enough dreams, you'll believe they're prophetic, and will convince your friends to sign up alongside you," Chancey explained.

"How dumb does she think I am?" I snapped. "And why me, out of everyone?"

"I mean... sorry to say, sweetheart, but nobody's gonna think it's weird if you start going around telling people you're seeing things." Chancey shrugged.

"Oh, of course, because *I'm* the crazy one." I crossed my arms.

"You said it, not me." Chancey got up from the table. "Anyways, I got a career counseling hour with Professor Jobe I'm already late for. See you later, losers... dollface."

Ivy snickered as he watched Chancey swagger off. "I think I called him a little weasel during one of our arguments a while ago. He got *so* bent out of shape about it. Guess that explains why."

I leaned forward. "So... are you two back together?"

"It's complicated," Ivy confessed, and he dropped his gaze. "We're taking it slow. It's... not like it used to be."

"It's going to take some time. You have to build that trust back again," Charlie said. "Taking it slow is probably good, for now."

"I guess so." Ivy sighed. "I just wish we didn't have to start over from the ground up."

"Ground up can be a pretty good place to start," I said with a smile, and put my hand on top of Charlie's.

"It feels more like ground zero, honestly." Ivy rubbed his face. "I wish these stupid headaches would go away."

"You've done a lot of good work, and we're all proud of you," I said. "If you feel like you're slipping, you can always talk to one of us."

"I really want to be done this time. The last round really fucked me up... and it nearly cost me Chance. Might still, if we can't find a way to work things out." Ivy poked listlessly at his food. "It's so awkward now. I love him, and I forgive him for what he did. But it's way harder to forget that he did it. But I can't say nothing, because what I've done is just as bad, if not worse."

"He didn't cheat on you because he wanted to sleep with somebody else. He did it because he was fucked in the head, and was really hurting," Charlie said. "Not that it makes it right, but I know Chancey loves you. It'll take some time, but you guys can move past this together."

"Yeah, well... I guess we'll see." Ivy gave a shrug and stood up. He dumped the rest of his food in the trash and walked away, clutching his textbooks to his chest.

"I feel so bad for Ivy," I said as I gave a sigh. "Cheating's the end of any relationship."

Charlie shook his head. "I don't think it has to be."

"No?"

"Infidelity is super hard to recover from, and they've made some pretty terrible choices, but at heart, they're both good people. I think if they can pull through this, it'll actually make them stronger."

"They don't just have that going against them. They're both fighting addiction, too."

It really looked like they were doomed to separate, but Charlie grasped my hand and said, "We know how they feel about each other. If they can recover from this, they'll be able to get through anything, and I don't think either of them can live without the other."

"Kind of like you and me, huh?"

"Maybe a little bit."

You two should stop being gooey and get me some more eggs, Oberi complained from under the table. *Five wasn't enough.*

After we were done eating, we headed to Hemlock's hidden room in order to partake in our demigod lesson at one o'clock. When we entered the room, the Christmas tree that Charlie had created was still there. It had failed to fade away or lose any signs of realness, thriving like a real tree would. When he'd imagined it, Charlie had put it into a pot, so the roots anchored the tree into the dirt. I touched it and found the soft needles of the tree gave actual feeling to my hand.

"It's been weeks since you created the tree, and it's still around," I told Charlie. "Illusions can be permanent, but magic has to be constantly funneling into them from a caster or an outside source to stay real. You haven't touched this tree in ages. It's completely self-sustaining."

"Guess I'm not as terrible at illusions as I thought," Charlie said, and he reached out to touch a white bulb hanging from the middle of the tree.

Marcus was working on a spray paint creation that spanned across the wall, which was over eight feet tall. It was a ghoulish-looking biped, with long fur all over its body, pointed ears, and claws that curled upwards instead of downwards. Fans stuck out of the top of its mouth, and it had a long snout with yellow eyes. It appeared quite fierce.

Kallie sat on top of the round table, shaking a toy mouse on a stick for Rishi to play with. I noticed Takahashi and Hemlock weren't here.

Marcus and Kallie both looked tired. They must've spent all day talking. Guess there was a lot to go over, after you learned you'd been together in a past life and had died trying to do the right thing together. I didn't know how they managed to handle the implications of such a reality. I mean, Marcus had already died for her and for one of the keys already.

Let's make sure that doesn't happen again, Oberi noted, catching my thoughts.

I described the painting to Charlie as we approached Marcus. Paint covered his skin, hair and clothes. He really lost himself when he was in the middle of a project.

"What is that thing?" I asked as we stopped beside the painting.

"Kallie told me about them. They're fae monsters called *grimsprites,*" Marcus informed me. "They spend their time picking berries and living in small communities. They're not typically malicious, unless you invade their grove. Then they pluck out your insides and cook them while you're still alive."

"On track for being fae-like, I see," Charlie said.

"Hemlock is going to kill you when she realizes you've ruined her wall," I said, staring up at the massive painting.

"It's illusion paint. It'll disappear," Kallie said. "We just wanted to try something."

Kallie wiggled her fingers, and Marcus stepped back. I observed in amazement as the *grimsprite* stepped out of the wall, becoming flesh and blood. A musty smell hit the air as the creature began stomping around, its massive weight creating small tremors. The loud, snuffling noises its snout made as it sniffed for berries invaded the room, and Rishi hissed, fur standing on end as it hopped around the *grimsprite.*

"That's super cool," I said as I watched the creature roam.

"Yeah, and it'll listen to us, which is important, because illusions usually take on a life of their own, but this one is completely obedient to our commands," Kallie said. "Watch. *Grimsprite,* smash the table."

The *grimsprite* loafed over, and with a massive fist, crushed the round table in the middle of the room. One hit was enough to completely smash it to bits.

"See, there's a difference when me and Marcus create an illusion using simultension, rather than when I just do it by myself, because it's stronger," Kallie informed me as she repaired the round table with her magic. "It'll last until we break the spell, and is basically impenetrable to other types of magic, instead of fading away with time. *Grimsprite*, return to the wall."

The *grimsprite* hurried back to the wall, where it melded together with the surface and became a painting once more. I was in awe of the power they could create. With this ability, they could summon whatever Marcus created at any time, and use them over and over again.

"The thing is, it has to be to scale," Marcus said. "Whatever I paint is going to be actual size, and I can't half-ass it, either. The more realistic the painting is, the better the illusion functions, so it's not exactly great in a hurry."

"Yeah, watch," Kallie said, gesturing to Marcus.

Marcus sprayed a stick figure on the wall. Kallie cast her magic, and the stick figure stumbled to life, peeling itself off the wall before taking a couple of clumsy steps and falling face-first on the ground, dissolving in a poof of red paint.

"It's still useful," I said. "We can come up with ways to use it."

"It's interesting, but I think my necromancy magic is where I should be focusing my energy," Marcus replied. "If I could make all those ghosts obey me last night, the potential to use that skill in battle if we get pinned in a corner is endless."

"Maybe we should ask Takahashi. He might have some insight," Charlie said.

"He and Hemlock aren't coming. They're wrapped up in an investigation," Kallie explained.

"Is the Warden trying to pin something on them?" Charlie worried.

"It's not that. They might've found someone else... like us," Kallie said.

"Another demigod here at the prison? Who?" I asked.

"We don't know. They didn't say," Marcus said. "But I hope they're right, because it would be great if they could convince another demigod to help us out."

"As long as we can trust them," I growled under my breath. I really hoped this guy was a new arrival, because everyone else outside of our little group of friends here was either an asshole, dangerous, or both. We couldn't have some loose cannon coming in and putting the team at risk.

"We've kept a pretty low profile," Charlie said. "The Warden knows what we are, but we haven't handed him any reason he can give to the Union as an excuse to do what he wants with us. He can't send us to Cellblock 9 unless we fuck up again, and we haven't gotten caught breaking any rules this semester, so he can't do anything to us yet."

"Marcus will give him a reason, if he keeps failing," Kallie shot at him.

"You're failing?" I asked. "What's the deal? You're one of the top kids in our grade."

Not that it took too much to be there, but Marcus was still pretty smart. He got mostly A's.

"Have you been slacking off again?" Charlie asked. "I'll kick your ass if you're being lazy."

Definitely possible. He'd been known to forget about homework more than once after getting absorbed into a painting.

"I really am trying, but I'm slipping in my Miriamic Magic class," Marcus said warily. "We've been working on herbs all semester, and I'm really shitty with plants. I've been asked to take care of a *meticulous miracula* plant, and it's not doing good."

"Give it to me for a sec. I can help it grow," Charlie offered.

"Uh, no." Marcus gave a nervous laugh. "You really don't want to."

"It's bad," Kallie added.

"Marcus, you're failing. If this helps Professor Warbright give you a better grade, you really have nothing to lose," I said.

He hesitated, before he gave a sigh and woefully conjured the *meticulous miracula*. My mouth fell open when I saw the dreadful sight before me.

There wasn't much left resembling a plant. A sad looking dry stem sat straight up in a tiny pot, with strands of twigs poking out the sides. The few leaves that were left on the plant were absolutely shredded, like Rishi had been chewing on the ends. There was no telling what the plant had looked like before, because it resembled nothing more than a shriveled-up shrub now.

Marcus deposited the plant into Charlie's hands. Charlie made a couple of astonished whimpering noises as his Earth magic wrapped around the plant. Green sparks touched the ends of the plant before it fizzled out helplessly.

"I was supposed to use the leaves in an alchemy experiment," Marcus said woefully. "But I—"

"You *killed* it!" Charlie yelped. He carefully touched a stem, and it snapped right off.

"I watered it!" Marcus said defensively. "But then, I think I overwatered it, and I forgot to put it in sunlight, so I left it alone for a month, then Rishi got his paws on it and ripped it all up... Then I put it in my stash, and well, there's no sunlight there..."

"I can't do anything with this! It's basically dead!" Charlie yelped. "You've *tortured* this poor plant!"

He was deeply offended. Oberi sniffed it and said, *Well, it certainly won't be winning any awards.*

"There has to be a way you can save it," I argued.

"I don't think there's a way. There's not even any roots that have enough life to help it out. Everything's limp in the soil," Charlie said.

"Let's use simultension," I offered. "Combine your Earth magic with my Spirit power. Maybe we can make it regrow."

He sat down and put the plant on the round table. I wheeled up beside him, and both of us put a hand on either side of the pot.

"We've gotta push our magic outward, instead of sharing it with each other," I informed him. "Let's use both at the same time."

Charlie attempted to grow the plant again, and once his Earth magic had wrapped around the *meticulous miracula*, I joined my magic with his. I didn't think my Spirit magic would have any effect on the plant, not unless I put it into Charlie's abilities, so I directed my healing power to intertwine with his Earth magic, giving it a boost. I could feel Charlie's energy willing the plant back to life, and I guided it along, instructing the plant to heal from the inside out.

It began to work. The dead parts of the plant blossomed into healthy new stems and vibrant green leaves. But that's not all that happened. I gave a gasp of excitement as I watched the plant grow tiny arms and legs. Miniature black eyes and a tiny mouth formed on a woody face.

The plant gave a *squee,* then pulled itself out of the dirt. It dizzily spun around in the pot before it noticed us above and started dancing.

Charlie could feel it moving with his Earth magic, and he reached out to touch it. The plant latched on to one of his fingers, and held on as Charlie lifted his hand up. The plant climbed upward onto the back of his hand, then scrambled onto Charlie's shoulder to give a clumsy hug to his cheek.

"Charlie, you made it come to life!" A huge smile spread across my face.

"Me?" Charlie was baffled. He reached up to touch the plant, but it'd taken a running leap from his shoulder back down to the pot, belly flopping onto the dirt.

"I think so? We healed it together," I said, leaning down to look closer. The plant reached up to bop me lightly on the nose.

A loud, obnoxious snort came from beside me. *I don't like it*, Oberi said, turning his nose up at it. *It's creepy.*

Marcus and Kallie hurried over to look. "Mother Miriam's bosom, she's alive!" Marcus exclaimed.

Rishi's tail flicked as he jumped onto the table to watch the plant. His eyes moved back and forth as he watched the plant run from one side of the table to the other, before he pounced. Rishi grabbed the plant, attempting to swallow it whole. The plant gave a *squee* of surprise.

"Don't hurt him!" Charlie yelled.

"Rishi," Marcus scolded, and he snatched up his cat. It was similar to watching Marcus tussle with a lion as he pried the plant out of Rishi's mouth. He set the plant down on the table, and it began wiping cat spit off his leaves. Rishi yowled, and the plant flipped Marcus off with one of his tiny leaf fingers.

"He doesn't remember you well." I snickered.

"Aw, it's so cute," Kallie sang. "It's like a little spriggan."

"What's that?" I asked.

"It's a demonic forest fae that's similar to a tree. My grandfather was killed by one when it speared him through the chest with a branch. Very noble way to go," Kallie replied simply.

"Charming," Charlie growled.

"No, I kinda like it." I giggled as the tiny plant tried to use a strand of my hair as a climbing rope. "We should call him Sprigs."

Oh, now you're naming *the thing,* Oberi said in disgust.

"There's no need to get jealous," Charlie said, and Sprigs tottered over to cling to Charlie's arm.

Oberi's beady eyes burned into Sprigs as it hugged Charlie's arm. *I should be the* only *pet.*

"Well, Familiars aren't really pets," Charlie replied. Oberi gave an insulted sniff.

Alette flew out from behind Kallie's hair. The white moth buzzed around Sprigs in tiny circles, observing it curiously. Sprigs cried out as he jumped onto Alette's back. The moth attempted to buck him off, but Sprigs clung into her feelers like reins, hanging on. It was like watching a miniature rodeo.

Eventually, Alette calmed down and let Sprigs sit on her back as she zoomed around the room. We watched them fly around for a long time, laughing as they did flips in the air.

After a while, Kallie whistled for her faekin, and Alette returned. Kallie put out her hand, and Sprigs hopped off of Alette's back and into her palm. She lifted it to her eyes to observe it, and the plant gave a happy wave.

"It's not an illusion. It's actually come to life," Kallie said breathlessly. "You made it sentient. You might've even given it a *soul.* I just... don't know how you managed to pull it off."

My eyes wandered to the Christmas tree. "Charlie... I think you actually *gave* the Christmas tree life, like you did with Sprigs. It's not just an illusion. It's a real, living thing."

"That's why it didn't fade away," Kallie marveled. "It's not a trick of the mind."

"Could you do that with other things?" Marcus wondered.

"I'm really good with plants," Charlie said. "But I'm not sure if I can actually bestow life on anything else. And Ava helped. I don't know if I could do it on my own."

Sprigs launched himself from Kallie's arm and back onto Charlie. He settled into the chest pocket on Charlie's uniform jacket and poked his head out.

"He really seems to like you," I said.

"I guess we can keep him," Charlie said, and he tickled Sprigs' leafy head. "As long as he stays hidden."

Guess I'm not good enough anymore, Oberi lamented.

I gave Oberi a sympathetic pat on the head. Marcus squeezed Rishi and said, "Sentient plants are cool and all, but you guys need to see what Kallie can do with her time powers."

"Did you make some progress?" I asked her.

She smirked. "Oh, did I. You'll want to see the sun for this."

Kallie gestured for us to follow her. Alette and Sprigs remained hidden as Kallie led us outside. It must've been close to two o'clock when we stepped into the prison yard. We kept close to the side of the building, where no one paid us any attention.

"Watch this," Kallie said as she snapped her fingers.

I watched the world around us go on rewind and into hyper speed. People became multi-colored blurs as we stood in place. I felt a churning feeling in my gut as we were caught up in the whirlwind, and I felt like I was floating, even though I knew we were on solid ground. The overall feeling was like being stuck in a car that was quickly going in reverse. I watched the sun overhead shift backwards in its place in the sky, and the light changed.

When Kallie stopped shifting time, the world halted. It was an abrupt shift, and I felt myself wavering in my chair as we were jerked to a halt. From what I could see, Kallie had taken us back about two hours in time.

Hm. Haven't experienced that in a while, Oberi said, turning around in a circle.

"You finally did it. You can turn back time!" I said in astonishment.

"I can," Kallie said, and her shoulders fell in exhaustion. "Only took a ridiculous amount of practice."

"How far have you gotten?" Charlie asked.

"I turned back an entire week, once, but that's as far as I got," Kallie said. "I think I can push myself further, but there's something I'm missing that'll help me access the magic."

"A week?" Charlie appeared baffled. "We didn't even notice!"

"You didn't, because I checked," Kallie said. "I popped in and out a few times, seeing if you'd spotted that I'd been messing with time, and none of you realized a thing. I've been practicing at night when people are asleep, so other demigods won't notice if I halt time. Then, once I mastered that, I tried stopping time in music class in front of you guys, to see if you recognized it. You didn't, so I'm learning that I can start moving through time alone, by myself, unless I choose to take people with me. It takes more effort, but I can prevent other demigods from realizing that I'm messing with time if I concentrate hard enough."

I was glad we hadn't noticed, because if she'd been able to conceal that she was messing with time from us, that meant any enemies wouldn't have realized it, either.

"Were you able to go forward, and speed it back up?" I asked.

"I was. I could return to the original moment from when I left, but couldn't go any farther."

"Did anything change?"

"Not that I saw. I was too afraid to alter anything," Kallie confessed. "I didn't know if it would fuck with the timeline, and didn't want to risk it."

She needs to watch herself, Oberi warned. *Time travel isn't anything to do on a whim.*

I repeated what he'd said, and Kallie shrugged. "I'll be fine. I'm not taking any unnecessary risks."

"That's dumb, Kallie. You need to be careful," Charlie pressed.

"I always am! Don't grill me. I won't screw anything up," Kallie hissed.

I looked around the prison yard again. My jaw dropped as I spotted Charlie and me on the other side of the yard, searching for Dante's grave like we had done earlier... except... *now* was earlier.

Past me glanced over her shoulder, then saw us. She did a double take, but as she did, Kallie snapped her fingers again. This time, a slight feeling of driving forward encompassed me. I watched as the world around me shifted into colors again, and people appearing as fast-moving blurs whizzed ahead.

When we finally came to a stop, I felt like throwing up. I gagged and held my middle.

"You okay?" Charlie said, crouching beside me. He laid a hand on my back, and I cringed away. His touch, as much as I wanted the comfort of it, hurt.

"I'm really sore," I confessed. "It wasn't pleasant."

"Time travel is apparently hard on the body," Charlie noted.

"I don't think I've got the magic right. The transition should be seamless, like stepping through one room and into another," Kallie worried. "I'm sorry I hurt you."

"I'll be okay. Just need time to rest," I said warily. I'd gone from fine to in really bad pain in less than five seconds.

"There's something else. I saw myself, just now, from before lunch," I stated. "My past self saw us standing there before we went forward in time, but I *know* I didn't see us this morning when Charlie and I were out here."

"We hadn't gone back in time yet, not until *this* moment, so that means things can change," Marcus pondered. "We can alter the timeline and add stuff at will."

"That sounds dangerous," Charlie said.

"It is. I'm worried about messing with stuff on the timeline. Do you feel any different, Ava, now that your past self saw us?" Kallie asked.

"No..." I pondered. "I know I went back in time now, at this current moment, but I don't recall it from this morning. That doesn't mean I won't down the line, though."

I grimaced, and put a hand to my side. This really hurt.

"Let's get you back to our room," Charlie said, and he began wheeling me toward the door. Sprigs poked his head out of Charlie's pocket, to see what was going on.

"No, Sprigs. There are people around. You have to stay hidden," Charlie told him. Sprigs dropped back into the coat pocket with a peep.

That thing's gonna cause us trouble, Oberi grumbled.

Kallie checked her watch. "Two o'clock, right on the dot."

"You're starting to get obsessive," Marcus grumbled.

"I have to keep track of the time, so I can have awareness of what I'm doing. It's too easy to get confused and fuck this up," Kallie replied.

We'd barely entered the building when the sound of arguing echoed from the cafeteria. It sounded like a group of people were about to get into a fight. I saw picket signs as inmates screamed at each other. There was some sort of protest going on, and counter-protestors had shown up to argue with the marchers.

I wasn't sure what they were arguing about; probably the same war stuff everyone got into every day. But down the hall and in the opposite direction, a nasty little voice sneered, "You need to join The Mission. It's the only way things are going to get better in this cruel world."

If anyone could make my day awful, it was Esther. I could ignore the shouting near the cafeteria, but I couldn't ignore her. Charlie tried to steer me the other way, but I grabbed my wheels and headed toward the sound of her voice, pushing through the burning agony racing through my spine.

"Ava," Charlie started.

"This bitch has been messing with my dreams. I'm giving her a piece of my mind," I snarled.

Up ahead, I heard someone respond, "I've already told you no. It's not for me."

That was Thaddeus. I rounded the corner, and saw that he and his hawk Familiar were cornered against a wall. Esther, Naya, and Mad Dog surrounded him, cutting off any outlet of escape. Thaddeus was bleeding from a cut on his head, where it looked like someone had hit him.

"You can't just live your life doing what *you* want all the time," Naya pressed. "It's selfish not to think of other people."

That was rich, considering Naya was the most selfish bitch I'd ever met on the planet. Thaddeus went to respond, but visibly sagged in relief when he saw me hauling ass down the hallway, followed by the rest of my gang.

"Can you take your bullshit parade somewhere else?" I asked loudly. "The rest of us can't fit our heads that far up our own asses to join you."

"Oh, great, *you*," Naya said.

"Our favorite fucking losers," Mad Dog added, giving Charlie a cold once-over.

Naya gave a revolting noise, then added, "Don't waste your time trying to convert her, Esther."

"No one's ever a waste of time, Naya," Esther replied sweetly. "Ava's soul is just as worthy of redemption as anyone's."

"Fuck off, bitch. I know you've been fucking with my dreams," I accused. "Cut it out, otherwise, I'll have to cut *you*."

"Those are some big words for someone who can't get out of their wheelchair," Esther replied coolly. "By the way, you never told me if you and Charlie managed to fix your little problem."

"What's she talking about?" Charlie asked.

I still hadn't told him anything about Esther's nasty comments at

The Devil's Playground, wondering if I could still have sex in my *condition*. My lip curled as I replied, "Don't worry, I'm getting laid. Pretty sure you aren't."

"I'm happy to hear you get to maintain that special relationship with your husband. Intimacy is such a vital part of marriage," Esther crooned. "Unlike *some people* around here, who fornicate with people they're not married to. *Worse,* people who they don't even *love,* just want to use for sex."

Her piercing gaze flickered to Marcus and Kallie, and the implication her words held was huge. Ancestors, this bitch could hone in on whatever was most bothering you and twist the knife in. What was with her, and how'd she even guess Marcus and Kallie were messing around?

"None of that's your business," Charlie replied. "If you're so busy running The Mission, do you really have time to be sticking your nose in other people's love lives?"

"The life of *every* student at the Institute is my business, due to the pathway of The Mission. I'm here to lead others into the light," Esther replied. "Please don't lecture me, Charlie. You and the people you hang with aren't doing any good for the world."

"I've given you my answer," Thaddeus said shortly, shoving Esther away. "Now leave them alone."

Esther's nose wrinkled, and she said, "I'm sorry we couldn't convince you, Thaddeus. But as my uncle says, some people think like the dead, so therefore, they might as well be so. Hopefully your soul will find its way to the light someday."

She slithered off with her nose in the air, and Naya copied her in due fashion. Geez, Naya really fell into the sidekick role when there was something in it for her. I bet the Warden had promised her graduating with honors and a free-flowing supply of victims if she palled around with his niece.

Mad Dog hardly said a thing the entire confrontation, but I didn't like the look in his eyes as he stalked off. It wasn't like him to keep quiet unless he had something dirty planned. He smirked at me, but left me alone as Oberi growled, warning him to stay back.

"Thank the ancestors they left." Thaddeus sighed once we were alone. "Esther's been grilling me all day about joining The Mission."

"You want me to heal that cut on your head?" I asked, gesturing to it.

"Nah, it's stopped bleeding already," Thaddeus said, touching it lightly. "Mad Dog punched me when I told Esther I didn't want to sign up for The Mission. He let me go, though, once Esther convinced him words would work better than fists."

"Why are they so insistent you join?" Charlie asked.

"Esther caught me spying," Thaddeus confessed. "You put me up to tailing our angel professors, and, well... I think I might've found something on Professor Mazur."

"What is it?" Marcus asked.

"Not here." Thaddeus shook his head. "Follow me."

Thaddeus' hawk flew ahead to lead the way. He roamed after his Familiar, although I sagged in my seat. Though I'd been fired up during the confrontation with Esther, now that she was gone, I was sorer than ever. My entire body ached in a way that made me want to cry.

"You want to go back to our room first?" Charlie asked gently.

"I can sleep later. We need to find out what Thaddeus knows," I replied weakly. "You're just gonna have to help me get there."

Charlie pushed me down the hall after Thaddeus, and Kallie started to complain. "What is it with Esther? Does she have a dictionary of everyone's biggest secrets?"

"I don't know how she figured that out," Marcus grumbled. A pink tint had come into his cheeks, and failed to leave since Esther had brought up the whole ordeal.

"I mean... not to bring this up, but it's pretty obvious you two have feelings for each other," Charlie pointed out.

"We've had a thing going on for ages, but nobody knows we've been messing around but you guys," Kallie shot back, and Marcus ducked his head.

"That must be her demigod power," I realized. "She knows people's greatest weaknesses immediately, and utilizes them."

"It's probably not limited to emotions. I bet she can sense the weaknesses in our magical abilities, which means she'll be able to counter whatever we throw at her in a fight," Marcus said.

"Let's not get in a fight with her, then," Charlie said.

Thaddeus had stopped near the fireplace in the foyer. Ivy was there, reading a book. He glanced up from the pages as he asked us, "You guys going to an orgy or something?"

"Can't really talk now, Ivy." Charlie stopped me beside Thaddeus. "Thad, where are we going?"

Thaddeus appeared mystified. His gaze wandered from left to right as he replied slowly. "I'm not sure. What were we doing?"

I looked closer at Thad's eyes, which had gone foggy. Overhead, his hawk Familiar flapped its wings in alarm and screamed, as if there was something wrong.

"You were saying you found something about Professor Mazur," I reminded him.

"Was I?" Thaddeus replied. "I can't remember."

"Shit. What's wrong with him?" I asked. Marcus waved a hand in front of Thaddeus' face, but he didn't even blink.

We need to help, Oberi said frantically. He began darting frantically around Thaddeus, barking in alarm as if he was as panicked as the hawk was.

Ivy stood up, tossing the book to the side. He did a slow circle around Thaddeus before lightly touching the cut on his head. Ivy jerked his fingers back, like he'd been burned, then grabbed Thad's elbow. Red blood magic wound up Thaddeus' arm as Ivy's powers worked over him. Suddenly, Ivy recoiled, grasping his wrist and taking a step back.

"He's under some kind of influence," Ivy said. "Vampire compulsion."

"Naya," I hissed.

"No, it's not her. She's wearing a noxite cuff, so she can't," Ivy stated. "A vampire can only use compulsion if they're talented, and the vampire doing the influencing usually has to stick around for the compulsion to work. This is one strong vampire, if he ain't anywhere to be seen."

"It's Mad Dog," Charlie said. "It has to be."

"Shit." I knew that malicious look in his eyes meant he was up to no good. Above his head, Thaddeus' hawk was pecking at his head, as if he was trying to snap his Elementai out of it.

"Can you break it?" I asked Ivy.

"I tried, but my blood magic can't stop this," Ivy said. "Damn, Mad Dog's got a good hold on him. I've never met a compulsion I couldn't break."

"Oh, gods," Kallie said in horror. "Mad Dog... he's..."

An icy chill swept through my veins as all of us realized the terrible truth. Mad Dog wasn't just a strong vampire. I'd seen him fight guards with noxite pulsing through his veins, which failed to do anything to him until he'd been shot with far more than the average dose. Ivy was a talented vampire, yet his abilities did nothing to stop Mad Dog's magic, which only meant one thing.

Mad Dog was a demigod. The Warden had one more ally to fight alongside Esther against us. Hemlock and Takahashi must've figured it out before we had, and were trying to figure out a way to minimize the damage. That's why they hadn't been at our lesson today.

Ivy hadn't realized what we had, and was still examining Thaddeus. "You should heal the cut on his head," Ivy stated. "Mad Dog won't be able to— *Thad, stop!*"

Ivy used his vampire speed to try and catch him, but it was too late. Under the power of Mad Dog's compulsion, Thaddeus reached up into the air, grabbed his hawk Familiar, and snapped its neck.

The bird gave a sharp cry, then went limp. Death instantly filled its eyes as it dropped from Thaddeus' grasp and landed on the floor.

I reached down and plucked the bird off the ground. "Come on, come on," I whimpered, tears beginning to fall from my eyes. They landed on the bird as I attempted to use my healing magic, forcing my magic into the hawk's body as it glowed with white Spirit power.

It didn't work. The hawk's wing twitched once, but that was all that happened. The bird had died, and I couldn't reverse death. The hawk dropped out of my hands, lying limply on the floor.

Ivy had yanked Thaddeus to the other side of the room with such speed, none of us had been able to catch it. Ivy's grip on Thaddeus slowly released as the fog began to clear from his gaze. Mad Dog's compulsion upon Thaddeus had ended, and why not? Thaddeus was already dead.

Thad staggered forward before he landed on all fours beside his Familiar, reaching out to clutch the hawk to his chest. Under the effects of the compulsion, he hadn't realized what he'd done until just that moment.

"No," Thaddeus whimpered. "*No.*"

Thaddeus began to sob. His shoulders wracked with sorrow, and he let out a bereaved scream that made guards and students come running.

Everyone, even the guards, came to a halt in a circle around Thaddeus as they watched the heart wrenching scene.

Mad Dog was certainly a demigod, because only a demigod vampire could have such strong compulsion abilities as to force an Elementai to murder their own Familiar, their living soul.

"I tried," Ivy rasped. "I wasn't fast enough, I—"

"It's not your fault, Ivy," I whispered. This wasn't anyone's fault but Mad Dog's.

Thaddeus' sobs began to turn into gasps of pain. He fell onto his side, still clutching the hawk to his chest.

"Thad." Charlie fell to his knees. He crawled toward Thaddeus and dragged him onto his lap. "Stay with us. Ava, please, do something."

Charlie called for me, but there was nothing I could do. My healing magic couldn't prevent this, either. No Elementai could live without their Familiar.

All I could do— all any of us could do— was watch as Thaddeus' grip on his Familiar slowly eased as he finally breathed his last.

The world spun around me when I felt the air leave Thaddeus' chest. I had the thought that this couldn't be real. I didn't trust my own senses— my own magic.

"Breathe!" I yelled. I forced air in and out of his lungs, but it wasn't the same as him breathing.

"Thad!" Marcus cried. He placed his hands on Thaddeus, and his whole body twitched. For a moment, I thought he was back... but it was only Marcus' necromancy magic trying to revive him.

Thaddeus was gone. Even Marcus couldn't bring back the dead.

Ivy sobbed. "I tried to stop it. Please forgive me."

"It's not your fault," Ava insisted.

"You don't understand, precious," Ivy pressed. "Long-term nightshade use slows vampires down. If I'd gotten off it sooner, I might've stopped Thad in time."

"Ivy..." Ava started, but they weren't hearing any of it.

"I'm sorry—" Ivy could barely get the words out. They were practically hyperventilating, and it got to be too much. Ivy fled.

Guards barked orders, but I couldn't make out what they were saying. Hands landed on me, trying to pry me away from Thaddeus, but I wouldn't let go.

Charlie, you have to, Oberi said gently. *There's nothing more you can do.*

This wasn't right. He was just a kid. I'd tried to keep him out of trouble... and now he was dead, because he'd followed *my* instructions.

The guards yanked me back, and Thaddeus fell from my arms.

"Everyone against the wall!" a guard shouted.

We followed their orders. Ava wheeled herself beside me as we were forced to stand in a line. Commotion filled the hall as the guards surrounded the scene.

"It was suicide," one of the guards stated. "I saw it with my own eyes."

"Like hell!" Kallie protested. "He was being compelled by—"

"You'll speak only when spoken to," a guard sneered, cutting her off.

I turned to Marcus and whispered, "What happens to Thaddeus now?"

Marcus lowered his voice. "He's an Elementai, so his spirit will hang around until he's ready to go with his ancestors. I suspect he'll be around for a while, because his death was traumatic and confusing. It'll take a bit before he can sort out what happened."

"So we should be able to talk to him?" I asked.

"If we can find him," Marcus said. "His ghost spooked the second he saw his Familiar's broken neck. I don't know when he'll be back—"

"I said quiet!" a guard roared.

Marcus and I both went silent. I didn't know how long they kept us there, but it felt like an hour before they'd documented the incident and wheeled Thaddeus' body toward the morgue. They asked us a series of questions, but most of it was to confirm what they already suspected.

What did Thaddeus say before he died? Had he told us he was planning this?

The questions made my guts churn. Thaddeus would never do this to himself. If anyone had a chance of graduating the Institute one day, it was this kid. He had a bright future ahead of him... and now he'd never get to live it.

I hated the Institute more than ever.

"Why is it that people end up dead whenever you're around, Wahkin?" one of the guards growled.

There will be more dead bodies before I'm done, I thought, though I held my tongue.

"Perhaps it's because a lot of people die here," I stated coolly.

"Get out of here," he snapped. "I best not find you around the next dead body we deal with."

It must've been three o'clock by the time the guards let us go. A large crowd had formed nearby. Oberi barked at people, and the crowd parted as I wheeled Ava through the hall. We turned a corner, where we were finally alone.

"I'm going to find Mad Dog and kill him," I growled.

Ava must've grabbed her wheels, because she came to a halt in front of me, blocking my path. "Charlie, you can't," she said sternly. Her thoughts slipped through our bond, and I was reminded of the conversation we'd had weeks ago. I'd already killed one person this semester. I'd promised I wouldn't go down that road again. Right now, though, it seemed like a pretty damn good option.

"Then what am I supposed to do?" I demanded.

"You're supposed to *grieve*," Ava said.

I crossed my arms. "How's what I said any different?"

"We're all pissed at Mad Dog," Marcus said. "But we can't bring Thaddeus back, and this isn't worth going down to Cellblock 9 for. We still have work to do."

"All right, then let's get to it," I said through gritted teeth.

"Charlie, we can take a minute—" Kallie started.

"I can't," I interrupted. "Thaddeus is gone, and sitting around wallowing in my *feelings* isn't going to bring him back. I need to do *something*. The least we can do is give his death meaning, so it motivates us to get the hell out of here."

Kallie hesitated. "What do you *want* to do?"

"Anything!" I cried. I just wanted to get the hell out of the Institute, no matter what it took.

Ava must've sensed my thoughts, because she quickly chimed in, "We should check out the next spot on the map."

"Kallie and I looked this morning," Marcus said. "Kallie sniffed around a bit, and I tried to use my Seer powers, but whatever used to be there must be long gone. We found nothing but trees."

"Good thing trees are my specialty," I said.

Marcus sounded uncertain. "If you want to check it out again, we can, but Kallie and I didn't have much luck."

"I think we should look again," Ava pressed. "Charlie might find something you missed."

She was trying to keep me busy and distracted. I could feel her intention slip through our bond. I didn't mind, because she wasn't wrong. I needed to act. It was better to distract me with this than to let me loose on the school, hunting down Mad Dog.

And well... I couldn't do that. At least, not now, in the middle of the day when I'd be easily caught.

"Show us the way," I suggested.

Kallie and Marcus led us out of the school and into the forest. It wasn't easy getting Ava's chair through the trees, but I used my Air magic to hover her a few inches above ground. We came to a part of the forest not far from the Lair, where the trees became thick and difficult to navigate. I used my magic to push back branches so Ava's chair could fit through.

Kallie and Marcus stopped ahead of us. "This is it," Kallie said.

Oberi sniffed a nearby tree. *I don't smell anything but dirt and pine needles.*

"We searched at least a hundred-yard radius, and we didn't find anything," Marcus added. "This part of the forest is pretty old, so we thought maybe there used to be a building here, but there were no remnants— nothing."

I splayed my hand over a tree trunk and focused my magic. Sprigs jumped out of my pocket and ran down my arm, until he could reach the tree, too. "This forest is old, but only a hundred-fifty years or so. These trees weren't around when Amalie and Dante were here. If there *was* a building here, its foundation may be deeply buried. Hold on."

I took a few breaths and focused deeper into the earth. I made it six feet before I felt a disturbance. It wasn't rock, or anything that felt like earth. I brushed my magic up against it, trying to map out its size and shape in my mind. It felt broken and decayed, whatever it was. It could be nothing, or it could be exactly what we were looking for.

I guided my magic outward, and that's when I realized there was more. Hundreds of small objects littered the area, all buried six feet below our feet. Tree roots curled around them— some roots pierced straight through the objects. My magic swirled around something round, and it hit me.

I jumped back with a gasp, and I nearly dropped Sprigs. I placed him back into my pocket before turning to my friends. "It's a graveyard."

There were no caskets, just endless bodies tossed haphazardly into the earth, like no one had cared to give them a proper burial.

"That can't be right," Marcus protested. "I would've felt that."

"Maybe you didn't know what you were looking for," I said. "These bones have decayed pretty badly. There may be nothing left in them for your magic to sense."

Leaves rustled as Marcus knelt to the ground. He must've been using his magic, because he gasped. "By Mother Miriam, you're right. It's so faint... but they're everywhere."

"This could be death row," Ava realized. "The records said their graves were unmarked."

"That means we've found Dante," I said. "That must be what the map is pointing to. The key could be with him!"

"We can't upturn a hundred graves," Ava said.

Oberi started digging, throwing dirt all over my feet. *We're going to have to if you want to find that key, sweetheart.*

"There may be a way to save us time," Ava suggested. "Marcus and Charlie could use simultension— Seer powers combined with Earth powers— to locate the proper grave."

"We might as well try," I agreed.

Marcus hesitated. "It might help if I meditate first, to get in touch with my past life. Come here, Charlie."

Marcus made me sit on the ground across from him, and we joined hands. Great. If he started singing *Kumbaya*, I was out of here. I didn't have time for this shit when there was a fucking murderer on the loose.

"Take a few deep breaths with me," Marcus instructed.

I gritted my teeth. I'd rather just dig up these graves one by one at this point. I wasn't in the mental space to do this right now.

"Just humor me, would you?" Marcus asked. "This isn't easy for me, either."

Reluctantly, I followed the pace of his breathing. *Deep breath in, hold it for three seconds, then breathe out.* Around us, I heard the sound of raindrops dripping from the trees, except it wasn't raining. I suspected Ava was using her powers to help us relax.

God damn it, it was working.

My shoulders dropped, and my jaw eased. When he was ready, Marcus guided his Seer magic up my arms, and it felt like a warm sweater surrounding me. I sent my Earth magic back to him, until our magic swirled together.

My perception of the graves beneath us suddenly became clearer, as if I was encountering Marcus' visions myself. I could perceive the bones with precision. I knew where every skull lay, and which bones belonged to which body, even if they were scattered yards apart. It was as if I could see underground through an X-ray, though there was no visual information, just an innate *knowing*. I'd never felt anything quite like it.

Marcus must've felt the shift, too, because he gasped. It seemed my magic had made his own stronger. It allowed him to explore the ground beneath us with greater clarity than with his own powers.

Our magic spread wider, until it honed in on a specific grave fifty feet away from us. The intuition that filled my chest became stronger now.

"We found it!" Marcus exclaimed. He scrambled to his feet and yanked on my arm. "I *know* it's him."

I quickly followed, and Oberi sniffed the ground at my feet as he hurried beside me. Rishi sprinted alongside Marcus. Twigs snapped behind us as Kallie helped Ava through the trees.

"Here," Marcus said, stopping in the place our magic had led us to.

I knelt to the ground and splayed my palm across the dirt. I could sense the grave beneath us, but if it wasn't for Marcus' magic, I'd never know this was the one we were looking for.

"What are you waiting for?" Marcus demanded. "Let's dig him up!"

Oberi started digging, and I heard sand and tiny rocks hit Ava's chair as she came through the trees with Kallie.

I grabbed him by the scruff and pulled him back. "Take a break, Oberi. I've got this."

I commanded the earth to shift beneath us, pulling the bones and anything else Dante might be buried with to the surface. I felt around, and my hands moved over the long-forgotten bones. I searched for a piece of metal, but I found nothing.

"Where's the key?" I asked.

"It— it's not here!" Marcus cried, before shaking me. "Check again. Are you sure you pulled up *everything*?"

I pressed my hands into the upturned earth and checked again, but I found nothing except worms. "I'm sure."

"This spot isn't marked on the map for nothing," Ava said. "There must be something here."

Unless the Warden had already found it, like he had with whatever had been in the lake. I didn't say that out loud, though, because I wasn't ready to give up hope.

"Let me try something," Marcus suggested.

We were still connected through simultension, because I felt his necromancy magic swirling around the skeleton. The bones twitched, but nothing else happened.

"What are you trying to do?" I asked.

"I'm *trying* to get him to speak," Marcus said. "I figured if he knew something, he could tell us. But he's been dead for so long, and his spirit has crossed over. I can't bring him back to talk to us even if I wanted to."

"What if we did a séance?" Ava suggested.

"Witches try to avoid them with crossed spirits, because it's hard to do and the messages are usually unclear," Marcus said. "We use them more often to commune with trapped spirits, in order to help them cross over to the afterlife."

"Would contacting him even work?" I wondered. "I mean, Marcus *is* Dante, so his spirit is already with us, just with different memories."

"I don't think that's how it works," Ava said. "When I was in the Ancestral Lands, my ancestors explained it to me. Every life you live is another fragment of your soul. Even though Marcus lived as Dante in a past life, there's a piece of him that still survives in the afterlife, and that piece is Dante, not Marcus."

"So how do we talk to him?" I asked.

"I don't know yet," Marcus said. "I tried to access Dante and his memories, to see if I could find the key, but it's all blocked off. I can't figure out why."

I frowned. "Check his bones. Amalie left clues behind for her future incarnation, right? If there's a clue here, she wanted it to last."

Kallie bent beside me, and the three of us reached out for the bones in unison. The moment I touched the bones, the world spun around me, like I was falling off a cliff.

My whole body lurched as I came to an abrupt stop, my feet planted firmly on the ground... except the ground wasn't firm at all. The earth rocked back and forth violently, and wind whipped my hair around. I tried to steady myself, but I stumbled sideways and caught myself on something round, like a barrel.

People shouted, and an ice-cold chill spread up and down my spine. I heard a loud splash, and water sprayed my face. I licked my lips to find it tasted like salt.

Holy shit. I'd been transported onto a ship in the middle of a storm!

The sounds of cannons exploded, and the ship rocked the other way as something smashed into its side. It was under attack!

"I hid the key!" A male voice cut through the roar of the wind, and intuitively, I knew it was Marcus... but yet, not the person I knew. "They won't find it. It's time! You must wipe our memories!"

"Marcus!" I screamed, before his hands landed on me.

"It's a vision," he said in a much calmer tone. I didn't understand how he could be across the other side of the ship a moment ago, only to appear at my side a second later.

"Marcus must've accidentally pulled us into his vision when we touched the bones," Kallie theorized from beside me.

It made sense. Marcus and I were still connected through simultension, and Kallie was bonded to him. I turned my attention to the scene playing out around me.

"I can't!" a man cried. I didn't recognize his voice.

"We may not survive this," a woman said. At first, I thought it was Kallie, only my friend was right beside me. "I'm begging you, Erasmus Morelli, by the gods you worship and the entire Arcanean pantheon, wipe my memory."

"You could forget him, Amalie!" the man argued.

"It's the only way," Amalie insisted. "This is the last fail-safe option we have left. If we're captured and tortured for information, we can't give up the key's location if we don't remember where it is. This key is more important than me or Dante. We must protect it at all costs. Promise me that you will!"

"If you forget, you'll never recover the key," Erasmus protested.

"We will live another life," she insisted. "The demigods will find the clues I've left behind in the lullaby. I'll leave more, as many as I can. You must be there to help us when we return. You're a vampire, so this storm won't take you. Swim back to the mainland if you have to, so that we can find you and recover our memories when the time comes. We must protect the key in this lifetime, so that I may find it another. Swear it, Erasmus."

"What about the ship?" the vampire protested. "They'll salvage everything if they manage to sink us."

"They won't find the key," Amalie promised. "I'll give my life to make sure that never comes to pass."

In the moment Erasmus hesitated, the ship lurched, and a large wave crashed over us. The water swept me off my feet, but in the distance I heard Erasmus say, "I swear it, Amalie. I will do my part to protect the key and help the demigods find it, whomever they are when they surface."

Thunder cracked overhead, and the ship lurched. Screams filled the air around us, until the whole world shifted and we were tossed into the frigid waters below.

I GASPED FOR BREATH, and my heart raced. It took me a moment to realize that I was back on solid ground, lying flat on my back. I clutched my chest, but my shirt was completely dry, and my skin warm.

"Are you all right?" Ava's voice sounded like it was coming from far away. I pushed myself to a sitting position, and she touched my shoulder, grounding me back to reality. "What happened? You all fell over. Oberi and Rishi freaked."

"Marcus had a vision and pulled Kallie and me into it," I said, rubbing my head. The dizziness quickly passed.

"What did you learn?" Ava asked.

"I remember now," Kallie said. "Amalie and Dante were sailing to Darke Island with the key. She asked her shipmate to wipe her memory. He was a vampire named Erasmus Morelli. The rest of the crew died, but Erasmus could've made it, because a sinking ship wouldn't kill a vampire. We didn't find any records of Erasmus in death row, so he could've escaped the authorities before Amalie and Dante were caught. They would've assumed him dead with the rest of the crew. But before he left, he swore to protect the key and agreed to wipe Dante and Amalie's minds, in case they were tortured for information."

"That must be why I can't access my past memories," Marcus mused.

"But Amalie knew she'd come back, because the fae believe in reincarnation," Kallie continued. "So she left clues behind. First, in *The Assassin's Destiny* story. Then she made the map. But... from what I remember, the map wasn't for the demigods, like the story was. It was for *her*, in case she managed to get a pardon, so she could go back to Darke Island and rescue Dante. Erasmus must've left behind what memories he could, so that she wouldn't forget her lover. The map doesn't lead to the key at all... it was a map back to Dante."

I groaned as I got to my feet and dusted the dirt off my pants. "Great. Another dead end. All this time we thought we were looking for clues to the merfolk key, and the map just marked where she'd find Dante— either alive in death row, or dead on prison grounds. No wonder we didn't find anything in the lake. She'd marked it because that's where they throw dead inmates, and she figured Dante might end up there, in the chance she didn't return quickly enough to rescue him."

"But it didn't matter, because they executed Amalie before she ever got the opportunity to attempt a rescue," Kallie added.

"We learned *something*, though," Marcus said. "Dante hid the key before their ship crashed on Darke Island. Erasmus was a vampire, which means he could still be alive today. He swore to protect the key, so he might know where to find it."

"And I suppose you just expect him to hand the information over," I said.

"He will if we can convince him of who we were in a past life," Marcus replied.

"Marcus is right," Ava agreed. "Erasmus should know what he wiped from their memories. I say we try to figure out where he is and go from there."

We agreed that was the only logical course of action. Kallie got a head-start leading Ava back through the trees, while Marcus and I reburied Dante's body. The bones sank deep into the earth with my magic. I didn't need Marcus's help, so I didn't know why he'd hung back.

He spread his hands over the grave, making the earth even again. "I *can* talk to the dead, you know," he blurted. "I didn't mess up this time."

"I know," I said. "I wasn't judging. I'm sure it's harder to contact people the longer they've been gone."

"I just didn't want you to think I couldn't... help," Marcus said timidly. "Because if you want to talk to anyone in the afterlife, I'm here."

My form stiffened and went rigid. He was serious. Marcus was offering me a way to talk to the people that I'd lost.

It wasn't the first time I'd thought about asking him to connect me with someone on the other side. I could talk to my mother, or to Marty. Before, I wasn't sure Marcus could actually do it, but his powers were growing. I was sure he could figure it out if I asked.

Marty was the first one I considered speaking to, but I didn't want to go there. He probably regretted being my friend. After all, he'd been shot because I was around. He might still be here if he hadn't chosen to help me out, and I was too cowardly to face him. I feared he might blame me for his death, because I definitely know I did, and hearing the truth out loud from my dead best friend that I'd had a hand in killing him wasn't something I thought I could handle.

Speaking to my mother would be even worse. It was hard, because I missed her, even though I couldn't remember anything about her. She was an absent piece in my life that nobody was able to fill. It was easier before I knew about the magical world, because I'd assumed there was no such thing as the afterlife, so I didn't have any fear that my mother would be ashamed of me for the choices I'd made.

Now I knew that our souls went on after death. That meant admitting to myself my mother was out there somewhere, and she probably knew about everything terrible that I'd ever done. She might've been watching over me all this time, observing as I stole from people, hurt others, and made mistake after mistake.

I bet my mom hated me. No one wanted their son to turn out like I had.

She probably didn't love me anymore. I bet anything she cursed the fact she'd risked her life to give birth to a useless fuck-up like me. Back when I was born, it was still illegal to have a child that was bred from two different elemental Houses, and she'd been executed for it. And though I was a grown man, inside of me, there was still a little boy that just wanted his mom. That little boy wouldn't survive if she turned away from him.

I was already in pain, and thinking about my mother made that pain worse, so I just shut it off.

"It won't necessarily be *clear* communication," Marcus babbled. "But I mean, we could at least try—"

"Okay," I said, just to get him to stop talking. "Sometime, I guess."

"All right, well, um..." Marcus stammered. "Let me know when you're ready."

It felt weird to think about. For the longest time, I believed that when someone died, that was it. You never got another chance to say what you wanted to. I hadn't thought about what I might say to the people who weren't here anymore. It wasn't exactly a chance you got every day, and if I was ever brave enough to face Marty or my mother again, I wanted to make it count.

Though I doubted I'd ever have the nerve to go through with it.

We finished burying the body, then made our way through the trees until we caught up with Kallie and Ava.

"We need to keep searching," Ava insisted, though her voice was tired. I felt through our bond that she was clearly exhausted.

"Pidge, you need to go rest," I stated flatly. "This is a lot for you to do in one day."

"I'm not ready to quit yet."

Tears nearly marred her words. She was clearly suffering at this point, and I wasn't going to let her stubbornness get in the way of her health.

I took on a direct tone, one I didn't use unless I was telling her I meant business. "That's not acceptable. You're at your limit, and you pushing yourself when I ask you not to is a *red light*."

Kallie and Marcus didn't understand the hint, but Ava clearly got the message, because I felt her give in.

"Fine," she grumbled. "I guess I could use a nap."

"Marcus, take Ava back to her room," Kallie said. "Charlie can help me carry books from the library so we can get started on researching this vampire right away."

"I can help you carry books," Marcus said, sounding offended.

"You, stringbean?" Kallie asked skeptically.

"I've been working out!" Marcus cried. To be fair, he *had* put on a lot of muscle since he started weightlifting with us.

"I don't mind taking Ava," I added.

"Except that *Marcus* needs to return to the scene and see if he can find Thaddeus' ghost in order to talk to him," Kallie emphasized. "I know it's not ideal right now, but we have to figure out what he found about Professor Mazur."

Marcus sighed heavily. "Okay! Geez."

Kallie plucked Sprigs out of my shirt pocket. "Take Sprigs, too."

Marcus wheeled Ava into the building, and Rishi followed them. Oberi remained at my side as I whirled toward Kallie, "Spill. What's this all about? You send Marcus after Thaddeus, but make me stay behind? You don't think I can handle it? Yeah, I feel guilty as all hell. I put Thad up to following our professors, and now he's dead. Add on to the fact that we found zilch out in the woods, and Thaddeus' death was for nothing. Don't act like reading books is going to help anything, because I swear if we spend one more second in that useless library—"

"Charlie, calm down," Kallie pressed. "I'm not keeping you away from Thaddeus. I *want* you to see him again. I just needed to get rid of Ava and Marcus to do it. You saw my time powers in action. I think we can go back and change it, but Ava and Marcus would never go for it. Marcus would say it's too dangerous manipulating death—"

That's because it is, Oberi said in my mind, but Kallie didn't hear him.

"— And I didn't want to give Ava false hope."

"False hope?" I asked. At first, I didn't understand. Then her words hit me full-on as I realized the implication of what she was saying. "Wait... you think if we do *this*, and stop Thaddeus from dying, that we can go back and stop the Underground from ever collapsing?

"Yes. That's what I've been planning on."

The entire world tilted on its axis. "If we can do that, Ava never would've ended up in the hospital and suffered the way she did."

"She could walk again," Kallie said softly. "None of what went down that night had to happen at all."

I would advise against this, Oberi warned. *It's dangerous to tempt fate.*

I should've carefully considered what this could mean, and the consequences we could expect from messing with time. If we went back and changed things, the last several months never would've happened.

But Ava wouldn't be in pain anymore, and Thaddeus would be alive. It didn't even seem like a question.

"If we can go back and change things, we might as well start at the Underground," I said. "If it never collapses, I'll never put Thaddeus up to tailing our professors. Esther never would've been following him."

"I'd love to, but I can't go back that far yet," Kallie said. "Thaddeus' death is fresh. We can still reverse it. If this works, then we can go back to the Underground once I can travel that far."

Her meaning was clear. She wanted to use Thaddeus' death as an experiment, to see if it could even be done. I didn't see what we had to lose. In this reality, Thaddeus was already dead. Either we changed it and he lived, or everything remained the same. At least with Kallie's time powers, there was a chance to save his life.

"Let's do it," I agreed.

Hellooo, Oberi said. *Is nobody listening to me? You don't want to do this! I'm telling you right now this is a bad idea. I'm a transdimensional being, and I happen to know a thing or two—*

Oberi's protests faded into the back of my mind while I focused on Kallie. She hadn't heard him, so she kept talking.

"It's three-forty-five right now," Kallie said. "We ran into Thaddeus at two o'clock, so we should go back to just a few minutes before that. We want to change as little as possible. We need to stop Mad Dog from punching Thaddeus and causing that cut, so he can't compel him."

"Okay— Wait!" I cried. "We were out in the prison yard at two o'clock. If we time travel from here, we'll run into ourselves."

"You're right," Kallie said. "Come on."

She grabbed my hand, and her wristwatch brushed against my skin. We ducked inside the building. Oberi followed, grumbling the whole way. The door clicked shut behind us.

"Three-forty-seven," Kallie announced. "Ready?"

I nodded firmly. "Yes."

The world spun for a brief second, before our feet landed on solid ground again. My stomach clenched, but I shook it off.

"It's just before two o'clock," Kallie told me.

The door creaked open a crack, and I heard the distant sound of

Kallie's voice. It was her past self, standing out in the prison yard. "Watch this..."

"I see ourselves in the prison yard," Kallie said from beside me. "It doesn't look like we've time traveled yet— wait! I just snapped my fingers."

Barely a beat passed before I heard my own voice outside. "You okay?"

Our past selves had time traveled and returned as if no time had passed at all. Any moment now, we'd walk inside and run into Thaddeus.

"We're barely a minute ahead of ourselves," I stated. "We don't have much time."

"You're right. We have to hurry." Kallie grabbed my wrist, and she led me down the hall as fast as she could. Oberi followed. We passed the cafeteria, where people were shouting protests like earlier, then turned the corner to where we'd found Thaddeus before.

I expected him to be right there, surrounded by Esther, Naya, and Mad Dog, but instead, their voices came from further down the hall.

"You're a *good guy,* Thaddeus," Esther practically sang, her voice getting closer. "I *know* you'll do the right thing and join The Mission."

Thaddeus sighed loudly, and it was like music to my ears. By the ancestors, he was alive! My knees shook with relief. We really did have the power to stop this.

"You can take your pitch elsewhere," Thaddeus said. "I refuse to be a part of it."

"Oh, you think so?" Mad Dog sneered. "One way or another, The Mission will have you."

Several things happened at once. Their footsteps stopped, and a *thud* sounded alongside a breathless *oof.* Thaddeus' hawk Familiar screeched.

Mad Dog's pinned Thaddeus against the wall! Oberi shouted to me.

Fuck, this was it!

"Hey!" I yelled, the same time Oberi's bark echoed down the hall. I threw my hands upward, and my Air magic swept Mad Dog's feet out from under him. Thaddeus gulped a greedy breath. Kallie and I rushed forward and helped steady Thaddeus on his feet.

"Oh, great, *you,*" Naya sneered.

I was definitely getting an intense case of déjà vu.

"Yes, *us*," Kallie seethed. "What were you going to do to him? Punch him? Make him *bleed*?"

I turned to Thaddeus and ran my fingers over his forehead. "You all right? Are you bleeding?"

"No," Thaddeus said in a trembling tone. "Just shook up is all."

Mad Dog got to his feet. "You're going to pay for that, Bandit."

I scoffed. "You've seen me in the ring. You sure you want to find out how dirty I play? Go pick on someone else."

Esther planted herself between Mad Dog and me, and like an obedient little puppy, he backed down. "I believe words fare better than fists," she said smoothly. "Let's talk this out."

"Forget about it," Kallie said. "Thaddeus said no. He has nothing else to say to you."

Kallie nudged me, and I knew we were running out of time. Our past selves would turn this corner any moment, then Esther and her cronies would know we could time travel. That was the last thing we wanted them to find out.

"Sorry, not interested," I told Esther, before we grabbed Thaddeus and ducked the hell out of there as fast as we could.

"You need to join The Mission. It's the only way things are going to get better in this cruel world!" Esther called after us.

It was like she'd been practicing that line, because it was the same thing she'd said our first time around.

We ducked around a corner, doing our best to ignore her. Hell, we had to move fast.

"Thanks for getting me out of there—" Thaddeus started, but Kallie hushed him. I shoved him back into the corner, so he couldn't see anything.

Kallie paused a beat, then whispered, "Esther's leaving with Mad Dog and Naya. They're heading toward the cafeteria."

Just in time, too, because a moment later, I heard the familiar sound of Oberi's paws padding along the carpet, along with several other sets of footsteps. It was the past version of Oberi, because the present version was standing right next to me, his fur brushing against my leg. Our past selves had narrowly avoided running into Esther.

"What's going on?" Thaddeus whispered. I held him back, or he'd witness two versions of Kallie and me roaming around. Even Ava and Marcus didn't know what we'd done. It was best if we kept it to ourselves.

Kallie turned toward him. "You have information on Professor Mazur?"

Thaddeus sounded confused. "Yeah... how'd you know?"

"Lucky guess," Kallie said quickly. "Wait here for five minutes, then come find us, okay?"

"Okay," Thaddeus agreed, sounding bewildered.

Kallie grabbed my hand, then yanked me further down the hall, into a quiet classroom.

You shouldn't have done that, Oberi demanded as he followed. *You don't know what effect this may have!*

"Why can't we stay to hear what Thaddeus had to say?" I asked.

"Because we want to change *as little as possible,*" she reminded me. "If he told us now, he'd never go looking for our past selves and tell Ava and Marcus. Now that he's safe, he's going to find us, tell us what he found, and everything will be back in place. We have to let this play out as it should have if Thaddeus hadn't been compelled."

"Okay. Let's go back to the time we left and find out what he learned," I stated.

Kallie snapped her fingers, and the world spun around me once more. I felt like vomiting, and I landed hard on my knees as the sound of screams filled the air.

Shouts echoed down the hall... but how could that be, when we were standing in a classroom a moment ago?

I didn't have a moment to make sense of my surroundings before I heard Oberi cry Ava's name. He barked, but his bark came from several yards away.

I didn't understand. He'd been at my side a moment ago.

"Charlie, what are you doing!?" Marcus screamed.

"Get to Ava, quick!" Thaddeus called.

I turned my head, trying to make sense of the noises all around me. Something shifted in my shirt pocket, and I realized it was Sprigs. I'd given him to Marcus before we saved Thaddeus. How did he get back in my shirt?

I realized in horror that Kallie must've transported us *too far* into the future. We weren't where we were meant to be, and had gone past the moment we'd left. I had no idea what was going on.

Someone grabbed the back of my shirt and yanked on me. I pushed my hands against the ground to get to my feet, but my palms landed in something warm and sticky.

Blood.

What the fucking hell?

"Charlie, get up!" Kallie barked in my ear.

I grabbed for her, not worrying about the blood on my hands. "Do you remember what we just did?"

"I remember everything, but something went wrong. There are dead bodies everywhere!" Kallie panicked.

My guts twisted into horrible knots. She yanked on me again, and I quickly followed. I heard the sound of Ava whimpering from beneath me, and my heart shattered into a million pieces. I dropped to the floor beside her and felt around. I expected to touch her, but my hands met something else. It was cold and round...

The wheel of her chair lay on top of her. I felt around, and I found the footrest and the handle. Ava's chair had been smashed to pieces.

Help me with this! Oberi barked, nudging his nose into my arm.

I flung the remnants of the chair off of Ava, then touched her warm, trembling skin. "Ava, you with me?"

"It hurts, Charlie," she croaked. "It hurts so bad."

She shook as she sobbed, and I feared drawing her into my arms, because I didn't want to make her pain any worse. I ran my fingers down her body, but I found no blood or wounds. Whatever pain she felt must've been internal. What the hell had happened here?

"Pidge, where does it hurt?" I asked, but I felt her consciousness shudder against our bond before becoming silent. She'd passed out from the pain and fell limp against the floor.

I went completely still as I surveyed our surroundings. I had to figure out what was going on.

"Keep the cafeteria doors locked, or I'll shoot you with noxite myself," Mad Dog sneered from nearby.

Across the hall, Esther shouted her own nonsense. "Join my uncle in The Mission, and you will be granted a place in the heavens for all eternity!"

I forced a gust of air to sweep through the hallway, and I felt bodies brushing against my magic. People shouted obscenities at one other, and others screamed as they fled the scene.

Oberi, what's going on? I demanded.

Mad Dog and his gang incited a prison riot. They stole noxite guns and overpowered the guards. They've trapped them in the cafeteria, Oberi rushed to say. He didn't sound like he was guessing, but like he *knew.* He must've grasped the scene instantly, unlike Kallie and me, who didn't have a clue.

I shook Kallie's arm. "Take us back! We went too far. Take us back!"

If we could go back to our real time, we could stop this from happening.

Kallie turned her wrist around, and her tone became hollow. "It's three-forty-seven, Charlie."

I felt all the blood drain from my face. "The same time we left."

"We returned back to the proper time, but in the *new* timeline," Kallie stated.

I told you this was a bad idea! Oberi growled. *You don't know how changing something small can affect the big picture outcome!*

My mind raced as it rushed to fill in holes. We'd stopped Mad Dog from punching Thaddeus, but Esther had continued toward the cafeteria, where we'd seen the protestors earlier. If I knew anything about Esther, she no doubt started preaching.

That's exactly what happened, Oberi confirmed. *The protestors got angry, Mad Dog threw a punch, and it turned into a riot. The Mission got the upper hand, and they took the guards hostage and killed the protestors.*

In our original timeline, the guards were busy investigating Thaddeus' death. In this one, they hadn't been sent to the great hall to deal with it. Mad Dog had the perfect opportunity to corner them in the cafeteria, steal their guns, and lock them inside.

Kallie yanked at me, but I shoved her off. "I'm not leaving Ava," I told her.

"We can fix this," Kallie hissed. "We have to go back and try again. If we succeed, this won't happen."

No! Oberi cried. *You could make things even worse!*

What's worse? I demanded of him. *Kallie's right. Ava's in critical condition. The guards are locked up. I'm not letting this happen.*

People are dead! Oberi shouted. *Ava could die if you press this!*

She could die if we let this happen, I argued. *She needs medical attention, and she's not getting it as long as Mad Dog's in charge.*

"Well?" Kallie demanded. "Are we going, or not?"

"We're going," I said through gritted teeth. It took everything I had to leave Ava-Marie behind, but if we did things right this time, Ava would be safely in our dorm room when we returned back to our own time.

I pulled Sprigs out of my pocket and set him on Ava's chest. "I'll be back for you soon, pidge," I said, before placing a kiss on her forehead.

"Three forty-nine," Kallie announced. She snapped her fingers, and the room seemed to flip.

The shouts died in a mere instant. Oberi barked, and the sound echoed off the hallway. Lively chatter came from the open doors of the cafeteria. Relief flooded my body.

"Where are we now?" I asked. My voice shook as I asked the question.

"I took us back to this morning, around breakfast," Kallie announced. "Thaddeus said Esther had been tailing him all day, and it's safe to assume Mad Dog was with her the whole time. We've got to deal with him first. That way, he can't go after Thaddeus, and he can't start the riots..."

Kallie's voice trailed off. "Oh, Charlie. You've still got blood on your hands."

I swallowed the lump rising in my throat. "So the riots still happened."

"In the timeline we just left, yes," Kallie said. "But we can change it. Quick, clean up, then we'll find Mad Dog."

I hurried to the bathroom and washed the blood off my hands, then met up with Kallie in the hall.

"What if we run into Ava or Marcus?" I wondered.

"We won't," she said. "At this point in the day, you and Ava are in your dorms sleeping, and Marcus and I should be searching the forest right now."

"How much time do we have?" I asked.

"At least an hour. Marcus and I came back inside around ten, then we split up. I went back to my dorm to grab my grimoire to look for clues. As long as we avoid the fae cell block and don't run into the past version of me, we should be fine. Let's go look for Mad Dog."

It sounded like a great plan... until I realized we didn't know where the fuck to find him. Kallie led me through a maze of hallways, but I didn't think she knew where she was going. She wasn't very helpful at navigating, either. I turned a corner and bumped into someone. She cursed at me, before strolling off. It sounded like a siren based on the way she hissed at me.

"Be careful," Kallie insisted. "Everything we do has consequences."

"I'm trying," I shot back.

Allow me. Oberi cut between us and nudged his nose into my hand. I placed my hand on his head to help guide me through the hall. Kallie walked in a calculated manner, as if trying to avoid setting off even the smallest change.

"This is taking too long," I complained. "The longer we stay, the more we risk changing."

Finally, someone's making sense, Oberi huffed.

I heard the sounds of the cafeteria up ahead. We'd just been here when we arrived in this timeline. It was like she was leading us around in circles.

I slowed my steps. "Where are we going, Kallie? We've been past here at least three times."

"No, we haven't," she snapped. "We went down the east hall, then turned around so we could search the west corridors. We've only been past here once."

I couldn't keep our location straight. It felt like I'd been walking by the cafeteria all day. It was like the timelines were bleeding into themselves, and I couldn't quite remember the sequence of events. I barely knew what time of day it was.

"We're not leaving until we find Mad Dog and stop him," Kallie said. "I've got an illusion in mind that will trap him for a few hours—"

"Kallie!" Marcus' voice came from down the hall.

This is bad, Oberi whined.

"Shit. It's Marcus from this morning," Kallie hissed. "He wasn't supposed to be here for another half hour."

"We must've accidentally changed something," I realized.

"Act natural," she said.

Marcus approached us, along with Rishi. "I thought you were going to your dorm to get your grimoire."

"I... did," Kallie said quickly.

"Already?" Marcus sounded shocked. He must've parted from past-Kallie only moments ago.

"Yep," Kallie stated confidently. "I ran into Charlie on my way back."

Marcus paused for a moment, as if he was looking me up and down. "You look like you slept well. I'm still wiped from last night."

Our night in death row felt like two nights ago, at least. Which didn't make a damn bit of sense, because Kallie and I had only been time-traveling for an hour, at most. This was so fucking confusing.

"Yeah, same," Kallie said quickly. "Have you seen Thaddeus? Or noticed Esther or Mad Dog roaming around?"

Marcus didn't get a chance to answer before a deep voice came from behind us. "Who's asking?"

Kallie whirled around. "Mad Dog. Just the criminal I was looking for."

"Fuck off," he growled.

"Kallie, do it now," I hissed.

I sensed her magic welling up inside of her, but Kallie never got a chance to blast off the spell. Mad Dog swept toward her in the blink of an eye. One second Kallie was standing beside me. The next, Mad Dog had pinned her to the wall. Oberi barked loud protests.

"Get off her!" Marcus went to yank Mad Dog off, but he must've thrown an arm back, because Marcus landed with a loud *thud* on the ground. Rishi hissed.

Magic crackled in my palm, but I didn't shoot it off, because I didn't want to hit Kallie.

"You don't want to mess with me today," Mad Dog warned.

"If you want to hold me down, you might as well buy me dinner first," Kallie said sarcastically.

Mad Dog drew a deep breath, as if taking in Kallie's scent. "Something's not right here. What kind of game are you playing, princess?"

Kallie spoke in a struggled breath, as if Mad Dog had her by the throat now. "No games... just saving lives."

Mad Dog laughed maniacally. "You can't save lives if you're dead."

We all reacted at once. I aimed my magic at Mad Dog's back, while Oberi rushed forward and bit him in the leg. Marcus shoved himself between Mad Dog and Kallie, but the vampire was already moving in for the kill.

Marcus gasped, and a warm, sticky liquid squirted over the front of my face. A heart-shattering scream filled the hall— the sound of a devastated lover. Kallie's horrified cry rivaled that of a siren as she screamed Marcus' name.

Mad Dog dropped Marcus to the ground, and I lunged forward to grab the motherfucker. I was going to siphon all this asshole's vampire strength and snap his neck in two.

But my hands met nothing but air. Mad Dog had vanished down the hall with his super speed, and I couldn't catch him.

Oberi whimpered. Beneath me, Marcus gasped for breath. For a moment, it was like the hall was filled with dead bodies all over again.

Kallie dropped to her knees. "*Marcus!*"

I hurried beside her and pressed my hands to Marcus' neck. Blood spurted from a huge gash in his artery, and there was nothing I could do to stop it. It wasn't the kind of vampire bite that could change him, but the kind designed to kill. Rishi yowled loudly.

"Oberi, you've got to be able to heal him," I barked. "Do *something.*"

"I— I was trying to save you," Marcus rasped. I felt his arm reach for Kallie before his entire body went limp, and he gasped his last breath.

"No, *no!*" Kallie screamed.

My whole body went numb. It was like losing Marty all over again. I'd already lost one best friend, and that had nearly shattered my world. Losing another felt like a black hole had opened up in my entire reality.

Guards flooded out of the cafeteria. "On your feet!" one of them yelled. I heard the click of noxite guns.

Fuck!

I grabbed Kallie's arms. "Kallie, we've *got to go.*"

Kallie sobbed hysterically, and I didn't think she'd heard me. This wasn't how things were supposed to go. We *could not* lose Marcus. We had to go back and stop this.

"I said *on your feet!*" a guard roared.

"*Now, Kallie!*" I snapped, and I shook her roughly. I had to get her to snap out of it, otherwise, there'd be no fixing this for sure.

Kallie snapped her fingers, and I felt the world spinning once more. Marcus' body disappeared beneath us, but I was still covered with warm blood. Chatter spilled out from the cafeteria, but the angry guards were gone.

"When are we?" I asked.

Kallie's voice trembled. I could hear tears spilling from her as she replied, "A little before nine."

I shook her. "Marcus is still alive. We can fix this, but we have to make the *right* decisions this time."

Oberi shoved himself between us. *No. No more changing things. You have to set things back to the way they were.*

"If we do that, Thaddeus will still die," I protested.

Every time you change something, it gets worse! Oberi pressed. *You have one last chance to fix this, and if you get it wrong this time, you could lose Marcus* and *Ava both. Do you understand?*

My stomach twisted into horrible knots.

"What's he saying?" Kallie demanded.

I drew a deep breath. "Oberi wants us to put things back the way they were. He thinks if we try to change anything else, more people will die."

"No. There's got to be a way," Kallie insisted. "Let's go through the timeline again. Marcus and I were outside this morning, checking out the grave site. When we didn't find anything, I came inside to get my grimoire, then Marcus found us at the cafeteria. Esther started tailing Thaddeus sometime this morning. We met up with you and Ava after lunch, then ran into the riots, then..."

Kallie trailed off.

"No," I said. "We ran into Thaddeus *before* the riots. Or was that in a different timeline?"

My memories of the day began to entwine together. I remembered walking in from the prison yard, straight into the riots, but I was almost certain Kallie and I had time traveled into that scenario. So how did I remember what happened before we reappeared in the new timeline?

I was *certain* I'd been time traveling with Kallie most of the day, but every reality seemed to exist just as equally as the others. "Marcus died this morning, but then he was alive when the riots started. It doesn't make sense."

Because your day is no longer linear, Oberi said. *It all happened. You're just remembering it as one day.*

"Oberi says we're remembering everything all at once," I told Kallie.

"Of course. The details are still fuzzy, but that's why you felt like we'd passed the cafeteria several times, because we *had* passed it several times today. Our memories must take time to integrate when we go back and change things, but we *will* remember, as if we'd been in both places, because we *were* in both places."

"But time's a line," I stated. I couldn't wrap my head around existing in two places at once.

"It's not," Kallie replied. "It's more like... folded on top of itself. That's why when we changed something and I took us back to the present, we ended up in a different spot than we left. Because we still experienced everything leading up to that new moment. There can be two of you in the past, and two of you in the future, but you can only exist at one point in the present moment— the time you leave and come back to. It's like... a checkpoint."

This is another reason time travel is so dangerous, Oberi said. *If you change too much, your mind can't make sense of what is and isn't real. It can drive you mad.*

"What about you?" I asked. "You seem fine, and you remembered everything before we did."

I told you, I'm a transdimensional being. I'm used to this kind of thing. Your mortal brain is not designed for such tasks.

"We must be able to use it for something, or Kallie wouldn't have this power," I said.

She has to utilize it properly. What you're trying to do is an abuse of her magic.

I turned to Kallie. "Oberi says you're abusing your power."

"I certainly have a lot to learn. Oberi's right. We've got to put things back the way they were. It's our only option."

"But Thaddeus will still die." My throat closed up.

"I know it's a tough decision, but what's the alternative?" Kallie pressed. "A bunch of other people die? *Marcus* dies? In every scenario, someone dies. It's not a choice I want to make, but an impossible decision like this comes down to the fact that it's clear we can't change things here. So we're going to put things back the way they were, to avoid them being even worse."

"How?" I asked.

Kallie got to her feet. "I have to stop myself from ever going back. We won't time travel at all, and everything we changed will be undone."

That's the best idea you've had all day, Oberi said.

Kallie led me out into the prison yard, and we snuck into the trees. We neared the death row gravesite. I could hear the past versions of Marcus and Kallie arguing from ahead of us. Rishi meowed loudly.

"There's nothing here!" Marcus insisted. It was a relief to hear his voice. His death still felt so real.

"There has to be *something*," Kallie replied. "You've got psychic abilities. Maybe you can figure it out."

"I can't just *make* my visions happen. A *clue* would be a great start."

"Well, I don't have a clue other than the dot on the map," Kallie shot back.

I placed my hand on a tree and stepped around it. Kallie— the Kallie from my timeline— snuck ahead of me. She lowered her voice and whispered, "I've got to get myself alone. Marcus would freak if he saw two of me."

She took another step, and a stick broke beneath her foot.

From ahead of us, Marcus gasped. "What was that?"

The tree beside me began to buzz with a strange frequency, and I felt my hand *melting into it*. The ground turned to jelly beneath my feet.

Kallie grabbed me and shoved me back. "Fuck! Change of plans. I spotted us, and we've created a paradox."

"What the hell is that?" I hissed.

"It's an impossibility in the timeline. Two of me can't exist together at the same point. It's fucking with reality."

Time to go! Oberi said.

Kallie grabbed my hand, and we hurried back through the trees.

"It's nothing, Marcus," past Kallie said, her voice fading as we scurried away as silently as we could. "Don't be such a worry wort."

We ducked behind a big tree trunk, and Kallie steadied her breath. "I'm lying to him. I remember seeing us. My memories are shifting as we speak."

"Is that enough?" I asked. "Will you avoid time traveling later today?"

"I haven't made the decision yet. I know something's wrong because you're covered in blood, but right now, I think that's the reason I have to go back. I still need to warn myself."

"How are we going to do that if approaching your past self creates a paradox?" I asked.

Kallie went silent for a moment, before she said, "I'll leave a note for myself to find when I go search for my grimoire."

I swallowed the lump in my throat and stood beside her. "I hope this works."

"It better, because this is our last chance," she said.

We snuck back inside, trying to not be seen. Kallie led me into the fae cell block, and hurried over to her desk. She tore a piece of paper and scribbled something down, then shoved it under the mattress where she kept her grimoire.

"It's done," she announced.

Great, Oberi said. *Can we go now?*

Kallie snapped her fingers, and that familiar tilting of the earth rocked my body. This time, when I landed back in the present, my stomach clenched into impossible knots. I felt like I was going to hurl.

I got the sensation that I was walking. Every instance we traveled *back* in time, we appeared in the same spot we left. When we returned to the present, we showed up where *the present version* of us was, based on what they experienced in the new timeline.

My feet moved beneath me, but I didn't know where I was going. My hands were curled around the back of Ava's chair, but the blood on was gone. Sprigs shifted in my shirt pocket, and Rishi purred as he rubbed against my leg.

"Erasmus..." Marcus mused from beside me. "Gah! I wish I remembered more about him."

I slowed until I came to a stop.

Ava reached over her shoulder to touch my hand. "Everything all right, Charlie?"

Her voice sounded strained. I remembered she'd been in pain earlier, but I was trying to place exactly where we were in the timeline.

We'd sent Marcus to take her back to her room, so what was I doing pushing her down the hall?

"Everything's fine," I told her. "Kallie, what time is it?"

"Three-forty-nine," she said in a detached voice.

Two minutes after we left the first time, but we'd spent two minutes in a *new* reality when Mad Dog had imprisoned the guards. I wasn't quite clear what had happened in this latest timeline.

Thaddeus is dead, Oberi filled me in. *You went to search for Dante's grave and found it. You're all headed back to your room together, since Kallie never pulled you aside and sent Marcus with Ava.*

I don't remember that yet, I told him. *How do you recall so easily?*

It's simple for me. You experienced each reality in a linear progression. I experienced them all at once. I explained this earlier.

Forgive me for being a little confused, I replied. *I've never lived a day multiple times, though I'm sure you're so used to it.*

Mock me all you want. I know a thing or two about this. You should have listened to me when I said you shouldn't go back.

We put things back in order, so I don't know what you're worried about, I replied.

Regardless of the way things are now, time travel comes with consequences, especially for demigods, Oberi pressed. *You and Kallie must both learn it's not as simple as it seems.*

We won't do it again, I promised.

Oberi huffed, like he didn't quite believe me, but he stayed close to my side and helped me navigate the halls.

Marcus groaned and staggered beside me. "I don't feel too good. I'm going to head back to my room."

I wasn't feeling well, either. I wanted to puke.

Kallie said goodbye to Marcus, then followed Ava and me back to our dorm. I sensed she wanted to say something, but couldn't in front of Ava.

We reached our room, and as I led Ava inside, I felt her barriers drop ever so slightly. What I saw on the other side was horrifying. Pain rippled up my back so intensely I nearly fell over, and my innards felt like they were being twisted from the inside out. My fingers tightened on the back of Ava's chair as I steadied myself. When she'd said she was in pain, I didn't realize it was *this* bad.

It's worse than you know, Oberi told me. *I told you there were consequences to time traveling.*

The nausea rolling around in my gut seemed to intensify. *Ava's sick because of what Kallie and I did?*

It affects you all, even if you don't realize it.

I turned Ava's chair around instantly. "We're going to the infirmary."

No! Ava protested in my mind. The pain must've gotten worse, because she didn't speak out loud, just gave a whimper of agony. *You promised you wouldn't take me back.*

This is bad, pidge. I was worried our time traveling had made her injury worse.

I just want to lie down, she insisted.

I lifted Ava out of her chair and set her gently on the bed. My stomach sank as she groaned with every minor movement. The ache in my gut couldn't compare to whatever she was feeling, though. Oberi climbed onto the bed beside Ava. He moved carefully and deliberately, which told me things were really fucking bad.

Kallie hurried out of the bedroom and came back a few moments later. She placed a wet cloth into my hands. "Warm it up, for the pain."

I drew Ava's Fire magic out of her, which was easier than ever, because she didn't resist my magical pull. I used the magic to warm the towel, then lifted her shirt and laid it across her middle. Ava didn't say anything, just gave a ragged breath as he laid her head back on the pillow.

While I helped with the warm compress, Kallie uncapped a bottle and told Ava to take her meds. Ava gagged as she forced the painkillers down.

Oberi, why isn't she healing herself? I demanded.

This is a magical affliction, caused by yours and Kallie's poor choices, Oberi said. *I daresay healing magic would barely counteract the effects of time travel. You should have listened to me. I tried to warn you.*

You should have been clearer about the consequences!

Kallie tugged on my arm. "Charlie, we need to talk."

I didn't want to leave Ava's side, but Kallie and I had a lot to talk about. Ava barely made a noise. I wasn't sure she was aware we'd left the room and shut the door behind us.

The nausea got worse, and I lowered myself to the couch. If *I* felt this shitty, I couldn't imagine how Ava felt.

"Clearly, we can't change things in the past," Kallie said bluntly.

I sighed heavily. "No shit. This whole thing was a mistake. We fixed nothing, and Ava's sicker than ever. Why did it affect her so much, when you and I were the ones who went back in time?"

"Even though I've learned how to travel at will, without affecting other demigods' timelines, it must give them a reaction. Ava's nervous system is already damaged, so it must be reacting worse than ours. I don't think my time powers can be used to manipulate events."

"Then what's the point of having them?" I demanded. The fact that we had the tools to go back and change what happened in the Infernal Underground and *couldn't use them* was infuriating.

"I can still go back, but only to observe and gather details," Kallie said. "We proved today that changing things is too much of a risk."

"What if you accidentally change things?"

"That's a gamble, too, which is why we have to reserve my powers for when we *really* need them. I still have a lot to learn. But I think there are ways we can still use my powers for good."

"What's there to learn?" I asked. "You change things, you make things worse. End of story."

"Maybe I can go back *without* changing anything," Kallie theorized. "The time travel we've experienced here on the Institute grounds is different than I thought it'd be. Time isn't supposed to be this linear thing. It's all happening at once. But here at the Institute, it acts differently, and I don't know why. It could be the noxite or inferichite— I don't really know. But today, we had to live out the day *before* we could go back. If I really understood my powers, I should be able to show up at any point in time without changing things, as if I'd been there the first time. I know time is happening all at once everywhere, but here at the prison, I can only work it on a line. I can't seem to go anywhere I want to go."

"None of this makes any sense," I said.

"That's exactly what I'm saying," she agreed. "Look, we pushed our limits today, but now we know better."

My shoulders dropped. "Yeah. We learned that we can't go back and change Ava's fate, no matter how much we want to."

I couldn't hide the devastation in my tone. What was the point?

Kallie sighed. "I can't manipulate destiny. That much is for certain."

"Then there's no point in *ever* going back," I said. "Not if it makes Ava this sick. We may have set things back the way they were, but we didn't— not really. We messed up our own timeline. We're in a reality where Ava's injury is flaring, when it wasn't this bad before. What happens if we can't restore things this close again? Every time we fuck with time, it makes her sicker. We did a lot of that today. We can't do it again."

"Unless we need to—"

"*No*," I stated bluntly. "Never. I'm not putting Ava in this much pain for anything. Do you understand?"

Kallie paused for a beat. "I'm not going to let that happen. I promise."

"Glad we're on the same page. You should head back to your dorm and rest," I suggested. "It's been a hard day on all of us."

Kallie got up to leave. The moment she left the room, I doubled over the trash can and spewed my guts.

Ugh. Fucking time travel.

I puked a few more times, before my body stopped trembling and I felt like I could stand on my feet again. I returned to the bedroom. The sheets rustled as Ava tossed and turned.

I knelt beside her and smoothed her hair back. "Pidge, I'm here."

She trembled beneath my touch. *Charlie, it's never been this awful.*

Tears leaked from her eyes, and I wiped them away. To say I felt guilty was an understatement. There were no words for the horrible blame I placed on myself. I wanted to take all her pain away and make it my own.

This is one of those unfortunate consequences I warned you about before we brought her back, Oberi noted sadly.

"I'm here, pidge," I said. It was all I *could* say, because there was nothing I could *do* to make this better. I hated that.

I wanted to comfort her, and I had the thought that I had to understand her first. Ava had granted me permission to enter her mind in dire circumstances, when I needed to help her. This felt like one of those times.

I didn't have to prod. For the briefest of moments, her barriers dropped, and I felt the agonizing pain throughout her entire body. It was like being impaled by a hundred knives from all angles. It felt as if someone had cut open my middle, set it on fire, then started tearing pieces out bit by bit. Every organ seemed to be folding inside out. My bones were like razor blades, cutting into my muscles. It was pure hell.

I drew away instantly, slamming the bond shut. I couldn't take another second. My hands trembled, but it was nothing compared to Ava's body shaking on the bed.

Guilt welled up inside of me. I was able to turn off the pain and retreat inside my own body, where I was safe. Ava couldn't, and I had the horrifying thought that *I* did this to her.

I can't endure this anymore. It's too much, she begged. *You have to end it. Just smother me.*

I went completely still. I didn't want to believe that she'd just uttered those words...

Except I *did* believe it, because I'd felt what she had, and it was unbearable. I found myself reaching for the pillow, but I didn't want to use it.

Ava wept. *If you love me, you'll kill me.*

I just sat there with the pillow in my hands, a million thoughts flitting through me at once. I could end her suffering and her pain. The last thing I wanted was my pidge to hurt like this.

Please, she begged silently. *I can't do this, Charlie. You have Air magic. You can make it quick. Don't let me linger on like this.*

Maybe there *was* a way to take her pain away... For one dark moment, I considered doing as she asked, if only because she wanted me to, and I would do anything for her.

I thought about the choice I'd made to bring her back from the Underground. This was a way to correct that mistake, because it *was* a mistake if she had to live like this. If anything, I didn't want my wife to exist in unbearable pain.

My fingers tightened on the pillow. I tried to move forward, but couldn't.

Oberi jumped between us. He knocked the pillow out of my hands and said, *Don't be silly, Ava. If you die, who's going to hide your body? Because we damn well know Charlie won't manage to carry you out to the prison yard without running into a few walls along the way.*

Ava let out a choked laugh that was more like a sob. Although the pain still resonated across our bond, it seemed to ease at the humor.

Oberi shoved me roughly, and I managed to force a smile onto my face. "You know, if I kill you, you're going to miss that opportunity to have that threesome Chancey won't shut up about. Never mind, that just gives you another reason to want to die."

"Oh, ancestors." Ava let out a hiss that became a snicker, and then a moan of pain. But at least she'd managed to say something.

And you'll miss all the wonderful *people here at the Institute, like the cheerful guards who think there's always something hiding up your anus,* Oberi said.

"Well, they'd be right with me. I shoved something up there this morning," I cracked.

"Oh, goodness." Ava giggled, then wiped at her face, sniffed, and giggled again.

I told every joke I fucking knew, and a bunch of really terrible jokes that I'd made up on the spot, just to distract her from her pain. She was laughing more than she was crying now, and at least that was something. Oberi was funnier than me, so he had Ava clutching her stomach in both discomfort and laughter within minutes.

Eventually, after what seemed like at least an hour of absolutely shitty comedy, Ava's flare up began to ease. She let out little snorts of laughter that turned into soft snores as she drifted off beside me. She didn't toss and turn, but rather, seemed at peace.

I checked in. She was still in pain, but it wasn't enough to prevent her from sleeping. Hopefully, she'd feel better in the morning.

Oberi lay at the foot of our bed, thumping his tail against the blankets as he watched Ava sleep.

"How'd you know what to do?" I asked him. "I was helpless."

There is pain you cannot stop. Merely endure until it goes away, Oberi replied. *And if the pain will not end, then laughter is the only way to ward off its effects. It's not necessarily difficult to make her laugh, though the situation wasn't at all funny.*

"No, it really wasn't. Let's hope it doesn't happen again."

Oberi didn't reply immediately. He seemed contemplative. *It has been a long day, full of some very hard lessons. Some rest will do well for all of us. And Charlie?*

I waited for him to go on. Oberi dropped his voice to a deadly tone before he warned, *If you dare to consider something like that again, you won't have to worry about ending your life once Ava is gone. Because I'll do it myself. Sleep well.*

ava-marie

FOURTEEN

Thad's death shook us all. It was one thing to watch a friend die in front of you, and completely another to stand by in horror as he brutally murdered his Familiar, the one thing that meant the most to them in this world.

I attempted to imagine hurting Oberi, and couldn't go there. It was an automatic response of revulsion. I'd sooner run myself through than harm a hair on my annoying Familiar's head.

It spoke to Mad Dog's power. No matter how strong his compulsion magic was, he shouldn't have been able to manipulate Thaddeus to harm his Familiar, and yet, he had. That meant he could compel *anyone* to do *anything,* and because he was a demigod, no one would be able to stop him.

Our group had fallen into a small bout of depression after the fact. We hadn't been able to prevent Thaddeus' demise, and on top of that, we were worried that Mad Dog would use his compulsion against us next.

I didn't think anyone was more bothered by it than Charlie, however. He'd taken to spending long periods of time by himself. I was afraid he was either drowning in misplaced guilt, feeling responsible for sending Thaddeus to his death, or plotting Mad Dog's imminent demise.

Both terrified me. Charlie wasn't afraid of Mad Dog, but I was— because I was terrified that Mad Dog could compel Charlie to do something crazy against his will. For the most part, it looked like Mad Dog was lying low. We hadn't heard or seen much from him since Thaddeus' death, so he was probably biding his time, making sure he didn't get caught and be taken to Cellblock 9.

Not to mention Charlie had been caught up in enough trouble since this semester started. The guards were already keeping an eye on him; they'd ruled Thaddeus' death a suicide, but suspected foul play, and the only reason they didn't pin his death on Charlie was because they had no proof Charlie had done anything to hurt him.

We needed to get the fuck out of here. Before our luck ran out.

I wasn't sure where to go next when it came to Erasmus Morelli, but knew I needed to find out more about him. I figured if it had anything to do with vampires, Ivy might know something.

"You look down, precious," Ivy purred as I rolled up to his table in the library. "Anything I can do to help?"

"Maybe. We've hit a dead end in our investigation," I told him. "Do you happen to know anything about a vampire named Erasmus Morelli?"

"Ah, good old Erasmus." Ivy gave a wicked smile. "I actually know him personally. He works for my dad. We did a couple of jobs together back in Chicago, before I landed in the pen."

"Can you contact him? We need to speak with him. It's urgent," I pleaded.

"I can try, but he's not an easy vampire to reach. My father often gives him the hardest jobs, because he's got the most skill. Some of these tasks for the mob take months," Ivy explained.

We didn't have that kind of time, but I reeled in my patience and replied, "Thanks, Ivy. The sooner you can get a hold of Erasmus, the better."

"I'll do my best," Ivy said in an apologetic tone. "I'm sure he'll be willing to help, once I'm finally able to establish contact. He owes me a favor or two."

I sure hoped so, because he was the only one who *could* help us.

A couple of weeks passed by in slow boredom. It was early June, and we were nearing the end of the semester. Once classes ended, all of us would be sent to work at our prison jobs full-time over the summer, and I wasn't looking forward to it, as it would definitely impede our search for the keys. Hemlock had written up some bullshit to get me out of work, so I could continue our search with her under the ruse that I was continuing my anthropology internship, but I couldn't do it by myself. If we were going to get anywhere, my friends needed time to look for the keys alongside me, and the Warden was keeping such a close eye on us it was difficult to search in secret.

To try and get everyone cheered up, Oberi had suggested we have a game night in the Villain's Den. When we arrived, Chancey was already setting up the board, while Ivy placed tiny plastic pieces out on the table. There were about a dozen other inmates in here, hanging out and holding conversation.

"This is gonna be fun and all, but don't you guys want to increase the stakes?" Chancey asked as Charlie and I came in. "I got a deck—"

"No cards," Ivy said sharply, giving him a harsh look.

"Yeah, yeah, no cards," Chancey grumbled.

Kallie lounged on the couch with her legs thrown over an armrest. She was alone.

"Where's Marcus?" I asked as I wheeled up to the table. Oberi rushed to grab a ball in one of the baskets by the television and started kicking it around with his paws.

"He's not coming," Kallie said, a little downhearted. She didn't offer an explanation why.

Marcus hadn't been around much since Thaddeus had died. I knew he was trying to contact Thaddeus' ghost, but none of Marcus' séances were working. That meant his soul had crossed over, so Marcus was trying to find a way to speak with him from the Ancestral Lands, which was difficult, because it wasn't a normal séance situation. Unlike ghosts trapped here on Earth, it was far more difficult to speak to a spirit that had passed. Marcus should be able to pull it off, but a spirit had to be willing to communicate, so it was obvious Thad didn't want to talk.

We were about to get started before a tinkling laugh pissed on my evening. I refused to look at her, but Esther came around to the table anyway, planting herself at my side. "Oh, what a lovely game! Can I join?"

"Go away, Esther. Everyone here fucking hates you," I spat as I continued setting up the game. If anything, I blamed Esther for what happened to Thad the most. Below us, Oberi let out a warning growl.

"You're such a mean girl, Ava. Don't you know it's not nice to put other women down?" Esther asked, leaning against the table.

"I don't like to hang out with murderers," I growled.

"That's pretty hypocritical, seeing as how your two best friends and your husband fit the bill. Hypocrisy is a sin, you know—"

"Fuck. Off." My fists clenched.

"Esther, I'm warning you, leave us alone," Charlie said coldly.

"Or what?" Esther gave another laugh, but instead of the fake cheer that usually infected it, the sound was chilling and cruel. "You know, Charlie, I find it so cute you still stick up for your wife."

"What the hell is that supposed to mean?" Charlie asked. His body stiffened, trying to hold himself back from erupting on the spot.

"I'm only saying that most husbands wouldn't be able to put up with her," Esther stated. "She's such a handful, and she's got so many *needs* since she's in a wheelchair. A lot of men wouldn't be able to handle the pressure of being their wife's caretaker, day in and day out. It's honorable you haven't left yet—"

The table shook, and pieces of the board game flew off as Kallie stood up and punched Esther across the face. Esther went flying, and she slammed into the wall.

Chancey laughed, but no one else did. Esther shakily pushed herself upward, although the movement faltered, as if it was difficult to do.

She flung her blonde curls out of her face. "You're going to pay for that, filthy mutt," Esther snarled.

"Go ahead and tell the Warden. I don't give a fuck anymore!" Kallie yelled as Esther got to her feet. The two girls faced off, ready to go to war.

Esther's chest heaved. Her arms shook, like she was seconds away from retaliating.

Then she noticed all the faces in the Villain's Den staring at her. The other students, most of them members of The Mission, waited to see what she would do.

She took a deep breath, then smoothed down her curls and put a smile on her face.

"I was only giving Charlie a compliment," Esther said calmly. "There's no need to resort to violence. I can see I'm not welcome here. I'll leave you alone."

Esther turned and walked out. Quite a few Mission members followed her. The inmates that didn't glanced at us, whispering under our breath. A couple of students who'd been near our table got up to move away to the other side of the room.

She looked like the victim and had painted us as the maniacs. It'd barely taken any effort.

Now the bitch was ruining our reputation. There wasn't any situation, it seemed, she couldn't turn to her advantage.

"You know I don't think that, right?" Charlie asked me softly. "You're not a burden. Nothing could make me stop caring for you."

Oberi laid his head on my lap, and I rested my hand there. "I know," I replied quietly. "Let's just play."

I tried to keep Esther's nasty words out of my mind as we played the first round. She didn't matter. She was just trying to utilize any weakness she could to get inside my head.

Didn't mean her words hadn't hurt.

"Hey guys!" Marcus' cheerful voice from the entrance lifted my spirits. When I saw him, I laughed out loud. Marcus had shown up wearing a wizard's hat and a sparkly robe. He'd put Rishi into a little bard costume. Rishi waddled up to the table in a wide-brimmed cap with a feather tucked into the side and meowed. I whispered to Charlie the details of Marcus' outfit, and he grinned.

Marcus stopped at the table and blinked when he looked at us. "Why am I the only one who dressed up?"

"What are you wearing?" Chancey snickered.

Marcus appeared baffled. "Are we... are we not playing *Dungeons and Dragons?*"

"No." I laughed. "I mean, we could if they had it here, but it's not approved by the Warden."

"Aw, man." Marcus dropped his gaze, clearly disappointed.

"You are *not* into role-playing board games," Kallie said scathingly.

"I won a competition once!" Marcus said brightly. "I was the dungeon master of my play group."

"He's the dungeon master of their bedroom," Ivy snickered under his breath.

"Marcus, that is the nerdiest thing you've ever said to me," Kallie said dryly. She hadn't heard Ivy.

"Come on, you haven't lived until you've tried an RPG. Please promise you'll play with me once we graduate," Marcus begged.

Kallie huffed. "Fine. *One game.*"

Marcus appeared thrilled. Oberi sat at his feet and looked up, banging his tail against the floor.

I am so jealous of those hats, Oberi said enviously. *I wish I could add them to my collection.*

Marcus plopped into a chair beside Kallie. "Okay, D&D is out, but you still have a chance to see my mad wicked board game skills."

"Why do I like you?" Kallie hissed under her breath, and I burst out laughing again. It was nice to spend time like this with friends, when we weren't trying to save the world or solve mysteries. I was glad we'd taken some time out to just chill.

We kept playing board games until around nine. We had about an hour before curfew, but hadn't wanted to leave just yet, so we'd stuck around the Villain's Den to talk. Charlie had helped me out of my chair and onto the couch, moving my legs so they were curled up on the cushion. My head lay against his chest, and he had an arm around me as Oberi slept over my feet. I felt very cozy and warm, snuggled up to my husband and listening to his heartbeats while Oberi let out soft snores.

This time of night, we were the only ones in here. I had been sleeping for quite a while, though I'd just woken up a moment ago. I dozed in and out of it, creaking my eyes open for just a moment to observe my surroundings. On the opposite couch, Ivy had fallen asleep with his head on Chancey's lap, and Chancey himself had his head thrown back against the edge of the cushions, off in dreamland. Marcus lay still on the floor, his arm around his wizard's hat while Rishi snoozed on top of him.

My eyes lulled, wanting to go back to sleep. Charlie and Kallie spoke lowly, their voices the only sound amidst the quiet.

"Ava passed out pretty quick," Kallie murmured.

"She gets tired easily these days." Charlie's fingers brushed my face lightly as he played with the ends of my hair.

"Do you think she's getting any better?"

There was a pause, until Charlie said, "No."

Kallie waited for a moment, before she asked, "Do you ever think she'll get back to the way she used to be, before she went down to the Underground?"

"Honestly? No. I don't think so."

I felt my heart break a little as he said that.

Kallie let out a soft breath. "That's gotta be tough."

"I don't care. She's still my girl."

I smiled just a little. Kallie shifted from her place on the floor and said, "She was pretty torn up about what Esther said. That bitch gets to her like none other."

"Fuck her. I'd never leave my pidge. She's mine forever."

I couldn't help it; I pressed into him further. He'd think it was me shifting in my sleep, but I wanted to be even closer to him than I already was.

Kallie's voice came closer. "Charlie... Ava's health is still up in the air. If something happens again..."

"It won't."

"But if it *does*. You can't go back to the way you were, you understand that? We all need you."

"She needs me more than anyone."

"Ava needs you to fulfill this prophecy if she can't. Promise me you're not going to go back there."

I didn't understand what they were talking about. This was confusing me.

Charlie moved slightly. "You wouldn't say the same if it were Marcus."

I dared to open my eyes again, just a little. Kallie parted Marcus' bangs away from his eyes and said, "We have to do what's best. For both of them."

I envied Charlie, and immediately felt bad for doing so. He'd lost his sight at a time when he couldn't remember it. He didn't know what it was to live without his eyes, because he had always done so.

I could still remember walking. I recalled how it felt to jump, to run, to have the wind in my hair as I carried myself from place to place, without having to think about the million and one things I had to consider now, just to get myself where I wanted to go. Everything had happened so suddenly. When I went down into the Underground, I could walk. By the time I woke up, that ability had been taken away from me. It was more than a shock. It was an inconceivable tragedy my mind couldn't understand.

I'd adjusted to life in a wheelchair as much as I could, but I still had a long way to go before I got to the point of acceptance.

Charlie gently shook me. "Wake up, pidge. It's time to go."

I barely stirred, though Kallie's words were still echoing in my mind. They haunted my sleep and continued to plague me throughout class the next day. I wanted to ask Charlie about it, but didn't have the courage. I wasn't sure if he'd be straightforward with me, or spew out some emotional bullshit he didn't mean in order to placate my feelings. Whatever Kallie had made Charlie swear to sounded serious, and I wanted to get to the bottom of it.

I took my opportunity to ask Kallie about it that evening. Charlie was on a four-hour factory shift and would be off soon, so I needed to ask quickly. She tossed a football back and forth with Chancey in the prison yard, practicing for an upcoming game. Chancey had joined the team, too, since he'd quit fight club, as he needed to get some energy out and— as he put it— *knock some heads without getting into trouble.*

Oberi stood at my side as a Fire unicorn. I clutched onto an alchemy textbook in my lap, trying to build up the courage for what I had to ask. Kallie jumped up to catch the ball, and I took a breath.

"Hey, Kallie..." I started, and she looked at me. "I overheard what you and Charlie were talking about last night. You said if something happened to me, Charlie couldn't go back there... but where is *there?*"

Kallie and Chancey shared a glance, like they weren't sure what they should tell.

"She has the right to know," Chancey said, like this had been a long time coming.

Kallie's expression twisted before she spoke. "I didn't want to be the one to tell you this. The night we came back from the Underground... Charlie kinda jumped off the deep end."

"What do you mean?" I insisted.

"He went fucking *nutty*, all that week," Chancey told me. "It was a rough sight to see."

I blinked. "Well *of course* he was upset, but—"

"You don't get it," Kallie replied. "He said he was going to kill himself if you didn't make it."

I felt the blood drain from my face as my body went ice cold. A wave of nausea pressed inward on me as each heartbeat became a stabbing knife in my chest. The thought of Charlie taking his own life...

I couldn't handle it. The very idea made me want to wither away. Charlie had spoken before in vague terms how he didn't want to live without me, but saying something like that and actually threatening suicide was a huge difference.

I always thought Charlie would be able to go on if I wasn't here, because he deserved a full life regardless if I got to live it with him or not. I knew he'd grieve, but I didn't think losing me would make him consider such extreme lengths.

I glanced at Oberi, asking if this was true. She bowed her head and confessed, *That is the honest truth.*

"Why didn't you tell me?!" I exclaimed. I gripped the armrests of my chair, so my hands didn't shake. This was shocking to me, because I didn't think I grasped how important I was to him until this very moment.

No one wants to hear words like that from someone they dearly love. Oberi reached out and nuzzled her soft nose to my cheek. *And it was hard enough to hear myself.*

I didn't know how Oberi managed, sitting there listening to Charlie's thoughts as he desperately looked for a way out of his grief. All, at the same time, while dealing with her own sorrow that I was gone.

I did it because he needed me, Oberi replied. *I had to put my own pain aside so he could survive that moment. It nearly did us all in.*

"What happened after the Underground collapsed?" I asked harshly. "I want *every detail* this time, not the story you guys edited to make me feel better."

Kallie glanced at Chancey, then launched into an explanation. She told me how they'd found my corpse, mangled from the explosion with my organs pouring out of me. She described, in a slightly detached voice, how Charlie had carried me to the infirmary, but the doctors had already told him I was gone, and there was nothing they could do. He'd nearly suffocated a doctor who'd told him so. Long minutes passed, and over my dead body, Charlie proclaimed he'd take his own life if they couldn't bring me back.

Then Oberi used her magic to restore my soul to my body, but it was a long fight of me struggling to survive. It appeared that I'd suffered so much there was no turning back, and Charlie wanted to spare me more pain, so he'd made the most difficult decision he ever could.

I remembered nothing of this, but knew it had happened. The story was like a scene out of some horrific tragedy. This had been *so* much worse than people had described it to me. I knew they'd been trying to protect me, because they didn't want to hold back my recovery with the truth, but I deserved to know what my husband had been through.

Slight tremors racked my body as Chancey added, "You can't imagine how fucked up he was until you woke up. The man completely lost his marbles."

"I really did worry he was going to do it. Marcus tried to talk him out of it," Kallie said softly. "The night you died, Charlie kept going on about how you were *his*, and he didn't want to live without you. He didn't eat, or sleep... he was a complete wreck. He told us if he had to end it all to be with you, then he would."

"He kinda came out of it, after he made the choice to take you off life support," Chancey said. "But I knew what his plans were. He was gonna fulfill his obligations to his people and the prophecy, because that's what he promised, but once it was all over, he wasn't gonna stick around. He didn't say it out loud, but I know Charlie. The guy's one of the best pals I'll ever have. And he loves you so much, right or wrong, that he won't go on without you."

This was so insanely hard to process. The thought of Charlie doing that to himself drove me to a place of incomprehensible sadness that was so heavy, I didn't know how to deal with it.

Without me being aware of it, that grief turned to rage.

I knew from my time in the Ancestral Lands that this life *meant something*. I couldn't believe Charlie didn't want to experience all this life had to offer, because this world was so much bigger than I was. Why didn't he realize how *special* he was, and how important he meant?

I'd heard enough. I grabbed the wheels of my chair and rolled toward the doors that lead inside.

"Where are you going?" Kallie called.

"To kick my husband's ass!" I yelled back.

"It's a long way down to the factory. He gets out in thirty minutes," Chancey added.

"I don't care!" This couldn't wait one more second. I wasn't sitting around waiting for him to get here when I was this pissed. Oberi changed into a phoenix and flew after me worryingly.

It *was* a long way to the factory, though. From here, it was all the way on the other side of the prison, and I'd never gone that far by myself since I'd been injured.

Fuck that, didn't care. I headed in that direction, determined to get there one way or another.

You shouldn't be angry, Oberi said as she soared overhead. *He was pushed to his breaking point.*

"I'm not shaming him for being suicidal, Oberi, fuck!" I snapped back. "I understand that night was awful for him. I'm not upset he couldn't handle it. But I'm angry he doesn't think he can go on without me!"

Well... could you?

I wasn't answering that question. "Screw him! Doesn't he realize how terrible it would be if he..."

I got choked up and had to take a breath all at once, and the effect made me gag. I ventured onward, refusing to lose my determination.

I was covered in sweat by the time I neared the factory. Oh, ancestors, it was so much harder getting here than I anticipated.

People flooded down the hall as the shift ended for the day. I spotted Charlie and made a beeline for him, giving a whimper as my middle ached. A couple of inmates veered out of my path, glancing at me like I was crazy.

Charlie felt me approach through our bond— or, at least, he heard my ragged panting. "What the hell, pidge? You shouldn't be down here."

"I... *you...*"

I took the book I had in my lap and threw it at him. It bounced off his chest and landed on the floor.

"Pidge, what are you doing?" Charlie bent down to pick up the book. "Just tell me what's wrong."

My lip trembled as I yelled, "I can't believe you! You said you were going to *kill yourself* if I died? How could you?"

Charlie stiffened. He looked a little sick, like he hated I'd brought up what had happened that night. A couple of people looked our way in interest at my raised voice, but students at the prison were long used to the daily Ava-and-Charlie drama by now. They moved around us like this was any normal day.

But this wasn't a normal fight. This was so serious.

Let's talk about this somewhere private, Oberi offered kindly.

I grumbled as Charlie moved to grab the wheelchair's handles, but I didn't have the energy to move any farther from this spot. I stewed as Charlie maneuvered us back to our cell, struggling to hold it in. The second he closed the door behind us, I absolutely erupted again.

"Why would you do that? Why would you say—"

I burst into tears. Charlie took a seat across from me in the armchair, then leaned over to put a hand on mine.

His touch was overwhelming right now. I felt overstimulated. He might as well be pouring salt into an open wound, because all I could think of at the current moment was the thought of that same hand, cold and stiff in a box six feet underground.

Walls immediately went up. I wanted to protect myself, and him, at the same time, and I didn't know who to help first, or if I could even help either of us. At the same time, his hand was comforting, so I let it sit there.

"Where did this come from? How did you even find out?" Charlie asked.

Kallie and Chancey told her everything that happened, Oberi explained, while I bawled like a baby.

I felt the guilt rolling off of him as he said, "I know what I said wasn't okay—"

"This isn't fair. I can't sit here and wonder if something happens to me if I'm killing you, too." I wiped at my face, and couldn't look at him, because doing so was just too painful right now.

Let's start from a place of compassion, Oberi offered. She perched on the armrest of the chair between us, looking back and forth. *Ava, I know you're upset, but let Charlie explain.*

I gave a loud sniff, but decided I'd let him talk.

Charlie took a breath and said, "You're my family, Ava. The only family I've ever had. My father and grandfather don't count. They're out there, but I don't really know them. I know you— you're the only person that's loved me, unconditionally, in the way I needed to be loved. I never got that growing up from *anyone* else. It felt like my dreams were coming true, then were shattered, because I'd had that love for such a short time, and I couldn't stand letting that go. Can you imagine how isolating that would be, and how absolutely terrible it would feel to lose that?"

A bottomless pit opened up in my stomach, and I felt my anger begin to ebb away. "I don't know if I can really understand, because I can't fathom what it would be like to live that way."

People can't live without love, Ava, Oberi said. *You've always had love all around you, from your family and friends, but Charlie hasn't. He's been starving for it.*

"But I can't be the only source of this... love. I can't be the reason you want to live," I pressed.

"Of course not. I know I have friends who care about me, and I have my own dreams I want to chase after. My life goes beyond you. But... you're the piece that holds it all together."

Charlie moved his hand farther up my arm. "I wanted to get married. I wanted the stability, and some sort of family unit around me I could lean on for support. You have no idea how difficult it was being alone all my life. Now that I know what it's like to have someone that means so much to me, I can't stand going on without it."

"I don't want you to be afraid to be alone," I pressed.

"Look at everything that's happened to me. I've been homeless, hungry, abused, and used by people. I was told I was trash all my life, and treated like it. Now I have someone who actually looks at me like I'm the sun, because I know you do, Ava. Then the world was asking me to let that go. When do I get to decide I've been through enough?"

"That doesn't mean you can just quit."

"Think about how you would feel, if you had to go through what I did when we came back from the Underground. You can't... sit here and say it wouldn't be unbearable," Charlie said.

This much is true. Just the mention of Charlie dying has you completely melting down, Oberi offered.

"It's more than that. The idea of you taking your own life..." I put a hand over my mouth, because it was too much to speak out loud.

"It wasn't a sensible reaction, I get it, but it was an understandable one, because my emotions were out of control. You can't realize the kind of damage that night did to me."

I couldn't, but I could guess. Charlie hadn't been the same since. He tried to hide it, but I caught little cracks here and there in the facade he put on. He acted like everything was fine, because I was still here, but the memories of that night would always haunt him.

"I know it must've been really hard for you," I said. "But it scares me you wouldn't go on without me, because you promised that you would. And knowing that you wouldn't makes me feel like if I was ever in that place again, I couldn't cross over knowing you'd follow. I would hold myself back because I don't want you hurting yourself, and that feels abusive."

"That's why I never told you, because I didn't want you feeling that way," Charlie said gently. "Because even though it felt true at the time— that I wanted to kill myself— I had decided to stay. I need you to know that if anything like that happens again, I'm going to keep living."

"So you're not still... thinking about it?" My voice broke. The thought that he might still be in that place terrified me to the core. I couldn't bear to see him hurting like that.

"No," he promised. "I never told you about it because I never tried to go through with it. It was just a thought, and it was a bad one. When your soul was gone, it felt like mine was, too. Maybe other couples can recover from that, but you're literally a part of me. Losing you felt like losing Oberi and myself, too— all the pieces of our soul all at once. It was the greatest pain I could imagine. So yeah, for a fleeting moment, I thought about ending it all. But that moment is over, Ava."

I wasn't sure if it was. I felt myself retreating away, becoming cold. This was just too much to handle. I wanted to help Charlie so badly, but at the same time, I mentally felt myself shutting down. I didn't think I was strong enough to have this conversation, even though I knew our marriage required it. I didn't wish for somebody to love me so much that they'd consider death a possibility over losing me... even though, I guess I'd done that in the Underground to save him.

Our love could kill us— *had* killed me. And when you had a love that powerful, it was scary.

Charlie caught my thoughts and added, "You want to know what I said to Oberi in that hospital room, right before I told the doctors to pull the plug? *I love her more than I need her.* And it's true, pidge. I wanted you to make your own choice, and I truly believed that you'd chosen to stay in the Ancestral Lands. I didn't think you'd want to live on machines. I promised you I'd go on, and I knew that I would, even if I didn't want to. I decided to stay here and fulfill the prophecy. So I was going to let you go."

"And if that *had* happened, what would you have done once you fulfilled the prophecy?" My guts twisted as I thought about what Chancey had said. "Would you have gone on any longer?"

Charlie wore a contemplative look. "I don't know for sure. If you hadn't come back, then maybe I *would* have fulfilled the prophecy and been done with it. But you *did* come back, and things changed. I'm not the same guy I was when I lost you. I'm glad you chose to come back to me, because even if I *could* fight without you, I didn't want to. It's selfish — I know. I hate what I brought you back to, but at the same time, I'm glad you're here with me. And if you ever chose to leave again, I'd let you go."

My stomach clenched, because I realized in that moment that I *had* wanted to give up not that long ago. I thought it was different when I asked Charlie to end my life, but maybe it wasn't. Emotional pain could be just as debilitating as physical pain. It nearly broke me knowing my husband had faced that kind of torture.

He kept reading my mind, and I didn't mind that he did, because I didn't have the capacity to form words. "I get it. I'd face that heartbreak all over again," Charlie continued. "And I'd do it proudly, because I know now that nothing can keep us apart, not even time. I would be with you again, as it should be. And if I couldn't, I'd find a way to move on."

"If something happens to me, I want you to find someone else," I said immediately. That fucking hurt, too, which didn't make a damn bit of sense, but I felt it deep down inside of me. I *wanted* him to move on without me, because I wanted him to be happy.

Charlie shook his head. "I don't think I could love someone again after you. You're all there is for me."

You two basically function as each other's internal organs now, Oberi said dryly. *I don't think it's possible for either of you to exist without the other. Not with this kind of soul bond. It's worse than losing a partner. It's losing part of yourself.*

It went against so much of what I stood for. I wanted both of us to have the ability to walk away if we weren't happy anymore.

Charlie added, "If you wanted a divorce, I'd let you have one. I wouldn't force you to stay by threatening suicide. You know I'd never do that. What happened after the Underground was different. If we split up, at least I know it was your choice, and I'd want you to find that happiness somewhere else, because that's what means the most to me. You'd be alive and thriving, because that's what Ava does. And even though I'd be brokenhearted, I'd be able to go on, because that's what you decided was best. It wouldn't be like what happened with the Underground, where we had our future ripped away from us."

"Nothing's guaranteed. We're never promised a future," I insisted.

"I don't believe that. I didn't believe in destiny, or any of that bullshit before I met you. But when you died, everything just felt *wrong*. You depend on your intuition all the time, but I never really had any of that guidance, until you were gone. My heart just told me we were supposed to be together, and no matter what, I had to set it straight so we could have that future."

"At what cost? Of losing ourselves?"

"I don't think it's a bad thing for us to be dependent on each other. We can admit that we need one another, and that's okay."

"I just don't want it to get to a place where it's unhealthy, for either of us." I wrapped my arms around myself, trying to ward off the chill that had come over me ever since this conversation started. "If something happens to me, I don't want you to die. I want you to move on, and be happy."

Charlie squeezed my fingers. "I couldn't do that. I'd try, for your sake, but it wouldn't happen. But maybe it could be possible for you."

His words weighed so heavily on my heart that it ached. He wanted to ask me to move on if something happened to him— I could feel that intent through our bond— but he was too afraid to say it out loud.

It would be really hard to be with another man after him. Trusting Charlie, being with him, after what had happened to me, had taken an immense bout of courage. I wasn't sure if I could let someone else into my heart like that.

I knew how I truly felt, though I'd never speak it. If Charlie died, I'd put up a good show for a while, fake the world into believing that I was okay. Then I'd die of a broken heart. If it wasn't him, it wasn't anybody.

I'd put it all on the line to love him. He'd done the same, in order to love me.

The terrifying reality dawned on me. I *was* dependent on Charlie. More than I wanted to admit. This idea of independence and being with someone because you wanted to be with them, not because you needed them, was my ideal. I'd seen my parents live it out, and I liked it that way.

I didn't think it could work that way with us. We'd both been so traumatized that it would be hard to pull away. After all the death I'd seen in my life, I didn't know if I could take much more... and I certainly couldn't handle Charlie's. How did we move forward when we were this interconnected, and life was this dangerous?

Charlie didn't say anything, because he was letting me think. I'd allowed him to observe my thoughts, because I didn't know how to get my feelings across to him any other way.

"What do you think, Oberi?" Charlie asked. "You have a better perception of this."

I think you can only take each moment as it comes. It is foolish to speak of something that has not come to pass, and may never will, she replied.

Then she ruffled her feathers. *But I also think it's okay to need each other. We all need each other. There are three parts to our bond that make it complete.*

"Why weren't you there for us when we were children, Oberi?" I asked bitterly. "You were alive. Where were you?"

If I knew that answer, beloved, I would tell you, she said solemnly. *I remember very little of my past, until the point where I found Charlie for the first time. But I am certain if I had the ability to be there, I would've.*

Charlie stroked her feathers, but I still felt cold inside.

I felt that my skin was going to peel off my body and crawl away. Being around people, around *anyone*, felt like exposing myself to the world. I couldn't even stand Oberi's presence. I needed to be by myself. I needed *space*.

Charlie stood. "I understand. I'll be back a little later, okay?"

"Okay," I mumbled. Oberi flew off to sit on his shoulder, and both of them left the room. When they were gone, I put my head in my hands.

I knew a lot of people wouldn't understand my need to be alone after that kind of conversation. They'd expect me to be falling into Charlie's arms, forcing some kind of resolution to come about, so we could kiss and make up.

But I just couldn't do that. I couldn't sit here and ask if we were okay when I knew that *I wasn't*. With all that he had been through, it would be selfish of me not to take this time to figure my feelings out, and get down to the core of why this bothered me. If I pretended like we were all right, I'd have to shove my feelings down, and that would make me resent him. I needed to be better than that, for him. If that meant I needed to take some time to myself for a moment, then I had to give myself that time, and really understand what was going on in my head... and my heart.

This was so unbearable. Admitting you cared about someone that much was terribly difficult. Because they could ruin you once they were gone.

Nobody got it. I'd *put* people in the ground. I'd seen my best friend's corpse. I knew all too well what it was like to lose people who died young. It was worse than a loss. There wasn't any way to describe just how terrible it was, and what a waste it felt like.

I knew Charlie had experienced that after I'd died. I was just worried he'd consider suicide again if something *did* happen. Imagining him dying like Monica was somewhere my mind just couldn't bear to go.

I wasn't really angry about what he'd said and done when I was in the hospital. I couldn't put a finger on what it was that really gutted me. It took me a while before I finally realized exactly what I was so angry about. And once I understood, the clarity was worth the pain. I loved Charlie so fiercely that I cherished him more than I cherished life itself, and I knew he felt the same way.

We couldn't live without each other. And no matter what that meant to other people, it was an undeniable truth about us I couldn't avoid any longer.

I didn't have the energy to do anything but sit around and try to process everything, for hours. The conversation didn't feel finished, but I was too afraid to take it any further when Charlie came back around curfew. We didn't say much, just got ready for bed. Oberi went to sleep on the couch, clearly giving us room to work it out ourselves.

When we laid down, he pulled me against his chest. I relaxed into him, because even though I didn't have the words to describe everything that was storming inside of me, I didn't need to. His embrace quieted everything down.

I slipped off to sleep fairly easily. I was woken up just as quickly a few hours later.

Charlie thrashed beside me. We'd slipped apart in the middle of the night to opposite sides of the bed. He tossed and turned, his brow furrowed as sweat beaded across his forehead.

I sat up slowly, unsure of what was wrong. I went to wake him, but before I could, he abruptly sat upright, giving a few ragged gasps.

His hands fumbled through the sheets, and even though it was dark, I recognized the panic splayed across his face. He kept searching the bed, until his hands found me. They traveled upward toward my face, palms resting on my cheeks as his fingers threaded through my hair.

He didn't settle until that moment. His shoulders relaxed; he visibly slumped forward. He let his hands fall from my face as he fell back onto the pillows, though he was still trying to breathe.

I'd overlooked everything. Before this moment, I didn't understand how bad it was.

I shut my thoughts off from him as I wondered who'd come back from the Underground more broken... me, or him.

"Did you have a bad dream?" I asked.

He didn't answer me, and Oberi's attention piqued up from the other room. She'd been listening in.

Those weeks you spent in the hospital were really hard, she said quietly, and added nothing else.

I thought of Oberi— rushing in to comfort Charlie in the dead of night, before getting up in the morning to put on a brave face for me, carrying in flowers from the hospital she'd grown for my enjoyment.

My Familiar had to be terribly worn.

Charlie took a short breath. "Sleeping without you was... I just... had these awful nightmares. I'd wake up in the middle of the night, thinking you were dead, and then when you weren't beside me, I'd think it was true. It took me forever to remember that you were in the hospital, and getting better. It was like that nearly every night until you came home."

I remembered the bruise on his forehead that I'd healed while I'd been in the hospital, and became still. Most people wouldn't describe our crappy, tiny apartment in the Institute as home, but it was, because that's where we were building our life. I reached out to hold his hand. He needed that grounding, the physical contact.

He rubbed his face with his free hand. "I hate talking about this. It brings up a lot of shit."

"I'm sorry about the conversation earlier," I whispered. "I just wanted to make sure you weren't going to hurt yourself."

"No. It was one moment that happened in a time when I was hurting. I'm not in that place anymore, and I don't think I could ever go back there. I want to leave that moment in the past... where it belongs."

"... Okay."

He curled away from me, and that hurt. This wasn't enough. Charlie and I had been doing so well, and anything that caused distance to grow between us was a threat to that connection. And in those hours, sitting alone with my thoughts, I'd come to a settlement between what my values were and what my reality was.

I needed Charlie. Right or wrong, I couldn't live without him. And no matter what I said, I understood where he was coming from, and was willing to accept his reaction to my death after the Underground, because I admitted to myself that I would've done the same thing. I needed him in the same way he needed me.

I couldn't tell him how I truly felt, because words didn't express everything I wanted to say. I wanted to prove to him that I could give him everything I had, so he could prove to me he could keep it safe. Show him that I could be obedient to all his desires, no matter what they were, because he lived and breathed for me. I longed to give myself over to him and completely submit, and I only had one idea how.

Charlie had curiously observed my thought process, waiting for me to come to a decision. I paused for a moment, before I said, "Dominate me."

"What does that mean?" He turned on his side toward me.

"I want to completely submit. In every way," I said. "I'm tired of trying to convince myself that I can live without you, so I might as well surrender to that desire. I can't keep fighting it. I want to give my whole life to you, in a way that deepens our marriage. You can make the decisions. I just want the freedom that comes with finally letting go."

"Are you sure?"

"I had a lot of time to think earlier." I raised my wrists together and offered them to him. "This is what I need."

Not even what I wanted— though I did. What I *needed*. I couldn't truly be his, or be free, when I was wrestling with this fear that loving him entirely, with all that I was, could end me. I knew it could, and I was willing to accept that now. He could have me in any way he wanted, so long as he took that burden from my shoulders.

I told myself that it was okay to need him. It was okay for him to need me. I wasn't afraid anymore.

Charlie sat up onto his knees. I was wearing one of his shirts, and he lifted it over my head and tossed it on the floor. He put a hand under my ass to lift me up, to support my weight. He then took my wrists gently and began kissing them, moving his lips up my arms and over my breasts. He kissed my neck, and I let my head fall against his gently as he parted my hair away, kissing the soft skin there before he ran his thumb over my lips.

"If you're giving yourself to me like this, I want to make you a promise." He gently lifted my chin with a finger and uttered, "I can't say I will never hurt you, but I will never do so intentionally. I will never abandon you, and I will never leave you alone. Whatever happens, you're always going to be safe with me. You don't have to worry about anything, baby girl. Just let yourself relax."

My eyes lulled shut as he caressed my neck lightly. He fisted a hand in my hair before he kissed me, and he tasted absolutely delicious.

Charlie sat me down and reached for the bedside table, where we kept the rope. He crossed my arms over my front, underneath my breasts, before he started tying. He bound both of my wrists together to my front before he wrapped the rope around my middle. The rope rubbed against my nipples, heightening the sensations there so the anticipation heightened. He crisscrossed the rope over my shoulders and fixed it in place, so I was wearing a simple chest harness. I couldn't move my upper body much. The restraint the rope gave sent a thrill of delight through my senses.

"Is that comfortable?" Charlie fixed the final knot and ran his hands down my arms.

I didn't respond. Instead, I focused on trying to rub my nipples over the rope, because it felt that good, but the harness made me stay in place.

"I asked you a question," Charlie said. "I always want to know the truth about how you feel. Don't make me ask again."

I wiggled a bit, then said, "It.. feels nice, but it's uncomfortable around my sides. Could you tie it a little looser?"

"Done." He adjusted the harness, then tied it again. "Better?"

"Yes." Charlie's knots were firm, but I was able to slip out of them if I needed to. The knot wasn't able to tighten down on itself, and he made a slip tie so he could pull the rope in an emergency to set me loose.

"Good. Now eyes on me," he said, and ancestors, that had to be my favorite fucking command. "Don't look away for a second."

Charlie got up from the bed and casually undressed. He removed his shirt at an unnaturally slow pace before messing with the waistband of his boxers. He was doing a little strip tease for me knowing I couldn't reach out and touch him, the bastard. I was loving this.

"Come here." He reached out and laid me on the edge of the bed, on my side. "Take my waistband down with your teeth."

I was happy to oblige, although the harness made that more difficult than I imagined. I strained against the bonds as I bit into the waistband of his boxers, and pulled them down.

I let my thoughts slip across our bond. *I want you to be aggressive.*

Charlie grabbed a handful of my hair, and ordered, "Put your mouth on me now."

"And what if I don't?" I leaned forward and planted a kiss on his dick, just to torment him. I could tease, too.

"Quit being a brat. I know you want it just as badly as I do, don't you?"

I did. I gave in and took him in my mouth, and Charlie let out a soft gasp of pleasure. I knew how to get him worked up with a really good blow job, so I took him all the way in, letting his length hit the back of my throat before I focused on running my tongue over the head. I took it slow, drawing out each motion so he fully enjoyed each movement my mouth made over him.

"I want you to moan, baby," Charlie said.

Oh, I moaned— loudly. The vibrations my mouth made over him increased the intensity, and I felt his hips buck forward slightly, like he wanted to fuck my mouth but was using all his self-control to hold back. I wanted to finish him off right here, because this was fucking hot.

He was about to come— I knew it, because I felt it across our bond. Charlie's fingers pulled back at my hair, and I withdrew. "That's enough. Now I'm going to pleasure you."

Initial disappointment flooded through me, but it was quickly overtaken as Charlie turned my body on the bed, so I was lying flat on my back. He climbed over me and sucked at my nipples, moving his tongue over both my breasts and the rope. The senses below my hips were dulled, but the sensitivity in my breasts was stronger than ever. He had me panting within minutes, though he drew out the movements as he nibbled and sucked at my breasts.

I attempted to wiggle away, but the harness pinned me down and left my breasts completely vulnerable to Charlie's whims. I couldn't move or do anything to stop him but use my words, and that accelerated my desire.

It snuck up on me and exploded out of nowhere. I tumbled unexpectedly into climax, and as I writhed on the bed, Charlie lifted my legs apart before he dove down and ran his tongue over my apex. Everything felt sensitive now, and my arousal was heightened. Since I'd been injured, it wasn't easy feeling him when he was giving me oral, but now I was so turned on that I could enjoy what he was giving me. This was like magic.

His mouth was off me for a moment, and I almost started begging him, before I heard the vibrator click on. He slid it inside of me, before kissing my apex again. Holy fuck, he was using the vibrator and his mouth on me at the *same time*, and I thought I might die of pleasure.

"Is that too much? Do you *want* it to be too much?" He sounded so amused. A wave of satisfaction washed through our bond, and I knew he enjoyed my struggle against the ropes as he forced my body to submit to more pleasure than it could tolerate.

"Green light," I managed to gasp out. It *was* too much, but I didn't want him to stop. It wasn't what he was physically doing that was driving me toward climax, but the mental state he was putting me in. A dreamy sensation overtook my thoughts, and I felt like I was floating as I fully allowed myself to succumb to that space.

The sexiest part about this was the way he got inside my head. In moments like these, Charlie completely invaded my mind and took control. I was forced to pay attention to him and direct my thoughts only on his commands. I was so aroused by the anticipation that he could do whatever he wanted to me like this, but wouldn't unless I asked for it. It felt so invigorating to be completely tied up and at his mercy, yet still be completely in control.

But I didn't want that control right now. I wanted him to take that control from me and mind-fuck me until I was sideways.

"You're such a bad girl," Charlie teased. "But you don't want to be bad, do you? You want to be my good girl."

I couldn't respond. I was too busy moaning as I fell into another climax.

"Tonight, you'll speak when spoken to. Answer my questions, and I'll reward you."

"Yes," I forced out. I was shaking so badly against the ropes that they dug into my skin, and I liked it.

"That's my good girl," he said, and I nearly died at the pleasure of hearing him call me that. "I'm going to fuck you until you scream. Do you want that?"

"Please," I pleaded. If he wasn't inside of me *right fucking now*, I was going to lose my mind.

"Good girl," he growled, and he turned me over on my side again, moving my legs upward so they were curled against my chest. We'd found a couple of positions I couldn't do, because it triggered pain points. But the rope actually helped with that, because it gave me some sort of physical support my legs could no longer provide.

Charlie got on his knees. He lifted me until my ass was against his thighs, and entered me from the side. He dove into me, and my eyes rolled back in my head. I gasped with delight as his thrusts rammed against me, and my body shuddered, getting ready to roll into another orgasm.

"Don't you dare come yet," he warned me. "You hold on until I tell you."

It was *so hard,* but I wanted to do what he told me *so badly*, so I made my body comply. I bit my lip and did my best to hang on as a mountain of pleasure loomed overhead, growing larger by each movement of his dick inside of me. I wanted to touch him, but I couldn't, and his hands were all over me, and I just couldn't take it anymore.

"Come, pidge," Charlie ground out, and I felt him give a gasp as he let go. The release was absolutely enthralling, but it was only multiplied by the feeling of Charlie's climax ricocheting beside mine. I felt two powerful orgasms all at once, and I nearly passed out. He kept fucking me through it, and I screamed so loud I was sure anyone walking by our cell was going to hear it.

It was over, but the remnants of all those *feelings* were still racing through my body. Charlie took a few deep breaths to recover before he picked me up, cradling me against his chest as he kissed my head and uttered, "That's my baby girl."

My head was *buzzing*. I was practically drooling. That had been the best sex of my life, hands down.

And we had so much more to experience together. I could hardly wait to get started.

"I love you, Charlie." I couldn't resist saying it. I nuzzled into his chest, feeling so cozy and warm.

"I love you too, pidge." He gave me another kiss, then set me down so he could untie me. The bonds came loose, and I winced as I felt my contracted muscles recoil.

Charlie's fingers moved over my body, to check I hadn't been hurt. He found the ridges in my skin the rope had made. His voice was disapproving as he said, "The rope cut into you."

"I'm not bleeding," I argued.

He reached for a bottle of lotion. "It might leave a bruise. No more struggling against the ropes unless I tell you to, understand?"

"Maybe."

"Ava."

"Fine." I scowled as he rubbed the lotion into the marks. "But you'd better let me do that every once in a while, because it was fun."

"As long as you don't get hurt."

He helped me stretch out, because being tied up for so long wasn't great on the muscles. As he rolled my arm back and forth, stretching out my shoulder, he said, "I miss your tongue ring."

"Yeah?"

"It felt good when you went down on me."

"Then I'll have to get another one." I was counting down the days, however many we had, until I got out of here and could rush to a piercing parlor.

I slept *good* that night. I woke up feeling refreshed, so much so that I didn't feel any pain. It was rare to have days like that.

"I don't feel like doing physical therapy today," I told Charlie after breakfast, as he wheeled me into the workout room he and the boys had set up. "I'm in a pretty good place."

Oberi huffed in irritation, shaking his furry ears. *Apparently whips and chains are all she needs to feel like a new woman.*

"That's not a good idea, pidge." Charlie closed the door behind us. "The exercises help you get stronger."

"Come on, skipping one day isn't going to set me back," I complained.

"I don't think so. You're doing those exercises."

His voice was gentle, but at the same time, unrelenting. I secretly got a whirl of delight at his command.

"Okay." I decided to give in— this time. Oberi barked, then went to the corner of the room to gnaw on a chew toy.

Charlie bent down to pick up some five-pound weights. He paused, before he said, "I just don't want you to get into a state like you were a few weeks ago. This helps prevent that from happening."

Sadness overcame me as I remembered begging Charlie to end it all. I'd felt awful for what I'd asked him to do that night, but in the moment, trapped within that spiral of incredible pain, it really had seemed like my only option.

"I'm sorry, again," I apologized. "I know that was horrible."

"You were suffering a lot. It's okay." Charlie placed the weights into my hands. "Now let's do twenty arm curls."

Charlie got a kick out of working out together. It was something he enjoyed, so I liked it, too. I wasn't as athletic as him and Kallie, and never had been, but I'd liked cheerleading and exploring caves before, so working out wasn't so much a chore as it was a fun activity for us to do as a couple.

We did some upper body strength exercises with the weights, before Charlie laid me down on a yoga mat to help me stretch. He lifted my knees to my chest and moved my feet back and forth, flexing my toes toward my calf.

"What's wrong?" Charlie noticed I was a bit uncomfortable the moment I realized it myself.

"I feel a cramp in my foot." I wrinkled my nose. "But it's probably just a phantom pain. I know I don't have any sensation there."

Charlie began rubbing the ball of my foot, flexing my leg to my chest and back out. "Can you feel anything now?" Charlie asked.

"No." I scowled. "The tension is still there, but I know it's not real."

Charlie helped me sit up and get back into my wheelchair. "Let's get the TENS out. That's seemed to help before."

The hospital had lent us a transcutaneous electrical nerve stimulation machine, often called a TENS unit, to help with my therapy. It was a small machine that had electrode pads attached to it, which delivered small electrical currents to my muscles. It was supposed to help release endorphins and encourage pain relief. Charlie lifted my shirt and placed the pads of the machine all over my lower back before he turned the machine on. The TENS unit was sort of loud, and it emitted a loud vibrating noise that sounded very much like... something else. I always snickered whenever it came on.

"I find it amusing you still think that's so funny," Charlie said.

"I *am* a child." As the machine worked, the tension in my back began to ease, and my shoulders slackened. I shifted in my seat as a sense of relief flooded through me.

"I guess I didn't feel as good as I thought," I admitted. "The TENS is actually helping me feel a lot better."

"I'm surprised you didn't notice."

"I'm just used to being in pain now. It's easy to ignore it if it's not completely overwhelming."

"Well, this will help with that."

He took a seat on the yoga mat in front of me, doing a round of push-ups before switching into sit-ups. I observed in appreciation. I loved watching my man work out.

Charlie took a deep breath as he finished a round, then said, "I'm sorry if we're not making good progress."

"What do you mean? I think I've come a long way since I was first injured," I said.

"We're able to manage your pain better, and some things have improved, but I don't want you to feel like you can't do things on your own."

I felt a lump rise in my throat. Oberi stopped playing with the chew toy and looked at me. "That's okay. It's what the doctors told us to expect."

"Are you sad that you still struggle with your wheelchair?"

I shrugged. "I mean... sometimes. But mostly, I'm tired of how people treat me."

"There are a lot of assholes here at the Institute," he agreed.

"It's more than that. Ez is still spending a lot of time researching my spinal injury, and I wish he wouldn't."

"He loves you. He wants to see you walk again."

"But I don't need to walk. I need... support."

Charlie waited for me to go on, and I rushed to explain. "People are always looking for some miracle that will make me walk again. But you know what would be simpler? Building more ramps." I sighed and looked up at the ceiling. "Or making larger doorways, or even just putting a minute of thought into how I can get around."

"I hear that," Charlie replied. "I don't like it when people act like my blindness needs to be cured, either."

"Right. It's like it's inconvenient for society to accommodate me, even if the solution is easy, so they'll go out of their way to find complex solutions to make me walk again. They want me to be just like everyone else, and *cure me*, rather than provide me with ways to make life accessible. Not being able to walk is hard, but it wouldn't be as hard if our society didn't keep putting barriers in the way that don't need to be there."

"I completely understand," Charlie said enthusiastically. "My reading glasses are great. They don't make me see, but they help me to read things. I didn't need to see back when I was on the streets— I needed *resources*, like access to housing, or a job, and affordable food. When it comes to my blindness, I don't need to be cured; I need tools. And I wouldn't want a cure, anyway."

"You don't want to be able to see?" I glanced over.

"No. I know some blind people would want to be able to see, and that's okay, but myself, I think it would be overwhelming," he replied. "This is the way I've lived my life since before I could remember. If I was able to see, I'd have to relearn everything, all while going through sensory overload. I'd even have to learn how to balance again, because there'd be so much visual stimulation that I wouldn't be able to process it all. I can do all of that stuff now, without sight, so why is being sighted considered automatically better? And I... like the way I am. I wouldn't want to change. Is it such a terrible thing for me to say that I'm okay with being blind?"

"It doesn't bother me that you're blind," I said. "But most people wouldn't understand, because they believe that being different is some terrible thing, like a punishment. I get why everyone wants me to walk again, but I don't know why I need to be cured. I'm perfectly whole, even like this. Why can't others see it that way?"

"They probably think that you miss walking," he suggested.

"Of course I do. Adjusting to this is really hard. But my perception of myself is changing, and I think I can be happy this way, as much as I miss my life before. I'm not seen as a person, but a problem. It's the same way with my bipolar. Nobody could accept that, either. Why am I something that has to be *fixed*?"

"I've always thought you were perfect," Charlie said softly.

I sighed. "I'm just... tired of hearing, all my life, that there's something wrong with me."

"There isn't anything wrong with you. What's wrong is what the world thinks about people like us. We're going to help change that."

The door to the workout room opened, and Kallie's boisterous voice called, "What the hell are you two doing in here?"

She put her hands on her hips as she looked down at the TENS unit, and I laughed. "Sorry to disappoint, but this isn't the kind of action you were looking for."

"I thought you'd taken your vibrator out for some exhibitionist fun, and figured it'd be hilarious to catch you in the act," Kallie teased.

Of course Kallie would think that would be funny, because she was a perverted weirdo like the rest of us. "Not yet." I snickered.

"I came to let Charlie know that Professor Jobe is looking for him. I know it's the weekend, but he wants an update on your criminal profile, right now," Kallie said, turning toward him. "He seems mad you're the only one in your class who hasn't turned in a report."

Charlie groaned. "We barely have anything new from last time. We've made no progress on this profile, and the final is due *next week*. I need to turn in *relevant* information if I'm going to pass, not just a bunch of bullshit we've guessed."

"We'll get together later and look over everything again," Kallie promised. "But in the meantime, if you don't want to fail, you should probably get down there. Just give Jobe some story until we can come up with something to turn in."

"I guess. You two going to lunch?" Charlie asked.

"Probably. I'm starving," I said, and Oberi gave an enthusiastic bark.

"Don't wait for me, I'll grab something from Commissary later." Charlie gave me a kiss, then left the room.

Kallie grinned. "You two are so adorable. And look, you have a hickey."

"That was from last night," I said enthusiastically. "Want to hear about it?"

"Do I!"

We got nachos from the cafeteria, and I was excited to find that Ivy and Opal had reserved spots for Kallie and me. Nobody else was there; I wondered where Marcus had gotten off to. I rolled up to the table and dipped corn chips into cheese as I retold the epic romance that had happened the previous evening. My husband didn't really care if I talked about our sex life, so long as I didn't go *too* far, and I wanted to keep a few juicy parts to replay in my mind over and over, just for myself. I didn't give them *all* the details— some things were reserved for Charlie and me — but I told my friends enough that they were swooning by the end.

"I am *so glad* that's working out for you," Ivy said. "See, I can give good advice every once in a while!"

Kallie wrinkled her nose. "Sounds like the fun times me and Scarlet had. The sex was great. The relationship, not so much."

"I haven't seen you sport that collar she bought you in a long time," Ivy purred.

"It doesn't really suit me. I'd rather someone else put it on," Kallie replied.

"I wish Charlie got *me* a collar." I leaned over the table and pouted.

"I think I'll make Marcus wear it." Kallie smirked. "If things progress."

I snorted. Nobody had to ask who was the dominant in *that* relationship.

"Did you guys end up talking about what I said yesterday?" Kallie asked. She didn't need to explain— everyone at the table had heard about it by now.

I hadn't told them anything about the conversation we'd had, just the rowdy times. "I did. We worked it out."

"I'm surprised you got anything out of him. Charlie's so quiet," Opal said.

I smirked. "Not in bed."

Kallie laughed, before she stood up. "Well, girls, as much as I'd love to continue this conversation, I've got somewhere to be. See you tonight, Ava."

Opal's cheerful disposition had suddenly dissolved into nerves. She wrung her hands under the table. When Kallie strode off, she asked, "Ava, can I talk to you?"

"Sure. What is it?" I asked. She must've wanted to talk to me about whatever this was for a long time, if she was this anxious.

Ivy sat back and remained silent, sipping at a cup of tea. Opal took in a short, quick breath. "Don't take this the wrong way. I know this is really awkward, but... how did you and Charlie manage to...?"

"Do it?" I raised an eyebrow.

"Yeah. You know, after... somebody hurt you." She dropped her gaze.

I was already aware of what she was getting at. Opal had killed her father after he'd molested her for years; it's what had gotten her sent to the Institute. The abuse had created a child, her daughter, Marina. Opal had to have good behavior here at the prison if she wanted to see her child after graduation. In the meantime, she was dating Ez, and she didn't seem to know how to take things further.

Opal blushed. "Ez is your brother, so it's kind of weird—"

"No, it's fine. He wouldn't mind, and neither do I," I said. "You haven't done anything?"

"No. We just kiss." Her lip trembled.

"But you want more."

"Kind of?" She twisted her fingers around each other. "I don't know. I thought I'd never be okay with it after everything that happened, but Ez makes me curious. The feelings are different."

"Of course they are. Sex comes from a place of love and trust. There isn't any fear or pain attached to it," I said. "It's not the same, Opal. Trust me."

"But how'd you get over it?" she pleaded.

"I didn't, really. I just wanted to feel special and loved. Charlie didn't make me feel like I had to protect myself. I can be intimate and vulnerable with him because sex is something I'm participating in, not something I'm being forced into. It's a choice out of mutual love."

She nodded slowly. "Does it hurt?"

"For me, it feels good. It's not painful. I don't know how comfortable it'll be for you, but you should take things at your own pace."

She twirled a strand of blue hair around her finger. "I'm so ashamed. Ez and I have been together almost as long as you and Charlie have, and we're not even close to taking clothes off."

"Don't feel bad that things haven't progressed as quickly with you guys. Charlie and I are... different in a lot of ways. You don't have to do anything until you're ready."

"I *am* ready," Opal said in frustration. "But I'm scared, too."

"You don't have to go straight from kissing to sex. There are other things you can do first, to build trust," I pointed out.

Opal put her arms around her torso and squeezed tight. "It's just... I love my daughter, and I'd like more kids someday. I think Ez would be a really good dad."

"I do too." Probably one of the best.

"I hope you don't think I'm moving too fast," she said quickly.

"No. I know how you feel about him."

I leaned in and dropped my voice. "Do you want to know a secret? I tried to force myself to do it with Charlie, because I knew he was the Elven heir and that he needed descendants for the throne. So I thought if I made myself do it, I could just get it over with, but he was the one who held us back, because he knew we both weren't ready. You and Ez have a long time to think about kids. What's important is that you get in touch with your own feelings, and trust yourself. Your judgment is the most important thing you have in this situation. You have the power to decide how much to trust him with, and how much to give him, at your own pace. This is all up to you, Opal. Not anyone else, and that includes the people you choose to sleep with... or not."

Ivy smiled slightly. It was the same advice he'd given me, long ago, and it had seriously changed my life.

"I'd like to share my body with him. But it seems overwhelming." Opal chewed on her lip.

"I was frightened, too. But I know you'll enjoy having that special connection with him."

Opal chewed on her lip. "Okay. So... how do we try?"

"Just start by touching him first," I suggested. "Take it slow, and eventually, you're going to want more and more. Ez is kind. He won't do anything without your say-so."

"But what if I freak out?" Her eyes sparkled with tears. She was really worried about upsetting him.

"Listen, Opal. Don't force yourself to be ready because you think you're going to lose him," I insisted. "Ez is a great guy, and you're safe with him, but you have power over this situation yourself. Only you get to decide how much you want to trust him, and you have the power to withdraw your consent at any time, even if you're in the middle of doing something. And if my brother oversteps that, know that I personally will beat the shit out of him."

"You and Charlie just seem so perfect." Opal sniffed, sounding close to bawling. "I don't think I could ever get that far with anyone."

"It wasn't that easy. I panicked with Charlie a few times, too," I said. "It's all right. Ez will be patient. And if you go to a bad place, take a break before you try again. It'll get better, I swear to you."

I hoped I wasn't giving her bad advice. But she seemed reserved as she straightened and said, "You're right. Being with Ez... it wouldn't be anything like what my father did to me. I trust myself enough to know that my boyfriend is nothing like my dad."

"Definitely not. I can't say it doesn't have an effect on our marriage, because it does, but we're able to get past it either way."

"You two are kind of... adventurous, aren't you?" Opal gave a giggle.

I smiled slyly and said, "You could put it that way."

"I envy you. I don't think I could enjoy being tied up. I'd freak out," Opal said.

I shrugged. "It's a personal preference. It turns sex into a conversation."

"Really?" Opal's eyes widened.

"Yeah. It's really helped our communication." We had to be open, if we were participating in activities like this.

"But isn't it dangerous?" Opal asked.

"Not if you do it the right way." Ivy spoke up for the first time, setting his tea down. "It's actually one of the safest ways you can have sex, because there's so much consent involved. You just have to make sure you have a partner who you can trust completely, and that you're always playing safely."

I nodded. "When I'm in that space, I have to tune into how I feel, and be completely present with Charlie in the current moment. When that happens, nothing else matters."

"I don't think it's for me," Opal stated. "But I'm really glad you found something that works for you guys."

"You can have that with Ez, too," I encouraged. "It'll just take some time."

"Thanks, Ava." Opal reached out and squeezed my hand. "You're a true friend."

Ivy gave me a wink, and affection for him rose in my heart. I was really glad we'd remained friends, despite everything. Without Ivy, Charlie and I wouldn't be as close as we were now, and I had him to thank for that.

I didn't do much the rest of the day, besides study for finals and take a nap. Charlie came back to get me that evening, and we headed to Hemlock's secret illusion room, both to practice our demigod powers and to work on Charlie's profiling project.

I was surprised that Marcus was sitting at the round table when we got there, dangling a cat toy in front of Rishi. Sprigs peeked out of Charlie's pocket, watching the cat toy swing back and forth.

"We didn't think you were coming," I started as I rolled up beside him.

"I think I've figured something out," Marcus began, and he stood. "I wanted to show you guys—"

He cut off, face going pale as a figure materialized in the room, six feet away from us. Kallie had suddenly appeared, as if she had teleported herself there. Her face panicked as she snapped her fingers once, then a second time.

Behind us, the door slammed. Marcus looked over his shoulder, and

I turned my wheelchair. I was gutted as I watched a *different* Kallie walk into the room through the hidden door.

Oh, shit, Oberi mumbled. *This isn't good.*

I couldn't believe my eyes. There were *two* Kallies in the room, and both of them appeared absolutely petrified. Before the Kallie that had walked in could face herself, the Kallie that had abruptly appeared in the room snapped her fingers once more. That Kallie vanished, blown away as if by a wisp of wind.

"What happened?" Charlie asked, clearly lost at our silence.

"There were two different Kallies in here, at the same time," I rasped. "And I don't think one was an illusion."

Charlie's expression immediately darkened in rage. Kallie strode toward us, her steps sharp on the marble floor.

"You guys don't know what you saw." Kallie's voice was ominous, warning Charlie not to go there.

"This is bullshit, Kallie! Have you been time traveling *again?*" Charlie yelled.

"It's not any of your concern," Kallie growled.

"You promised me you wouldn't!" Charlie cried. "You swore to me!"

"I *promised* nobody would get hurt," Kallie snapped viciously. "And so far, nobody has."

"Yet!" Charlie screamed. "You're fucking around with shit we swore not to mess with again. I trusted you not to go there, after the last time we tried!"

"You act like you don't know me," Kallie seethed.

"Clearly I don't, if you're just going to lie to my face!"

Kallie shifted into a wolf and launched at Charlie. Her paws hit his shoulders with a snarl and knocked him to the floor. Charlie siphoned her shifter strength out of her and threw her off, tossing her across the room. Kallie rolled as she fell before she got up again, charging at Charlie and tackling him to the floor. The two of them wrestled, while Marcus and I looked on in shock. What the hell was going on here?

Oberi changed into a unicorn and charged between the two of them. She forced them apart with brute strength before she cried, *Time travel isn't anything to toy with! I warned the two of you consequences like this could happen!*

I was completely lost. Kallie morphed back. She and Charlie stood at a distance, both breathing heavily and ignoring the other.

"Okay, what's going on?" Marcus demanded. "Ava and I are in the dark. Did you two do something you weren't supposed to?"

"We tried to fix the past," Kallie said heavily. "And I've been trying to fix it ever since things went wrong."

Kallie and Charlie had gone behind our backs and done something huge, without telling Marcus or me about it. We needed to know what was going on *now*.

Charlie paused. He was contemplating telling us the truth, until I gave a harsh nudge across our bond that told him I was his *wife*, and I needed the fucking truth.

Charlie took a breath. "When Thaddeus died, Kallie, Oberi and me went back in time to try and stop it. We relived the day several times, but whenever we tried to change something to save Thad, things got worse."

"Are you kidding me?! You did this without us?" Marcus burst. Rishi gave an indignant yowl.

"Yes. We saved Thad the first time, but then Ava got hurt, and Mad Dog took guards hostage inside the prison," Charlie said harshly. "We tried changing things again, and lost Marcus."

"Lost?" I squeaked. I didn't have memories of any of this.

"He *died*," Kallie said harshly. "So we went back again to put it right, and had to leave things as they were, and let Thad die so everyone else could live."

"But you weren't good with that, huh?" Charlie demanded, rounding on Kallie. "You decided you had to keep trying."

"Wouldn't you, if you had this kind of power?" Kallie asked.

"You need to start from the beginning," I said. "Tell us everything you remember, and don't leave anything out."

Charlie told us everything. Kallie leaned against the wall and looked surly as he recounted it all. The story was confusing, and I could barely keep the facts straight. According to Charlie, his memories of that day were muddled, and running together.

"When we got back, everyone was sick, especially you, Ava," Charlie said. "We saw how much pain you were in, and Kallie vowed not to do it again, because time travel obviously causes consequences for all of us."

"I had the flu for a week. Or at least, I *thought* it was the flu," Marcus accused. "What you guys did seriously fucked with my health."

And mine. I'd wanted to die that night from pain. "I haven't had any symptoms lately, though, and Kallie's still time traveling," I objected.

"I figured out if I go back, and don't mess with anything, it doesn't make anyone sick," Kallie said. "So I thought if I could be smart enough to figure out a way to change what happened, but not actively interfere myself, then Thad could be saved."

"Has it worked?" Charlie asked. "Apparently not, because you've come back to this reality where he's still dead."

Kallie dropped her head. "I'm just trying to perfect it. See how it works. That's why I keep popping up in this room a million times, because I can practice here without being caught. If I have this ability, I need to be able to use it so we can find the Divinity Keys and prevent other people from dying."

"We don't have the power to stop people from dying, Kallie," Charlie muttered. "That should be pretty fucking clear to all of us by now."

Silence rang throughout the room, and I asked, "What's it like, seeing yourself at the same point in the timeline?"

"I can't confront myself, because it creates a paradox," Kallie explained. "But even if I'm on the same spot in the timeline, I experience that moment from both angles. I'll eventually remember both realities, but since they're happening *together*, it takes a moment for the memories to integrate, and I can't remember which one is correct... that is, which memory happened most recently, or what I tried to fix."

"But you aren't going to do it again, *right?*" Charlie growled.

"I don't know. I'm worried I still haven't caught up to myself," Kallie said. "I won't remember anything that happened until I get to that point in time where I went back and changed things. There could still be a point in the future, as we see it from today, where I went back to alter our reality, and that tampering has a ripple effect on what's happening now. The version of me you just saw was me from the future, and I don't know what I came back to change. The fact that I came back at all to this moment already changed things, because we wouldn't be having this conversation if I hadn't."

"But what reality is the right one?" Marcus questioned.

"It's all real," Kallie said hollowly. "I just can't recall the reality that I most recently changed, so I'm not sure what timeline I'm actually on."

"This shit is going to drive you insane," Marcus muttered.

"It may have. I'm just not at the point yet where I've actually lost it."

That was a terrifying statement. Marcus shook his head and said, "From now on, we don't go back in time unless all *four* of us go back. It's not safe."

"Then what do you want us to do, Marcus?" Kallie asked, on the verge of tears. "Because I'm damn tired of running into nothing but dead ends. We have all this power, but we can't use it to change the past."

"We can't change the past, but we can speak with the dead," Marcus replied. "I've been trying to get in contact with Thaddeus for several weeks, but since he's already crossed over, I couldn't just summon him back at any time... that is, until now. I created a spell that will help us communicate with anyone who's crossed over, and that includes Thaddeus' spirit."

"So what are you saying?" Charlie asked.

"We need to bring him here," Marcus replied darkly. "Because it's the only way we're going to get answers."

charlie

FIFTEEN

"What do you mean you found a way to talk to Thaddeus?" I asked. "I thought we couldn't hold a séance because he'd crossed over."

"A normal séance isn't enough to contact Thaddeus," Marcus confirmed. "I know, because I've tried. But I've developed a spell that's stronger— like a séance on steroids. Usually, once a spirit has crossed over, it's difficult to connect with them. I've been practicing with my powers, though, and I figure if I'm a demigod with control over death, I should be able to pull this spell off."

Marcus knew more about Death magic than I did, so if he said he could successfully cast the spell, I believed him. We *had* to find out what Thaddeus had learned about Professor Mazur.

"We shouldn't do this," Ava protested. "Thad would've spoken to us by now if he wanted to. Forcing him to communicate is wrong."

"I think he *does* want to communicate," Marcus argued. "My magic can sense something isn't quite right. It must be the wards on the prison that are preventing him from coming in. Thad wouldn't leave us hanging like this."

"Marcus, you have demigod abilities that specialize in death. If it's not easy for you to bring Thad here, we shouldn't be doing it at all," Ava said.

"*Exactly*. I have demigod abilities, so I'm going to use them." Papers rustled as Marcus brought out a book to consult for his spell. "I'm going to draw an alchemy circle on the ground with chalk. It's basically a circle of symbols that will help direct the energy of the spell. I'll place quartz crystals and an herb blend of lavender, agrimony, and sandalwood inside. This will help amplify our connection to the beyond, while warding off unwanted energies. You'll all want to be inside the circle, because Thaddeus' spirit will be protected within it. Are you ready?"

"Marcus is right. We have to get this information," Kallie said.

"You're just backing Marcus up because he's your mate. Charlie, help me out here," Ava stated.

I wasn't thrilled she'd put me on the spot. "I wish I could, but Marcus is the one with Death magic, so we should trust him."

Ava huffed. "Whatever."

I wheeled Ava to the center of the room, and Kallie joined us. Marcus circled us, scratching lines of chalk across the floor. He placed crystals around us, and the sweet scent of lavender filled my nose as he sprinkled the herbs at our feet.

"Brace yourselves," Marcus warned.

I didn't think much of it, until a gust of wind swept through the room so fast it nearly knocked me over. I grabbed the back of Ava's chair so I wouldn't fall. She squeezed my hand, and I felt a moment of fear flicker through our bond, because we didn't know what to expect. Sprigs cowered deeper into my pocket.

The lights have gone out, Ava told me.

Marcus muttered Latin phrases under his breath, and the spell grew in intensity. The ground began to shake beneath our feet, and I could feel the magic rolling off him in waves. Blasts of heat pulsed throughout the room. I'd never seen Marcus perform magic like this before.

Oberi barked loudly. *Tell Marcus to stop!*

"This is intense!" Kallie cried over the sound of the room shaking around us. "Marcus, are you sure about this?"

"I can feel him!" Marcus shouted. "Thaddeus, is that you?"

A muffled voice came from somewhere in the distance, but I couldn't understand what was being said. It sounded like the voice was coming from the other room, only it surrounded us from every angle.

"Thaddeus, we just want to talk!" Marcus said. "You had information about Professor Mazur that could help us. We need to know what you found!"

In a split second, the heat warming my skin turned into an icy chill. The hairs on my arms stood up, and a shiver rocked my whole body. The floor stopped shaking, and the wind settled. Ava breathed a sigh of relief.

"*I'm here,*" a voice said, filling the room. It sounded like he was standing right in front of me.

My heart became so full when I heard Thaddeus. Without thinking about it, I reached out to feel him, ignorantly thinking I'd be able to touch him. What I found instead was unexpected.

My hand went straight through his spirit, but an image of him formed in my mind, like it had when I touched my ancestors' spirits before. Normally, only Marcus could see ghosts, but his powers had allowed Thaddeus to appear to us all.

Thaddeus stood in front of me, his form glowing with ethereal whisps. His Familiar perched on his shoulder. I'd never seen Thaddeus in the flesh, but I was shocked by how smooth his skin appeared. I knew he was just a kid, a teenager barely old enough to have his magic, but seeing his young features reminded me of just how short his life had been cut. When I pulled my hand away, the image in my head vanished.

"Thad!" I cried in relief. "It's so good to hear your voice! I'm so sorry about what happened—"

"*You don't have to apologize,*" Thaddeus said gently.

"But I sent you after Mazur," I argued.

"*That's not the reason I'm dead,*" he pressed. "*I'm dead because of Mad Dog. Don't beat yourself up about it, Charlie, because it's not your fault, and you can't change it.*"

My guts twisted, because I *had* changed it, only to have to go back and let him die all over again. It felt like I'd chosen my friends over Thaddeus, but he was my friend, too. It was an impossible decision to make, and no matter who had wound up dead that day, I'd still blame myself for making that call.

Kallie didn't waste any time. "What did you learn about Professor Mazur?"

"*I overheard her talking to the Warden,*" Thaddeus explained. "*She knows where the Elven concentration camps are.*"

"Where?" Ava asked eagerly.

Thaddeus hesitated. *"She didn't say. But one thing I do know... Eddie was moved from the camps. He's not there anymore."*

My stomach dropped, because that meant Eddie was further from our reach than ever before. "We have to find him once we get out of here. Did she say where he was taken?"

"No. But I thought you should know," Thaddeus said.

"That isn't helpful," Marcus complained. "Not unless we know where he is."

Thaddeus paused for a beat. *"Maybe I can find out. I'm a ghost now, so I can sneak around without being seen. I could get into the Warden's office."*

"That'd be great!" Marcus exclaimed.

I don't think this is a good idea, Oberi warned.

"No. Thad, you can't do this," Ava protested. "Marcus summoned you into this circle, but the spell is temporary. If you want to get into the Warden's office, we'd have to break you out of the Ancestral Lands, so your ghost could stay here to search."

"I can do it," Marcus said confidently. "His spirit is really strong here. It wouldn't take much—"

"I'm *sure* you could do it," Ava said. "And that's the problem. I've come back from the Ancestral Lands, and I was lucky enough to have a body to come back to. Thaddeus doesn't."

"He's already crossed over once," Marcus said. "He can cross over again."

"You don't realize the risk you're taking," Ava pleaded. *"None* of you comprehend how hard it is for a soul to come back after they've crossed over. I've been there— it fucking sucks. It messes with your spirit in a way you can't understand. I still haven't gotten over it."

Ava wheeled closer to the center of the circle. "Thad, don't do this. Just stay in the afterlife. We'll find another way to get information."

"We *need* to get into the Warden's office, Ava. Thaddeus can do that without tipping off the wards. If Thaddeus wants to help, you can't stop him," Marcus argued.

"I do want to help, and I don't think you guys can get the information without me," Thaddeus said. *"But I have to return to the Ancestral Lands as soon as possible."*

"Yes, of course," Marcus said. "We won't keep you here any longer than necessary. Once I break the circle, you should be able to roam free around the Institute."

Marcus went to the edge of the circle, and his toe scraped against the ground as he broke the sigil. A distant, high-pitched squeal filled the room as his spell broke.

A chill spread over my skin as Thaddeus passed by me. His voice came from outside the circle. "*I know how important this is to all of you. I want to make this right and finish the work I didn't get to wrap up before I died. I'll do my best.*"

"Find out where Eddie was moved to," Marcus instructed. "Oh—and Thaddeus. Keep an eye out for any clues mentioning keys or the siren lake. We think the Warden found something in the lake, and it would help us a lot to learn what it was. Let us know when you've found something."

"*I will.*" Thaddeus must've vanished, because the chill in the air receded.

Marcus is entering dangerous territory, Oberi warned.

Oberi had me worried at first, but I figured he was just concerned about what happened last time we used our demigod powers. He didn't want to see Ava get hurt again.

"Thaddeus wants to help," I replied. "Don't act so concerned."

I wouldn't if the last time we attempted to tamper with things had ended better, Oberi sneered. *You two can't keep out of trouble, can you?*

I scoffed. "It's not like we're criminals. Oh, wait. We *are*."

There's no need for your sarcastic sass, Oberi scolded. *Don't come running to me when this gets messy. Death isn't something that should be dabbled in lightly.*

"Like time?" I asked him. "It's like you don't want us using our demigod powers at all."

Your powers are dangerous.

"Yes, but we're not going to get anywhere without them," I argued.

"What's he saying?" Kallie asked, and Ava quickly translated.

"If Oberi wants to go inside the Warden's office himself, he's more than welcome," Marcus said. "But otherwise, this is our only option."

"That may be the case, but we have to be careful," Ava said. "Oberi's is right. The three of us are still fucked up from bringing me back. It was a lot for our soul to take. I'm glad that I'm still here, but we need to be careful about any consequences to bringing others here."

"We'll be careful," I insisted.

We trained for a while after that, but nobody could pull off a feat quite like Marcus had. I managed to create a solid illusion of a tiny throne made out of twigs for Sprigs. Then I made him a flower crown, which he wouldn't take off.

"I want a throne, too," Marcus whined.

Within minutes, I'd made three separate thrones for my friends, made out of elements of the Earth like gold and silver, because those were the easiest to conjure with my Earth magic. We were getting better by the day, and I felt we were getting closer to busting out of here.

I was pushing Ava back to our room after practice when I heard the sound of a familiar voice. "I made an honest mistake, Professor. I didn't mean to hand in the wrong paper. I swear it."

Ava grabbed her wheels, bringing us to a complete stop. That was Ez, and he sounded really upset.

"There's no use in lying to me," a woman sneered. Her voice grated on my nerves. "If you spent less time on your *extracurriculars* and more time studying for my class, perhaps you'd scrape by with more than just a measly D."

Professor Mazur.

"You've got to let me resubmit," Ez begged. "I've got the essay saved. I can reprint it and submit the *right* paper."

"I'm afraid it's too far past the deadline," Mazur stated.

"Oh, this bitch didn't," Ava mumbled under her breath.

Her wheelchair started moving, slipping out from under my fingers.

"Let me see that." Ava must've ripped the essay out of Mazur's hands, because papers rustled as she flipped through them. "A paper on spinal injuries? Hey, it's actually really good! You can't fail my brother. This is ridiculous."

"This is no matter of yours," Mazur snapped. "He can still pass the semester with a failed exam paper. Consider me generous for not kicking him out of my class for pulling a stunt like this."

"This affects my total grade!" Ez cried. "Professor, I'm doing my best. I haven't gotten much sleep lately. You've got to help me out—"

"Your *best* would be to focus on your coursework," Mazur stated harshly. "If your lack of sleep affects your attention to detail, perhaps you should reevaluate what you're sacrificing your sleep for. Compiling information on spinal injuries isn't going to fix your sister's condition. She's a lost cause."

How *dare* she say something so vile! Rage flared in my veins, and I didn't think. I just acted. I stomped straight up to Mazur, my hands curled into fists at my side. Before I could raise my arm, Oberi bit my sleeve, pulling me back.

You'll go to Cellblock 9 for assaulting a professor, he warned.

Fuck, I grumbled. Didn't make me any less willing to punch her face in, though.

"You take that back!" I warned.

"Guards!" Professor Mazur screamed, and heavy boots immediately sounded down the hall.

I pointed a finger at Mazur. If I couldn't fight her with my fists, I was still going to give her a piece of my mind. "You think you're a saint, but you're nothing more than a worthless pawn in the Warden's sick game. You kidnapped those Elves and moved them to ancestors-know-where. Where'd you send them!?"

"I have no idea what you're talking about," she said coolly.

She was a fucking liar! "One day, you're going to tell us where to find them—"

Someone grabbed my wrist and yanked it behind my back, cutting me off. Cool metal touched my skin as they slapped cuffs on my wrist.

"Threatening a professor has earned you a ticket to solitary," a guard sneered in my ear.

I wished Oberi hadn't stopped me. If I was headed to Cellblock 9, I should've got at least one blow in. At least I'd walk away a little more satisfied.

"He wasn't threatening her—" Ava started, but Mazur cut her off.

"No!" the angel professor said almost too quickly, before her tone softened. "There's no reason to pull them away from their coursework. Take them back to their rooms, and lock them in for the rest of the night. That should give them plenty of time to think about their actions."

I heard the sound of Ez's paper fluttering to the ground, forgotten.

"You didn't have to do that," Ez said under his breath as we were guided down the hall.

"I'm not going to stand by and let someone bully my brother," Ava argued. "I don't care what kind of authority they have. Are you okay, though?"

"Yeah, I just made a mistake," Ez admitted. "I grabbed the wrong paper and didn't realize it until I handed it in."

We didn't get a chance to say anything else, because the guards dragged Ez off in the other direction toward the Elementai cell block, while we continued on toward our room. The guards tossed me inside so quickly that they forgot I was still cuffed. They shoved Ava's chair in behind me. The door slammed shut, and the sound of the lock slid into place.

"Ugh, I hate that bitch!" Ava screamed.

At least she didn't throw you in Cellblock 9, Oberi said as he hopped onto the couch.

"Yeah, why didn't she?" Ava wondered. "She's not the type of professor to stick up for us. She's nothing like Hemlock or Warbright."

"Because if we're down in Cellblock 9, we can't go searching for clues like the Warden wants us to," I pointed out. "He wants us to find shit for him so he can come and steal it from us."

"You don't think he knows how many Divinity Keys we have?" Ava asked.

"If he does, he doesn't know where we're keeping them," I said. "He'd have indicated something if he did, or Esther would've slipped up. She doesn't miss a chance to make others feel inferior."

"Well, I'm feeling fucking inferior right now," Ava complained. "I *hate* being locked up."

Mm... I'm not sure about that, Oberi cracked. *Judging by the sounds coming from the other room every night, I'm pretty sure you* love *it.*

"Hey, if you're that annoyed, cover your ears," Ava shot back. "And consider yourself lucky, because I'm too tired to do any of that tonight."

Thank the ancestors, Oberi said flatly.

"Charlie, can you help me into bed?" Ava asked.

"Yeah. I'll be right there."

Ava went into the other room, and I turned toward Oberi. "You don't have to be such a dick."

I know no other way of being.

"I've noticed," I said sarcastically. I conjured a small key in my hand, then twisted it. The illusion was easy, because it was made of metal. A light *click* filled the room, and I pulled the handcuffs from behind my back.

What are those— Oberi gasped. *The guards forgot your cuffs!*

I smirked. "Lucky for me, too. Ava's going to love these."

Oberi's tone was curious as he stated, *I understand why this is appealing to Ava. But as for you, I do not quite understand. You don't seem like the kind of person who gains enjoyment out of dominating others.*

"It's good for us," I stated.

How so? Oberi laid by my side and crossed his paws on my leg.

I had to think about it for a moment, because I wasn't sure how to put my feelings into words. "Neither of us ever had safe sex until each other," I explained. "It was always scary, or violent, or something that had to be done out of necessity for survival. But with Ava and me, it's enjoyable, because we trust each other. Playing out these scenarios builds that trust, and it changes every idea we've ever had about what sex is and what it can be. We can act out these scenarios without anyone getting hurt, so we can feel safe with sex again."

I decided to get really vulnerable, and dropped my tone. "I didn't really get any control when I slept with other people. I had to give that control up to get by, and let others use my body how *they* wanted, whether I asked them to or not. But with Ava, she's willing to hand me that control. She gives me back that piece of me I had to let go of, and it's very special, because I know what she went through. She's chosen me to be her protector and provider, even after she suffered at the hands of someone else. So I want to be that safe haven for her."

Isn't it safer if you don't tie her up? Oberi asked.

I shrugged. "I like tying Ava up because *she* likes it. It shows me how much she wants me and trusts me. She's consenting for me to please her in any way I want, and showing me she's not going to run away— even though she has that option, *always*. But she doesn't ask to stop; in fact, she encourages it, and that really turns me on. I know if you hold on to something too tightly, it runs away, but me tying Ava down is my way of holding on tight to her, and her telling me she's not going to leave. When I've tied her up, it means she's mine, and her doing what I ask confirms that. Because Ava wouldn't unless she was willing to give herself to me."

It seems like you're playing out dark fantasies.

"So what if we are? The darkness is all we know, and our thoughts are only turning darker. In the bedroom, we get to explore that darkness in a safe environment, without it being dangerous. It's a place we've created that no one else has to know about. Darkness doesn't have to be something evil or bad. It can be revolutionary, and even freeing. And we can expose the worst parts of ourselves without anyone getting hurt. It's enjoyable that we both like that dark side of each other. It's not something we have to try and change, or hide. We can let each other be who we truly want to be without judgment."

So you fantasize about dominating her?

I sighed. "That's not really the point. It's not about acting out sick fantasies. I would *never* touch Ava without her consent, and even thinking about doing that makes me sick. This is different. Every time she asks me to tie her up, she's showing me how much she trusts me. I love that I get to reciprocate that trust."

I almost stopped there, but then I realized there was more to it. "I like dominating her because it helps her calm her mind and focus on her pleasure, not just what makes me happy. I know Ava struggles with making healthy decisions, and it's only gotten worse since her spinal injury, because she no longer has the energy to. She's fighting against her bipolar and trying to recover all at once. But when we're in bed together, she gets to leave all that behind and ground herself again. It takes the pressure off of her. I'm honored that she wants me to make the decisions, because it shows me she trusts me to make the choices she can't. Me dominating her is me taking care of her."

I believe I understand, Oberi said simply. *I only want what is healthy and happy for the both of you, and I do think this helps rather than hurts. Avoiding the darkness inside leads to ruin. And it is a good thing that you are transforming that darkness into love.*

I bent down and tucked the cuffs under the couch cushion. I didn't want Ava finding them before we were ready to use them. "*Don't* mess with these. If you want Ava to be happy, you'll let us have our fun."

Oberi grumbled. *Yeah, yeah. Whatever you say. I won't touch them.*

I patted him on the top of the head. "Good dog."

SEVERAL DAYS PASSED, and I was a little disappointed we hadn't had a chance to use the handcuffs yet. We'd been swamped with finals, and Ava spent most afternoons resting.

She wouldn't admit it, but I could tell she was having a hell of a time with exams after she'd spent half the semester in the hospital, not to mention she kept forgetting information that I knew she'd already learned. I couldn't give her the answers through our bond, either, because we weren't taking them together. My exams were scheduled after hers, so my professors could read the questions out loud to me. At least she had Oberi, but I didn't know how much help he'd been.

I met up with my friends in our secret gym after one of my finals. The four of us decided we needed to blow off some steam, and lifting weights felt like a pretty good way to relieve some stress.

Marcus lay on the bench, groaning as he lifted weights. Ava and Kallie were in the other corner.

"Kallie, I can't!" Ava complained.

"We'll have to try something else," Kallie said gently.

"Hey, what's going on?" I asked, making my way over to them. Oberi was in her unicorn form, and I could feel the heat of her Fire mane rolling off her.

Ava huffed from Oberi's back. "I'm trying to ride Oberi, and I... can't."

"How so?" I wondered. "It seems you're riding her now."

"*Sitting* on her and riding her are two different things," Ava stated. "Without use of my legs, I can't hold myself on when she moves, and if you're not riding her with me, I can't stay on."

This was a major problem.

"We've been building up your core all semester," I stated.

"My core isn't going to help me here," Ava said. "My core will help me balance, but my legs keep me on. If I can't hold myself in place, I can't ride Oberi."

This really sucked because I didn't feel like I could help. Ava needed *some* sort of help or accommodations.

That's when it hit me.

"I have an idea." I reached up for Ava and helped her down, then set her back in her chair. I ran my hands over Oberi's back, getting a feel for the curve of her spine. The idea formed in my head like an architect sketching out the blueprints for a building. I ignored reality when I touched her fur, and instead, pictured that I was running my fingers across smooth fabric. The cloth formed beneath my fingers, and within moments, a saddle appeared.

Ava gasped. "Charlie! It's beautiful!"

Kallie came up beside me and ran her fingers over the saddle. "How did you *do* this?"

I shrugged. "With all our practice this semester, I've been getting better at illusions. This one should be permanent."

"Yes, but all your illusions have been made with your Earth powers," Kallie pointed out. "This is like a real saddle!"

"Oh, um... I guess I didn't really think about it," I admitted. "I knew Ava needed a saddle, so I just did it."

It feels really nice, Oberi remarked. *It's comfortable.*

"It's a bareback pad," Kallie said. "I thought you didn't know anything about horseback riding."

"I don't know much, other than what I've learned from riding Oberi," I said. It wasn't leather, like most saddles. It was made of nylon cloth, so it was thinner and more comfortable for two riders. It only had one set of stirrups, which I'd made thick to support Ava's legs. "My idea was to create something that would keep Ava secure, but also allow me to ride with her."

"Charlie, it has straps for my legs!" Ava sounded really touched by the gesture.

"I figured you'd need some adaptations," I said.

"Can I try it?" she asked.

"Absolutely." I double checked that the strap was tight around Oberi's belly, then lifted Ava onto the saddle. I situated her feet inside the stirrups and secured each leg with Velcro straps— three for each leg. Then I draped another strap across her thighs, like a seatbelt, and secured that, too. I held on to her and tugged lightly on the saddle to make sure she was secure. She barely moved.

"Ancestors, it's perfect!" Ava cried. "Oberi, let's go for a ride!"

I held the door open as Oberi went into the abandoned hall. Kallie and Marcus followed to watch. Her hooves clicked across the ground slowly and deliberately. I stayed by Ava's side, holding her hand so I could catch her if she fell.

"I want to go faster," Ava said.

Oberi increased her speed to a brisk pace, and I followed along beside her. Ava laughed gleefully. "It's working! Oberi, faster!"

Oberi turned at the end of the hall, then took off at a quick trot. My hand slipped out of Ava's grasp. She screamed happily as Oberi jogged to the other end of the hall.

"Ancestors, I stayed on the whole time!" Ava cried as Oberi slowed.

"This is wonderful," Marcus said.

"I couldn't have created a better illusion myself," Kallie added.

Oberi walked back to me, and Ava brushed her hands across my shoulder. "I want you to ride with me."

I braced myself against Oberi's back, then leapt upward, tossing a leg over her. I sat behind Ava and curled my arms around her.

Ugh. You two are heavy, Oberi complained.

"Shut up," I said. "You're a mutabeecha. You can bench, like, a thousand pounds."

More, actually, Oberi replied proudly.

"Then what are you complaining about?" I asked.

Oberi blew a breath. *Just giving you a hard time. Though, I don't appreciate your junk rubbing on my bare back like that!*

"Yeah, I'm sure you can feel that," I said sarcastically.

Ava leaned back to say in all seriousness, "You're very gifted."

"Is this better?" I resituated myself and slid closer to Ava, keeping our weight as close together as possible.

"Much better," Ava said.

Oberi took a few steps. *I think it'll work.*

"It'll work?" I repeated. "I just pulled off the biggest illusion I've ever done, and that's all you have to say."

Well, it's the truth! Oberi nickered. *Very well done. Is that better?*

"Much," I replied, before turning my attention to Ava. "This is a good next step in physical therapy. We can practice getting up and down from the saddle."

"I think with enough practice, I can do it," Ava said. "Though I might have to start with some magical assistance."

"We'll learn. Together," I offered.

Oberi took off down the hall again, and my hair whipped around my face. For a brief moment, it felt freeing, and I could imagine we weren't locked in the Institute at all. If I could create illusions this strong, we might actually find a way out of here soon.

We rode Oberi up and down the hall a few more times, before we returned to our secret room. I hopped off her back and helped Ava back into her chair.

"There's just one problem," I said. "How are we going to transport the saddle with us? We need it to be available at a moment's notice."

"I can subconjure it and keep it in my stash," Marcus offered.

I pressed my lips together. "Strapping it on will take time we don't have if we're attacked. There's got to be a better way. Hang on— I've got it!"

I ran my hands over Oberi's back. "What if Oberi and I use simul-tension and combine shifter magic with my illusion magic? We can make the saddle shift with her."

"That might work," Ava said. "Why don't you try it?"

Oberi nickered, and I felt her shifter magic flowing through me. I ordered it to tangle with my illusion, and the saddle buzzed with energy.

"Try it now, girl," I instructed.

Oberi shifted, her form shrinking beneath my hands. Oberi let out a bark.

The saddle's gone, he said.

"Incredible," Marcus mused.

"Try shifting back," I suggested.

Oberi's energy changed as she became a unicorn again. I ran my hands over her back, and the bareback pad was still there.

"This is amazing!" Ava raved, sounding thrilled. "Now we won't have to worry about this."

I paused when I heard the sound of footsteps in the distance.

"Someone's coming!" Marcus hissed.

The door to the abandoned cell block opened, and we all held our breath. Rishi meowed and pawed at the door to our secret room.

"Yo!" someone shouted. "Anyone here?"

I relaxed. "It's just Alistair."

I opened the door and called down the hall. "We're in here."

"Is Marcus down there?" Alistair asked.

"He's here," I said.

Alistair's cane clicked louder and faster against the ground as he hurried toward us. "Marcus, I need some damn answers."

Marcus groaned as Alistair entered the room. "I told you, we can't cheat on our final. If we're caught—"

"I'm not talking about cheating," Alistair interrupted. "I'm talking about Eddie! What did Thaddeus find?"

We'd told our friends we'd summoned Thaddeus, and that he'd learned the Elves had been moved. They knew Thad had gone looking for answers, but so far, we didn't have an update. It'd been a few days, and that worried me.

"He's still looking for information," Marcus said.

"Well, he's taking too long!" Alistair shouted.

"He's a *ghost*," Marcus shot back. "He can't exactly shift through paperwork."

"He must've found something," Alistair insisted.

"That's not fair," Marcus said. "We've been searching for answers all semester. Thaddeus has only had a few days."

"That's a problem. How much longer are we going to hang out waiting on answers?" Alistair demanded.

"Look, I'm sorry, but Thaddeus doesn't have any answers for us," Marcus said harshly.

"That's not good enough, Marcus," Alistair spat, before turning to leave.

"Alistair, come on!" Marcus called.

"Don't want to hear it," Alistair shot back as he kept walking.

The atmosphere in the room turned melancholy. None of us knew what to do. Until we got more information, there wasn't much *to* do.

"I'll talk to Ivy and see if he's reached out to Erasmus Morelli," Ava offered, and I heard her begin to wheel away. "If we don't have answers on the Elves, perhaps we could find out more about the merfolk key."

ava-marie

SIXTEEN

We were no closer to information on Eddie's location than we were when we first contacted Thaddeus' ghost. It was terrible, waiting around knowing the Elves were in trouble when we knew there was information within our reach to help them, but at the moment, there was little more we could do.

My nights had been fragmented with dreams of Eddie— realizing that he could be close by, while at the same time, admitting to myself he could be under torture right now, if he wasn't dead already.

Thinking about my friend like that tormented me, so I tried not to. Instead, I focused on solving the mystery of the merfolk key. The quicker we got it, the quicker we could find a way out of here and go looking for wherever Eddie had been taken.

The following day, I went to the Villain's Den to speak with Ivy, to see if there was any progress on Erasmus Morelli. Ivy was sitting at a table, a textbook spread out in front of him while he sipped on tea from Commissary.

"Hey," I asked as I rolled up to the table. "Have you heard from Erasmus yet?"

Ivy shook his head. "Sorry. I'm still waiting."

"What kind of job does your dad have him on?"

"Knowing my old man, it probably ain't pretty. Erasmus has gone completely off-the-grid. We might have to wait a few more weeks before we hear anything back."

"Ugh. This is pointless." I scowled as I tossed my bookbag on the table.

"He'll contact us eventually." Ivy laid a hand on mine. "I have a feeling we're close. Just hang on."

"I know we hate your dad, but could you ask him for a favor, and see if he can reach out to Erasmus for us?" I despised Salvatore Bianchi with a passion, but it was taking way too long to get answers. If we could manipulate Ivy's crummy father in order to get some, then I was all for it.

"Well, seeing as how my father isn't going to like the way I've decided to live my life, I'm pretty sure that option is off the table." Ivy blew a lock of hair away from his eyes.

"What do you mean?"

"I've made some pretty big decisions lately," Ivy confessed. "Decisions my family isn't going to like, but I figure I'm tired of trying to make them comfortable for the sake of making myself *uncomfortable*. This is my life. I've decided I get to choose how to live it."

"How so?" I leaned forward, interested in this new development.

"Well, for starters, I decided I want to be completely called *they* and *them*. No more he and him," Ivy began. "This is who I am. I'm not one gender or the other; I'm a million different things, and all are true at the same time."

"Ivy, that's so great!" I leaned forward to give them a hug. I was so thrilled that Ivy was taking this moment to truly be who they wanted to.

"Thanks, precious. It's been a long time coming." Ivy withdrew from the hug and took a breath. "Secondly, I've declared my major, and I have you and Charlie to thank for that."

"What did we do?" I was bewildered.

"I found out I really like helping couples grow closer together. Seeing how my advice helped you guys really made something come alive in me. I've decided I'm going to pursue being an intimacy counselor." Ivy crossed their legs, appearing resolute.

"I can't believe it. That would be so perfect for you," I insisted.

"I'm not sure what path I'm going to take yet. I love entertainment, and running the club was so much fun, so I think it might be a blast being an intimacy coordinator on film and theater sets, to make sure the actors are comfortable and to help stage romantic scenes." Ivy tapped their pencil on the table. "But I also considered becoming a sex counselor, so I can help couples find their way back to each other again."

"You'd be amazing at that. Your advice was great for Charlie and me. Imagine all the other couples you could help!"

"Exactly. I'm pretty torn." Ivy stirred their tea. "I'm taking psychology courses next semester, even though I can't *really* say what I'm striving to be, since we both know the Warden wouldn't allow it. I just put down that I wanted to be a therapist on my major declaration sheet. I'm actually going to be doing an internship with Professor Takahashi over the summer."

"I am so proud of you." My eyes began to water.

"Aw, don't you cry. I'm not anything to fuss over." Ivy leaned over and wiped a couple of tears away from my eyes.

"It's just so nice to see my friends succeed and want to achieve their dreams."

"It gives me a distraction, something to focus on. I kinda need it, because it takes my mind off the juice, and I ain't opening the club back up again," Ivy stated.

"You've shut down The Devil's Playground for good?" I asked sadly.

"Yeah. Me and Chance decided it's just too much temptation for me, and though it's fun and all, it's not worth the risk of me going back on drugs."

I was a little upset, but at the same time, the loss of the club meant nothing so long as Ivy was healthy. "This is great you're finally getting back on your feet. I know you're going to be amazing at whatever you do."

Ivy smiled and went to respond, but before they could, there was a soft, "Eh-*hm*."

Esther had come up to our table— without an invitation. She tapped her foot against the rug, and Ivy sneered, "Can we help you?"

"I just came over to make a correction," Esther replied. "There are only two genders, which are male and female. And since you were born a male, you're a he. That's biology. You can't get around science."

I rolled my eyes, but Ivy said, "Biological sex and gender are different. Gender is a state that you choose by what feels most authentic to you. And I choose to be both."

Esther wrinkled her nose. "You're just making things up. There's no such thing as nonbinary people, or trans people, or any of that nonsense. If you're *that* mentally ill you can't accept that you're a man, you need to go to the infirmary, before you poison the rest of us with your little freak show."

Esther had never been so actively accusatory. Usually, she hid behind a fake smile and a bunch of backhanded compliments that were actually mean taunts, so people couldn't accuse her of being an ass later. Right now, she was putting her hatred on full display, and I wasn't about to put up with it.

"Ivy can be whoever *they* want," I said coldly. "Just like you have the right to be a massive bitch to everyone you see."

"It's against the laws of The Mission!" Esther yelled.

"I suppose the rules don't apply to me, because I don't follow your religion," Ivy said snidely.

Esther sniffed. "The laws of The Mission apply to *everyone.*"

I had a grip on a book, ready to toss it at Esther's head. But Ivy slowly stood and said, "This is who I am. I accept it, and I love myself this way. I don't need to change who I am, but embrace it. And anyone who doesn't approve of it, or tries to change me, doesn't have a place in my life. Maybe if you accepted yourself as you are, then you wouldn't feel the need to go around and make other people feel bad about being authentically themselves."

"Are you serious?" Esther let out a laugh that sounded insecure. "I think I'm an awesome person."

"I don't think so, Esther. Bullies pick on people to get some sort of validation, because inside, they hate themselves," Ivy spat. "And I've never met anyone who despises herself more than you do."

Esther's lip trembled, and it was the most honest response I'd seen from her all day. "Well, I'm not surprised something so crazy would come out the mouth of a *freak.*"

She whirled around on her heel, dramatically exiting the Villain's Den. It was at that moment Oberi walked in, hopping on his paws.

It's a good day. I just saw Esther cry, he noted gleefully.

"Holy shit, you destroyed her," I said, baffled as I turned back to Ivy.

"It's the truth. I'm sorry she can't handle it." Ivy shrugged. "The laws of The Mission teach that we're all terrible people who can only be redeemed by guilting ourselves into doing whatever the doctrine tells us to without question. You can't follow a religion like that without having some sort of inner hate. Esther wouldn't be spending all of her time going around making people feel awful if she didn't feel shitty about herself."

"Maybe she just gets a kick out of being evil."

"Well, she does, but you have to ask yourself the reason *why*."

Ivy set down their tea and brushed off their skirt. "Wish me luck on my Vampiric Magic final. And if luck won't do it, the answer sheet I stole from Professor Cyrus might do the trick."

I smiled and shook my head as Ivy strolled away. Some things didn't change.

"Why are you here? Shouldn't you be with Charlie?" I asked Oberi.

The professor proctoring the exam wouldn't let me go in there. She figured he'd use me to cheat, as silly as that is, Oberi replied. *So I came to bother you.*

"Well, you might as well get comfortable, because I'm not going anywhere."

I spent the next hour prepping for my own exam that afternoon, while Oberi napped on the rug underneath the table. With a quick check of the clock, I realized I had to leave in order to get to my exam on time.

I had packed away my things to go take it when I felt a warm, wet sensation flood my skirt and my wheelchair seat. I wasn't sure what it was, because the feeling in my legs was dulled, so it took a moment for me to put the pieces together.

I froze, before I realized what had happened and started to panic.

Oh, *shit*. Not fucking *here*.

Oberi woke up, and gave a whimper of concern. *It's okay. Just stay calm.*

I reddened profusely, and prayed that nobody saw me blush. People weren't looking my way, but if they did, they might put together what had happened, and then I'd die of humiliation.

Please don't let anyone notice. I slowly rolled my chair out of the room, praying no one knocked into me, because if they did, it'd go spilling all over the rug. Oberi walked near my chair, blocking it off from sight.

Pidge, you okay? Charlie was across the prison, taking an exam, but he'd paused when he felt my embarrassment seep across our bond.

Yeah, just spilled something, I lied, before shutting my connection to him off. I wanted some fucking privacy, thank you, after pissing myself.

I rolled to the closest bathroom and struggled with getting into the disabled stall. It was a pain in the ass. The walls were still too narrow for me to turn around, so I ended up getting stuck a few times. I had to maneuver around the stall in my wet skirt before I was able to use the bars to lift myself onto the toilet seat, but I was still too late.

"Fuck." I dropped my head and started to cry. I hated this. It was probably one of the worst parts of my spinal injury. I couldn't sense when I had to use the bathroom anymore. I hadn't had an accident since I'd been in the hospital, with nurses who were around to help me clean up. There'd been a few close calls, but nothing like this. I'd managed to get around the problem by scheduling bathroom breaks at the same time every day and never being too far from a restroom, but I'd been so eager to talk to Ivy about contacting Erasmus, I'd forgotten to take one after lunch. Oberi whined outside the stall, unsure of how to help.

It's not your fault. You shouldn't be ashamed, Oberi objected.

Sure feels like it. I sniffed and wiped my face. I didn't know what to do. I needed to change, but my exam was in ten minutes, and I couldn't miss it, or I'd fail. That wasn't enough time for me to go back to my cell and change, but I couldn't go to class and take a test while sitting in my own mess, either. Completely overwhelmed, I put my hands over my face and cried.

Someone shut off a faucet outside. "Ava?" Kallie's voice echoed over the stalls.

She knocked on the stall. Oberi's nails clicked on the floor as he stepped aside. I felt degraded, but I needed *someone* to help me, and I'd pick Kallie over anyone. I leaned forward and unlocked the stall door. She opened it, but the door banged against my wheelchair and wouldn't go any farther.

"Are you okay?" Kallie poked her head in, and her face fell when she saw my soaking wheelchair and my wet skirt.

"I feel like an infant." Tears bubbled up over my eyelids and ran down my face.

"It's okay," she rushed to say. "I'll help you clean up."

"My Anthropology exam is right now!" I whimpered.

"I'll tell Professor Hemlock you need an extension. Just stay here, I'll be back in a second."

I wasn't going anywhere like this. I locked the door again and waited an eternity for Kallie to return, while Oberi guarded the door. When she did, she'd come back with a couple of towels, some wet wipes, and a fresh change of clothes.

"I told Hemlock you weren't feeling well. She's pushing your exam until tomorrow," Kallie said. She squeezed herself into the stall and shut the door behind her. She barely had enough room to maneuver around. Screw the Institute and its half-assed attempts to make things accessible. Kallie did her best to move my wheelchair out of the way, and she handed me a few wet wipes. I cleaned myself off while she worked on wiping down my legs.

"I'm so sorry you have to do this," I apologized. My friends shouldn't be helping me this way.

"You'd do the same for me in a heartbeat," Kallie replied. "What are friends for?"

My lip wobbled. "It's embarrassing, you know, relying on your help like this."

"Hey, look at it this way, from this angle, I get a great view of that famous bikini wax you're always bragging about," Kallie joked. "And it does look good, by the way. Can you do one on me? I'm sure Marcus would love it."

I let out a choked giggle. "You steal the supplies from the cafeteria, and you've got yourself a deal."

"Done." Kallie tossed the wipes away, then looked at my wheelchair with a frown. "What do you want to do about that?"

"I'm not sure." When I'd first gotten out of the hospital, Charlie and I had a *major* blow-out argument about using disposable underpads to protect the wheelchair, and the gel cushion it had come with, in case something like this happened. I'd felt completely insulted, and complained he wanted me to use a puppy pad, but he wanted to play it safe just in case. Apparently, he'd been right.

"You could use your Water magic to get rid of it, then we can disinfect the chair and the gel cushion with the wipes," Kallie suggested.

"You're right. Ugh, this is terrible."

"Hey, it could've been worse," Kallie pointed out.

I shuddered to think. Definitely could've.

We managed to get everything else clean. The chair wasn't ruined, but that was a stroke of luck. Kallie helped me into a new skirt, and put on new socks and shoes, since I still struggled to get them on by myself.

"Are you okay with me doing this?" Kallie asked as she finished knotting a bow on those awful, deplorable, no-good Mary Janes.

"I have to be. But sometimes, it makes me feel like a toddler," I confessed. "Charlie has to get up even earlier now, because he's got to help me dress after he gets ready, too. I'm still working on doing things by myself, and I think I'll get the hang of it eventually, but I still haven't mastered stuff that requires me to bend over, because my middle is so scarred. I'm shit at tying shoes."

"Meh, Chancey can't tie his own shoes either. The angel struggles to learn his colors and shapes. You can count to five, so you're already way ahead of him."

A loud laugh bubbled out of me. "I love you, Kallie."

"No love needed for telling the truth. He's a big, dumb idiot."

Kallie pushed me out of the bathroom, and I felt a little lighter. What happened was horrible, but it was made a little less so by having a good friend at my side. Oberi panted, happy that we'd solved my latest crisis of the day.

"I definitely need to repay you for this. I owe you one," I told her as she pushed me to the library.

"You don't owe me anything. You needed me," Kallie insisted.

I did. I'd needed her, and she hadn't hesitated to step in. How could I express the immense gratitude I had for her? There wasn't a way to show her how thankful I was.

Marcus was scribbling in a notebook while Rishi purred on top of a stack of books. Kallie pushed me to his table and plopped down in the seat next to mine.

Marcus glanced at me. "Don't you have an exam right now?"

"It got moved," Kallie said shortly. "We're just hanging out."

Kallie's tone told Marcus to stop asking questions, so he changed the subject. "Professor Mazur caught me following her around. She gave me an infraction and threatened to send me to Cellblock 9 before she finally let me go. She knows we're tailing her for information. She's not going to slip up and talk about where Eddie is if she's aware we're following her."

"We've gotta find a way to get through to her," I mumbled.

"Pain works," Kallie said, and she smacked a fist into her palm.

"Yeah, right, like we could get away with that." I sighed, placing my chin into my hand. "Maybe we could negotiate. There's gotta be something she wants. Or we could pay her off—"

"Don't think so. She subscribes to The Mission's cause like it's her own personal vendetta," Marcus replied.

"I bet she's already told the Warden. He's gotta be getting off on the idea that he knows more than us," Kallie complained.

"Forget the Warden," Marcus said. "My next idea is to rifle through her office. She's outside giving an exam in the prison yard next period, so I figured I could do that now. Unless you girls have any other concerns."

I paused. "Actually, Marcus... I wanted to ask you something unrelated."

He turned toward me in interest, and I said, "I overheard your offer to Charlie, to help him talk to his mom. I know he's not ready for that yet. But..."

I took a deep breath. "I want to talk to Monica. That is, if you're willing."

He blinked, and Rishi gave a low meow before Marcus stated, "If you think you're ready, I can definitely do that for you, Ava. If I send her an invitation and she accepts, she'll speak with us. She didn't die that long ago. She should be easy for me to contact, now that I have a better handle on the spell after we contacted Thaddeus."

Complicated emotions raged inside of me. Hope. Regret. Heartache. I didn't think I'd get the chance to speak with Monica again until after I died— and even then, I hadn't gotten that chance. The gift Marcus was giving me was incredible.

Oberi's ears had perked up. *This is a good plan, Ava. It's not like bringing Thaddeus here to the Institute. Speaking with Monica might help you heal.*

"Then I'm ready," I said. "When should we begin?"

"Let's go to the Witch Tower now. The supplies will be there." Marcus subconjured his things, and turned toward me.

The three of us made our way there. After Kallie had lifted my chair up the stairs with her telekinetic magic, Marcus got to work setting up the area.

Oberi changed into a Fire unicorn and dipped her head as Marcus buzzed around the room, furiously getting things in place. He drew a chalk alchemy circle on the floor, placing herbs around it like he'd done with the ritual to summon Thaddeus.

When he was finished, Marcus faced me. "Okay, Ava, enter the middle of the circle."

I rolled into the alchemy circle, and Marcus said, "I'll be the conduit. Monica's spirit is going to come through me and into the circle, but she won't be able to leave it. Once you come out of the circle, the communication will be over, and she'll return to the Ancestral Lands. You ready?"

"Yes." My voice shook. Now that the moment was here, I wasn't sure how to feel. I'd been living without her for so long that she'd become a distant memory, almost like something my bipolar had made up. I wasn't sure how to continue our relationship after her death, as I'd struggled so much without her. This wouldn't be like when I'd seen her image in the caves that led to Forevermore. That was an illusion meant to trick me. This would actually be the *real* Monica. I had no idea what she would say. It was honestly really scary.

But I wanted to speak with her more than anything, so I'd take this chance, even if what she said hurt. Marcus knelt by the edge of the alchemy circle and placed his hands upon the edge. The alchemy circle lit up, glowing amethyst and igniting the room. Kallie watched the display from afar, her hair blown back by the burst of power the circle emitted.

The alchemy circle continued to glow, and Marcus' eyes took on the same color, shining a deep purple. Rishi walked the edge of the alchemy circle and meowed, while Oberi stood cautiously at my side.

I didn't see a ghost materialize, as I'd seen Thaddeus. "Is she here?" I asked, looking around. I expected her to pop right up in front of me, and yet, nothing.

"She is," Marcus replied, though his voice echoed strangely. His face reddened, and he added, "Oh, wow. No wonder she's your friend, Ava. She sure doesn't hold anything back."

"What'd she say?" I asked eagerly.

"It was inappropriate," Marcus said distastefully. "Ghosts aren't usually so... brutally honest."

I can hear her, Oberi said lightly. *She's quite funny.*

"Why can't I hear her? Or see where she is?" I was getting impatient.

"She doesn't want to show herself to you."

"What the hell!" I threw my hands up.

"She won't cross over from the spirit realm. She's remaining there while sending messages straight to me."

"If she's going to relay everything she says through you, anyway, why not just show her ass up and talk to me in person?" I demanded.

"She doesn't want to." Marcus cocked his head. "It's weird. I have the ability to bring her spirit over, but she's resisting. I don't get it."

I felt rejected. She hadn't come to speak with me in the Ancestral Lands when I'd died, now she was refusing to come talk to me. Wasn't I worthy? Didn't she miss me at all, like I desperately missed her?

"Ava, I can't do this forever," Marcus reminded me. "This takes a lot of magical energy. So if you want to talk to her, I suggest you start, instead of complaining about the methods involved."

I huffed. "Fine. I'll take what I can get."

I swallowed a lump in my throat. "I'm sorry for what happened. I go over that night all the time and wonder if I could've changed anything, and if it was possible to save you. Maybe if I had done something different, you'd still be here today."

I thought about it all the time— what would've happened if I had stopped us from running away, if those men hadn't tried to pull me into that van, if Monica had tried to save herself instead of attempting to rescue me. There were a million variables that could've made things turn out differently.

"She doesn't blame you for what happened," Marcus said quickly. "She thinks it was *her* fault."

"It wasn't," I insisted. "The only people responsible for her death are the men who killed her."

"She knows that, but she regrets not going back home when you wanted to," Marcus replied. "But what she doesn't regret is trying to save you. She wouldn't have run away, Ava. She couldn't leave you behind."

"She should've," I whispered. So many times, I'd had the thought it was wrong Monica was gone and that I was still here. I figured it should be the other way around.

"She knows you have a great destiny ahead of you, and a prophecy to fulfill. I guess it was in her soul contract to help you fulfill it, but..." Marcus paused. "Things changed when she died, and someone else had to step in. But she really wants to press that it was important for you to stay on Earth, because you're going to do some great things... like helping Charlie save the Elves."

I snorted. "Yeah, we're making great progress on that."

Marcus let out a nervous chuckle. "She said, *If you stopped paying attention to the voices in your head and listened every once in a while, you might get somewhere.*"

"That bitch!" I yelled, giving a choked laugh. I thought this was going to be a tender, emotional reunion, not a snarkfest.

I shouldn't be surprised. This was Monica, after all.

Marcus smiled, before his grin faltered. Oberi let out a gentle nicker, and Marcus added, "Monica's showing me something. Lessons that she's learned about her life while living in the Ancestral Lands, lessons that she wishes she could've had more time to learn on Earth. She doesn't want you to make the same mistake. She's not... upset that she died, and she doesn't necessarily want to come back, but she thinks your life could be so much better if you took the time to listen to what the world is trying to tell you. Because she spent her whole life running from it, instead of facing it."

"Well, sorry I'm screwing up." I crossed my arms, feeling bitter. This wasn't how I wanted our conversation to go.

"She's not angry at you, Ava."

"If you tell me she's *disappointed in me*, I'm gonna find a way back into the spiritual realm so I can rip her hair out," I threatened.

"No. She's... sad."

My heart fell out of my chest, and Oberi rested her nose on my shoulder. "Why is she sad?"

"You aren't honoring her life. You're so upset about her being gone you've forgotten all the great times you two had together," Marcus continued. "It hurts her to see you so lost in grief. She wants you to keep the memory of your friendship alive by doing the things you two loved. She's really excited you and Charlie started making music again, and that you started up your vlogging channel. She wants you to continue that."

I bunched my hands in my skirt. We'd put off making more music videos because we'd been so wrapped up in investigating the mystery of the merfolk key. I'd missed it, but in the face of everything else, it seemed... unimportant.

It is important, Oberi insisted. *Doing the things you and Monica loved will give you inspiration to solve the problems in your life.*

"She's saying to keep telling the jokes she always liked to make. Do the things she enjoyed, and advocate for the causes she cared about," Marcus said. "She's frustrated because everyone has made her memory all about her murder, and the tragedy of dying young. No one remembers the life she lived, and that's what's really important. How she died is a footnote compared to how she lived her life. So because she can't, she wants you to continue that work— to be young, wild, and free."

An overwhelming sensation of grief welled around me, and I tried to hold it in as I said, "I'm doing my best every day to make her proud."

"She *is* proud of you, Ava. She knows you do everything you can to fulfill the dreams the two of you had together. She said she was at your wedding, sitting in one of the pews— you just couldn't see her. Oh, goddess, she *loves* Charlie. He's one of her favorite people," Marcus said.

Then Marcus' eyes widened, and he said, "But Monica wants you to know that since she can't be there, she sent someone along to you to take her place."

My lip wobbled, and I whispered, "Kallie." Across the room, Kallie pushed herself off the wall and approached the alchemy circle curiously.

Marcus stuttered, then added, "I guess she hand-picked Kallie. She says she knew you needed someone by your side who was as big a bitch as she'd been."

Kallie laughed out loud, and tears welled in my eyes. I was so honored Monica cared so much about me that she'd done her part from the Ancestral Lands to make sure I still had friends... *best* friends.

"Kallie took over Monica's part of the soul contract," Marcus said in astonishment. "Kallie was always supposed to help us with the prophecy, because she was a demigod and it was in her life plan, but after Monica died, Kallie offered to take on Monica's role."

"I don't have any memories of this," Kallie said.

"You wouldn't. It would be your highest self, the piece of you that always remains in the spiritual realm, who'd take on the negotiation," Marcus explained. "Monica knows that Kallie had the ability to love you just as much as she did. Maybe... even more."

I hugged myself as I looked at Kallie. Our friendship was special, but now it felt even more sacred, because I knew my best friend who'd passed on had set this connection up for me.

Marcus blushed even harder, and he shouted, "Okay, this isn't about me!"

"What'd she say?" I asked Oberi.

She told Marcus to stop being a pussy and make Kallie his girlfriend, Oberi gushed.

Marcus huffed. "She... *ugh*... she wants you to know that the guys in the Ancestral Lands are easy on the eyes. Her words, not mine. She wanted me to say it exactly like that."

"She hooked up with somebody? Who?" I demanded.

"She won't say. She's teasing you about it." Marcus scowled. "Okay, so *you* won't tell us anything about *your* love life, but mine is on the table for group discussion?!"

The alchemy circle flared, losing its glow for a few seconds before lighting up again. Around me, the amethyst color began to dim.

"The connection's getting faulty. We only have a minute or so left before I can't hold the connection any longer," Marcus said sourly. "Is there anything else you want to say?"

"Just that I love her," I noted softly. "And that I miss her. So, so much."

"She knows, Ava. She really does."

Marcus held a breath. "She's saying something else. Hold on, it's unclear..."

"What is it?" I leaned forward, needing to hear every word she had to say.

The alchemy circle abruptly died, losing all of its light. A hollow feeling opened up again in my chest, and I knew that Monica was no longer with us.

Marcus dropped his arms. "She's gone now. But... before she left, she wanted me to tell you to *make that bastard pay*."

An icy feeling wrapped around my insides and began freezing me outward. Monica had known exactly what had been suffocating me, and the advice couldn't have been any clearer.

Marcus stood, brushing off his clothes as Rishi wrapped around his legs. Kallie stepped into the alchemy circle. She approached me slowly, as if recognizing me in a whole new light. "Seeing what you and Monica shared, even in a context like that, was just... beautiful. I never had a friend who loved me like she loves you."

"Now you do, because I love you." I reached out and took her hand. "Losing Monica will always hurt, but you've made that pain bearable, because I have you. I don't think I could get along without you."

Kallie gave me a watery grimace, and I could tell she was struggling to find the words. She wasn't someone who showed emotion often, so when she teared up, I knew whatever she was feeling, she felt deeply.

"I hoped it gave you some sort of peace," Marcus said as he went around the room, erasing the edges of the chalk alchemy circle with his shoe.

"It was great, but I still don't feel like I have closure about all of this." I dropped my gaze. "Talking to Monica helped, but everything still feels unfinished."

Kallie bit her lip. "If you're looking to tie a bow on the stuff that happened in your past... I might have an idea."

"What is it?" I squeezed her fingers, telling her I would be open to anything.

"It's a fae ceremony. I can perform it for you, but it's a little... dark," she confessed.

"Isn't everything that involves the fae morbid?" Marcus complained.

"It depends on how you view it culturally," Kallie said. "To my people, death and the cycles life takes are beautiful. If you're interested, we could do it tomorrow night."

I lifted an eyebrow. "So what does it entail?"

Kallie explained the ceremony to me. Once I had the details, I was certain it was something I wanted to do. We planned to go forward with it the following evening.

"I'll invite the others," Kallie said before we left. "And Marcus— we're going to need some music."

"Ooh, I get to use my harp again!" Marcus squeaked. He seemed positively thrilled.

"How are you going to break the idea to your husband?" Kallie asked as she used her telepathy magic to levitate my wheelchair down the stairs of the tower.

"I don't know. I'm not sure how he'll take this," I said slowly.

Agreed, Oberi replied, and her hooves clip-clopped on the stone stairs. *But I think it is something that must be done.*

When we got to the ground floor, I parted from Kallie and Marcus, and went with Oberi to the phone room. We still had some time before curfew, and I'd finally made up my mind about what to do about John.

The second I arrived, I dialed the number. My father picked up immediately.

"Daddy? Send a legal notice to the Institute that I've been summoned to court. I'm going to testify."

♂ ♀

I FELT secure in my choice when I ended the phone conversation and returned to my cell with Oberi. I'd been going back and forth for days on what to do, but with Monica's support, I knew that I could summon the courage and face John again— and give my testimony, which would hopefully put him behind bars.

It wasn't fair, or just, that I was in prison and he was roaming around free. Fuck John. I was coming for him.

Charlie was lounging on the couch when I rolled in. "Hey. Where have you been?" he asked as Oberi changed into a husky, and shut the door behind us.

"I was in the Witch Tower with Marcus and Kallie," I said. "I... Marcus was able to help me talk to Monica."

"Really?" He sat up, leaning over his knees. "That must've been really hard."

"Not as hard as I thought, but it... brought up a lot of stuff, honestly. I wanted to talk to you about it."

"What's up?"

I said apprehensively, "Well... we never had a funeral for me, and I *did* die."

Charlie's eyebrows knitted together. "That's crazy, pidge. Why would you want to hold a funeral for yourself if you're still alive?"

"But that's the point— Kallie suggested it. It's a ritual for fae who've seen the devastating effects of battle, and don't know how to get over it. They have to kill the old self in order to be born again into someone new," I explained. "I've gone through such a big transformation over the past two years, so much so that I don't feel I'm the same person I used to be. I want to lay that to rest, so I can grow to be the woman I'm meant to become."

"Don't you think having a funeral will make things more difficult for you to get over?" he questioned.

"I don't think so. It might be painful, but she also reassured me that it's... freeing. It needs to be put to rest."

"If you're going to do this, I need to be there," Charlie said firmly. "You need my support."

"Charlie, one of the reasons I came back was because I knew you needed me. I don't want you to come if it's going to be triggering for you. This could put you through more unnecessary grief."

"No. I want to be there," Charlie said. "It's sort of like... burying the past. I think we both need to do it."

I was still uneasy. I wanted to protect him, and this could bring up a lot of trauma both of us didn't want to deal with.

But I also wanted him to be there, and I think he needed this as much as I did. "Okay. Thanks for being there for me. But if it gets to be too much, you don't have to stay."

"I'll be there, pidge," Charlie promised. "As much as it sucks to admit, I think I've got parts of myself that have died, too. We can let our old lives go, together."

I was glad he was backing me up, and that he hadn't freaked out about this idea like I'd worried he would. I wasn't sure if this was the right decision, but I was sure that I couldn't continue living my life wishing for things to go back to the way they had been.

So tomorrow night, I'd have to say goodbye.

THE ATMOSPHERE WAS SOMBER the following evening. My friends arrived at the chapel at sunset, wearing all black. Oberi, who insisted the event needed even more drama than what was already involved, had donned a long black veil over her fluffy ears and around her horn. I wore a matching veil over my face, to compliment my black dress. We'd made them in the Arts & Crafts room earlier, and they definitely suited the mood. A couple of inmates had heard about what we were doing, and called us *fucking freaks* on our way to the chapel.

Who cared what they thought. This wasn't about them.

A small black box sat on the altar, surrounded by a collection of flowers that Charlie had bloomed. Sprigs played in the petals, hopping from flower to flower with no awareness of how grim this all was.

Beside the box was a photograph of me, one I'd brought with me from home the first time I'd arrived at the Institute. The photograph was from high school, and depicted me smiling in front of the seaside on Kinpago's shores.

I stared vacantly at the photograph and felt nothing but regret. I could look at that girl in the picture, and have her memories, but I didn't identify with her anymore. It was almost like looking at a depiction of a stranger, because I was so different now.

I took a deep breath and gazed at the swaths of black fabric hanging from the chapel's rafters that Kallie had conjured. In the loft, Marcus played his harp, while Alistair— painfully— accompanied it with notes from the organ, creating an aching funeral march.

My life had started here in this chapel, with the confession of my darkest secrets to Charlie on the balcony, with our wedding... and that life was about to end here, because Kallie promised me that after this, I'd be someone totally new.

"This is weird," Chancey complained as he looked around. He'd shown up, but not without a lot of whining that this was dumb and unnecessary. Beside him, Opal and Ez whispered lowly to each other.

"Shh. It's starting!" Ivy whispered.

Kallie walked up the center of the aisle, wearing a long black robe. Oberi strode behind her, and Charlie pushed my chair to the front of the room so I was positioned next to the box, beside the altar. Oberi stood beside me, and Charlie took a seat in the first pew, while Kallie went up to the preacher's stand.

Charlie had been tense since we'd arrived, but I couldn't read anything else across our bond. I knew he had to be thinking that this could've been real, and this enactment of my funeral hadn't been so far from what had really taken place. He could've experienced this— they all could've. It was only by magic and faith we'd managed to escape it.

Kallie lifted her hands, and the music in the pews above ceased. "Good evening, everyone. I want to thank you for coming tonight, for your presence is deeply cherished. We are here to celebrate the life of Ava-Marie, all that she was in this life, and to part with that memory so she can begin her world anew, in a new state of being."

Kallie shuffled a couple of papers, as she'd prepared something. "Ava meant so much to us all— she was a friend, a sister, a beloved wife. She was impulsive, yet intelligent, cruel, but kind. And when she went down into the Infernal Underground to save a friend, she did so willingly, knowing the consequences she was risking. That risk took her life, and though she came back to us, she didn't return the same. She didn't just lose pieces of herself— she lost her ability to walk, and gained a whole new world of pain."

Kallie cleared her throat. "But the Ava I've known since that day is a woman renewed. You're different, in a way that brings more light to all of us than you ever have before. You've always been a beacon for us, Ava. And I'm glad I get to aid you through this transition in life."

She stepped aside, allowing others to come up to the stand to speak. Ez came up after Kallie. He adjusted his suit jacket, tripped on the stair that led up to the preacher's stand, and blushed before he leaned in to speak.

"When you told me about wanting to do this, I understood immediately why," Ez began. "You're my sister, and you're still here, but I have to admit the sister that grew up with me in my childhood is gone. And I know all we're doing is playing pretend, a game like children do. Still, though... a part of this feels real. This day could've happened, if Oberi hadn't saved your life. But I know, as everybody in this room does, that a piece of you died when you went down into the Underground, and that's a part of you none of us are going to get back. We all see it."

Ez's voice became lonesome. "You aren't as daring as you used to be. You're more scared; I've seen more fear in your eyes over the past six months than I've seen from you in my entire life. You were always my brave big sister, ready to take on the world, and I never thought I'd have to watch as that courage within you slowly faded away. I *hate* the Warden for that."

Ez gave me a smile that was full of so much love. "But I'm really glad you're still with us, and I'm super excited to see what new pieces of yourself come up to replace what you lost. I think I'm going to like my new sister. Because even though she's changed, she's always been braver than I could ever be."

My brother stepped back, and Opal dotted her eyes with a tissue. He returned to his seat, and Ivy came up to take his place.

Ivy adjusted the black birdcage veil they were wearing, and began to speak. "I know what it's like to kill a piece of yourself— to bury who you were in an attempt to please other people. But I also know what it's like to kill the person who everyone else *wants* you to be, so you can decide who you want to become. And I'm really proud of Ava for seeing the parts of her that need to be let go, and welcoming the parts that beg to thrive within her. You aren't the only one who's died lately, Ava— the old self in me died, too, when I decided to stop using. And I'm really glad we get to be reborn together."

Chancey gave a loud whimper from the pews that he clumsily turned into a cough. Ivy gracefully sat down, and the chapel became silent. No one immediately got up after Ivy, and I went to open my journal, until my fingers paused on the pages as I watched my husband slowly rise.

Kallie appeared just as shocked as I did. She bowed her head as she helped Charlie up to the stand. Sprigs, who'd noticed, jumped off the flowers and raced to Charlie, where he climbed up Charlie's suit and perched on his shoulder.

Charlie cleared his throat, before adjusting his tie and hoarsely saying, "This isn't easy for me. I wasn't even sure if I was going to say anything. I didn't think I was strong enough. But something's occurred to me, and I think it needs to be said."

He drew a deep breath. "When Ava-Marie died in the Underground, a piece of me died with her. It wasn't to the same extreme, and it was a much slower, progressive death, but it had died nonetheless. I'm not talking about the piece of her soul that she shares with me, though I felt that death permeate every cell of my body. There was a darker piece of me that clung so tightly to her soul that I wanted nothing more than to follow her. It's rare for me to fall in love with anything, so when I do, I hold on as tightly as I can, for fear of losing the thing I love. But when you hold on too tight to someone you love, you suffocate them."

He paused for a moment to collect himself, then continued. "Ava's death showed me that I don't have to hold on so tight anymore— because no matter where she is, in this life or another, I will always love Ava-Marie. I don't need to cling to her to know that. So today, I let go of the Ava-Marie who existed before we entered the Infernal Underground. I see her for the wonderful woman she was, and grieve for her loss. But I know now that I don't have to follow her into the grave. I get to follow this new, amazing woman into a new life. While there are remnants of our old life left behind, I see a renewed woman who can stand against anything— and a new man who will stand beside her. Thank you, Ava-Marie, for showing me what we can be together... and apart. Today, we part ways with the Ava-Marie that once was, and know that she was incredible in every way. Through this process, we come together with the Ava-Marie that is now, and know that she hasn't lost anything in her death, but gained everything."

Charlie sat back down, and Kallie gave me a nod. My hands shook as I opened the journal my Aunt Maddie had given me. It was filled with clues about my prophecy, but I'd found some spare pages in which to write my farewell to my old life. For some reason, that's just where I felt like it fit.

"I look back on the person I used to be, and I cringe," I began. A couple of people laughed, and I smirked. "Yeah, shocking, right? We all do that."

I swallowed, and went on. "The old Ava-Marie was loud. She was obnoxious, and rude, and sometimes, she only cared about herself. She was selfish, as much as she didn't want to be, and she allowed her emotions to run the show as her rampant feelings bowled over every-thing in her path. She got jealous, and mean. Sometimes, she could say the worst things to people, because she was hurting so badly. She just wanted someone to understand how she felt, so she'd say something awful to cut someone else. She put her family and friends through a lot — she put her husband through *hell*. And a lot of those parts of me are still there, but some of those traits aren't. So instead of grieving over the person I once was, I want to focus on what I wish to do better."

I parted a lock of hair back, so I could read the words on the page. It was hard, because teardrops kept falling from my nose onto the page, ruining the ink. "The new Ava is not only smart, but wise. She uses her anger for good, instead of using it to destroy relationships, because she's no longer afraid of people getting too close. She's loud and obnoxious in a way that gives people joy, not in a sense that purposefully drives them away. She speaks with honesty, but not brutally. She understands her bipolar is something to work with, not fight against. She is willing to accept the truth about who she is... all the despicable parts of her villainy that she no longer wishes to escape."

I had to choke out the next part, because admitting it out loud was terrifying. I could never say any of this to the people who weren't in this room, but they were all here, and I was certain that each of them would understand. "I'm not afraid to admit it. I *liked* killing those guards in the Underground. I *enjoyed* taking Jaymin's life, and watching her die."

Ivy began clapping in the pews in a show of support, but they were the only one who did.

I went on. "Ending those lives... it felt freeing, and that awful act of murder fed my soul in a way nothing else ever has before. When I caused that explosion in the Underground, I didn't have to turn away from that part of myself. For the first time, I could accept it— I liked killing people. Before, I kept pushing it away, insisting that wasn't who I was. But now, I'm embracing it. I've always been afraid of being a monster, because I know inside that's what I am, deep down. But if I'm a monster, I'm the kind that hunts the shadows in the dark, so I can prevent them from hurting others. I can be twisted, evil, and malicious, but only toward those that dare to harm my loved ones. I will defend innocent people out there that don't have the capability to become something terrible in order to keep away the devil. I do; I have that ability to become my enemy's darkest nightmares, and I will no longer flinch away from it just because it's dirty, or nasty. I'm no hero, no matter how badly I want to be. I'm a bad person who can also be a good person, because the two aren't mutually exclusive, and I know I'll have to give away my soul to fulfill this prophecy. So why not have some fun along the way?"

Oberi nuzzled my cheek, and I continued on. "It has been really, *really* hard accepting that I am never going to walk again."

My voice cracked, and I heard Charlie give a sob from the front row. "I don't know where I am with all of that yet. But I know that this is my life now, and I'll find a way to be all right with living it this way. I can be a better— and worse— person from here on out. Because though I'm more scared than I ever have been in my entire life... I'm also more fearless than ever before. And I think the old Ava would be proud of me. At least, I hope I can be someone she can look up to."

I glanced to Kallie, to signal that I was done. She wiped her eyes, and said, "We will now commence with the burial. If everyone could please follow me out to the prison yard."

She picked up the box, while I grasped the photograph in my hand. Charlie got up to push my chair behind Kallie, while the rest of our friends fell in line behind us. Marcus remained at the back, still strumming his harp. Though this was very sad, I think he was getting a kick out of this.

"That was a really good speech," Ivy complimented, laying a hand on my shoulder as we left the chapel.

"Thanks," I told him. "It came pouring out of me earlier."

"Death is... interesting for us immortals," Ivy murmured. "Vampires and angels don't die unless they're killed. Funerals aren't something we often attend. But this is special."

That much was true. And it wasn't like I was the only one who'd changed. All of my relationships would morph and grow over the years, continually dying and reblooming again. Kallie had told me this was the circle the fae honored on this Earth, and I was just beginning to understand that death wasn't a permanent state. It was flowing, much like birth was. It was only our perception that made it seem final, inevitable, instead of a seamless transformation, just like Oberi shifting from one body to another. To change was to stay the same. That was a comforting thought.

The cemetery was still ruined from the Underground caving in, so we went to a piece of the prison yard that hadn't been disturbed by anyone yet. Charlie used his Earth magic to create a hole, and Sprigs jumped in, rolling around in the dirt.

"Sprigs, no," Charlie scolded gently, then lifted him back out. Kallie placed the box in the ground— inside were a collection of objects from my old life. There wasn't a lot in there, as the Institute didn't allow us to have much, but I'd managed to find a few tokens that I'd saved over the years. I gave the photograph to Kallie, and she laid it on top of the box before bowing to me.

I lit the box and the photo aflame. My Koigni magic was hot, and turned everything inside the shallow grave to ashes instantly. I observed the face of the girl in the photograph, watching the edges of the flames devour up her visage, and I felt sorry for her. There was so much she would have to endure to get to the point where I was at now, and in the end, it would kill her. I knew there was no going back and changing the past, but the future I was looking to create was bright. I had to rebuild myself from the ground up. After such a long time, I finally felt ready to start.

Once there was nothing left to burn, Charlie moved the dirt over the ashes, immersing them completely in the ground. As the grave was closed, I gained a sense of heavy relief, and released a long-held breath.

"It is done," Kallie said. "The old you has died, and been committed to the earth. You have been reborn."

A tremendous warmth welled inside of me, growing warm in my chest. I felt lighter. More than that, I felt... transformed.

Behind me, Chancey wailed. "You can't get me like that, man!" Chancey sniffed. "It's too much!"

"And you thought this was silly," Ivy scolded, taking out a handkerchief and wiping Chancey's face. "You're crying more than anybody."

A couple of people laughed. Charlie knelt beside me. "How do you feel, pidge?"

"Renewed," I told him. "What about you?"

He patted Oberi on the back and said, in a way that set my soul free, "Like we can finally put the past behind us."

SEVENTEEN

Burying the past was a profound experience for all of us. I always thought leaving things in the past meant ignoring them until you forgot about them completely. But that only left wounds that festered, until you couldn't ignore them any longer and one day they consumed you. Ava's funeral felt healing in a way that didn't make any sense. It should be sad— and it was, but not in the way I'd become accustomed to. We could look back and grieve on the Ava-Marie we lost — and the parts of ourselves we had lost with her— but we could honor it, too, and be happy about the new person she was becoming.

Honoring our past didn't mean forgetting about it. It meant remembering it with reverence, while still being able to move forward with those memories and lessons in our hearts.

Obsessing about the past used to feel like honoring it. It was like if I forgot about what happened for one moment, it didn't matter at all. Ava showed me things could be different. For the first time, I didn't feel shame for not holding on to the past long enough.

I would always remember the old Ava. I grieved for the woman we lost. But I damn sure loved the Ava who'd been born from the ashes. I could love them both, even if I only got to exist alongside one of them.

There was so much I wanted to say when I stood at that pulpit, but I didn't know how. Maybe that was okay, though. I didn't have to get all the words right to know it was okay to move on. I was certain Ava could feel everything I couldn't find the words for, and that was good enough for me.

Ava and I seemed more in sync than ever. I didn't know if it was something that happened at the funeral, or a slow process that had taken place over the last several months, but it seemed that our bond had never been stronger.

I dodged Marcus' stunning spells as we trained in Hemlock's secret room once finals week was over. Ava gave instructions through our bond. It was like we didn't need language at all anymore.

Left! Right! Duck! she instructed, only it was more a *feeling* than actual words. I reacted so quickly it shocked me. I didn't have to think about her instructions; I followed them as if they were my own thoughts.

Oberi had been the one to suggest the training exercise. I needed to learn how to fight on his signals, so I didn't hurt my friends during battle like I did in Forevermore. Oberi had started by barking once to move left and twice to move right, but Marcus' spell had taken me down in a single blow.

Ava had quickly cut in with a better idea. Our bond was definitely a quicker method.

Jump, Ava instructed.

I jumped as high as I could, and my hands landed on the table in the center of the room.

Duck! Ava yelled in my mind.

I dove into a summersault, and Marcus' spell whizzed through the air overhead. I'd narrowly dodged it and came away unscathed. I scrambled to my feet and raced forward, until Ava told me to jump again. I leapt off the table and landed on my feet.

Ava and Kallie clapped. "See?" Ava said to Oberi. "It's better to utilize the bond. That way, we don't alert our enemies."

I wiped the sweat from my brow. "It's much faster, too."

Takahashi stepped forward. "This is excellent progress. However, Ava can't be giving instructions when she's distracted defending herself."

"Oberi will have to be my main point of communication," I decided.

"Mm..." Takahashi sounded thoughtful. "I wonder how you would fare in an offensive position. Perhaps we should try some target practice."

I shrugged. "Sure. I'm up for anything."

"Let me help," Kallie offered. The air shifted in front of me. "Take a moment to get a feel for it first."

I reached out, and my hand landed on some sort of large cube. It was pretty hard, but had a little give to it— almost like a punching bag. "What is it?"

"It's an illusion I made solid," Kallie said. "A target."

I smirked. They were talking *literal* target practice. This was going to be easy. "I should be insulted. You underestimate me."

"Why don't you show us what you've got, then?" Marcus challenged.

My friends and I went to the other side of the room, then faced the target. Magic swirled in my hands, and I used my Air to feel where the target was. I blasted the magic outward in a stream, but instead of landing against the target, my magic slammed into something hard. Stone cracked, and I realized it'd been the wall.

I stood up straighter, trying to get a feel for my surroundings. I didn't know how I could possibly miss that. My Air magic swirled around a large object nearby, but it was at least five feet to the right of where the target had been.

"That's cheating!" I accused.

Kallie snickered. "Hey, no one said anything about stationary targets."

"That moved way too fast," I remarked. "You undid the illusion and reformed it over there."

"Look, you're going to have to deal with a lot worse in battle," Kallie pointed out.

She wasn't wrong. I had to learn how to react quickly to a fast-paced environment, because the battlefield wasn't the place to take it slow.

I rolled my shoulders. "Let's go again."

I sensed the void in the room as Kallie's illusion faded, then the shift in the air when it reappeared several feet to the left. I blasted my magic at it again.

Left, two feet! Oberi barked in my mind.

I shifted my stream of Air to Oberi's commands, but Kallie's target was gone before my magic made it there.

Right! Oberi instructed. Somehow, without a clear answer on how *far* to the right, I just knew what he was referencing. I swung my hand out, and my magic shifted course, slamming straight into the target.

"Great job!" Ava cried.

"Again," Takahashi pressed.

Left. Right. Higher. There's two of them! Oberi continued giving instructions.

I threw my hands apart. Battle magic sizzled out of my palms, landing in the middle of both targets. The illusions shifted again, morphing into a single target. I threw another spell but missed it.

Closer. Farther. Lower, Oberi continued.

I missed more times than I hit, which was concerning, because if this was a person fighting back, I'd be dead already. It was a miracle I'd survived Forevermore at all.

Kallie's illusions continued shifting. The more targets I hit, the harder the exercise became. Targets popped in and out of existence, and morphed together and broke apart like a kaleidoscope. I started throwing battle magic at random, trying my damndest to hit *something.*

Be careful! Oberi yelled.

A spell bounced off the wall and ricocheted in our direction.

"Everyone down!" I cried. We all ducked, and the spell hit the wall behind us and fizzled out.

"Um..." Ava sounded nervous. "Maybe aggression isn't the answer. That was dangerous."

"Aggression is what gets things done when you're in battle," I countered.

"Not at the expense of your teammates," Marcus pointed out. I smelled the faint scent of burnt hair and realized the spell must've nicked him.

"If I may offer some advice," Takahashi said kindly. "Your goal is not to hit the target. It is to *not miss.*"

I paused. That was definitely a fresh perspective I hadn't considered before. I had to stop thinking like some guy in the ring throwing punches and playing dirty. I had to start thinking like a demigod. "All right, Kallie. Give me your worst."

The air shifted again. It seemed there were at least a dozen targets hovering on the other side of the room, moving at random speeds and directions. It was a lot to take in with my senses alone. I couldn't tell where they'd end up by the time my spells made it to them.

Instead of shooting off spells right away, I turned my focus inward. When I tapped into my Elven magic, I could sense the energies around me. It was easy to pinpoint Kallie's fae illusions. I tangled my Elf magic with hers, until I could physically *feel* the targets on the other end of the room. Kallie must've not noticed what I'd done, because she didn't pull back.

In one swift motion, I blasted battle magic toward the targets. Oberi shouted quick instructions in my mind, and I instinctually split my magic into twelve pieces. The magic slammed into the targets so hard that Kallie's illusions broke instantly. The targets disappeared on impact, and Kallie stumbled back a couple steps.

Marcus grunted as he caught her. "Holy shit. What happened?"

Kallie groaned, like my magic had been too much for her. "Charlie cast one hell of a spell. That's what happened."

I reached out for her. "Did I hurt you?"

"No, you did a great job, but fuck, that tired me out." Kallie slumped into a nearby chair. My last spell was stronger than I realized, and I must've siphoned some of her powers to do it.

"This method shows promise," Takahashi said. "You've shown you can dodge spells and hit targets, but you will be required to do both in battle. Let's see what happens when your target fights back. Let's get Ava on Oberi's back, and see how the three of you fare against an opponent. Marcus, if you will."

Marcus took a spot on the other side of the room. Oberi shifted into a unicorn, and her saddle appeared on her back. I helped Ava out of her chair and hoisted her up. She was wearing a dress today, and the hem caught on the edge of the saddle. My hand accidentally slipped beneath the fabric as I was positioning her, and my heart skipped a beat when I felt nothing but smooth skin.

I smirked as I leaned forward and whispered, "No panties?"

She snickered lightly. "You like that?"

"Hell, yeah," I whispered. It'd been a while since we'd had sex, and she really knew how to tease me. She'd skipped the panties on *purpose*, waiting to see how long it'd take me to notice. I sure as hell noticed now.

I straightened her dress, then secured the straps around her legs.

"You're going to have to be quicker than that," Marcus pressed. "A battle could break out without warning, and you're not going to have time to get it perfect."

He shot a stunning spell across the room. I shot another spell back, and they collided mid-air and exploded in a loud *boom*.

"Let's keep our spells safe for training," Takahashi reminded us. "We're not here to hurt each other."

I threw my leg over Oberi's back. Marcus had already shot another spell across the room, and Oberi jumped out of the way, nearly knocking me off her back. I quickly settled in, then started shooting off spells at Marcus. Oberi focused on dodging spells, while Ava and I cast our own magic back at Marcus. We weren't trying to hurt him, so the spells weren't very strong. It was like throwing tennis balls at him, at best. It was child's play compared to a real battle, but I found that we were working in sync more than ever.

Ava opened her mind to me. As spells whizzed around the room and my senses became overloaded, her perception filled in the gaps. I could make sense of where the spells were, and how much of a threat they posed with greater accuracy. I no longer had to rely solely on sound and Air magic to pinpoint Marcus' location as he dodged our spells and moved around the room, because Oberi's commentary and Ava's aware-ness made it easy.

"Again," Takahashi instructed as Oberi slowed to take a breather.

We fell into a pattern. Marcus threw up shields to deflect our spells, but Ava quickly let me know. She didn't speak in words, *per se*, but I instantly got a sense of what she was feeling. I tossed spells overhead, bypassing Marcus' shield and bouncing them off the walls. I must've hit him in the back of the head, because he cursed and dropped his shield. Ava blasted off a spell, and he gave a heavy *oof* as she hit him in the chest.

"I think that's enough for the day," Takahashi said.

Ava, Oberi, and I could easily keep going, but Marcus panted like we'd tired him out. It *was* three against one.

"You all did an excellent job," Takahashi commented.

"That was fun!" Ava said as I helped her off Oberi's back. "I think we work really well together when we're focused on one target."

"Then that's what we'll have to do during battle," I decided. "We'll work as a unit, focusing on one enemy at a time."

"Marcus, how do you feel?" Takahashi asked.

Marcus sighed heavily. "Fighting my friends is a piece of cake."

Yeah, okay. It sure didn't sound like it, with how winded he was.

"As for my own powers, they're getting stronger," Marcus added. "But I can't help but feel responsible that we haven't gotten anything from Thaddeus yet."

"If you have not found him yet, I'm afraid to say he's likely moved on," Takahashi said.

"Oh, he moved on," Marcus said nonchalantly. "That's why we summoned him back, to learn what he knew. He's gone to find more information for us."

Takahashi went silent for a beat, then stammered, "Y— you summoned your friend from the Ancestral Lands and *released him* inside the prison?"

"Yeah. We *had* to talk to him," Marcus said. "He wanted to help."

Takahashi sighed heavily. "Marcus, you act like this is an inconsequential act. This isn't the same as contacting a spirit who's already trapped on Earth."

"Why not?" Marcus asked. "He can go back to the afterlife at any time."

"You don't know that," Takahashi protested. "You have incredible power, Marcus, but it is not to be abused. There is a reason spirits don't come back once they've moved on."

"Yeah, because they don't have a demigod to make them return," Marcus insisted. "If I can bring him back here, I can send him back where he belongs. Don't you want answers?"

"Of course, but not at the expense of others," Takahashi pressed.

"Thaddeus *wanted* to help us," Marcus retorted. "I don't get why you're so against this."

"Takahashi's right," Ava cut in. "We don't know the full extent of our demigod powers, or what bringing back a soul could do."

"Well, what do you want me to do about it now?" Marcus asked. "I can't change that we already brought Thad back, so we might as well utilize the tools we have and get answers from him."

"Every time you summon him, you tear him from the spiritual plane," Takahashi said. "You don't know what the consequences of that could be."

"So enlighten me," Marcus challenged.

Takahashi didn't have all the answers. Instead, he said, "The best thing you can do for your friend is let him find his way back to the Ancestral Lands."

"Okay. I get it," Marcus caved.

Takahashi seemed to relax. "I think we've covered enough in our lesson today. You should all get some rest."

Takahashi excused us, and the four of us left the training room together with Oberi and Rishi at our heels.

"Takahashi's blowing smoke," Marcus huffed. "He doesn't know what he's talking about."

Ava's wheels screeched as she grabbed them and whirled around toward Marcus. "He's our mentor. You should listen to him."

"Listen to a man who doesn't even have answers?" Marcus balked.

"He knows there's a risk involved," Ava pressed. "Just because he's never seen it first-hand doesn't mean he can't sense when something's wrong."

"Of course something's wrong!" Marcus practically shouted. "Thaddeus is taking too long to give us answers, and that's a problem. The least I can do is summon him and see what's up."

"Or we could give him more time," Ava argued. "Even on Earth, spirits experience time differently. A ghost's consciousness isn't defined by time the way mine and yours are. I'm sure Thaddeus is putting forth his best effort."

"Best effort or not, how does Takahashi expect me to send Thaddeus back to the Ancestral Lands if I don't know where he is?" Marcus asked. "We need to do this."

"You promised Takahashi you wouldn't," Ava protested. I caught her thoughts slipping through our bond— she was hoping to buy Thaddeus enough time to get to the Ancestral Lands by himself. She worried what kind of pressure Marcus' summonings would put on him.

"I mean... I didn't *really* say that," Marcus said.

Ava was becoming increasingly frustrated. "You're going to do this with or without us, aren't you?"

"Someone has to," Marcus insisted.

Ava turned her chair back around. "I'm coming with you. Someone has to make sure you don't fuck it up."

"If all I am to you is a fuck-up, then you don't have to join me," Marcus spat.

"That's not what I said," Ava replied coldly.

Kallie quickly cut in. "Can we not do this here?"

My friends got really quiet. I didn't hear anyone else in the hall, but that didn't mean no one was in nearby classrooms.

"Let's go to the Witch Tower," Marcus suggested. "It's usually pretty quiet there."

We hurried to the Witch Tower, and I used my Air power to levitate Ava's chair up the stairs. No one was there when we arrived. We gathered around a study table, and Marcus quickly got to work arranging the items for the séance.

"I've got my summoning herbs..." Marcus mumbled. "Ava, can I have a light?"

Ava grumbled. She wasn't happy about it, but she lit Marcus' herb bundle with her Fire magic.

"Thaddeus?" Marcus called. "Thaddeus, how you doing, buddy? Are you there? We just want to check on you."

Nothing happened.

"Thaddeus Blake, I don't want to force you out," Marcus stated harshly. "It's Marcus. I need to know you're all right."

Another moment of silence passed, and Marcus shifted uncomfortably.

"Maybe he's already moved on," Ava suggested.

"No, I can feel something," Marcus said. "He just needs a bit of a nudge."

Marcus began muttering words I didn't recognize under his breath. The table began to shake, and the chair beneath me wobbled. Oberi barked, and Rishi hissed.

The sound of a hawk's cry came from overhead, and it dove for me. I covered my ears and ducked, but the hawk spirit passed straight through me. For a second, I could see the visual outline of Thaddeus'

Familiar. Then his spirit shifted into a man, and he vanished from my mind.

A sharp, pained breath came from behind me, and a chill spread over my spine.

Marcus gasped. "Thaddeus! You look... ah... you don't look well."

What's he talking about? I asked Oberi.

Thaddeus' spirit appears sick, he explained. *His form has an ill sheen, and he has dark bags under his eyes. His energy is... chilling.*

Yeah, I could feel that for sure.

"*Marcus?*" Thaddeus' voice filled the room, but something was off about it. It sounded distant and ethereal. It didn't quite seem like he was standing in front of us, but rather, was stuck between two different places. "*What's going on?*"

"This is what I was talking about," Ava said. "Marcus, he's confused! We need to send him back to the Ancestral Lands!"

"Not until we find out what he knows," Marcus insisted. "Thaddeus agreed to help us. You remember, don't you, Thad? You were supposed to sneak into the Warden's office and learn what you could about the Elves."

"*I did,*" Thaddeus replied. "*I've been tailing the Warden...*"

He groaned, like being here pained his spirit.

"Marcus, this is obviously too much for him—" Ava demanded, but Thaddeus cut her off like he didn't hear her.

"*I found records of a ship in the Warden's office,*" Thaddeus told us. "*The records only go back a few months. But from what I found, he's looking for a ship by the name of* The Assassin's Destiny."

We all shared a collective gasp. "*The Assassin's Destiny* is a children's story," Kallie said.

"*A story named after the ship,*" Thaddeus clarified. "The Assassin's Destiny *was an Elven ship that launched from an Atlantean dock, with plans to come to Darke Island... but it never made it. It's believed to have carried a great treasure, which the Warden thinks is some kind of key.*"

"That's the ship Amalie and Dante took to escape Atlantis," Marcus said, before he began reciting lines from the children's story. "*Into the dark she ran, with her treasure of the sea. The key to her riches lies with* The Assassin's Destiny."

"The story was being literal," Kallie realized. "It's the name of the ship from our vision!"

"They brought the key aboard," Thaddeus said. *"But the ship was caught in a storm, and it was lost to sea, along with the key. There were two survivors— a merman named Dante, who was imprisoned on Darke Island, and a sorceress named Amalie, who was sent back to her people to be executed."*

"Plus Erasmus," I noted. "But he escaped the authorities. The Warden must not know he's still out there."

"I found no records of anyone by that name," Thaddeus said. *"What I do know is the ship itself was never found. The Warden is searching for it."*

"Fuck," Ava mumbled as she grabbed my arm. "Charlie, this is my fault. Remember when I told Jaymin we were investigating Atlantean shipwrecks last semester? It was a lie meant to throw off the Warden, but now we *are* searching for a shipwreck. That means he's way ahead of us."

"It must've been your intuition," Kallie realized. "You randomly came up with the lie when Jaymin was prodding us for information, but your insight was actually giving you hints on what we needed to look for next."

"And I just handed that information to the Warden, months before we knew what we were looking for," Ava grumbled. "Fucking perfect."

"Does the Warden know where the ship is now?" I asked Thaddeus.

"Not that I could find," he replied. *"But he's getting close. He's got teams of merfolk searching the waters surrounding the island."*

"Damn it," I growled.

"No, this isn't a total loss," Kallie insisted. "The Warden may know about the ship, but he doesn't know where it went down or where to get that information. We know Erasmus is still out there, which puts us a step ahead of him. Not only does he know what memories he wiped from Dante and Amalie, but he knows where the ship crashed— and where the key is. The second we get that information from him, we can search the waters and get the key before the Warden finds it."

"That involves contacting Erasmus, and he's off the grid," I added. We'd learned the name of the ship, but that didn't help us track it down. We knew most of this information already, so none of it was particularly helpful— not until we could get in touch with Erasmus, at least. Maybe Ava was right and Thaddeus wasn't really ready, or even capable, of helping us. Talking to him one time was different than harassing his soul for answers, and he couldn't be at rest when we were constantly calling him up like this.

"We can't wait around," Marcus insisted. "You need to get us more information, Thaddeus."

"*If you want more, you'll have to go to Cellblock 9,*" Thaddeus told us. "*I discovered that's where the Warden is keeping information on where the Elven camps are, and where Eddie is. What more do you want from me? This isn't as easy as I previously believed... I offered to help you before, but I've done all I can.*"

"That's not true," Marcus replied. "If *we* go down to Cellblock 9, we'll never come out. You have to go for us and see what you can find."

"Marcus, we can't keep him here," Ava argued. "Can't you see that the longer he's here, the greater toll it has on him? Thaddeus' spirit deserves to be free!"

"So do the Elves!" Marcus demanded, shooting out of his chair. "Sorry these decisions aren't easy, Ava, but this needs to be done! Thaddeus agreed to help us, and he's not leaving until he finishes the job."

"You can't *make* him stay here," Ava shot back.

"I'm not forcing him to do *anything*," Marcus insisted. "Thaddeus wants to help us."

"*Ava's right,*" Thaddeus said in a strained tone. "*Staying here is harder than I thought it'd be. I need to return to the Ancestral Lands, but I'm not sure I can do it on my own anymore. I need your help, Marcus.*"

"Then go down to Cellblock 9 and find what's in those records," Marcus said.

Thaddeus hesitated. "*I'll help you this one last time, but then you need to help me cross over again.*"

"I'm not doing anything until you get us what we need," Marcus seethed.

"*This is unfair. I don't belong here, Marcus. You need to let me go!*" Thaddeus begged. "*Please, send me back to the afterlife! It's torture being stuck here when my soul should be somewhere else!*"

"I'm in control here. You *have* to do what I tell you, otherwise, I'll never set you free!" Marcus shouted. "Now *go!*"

A rush of cold wind chilled my skin, and the heavy presence in the room lifted from my shoulders as Thaddeus vanished.

"That was cruel, Marcus!" Ava's rage flared across our bond as her voice grew louder. "He's pleading with you to go back, and you're making him stay here? You're better than this."

"Thaddeus is *dead*. There's nothing more we can do for him, and using him to find out information can prevent the deaths of others, including ourselves!" Marcus snapped. "Do you want to end up like him?"

Marcus realized his horrible choice of words and inhaled a gasp to take it back, but Ava was already blowing up.

"You have no fucking idea what I've been through, what you're putting *Thaddeus* through," Ava seethed. "Do you understand what it's like to be torn out of such a wonderful place like the Ancestral Lands and forced back here, into this agonizing existence? My mind's half gone, because something doesn't feel right with me. I don't regret the choice I made to come back, but I sure as hell feel the effects every day of what it's like to have one foot in the grave and the other here on this Earth. And I'm *still alive*. Thad is gone, and his ghost is confused, wondering why the hell he's still stuck here when he should be at peace in the afterlife!"

I'd forgiven myself for the guilt I felt over bringing Ava back, but I couldn't help but feel sympathy for my wife as her words bled out of her and over all of us. She *was* confused, and I knew some of her memory struggles were due to her spinal injury, but it was more than that. She'd seen things the rest of us hadn't, and gained an understanding of death we couldn't grasp, because she wasn't able to put it into words. Being gone had given her a sense of satisfaction none of us had ever felt, and that peace had been ripped away from her when she'd decided to return. It was terrible that Marcus was forcing Thaddeus into such an existence against his will.

"He's useful to us. Until his usefulness runs out, he stays," Marcus growled.

"Okay, *Doctor Taurus*," Ava sneered back.

"You wanna compare me to the Warden? You want to win, we're gonna have to become just like him, because I'm sick of trying to be the nice guy," Marcus spat. "Thad can get into places we can't, and get us information that's out of our reach. If we've got any chance at all of saving Eddie, or getting our asses out of here, he's our only option."

"So you're going to use his soul to get us what we need," Ava replied shortly. "I didn't think you were like that."

Marcus gave a mean laugh. "You've used people too, Ava. Sorry this one wasn't your idea."

Ava whispered, "Fuck you, Marcus."

"Break it up." Kallie's loud steps echoed through the chamber as she came between them. "This isn't going to help."

"Marcus needs to let Thaddeus go," Ava insisted. "This is *wrong*."

Marcus' words were cold as he replied, "Well, you don't have the ability to stop me. I'm the only one here who has power over Death magic, and nobody can prevent me from controlling Thaddeus. So protest all you want, Ava. I'm not going to quit until this gets us somewhere."

I was horrified at Marcus' words. On one hand, I sided with Ava. I knew acclimating back to life here after her experience in the Ancestral Lands had been far from easy, and she was still suffering for it. What Thaddeus was going through was even worse.

On the other hand... Marcus was right when he said Thaddeus was our only option. Life at the Institute got more dangerous every day, and the Warden was closing in. I felt sorry for Thad, and knew it was awful we were putting him up to this.

But what other way was there? We had to sacrifice Thad's peace in order to protect others.

Even if it tasted bitter going down. I for one couldn't wait for when we finally had the information we needed, because none of us should be fighting like this.

Marcus bitterly left the room, and Kallie rushed after him. Oberi's tone was hesitant.

I am concerned about Thaddeus, Oberi worried. *As a mutabeecha, I can communicate with ghosts. I must find Thaddeus' spirit and speak with him, in order to help ease the effects of being torn between the two realms.*

"If it helps," I said. I wasn't sure what else we could do.

Oberi hurried off. Ava held it in on the way back to our cell, but once we got there, she nearly broke into tears.

"I can't believe he'd do something so cruel. This isn't Marcus!" Ava protested.

"Maybe not before," I pointed out. "But we're all getting darker now. He has a point, pidge. The Warden's ruthless. We might have to be just as terrible as he is in order to beat him."

"I *refuse* to believe that. He's just being a stubborn asshole."

We kept tissues on the counter. I handed one to her, and she mumbled, "I'm not gonna forgive him for this."

"Just give it some time. If Thad locates what we asked for, Marcus will set him free, and we can put this behind us."

"Whatever. Like he said, I don't have the power to stop him."

She gave a resentful sniff and growled, "Yet."

I had to get her mind off of this somehow. She was triggered— I could tell by the emotions swelling through our bond. Her mind was disoriented, trying to piece together fragmented memories of what had happened in the Ancestral Lands, and what had happened in the hospital, attempting to figure out what had been real and what her mind had potentially made up to fill the gaps in her memory.

I didn't know what was real, either, and sorting through the chaos in her head was a task neither of us were equipped for, so I went with something simpler. "We should get our minds off of it. We never finished writing the song we were working on last weekend."

Ava huffed resentfully. "That would be great if I could remember where it is. I put it down and don't recall where."

"We'll find it."

Ava started shuffling items around, and I went to help. When I misplaced things, I worked in a grid pattern around the room to locate them. I started in the farthest left corner, and worked my way along the wall, where the counter was. When I didn't find it, I moved a few feet down and moved my way to the back of the room.

I couldn't help but admit this had been an easier process when I'd lived alone. Ava was doing her best, but she'd been a messy person *before* she'd gotten injured, and memory issues aside, she had a tendency to misplace our belongings. Our apartment wasn't very large, so I was sure we'd find the folder we'd kept our sheet music in eventually.

Ava sounded intrigued as she asked, "Charlie, what are these?"

I heard the clink of the handcuffs, and froze. "I... uh, stole them off a guard."

"Why?" Her voice raised a pitch.

"I thought you'd like them. I was saving them for the right time."

"Now's a *great* time."

At the mention of sex, Ava's anger completely flew out the window. I saw it as an opportunity to quiet her mind, and she needed to focus right now. There was nothing that calmed her thoughts better than bondage. Right now, I couldn't focus on much other than those cuffs. I'd been waiting a long time to use them.

I gently took the cuffs out of her hands, teasing her as they jingled above her.

She reached out to grab my shirt, keeping her wrists close together, as if offering them to me. "I've been a bad girl, haven't I, Charlie?"

"The worst," I agreed. "Someone needs to make an arrest."

Ava giggled. "Officer, please, you've got the wrong girl."

"Oh, I've got the right girl. Only someone as hot as you could walk away with the smoking gun." I slapped the cuffs on one of her wrists. "I need to restrain you."

Ava used her free hand to try rolling away, but I held on to her cuffs. I was gentle, and she laughed lightly. "Stop resisting," I ordered.

I grabbed her other wrist. Her hand slipped from my grasp as she struggled away, but I caught her again and cuffed her hands together. "You have the right to remain silent."

"You have the right to suck my dick," she said as she tried to elbow me.

I grabbed tight to her wrists and leaned down to whisper firmly, "Remain. Silent."

"I don't take orders from cops."

Ava was being a *really bad* girl. I picked her up and tossed her over my shoulder. She let a snicker escape as I carried her to the bedroom and threw her on the bed.

"Put your hands above your head," I ordered.

"Make me."

I jumped on the bed and straddled her, then grabbed her wrists, which she was keeping close to her chest, and pinned them above her head. I leaned down until my breath brushed the side of her face. "Do you have anything on your person?"

Ava shivered in anticipation. "No, sir."

"I'll be the judge of that." I began running my hands down her body, patting her down. She lowered her wrists to her chest to see if I'd notice, and I heard the jingle of the cuffs. "Hands above your head, sweetheart, or I'll hold you for defying an officer."

Ava lifted her arms at my command. I continued exploring her body with my hands.

"I'll have to do a strip search," I stated. "You could be hiding anything."

"Yeah, I'm hiding a gun up my skirt," she said sarcastically.

Ava was wearing a dress today, but with the cuffs on, there was no way to take it off over her head. Instead, I tore the sleeves, then ripped the dress off of her completely.

"This is police brutality," she said with a giggle.

I smirked. "I'll do what I want with you, criminal."

"I haven't been convicted yet."

"You'll be begging to be released by the time I'm finished with you."

Ava wiggled beneath me, obviously enjoying the foreplay. My hands roamed over her naked body.

"Oh, I forgot," Ava added sarcastically. "The gun's not up my skirt—it's up my vagina."

I stifled a laugh and almost cracked, but I put a stone-cold expression on my face and said, "I've got a warrant for a cavity search."

"Who's enjoying this more, you or me?" Ava teased.

"This is your last warning to remain silent," I said in a serious tone.

Ava kept quiet as I parted her legs and slid my fingers inside of her. She let out a tiny moan as I rubbed her G-spot.

"You like that, you bad girl?" I asked.

Ava responded only with a moan. I continued rubbing her, inside and out, until I felt through the bond that she was close to her peak.

I withdrew my fingers. "The cavity search is complete, and I found no incriminating evidence. Do you have anything to say for yourself?"

"Are you going to let me go now, officer?" She sounded so disappointed.

"I've got other charges I can keep you on," I replied. "How can I be sure you'll behave yourself?"

"Perhaps if I give you something in return, you'll let me go," Ava offered.

"And what would that be, darling?"

"You can fuck me any way you want."

"Mm... that goes against my code as an officer of the law. You're going to have to convince me."

"Please," she begged breathlessly.

I leaned over to our bedside table and retrieved the vibrator, then turned it on. I could feel Ava buzzing with anticipation through the bond. "I'm not convinced you want it bad enough."

I pressed the vibrator to her clit, and Ava inhaled a sharp breath. She began moaning the longer I played with her. To intensify the sensation, I leaned down and drew her nipple into my mouth as I worked her clit with the vibrator. Ava squirmed beneath me. I felt her on the edge of orgasm once again and pulled the vibrator away.

"Do you regret being a brat now?" I asked.

"Yes, I regret it," Ava pleaded. "Please, I can't take it anymore."

I tossed the vibrator aside, then placed a hand under her back and the other under her knees. I flipped her over, tossing her onto her stomach effortlessly. She kept her hands over her head like a good girl. I jumped on top of her, tangling my fingers in her hair. I tugged slightly, and she let out a pleading breath.

I placed my lips to her ear and whispered, "Convince me to let you come."

Ava bent her elbows, reaching behind herself to grab my hair in both hands. She tugged hard and whispered, "I *need* this. I need *you*."

Hell, we both needed it. I positioned myself and slammed into her aggressively from behind. Ava and I tugged on each other's hair. The deeper I went, the harder she tugged. The pain was exhilarating, heightening my senses and grounding me to the moment so that all I could possibly focus on was her— the high flowing between our bond as our bodies connected.

We reached the peak of orgasm together, and Ava contracted around me as I buried myself deep inside of her.

I rolled off of her as I came down from the high, then helped Ava roll onto her back again. We panted as the buzz of the scene wore off.

"You were a *very* good girl," I told her.

Ava broke character and started laughing. I joined in. That had been way more fun than I anticipated.

Ava curled into me. "Out of all the times I've been arrested, that was the most fun."

I created an illusion of a key and reached for her cuffs.

Ava drew away. "What are you doing?"

"Taking the cuffs off."

"I really like them," Ava protested. "They were a gift from you. They're the prettiest bracelets I've ever worn!"

I knew if she didn't get out of them now, she'd never take them off. She was the kind of girl who'd go to Work-Study cuffed just to show them off. That was nothing but a recipe for trouble. I didn't want her sleeping in them, either, because wearing them too long could damage her wrists.

"Ava, take them off," I ordered.

Like my good girl, Ava offered her wrists to me. I undid the cuffs, then cleaned up and put them in the drawer next to the vibrator. We were *definitely* using those again. The Warden couldn't pry those cuffs from our cold, dead fingers.

I returned to the bed, and Ava was sitting up. "Should we finish that song we were working on?"

"Absolutely," Ava said brightly. "I have a lot of inspiration now."

I grabbed a notebook and crawled into bed with her. I leaned against the wall and pulled her into my lap. Her skin felt so soft on mine.

We worked on the song for an hour, and we were almost finished when we heard Oberi open the door and enter the apartment. Ava and I sat up straighter, and I quickly grabbed the blanket and pulled it over us.

Is that all you guys do when I'm not around? Oberi huffed as he trotted into the bedroom. He jumped onto the bed, and his tail batted against the mattress. *Is that blanket necessary? I'm naked around you guys all the time. What you've got ain't that special, Charlie.*

I scowled. "Don't act like you're upset about this. You feel everything we do through the bond."

Yeah, so much fun. Here I was, running around the Institute, trying to save Thaddeus' poor soul, and there you two are, having a no-pants party.

"Sorry we were having fun," Ava said. "What'd you find?"

Nothing, he grumbled, laying his head on his paws. *This is concerning. We have to do what we can to convince Marcus to send Thaddeus back, because if this continues, it's not going to work out the way we are hoping.*

"I understand where you're coming from, but this is a necessary evil," I said.

Evil is never necessary, Oberi replied.

Oberi and I had very different ideas of evil. He could see the gray areas, but his gray was more defined than mine. I was leaning more and more into the darkness every day. What once seemed evil didn't seem so bad anymore.

Though maybe Oberi was right, and we'd gotten ourselves into something we couldn't turn back from.

ava-marie
EIGHTEEN

The first football game of the summer was today, and I was looking forward to it, since I'd finally get an opportunity to see Kallie play. She'd finally been made the team's quarterback, like her coach had promised her last semester, and I knew she was going to be amazing out there on the field. It would be nice to go to a sports game and get our minds off everything for a while.

There were four football teams made up of inmates at the Institute, and they played against each other, with games every other week. They were composed of mixed genders, since supernaturals were typically equal in physical strength. In previous years, I'd heard the teams had sucked, but the lineup from the past two semesters had become decent enough that there were rumors teams from other supernatural schools might be bussed in to play against us in the fall. That was very exciting, seeing we didn't get to talk to anyone outside the prison. It almost felt like we had the potential to become a real college, and shake off the dumpy reform school reputation that we so totally deserved.

Charlie pushed my chair through the crowd in the prison yard, while Oberi carried a little flag we'd made in his mouth, wagging his tail. At the entrance to the football field, Mission members were handing out pamphlets.

"Seek salvation from the God of The Mission! Don't wait to make this world a better place!" a boy shouted through a megaphone. The girl beside him shoved a pamphlet into my hands without asking if I wanted one or not.

I scowled as I gazed at the pamphlet's cover. It had an illustration of a group of people moving toward a great light, while a second group walked in the direction of what looked like a building that was on fire.

Whoever this *God of The Mission* was, I didn't like what he was trying to sell. I handed the pamphlet back to Charlie, who waited until we were away from The Mission members before he tossed it in the trash.

"This place is turning into some kind of religious private school," Charlie said.

"More like an indoctrination center," I replied. Mission members were *everywhere* now. You couldn't walk to the cafeteria anymore without getting swarmed by a group of Mission kids, begging you to sign up.

I guess they *had* done some good. The school was cleaner now, because Mission members volunteered to help clean it up, and there were more extracurricular activities after classes and Work-Study, so it kept inmates out of trouble and prevented them from getting into fights.

Problem was, you had to be a part of The Mission to participate, and it felt exclusionary. It was definitely clear that Mission members were the favorites around here.

The stands had been set up around the field so people could watch the game, but there wasn't really a place for me to put my chair. We managed to find an empty spot on the side of the stands, and Charlie took the lowest seat next to me. People kept standing in front of me, so it was hard to see. If I couldn't watch the game, Charlie wouldn't be able to enjoy it, either, because I wouldn't be able to describe it to him, and there weren't any announcers at this crappy school.

"I'm sorry, can you please move?" I asked the people in front of us—though, what I thought was, *Bitch, move your ugly ass.* They turned around, and my stomach soured when I realized it was Brianna and Edwin.

"We like our spots," Edwin said. "Why do we have to be inconvenienced just so you can see? It's not like Wahkin's gonna notice anything, anyhow."

"Yeah, why is he even here?" Brianna asked. "He can't watch the game, and *you* can't play, so why do you have an interest in sports?"

I'd felt bad for Brianna after her cousin had died, but clearly, the loss hadn't done much to change her perspective on life, since she was still terrible to everyone she met.

"We're allowed to be here just as much as you!" I shouted.

"You two get enough perks for being cripples. We should get some benefits, since you're living it up in the *Conjugal Visit Wing*," Brianna quipped.

"What the hell is that supposed to mean?" Charlie snapped.

"You guys don't even love each other. You just got married so you could get a bigger dorm than the rest of us," Edwin sneered.

"It's honestly not that much bigger," I argued. "It has two rooms, but it's hardly enough to move around in."

"Maybe in that clumsy chair," Brianna said.

Edwin gave a nasty laugh. "You two are the running jokes of the prison, the blind guy and his legless wife. Talk about a charity case. What, is your dog gonna start limping around next?"

Oberi gave a pathetic whine, and began limping toward Edwin. When he got close enough, Oberi lunged to bite. Edwin let out a shriek as he cringed away from Oberi's teeth.

Charlie stood up. "Look, my eyes don't work, but my fists sure do, and if you don't shut up, you're going to get one to the face."

Brianna scoffed, but Edwin lost a bit of color. "Let's go," he grumbled under his breath, then grabbed her by the arm to drag her off.

"People here are such dicks," Charlie growled as he plopped down next to me.

"Don't mind them," I said. "Here comes Alistair."

Pig meowed as she led the way, ahead of her warlock. I shouted his name, and Alistair turned, reaching out for a seat so he could sit beside Charlie.

"Wow, it's so loud. Everybody's out here today," Alistair said. "The crowd could've moved a little faster, you know, so I didn't have to whack my cane against their ankles."

I giggled. "How are you, Alistair?"

"Wonderful, considering I shoved a battle orb up the ass of a vampire this morning who thought it'd be funny to call me short. He ain't gonna be sitting for a few weeks, that's for sure."

"You're so evil," I replied with a wicked grin.

"Well, justice is blind and all that."

Charlie let out a laugh, until Oberi nudged his knee. Alistair sat back and asked, "So what's up with you two? Learn anything new?"

"We found out *The Assassin's Destiny* is the name of the ship Amalie and Dante sailed to Darke Island on," Charlie said in a low voice, but his tone was hesitant. Charlie and I never told Alistair about Mazur, because we couldn't trust Alistair to keep a level head.

"What about the Elves?" Alistair pressed. "What else do you know?"

"We told you everything," Charlie insisted. "We don't know where the Elves were moved yet. Thaddeus found out the records we need are sealed in Cellblock 9."

"You're such a fucking liar, Charlie. You know how I can tell when you're lying? When your mouth is moving," Alistair sneered.

"Hey, don't say that about my man," I snapped.

"How did Thaddeus get his hands on this information in the first place?" Alistair asked. "I know you're keeping it from me."

Charlie's shoulders sagged. *Maybe we should tell him, pidge,* he said through our bond. *I would want to know who had information if you were missing.*

Yeah, and you'd go off the rails if you did, I replied.

I think Alistair's just looking for some peace, Charlie argued. *It's wrong to keep this from a friend.*

All right, but I hope you know what you're doing. Alistair's going to be a wreck.

Charlie took a breath. "Thad was trailing Mazur. She was the one in charge of moving the Elves from the concentration camp."

Alistair's expression betrayed no emotion. "Really."

"She's been helping the Warden run the camps secretly, from inside the prison," I explained. "We're not sure how, but Mazur's giving the orders on where to send people and when. We've tried confronting her, but she won't tell us anything about where she sent Eddie."

Alistair gave a slow nod. "I see. Thanks, guys. For telling me."

He got up and walked away. Pig followed, trotting at his heels.

"Wow. He handled that better than I thought," I said.

"Should we go after him?" Charlie asked.

"He needs some time alone. That news about Eddie was hard to take," I said. "We should leave him be. Oh, look, the game's starting!"

The crowd cheered as the two different teams rushed onto the field. Kallie was at the head of her team, carrying the ball. Chancey jogged beside her, and I heard Ivy give a cheer from the top of the stands. I spotted Marcus among a group of girls, wearing Institute colors and performing a cheerleading routine.

Marcus had joined the cheer squad. He'd said it was because he was bored, but I was certain it was more because he wanted to watch Kallie at football practice and needed an excuse to be around without looking creepy.

I still hadn't forgiven him for our argument. In fact, I was pretty fucking pissed he was making Thaddeus stick around to do our dirty work. We'd talked about joining the cheer team *together*, because I'd been head cheerleader back in high school, and I somewhat missed it. I was sure the squad could come up with adaptations for me to do the cheers. Marcus and I had discussed making it a friend activity, but now that we weren't getting along, I'd lost interest... not to mention he'd signed up for it behind my back, without telling me. So obviously he didn't want me there.

He glanced at me, but I pointedly looked away. Marcus scowled and went back to performing the cheer routine.

Whatever. I didn't care that we weren't talking right now. He wasn't a very good friend if he was forcing Thaddeus to stay here when he wanted to cross over.

The two teams squared off in the middle of the field. I watched the game closely, recounting the details to Charlie.

"Kallie's team won the coin toss. Her team's running the ball, but they couldn't get past the forty-yard line. She tosses it, it's a miss, ball bounces out of bounds," I told him quickly. "Third down, Kallie runs the ball, they get back to first down, start up the play again— oh, shit, I missed what happened there, sorry."

"What's going on now?" Charlie asked.

"Second down. Kallie's going for a Hail Mary!"

The crowd gasped as Kallie launched the ball into the air, all the way down the field. I thought there was no way anyone could catch it, but Chancey sprinted down the field and jumped up, snagging the ball in mid-air. He ran the rest of the way, crossing the goal line.

"Chancey caught it! First touchdown!" I said in excitement.

"All right!" Charlie smiled. "Football's been really good for him. So much better than fight club."

Hooray! Oberi waved the flag in his mouth.

There was a cry of surprise from someone on the cheer squad. Marcus had been so busy watching Kallie toss the ball, he'd ended up dropping the girl he was supposed to be lifting.

"Ow! Hey!" Melody snapped.

"Sorry!" Marcus yelped, and he rushed to help her up. Melody shoved him away.

The game went on. It was exciting, watching supernaturals play sports. Nobody used their magic, but sometimes, players cheated and utilized their incredible strength or insane speed to score points. I had a hard time keeping up so I could relay all the details to Charlie, because the game moved so fast.

During the second quarter, one of the linebackers tackled Kallie to the ground— *hard.* She lay there for a while, and I started to get scared, worrying she'd been hurt.

Kallie winced as she slowly got back onto her feet, and the crowd applauded. The linebacker who'd tackled her lifted off her helmet to fix her hair, and I realized, with disgust, that the person who'd sacked her had been Scarlet.

"Scarlet hit Kallie. It looked bad," I told Charlie. "She's making the next play, but moving slow."

Even through all the gear she was wearing, I saw Kallie's body stiffen as she stood across from her ex-girlfriend. Clearly, Scarlet was out for blood.

"Kallie's calling the play. She's got the ball, but there isn't an opening," I said quickly. "She's tucking the ball to her side— she's making a run for it!"

She was still thirty yards from the goal line, but went for it anyway. The crowd went nuts as the opposite team's defense gave chase, but Kallie crossed the line and ended up scoring another touchdown.

"She did it!" I shouted. If I could stand, I'd be out of my seat. "That was incredible!"

"*Go Kallie!*" Marcus jumped up and down, waving a pair of pom-poms. He'd stolen them from Melody, and she looked *pissed*.

There were a couple of boos from people rooting for the opposing team. I looked across the field and saw Esther sitting with Naya near the water coolers.

Esther was finally leaving us alone after Ivy had ripped into her. She wrinkled her nose when I looked her way. Mad Dog was the quarterback on the opposing team, and they were here to cheer him on.

I was pretty sure Mad Dog had bullied his way into the star position on his team, because he fucking sucked. Every pass he threw missed, he called stupid plays, and his team only scored a touchdown because Kallie threw an interception that an opposing player caught and got across our goal line. Kallie's team absolutely slaughtered them, with a final score of forty to seven.

The fans of the opposing team were pretty pissed at the blowout score, so naturally, a fight broke out. A couple of kids started punching, and eventually, the entire stands were tossing blows back and forth. Charlie wheeled me out of it quickly, while Oberi watched from a distance.

Now this is entertainment! Oberi said in appreciation. He gave a happy bark as he watched Ivy pick a guy up and toss him over the stands for leaving a scuff mark on their shoes.

The guards rushed in to break it up. Inmates were yanked off of each other and separated as one of the head guards stormed to the middle of the fight to start shouting at people.

"I'm sick of being a babysitter to you fucking kids!" the guard snapped. "This is your last warning!"

I wasn't sure who he was talking to, since about fifty people had been involved in the fight, but the crowd dispersed anyway. The guard reached down and grabbed Ghost, who was the closest person nearby. He hadn't even been in the fight, just got caught up in the turmoil.

"I've had about enough of you!" the guard said as he shook Ghost by the collar. "Should've known *you'd* start this."

"I didn't, I swear! Please, don't send me back to solitary!" Ghost whimpered.

I was shocked. Usually, nobody got in trouble during these fights, because a brawl broke out on campus every time there was a football game. It was never serious, just a bunch of inmates letting off steam.

"You aren't going to solitary; you're to report to The Mission office," the guard ordered. "Immediately!"

Ghost's face slackened, like he was confused. The guard shoved him forward, and Ghost started toward The Mission office with his head hung low.

Ghost had told me the other day that he'd refused to join The Mission because he felt like it went against his beliefs in Mother Miriam. The guards were purposefully targeting people who weren't in The Mission and punishing them by forcing them to join anyway.

"Let's get out of here," I told Charlie. I didn't want to get dragged down to The Mission office and forced to sign up against my will.

We met up with Kallie and Chancey near the double doors, who high-fived each other as we approached.

"Good game!" I called out. "You made Mad Dog's team eat dirt."

"That was the plan," Kallie replied with a snicker.

"It was almost too easy. What a bunch of chumps," Chancey said with glee.

"Bet it was easy to win, with Marcus cheering you on," Charlie teased.

"If he wasn't too distracting," I grumbled. I was still too mad at him to joke around.

"He's bulked up since he started working out with you and joined the cheerleading team," Kallie said in appreciation. "He's actually got some pretty big muscles."

I hadn't really been paying attention, since I'd always considered Marcus kind of a skinny guy, but on second thought, I guess he *did* look more muscular. "I bet they feel nice."

"Oh, they *do*." Kallie smiled. "Trust me."

"All right, enough of that crap. We gotta hit the showers," Chancey said. "You guys wanna come to a party tonight in the Villain's Den to celebrate?"

"Wish we could, but Kallie and I have to finish up my project for Criminal Justice," Charlie said reluctantly. "Unlike you, I still haven't turned in my profile."

Chancey laughed loudly. "Bet that's the first time I've ever beaten you on homework."

"It's never happening again," Charlie deadpanned.

"If you weren't such a perfectionist it'd be turned in already. I was perfectly happy with a C minus," Chancey drawled.

"I want to do it *right*," Charlie grumbled. "I already had to lie to get Professor Jobe to give me an extension."

"Yeah, that was pretty funny." Chancey snickered, and did an impression of Charlie. "*I've got all the info. I just need help typing it up. I can't do it, because, you know, I'm blind.*"

"I don't sound like that, jackass." Charlie scowled. "And for the record, I can use a computer, but Professor Jobe doesn't need to know that."

"We really do need to finish that profile. It was due over a week ago. Sorry, Chancey," Kallie replied.

"Aw, come on. Semester's over, and you're our star girl!" Chancey said, slinging an arm around Kallie's shoulder. "You can't turn down a reason to celebrate!"

"Charlie's right, I promised I'd help him," Kallie said. "But *next time* we win, that party is definitely happening."

We split up, and I went back to our cell with Charlie to grab the materials we needed to complete the criminal profile. On our way to the library, we passed Professor Warbright, who waved us over.

"Ah, Mister and Mrs. Wahkin, I'm so glad I found you," Warbright said cheerfully. "I'm putting together a little summer music group for some of my best students, and I want you and your friends to join. You were all so wonderful this semester, and I think we should keep the fun going. I'd like to have our first practice, say, tomorrow after Work-Study hours?"

"We'd love to, Professor," Charlie responded. "We'll definitely be there."

"Excellent." Warbright gave us a wide smile. "See you then!"

My spirits lifted. I was glad Warbright was giving us a reason to continue our music lessons. I hadn't uploaded anything to my vlog all semester, but I had some ideas rattling around in my head. Maybe we'd get some time during the summer music group to make new songs.

When we got to the library, Marcus was already waiting for us.

Neither one of us needed to be here, but Charlie had asked us to look over his and Kallie's work before he turned the profile in, just in case there was something they'd missed.

I didn't need to talk to him. I rolled down an aisle and pretended to be engrossed in books about incurable fungal growths. Marcus acted like my sudden interest in magical mushrooms was completely normal and conjured a cat toy for Rishi to play with.

Thankfully, Kallie showed up right after that, so it felt a little less awkward. Oberi changed into a phoenix and sat on the back of my chair, preening her feathers.

We'd all been in a pretty good mood after the win, but that mood quickly soured as Kallie and Charlie got to work on their criminal profile. I thought that they'd be able to wrap this up quickly— you know, seeing as this project was literally due *a week ago*, but clearly, it was far from finished as the two of them bickered across a library table. We were the only ones in here, and I was glad for it, because their argument was really loud.

"Finals week is over. The extension Professor Jobe gave me is already past due, and final grades have to be in *tomorrow*," Charlie moaned. "If I don't turn this in first thing in the morning, I'm going to fail."

"We're not going to let that happen," Kallie insisted.

"I don't have enough here to pass!" Charlie argued. "Our profile barely lists anything about the killer that the police don't already know!"

"Calm down. We can figure this out." Kallie's fingers drummed against the table as her eyes scanned the evidence, but she appeared just as puzzled as he was.

"Mind if I have a look?" I suggested. I knew about Charlie's project, but it was kind of his and Kallie's thing, so I hadn't paid any attention to it. But clearly, these two were stuck.

"Go ahead. Maybe fresh eyes will give us some insight," Kallie suggested as Charlie rubbed his face tiredly.

"I want to help, too." Marcus sat beside me, and we flipped through the collection of evidence the two of them had collected.

To be honest, there wasn't much, which confused me. Kallie and Charlie had been working on this thing for months. Why hadn't they gotten anywhere?

"Tell us everything you know about the Dollmaker, from the beginning," I insisted.

"Kallie and I have been over this a hundred times," Charlie complained.

You're very whiny today, Oberi commented. *Just tell your wife what you know.*

Charlie huffed, and Kallie said, "We know the Dollmaker targets women in their late teens or early twenties. He kills them through bloodletting, then after the murders are complete, he dresses them up in navy gowns and poses them like dolls. He used to commit the murders in secluded areas of the city, but he's gotten bolder, and has moved on to targeting girls during events, where he'll have an audience that will be shocked by his work."

"He likes creating a spectacle..." I murmured. "It's how he gains pleasure from the killings. He wants attention."

"What does the profile say?" Marcus questioned.

"We think the killer is young, possibly early twenties to mid-thirties," Kallie continued. "We're almost certain he's a member of the noble class, because he's the only one who can gain access to some of these locations where these girls were killed."

"We *think* he kills women because he's traumatized from a situation in his past, and he's trying to impress a girl he associates from his childhood with the killings, but that's just a guess. We don't have anything to back that up," Charlie said.

"You don't commit crimes like this without a deep-seated hatred of women," Marcus replied. "This girl the Dollmaker was obsessed with must've really messed him up."

"That doesn't mean it was her fault. She could've done something innocent he might've perceived as an insult," I replied.

"So he hates her as much as he wants to impress her," Charlie said thoughtfully. "He's vying for her to give him attention, but what kind of girl would be impressed by *murder?*"

"It's about power to him," I replied. "Whatever this girl in his past did, it took away the power he wanted over her, so he's trying to regain it by using the victims as a replacement for her, so he can act out the dominance over her he wants to exert so badly."

"How can you be sure?" Kallie asked.

"I just know." I'd been a victim of someone like the Dollmaker—John wasn't a serial killer, but his intention in luring me out to the woods that day was to feel like he'd gained power over me. I'd been fortunate enough to keep my life, but I could've just as easily been murdered, like these girls had been. This guy had similar motives.

I flipped open a folder, which contained photographs of all the victims. I began laying them out on the table, one by one. As I did so, a pit of dread grew in my stomach, and I began to feel ill. Marcus stopped what he was doing and paused to observe the photographs, eyes locking on the similarities. Rishi hopped up on the table, giving a low mewl.

Marcus and I shared a glance. We didn't have to speak to understand we were thinking the same thing.

I swallowed a lump in my throat. "Kallie... all of these girls look like you."

"What?" Kallie visibly startled. She jumped to hover above us, observing the photographs. "That's... it's impossible!"

"They all have blonde hair and blue eyes," I said quietly.

"That's not enough," Kallie stammered. "It's a coincidence!"

"The bone structure in the face is the same," Marcus said, sounding like he was going to be sick. "And they're all wolven girls of the noble class, just like you."

Kallie's face became stark white, while my husband sat forward in interest. Charlie wouldn't have noticed, because he couldn't look at the pictures, and from Kallie's perspective, this would've been something easy to overlook, because she wouldn't consider herself part of the investigation. But to Marcus and me, it was obvious.

"I... this isn't real. I *can't* be the object of this bastard's obsession," Kallie insisted.

"I'm sure others have said the same thing about other serial killers," I pressed. "These people aren't hermits, Kallie; they live normal lives when they aren't out destroying people, in order to stay hidden behind a mask."

"Let's play along with this theory," Charlie said. "Kallie, if the girl the Dollmaker is trying to impress *is* you, then who could he be?"

"She might not know him personally," Marcus objected. His tone became protective. "Kallie was a princess back home, and one of the most famous people in her country. The Dollmaker could be some stalker she's never met."

"No," Kallie said hollowly. "He's not."

The defeat that had overcome her form made her shoulders slump forward, and she staggered into a chair. In the few seconds since we'd come up with the theory, she'd figured it out.

"I can't believe it," she whispered. "I can't believe I didn't realize..."

"Who is it?" Charlie insisted. "Kallie, come on. If you don't tell us, we can't catch this guy."

"It's Valen," she said miserably. She put her face in her hands and leaned forward, completely falling apart.

"What?" I was shocked. "The guy you participated in the King's Contest with? Your *ex*?"

"Yes! It has to be him!" Kallie wiped frantically at her eyes, which were starting to tear up. "And because I was so *stupid*, I let him get away! It's *my fault* he killed those girls!"

"You seem so sure," Marcus said. "How do you know?"

Kallie sniffed. She steadied herself as she said, "I gave him a dagger before the King's Contest. One I'd made. It had an edged blade. There wouldn't be any other like it."

"Do you think the edge of the dagger could match the wounds the Dollmaker gave his victims?" I asked.

Kallie swallowed, and Charlie said, "If it does, we have our killer."

"I never got to inspect the bodies. If I did, I might've been able to piece it together," Kallie whimpered.

"This still seems like a long shot," Marcus said. "What else do you know?"

"I know what traumatized him." Kallie gave a bitter huff and said, "Well, *he* must consider it traumatizing. A normal fucking man would consider it a simple no."

"You're gonna have to clue us in," Charlie said.

"When I offered Valen the opportunity to be my partner for the King's Contest, I made it clear I strictly wanted a business relationship, but he didn't see it that way," Kallie said. "I can't describe it, but shifters *know* where their mates are, even before they've met them. I sensed my mate wasn't in Malovia, but I misinterpreted what I felt. I believed that my mate didn't exist at all, and there wasn't anyone out there for me, so I could pick and choose who I wanted. I was the only female shifter, so this idea made sense to me. I had no idea my mate was all the way across the ocean."

She gave a miserable look to Marcus. "After the date for the King's Contest was set, I knew I couldn't wait to find a proper mate, because I couldn't compete for the crown without one. So I went with the strongest male of the noble class I could find, one I knew somewhat well. I figured if I couldn't have my true mate, it didn't matter who I married, so it might as well be anyone. What a colossal mistake that was."

"Let me guess, he couldn't take no for an answer," I said flatly.

"That's putting it lightly. His behavior was downright creepy," Kallie replied. "My brother had to scare him off a couple of times. You guys remember I told you in group therapy that he'd cornered me once. I'd gotten my magic by then, so I was able to get him to back off, but he still wouldn't leave me alone. And it wasn't like I could get rid of him, because we were competing in the Contest together, and after that, we were supposed to become king and queen. A crown wasn't good enough for him, though. He didn't just want Malovia; he wanted me."

"So what was the inciting event that made him start killing?" Charlie asked.

"I rejected him," Kallie stated. "A couple of months before the Contest, while we were still training to win, he demanded more. He didn't want to act like a couple for the public's sake. He wanted to *be* a couple, and he had no interest in taking it slow."

"What are you talking about?" Marcus sounded deadly. I heard his knuckles crack under the table.

"I'm *saying* he was trying to manipulate me into sleeping with him. I had absolutely no interest, and made that clear. He changed into a wolven and attacked— but I was able to shift, and I was stronger, so I put him in his place. I don't think his ego ever recovered."

"Defeating him in battle, after he wanted to conquer you, must've driven him into a rage," I replied.

"I think so," Kallie said quietly. "The first victim of the Dollmaker was discovered that night. I didn't connect the two events, because they didn't seem related, but it's so obvious now."

"But Valen couldn't have known you were out protecting the city.

No one knew you were a vigilante until you got caught trying to assassinate your brother," I said.

"That's the thing— he *did* know. Valen found out about my assassin work before this happened. I had to tell him, because he discovered my things while he was snooping around in my room. When I confronted him, he swore to keep it a secret," Kallie said. "I couldn't figure out why he didn't use it against me for leverage."

"If he's the Dollmaker, exposing your assassin work could potentially expose him as well, and this is a game to him, one he doesn't want to stop playing," Charlie said.

"Exactly. He's looking to impress me with these killings because he was one of the few people who knew I was hunting predators," Kallie said in disgust. "And because he *knew* I'd give him attention if he became a serial killer, he started slaughtering girls that looked like me, in the hope that I'd start pursuing him. He wanted the thrill of the hunt, the excitement of the cat-and-mouse chase."

"He sees you hunting him down as a romantic pursuit, a reversal of the courtship that had failed on his end," I said sickeningly. This shithead was a real piece of work.

"But the killings haven't stopped since you came to the Institute. If anything, they've ramped up," Charlie said.

"Because he's trying to taunt me. It's a part of the game he plays," Kallie said. "When we were together, Valen liked to push my boundaries, especially in public situations where I couldn't freak out on him without causing damage to the reputation of the royal family. This is probably some sick fantasy of his— me locked behind bars, unable to stop him while he slaughters a facsimile of me over and over, to fulfill his sense of revenge and get back at me for rejecting him. He's pushing my boundaries again, and since I'm locked up, I can't say no."

Kallie glanced at Marcus, almost in a needful way. "You're being awfully quiet."

"I just... don't understand why you felt like you *had* to win the King's Contest in the first place. Valen sounds like a horrible person. Why did you want the crown that badly? It wasn't worth it to be with someone so vile," Marcus said. It sounded like it physically hurt him to imagine her being mistreated.

"I didn't want to be queen. I wanted the opportunities it presented," Kallie replied. She stood from her chair, irritated he'd asked.

Marcus pressed on with more questions. "How'd you begin your assassin work? You were barely a teenager when you started your vigilantism. Teenage girls don't start going around killing people randomly. We need to know."

Kallie took a slow, deep breath. She paused for a moment, contemplating what to say, before she finally spoke. "The first time was an accident. I didn't mean to kill anybody, I just *did*. But when I saw the effects it had on other people, how someone dying meant someone else could live... I realized there was a chance for me to make a difference. Maybe not in the most virtuous way, maybe not in the way I wanted, but what I could do to help my country *mattered*. So I put aside any sense of self-morality and started on my work."

"Tell us everything," Marcus said gently. His tone remained open, telling her he was okay with whatever she had to confess, no matter how terrible it may seem to say out loud.

"When you're a part of the royal family, or even in the noble class, people are always looking to take advantage of you. If they can't manipulate you, they'll use violence," Kallie began. "When I was fourteen, a group of political terrorists had attacked one of my own. A person I dearly love— my cousin, Theodora. They abducted her and sent a ransom note to our family, trying to force my father to pass a decree he found abhorrent."

Kallie began to pace. She moved quickly back and forth, her eyes staring at the floor, as if she was talking to herself more than to us. "My father had sent soldiers to find her, but it'd been days, and nothing had come up. My brother and I did what we could to rally our friends behind our parents' backs. We were still kids, really, but I knew we had to get together and do *something* to bring her back."

Kallie quickly spun on her heel. "We were able to figure out where Theodora was. My brother was always excellent at research, and I quickly found out that I was good... *really* good... at finding clues and putting them together. Because we were kids, we had ideas about things the adults didn't think of. We figured out where she'd been when she was taken, and where they were keeping her at the time."

Kallie's voice got darker. "My brother wanted to go to our parents, get their people on it. But I was worried if he did that, they'd kill Theodora before the soldiers managed to rescue her. I was sure I could save her, so I went off alone."

Her words turned vengeful. Almost like she enjoyed this part of the story just as much as she hated it. "My parents... they gave me the best training available. I'd had a blade in my hand from the moment I could stand, and even back then, I knew how to wield it. I realize now that my parents knew I was a demigod, and wanted me to be prepared for whatever I had to face in the future. But in doing so, they'd unknowingly created a superweapon, a little girl who was able to slaughter anyone she wanted to, and slip unseen into the shadows, because who would suspect such a terrible thing could be done by a teenage princess? I didn't have magic, because I wasn't old enough, but I had a dagger, and I had my rage. That would always be the best weapon I could ever ask for."

Kallie shrugged. "I snuck in... managed to sneak Theodora out. But as we were escaping, we got caught. The kidnapper tried to kill us. So I killed him."

She turned away from us as she went on. "I should've felt remorse... some sort of regret for taking a life. But I didn't. All I felt was relief that Theodora was safe, and that the person I killed could never hurt anyone else."

Kallie crossed her arms, spinning around to face us again. "I thought that was the end of it. Then I saw on the news there was a murderer on the loose— someone who had killed his mate and kids. For *days*, that ate away at me. I knew I could do something about it, because I'd already done it once. So... I did. I told myself that after that, I was done. Yet I found him, and killed him too, and it wasn't enough. It dawned on me that this didn't have to be the end. I could stop all kinds of hideous people from doing awful things. And once that hit me, it seemed selfish to turn away, just to save my own soul."

"It wasn't your responsibility to save everyone," Marcus said kindly.

"It became my responsibility once I realized I could do some good in the world, despite knowing the kind of sick person I was turning into. Worse than that, I realized I was the only person who had the stomach to do the job," Kallie said spitefully. "Do you know how many people I had to *allow* get hurt, because the person I was hunting ended up working for someone else, someone who was going to do something even *worse*? Do you know how many monsters I had to let go, so they could lead me to someone who was truly evil?"

Kallie's voice shook with fury. "I broke into the Arcanea Alliance station so many times, and I reviewed so many tapes— so much gruesome footage, so many horrible crimes. And we're not talking petty shit. This kind of stuff involved innocents... *children*. Police in the Arcanea Alliance were quitting their jobs or killing themselves because they couldn't stand to watch what was on those tapes. That kind of stuff changes you on a level you guys can't understand. Yet I sat there and forced myself to watch, because those videos contained evidence, which I needed to put these sick bastards down. I told myself I was strong enough to handle it. The *only* person strong enough to do what no one else could, and exterminate these beasts like the roaches they were."

Kallie punched a pillar. Her hand went straight through the concrete, creating a hole, yet she kept on going.

"But it wasn't enough. No matter how many psychos I put in the ground, more always cropped up. That's when I realized... these kinds of people were *common*. They were everywhere, in every community. Yeah, you had your run-of-the-mill criminals, who you could just look at and tell they were no good. But so many of them were blatantly average. They were involved with schools, had regular jobs, shit, they were in the fucking *priestesshood* for the gods' sakes. And nobody looked at them. Nobody knew who they were, except me, and even if I duplicated myself a hundred times, I could never catch them all. And that's where the King's Contest came in."

She put a hand to her mouth, contemplating the past. "I knew if there was any chance— any chance at all— of stopping the horrors that I'd seen, I needed a crown behind me. I needed armies... money... unlimited power. I needed people who would comply with what I asked without question, because I would be their queen and that's what duty would demand of them. I never wanted *the throne*. I wanted the resources it could provide me, resources that I'd attempted to get on my own and couldn't as a princess."

Kallie gave a noise of disgust. "My parents had tried and failed for years to stop the underground crime rings in Malovia, but they weren't willing to go to the lengths I was in order to put a stop to this. So I chose

Valen as my partner for the Contest, and used him in order to win, because I knew I had to do so at any cost. But during my Trial of Competency, I made a mistake... I was too honest. I told the governing members of the Circle what my plans were, how we could put an end to the people's suffering. I really thought they'd be behind me, that they'd think I was a visionary."

Kallie shook her head. "All of them betrayed me. The Circle called my methods disturbing, even insane. Yet I'd dealt with this firsthand, and I was certain that only someone who had the balls to be just as twisted as these predators would be able to exterminate them for good. I wanted to haul each of them out one by one, every name on every list I'd compiled, and behead them in the public square, without a trial. That's *exactly* what they deserved, and it would send a message to everyone who dared to think about harming an innocent. Yeah, I wanted my people to love me. But I *needed* them to fear me. Because when you're dealing with monsters like the ones I slaughtered, that's the only language they understand."

She dropped her gaze. "It didn't work. The Circle deemed me unfit to rule, took what I'd rightfully won away, and gave it to my brother."

"I know this is really important to you. But it didn't mean you had to throw your life away and promise yourself to someone you didn't even like, let alone aren't mated to," Marcus protested.

"You don't get it. I'm already lost because of what I've done. Damned to hell, sentenced to a fate of eternal torment, whatever. My soul and my life doesn't matter. It made me sick to stand up there at my Choosing ceremony, and swear to my goddess to be bound to someone that I didn't love," Kallie choked out. "But I *did*, because Valen was my best option to win the King's Contest and gain the throne. His magic was the strongest I'd ever seen in a shifter, and I'd never witnessed him lose a fight. I knew if anyone could get me through that competition and place me in a position of power, it was him. So I sucked it up and proclaimed Valen to be my mate, even though he wasn't, because my destiny to protect the people I was responsible for came before my happiness. If it meant getting these depraved pigs off the streets, then yeah, I'd do anything. I'd marry him, I'd *fuck him*, I'd even push his heir out of me, as much as I despised the thought, because my mission to stop suffering in my country was more important than whatever I wanted."

I gained a deep understanding of Kallie. She'd seen the worst horrors imaginable, and hardened herself to the darkest parts of society. She seemed so strong, emotionless, even, save for her anger, but her anger was her weapon, and she used it to protect herself.

Kallie struggled with being vulnerable and having emotions other than rage, because she'd kept everything inside for so long. She was worried if she felt an emotion other than anger, she'd break.

Marcus stood. He walked to Kallie and grasped her hand. "Kallie, you're so lucky. This work could've killed you."

"Do you really think one of those parasites would've been strong enough to end me?" Kallie hissed. She attempted to rip her hand away.

Marcus didn't let go. "I don't mean that. I mean... if you hadn't come to the Institute, you would've kept doing it. One day you wouldn't have been able to stand it anymore."

She resisted holding his gaze, and I had to admire her strength in the remnants of everything she'd done for her country, and all that she'd sacrificed to protect other people, people who, most likely, would never know what she'd done. Not a damn one of us in this room was strong enough to do that, besides her.

But even she wouldn't have been able to pursue hunting down these nightmares forever. The overwhelming effort it would take to put a dent in the world's predators would drown her.

Eventually, she'd look for a way out.

Oberi had been listening to all this carefully. Her head lifted as she said, *Is there a possibility that the attempt on the life of the fae king wasn't all it seemed to be?*

My heart pounded against my ribcage. I wanted to hurl. Kallie caught the stricken expression on my face and asked, "What?"

I told my constricted throat to relax. "Kallie... what if you didn't try to assassinate your brother?"

A clearness came into her eyes. "But... I *know* I did. Everyone saw me try."

"You've told us before you don't remember doing it. You could've been compelled," Marcus pointed out.

Kallie began shaking her head madly. "No. I... I lost myself in a fit of rage, I—"

Marcus grabbed her shoulders and shook her. "You *would not* have killed your twin. I know you! No matter how mad you were at him for taking the crown, you wouldn't have done something like that."

"If you were compelled to kill your brother, there's only one person with motive," Charlie said. "Did something happen to make Valen angry the night of the assassination attempt?"

"I broke up with Valen during my brother's coronation, the same day I tried to kill Kaz," Kallie said, near madness. "If I couldn't have the crown, there wasn't a point in being with him anymore. It was a relief, because I just wanted out of it."

"How'd he take it?" Charlie asked.

"At first, Valen flew into a rage. Then all of a sudden, he just... walked away. I couldn't figure out why he didn't make a bigger deal out of it, after he tried to force me to be with him," Kallie mused.

"Because he decided he was going to compel you. He knew if you killed your brother, the guilt alone would be, in his eyes, a just punishment for breaking up with him," I said. "Kallie, you were sentenced to the Institute for this specific crime. You didn't commit it of your own free will. If we can prove you're innocent, you could go free."

"Free?" Her eyebrows lifted, stunned by the possibility.

"If you get released, you *have* to search for the Divinity Keys while the rest of us figure a way out," Charlie pleaded. "This could be an opportunity for us."

Kallie said nothing. Charlie began gathering the evidence, suddenly in a hurry.

"I'm going to turn this in to Professor Jobe right away," Charlie said. "You should come too, Kallie. He'll want to hear what you have to say."

She hesitated for a moment before rushing after him. I turned to Marcus, who seemed very sad. Rishi jumped into his lap and began purring, rubbing his head on Marcus' chin.

"What are you going to do if Kallie gets released?" I whispered.

"I want whatever's best for her. It's certainly not this place," Marcus hushed.

"If it happens... you might never see her again."

The prophecy we were attempting to fulfill was dangerous, and we'd all realized getting out of the Institute alive was damn near a miracle for regular inmates, let alone us. But Marcus stroked Rishi's fur and said,

"I'd rather she be alive and safe than with me. She needs to go home. Whatever happens to me doesn't matter."

"It matters to all of us, Marcus, especially her."

"I can't be happy unless I know she's okay. This is her golden ticket out of here. She's gotta take it, even if I have to stay behind."

His tone said to drop it, so I didn't say anything more about it. I didn't agree with his choices lately, but I didn't want him to live without his mate.

At the same time, Kallie was one of my closest friends. I wanted her to be safe just as much as he did.

Even if we had to let her go.

⚭

CHARLIE DIDN'T COME BACK to our cell until it was nearly past curfew. He told me Professor Jobe had believed them, and was going to send what they'd put together to the Arcanea Alliance straight away. We'd just have to wait and see if the theory actually panned out.

It was hard to sleep that night. I couldn't rest with everything that was going through my head. Was there a chance the Dollmaker would be arrested, and made to answer for what he'd done? Would Kallie be released from the Institute once the Malovian officials knew her crime wasn't her fault?

I had an absolutely dreadful day of Work-Study. Transcribing all day in the Institute's office bored me to tears. I kept glancing at the clock, waiting for it to be five so I could go to summer music group. My constant checking made the day even longer. Oberi lay at my feet, snoozing the afternoon away. He sure wasn't in a hurry to get out of here.

Finally, I was released. Charlie was already waiting for me outside of the office.

"How was your day?" Charlie asked. Oberi yawned, transformed into a unicorn, and trotted ahead of us.

"Long. What about you?"

"Alistair was acting... weird," Charlie said. "He barely spoke to me all day."

"Strange."

"He's really bothered by what we told him about Mazur. Maybe we shouldn't have said anything."

"He loves Eddie. He deserves to know. We did the right thing."

Ez and Opal were already in the music room. Opal was strumming a harp, while Ez was busy working on setting up a camera. Tahoma pressed piano keys with his antlers.

"What are you doing?" I asked curiously.

"I thought we should film a video for your vlog, since we haven't in so long," Ez said.

I was excited, but at the same time, trepidation weighed down my limbs. "My fans haven't seen me in a wheelchair yet. They'll want an explanation."

"You don't have to give them one. They'll see it, and realize why you've taken so long to upload anything new. Just let the music speak for you," Ez suggested.

I really wanted to get back into my vlog, so I guessed Ez's advice was the best way forward. Marcus came in almost immediately after, but instead of saying hi to us, he sat in the corner with Rishi and flipped open a sketch book.

"Why did you come if you're not going to participate?" I grumbled under my breath. He acted like he didn't hear me.

Charlie and I got to warming up on the piano. He was halfway through playing a song when Kallie walked in. "Hey, everyone."

Charlie stopped playing, and Marcus looked up from his drawing. Everyone went quiet.

"I received the news," Kallie said heavily. "The Malovian government is clearing me of all charges, but the Warden won't let me go."

"*What?*" Several of us shouted at once. Rishi gave a low mew.

"He says I've committed crimes during my sentence here at the Institute, so that's grounds to keep me behind bars," Kallie admitted. "And because he's the authority here and has the Union's backing, nobody can override him, not even my brother's legal decree of my innocence."

"He just wants to keep as many demigods as he can within his reach," I spat bitterly, crossing my arms.

"I'm really sorry you didn't get pardoned," Charlie apologized. "I know you wanted to get out."

Kallie let out a breath. "Yeah, well... maybe it's a good thing I'm staying."

She glanced at Marcus, and I knew. Kallie was disappointed, but she hadn't wanted to leave her friends, nor her mate.

"Anyway..." Kallie straightened up. "I'm stuck here as long as you guys are, so might as well make the most of it. What are we doing today?"

"Making a video," Ez responded. "Do you want to be in it?"

"Sure."

We got into our places, and Professor Warbright came in.

"I'm glad you're all taking initiative," Warbright said pleasantly. "Mrs. Wahkin, I hope you don't find this odd, but I've been a fan of your vlog since you showed it to me early this semester. It's smashing you're getting back at it."

"Thanks, Professor." Nicest teacher ever, I swear.

"I'm here for supervision and guidance only, so go ahead and play what you wish," Warbright said.

Ez pressed the *record* button on the camera, then narrowed his eyes. "Hold on. The angle's off." He took the camera off the stand and began adjusting the settings.

The door burst in. Our heads snapped to the side as the sound of stomping boots rampaged into the room. Twelve guards burst in, carrying noxite guns and fully armed.

"Get up against the wall!" a guard shouted. He grabbed Kallie by the back of the neck and shoved her forward. She smacked against the concrete, and another guard lunged for Marcus. He yelped and dropped his sketchbook as he was pinned beside Kallie.

The guards ripped me out of my chair and threw me on the floor. I cried out in pain as my side hit the ground. Oberi and Charlie both rushed to help. The guards kicked my chair over, and Charlie dragged me to the wall before they could touch me again. Oberi and Tahoma stood in front of us, flaring their nostrils in a warning for the guards to stay back.

Opal started crying as she turned toward the wall and put her hands behind her head. Ez followed her lead. I watched his hands shake as he took them out of his hoodie pocket and placed them against the stone.

"This is unjust!" Kallie screeched. "We weren't doing anything wrong!"

"Do as they say, please," Warbright said hurriedly, appearing both terrified and bewildered. "What is the meaning of this?"

The guards didn't answer him. Instead, once they had everyone up against the wall, they forced us to turn around. I remained on my place on the floor, completely helpless as I clung to Charlie's legs.

There was a loud ripping sound as guards began to tear apart sheet music. The papers fluttered in the air like rain as the guards tossed them into the air, then grabbed the instruments. A whistling sound pierced my ears as a flute flew across the room and broke against the wall. One guard put his gun through a drum, and another swung a saxophone in the air, smashing it against the floor. The acoustic guitar Ez played was broken in half as a guard slammed it up against the piano bench.

They were destroying our instruments. Every last one.

"Please stop!" Warbright begged, waving his arms. "Stop, stop, *stop!*"

"Music is hereby banned at the Institute," the guard growled. "By order of the Warden."

Charlie went to take a step forward, but I grabbed his legs tightly so he couldn't move.

Pidge, let me go! I'm going to stop this, and I don't want to hurt you, Charlie insisted.

You can't. As badly as this was tearing me apart, we had to let this happen.

We're demigods, and we're stronger than them! I'm not letting them get away with this, he seethed.

If you stop them now, we'll be sent to Cellblock 9 for assaulting the guards. Even demigods can't get out of there. Then we'll never find the merfolk key, and everything we've been working for all semester will be ruined.

There was an absolutely awful sound— the mournful melody of keys being smashed.

The guards began ripping apart the piano. Their guns smashed holes in the wood, while their hands ripped out strings. The piano made a sad sort of song as the keys were repeatedly mashed by the boots of the guards, until it could sing no more.

I felt Charlie's chest compress through our bond, and his shaking hands flew over his mouth.

I felt Charlie's devastation through our bond— the way tears stung his eyes as he heard them destroy the piano. I stared up at him, and I no longer saw my husband. He was no longer a fully-grown man, but a little boy who was having his instrument smashed in front of him. Piano had been his way of escaping from abusive situations as a child, and in that moment, he was back in the brothel he'd been raised in, losing his way of disappearing from places he couldn't leave.

Just like the Institute.

Ava, I'm begging you.

This was one of the most difficult choices I'd ever made. Choosing the world over Charlie's suffering. But we'd come too far to turn back now.

Please... don't.

Warbright whimpered, but his pleading did no good. A broken violin hung limply by its strings as a guard threw it into a pile of busted trumpets. The heads of microphones were smashed. The stereo at the front of the room was crushed to pieces.

I observed the heap of wood lying on the floor where the piano had been and started to cry.

We'd spent hours here, playing that piano. I'd let Charlie touch me for the first time on that piece of art. It'd been one of the ways we'd reconnected after we'd broken up, and it had been an escape from prison life after what had happened in the Underground.

I reached up to grab Charlie's hand, which had gone cold. His whole body was stiff. He was in disbelief this could really be happening. I remembered all the amazing songs we'd created and the good times we'd shared with that piano.

It would never make music again.

Opal sobbed so loudly that we could hear it over the sound of the guards tearing things apart. Through it all, they made us watch, being deliberately cruel. By the time they were done, all that was left was one big, giant mess.

I didn't think I had much of a heart left to break, but even still... I was *devastated.*

When the guards had broken everything in the room, they pointed their guns at us. "The chapel. Now!"

Marcus fumbled to get my capsized wheelchair upright. Charlie's arms quivered so badly he almost dropped me as he tried to lift me back into it. Oberi caught me, and her neck lifted me up. Somehow, I was able to roll myself forward as the guards marched us out of the music room and into the chapel beside it.

They made us line up underneath the balcony, then grabbed Charlie by the front of his shirt. "You! Come with us!"

My throat seized up in terror. Why had they singled out *Charlie?* I tried to force myself to say something, but couldn't find the words. They'd gotten caught up inside of me, until I was gasping for air. A panic attack, shock, I wasn't sure *what* was happening to me. I felt powerless to protect him, and by far, that was the worst feeling I'd ever experienced.

They hauled him up the staircase. Although she hadn't been summoned, Oberi trailed behind with a worried nicker, her hooves clopping up the wooden steps.

We looked up to observe whatever horrifying thing was about to take place on the balcony. The guard shoved him forward, and Charlie fell against the organ. The instrument screamed in protest as he pushed himself off of it.

"Destroy it," the guard said, and nothing more.

"What?" Charlie's tone was full of astonishment.

"You heard me, *boy*! Destroy the organ!" the guard screamed.

"I'm not fucking doing anything!" Charlie bellowed.

"You don't take apart that organ, there will be hell to pay," the guard threatened.

Charlie's chest heaved in rage as he replied, "You're going to have to kill me, you bastards."

He wouldn't let this happen. He wouldn't allow the guards to rip apart our dreams and treat us like this.

I adored his bravery. But more than that, I wanted him to comply. I knew these guards would go to unimaginable lengths to force Charlie to submit, and nobody in this prison would stop them.

Just do as they say, I begged, but a fierce resistance rose up inside of him, threatening to spill over.

He wasn't going to give in. Not even if they killed him. He was done watching us suffer at this prison, and was going to make a stand.

If he did, the rest of us would, too. Nothing mattered anymore, not if we could be abused like this. Charlie would go down... we'd all go down. If this was an acceptable way to treat us, and we couldn't escape it, we might as well die.

The guard smacked him across the face so hard that he fell to the floor. "Destroy it!"

I gasped, tears brimming over my eyes as my hand went to my mouth. Charlie's voice was shaking as he said, "*No.*"

The guard went to reach for Charlie again, but a loud, resonating sound echoed through the chapel. One of the organ's pipes fell to the floor. I shuddered as I watched Oberi's hooves collide into the organ, smashing the keys to pieces. She used the bulk of her body to tear the organ apart, bending over pipes and ripping apart keys with her horn.

When it was done, Oberi stood over the shambles and gazed at Charlie. He looked like his world had ended.

I'm sorry, Oberi said. *They were going to hurt you.*

Something detached inside of me, then. I stopped being sad... stopped feeling like I was worth nothing, stopped drowning in this endless sorrow.

I stopped feeling *anything*.

But at least it was over with. There was nothing left for the guards to destroy.

Maybe it wouldn't have been so bad if they hadn't made us clean up the mess.

I'd only seen Charlie cry three times in my life. Once, when he found out his father was still alive. The second, when we'd been down in the Underground, and after I'd woken up from my coma. And now, when they forced him to pick up the smashed pieces of the organ and toss it in the trash. Once that was done, the guards took us back to the music room and made us clean up the fragments of the piano, and the rest of the broken instruments. Warbright watched with a trembling lip, failing to intercede.

I hated him, too. Just another adult who'd failed to protect us. Even if he'd been outnumbered, he should've done *something*.

After we'd picked up every fragment and shoved every music sheet into garbage bags, the guards dragged it all out to the prison yard and put it into a massive pile. They made us gather around it, then opened the doors to shepherd others out.

We weren't the only ones who were made to watch. The guards dragged a bunch of kids out here and made them stand witness, too. Hundreds of students stood in a circle around the pile of broken instruments.

A guard sneered at me, poking the barrel of their gun into my shoulder. "Light it on fire."

I didn't resist like Charlie had. What was the point? There was no fixing what had been broken. Might as well give the instruments an honored funeral on a pyre of dignity, as a farewell to the joy they'd provided us.

The instruments ignited into flames. So great was my rage, and so hot was my Fire, that the instruments were consumed in seconds.

Some cruel inmates cheered, even laughed. Most just stared at the flames like this was to be expected.

Everything we loved was destroyed around here.

When the fire burned out on its own, the guards left us alone. They went back into the prison, abandoning us there.

I turned my head to glance at the balcony that overlooked the prison yard. Standing beside Esther was the Warden. He'd been watching.

The Warden locked eyes with me, then put his hands behind his back as he turned to leave. Nothing else had to be done.

Charlie sniffed, then wiped his face. Everybody was crying. Nobody said anything. What *could* you say, after going through something like that?

I moved first. I needed to get out of here and away from the smell of the ashes in the prison yard. I rolled my chair forward, and the rest of my friends followed me.

I didn't know where else to go but the library. It was the quietest place in the prison, and we needed somewhere to grieve. We got a table in the back corner and sat around it, staring at the carpet for at least a half hour before somebody spoke.

"We have to do something," Kallie said quietly. "The Warden can't get away with this."

"He already did." Charlie's voice was almost a sob. He was more broken than anybody.

"No," Ez whispered. "He didn't."

Ez reached into his hoodie pocket and withdrew the camera. I didn't realize he still had it.

I stared at it. "You were filming?"

"The entire thing."

"Did the guards see it?"

"No. But they're going to."

A hardness grew in my stomach as I understood what he was suggesting. Marcus shook his head. "That's risky. If Ava posts that video to her vlog, she'll be sent to Cellblock 9."

"He can't send me to Cellblock 9 for exposing prison brutality," I hushed. "There'd be a public uproar."

"We already have a target on our backs," Kallie said tiredly. "What's uploading the video going to do, make the Warden want to kill us even more than he already does? We need the public on our side. This could help."

I took the camera from Ez and placed it on my lap. I rolled to a nearby computer and began the process of uploading the video.

"Ava, please think about what you're doing," Opal pleaded. "You can't take this back once it happens."

I didn't respond right away. If I made this video go live, I knew within hours that I'd lose my vlog. All the hard work me and Monica had put into it over the years, all the memories we'd captured, would be gone. The video we'd uploaded would be deleted and taken down.

But by that time, it'd be too late. The video would be saved by my fans and be circulated around the web, in so many places that it would be impossible for the Warden to stop it from being seen.

Monica would want me to do this. She'd have no problem with sacrificing what we'd built in order to make the Warden pay. In fact, she'd be ashamed of me if I didn't.

I needed Charlie to give me the answer. I couldn't make this decision on my own. I reached out to him through our bond, and he said, "Do it, pidge. I'll protect you from whatever happens."

"There are going to be consequences."

"Damn the consequences. I don't care anymore."

I didn't really care, either. The Warden had pushed us beyond our limits, and he was going to find out the repercussions of that.

The upload was complete. I pressed the *Enter* key.

And the video went live for the entire world to see.

BY THE NEXT MORNING, Union representatives were swarming the property. Access to the Internet had been completely restricted. Inmates no longer had any computers, as the guards had destroyed those during the night, too. But by then, the damage was already done.

My friends and I were in the prison yard, enjoying the rare sunshine before breakfast. The ashes from the night before had been cleaned up. In fact, *all* evidence of what had happened had miraculously vanished into thin air.

"Gentlemen, this is an outrage! I'm being falsely accused!" The Warden's brusque voice betrayed impatience— worse than that, rage. My eyes followed him as he tailed a group of three men across the prison yard, who were dressed in suits and carrying clipboards.

"We don't doubt that you run a fine institution, Doctor, but an investigation was unavoidable after that video circulated through the news," a Union representative replied. "We must look into this, even as a formality."

"This is ridiculous. Many members of the Union's council agree that I am in good standing to be in charge of this school," the Warden raged.

"Of course you are, Doctor, but it's clear you've lost control of your staff," another representative responded. "We've had angry calls from parents all morning who are close to busting down the Union's door. This is the last thing the supernatural community needs in a time of war."

"I've told you, I'm extremely qualified to be in charge of the Institute, and have a perfect record for running this school. Those guards were out of line. Disgruntled employees, looking to ruin the Institute's outstanding reputation," the Warden stated harshly. "They've already been fired, and the school is pursuing legal action. I gave no order for them to commit such heinous acts. They acted outside my authority, and if they had the kind of training that *I* received, none of this would've happened."

"Be that as it may, this did happen on your campus, Doctor Taurus, and despite being *unaware* of the situation, it was your responsibility to *become* aware and put a stop to it," the representative responded. "We shall give you an update on the Union's investigation once we are satisfied we have all the evidence required."

"How long will that take?" the Warden demanded.

"As long as we determine," the Union rep said coolly.

The suits strolled away, acting like the Warden was of no importance— and I know he *hated* that. His lip curled as he saw my friends sprawled out in the grass. His eyes narrowed in rage as he once again caught my gaze, but I held it.

The Warden looked away, and his sights landed on my brother. The Warden's hands became fists that shook at his sides, before he brushed off his jacket and turned back into the school.

"He knows I filmed the video," Ez said quietly. "He's not going to let me get away with it."

"Let him try," Kallie replied simply. "We're done."

I parted back my hair, completely unbothered. The Institute's threats meant nothing anymore.

The Warden needed to know we were the type of people to set ourselves on fire just to make sure he burned.

charlie
NINETEEN

The Warden had made it pretty damn clear upon our arrival at the Institute that he would try to break us. Despite blow after blow, we had yet to completely fall apart. It either had to be the demigod genes in us or a total miracle, because I didn't know how anyone could be expected to hold it together this long.

Music had been the one thing that made the Institute bearable. It brought the whole gang together, and it was one of the few ways we could express ourselves when the Institute tried its damndest to stomp out all self-expression from its inmates.

I could still hear the clang of metal smashing against the floor. The clash of piano keys and sickening snap of its strings would forever haunt my memories. And the organ pipes— dear ancestors, the pipes. The deafening sound of the pipes crashing to the ground would ring in my ears for life.

If there was one thing that could make it better, it was listening to the Warden grovel at the feet of the Union representatives. It almost made losing our instruments worth it.

"Did you *see* his face?" Kallie laughed as the Warden returned inside with the Union reps. "That was golden!"

"He might think twice about messing with us again," Marcus added. "The Union seems to be the only thing that scares him."

"Oh, he's scared of much more than that," Ava stated coolly. "A fall from his throne would be a travesty."

I smirked. "You'd think a man with wings wouldn't be so afraid of heights."

"His real fear is having those wings chopped off," Ez said. "And I think I just ripped out some feathers."

Ava gave a dark laugh. "Be that as it may, we only have an hour until Work-Study begins. We should grab some breakfast."

I placed my hands on the back of Ava's chair, and we started inside. We were halfway to the cafeteria when I heard my name.

"Charlie Wahkin? Kalina Nowak?" A deep voice came from down the hall. It had to be a guard.

"Great," I said flatly. "What'd I do wrong? Forget to tie my shoelaces?"

Kallie nudged me. "These guys have visitor passes."

My friends and I stopped in the hall, and two pairs of footsteps approached.

"I'm Charlie," I stated diplomatically.

"Mister Wahkin! And Miss Nowak, I presume. It's great to meet you both," one of the men said.

Shake his hand, Oberi told me.

I reached out, and the man shook my hand firmly.

"I'm Killian Ryan. This is my partner, Colter Kaminski," one of the men introduced. "We're supernatural bounty hunters. We came to thank you both for the criminal profile you completed this semester."

"You work for the United Supernatural Union?" Kallie asked.

"We work *with* them," Killian clarified. "As freelancers."

I didn't vibe well with authority, but these guys were different— more approachable. They sounded like the kind of guys who you'd want to have a cold beer with and share stories.

"Thanks to both of you and your report, we were able to get a warrant for the Christoffer family mansion," Killian continued. "The Arcanean Alliance uncovered quite the mountain of evidence, including the murder weapon."

"An edged-blade dagger," Kallie muttered.

"Yes," Colter confirmed.

It was Kallie's blade, the one she'd made for Valen before the King's Contest. The theory had been bad enough, but to know we were right had to be devastating to her.

"So the Dollmaker's behind bars?" I asked.

Killian cleared his throat. "Not yet. Valen Christoffer got word of the search and fled the country before the Arcanea Alliance could arrest him. My partner and I have been assigned his case. We're working diligently to track him down, but as of right now, he's on the run."

I felt my heart harden in my chest. The Dollmaker had been unmasked, but he was still at large, which meant he was incredibly dangerous to anyone who ran into his path of escape.

"We came to speak with you personally, to see if you had any more information that would help us track him down," Colter said.

My blood ran ice cold. I *wanted* to help them, but there was nothing more I could do. "Everything we learned is in that report. Unless... Kallie, do you have any ideas where he would run?" I asked.

"No," she said, her tone sounding hollow. "He wouldn't stay in Malovia, I know that much. He must've fled the country. Most likely, he's in Europe, but even that's a long shot. He's got money and connections. He could be anywhere."

"If you think of *anything*, give us a call," Killian said, before placing a business card in my hand. "We want to catch this guy as much as anyone, and we'll chase him halfway around the world if we have to."

"By the way, Charlie, we heard you're studying to be a supernatural bounty hunter," Colter added.

"Yes. Criminal Justice is my major," I replied. Even as I said it, my stomach dropped. I was waiting for him to tell me that I couldn't do it, or that I needed to look into other career options, because I wouldn't be capable of performing the job.

"Fantastic. Looking at the profile you compounded, you've definitely got the skills to land the job. We think you've got the talent to hunt some of these criminals down," Colter replied.

"Really?" I was completely blown away. I almost felt myself wavering.

"Absolutely," Killian confirmed. "Save our number for when you get out of this place. You'd make a great part of our team."

The men shook my hand again, but I was too starstruck to say anything. Hell, I barely realized they'd left, because I was still reeling from the offer. Everyone at the Institute said I'd never make it as a bounty hunter, but these guys who *actually worked in the field* thought I had it in me. They didn't care that I was blind, or that I had a record. They wanted me on their *team*.

Take that, *Professor Mazur,* and anyone else who doubted me. I'd survive this place, and I'd have a *job* when I got out. It was my shot at a semi-normal life.

We continued on our way to the cafeteria, but I was more floating than walking.

"Charlie, that was really exciting!" Ava raved, and she reached out to squeeze my arm. "I'm so proud of you!"

"We're proud of *both* of you," Marcus said, a bit too harshly. Ava gave an exasperated huff.

It was getting really fucking annoying that they were still fighting. After what we'd been through in the music room, I wished they'd just make up already.

"I couldn't have done it without you guys," I said, trying to lighten the mood.

It wasn't working, apparently, because Kallie said bitterly, "It does us no good if Valen isn't caught."

I tried my best to comfort her. "At least the Dollmaker's identity has been revealed. Everyone knows who he is now. He can't keep killing people and living a normal life. Eventually, the police will catch up to him."

"I sure hope so," Kallie said. "And if they don't catch him by the time I get out of here, I'll hunt him down myself. He can't run from me."

"Hold up!" Ez grabbed the side of Ava's chair, drawing us all to a stop. I nearly ran into him, and my shoe slipped on something sticky and wet.

Everyone went quiet. "Is that... blood?" Ava asked in a chilling voice.

Ez and I knelt down beside each other. I wiped my fingers across the carpet and felt tiny warm droplets, then ran my fingers over a puddle the size of my hand.

"I'm sure it's nothing," Marcus said. "Fights break out every day. Someone's bound to walk away with a bloody nose."

"Not today, they're not," Ez replied. "No one's going to risk starting a fight with the Union reps roaming campus. This is more than just a bloody nose. Someone's hurt."

I rubbed the blood between my fingers. My Elven abilities could sense the angelic magic still pulsing through it. "It's an angel."

"You don't think Chancey got caught up in something?" Ava wondered.

I shook my head. "I don't know who it is, but we should check on them, just in case. This is a lot of blood to lose."

We began following the blood trail, and the droplets led us through a maze of hallways. I couldn't be sure where we were until Kallie uttered, "This is leading us toward death row."

"No one knows about that place but us." Ava sounded confused.

"Except the Warden," I theorized. "Maybe he ran out of room to torture people in Cellblock 9."

The thought of him taking a student and dragging them down here made my blood run cold. The ghosts alone were enough to frighten someone to death.

We continued down the twisting hallways, until we heard the faint sound of a tortured scream. It didn't sound like it came from one of the ghosts, either, but someone living. We ran down the hall as fast as we could, until we came to the curved hallway leading to death row. We slowed, because we had to assess the situation before we came in guns blazing.

"I'd sooner kill myself than tell you anything," a woman snarled. It sounded like Professor Mazur.

Holy shit, what had she done? I wouldn't put it past the Warden to torture one of his followers if they stepped out of line. After all, he'd killed Professor Cusak. But I never imagined Professor Mazur would defy the Warden. She was one of his most devoted followers.

A hollow laugh echoed down the hall, followed by a cat's hiss. "I'm not allowing you to die until you tell me what you know."

"That's Alistair!" I realized.

"It sounds like they're alone," Ava remarked. "What the fuck is he doing?"

Ava grabbed the wheels of her chair and rushed into the cell block. Oberi barked, and the rest of us followed closely behind.

"Tell me where to find Eddie!" Alistair roared. Pig growled lowly.

I heard a fist crack, and it sounded an awful lot like the fights at the club. Mazur cried out, but I couldn't make sense of the scene. Alistair sounded like he was at least several yards away from her.

Mazur spat, and it sounded like she was spitting blood onto the floor. "Oh, look. Your friends have come to stop you. How ironic."

"What the hell is going on here?" I demanded.

There's blood all over the floor, Oberi explained. *Mazur's on her knees, and she's covered in bruises. Her right eye is swollen shut, and there's a gash across her forehead. I barely recognize her through all the injuries.*

"I'm doing what has to be done," Alistair said calmly, like he didn't care he'd been caught.

"Torturing a professor?" I balked. "Alistair, you won't just be sent to Cellblock 9 for this. You'll be executed! The Warden isn't going to let this go!"

"So let them hang me!" Alistair snapped. "I'm gonna die to find Eddie. Don't act like you'd do any different if they took Ava."

Ava wheeled forward a few feet. "Alistair, perhaps we should talk about this—"

"Don't come any closer!" he yelled.

My friends and I all backed away, but we hadn't intended to. I suddenly felt like a puppet on a string, being forced to move in ways I hadn't decided to. I tried to take a step forward, but my legs had turned to stone. I realized I couldn't move unless Alistair pulled the strings, and that was terrifying.

"Alistair, let us go," Marcus demanded. "You can't use your Mentalist powers like this."

"I obviously can," Alistair replied with a bitter laugh. "So I will."

I'd always known Alistair was from the Mentalist Cast of the Miriamic Coven, but I didn't know what powers he possessed until now. From what Marcus had told me, Mentalists were witches and warlocks who could control the mind and perform telekinesis, though their exact specialties varied. It looked like Alistair had the power to play puppeteer. It was different from vampire compulsion— like the powers

Mad Dog had used on Thaddeus. Each one of us were fully aware of what was happening, but nonetheless, we couldn't stop it.

Marcus had warded us from mind reading from other Seers, but this was mind control cast by a Mentalist. There was so much going on that we couldn't account for every variable, and it was difficult figuring out every possible way that our enemies could hurt us. We couldn't think of everything. But Alistair was a friend, and I never thought he'd use his powers against us.

"The Goddess didn't give me these powers to sit on my hands and not use them," Alistair said. "I've been hiding my magic from the Warden because I didn't want to wear one of those damn noxite bracelets, but I can't hide it anymore. This bitch needs to fess up."

A heavy *thud* sounded as Mazur's fist connected with her own face. The sound of gagging met my ears, followed by the scent of stomach acid as Mazur vomited. Alistair must've made her shove her fingers down her throat.

"Tell us where you moved the Elves!" Alistair demanded.

When she didn't answer, Alistair continued his torture. Mazur's scream echoed through the cells around us.

It's gruesome to watch, Oberi remarked apprehensively. *Alistair's making her scratch her own face raw with her nails.*

Ghosts wailed above our heads. To be honest, it sounded like they were cheering. This had to be the most entertainment they'd had in over a century.

I couldn't say I didn't get *some* sort of satisfaction witnessing Mazur's torture. It was sick, really, standing there listening without really *wanting* to intercede. Mazur had been horrible to all of my friends. She'd bullied me about my disability, and she'd shamed and manipulated countless students into joining The Mission. She'd played a hand in the experiments the Warden had conducted in the Infernal Underground, and she'd helped to send the Elves to the concentration camps. She deserved the torture Alistair inflicted upon her.

My only protest was my friend had to be the one to administer it. I didn't want this coming back to bite him in the ass one day.

"If you don't want to tell us about the Elves, tell us what the Warden knows about *The Assassin's Destiny,*" Alistair growled. "What does he know about the keys?"

"Why don't you ask him?" Mazur said through ragged breaths.

"I'm getting real fed up with your attitude," Alistair said. "Looks like we'll have to kick it up a notch."

Mazur began crawling across the floor against her will. Disgust twinged through the bond, and I knew she must be dragging her body through her own blood and puke.

Mazur reached the nearest cell, and the metal sang softly as she pulled herself up. Then came three loud *clangs* that echoed all throughout death row. The crack of her skull filled the air. Alistair had forced Mazur to smash her head into the bars over and over again.

"Stop!" Mazur screamed in agony, before I heard her slump to the floor. "I'll tell you what I know!"

"That's better," Alistair seethed. "Might as well get talking."

Mazur took a rattling breath. "From what I've heard of the ship, it sailed to Darke Island, and was never seen again. That's all I know."

"You're going to have to give us more than that," Alistair insisted.

The cell door rattled, like she was getting ready to slam her face into the bars all over again. Mazur let out a pained whimper. "The ship went down in the waters around Darke Island, and the crew drowned at sea. The only survivors were a merman named Dante Winselt and his mate, a fae sorceress named Duchess Amalie. Dante was kept prisoner here, while Amalie was sent back to Malovia—"

"We know all this," Alistair growled. "If you're not going to be useful, you can go to hell right now."

"I— I don't know anything else," Mazur stammered. "All I know is the Warden has searched the south side of the island and found nothing."

"Is that all?" Alistair demanded.

Mazur gave a wheezing breath.

"*Where else has he searched!?*" Alistair screamed.

Mazur gave a choked cry, like Alistair had put her hand over her throat and squeezed. "The west and east sides as well," she rasped.

"Very good," Alistair said proudly. He must've released her, because she took a greedy gulp of air. "Play your part, and I'll stop torturing you. That's how this works, you see? So if the Warden's searched everywhere else, that means the ship wrecked off the north shore of the island."

Mazur gave a wild laugh. "What are you going to do? Go looking for it? If you want to narrow down the location, there's only one way to get your hands on the Warden's records, and that's to go down to Cellblock 9 yourself. Even *I'm* not privy to all the information the Warden has gathered. Search the records in Cellblock 9 all you want, but we all know no one makes it out alive. You'll never find that shipwreck unless you get out of the Institute, and the only way you're leaving this place is a body bag."

"Funny you should bring that up, because I was thinking the same about you if you don't tell me where Eddie is," Alistair threatened. "You told us about the ship. That wasn't so hard, was it? Now tell us about the Elves!"

"I know nothing about the Elves—"

Mazur was cut off as the heavy clangs started up again. Alistair forced Mazur to bash her head into the cell bars. This time, she didn't cave, so Alistair went for another method. Mazur smashed her fist into the wall, until a broken bit of concrete clattered to the floor.

Oberi cringed. *He's making her slice the skin on her arm with the sharp edge of concrete.*

"Alistair, stop!" Ava insisted. "She's going to bleed out."

"Not until she tells us where Eddie is!" Alistair shot back.

She's going for the eye! Oberi barked loudly.

I cringed, knowing that Alistair wouldn't stop. He'd forced Mazur to gouge her own eyes out if it meant telling him where Eddie was located.

This was going too far. I was about to say something, before Mazur wailed, "They're dead!"

The cell block went dead silent. Even the ghosts had stopped making noises.

"*What* did you just say?" Alistair demanded.

Mazur took a few ragged breaths before continuing. "The Elves were being kept at a camp across the island," she confessed. "We were moving them to the mainland when our guards were attacked. There was an explosion, and the Elves fought back. They died— each and every one."

My heart turned to stone before it crumbled into a million pieces. I always thought we'd have more time to find Eddie. I didn't know what the hell they'd done to him at that camp, but I thought for sure they'd keep him alive until we could finally break him out. It seemed too soon to lose him.

This wasn't real. I didn't want to believe my guard— my friend— was gone for good.

"I don't believe you," Alistair accused. "If they're really dead, where are the bodies?"

"There were no bodies left to recover," Mazur admitted. "All that was left after the explosion was a crater in the ground. Your friends disintegrated on impact, as they deserved for the vile beings they were!"

"*Vile!?*" Alistair roared. "You're the vile one, for the hand you played in exterminating the Elves. You deserve a far worse fate than theirs!"

"You'll never understand," Mazur wheezed. "Doctor Taurus has sworn to create a world without suffering, and as long as people like *you* and your crippled kind continue to exist on this planet, it will never be so! This Earth deserves to be mastered by perfect people, instead of infested with a bunch of sickly freaks!"

Professor Mazur had always hated me from the beginning, for seemingly no reason. Now I understood why. She hated everyone who had an illness or a disability, because they didn't fit into her vision of a painless utopia. Disabled people didn't live in her idea of a blissful paradise. She wanted us— me, my friends, and people like us— eliminated and exterminated.

Alistair's rage could be felt in our bones as he screamed, "You're the one who deserves to suffer! I don't want to live in your perfect world, and you'll never get to see it!"

Mazur screamed so loud that it shook the entire cell block. Alistair's anger permeated the air, fueling a spell he shouldn't be able to pull off. My Elf magic sensed his power as Alistair forced Mazur to siphon her own life energy out of herself. He wasn't like me, who could steal someone's energy. Instead, he used his mind control to force Mazur to drain her own life force using her angel magic.

Her screams turned to desperate rasps as she gasped for breath. Mazur's voice aged decades with each passing second.

None of my friends protested, and I remained surprisingly calm. It should have bothered me that I showed no remorse for letting this happen, but to be completely honest, I was kind of glad Alistair had made us keep our distance.

Professor Mazur slumped to the ground. "The God of The Mission will punish you for this," she rasped in a dying breath. She gave one last sigh, then... nothing.

Alistair heaved and dropped to his knees. "You *bitch!* You *killed him!*" he screamed, though Mazur could no longer answer. Sobs filled his chest, and his breath became unsteady as he slammed his angry fists against the ground.

He was so enraged that his hold on us loosened, and we could move to our own will again. We all felt the tragedy of death filling the room.

Except it wasn't a tragedy at all. Eddie was gone, and it felt fitting that we'd enacted revenge for his death. I didn't fault Alistair in the slightest.

Ava was the first to speak up. "We have to do something with the body."

"Leave her here to rot," Alistair spat. "She doesn't deserve a proper burial."

"The Warden's going to notice she's missing!" I said. "He knows about death row, and he'll send guards all over the prison to find her. This was a sloppy job, and the Warden will find evidence of who's responsible. Ava's right. We have to clean this up if we don't want to get caught."

"Let him do his worst," Alistair raged. "If Eddie's gone, none of it matters."

"Then get your revenge!" Ava yelled. "You just proved that you can kill an angel, which none of us thought we could do! Let's use your power to kill the Warden, and have this over with!"

Alistair scoffed. "The Warden's way stronger than this bitch, and he's got protection spells up the ass guarding his mind. You all know it, because Marcus has been trying to read his mind all semester, and he hasn't got a single peep out of him! But even if that wasn't true, you know what? I don't really give a shit anymore. Eddie's dead. So as far as I'm concerned, I couldn't be bothered to give a fuck about who lives or who dies. You want the Warden dead, kill him yourself."

His cane clattered as he got to his feet. He pushed past us, and Pig followed behind him.

"Alistair, stop," I begged.

"Don't follow me, Charlie," he snapped. "You promised we'd rescue

Eddie, but your promises are as empty as the Warden's. You all can fuck off. You want this mess cleaned up? Clean it up yourself. You're the ones who exposed Forevermore and got Eddie locked up in the first place. I suggest you get to work, before the Warden finds you missing from your shifts."

With that, Alistair stomped out of the room.

For fuck's sake, I knew he was grieving, but comparing me to the Warden was a low blow.

Ava took my hand. "He didn't mean it. He's angry, and rightfully so."

I understood, perhaps far too much. The news about Eddie had devastated us all, but Alistair took the brunt of the blow. Eddie had been his partner, and I knew how it felt to lose someone you cared so much about.

"He'll come around when he's ready," Ez said gently. "In the meantime, we have to clean up this blood trail before anyone follows it here."

"If we all ditch Work-Study to clean this up, the guards will come looking for us," Marcus pointed out.

"We'll stash the body in one of the cells," I decided. "We can't dump it in the middle of the day anyhow, or we'll be spotted. We'll clean up the blood trail and come back tonight for the body."

I'd never dumped a body before, but that's what you did for your friends. Alistair would be caught and sentenced to death unless we wiped all traces of evidence. The Warden would be suspicious about Mazur's disappearance, but we had to make sure he wouldn't be able to trace it back to us.

I expected dumping the body to churn my guts, but I'd gone oddly numb to the whole thing. I guess I really did belong in this place amongst criminals, because I'd certainly become one.

Marcus and I dragged Mazur's body into one of the cells, while the others got to work on cleaning up the blood trail. Ava and Ez used their Toaqua magic to draw the blood out of the carpet in the hall, and Kallie used illusions to cover what was left behind.

We had to be quick about it, because we were cutting it close to Work-Study. We cleaned up as quickly as we could, then rushed to the showers to get any remnants of blood off our bodies.

I ended up leaving Oberi with Ava, then running to the factory after we finished so I wouldn't be late for my shift. I drew a deep breath before entering the printing room, trying to calm my anxiety and nerves. It didn't help curb the paranoia, though. My hands shook as I worked my table, and I kept messing up as I focused my attention on the door. I thought for sure guards would come in at any moment and haul me away, then toss me into Cellblock 9 with my friends. I wasn't sure we'd gotten all the blood, or that Kallie's illusions would hold, or that no one would stumble across the body in death row.

Alistair was supposed to be working beside me, but his table remained empty. He either figured an infraction was better than going to work, and he'd locked himself in his room to grieve, or the Warden had picked him up.

I was a bundle of nerves when I left my shift. Every time I heard footsteps, I ducked into an alcove or around the corner so the guards wouldn't spot me. We waited until darkness fell, then my friends and I met up at death row.

"Anyone else paranoid as shit?" Marcus asked.

Ez seemed agitated. "I was glancing over my shoulder all day."

"Was anyone followed?" Kallie questioned.

"I didn't let anyone see me while I was coming here," Marcus said. "Stopped by the witch dorms and checked on Alistair, though. He doesn't handle grief well."

He's in a bad place right now, Oberi agreed. *Pig says he's seen better days.*

"Let's finish this before he ends up in a worse situation," Ava said.

Marcus, Ez, and I lifted the body, which had gone cold and stiff. We snuck through the halls, and Kallie used illusions to help conceal us. Marcus' shoe squeaked, and we all went dead still.

Footsteps started in our direction.

"Guards," I hissed.

I've got this, Oberi said.

He walked around the corner, panting like he was having a good time. He sat in front of the guards, his tail thumping on the ground.

"It's just a stupid Familiar," one of the guards said.

"Leave him be," the other stated. "He's not hurting anyone."

As soon as the guards left, Oberi ushered us forward. *Come. We don't have much time.*

We reached the prison yard. "Stop!" Kallie hissed. We all ducked around a corner, then quickly she said, "This way."

We made our way across the yard as fast as we could, using the darkness of night to conceal us. We'd made a deal with the sirens to deliver them a body, and we intended to fulfill that promise.

Once we got to the lake, we tossed the body in. Within moments, sirens were swarming the surface, their heavy fins smacking against the water as they viciously fought over their next meal. We could hear the tearing of flesh as their sharp teeth sank through the muscle and tore Mazur's limbs apart.

The sirens were ruthless, and they couldn't resist the scent of blood as it filled the lake. They'd been denied fresh meat for so long, I had no doubt that they wouldn't leave a single trace of the body behind.

Marcus gagged, and Ez had to distance himself from the scene.

"It's done," Ava finally said as the sounds of sirens quieted. They ducked back underwater, and the prison yard went quiet again.

The silence continued, even after we returned to the building. Nobody wanted to say anything, because we were all grieving.

Me, especially. Eddie and I were connected by a magical bond. It wasn't the same as the bond I shared with Ava and Oberi, and not nearly as strong. But it was a bond nonetheless, like a connection between brothers. I hadn't felt that connection in a long time, and it killed me to know that I hadn't been there for him.

Worse than that... I'd *failed* him. Eddie had sworn to be my protector, but he and the other Elves were dead because I hadn't been able to keep them safe.

I tossed and turned in bed that night. Every so often, I'd drift off, only to be jolted awake when I remembered that Eddie was gone.

He was just another friend that had died because of my actions. It wasn't possible to hate myself more than I already did. When would the bodies stop piling up?

Ava and I moved slowly the following morning. It took us longer than usual to get out of bed. When we finally managed, we made our way to the secret training room. Kallie and Marcus were already there, chatting with Takahashi. We joined them around the table.

"I'm tired of staying here," Marcus said in exhaustion. "We have to get out as soon as possible."

I agreed. We'd all done bad things here, but what had happened with Mazur crossed a line. We couldn't keep expecting to get away with murder, because at some point, the Warden would find out.

"The Demigod Guardians are prepared to help whenever you're ready," Takahashi said. "But we'll need a solid plan to get you out. We may be able to break Ava free when she's escorted to the mainland to testify in John Smith's court case. If we can distract the Warden long enough, we could get the rest of you out. The Demigod Guardians have safe houses where the Warden won't find you."

"I know what we have to do," Marcus stated. "It was Mazur's idea, really. She said the only way out of here is in a body bag, so... why not do just that?"

"Oh, gee, why didn't we think of that before?" Ava said sarcastically. "If we die before the Warden decides to kill us off, at least we get to do it ourselves. Absolutely genius idea!"

"I'm not talking about *actually* dying," Marcus shot back. "I'm talking about faking it. I've got Death magic. We should be able to brew a potion that *mimics* death, along with an antidote that the Demigod Guardians can administer once we're out."

"An antidote?" Kallie asked. "So... that means the potion could kill us?"

"We'll have twenty-four hours," Marcus said. "The first potion will slow down our bodily systems, so that we *appear* dead. The antidote will kick-start them again."

"How long will it take to make the brew?" Kallie asked eagerly.

"A week, at most," Marcus said. "We'll need a few ingredients we can't get on campus, but Hemlock should be able to get them for us. Once we have everything, we can get started right away. After it takes effect, our parents can petition to have our bodies returned home. It's within our religious protections. Professor Takahashi can come up with a story to explain our deaths."

"I say we frame Naya," Kallie said with an evil laugh. "Let the Union think she poisoned us."

I drummed my fingers on the tabletop. "This might actually work. The Warden won't let our bodies go without a fight, because he'll want to experiment on them, but if the Union steps in, the Warden won't have a choice. It won't matter what the Warden thinks happened, because it'll be out of his jurisdiction. Seeing as the Union's taking their time with their investigation, they'll be hanging around until the next ship off the island leaves. We'll have to be put on that ship out of here."

"No," Ava stated firmly. "I have to testify against John first. The trial is next week. If I take the death potion before the case is finished, I won't be able to get on that stand. I need my voice to be heard. I'll testify first, then, once I return, we can talk about taking the potion."

We all understood... perhaps too deeply.

"Then we'll leave after the trial," I decided. "We'll take the potion right before another shipment arrives, so we can get off the island the same day."

"The Demigod Guardians can be on the ship to administer the antidote and smuggle you to safety," Takahashi said.

"Which will put us in the perfect position to search the waters for the merfolk key," Kallie added. "But we'll have to be quick, before the Warden suspects anything."

"What about our friends?" Ava asked. "We can't leave them here."

"The Demigod Guardians will execute a plan at a later time to rescue your loved ones, but you four are the priority. It's imperative we get you out of here first. At the same time, it'll be safer for your friends if you're not around, for the Warden's focus will be on finding you," Takahashi replied.

"That brings me to my next point," Marcus said. "The Warden has narrowed his search for the shipwreck further than we know. Mazur said those records are in Cellblock 9. Thaddeus has been searching those records for us, so I say we summon him to get our info, then help him cross over before we leave."

"By the gods," Takahashi breathed. "You haven't helped your friend cross over yet?"

"He agreed to help us," Marcus insisted. "Whatever he found in Cellblock 9 could be crucial. If we can narrow down the site of the shipwreck, we can do this all in one go and get off the island *with* the merfolk key undetected."

"I'm in," I decided. I'd do almost anything to get out of this place.

"It's our best way out of here," Kallie agreed.

"No!" Takahashi protested. "You need to stop summoning your friend so he can *move on*. Marcus, you can't do this again."

"Technically, I *can*," Marcus said.

"But you *won't*," Takahashi insisted. "Not as long as I'm around."

It was meant to be some sort of a threat. Marcus grumbled and said, "All right, fine. I won't."

Takahashi took that as the end of the conversation. "Let's focus on the task at hand. Marcus, I'll need a list of ingredients for the potion. I'll begin gathering them right away while you work on your demigod practice this morning. We'll start brewing, so we can be sure the potion is ready the moment Ava returns from her trial."

Marcus scribbled a few things down on a sheet of paper, then handed it to Takahashi. Takahashi thanked him, then left the room.

He wasn't gone two seconds before Marcus conjured a bundle of herbs, the scent filling the room as he lit them.

"Marcus, what are you doing?" Ava demanded.

"Summoning Thaddeus. What does it look like?" he asked innocently.

"You said you wouldn't!" Ava insisted.

"I said I wouldn't *as long as Takahashi was around*," he emphasized.

Kallie almost sounded *proud*. "You make promises like a fae."

"I've learned a thing or two," Marcus said nonchalantly. "Are you guys staying, or not?"

"I'm not going anywhere," Ava growled.

"But you're not going to stop me, either." Marcus waved his herb bundle around and began calling out Thaddeus' name, but nothing happened.

Oberi barked a few times, like he was trying to help. *Something feels awry*, he added, and I mentally felt his consciousness bristle.

"Thaddeus, show us a sign that you're here," Marcus demanded.

A chill spread over my arms, but that was as far as it went.

Marcus tapped his foot. "He's around, but for some reason, he's not appearing in full form. It seems he needs a bit of help."

Marcus began muttering words in Latin, and a cold breeze swept through the room. A hawk's cry came from overhead, and my heart leapt as the bird's scream came closer to my ear. The bird swept past me, and I clutched my chest as my heart rate slowed.

"It's Thaddeus' Familiar," Ava said.

The hawk flew around the room in a chaotic pattern, as if it was trying to escape from a cage. Its continuous squawk filled the room. Oberi whimpered, like he was trying to calm the bird down.

"Thaddeus is confused," Marcus said. "He doesn't know where he is, or how to shift his spirit from Familiar to man. They are two pieces of a whole, but his soul is disturbed."

Oberi continued barking. The hawk swooped down toward him, and Oberi jumped. His jaws snapped, and the hawk cried out from the floor. Oberi must've pinned the spirit under his paw. I didn't know he could do that, but he was a *mutabeecha* with one foot residing in the spirit plane.

Be still, Oberi ordered the bird.

The hawk's cries died down, then came the sound of Thaddeus' screams from below us. He was lying on the ground. His spirit must've shifted to his human form. The cries were deafening, echoing off the walls and vibrating the rafters above us.

Marcus raced over to him. "Thad, it's just us!"

This isn't right, Oberi said as he stepped back.

"Thad!" Marcus kept trying to get his attention, but all Thaddeus could do was scream. "It's Marcus. I sent you down to Cellblock 9, remember? You've got to tell us what you learned!"

"Can't you see he's incapable?" Ava yelled. "Marcus, you've got to send him back to Ancestral Lands. Staying here is killing him!"

"He's already dead," Marcus shot back.

"You know what I mean," Ava snapped. "The longer he stays, the more tortured he becomes. Tortured souls can't move on alone. Send him back *now*!"

Several beats passed, and all that seemed to exist was the hollowing cry of Thaddeus' tortured spirit. He sounded in so much pain— like his soul was being torn apart from the inside out.

"I can't—" Marcus rasped.

"You can, and you will," Ava growled. "He can't help us in the state he's in! The least we can do is help him!"

"No, I mean... I'm trying, and I can't!" Marcus said. "Thad should be able to move on, but my connection to the other side is... gone. I— I can't send him back."

Terror festered within me, but I refused to accept it. We damn sure were going to find a way. We'd break down the gates of the Blessed Haven ourselves to send Thaddeus through, if we had to.

But we didn't get a chance to discuss it, because Thaddeus' screams came to an abrupt halt. A blast of ice-cold air nearly knocked me to the floor, then... everything became silent. The room returned to its normal temperature, and the sound of ghostly wails ceased. It was like Thaddeus had never been there in the first place.

Then, we heard it— the banging above our heads, and the faint shrill squawk of his hawk. The whole room groaned, and clanging came from inside the walls.

"What *happened?*" Kallie demanded.

Marcus' voice shook as he got to his feet. His footsteps were light and timid as he took several steps back. "Thaddeus transformed into a poltergeist."

"What does that mean?" I demanded. We were all panicking, and it certainly wasn't helping the situation.

Marcus was on the verge of tears. "It's what becomes of a tortured soul. When they can't contain their energy, they become a spiritual being who can influence our surroundings. Poltergeists can bite you or move things around the room. His spirit has basically been torn to pieces, and although he can return in spirit every now and then, he'll have no choice to do so. His spiritual presence is left up to chance."

Nobody spoke as the horror of what Marcus said sank in. It was like watching Thaddeus die all over again. If there was any chance of helping him move on, that just went out the window.

"I... never intended for this to happen," Marcus rasped.

"Intention or not, your poor decisions led to this," Ava bit at him.

"I'm not an idiot," he snapped. "Obviously, I fucked up. What do you want me to say, Ava? That you were right? Because you were. You don't need to rub it in, okay?"

His voice cracked, and Ava didn't say anything. Then I felt her sorrow slip through the bond. Something changed in her when he admitted he fucked up.

I heard her roll forward and lean in to give Marcus a hug.

Marcus was silent, before he let out a sob. I felt his embrace through our bond as Marcus hugged her tightly and cried into her shoulder. "I'm really sorry, Ava. I should've listened."

"It's okay," she whispered. "Sometimes we make bad choices."

She held him for a moment, before Marcus gave a sniff and drew away. "I made a really bad choice this time."

"None of us are innocent," Ava replied. "We'll get through it. We're getting out of here."

I heard her think, *Even if Thad didn't.*

Marcus was pretty torn up, so Kallie took him back to his room. She promised us she wasn't going to leave him alone before they left. I wheeled Ava back to our cell, but she must've felt I had more to say, because she turned to me and said, "You've been awfully quiet."

I sat on the couch, and Oberi hopped up beside me. "I'm thrilled we're getting a chance to leave, but that's all it is right now. A *chance.* We don't know for sure if this will work. We're putting our lives in other people's hands to pull this off, and that scares me."

"I don't think we have another choice," Ava said.

I nodded. "*I* don't, but if you see a chance to run during your court case, you do it. You'll be far away from the Institute and the Warden during that trial. Me and the others will be fine. We'll take the potion and get out of here, but I don't want you to take that risk if you don't have to. You're getting outside these walls and back into Kinpago to testify. You have the best chance of escaping."

"I don't want to leave you behind," she insisted.

I took her hands in mine and squeezed. "I'll be right behind you."

Ava choked up. "If you meant that, you wouldn't be asking me to do this."

"I need you to think about yourself first, for once," I begged. "Please, pidge. One of us has to survive this."

"No!" she argued, squeezing my hands back. "We *both* will. If I can run, I'll do it. But otherwise, we're getting out of here together."

"If that becomes an opportunity. But you'll be outside the Institute next week for that trial, and we can't count on this death potion to work. One of us *has* to get out of here. It's not an option for all four of us to fail. So if you see a chance to break out while you're testifying, take it. *Promise me*, Ava."

Her tone wavered, but she replied, "I promise."

Ava wasn't the best at keeping promises, but I hoped she wouldn't break this one... for me.

Even if I had to be without her, I'd rather she be far away from me and safe then here by my side and at risk. Every day, my friends and I were doing something that put us in even more jeopardy than we already were, and Ava couldn't keep being involved. We wouldn't keep getting away with this. One day, there'd be a cost.

Ava needed to be nowhere near me when it was finally time to pay the price.

ava-marie

TWENTY

There were screams... dozens of screams.

I found myself standing in a darkened room, a room that was without end, a room without light or color. All around me were thousands of people, pressing in on each other and crying out. I attempted to move, but no matter which way I went, another person pressed into me. I began to feel suffocated as all those bodies squeezed in around me, and claustrophobia overtook my senses. I couldn't see where I was, or what was going on. All I felt was this terrible fear, and the inability to escape it.

A sliver of light shone through a crack, like there was a door up ahead. People stampeded over each other to get to it, and the cries of agony grew louder.

I felt someone shove me forward. I hit the ground hard, and felt footprints embed into my back as the crowd crawled over me to get to the opening.

I gasped, struggling to make air fill my lungs. I couldn't breathe, and my spirit started to slip away as the door ahead of me closed, sealing off the light.

"Pidge? You okay?"

Charlie was trying to get me to eat breakfast. I'd gotten some food down, but it was difficult taking another bite. The cafeteria around me was full of conversation, but inwardly, I felt nothing but detached... cold.

"I had another bad dream last night," I said, turning toward him.

"Esther manipulating your dreams again?" He scowled.

"No. I didn't see the cardinal. I think this was more like... a vision."

Charlie's eyebrows knitted together, but he said, "It must be the stress of the trial. It'll be over soon."

I shivered, but I wasn't sure that's what it was. Though I had to admit I *was* under a lot of stress.

I was being summoned today to testify. This afternoon, I'd go into the Kinpago courthouse and tell my story for the whole tribe to hear.

Telling Charlie what little he knew had been gut-wrenching, and that had been him, alone, in a private place where I knew I wasn't going to get hurt. My testimony was going to be ripped apart and examined piece by piece by strangers, and I knew details would come up that I didn't want to recount.

I told myself it would be worth it if we could get John behind bars, but still, I wasn't sure.

All you have to do is get through the day, as you've gotten through every day before this, Oberi said, putting a paw on my knee. *Then you will be home with us once more.*

The idea of going up against John, and publicly declaring what had happened to me, made me feel absolutely sick. I'd almost rather go down into the Underground all over again. It was Monica's encouragement to make him pay, and the thought of protecting other women, that made me stick to my decision.

"I wish I could come with you," Charlie said sorrowfully. "I hate the thought of you being in the same room with him."

I will be there with her, Oberi said. *We will get through this together.*

I wanted to stay with Charlie longer, but I had to leave now if I was going to make it to the courthouse on time. We ventured toward the drop-off room at the front of campus, which was the same room we'd come in when we'd been bussed here, and the same room graduates left through once they got out.

The room was empty, save for Professor Takahashi. He turned toward me as we entered, giving a slight bow.

"It's nice to see you, although I wish it was under better circumstances," Takahashi stated.

"I will be your escort to the trial today."

"Really?" I couldn't be happier that Professor Takahashi was escorting me to the courthouse, instead of a bunch of stupid guards.

"Yes. I have promised to take full responsibility for you, and accept the consequences should you escape outside of the Institute's walls," Takahashi said.

"I can't believe the Warden allowed it." I was certain he'd send a whole battalion to guard me, his precious little gem, and make sure I didn't get away during the trial's proceedings. I was still wearing the tracker cuff that followed my movements, but if I got a moment to run outside of the prison, Oberi would break it off.

"It was rather unexpected," Takahashi admitted.

The doors behind us opened, and Hemlock's sharp footsteps resonated behind us. "I am here to see you off," Hemlock said, whirling her cloak behind her. "As I am the only teacher on campus authorized to cast portals, my magic will work on school grounds to transport you to Kinpago. Mister Wahkin, I have obtained exemptions for Work-Study for you and your friends today, and have set up streaming services in my office for your group to watch the trial live. Your wife will need support, and it is best that everyone knows the details as they happen, rather than asking her to recant them upon her return. This trial will be highly publicized, and her friends should know the facts before rumors begin flying around the school."

Charlie gaped for a moment before shutting his mouth. "But the Warden's shut down internet access all around campus. Are you sure it's safe?"

Professor Hemlock gave a short laugh. "It is quite hilarious you believe the Warden is capable of outwitting me. I am very good at what I do, Mister Wahkin. Trust that I have the situation handled."

Hemlock handed me a small, folded up note. "By the way, Ava... I was told to give you this. Do not read it until you are outside school grounds."

Her mouth was completely flat, like she hadn't wanted to deliver this letter to me, but had no choice. She cast a portal. As it bloomed before me, I saw Kinpago's warm streets be illuminated before my eyes.

"Remember what we talked about," Charlie said as he squeezed my hand. I tucked the letter into my pocket.

"Okay," I whispered. I didn't want to wish him farewell, because that could be something final. If we never said goodbye, we'd *have* to be together again. This wouldn't be the last time.

I wouldn't let go of his hand, so he had to withdraw his fingers from mine. I rolled my chair through the portal, and Oberi walked beside me as we entered through it. Takahashi strolled behind me, and once his feet hit solid ground, the portal vanished behind us.

I'd traveled hundreds of miles in mere seconds, but the journey through the portal wasn't difficult. It was like exiting one room and entering another. The atmosphere around me immediately warmed, and the sun shone on my face. It was rare for Darke Island to get any sort of sunshine, so I absorbed the light and took in a deep breath of fresh air.

I was *home*. I'd missed California— missed Kinpago, so fucking much. The cries of Familiars rang throughout the skies all around me, and the colorful streamers that hung off of buildings waved in the sea breeze. Compared to the bleakness of the Institute, Kinpago was a world full of wonder.

We'd been transported directly in front of the courthouse. I expected to see the center of Kinpago look just as it always had.

But it didn't. Multiple buildings were capsized, or lay in rubble. A couple of complexes had been destroyed, along with a few stores. People walked by the devastation with their Familiars like this was completely normal, as if they'd all gotten used to the mess.

The angels had definitely retaliated for the bombing on Celestial City. The Hawkei were rebuilding, but there was tension in the air from everyone who passed by on the street. The tribe was once again in a time of war.

Oberi nudged my hand, and I rolled up the ramp that led into the courthouse. I couldn't stay here and be sad for what the war was doing to my home, because according to my prophecy, I was the only one who could stop it. That wasn't going to be today, and I'd come here on unfinished business, so my destiny would have to wait.

Daddy and Mama were already waiting for me inside the courthouse. Relief shone on their faces when they watched me roll in. Takahashi stood nearby, but at a distance in order to give me space.

"There's my peanut." Daddy immediately ducked down to give me a hug. His embrace was a bit too careful, like he thought I might break if he held me too tightly. "How are you feeling?"

"Well enough to put this jackass away," I responded.

"That's my girl." Daddy puffed out his chest. "You've always been my little fighter."

"You look so much better!" Mama stroked my hair back.

"Six months of recovery will do that." I was glad I'd healed up since my injury. The last time they'd said goodbye in the hospital, I knew I hadn't looked great.

Daddy moved aside, and I saw that my little sister had been standing behind him. My heart fell from my chest into my stomach.

"Alana, you shouldn't be here," I said. I didn't want her to watch this circus.

"I'm almost the age you were when this happened to you," Alana said. "If you can get up there and be strong enough to tell your story, I can be strong enough to hear it. You need my support."

I wanted her to go home, but at the same time, didn't want her to leave. "So how is this going to go down?" I asked. I'd been in court plenty of times, but I'd never been on the side of the prosecution, so I didn't know what to expect.

"There are six women in total that are testifying, yourself included. The testimonies will be going in the order of crimes committed, so unfortunately, you're up first," Daddy said reluctantly.

"Not unfortunately. I just want to get this over with. Who's judging the trial?" I asked.

"John waived his right to a jury, so they asked Judge Tellus of Nivita to preside," Mama said, with a glance at Daddy.

My mouth ran dry. "They picked someone from John's own House to give the verdict?"

"He probably thinks it'll be easier to convince one person he's not guilty than a whole jury," Alana added, crossing her arms.

"Judge Tellus is fair. I've worked with him before, and he'll want to hear the truth over being loyal to his House," Daddy insisted.

I wasn't about to buy that. "And what's the bastard pleaing?"

"He refused to take a plea bargain and is maintaining his innocence," Daddy said, a sense of pure hatred in his tone.

"Good," I growled. "I don't want the Elders cutting this psycho any deals."

"They weren't going to press charges, until the evidence of his assault against the last girl was too overwhelming to deny," Alana said quietly.

"We still have to prove that he committed five other assaults," I mumbled.

"You don't have to prove anything," Daddy encouraged. "Just do the best you can, peanut, and leave the rest up to the judge."

The doors to the courtroom opened, and I knew we'd be starting soon. I managed to steady my shaking hands enough to roll myself forward. Oberi walked in front of me, keeping his ears perked.

At the entrance to the courtroom, the bailiff stopped me and withdrew a set of handcuffs. The bailiff went to put the handcuffs on me, glanced at my chair, then shook his head and pocketed them away.

Look, buddy, I can still make an escape in this thing, I thought sourly. But I wasn't going to complain, because I didn't want to look like some sort of criminal while I was stating my testimony... even if, you know, I was one.

Daddy sneered at the bailiff, who quickly looked down. I moved to the front of the room, while my family took a seat in the row behind me. As I parked my wheelchair, I looked down the row at the girls sitting on the bench next to me.

They had to be the other...victims. We all shared the same look as we shared glances. *He got you too, huh?*

There weren't any resemblances between us, except I knew we were all Toaqua girls. That was where the similarities ended, it seemed. I'd been told the rest of them had been introduced before this trial, but seeing as how I'd been at the Institute, I hadn't met any of them yet.

The girl next to me held a wadded-up tissue, but she wasn't crying. The faces of the other girls were somber, save for the small one at the end, who was already weeping. She appeared a nervous wreck. I didn't think she was going to make it through this trial.

I steeled myself. I had to be strong for the rest of these girls. I was going first. I needed to set an example and help them be able to testify.

None of these girls had a Familiar but me, which meant they were all really young. If they were sophomores at Orenda Academy, I'd be shocked.

"Mrs. Wahkin, I'm glad to see you here." A woman stood in front of my chair and outstretched her hand. "I'm Alexa Walker. I'll be the prosecuting attorney for these proceedings."

I shook it, taking in her no-nonsense stance. She certainly seemed capable. "Thank you for doing this."

"There's no need to thank me. It's my job to prosecute the worst of the worst, and from what I've read from your case file, the defendant certainly fits the bill."

"You read my case file?" I shouldn't be surprised— she had to, in order to try the case, but at the same time, it felt extremely revealing to be speaking to this woman for the first time when she already knew all about one of the worst days of my life.

"Yes. I'm sorry we didn't get a chance to be formally introduced and go over the evidence together, but the Warden of your school made it all but impossible to meet you before this moment." Walker frowned before she went on. "However, I want you to know that this trial is in my very capable hands, and I will do my best to obtain the optimal result for all parties involved."

Of course the Warden had been a jerk about this. As a victim, I should've received an interview, along with a thousand other things before this trial, but he'd illegally prevented me from having them.

No matter. We'd get this done regardless. Walker gave me a short nod before she proceeded to the prosecutor's desk, and that's when the door opened, causing my insides to melt as my darkest nightmare entered the room.

John was escorted by a couple of officers. The feeling that came over me when he entered was akin to being dunked in a tank of ice water and having my insides ripped out all at once— and I knew, because I'd had my organs outside of my body before, and the nauseated, wrecked feeling I'd felt back then was the same I was experiencing now. He was wearing a suit, which was irksome— he'd been doing time in the Kinpago jail while waiting for his trial, and I wanted him to look like the criminal he was, not the clean-cut hometown boy he appeared to be.

He looked down the row of victims, before his gaze landed on me. Horror flooded through my bones, but I told myself I had to hold his gaze. I'd seen scarier things in my day than him. I wasn't going to allow him to frighten me anymore.

He *smiled*, before he sat down. The absolute nerve of this piece of shit. Did he think this was funny? He probably assumed he was going to get off, but myself, Walker, and the five other girls next to me were going to hold him accountable.

There were a couple whimpers from the audience that sounded pathetic. I glanced over my shoulder and saw that Rosary was here, dressed in all black and looking like she was attending a funeral. My brother's abusive ex-girlfriend had a hand on her heart as she gazed at John, playing the part of the astonished partner.

I still couldn't believe she and John were together. I bet she'd bought his story that this was all made up and we were just a bunch of whores who wanted attention. That idea was confirmed when Rosary locked eyes with me, then gave me the cruelest look I'd ever received.

Ancestors, what some women would do for some dick. This was below even her.

The audience rose to their feet as the judge entered. The legal proceedings began, but I couldn't pay attention to what was being announced. The words fluttered over my head and out the door as my eyes fixated on John. I was as fascinated by him as I was disturbed and disgusted by him. And that terrified me.

Don't be ashamed. We're all intrigued by what goes through the mind of a monster, Oberi told me. *I'm not sure if we'll get any answers today. But we* will *have justice, one way or another.*

Oberi was right. As much as I wanted to understand the motives, and get to the bottom of the *why* that had happened to me, I wasn't even sure John knew himself. I could look for answers today, but if none arose, I'd have to settle for the idea that he was a beast driven on by his twisted urgings, and nothing more.

I wasn't sure if I could live with that. I didn't want to be an *opportunity* for this depraved individual, though perhaps that's all I had been. Either way, I'd find out.

"We call to the stand the individual known as Victim Number One; Mrs. Ava-Marie Wahkin," Walker declared. She turned to me, and my hands shook as I went to move forward.

They must've been talking for at least forty minutes, maybe an hour, but I'd been so absorbed in my thoughts that it'd gone by in a flash. I took a deep breath as I rolled to the front of the room, up the ramp and onto the witness stand beside the judge.

I reminded myself what I was here for. I wasn't just doing this for me. I was doing this for Opal, for Ivy, and for all the other people who'd suffered at the hands of a monster. It was time for some payback.

Oberi growled as we passed the defendant's desk, the hair on his spine standing upright. He bared his teeth in a warning to stay back. John gave my Familiar a look that said he'd kill him if we weren't in a crowded courtroom.

Yeah, right. I'd rip open his innards and eat each one, and enjoy it, Oberi replied to my thoughts.

The eyes of every person in the room were on me as Walker approached. I didn't know where to put my gaze. John bore his stare into my body, to try and intimidate me, and the act made me feel slimy. I refused to give him any attention as I attempted to find some other place to look. I tried to look at my family, but I couldn't hold it. Despite knowing I didn't have to feel ashamed, I still did, and it was going to be too hard to look at them while recounting my story. I knew they were going to get upset, and I didn't wish to watch their devastation in real-time.

I ended up holding my gaze with Alexa Walker, and no one else. She was a professional.

"Mrs. Wahkin, can you please state your name, as well as give your account of what happened?" Walker asked calmly.

I did as she asked, then gave the date and approximate time of the event before I dove into my explanation. I tried to keep it simple; said I'd suffered a recent loss at the time, that John had known of that loss, and taken advantage of that, waiting until we were alone to attack. I stated I'd gone to the women's shelter afterward, and completed an examination to gather evidence.

"Is there a reason you didn't come forward until a few months prior to this trial date?" Walker asked, although the question wasn't cruel. She was trying to divert what accusations the defense was going to throw at me.

"Yes. I was afraid of the accused, and concerned about my family, as well concerned for my reputation within the tribe," I replied.

"You are a daughter of a chieftain, correct?" Walker asked.

"Yes. Liam Mitoh is my father, and the chief of Toaqua. I am not just any child of his— I am his firstborn, which means I'm supposed to take ownership of the Water tribe someday. I didn't want my father's position within the tribe questioned because of what happened to me, and at the time, I didn't want to tarnish my own reputation with the judgements I knew would come. I felt humiliated by what had happened," I replied.

Walker nodded. "Very well, Mrs. Wahkin. No further questions on my end."

The defense attorney rose, approaching the witness stand to begin cross-examination. I think I'd heard somewhere during the introductions that his name was Gary Bernard. He looked like a jerk.

The expression on his face was hard as he contemplated what to ask. The DNA in the kit didn't lie. In order to get his client off, he had to prove what had happened was consensual. Good luck, loser.

Bernard cleared his throat before he set his eyes on me. "Mrs. Wahkin, what were you wearing that night during the encounter between you and Mister Smith?"

Gee, I didn't know that *question was going to come up.* I resisted rolling my eyes as I responded, "What I was wearing has no consequence to this case."

"Is there a particular reason you refuse to answer the question?" Bernard asked.

"Because what a woman's wearing when she's attacked doesn't matter," I responded shortly.

"Or is it because you're seeking to evade responsibility?" Bernard turned to the judge. "Mrs. Wahkin is someone who has, as I'm sure the court knows, a particularly long record. She is a convicted criminal who has been caught lying under oath more than once. Why should we believe her testimony now?"

"I'm not lying about this," I hissed.

"I'm sure that's what you want the court to believe, Mrs. Wahkin, but the judge is aware that you're currently serving time at the Darke Institute for Supernatural Offenders on multiple charges," Bernard stated. "Meanwhile, my client has never been accused, let alone convicted, of a crime in his life up until this trial. Why should we believe your story over my client's?"

"No one has to have faith in any *story* I might be telling. The evidence shows what happened to me," I said. It took everything I had inside of me to remain calm. "It's your job to prove that the evidence is insufficient, not mine. So far, you seem to be doing a poor job of that."

Bernard flushed, and Judge Tellus said, "Please refrain from being antagonistic with your answers, Mrs. Wahkin."

"Yes, your honor." I folded my hands in my lap. A wave of glee rushed through Oberi and to me as Bernard clumsily flipped through a few pages of his folder, then changed angles.

"How did your parents not know what happened to you?" Bernard asked, intensifying his tone. "The so-called injuries you sustained would be impossible to hide."

"I'm very good at applying makeup. I went to Cosmetology school. I was able to cover up the markings," I replied.

"Do you really expect us to believe that *makeup* is enough to conceal these kinds of markings?" Bernard asked skeptically.

I wasn't going to play this game. "Well, the evidence is there, so you tell me."

"Why would you feel the need to hide something so horrific from your parents? Seems strange you wouldn't tell them straight away," Bernard said. "The only reason I can think to hide this from your family is because you didn't want them to know about it— because you were compliant. And if you're as good at disguising your injuries as you say, all that proves to the court is you're exceptional at twisting the truth."

I heard the sound of Daddy starting to get up. I knew it had to be him. But I rushed to answer before he could say anything. "Do you want to know the first thing I thought— the first thing *a lot* of girls think after they've been through something like this?" I demanded. "I wanted to make sure no one ever told my father. He was the last person in the world I wanted to know about this, because I knew he'd be heartbroken, and I was afraid that after he discovered the truth, I'd feel like I'd let him down, even though what happened wasn't my fault. I couldn't take the thought of making my father— my *chief*— be in that kind of pain, no matter what I was personally going through. I hope everyone here can understand that."

There were a few nods from the audience. I saw dottings of sweat break across Bernard's brow as he rushed to say, "Or perhaps, Mrs. Wahkin, you injured yourself during a psychosis episode. You have a well-known diagnosis of bipolar depression. This *assault*, as you call it, might have been a conjuring of one of your delusions, and you could've harmed yourself as a result of this psychological fantasy."

"That doesn't explain why John Smith's DNA was found inside me. Try again." My voice was flat. This lawyer was a joke. Was this really the best John could do?

"I'm not suggesting you didn't have sexual relations with Mister Smith," Bernard rebutted, and I felt my insides curl up and wither at the suggestion. "I am merely implying that you *did* agree to have an intense sexual escapade during one of your psychosis episodes, don't remember agreeing to it, and are now crying *rape* hereafter."

Oh, great, he was trying to make the court think I was crazy. And that wasn't a hard stretch.

"I *do* have a bipolar diagnosis. But I was in my right mind, and able to consent, the night of my assault, and I did *not* give consent whatsoever. John Smith didn't care, and proceeded to attack me," I replied.

Bernard took a step closer to the stand. "You are married, is that correct, Mrs. Wahkin?"

"Yes." Why did that matter?

"In your estimate, how many sexual partners have you had?"

I bunched my hands in my lap as I replied harshly, "I've only been intimate with my husband."

"Is that something you're willing to stick to under oath?" Bernard challenged. "It's difficult for the court to imagine that a girl with your criminal background and struggles with mental health isn't promiscuous."

What did this guy want to portray me as, a loony or a whore? Pick a lane, for ancestors' sake. I frowned and said, "Well, I have to say, a violent sexual escapade wouldn't have been my first choice, seeing I was a virgin at the time of my assault."

"Can you prove it?" Bernard asked.

"Your honor, *please*," Walker said, cutting him off. "This is out of line."

"Stick to the facts of the case," Judge Tellus said.

"But your honor, this *is* a fact of the case," Bernard replied. "To gain a full understanding, we must have a full picture of Mrs. Wahkin's life."

The judge nodded. "Very well. Proceed."

Walker didn't show any emotion, and I decided to follow her lead as Bernard continued with his asinine questions. "And how is your intimate life with your husband, Mrs. Wahkin? Do you participate in any *unusual* sexual endeavors?"

I knew what kind of trap he was attempting to lure me into. "No. We don't."

This was one of the reasons Charlie and I didn't share a lot of details about our sex life, not even with our friends. If the court knew I liked being tied up and bossed around, no matter what kind of evidence I had, my testimony would be thrown out the window. I wouldn't be able to explain, and get people to understand, that what Charlie and I shared together and what John had done to me couldn't be more different.

Bernard's lip curled. "What I and the court are having trouble understanding, Mrs. Wahkin, is how you're able to be married at all. That is, how you're able to have a consensual sexual relationship with your husband, if you're as *traumatized* as you say. One would think that you'd be unable to participate in martial acts if you truly were raped. Are you going to accuse your husband of assault, too?"

It wasn't like I didn't know questions like this weren't going to come up, because as a sexual assault victim, I'd heard it all before. But the reality didn't quench the rage inside of me. I couldn't fucking see straight when he insulted my marriage like that.

Walker protested immediately. "These invasive questions are not relevant to this case!"

"Your honor, what Mrs. Wahkin is accusing my client of can't possibly be taken as valid by the court," Bernard insisted. "Keep in mind this is the same girl that, no less than three years ago, had a warrant out for her arrest by the court for grand theft auto—"

"Previous and other crimes can't be submitted as evidence, even in a case of portraying character, Gary, you know this," Judge Tellus said tiredly.

"But your honor, Mrs. Wahkin only walked away from that crime because her grandfather was able to make a financial settlement with the victim of the stolen vehicle!" Bernard insisted. "Mrs. Wahkin's DNA was found at the scene of the crime after the vehicular accident—"

"How'd you know that?" I said abruptly, without waiting to be asked. "I've never voluntarily submitted my fingerprints or DNA into any criminal justice system until I was admitted to the Institute. How was the court able to match my DNA to the crime scene?"

Bernard suddenly shut up. The hair on the back of Oberi's neck stood up, and an awful truth began pressing in on me from all sides.

John's DNA wasn't the only genetic material in the kit. Mine was included as well.

"The court used my rape kit to convict me of other crimes," I whispered. I couldn't *believe* this was real. They'd taken my DNA from the kit and entered it into a database, illegally. I'd never been more ashamed of my tribe. Tears threatened to spill over, but I'd be damned if I let them fall here.

"I... well." Bernard failed to elaborate. "That is what the record shows."

Even as my life felt like it was caving inward, I realized that for the first time, John looked uncomfortable.

And I reveled in that. It was the one thing that kept me from completely exploding on the witness stand.

Bernard backed off. "No further questions for Mrs. Wahkin, your honor."

I was more than happy to get off that stand. I kept my eyes on the floor as I rolled back to the bench where the rest of the girls sat. I felt beaten up, run over, and exposed for the entire world to see. Now all I wanted was some damn peace.

Walker stood. "We have expert testimony to add to Mrs. Wahkin's account, your honor."

"Very well. Bring them forward," Judge Tellus replied.

"We call to the stand Mrs. Mia Bylilly, to aid in the victim's testimony," Walker stated.

I recognized the woman that approached the witness stand. She'd been the lady who'd been at the women's shelter the night of my assault. I'd never forget her. She gave me a comforting smile before she sat down, which put me at ease.

"Can you describe what you do, Mrs. Bylilly?" Walker asked.

"Yes. I am the executive director of the Kinpago Women's Shelter. I provide resources and aid to victims of domestic violence, as well as sexual assault," Mia responded.

"Can you state your qualifications?" Walker said.

"I have a master's degree in psychology, and a bachelor's in nursing. I have run the shelter for over fifteen years. During that time, my staff and I have seen thousands of cases of domestic violence and assault."

"So you are certainly qualified," Walker stated. "Mrs. Bylilly, it is stated on the report that you were the one to put together the sexual assault forensic exam on Mrs. Wahkin, more commonly known as a rape kit?"

"Yes. I performed the analysis myself," Mia replied.

"Can you testify to her injuries?"

"Yes. She had lacerations on her arms and upper torso, multiple bruises on her face and both eyes, along with markings on her neck, ones that appeared to be caused by both teeth and minor strangulation."

A murmur went up throughout the courtroom. Walker gestured to a large screen, which had been set up on the side of the room, along with a projector. She clicked the projector on, and said, "Are these the photographs you took that night of the victim's injuries?"

"Yes," Mia confirmed, though her voice wavered slightly. "It wasn't a night I'll soon forget."

I didn't look at the photos the prosecutor displayed on the screen. I had no wish to remember that.

"Can you tell us more about the injuries sustained?" Walker asked.

"The victim did sustain blood loss," Mia confirmed. "Not enough that she required immediate medical attention, but enough that she had to be treated by my staff. The following photographs will give context to the injuries sustained."

The prosecutor clicked onto the next slide. Multiple people in the audience gasped. A couple of them started crying.

"As you can see, your honor, this wasn't your typical assault. This was a particularly violent act, driven by the motives of someone who is clearly disturbed," the prosecutor stated firmly.

My gods, Ava. I had no idea, Oberi whimpered in horror as he observed the slide. I still refused to look, either at the slides, or my family. It took a tremendous effort not to melt into the floor.

The only person in the room who didn't appear even slightly bothered was John. He sat there like a pompous asshole, acting like he didn't understand what the big deal was. *Self-righteous prick.*

Walker crossed her arms. "According to the file, DNA evidence was also compiled from the kit, with a ninety-nine-point-nine accuracy match to Mister Smith's DNA. What are the chances that the DNA recovered from the kit is not Mister Smith's?"

"Basically zero, your honor," Mia confirmed. "And in my professional opinion, recalling the mental state of the patient as she entered my shelter, there is no possible way that this act was consensual."

Walker asked Mia a few more questions before she ceased questioning.

Bernard droned on as he went to cross-examine Mia. "Mrs. Bylilly, it's well established by the court that you are the director of the women's shelter. But is the court also aware that a little over twenty years ago, you were engaged to Mrs. Wahkin's father?"

My mouth dropped open. I'd never heard of this before! I didn't know my dad had been engaged to someone else! My head swiveled to the side, but neither Mama nor Daddy showed any type of reaction. By the blaise looks on their faces, they definitely knew Mia personally, but she didn't have any standing on their relationship today.

Mia didn't even bat an eye, as if this was old news. "It's true. Liam Mitoh and I were arranged by our parents, as was Toaqua custom. We dated for a while, but the relationship didn't last."

"Because you cheated on him," Bernard accused. "Is your testimony today some sort of favor to Mrs. Wahkin's father, to make up for your past infidelity?"

Oh, wow. It got even *more* dramatic. I peered at my father, but Daddy appeared more annoyed than anything, like it was irritating to him that ancient history was being dragged back up. If I had to guess, he and Mia had dated before my mother had met him.

"No," Mia said simply. "We simply didn't work out. I helped Ava-Marie because I would help any woman that came to me in the state she did that night."

"But you had to know who she was when she came into your facility," Bernard accused. "Why didn't you reach out to her father?"

"Because it's not my place to reveal the worst days of my patient's lives. I'm bound to patient confidentiality, regardless of personal relationships," Mia replied sharply. "I did know who Ava-Marie was when she entered my office, but whatever relationship I previously had with her father didn't matter. To me, she was a hurting child who was in trouble. I assisted that child and did the best I could to get her help."

Mia glanced at my mother, and I saw Mama whisper a *thank you.* The emotions coming from my parents toward Mia were full of nothing but gratitude. Whatever bad blood had been between them, if any, I knew my parents forgave Mia for it now, because she'd helped me.

"Very well," Bernard grumbled, clearly pissed his angle hadn't worked out. Bernard asked Mia a bunch of stupid questions about the DNA and photographic evidence that didn't go anywhere. By the time she left the stand, he'd made the defense look absolutely terrible.

The three girls who went after me all had similar stories. John would talk to them for a while, grow a relationship, make them think that they were friends. Then, something terrible would happen in their lives—they'd break up with a boyfriend, or someone in their family got sick, or they'd fail a class. John would reach out, pretending like he wanted to help. Once he got them alone, he did what he wanted to them and lost interest after that.

None of them had any evidence, since nobody had done a rape kit like me, nor reached out for medical help. Like me, each of them had been too scared to come forward. At the time of their assaults, two of the girls didn't have any magic to defend themselves, and the other two had just gotten their powers, so they didn't know how to use them for protection.

I phased out during the other testimonies. I got the gist of what was going on, but I began disassociating almost immediately after I'd left the stand. I caught major details, yet everything else faded into white noise amongst the voices in my head.

The fourth girl had a different story. She'd been dating John at the time, so the specifics seemed unclear, though I knew exactly the angle the defense was trying to portray.

"Miss Welch, you say that Mister Smith assaulted you, but you continued to remain in a relationship with him afterward, even continued to have sex with him for months later, until the time he ended your relationship," Bernard said.

"Yes. The times after that were consensual," she confirmed. "But the first time was not. I said no."

"Then why didn't you turn him in, or at least attempt to break off the relationship?" he asked.

"He... he made me feel guilty," she insisted. "I wanted to tell someone. But after it happened, he just laid there and cried in my arms, and kept going on about what a bad person he was. I didn't know *what* to do."

I understood. She'd fawned in order to keep herself safe. Her assault hadn't been as violent as the rest of ours, so she'd found excuses and tried to tell herself it hadn't been rape. At the time, part of her loved John as much as she feared him, and the two had combined to make her comply with whatever he demanded. John, worrying that she'd expose him, put on a show of being some tortured soul to guilt her out of turning him in.

I was fed up with this trial by the time the last girl was approached by the defense. She was the girl who'd been sobbing the entire time, and she was still crying as Walker nailed her with questions. He was harder on her than he'd been on the rest of us, as he was clearly frustrated this wasn't going his way.

"Miss Flynnia, is it true that you terminated a pregnancy after your encounter with Mister Smith?" Bernard asked.

I felt my skin grow cold, and beside me, Oberi recoiled. Something hollow opened up inside of me, blooming a void in my pelvis that sank further down and ruptured.

"That's... yes," she whimpered. She wiped at her wet face as she sank lower in her seat.

"Why was that decision yours alone to make? Doesn't Mister Smith have a *right* to decide what happens to his child?" Bernard ranted.

A crawling sensation, one of cockroaches scuttling over my skin, overtook my entire body. The girl next to me went green. Similarly, I thought I also might hurl.

Bernard kept on grilling this poor girl, and every accusation he flung at her made me want to crawl into a hole. I wondered who was on trial here; John, or us.

Oberi, I don't know if I can do this. The crawling sensation that had spread over my skin was getting unbearable. If I opened my mouth, I was afraid I'd scream.

Just think of something nice, Oberi encouraged. *You don't have to be here.*

Mentally... no, I didn't. I'd testified— my part was done. My thoughts could float on out of here, and no one but Oberi would be the wiser.

And they had to, because if my spirit remained in this suffocating courtroom, with my torturer sitting twelve feet away, I'd absolutely lose my shit. I couldn't do that. I had to appear sane, because I had to get the judge to take me seriously. Even though breaking down would be totally understandable in a situation like this, it wasn't something women could afford. Showing emotion here would be considered a weakness or a lie.

I had a really hard time shifting out of my current state of mind. I attempted to take breaths, but they were shallow, and my lungs tightened with each inhale.

Oh, shit. I was about to have a panic attack.

The judge banged his gavel and said, "I would like to remind the defendant to keep his eyes forward, please."

John was looking at me. I *knew* he was. I did *not* want to give this bastard the satisfaction of watching me have a meltdown. He didn't own me. I wouldn't let him know his actions had affected me this badly.

Breathe, Oberi said gently, laying his head on my lap. *Pick a spot, focus your sight, then allow yourself to float away.*

I gulped another shaky breath, then fixated my gaze on a speck on the floor. I didn't allow it to move, and I forced my quickening heartbeat to steady. Ancestors, I wished Charlie was here.

Charlie. He *was* here. There wasn't an ocean between us. In fact, I wasn't in this courtroom at all. I was on the beach at my grandmother's house in *Hok'evale*, lying on a blanket next to him in the sand. Oberi was playing in the waves, and Charlie was laughing. I must've said something funny. The sun was bright and warm, and I could smell my grandmother's cooking wafting from the open windows of her home. Charlie reached out for me and cradled me against his chest, and I buried my face in his t-shirt, indulging in his scent as I counted the beats of his heart. He placed a kiss in my hair, told me I was his pidge and it would be all right.

I didn't care that we'd never been there together, because it was real to me. I think I spent a few hours absorbed in that vision, soaking up the rays and locked in Charlie's arms, because that was the one place on Earth I wanted to be.

It was the only way I got through it. If I didn't love him so much... I wouldn't be able to endure this.

By the time I came out of it, I realized that a warm, firm hand was grasping mine. I looked down, and saw that the girl beside me was clutching her fingers tightly in my own. She gave me a wavering, but encouraging, smile.

I returned the gesture and squeezed her hand back. This girl was a stranger to me, but we'd manage to make it through this together.

I saw my Uncle Jonah cross the room. I hadn't even recognized that he'd entered. He must've just got done testifying. He gave me a wink as he went to sit back down, telling me things were going to be all right.

Oberi, what happened? I asked. *I totally blanked out.*

Your uncle testified that he walked in while John was attempting to suffocate Miss Flynnia. The evidence your uncle gave was too damning to deny. Walker has been portraying John as a sexual sadist to the court, who needs to torture his victims to gain a sense of relief from his inner longings. He doesn't mean to kill, but he's ceasing to derive pleasure from the assaults themselves, and is pushing his victims further and further to satisfy his urges, Oberi replied.

Sounds about right. John wasn't quite the Dollmaker, but he still enjoyed torturing women, and he needed to go down for it.

After the last terrible round of questioning, John was up next, in order to defend himself for what we'd accused him of. Oberi told me not to listen, and I tried not to, although it wasn't easy.

Everything he said, about that night and about me, was straight bullshit. Worse than that, it didn't match up. John started off his story saying that I was the one who'd come on to him, then changed it mid-way through, saying that we'd been in a secret relationship for a month before that night in the woods.

Was he really so arrogant to think he'd avoid charges on a half-assed lie? It shocked me he hadn't put more effort into thinking this through. For as sick and twisted as he was, John was no criminal mastermind—

just a violent moron who thought he could commit terrible things and get away with it.

I studied John as he gave his testimony. I couldn't help it— Charlie had been working on criminal profiling over the past semester, and I'd picked up things from him as I'd watched my husband study his work.

And from what I could see, there was nothing distinguishable about John Smith. He was hardly a person... he was a *caricature*. He had no features that could distinguish him from most guys walking the street today. His appearance and personality were just as bland and common as his name. He could be any man, anywhere.

He was utterly unremarkable. A person so incredibly average that his banal normality could mark him as anybody.

And that's exactly what made him so terrifying. John could blend into his environment. He could play the nice guy, act like one of the good old boys and pretend to be the town hero, while his mind went down to dark places even hell was afraid to go.

Everybody thought that criminals could easily be spotted amongst civilized society. A scar across the eye, a swooping black cloak, and a toothless grin to match. Meanwhile, their worst nightmares roamed the streets, sleeping in their homes, attending their sports games and eating their family dinners.

The real monsters had camouflage. And you never saw them coming.

It was easy for people to doubt what he truly was. He played the part of the accused innocent so well. It was hard to believe that someone so active in the community, so seemingly generous, so polite and well-mannered, could commit a crime so heinous. Because if that were true, and someone like him could be so vile... who else was hiding in the shadows?

Rapists weren't always the terrifying men hiding behind the corner, waiting for some poor soul to walk by. They were our brothers, fathers, uncles and friends. They were the very people no one wanted to accuse.

John Smith wasn't a character, a person, or even a hideous beast. He was an unfortunate product of society, an ideal of masculinity placed on a pedestal.

And society had never been very kind to people like me.

The prosecutor poked a lot of holes in John's story, which I was thankful for. I was impressed with Walker's analysis— despite this whole situation being really tough, I had to appreciate how she performed her job like a master.

Of course, the defense pounced on any opportunity to make the victims look bad.

"Why do you think Miss Welch is testifying against you today, Mister Smith?" Bernard questioned, whirling on his client for dramatic effect— which looked phony as fuck.

"She's mad because I broke up with her," John said offhandedly. "What else is there to say?"

They moved on to character letters. John's dad came up and read a stupid letter about how John had been *depressed* since the accusations had gone public, that his reputation in town was ruined and that he wouldn't be able to get a good job now because of *all these misunderstandings*. He went on that before his arrest, John hadn't even been able to grill a steak, one of his favorite foods, because he'd been so worried about the upcoming trial.

Wow. Sorry he couldn't eat like a king, when I'd starved myself for years after the fact.

"My son's life is ruined due to these women," John's father went on. "When does it end, your honor? When does the crucifixion stop?"

My knuckles cracked as my fists shook. *His* life was ruined? What about my life, the lives of all these girls sitting next to me? Why did *his* life matter, and ours were disposable?

Rosary was the next person to petition for the freedom of this complete piece of filth, singing to the world what a good boyfriend John was and insisting the only reason any of us were here today was because we were all jealous he was dating her and not us. She completely refused to admit that John had committed these crimes while he was dating her. After all, he'd never treated *her* like that, so the rest of us had to be lying, evidence be damned.

"If there are no further witnesses, we may proceed with closing statements," Judge Tellus said as Rosary completed her saintly monologue of one of the worst people on Earth. "The court will take a short recess before I render the verdict."

Takahashi immediately swept forward and grabbed the handles of my wheelchair. "Would you like some privacy, Ava?"

"Please." I was worn out. I could tell my family wanted to speak to me, but one devastated expression from me was all it took for them to hold off. We could talk later. I just wanted a moment alone with me and Oberi.

Takahashi wheeled me into a nearby waiting room that was completely devoid of people, down a hallway that was isolated and bare. The noise of the courtroom was gone, replaced by silence and still countenance.

"I find myself rather thirsty. I believe I must find something to drink," Takahashi stated. "Do you want anything, Ava?"

I shook my head. Without another word, Takahashi left me alone.

I took in my surroundings. The window was open. Takahashi had left the door unlocked. For the first time in two years, no one was here to guard me.

He was providing me with an opening. Saying he was willing to bear the consequences should I make a break for it.

Maybe this had been an agreement with the Demigod Guardians... some sort of plan to get me out. But he didn't want to mention it to me, because after what he'd witnessed in court today, he wanted it to be my choice.

Oberi shifted into a unicorn. Her Fire mane blazed softly as she knelt beside my chair.

I could have you on my back and into the woods before they realize you're missing, Oberi offered. *And by the time they begin the search, the Demigod Guardians will have you in a safe place. The Warden and his men will never find you.*

My throat tightened as I tasted freedom. It'd be so easy... the simplest run from the law I'd ever made, and here it was, right within my grasp.

Charlie had told me to leave if I had the chance. He'd made me *promise* to escape if there was even a slight possibility that I could.

It's up to you. Oberi blinked at me with her full, black eyes.

Something crinkled in my pocket. I looked down, opened the letter that Hemlock had given me. I read the scrawled handwriting, before I wrinkled my nose and crushed the paper within my hand.

I rolled toward the window. I leaned out and tasted the salty air, inhaling a fresh, cleansing breath as the wind kissed my face.

The way the breeze caressed my hair away from my eyes reminded me too much of him. In one brisk movement, I put my hands on the pane and slammed the window shut.

A HALF AN HOUR LATER, I rolled back into the courtroom with Oberi at my side. Takahashi followed behind solemnly— he'd been sad, and yet, understanding. We hadn't spoken a word, but I knew how that's how he must've felt. At the same time, a semblance of pride had shown on his face when he'd found me still hanging around the waiting room. Maybe his counseling sessions had done some good after all.

A sour taste muddled the effect of any moral high ground I might've felt from my decision. I remembered the words the Warden had written on the letter Hemlock had given me.

It doesn't matter you're outside my walls. No matter where on this Earth you go, no matter where you plan to hide, you will never be able to outrun me.

I will always be inside your head. And for the rest of your days, that will be a prison you will never escape.

The Warden knew me better than I thought he did. That's why he'd agreed to allow Takahashi to be my only escort. He was certain I wouldn't be able to let this go, and I'd have to see this trial through.

He knew, above all, I couldn't leave Charlie behind. I would never run from the Institute, not without my friends or my husband. That's why he didn't send a guard with me. He wasn't worried about me breaking free, because he knew I'd come back.

And he was right. I was still his prisoner. No matter where I was, I'd never be able to escape the Warden, because he was a part of me now.

But I was a part of him, too. And I hoped that piece of Ava-Marie that festered inside of the Warden poisoned him every day.

The judge called everyone to order, and John stood, waiting on the verdict. Tension filled the courtroom, and it infected my limbs like ice. I knew if anyone were to touch me at that moment, I'd shatter. *Ancestors, please, hear me. Don't let him get away with this.*

Judge Tellus opened his mouth, but all I heard was white noise, and the sound of the whispering voices in my head. There was action in the courtroom— applause, people jumping to their feet. I heard the distinct sound of Rosary wailing, and I watched as the judge left the stand, almost in slow motion. The feeling in my veins changed from ice to wading through water.

Wha.... what? I thought vacantly. *What did he say?*

Thirteen years in Kinpago Penitentiary, Oberi said, satisfied. *Eleven for the attempted murder on Miss Flynnia, and two for the crime he committed against you.*

He didn't give John any time for the four other girls he attacked?

Unfortunately not, Oberi replied grimly. *He stated there wasn't enough evidence.*

I fixated on John's expression. His mouth was slightly open, and the color had completely drained from his face. Fear shone in his eyes as the bailiff proceeded to put his shaking wrists in handcuffs and take him away.

He glanced back over his shoulder at me. The terror left his eyes for a brief moment, to be replaced by the darkest flash of hatred I'd ever seen. He blamed me for this.

I didn't look away this time. Instead, I allowed our gazes to connect. *I'm not afraid of you anymore,* I thought. *And now, you're finally getting what you deserve.*

I gave my signature Ava-Marie smirk to send him off, because I wanted it to be the last thing about the free world that he remembered. Then, he was gone from my life forever.

The girls around me had mixed emotions. Two of them were hugging. The girl who'd nearly been killed cried harder, clearly out of relief. The girl beside me clenched on to her tissue, her lips set in a thin visage of rage, like she believed John had gotten off easy.

I touched her arm. She looked down at me, then gave a short nod.

"I guess it's something," she replied. "That's what matters."

"It is," I said. "And it took all of us to bring him down together. I'm glad that you were brave enough to come forward."

"So were you. We all were. Now the world is a little safer."

She moved around me to leave, appearing like she was ready to put the past behind her. For the first time in almost five years, so was I.

I turned my chair around, wheeling out of that courtroom with my head held high. I felt invigorated... almost like a new person. Takahashi approached, giving me a quick bow.

"Well done, Ava. Well done." He gently clapped me on the back, and we proceeded out of the courtroom together, Oberi strolling forward proudly.

We met my family in the hallway. My mother and Alana gave me worried smiles, but Daddy fumed, his hands fisting in rage.

"Two years. What a fucking insult," Daddy growled. "That bastard deserves a lifetime in hell for what he did to my daughter. I'll be waiting outside the penitentiary the day he gets released, you can bet on that."

"Liam, not now." Mama laid a gentle hand on Daddy's shoulder. His shoulders relaxed, and Mama turned toward me, holding her breath.

"I'm so sorry, sweetie. I know you wanted him to get more time," Mama apologized.

A huge smile spread across my face. "No. This is *great!*"

"What?" Mama glanced at Daddy, clearly concerned.

"You guys don't understand. I didn't think he'd get any time at *all*," I emphasized. "But people *believe* me! He actually got convicted and is serving time for what he did! The judge didn't think I was a liar!"

"You're right, Ava. He was held accountable, and for that, we need to celebrate," Alana insisted.

The reporters pressed in, and Mama said, "Let's get away from the press."

The news media was already swarming the courthouse, trying to get me to do an interview. Daddy bullied them off, while Mama summoned a carriage.

There was a crowd around the courthouse, but they respectfully kept their distance. I waited by the fountain in the middle of the square, while Alana sat beside me. Oberi changed into a husky to frolic in the fountain, while Takahashi went to speak with my mother.

"Do you feel relieved?" Alana asked as her fingers skimmed the fountain's edge.

"I feel... justified. Like the people in my tribe finally see me as something other than a monster," I responded.

Alana seemed intrigued by the thought. Before she could respond, a screech rose over the square. Rosary stormed toward me, appearing absolutely deranged.

"You psychotic bitch!" Tears ran down her face and ruined her mascara as she directed her rage at me. "Do you realize what you've done? You've *destroyed* my future!"

"You're better off without him, Rosary," I replied simply.

"I love him, and now we're not going to be together, because you and a bunch of other sluts made up some bullshit!" Rosary sloppily wiped at her face, and her lip rose into a sneer. "Your whole family's trash. I couldn't be happier that I dumped Ez when I did. The idiot couldn't even figure out the baby wasn't his!"

Rosary could've punched me in the face and the effect wouldn't have been as strong. I reeled in my chair. Rosary had *lied* about Ez being the father of her baby? I'd say I couldn't believe it, but I hated her, and I knew she was the kind of person who would do such a thing.

Alana immediately jumped to her feet. Her face turned redder than her fiery hair as she exclaimed, "You cheated on my brother with John!?"

"Of course I did! It's *always* been Johnny. I've wanted to be with him *forever*. I just told your moronic brother that *he'd* gotten me pregnant, because Johnny didn't want to be a dad and I knew Ez would step in to raise it," Rosary sneered.

I glanced to the side and saw, with horror, that a full news crew was standing only a few feet away. The cameras were still rolling. They'd captured the whole thing live.

Ancestors, Ez was back at the Institute, and the trial had just gotten over with. I knew he had to be watching this. I couldn't imagine what was going through his head right now.

"I hate you, Ava. You're going to get what you deserve," Rosary seethed. She reeled her hand back and used her Earth magic to rip out bricks from within the street. She hovered the stones in mid-air and sent them flying at me, straight for my head.

Oberi jumped out of the fountain to protect me, but he was still too far away. My hand twitched, and I almost called upon my magic, but a thought stopped me. If I messed up— if I even defended myself outside of Institute property— the Warden would use it as an excuse to send me to Cellblock 9 the moment I got back. I couldn't use my powers, otherwise, I'd pay for it after I returned to the prison. I'd have to let Rosary hurt me.

Jets of water came shooting out of the fountain, forming a large, protective wall. The wall of water froze to ice instantly, stopping the flying bricks in their tracks. They fell to the ground, unable to penetrate the thick, icy shield.

I thought my magic had taken over without me attempting to command it, but a wave of surprise flooded through my body as I saw Alana standing before me, her chest heaving and her hands held out. She appeared absolutely enraged. She let her hands fall, and the wall of ice melted away, water flooding the city streets.

I'd never see my sister perform magic before, and that had been *strong*. She must've just gotten her powers!

Alana shook her red hair out of her face. There was a low growl, and a couple of people gasped as a tigress emerged from the middle of the crowd. It was a beautiful animal, with shining orange fur and dark black stripes. As the tigress prowled, I watched the colors on its coat change, from white, to purple, to green, with multi-colored stripes like a rainbow. With a low, guttural sound, the tiger planted herself by my sister's side and refused to move.

Alana stroked the tiger's head and stated, "Attack my sister again, and we'll put you in the ground."

Rosary gave a choked laugh. "You want to fight? I'm all in."

She went to raise her arm again, but Daddy had stormed into the middle of the argument. He grabbed Rosary's wrist and didn't let go.

"Rosary, you need to leave," Daddy said firmly. "Or there *will* be consequences."

Rosary ripped her arm out of my father's grasp. "Whatever. I'm done with *all* of you."

She ran off. As Rosary sprinted away, a towering figure loomed over my chair.

"Ooh, that was very exciting." Uncle Jonah inched forward, appearing giddy, while his hippogriff Familiar chirped happily. "Almost as juicy as what happened back in my day."

I laughed and leaned over to give him a side-hug. "You're always around when the drama happens, aren't you?"

"Always, boo. The *tea* is what keeps me young," he replied, fluffing his hair.

I did the math in my head. Rosary had gotten pregnant when she was sixteen. John was older than I was— he was already an adult at the time she'd conceived. He'd definitely groomed her to get what he wanted.

Though she didn't want to admit it, Rosary was a victim, too. Just in a different way. I was lucky enough not to be in love with my abuser, and though she was an awful person, I felt sorry for Rosary... because she wasn't mature enough to understand the consequences John's behavior would have on her.

It was a good thing John was behind bars. Now Rosary would be safe from him, too.

"I can only buy you a few more minutes," Takahashi said quickly. "Please say your goodbyes, Ava."

Alana turned toward me. She laid a hand on her Familiar's head, who gave a chuffing noise. I couldn't believe I'd watched my sister get her magic and find her Familiar, right before my eyes. It was such a special and magical moment.

"What a cool Familiar," I said as I gazed at the tigress. "She's like a chameleon. Her coat color changes with her mood and her environment. What's her name?"

"Zareen. And she *is* pretty cool. At least she knows who she is," Alana said glumly. "I can feel it through our bond. It's so new, but she's confident. I have no idea who I'm supposed to be."

"It's not unusual to feel lost at seventeen," I told her. Hell, I felt lost all the time at twenty-one.

"I just... didn't expect this. I always thought I'd have Fire magic, like Mom, but I can't be Koigni at all. Fire burns me," Alana confessed. "And I know I don't have healing powers like you or Ez, so I must be full Toaqua."

"I guess so. But you should be proud! You're still in high school. Very few people bond or get their magic that early in the tribe," I praised.

"But I'm *afraid* of water. It doesn't make sense. I don't even like to swim!" Alana said in frustration.

"Sometimes our magic doesn't make sense when it first comes into our lives. I was upset when I found out I was a dual-caster, and overwhelmed when I realized I was actually a tricaster, but now, I think it's one of the best things about me. You'll grow to love your Water magic, too," I insisted.

Alana looked away. "I sure hope so. I just... don't understand why I have magic that feels so disconnected to who I really am."

"One day you'll learn that it's not a disconnect. It's actually who you are," I promised. "Things in life don't always make sense when they happen, but once you get some distance and look back, I swear it'll all make sense."

Alana's Familiar gave a slumbering sigh. The rest of my family and Takahashi neared, signaling I had to leave.

"Professor Hemlock is waiting for us. It is time to go," Takahashi said, placing his hands behind his back.

"Are you okay, Ava, after everything that happened today?" Mama asked.

"It's been amazing, being with all of you," I stated. "But I think I'm ready to go home."

Daddy's expression seemed quizzical. "You are home, sweetheart."

"No, I mean... back to the Institute. I miss my friends." *I miss Charlie.*

Mama and Daddy shared a glance, like they understood. I said my farewells, but they weren't as hard to make as they'd been before. For some reason, my intuition told me I'd see them very soon... and I believed her.

Takahashi tapped on his wristwatch. He whispered something into it, and before us, a portal bloomed once again. Through it, I saw the stony walls of the Institute waiting to devour me.

They hadn't, not since the day I'd stepped foot in that place, and never could.

Takahashi rolled me through the portal. Instantly, my family was gone, and the portal shut behind me as I inhaled the musty, stifling air of the Institute's inner halls.

Hemlock was standing in the Institute's entrance hall. Her mouth tilted downward as she looked at me, taking me in. "Oh, my dear."

Hemlock knelt down to give me a hug. At first, I was surprised. Hemlock wasn't the kind of person to show any sort of affection, but here she was, embracing me.

Hemlock didn't talk about any kids she might have, so I hadn't been sure up to this point if she was a parent. But her hold was one only a mom could give, and it was nearly as comforting as my own mother's.

"It's over now," I said as Hemlock drew away. "I can finally move on."

"Indeed you can," Hemlock said, and she gestured forward. "Come along. Everyone's waiting for you."

Takahashi wheeled me behind Hemlock, who led us to her secret office. When we opened the door, everyone was still looking at the widescreen television anchored to Hemlock's wall, which was playing the Hawkei News Network.

Heads immediately turned in my direction when I came in, and there were several cries of joy. I was immediately swarmed by a huge group of people, who were talking all at once. It reminded me of the noise that had been made when I'd woken up from my coma.

"Godsdamn, girl, you're so brave," Kallie praised. "Good for you, for telling your story."

"He got what he deserved," Marcus affirmed, giving a nod. "Nobody's gonna miss him."

Opal's eyes were wet, and she wiped at them as she whispered, "Thank you, Ava. Watching you obtain justice... well, it was healing for me, too."

Ivy was absolutely bawling. They didn't bother to hide their outpouring of emotion as they screamed, "Precious, you did it! You got him!"

My lip wavered as I observed Ivy's tears. I knew I hadn't just gotten justice for myself. I'd done it for them, too.

Charlie took my hands in his and squeezed tightly. He leaned down to whisper, "I'm so proud of you, pidge." Then he placed a gentle kiss on my lips.

I felt his emotions through our bond, and it was far more than he could communicate in words. Charlie had a way of clamming up when things got really emotional. Right now, he seemed overcome with pride that I'd had the courage to speak my truth, and relieved that it was all over.

Ez sat in a chair at the round table. His eyes were conflicted as I approached. "Hey, sis. I'm sorry you had to go through that. But I'm happy you got the outcome you wanted."

"Thanks, Ez." I paused, before I added sadly, "Sorry about Rosary."

Ez scowled. "I *knew* that condom didn't break."

"Oh, Ez." I felt myself sink in my seat. "Did you suspect Rosary cheated on you?"

"Not really, but I was definitely confused when she told me she was pregnant, because I knew we were being as safe as possible," Ez admitted. "But I figured she wasn't sleeping with anyone but me, so I thought the baby *had* to be mine. Guess it's just another lie."

Opal wrapped an arm around him, and Ez gave a huff. "Anyway, that's in my past. Guess we can all move forward with life now, right?"

"Absolutely," I agreed. I knew that the dark memories of my past could finally be laid to rest. For a long time, I'd been afraid of John and what he'd done to me, but I wasn't any longer. In the same way that I'd conquered the pain of my past, I knew that I could overcome my fear of the Warden.

I wasn't afraid anymore. Not of the Institute, or the monsters that lurked here, or even the Warden himself. I'd conquered everything that had tried to tear me down, and came out on top. I'd had my funeral, and accepted the new woman I was becoming, laying the old me to rest. I'd fought back against the Warden by putting that video of his abuse out for the world to see, and I'd sent my rapist to prison to pay for his crimes.

The only thing to look forward to now was my future, and the life Charlie and I would create once we busted out of here, because once that potion was ready, we were breaking out.

As I'd done with everything that had attempted to destroy me before, I'd make sure to leave a trail of ashes behind me.

TWENTY-ONE

"That's it!" Ava said proudly as she dropped the last ingredients into the potion. The recipe she'd developed with Marcus was potent, and it took days of simmering before we could add the finishing touches. The cauldron bubbled as she sprinkled the last of the herbs inside.

We sat in the Witch Tower the day after Ava's trial. Ava stirred the potion over the fireplace. A few other witches chatted at a study table across the room, but they paid us no mind. It wasn't unusual for students to brew all kinds of things in the Witch Tower, so it was the best place in the Institute to prepare the potion without drawing attention to ourselves.

Most witches at the Institute couldn't brew anything more than a simple study potion to help them focus. The Warden kept more potent ingredients on tight lock-down. But Takahashi had smuggled us the ingredients we needed, and the true potency came from Marcus' Death magic.

"Just a few more hours of simmering, and it will be done," Ava said.

Finally, I'll be free to run! Oberi raved.

A loud *thump* came from overhead, and the girls across the room shrieked.

"What the hell?" one of the girls yelled. "I've been hearing noises like that all day."

Marcus raised his voice to say, "It's just a friendly poltergeist!"

"Like a ghost?" The girl's voice raised a few pitches.

"Don't tell me you're scared of ghosts," Marcus said.

Rich coming from him. The man used to nearly piss his pants at the mere *mention* of spirits.

"Ghosts don't scare me!" the girl insisted. "I can see ghosts. I can't see... whatever the fuck *that* is. It's freaking me out!"

The *thud* came again, louder this time, which prompted another round of screams.

"Let's get out of here," one of the girls suggested, her voice trembling. "I don't mess with spirits I can't see."

The girls quickly gathered their books and fled.

Marcus sighed. "It's just Thaddeus. I don't know what they're so afraid of."

"Don't worry about them," Ava said. "The fewer people in the Witch Tower, the better. Our brew is almost done."

"I can't even communicate with him anymore," Marcus said in a depressed way. "He's so confused he doesn't respond. He just floats around all day, aimlessly trying to scare people, because that's what he thinks he's supposed to do. I don't think he remembers his life, or how he became what he is."

"It doesn't matter now," Ava replied softly. "There's nothing more we can do for him."

The cover clanged against the cauldron as Ava placed it on top.

"Does this mean we're getting out of here tonight?" Kallie asked.

"According to Takahashi, the next ship off Darke Island leaves in the morning," Ava said. "We'll take the potion tonight, and they'll discover our bodies before breakfast. Then we'll be out of here."

"And the antidote?" Kallie asked, sounding a bit nervous.

Ava's spoon *clanged* as she stirred a second cauldron. "We'll hand over the antidote to Takahashi tonight, so the Demigod Guardians can administer it on the ship and wake us up."

Rishi growled. I didn't think he liked the idea of drinking a death potion, but he was going to have to suck it up, because he needed to get out of here, too. Legally, the Warden couldn't separate us from our animal companions, so Rishi and Oberi had to take the potion with us.

This whole plan was risky. If the Demigod Guardians were

somehow intercepted and we didn't receive the antidote within twenty-four hours, we would die. But we had to risk our lives to get out of here. It was the only way.

"We should eat before we take the potion," Marcus suggested. "It will help curb the side-effects once the antidote is administered. We'll be tired and confused when we wake up."

We left the potion simmering as we headed down to the cafeteria. Marcus and Kallie laughed and joked a few paces ahead of us, but Ava and I said nothing. I hadn't been able to feel her emotions through our bond since the trial started, and that worried me. I wasn't going to pry into her head, but I needed to know she was all right.

How is she, Oberi? I asked.

That's not for me to tell, he insisted. *Don't use me to bypass tough conversations. If you want to know what she's feeling, why don't you just ask her?*

Fair enough.

I needed to steal a moment with her alone before we took that potion, and I wasn't going to manage with our friends hanging around. This couldn't wait any longer.

I stopped in the hallway. "You guys go on ahead," I told Marcus and Kallie. "We'll catch up with you later."

They continued on their way. Ava stopped beside me, and Oberi nosed my hand.

"Is everything all right?" Ava asked.

"Pidge—" I started, but I cut off when I heard footsteps coming in our direction. This wasn't the type of conversation to have out in the open. The Angel Aviary wasn't far from the Witch Tower, and Chancey had said he and Ivy had worked out a lot of stuff there. It seemed like the best place to have a hard conversation.

"I wanted a moment to talk before we leave," I said. "Let's go somewhere private."

I led her down the hall and through a doorway. We stood in what appeared to be an open field, though it was only an illusion. Birds chirped overhead, and the sun shone on my face. A soft breeze passed through the room. The sound of a harp played overhead, but I didn't hear any voices. It sounded like we were alone.

Ava gasped. "I haven't been to the Angel Aviary before. It's lovely.

The tower is massive. It appears like there's an expanse to the clear sky. It's an illusion of a sunset, with fluffy clouds passing overhead and purple, orange and pink colors reflecting off the clouds. It almost makes me feel like we aren't in the Institute at all."

She took a breath. "To think, by tomorrow, we'll be able to watch a real sunset together. I mean..."

"No, it's fine. I may not be able to *see* a sunset, but I'll watch it with you. Sunsets are amazing— the way the sun hits your skin differently, and the shift in the air. I agree. It's beautiful."

And fluffy! Oberi said as he raced across the grass. I felt the shift through the bond as she became a phoenix, flying high into the clouds.

Ava snickered. "Oberi looks like she's having fun."

I took her face in my hands, then bent down to place a kiss on her forehead. This was our last night here, and although this place had been nothing but cruel to us, it was our home. It was strangely bittersweet to be leaving. She'd never been to the Angel Aviary, and I wanted her to experience its magic properly before we left.

"I can take you to the sky, my dear," I whispered.

"Please do."

I swept her into my arms. Her proximity made my heart soar— quite literally. We hovered inches off the ground as my Air magic swirled around us. I wanted to take her away, to a place where nothing could hurt her *ever* again. This room may be an illusion, but for just the briefest of moments, we could pretend that it was real.

Air magic swirled beneath my feet, and I flew us up into the clouds. Ava reached her arms outward, laughing as her fingers passed through the water droplets. The air got colder the higher we flew.

"The sky is so pretty up here above the clouds," Ava said dreamily. "I can see the stars. It reminds me of what the sky looked like in the Ancestral Lands... the day and the night, combining all at once."

She sounded happy, as if I *had* actually managed to fly her far away from all her problems. I sensed a cloud passing by beneath us, and I used my illusion magic to make it solid, like a giant ball of cotton in the sky. Gently, I lowered the two of us onto the cloud. My feet sank into it without making a sound, then I set Ava down.

She sighed as she melted into the cloud. I sat beside her. The cloud was soft as velvet and cozier than anything I'd ever felt.

Ava ran her hands over the gentle texture beside me. "This feels amazing."

I gently caressed the side of her face. "It does. But that's not why I brought you here. I know the trial was a hard day for you. It killed me that I couldn't be there."

It's a good thing they didn't let me go. I didn't think John would've survived the trial if I'd have been there. I couldn't get all the things he'd done to her out of my head. I was grateful I couldn't see the evidence they'd presented, because it sounded horrifying. Ivy had to describe the photos to me, because they were the only person who could stomach doing so.

As the trial had uncovered every gruesome detail, I wanted to smash that TV on the ground, as if that would bring it to an end. The only thing keeping me in that chair, forcing me to listen to the evidence, was knowing that no matter what I did, Ava would still be in that courtroom. Turning away from the TV meant leaving her alone in this, and I'd never do that to her.

I remembered wanting to cover my ears, just to make it stop. I'd tugged on my hair instead, sinking down in my chair as I tried to hide my sobs from my friends. The defense made my wife out to be a liar and a whore, and I hadn't been able to do anything about it. I'd wanted to save her from that pain... but I couldn't, and that was a really fucking hard pill to swallow.

"It was difficult. But it's over now," Ava replied gently. "It would've been wonderful if you'd been there in the past to protect me, but you weren't able to, so I don't want to torture us with what-ifs."

"It's more than that. I didn't get to be there for you then, so I want to be here for you now. I'm not trying to pry. You don't have to tell me anything you don't want to. I just need to know that you're okay, and if you're not, I want to help you."

Ava squeezed my hand. "You *are* helping, Charlie. Just being here shows me how much you care. I'm not shutting you out because I'm not okay. It's more that I don't really understand how I feel— in a good way. I used to break down all the time because this terrible thing happened to me. Now I feel fucking victorious, because it's finally over."

She drew a deep breath before continuing. "It's so new to feel this way about it, and I'm still processing. The trial opened wounds that I've been trying for years to heal, and somehow, that itself was therapeutic, because for the first time, I realized I *was* healing. Speaking it out loud and facing him changed something in me. I'm not going to let it have power over me anymore."

She turned toward the sunset. "John was sentenced for his crimes. Would I have liked to see him get a harsher punishment? Absolutely. But I also got this sense of closure, and that was more than I felt I could ever ask for. I feel a tremendous relief that I'm finally *justified*. I've been called a liar my whole life, yet people believed me when I told them about this. That was all I wanted, in the end."

That was such a relief to hear. I didn't want her to hurt anymore.

"I'm here for you every step of your journey," I told her. "I may not have been there at the trial—"

"But you *were*," she interrupted. "You watched the trial all day, and you were there for me when I got back. You may not have been there *physically*, but you were there for me, like you always are."

"I wanted to be there to hold you when you got off that stand."

Ava gently brushed the hair out of my face and whispered, "So hold me now."

An intense sense of desire came through our bond, and I wasn't sure if it'd come from her, or me, or both of us. I curled her in my arms, then gently laid us both down.

Ava giggled, like my touch tickled her. "It's like a dream here."

I smiled. "I never let myself think of the future much. It's strange, having dreams."

"It's strange *not* having them," Ava said. "I've always used my imagination. Problem is, my imagination is sometimes bigger than life, and that gets me into a lot of trouble."

"I've always admired that about you," I told her. "You always believed anything was possible. I was so focused on surviving the next day that I never let myself entertain the possibilities. What's strange is that it took going to prison for me to finally accept the possibilities. It took meeting *you*."

"You don't have to just *survive* anymore," Ava said gently. "This time tomorrow, we'll be on a boat, and on our way to a new home. When we get out of here, Charlie, I'm going to show you how to live."

"You already have. I may be locked up at the Institute, but I'm not locked up in *here* anymore," I said as I tapped the side of my head. "The guy I was before never would've thought of breaking out, because he wouldn't think it was possible."

Ava took my face in her hands. "Anything's possible when we're together."

I kissed her gently, and Ava's lips parted. She didn't let go of me, and I didn't want her to. She tugged me closer, and I carefully climbed on top of her. I kissed her over and over again, and passion built inside our bond. My heart hammered as I took in my wife's sweet scent and delicious taste.

"Kiss me," Ava begged. "Everywhere."

She didn't have to say anything else. I could feel the wanting through our bond and knew exactly what she needed. I was eager to oblige. All I wanted was to pamper her— to shower her with love and show her that *nothing* would ever hurt her again as long as I was around. When she was in my care, she would always be safe.

My kisses trailed down her body. Ava tilted her head back, taking in shallow breaths as I pressed my lips to her skin. My hands slid under her skirt, roaming over her soft skin.

Ava's skin grew hotter from her Fire magic, and I could feel desire pulsing through her. I pushed her skirt upward, until it was around her middle. Ava's fingers roamed through my hair as I ducked my head and pleasured her with my tongue. This wasn't the playful, rough sex we'd had over the past few months. This was gentle and sweet, though it surged with passion that made my heart pound like a drum in my chest. Her moans were like music, keeping in time with my heartbeat. It seemed we'd composed a glorious tune inadvertently.

We fell into sync with one another, and the composition seemed to move in a pattern. We played out verses and choruses with the rhythm of our bodies, going from soft and sweet and to intense, then back again. We did this over and over again as passion built up inside our bodies. I didn't know how long it lasted, but I didn't want it to end. Then the song transformed into a bridge, until reaching a crescendo that peaked with Ava's climax. She tugged my hair lightly, begging me to fill her with my love. I undid my pants, then slid into her effortlessly, moving to the rhythm of the gentle harp above us. It was slow, and I felt every intoxicating sensation as I slid in and out of her.

I wanted to go longer, to never let this beautiful dream end, but I couldn't take it anymore. I spiraled into an earth-shattering orgasm, and she gasped as I filled her all the way up.

I sagged into the cloud beside her, and Ava leaned over to run her hands over my chest. "You're always gonna be my safe place."

"That's what I'm here for. You'll always be safe with me." I couldn't do anything to defend her during that trial, but I damn well could make sure she would never have to go through anything like that again. It was behind us now. I'd made peace with how badly she'd been hurt, and how powerless it had made me feel to know I couldn't change it, but what drove me on is knowing we had a future together, despite everything that had happened. I'd do everything I could to make sure I could give her a full life from now on, because my wife deserved it.

We remained in the clouds a while longer, before deciding we should get to dinner before the cafeteria closed. I floated Ava down from the clouds and set her back in her chair again. Oberi squawked from the clouds, like she didn't want to come down.

"Time to go, Oberi!" I called up to her.

Oberi grumbled in our minds, but she swooped down and landed on the back of Ava's chair.

"What do you want for our future, Ava?" I asked as I pushed her out of the room. We were actually getting out of here, and I liked this idea of dreaming and planning for what was ahead.

She thought about it for a moment. "I don't know. It's hard to think of life outside of the prison, one that doesn't have to do with all these prophecies."

"One day it'll end. Then what are we going to do?" I asked.

She sighed. "I don't know if our destiny will ever be over. But I still want to do anthropology. I don't know how, seeing as it's going to be difficult investigating ruins and caves when I've got this wheelchair, but I'll make it work somehow. What about you?"

"I know I want to be a supernatural bounty hunter, but I've never really thought of how that would fit into our lives," I admitted. "I'd be traveling a lot. I couldn't do that if we started a family."

"You want kids?" she asked curiously.

I shrugged. "Maybe. I haven't really thought about it. But yeah, if we could make it happen, I don't see why not."

If anything seemed like a far-off dream, it was children. I never thought I'd be a father, because I never had the resources to provide for anyone else. But once we got out of here, we could get real jobs and make real money. I could put food on the table and actually provide for my family. I knew Ava wanted to go wild and travel around the world and all that, but eventually, I figured we'd both want to settle down.

"I don't think I could be a mother," Ava said. "It'd be too hard. I'm in a wheelchair and have bipolar, and you're blind. How are we supposed to be good parents?"

"Our disabilities have never stopped us before," I told her. "We'll find a way to parent *our* way. Society doesn't get to tell us what we can and can't do. But we'll only do that if it's what you want."

Ava thought about it for a moment, before she whispered, "Perhaps someday."

I didn't *really* know if I wanted kids or not. Ava made a point about our disabilities, but I didn't see them as something that held us back— just something we had to adapt to. Ultimately, it was her decision, because it was her body. And if her body was too damaged to have kids, there were other ways to do it.

But I wanted that to be her choice. Yeah, I thought it would be cool to be a dad, but I wouldn't push it if it wasn't what Ava wanted. She was enough for me.

A loud scream came from down the hall, and I stopped in my tracks.

"That sounds like it came from the Witch Tower," I panicked.

I whirled Ava's chair around, and we rushed to the tower. We could hear Kallie and Marcus shouting at someone, but they spoke so loudly I couldn't make out what they were saying. We'd been in the Aviary so long, they must've been done with dinner already. I heard another voice — Ivy, by the sound of it. They must've been the one who'd screamed.

"Oopsies," a girl said innocently. "If you didn't want anyone to touch your potion, you shouldn't have left it lying out."

"What the hell is going on here!?" I shouted when we reached the top of the stairs. I heard the sound of hissing. At first, I thought it was Rishi, until I realized it was the fire we'd been brewing over. The bubbling sounds of the cauldron were gone. I felt all the blood drain from my face when I realized what must've happened.

Ava reacted quicker than me, and she wheeled across the room so fast I lost my grip on her chair. "Esther, you *bitch!*"

"I didn't mean to!" Esther insisted. She was really good at playing the innocent party, but we all knew she was *far* from innocent.

"She knocked the potion over on purpose!" Ivy insisted. "I saw her."

"How was *I* supposed to know it was yours?" Esther pouted.

"What are you even doing in the Witch Tower?" Ava demanded. "You're not a witch."

"Neither are you," Esther shot back. "*All students are permitted to use all recreation rooms, regardless of their magical abilities, without discrimination against age, gender, and race.*"

It sounded like she was reciting a line from the handbook. She had to be the only person in this place to have ever read it.

My hands curled into fists. Esther had poured out our potion— our ticket out of the Institute! That was our only shot out of here!

Esther continued to justify herself. "All students have access to these cauldrons and ingredients—"

"*GET OUT!*" I roared.

Esther's demeanor faltered. "I beg your pardon. I'm allowed to be here as much as you—"

"Get the fuck out, Esther!" I pointed to the door, and Oberi growled. "Leave! Before I make you!"

"That's a threat!" Esther cried. "I'm reporting you to my uncle!"

"Go right ahead." I fully expected her to report us, anyway.

Esther fled the room, like she was hell bent on finding the Warden. Truth be told, I think I scared her, but that was a poor consolation.

"Esther knocked our cauldron over!" Marcus spat. "She did it on purpose. She must know what we have planned."

"I doubt it," Ava said. "She would've made worse threats if she knew. I bet she saw us leaving the Witch Tower and snuck in behind us. When she couldn't figure out what we were brewing, she dumped it to make sure we couldn't use it."

Marcus paced around the room, sounding distressed. "This changes everything."

"The potion isn't our only problem," Ivy said in a chilling voice. "I've got news."

It better be fucking good news, because Esther's little *accident* had pissed me off to high heaven. We had no back-up plan, which meant our attempt at escape had failed. We were supposed to be getting out of here in the morning, and now, we were fucked.

Ivy drew a deep breath, then said, "I just got word that Erasmus was found dead this morning— tortured, by the looks of it."

Fuck! "I thought vampires were immortal," I growled. How the hell had this happened? And what else could go fucking wrong?

"There are a few ways to kill them," Ivy said. "Which means this was a targeted attack. Witnesses couldn't identify the men they saw fleeing the scene, but they looked like angels. My father doesn't believe this had anything to do with the job Erasmus was on."

"The Warden did it," Marcus blurted.

I gritted my teeth. "I wouldn't put it past him. The phone lines are tapped. If he got word we were trying to contact Erasmus, he might've put two and two together."

"And he killed him before we could get answers!" Ava raged.

"I came to tell you, but... then we found *her* here," Ivy sneered.

"We can't sit around here and talk about it," Kallie said. "Esther's gone to get the Warden, and he'll be back any minute with guards."

"Kallie's right," Ava agreed. "We need to go somewhere private."

We ditched the Witch Tower as fast as we could. My friends and I avoided the guards and made our way outside, then snuck into the trees. After making sure we weren't followed, we ducked into the Liar.

We hadn't been here in what felt like ages, because for the longest time it didn't feel safe, not with the Warden's eyes on us. Right now, it was the only place we were getting any privacy.

Ivy hadn't been there before. The Lair had always been a place just for the four of us. Ivy gasped as Marcus lit a witch light, and I heard their skirt swish as they spun around to take in all of Marcus' paintings. The rocks here had become Marcus' own personal canvas, and he'd covered the Lair from floor to ceiling with his art.

"This place is beautiful!" Ivy raved. "Marcus, you're so talented. This door you painted looks as if I could open it and step into another world."

"It's even better when Kallie uses her illusion magic to make my art come to life," Marcus said.

"Ooh, can I see?" Ivy asked. They were trying to lighten the somber mood, but it wasn't exactly helping. We were supposed to be breaking out of here in the morning. That wasn't possible anymore without the potion, and I was kind of pissed that Ivy was more concerned with the artwork than the problem at hand.

I hated Esther for a lot of reasons, but I hated her even more now. I should've ripped her head off before she had a chance to leave the Witch Tower. I couldn't contain my anger, and I slammed my fist into the rock wall. Pieces of rock chipped and clattered to the floor.

Fucking hell!

I whirled toward Ava. "What are we going to do?"

"I don't know." Ava sounded calculating, like she was trying to work out the pieces in her head.

I felt completely hopeless. "Oberi, any ideas?"

If I had any, I'd have offered them up a long time ago. This potion was our best shot.

"Can we recreate it?" I asked Ava.

"We're out of time," she said. "Esther's gone to tell the Warden we're brewing something. Even if we *could* get enough ingredients again, the Warden will know what we're up to. We were supposed to be on the ship *tomorrow*. The Union reps leave campus in the morning, and if they're gone before we are, we'll no longer be protected by their protocols. The Warden will find excuses to keep our bodies at the Institute until it's too late. We've got to find another way out of here."

I pressed my fingers to my temples. "So we return to the drawing board. Great— the drawing board is blank. Where do we even start?"

Perhaps you have more information than you realize, Oberi said.

"Yeah, let's just find another way to fake our deaths," I replied sarcastically.

That may not be the only way out, Oberi added.

"We've tried everything," Ava insisted. "All I've got is my Aunt Maddie's journal, and there are no clues in here about escaping. Unless..."

Ava rifled around in the bag that hung on her chair, then pulled something out of it. Pages rustled as she flipped through it, looking for a hint. "Let's review this one more time. We have drawings of my Aunt Maddie's visions, along with some cryptic messages that don't make sense. Then there are the blood stains—"

"Blood stains?" Ivy overheard our conversation, and their interest piqued. They abandoned Kallie and Marcus, who were still playing with Kallie's illusions. Ivy hummed lowly as they examined the journal.

"I can't seem to figure out the blood stains," Ava admitted. "The page here seems older than the others, which has to mean *something*. But is it a clue, or an accident?"

"Oh, it's a clue, all right," Ivy said. "Spilled blood can leave behind information, like what the individual was doing at the time the blood was spilled, or even convey thoughts they were thinking."

"How do we access that information?" I wondered. "None of us have ever worked blood magic before."

"I'm a vampire, my dear. Vampires are quite intimate with blood magic. Let me see." Ivy took the journal from Ava.

"Ew, are you licking—?" Ava started, but Ivy shushed her. A heavy darkness entered the room... like we were in the presence of something disturbed.

Ivy's eyes are turning black, Oberi muttered beside me. I froze in place, waiting to see what Ivy's blood magic would uncover.

"It's Erasmus," Ivy said breathlessly. "It's *his* blood."

"The same vampire who wiped Amalie's and Dante's memories?" I asked.

"The very one," Ivy said.

I tilted my head. "I thought vampires couldn't bleed."

"They can," Ivy explained. "When you become a vampire, your blood freezes in your veins. *I* bleed, because I'm half-merfolk, but most vampire blood is thick like lead, and it doesn't flow well. They'll still bleed if you cut them open, but it doesn't spill as fast, and it's not going to kill a vampire that's already been changed."

"How did Erasmus' blood end up in my journal?" Ava wondered.

"I don't know," Ivy replied. "Your aunt must've run across it on her travels and knew it was important to your prophecy. It looks like it's been sewn into the journal."

"What clues did he leave behind?" Ava asked.

"Under the water, yet on land," Ivy said.

I furrowed my brow. "What does that mean?"

Ivy handed the journal back to Ava. "I don't know. That's all I heard. It's got to mean *something*, right? I mean, if Ava's aunt thought it was important enough to leave in the journal, it has to be leading you somewhere."

"It's code— some sort of clue. The Divinity Keys..." Ava said thoughtfully. "Erasmus knew where Dante hid the key."

"We know the merfolk key was left on the ship," I added, putting the pieces together.

"Right, so the clue must be telling us where the ship is..." Ava trailed off. "But of course it's under the water, because it sank. What could *yet on land* mean? The ship can't be underwater *and* on land at the same time."

"Maybe some sort of cave you can only get to underwater?" I wondered. "Except... how would the ship get there? Unless the cave entrance was big enough..."

I repeated the clue out loud, as if they would help us decipher it. "Under the water... on land. Under... the island?"

Ava drew a sharp breath. "*The lake!*"

The same time she realized it, Kallie shouted from the other side of the Lair. "Holy shit! You guys need to see this!"

Something creaked, like a door opening on hinges. The air in the Lair shifted, like someone had opened a hole in the rock. I felt my stomach bottom out as I heard the *thrum* of magic echo through the Lair.

"Ancestors, Kallie, what did you do?" Ava gasped.

"She brought my painting of a door to life and opened it. It's a portal!" Marcus cried.

Oberi barked, and his tail whacked me on the leg as he spun in a circle. *We can get out of here!*

I felt the whoosh of the portal's air upon my face as we approached the door slowly.

"Is it safe?" Ivy asked.

"It feels stable to me," Kallie said.

Ava wheeled forward. "This looks like it's leading outside the prison. I don't recognize this forest. Those trees don't grow here on Darke Island."

"How'd you get past the prison wards?" Ivy questioned.

Kallie replied, "I was messing around with Marcus' art, combining our magic through simultension. Our magic must be strong enough to overpower the wards. I can't make a portal on my own, but if Marcus' magical paintings combine with my portal magic, it's strong enough to get past the boundaries holding us here. I don't think I could create a portal with anything— just a doorway. I brought the door to life, and it fused with my portal magic."

"What are we waiting for?" Marcus asked. "Let's go!"

"Not yet," Ava protested. "We think we found the merfolk key. *Under the water, yet on land.* It's got to be in the siren lake."

"We already searched the lake. There was nothing in there," Kallie argued.

"Because that's what Amalie *wanted* everyone to think," I said quickly. "In our vision, Amalie promised Erasmus the authorities wouldn't find the ship. She had a plan to hide it."

"When the ship went down, Amalie must've portaled it to the closest inland body of water, to throw off the authorities," Ava said. "She knew the people looking for the ship would search the ocean, just as the Warden's been doing."

"Then why didn't we find it when we searched the lake the first time?" Marcus questioned.

"Amalie must've put an illusion on it, to hide it," Ava explained. "But I think it's more than that."

"The giant squid," I added, piecing it together. "It becomes aggressive, but only in certain parts of the lake. That must be where the ship is."

"This sounds like a long shot," Marcus protested.

"Maybe, but it's possible. Kallie, do you think that's something Amalie would do?" I asked her.

"I... I think so," Kalie said slowly. "I know, because it's what *I* would do. This explains why the Warden hasn't found it yet— because he's looking out at sea, in all the wrong places."

Ava gasped. "Or he was looking in the *right* place, and he missed it! The Warden was searching the lake for weeks. He *knew* something was down there, but I bet he didn't know what he was looking for, just like us. We assumed he stopped looking because he found something, but what if he gave up like we did? To find what he was looking for, the Warden would have to break the illusion to find the ship. That's why the sirens can't see it, either. Think about it. Our first clue was leading us to the siren lake, but Amalie was leading us to the *key*."

Marcus considered this for a few moments. "All right. Let's say the ship *is* in the siren lake. How do *we* break the illusion and find it?"

"I can do it," Kallie said. "A fae illusion can be broken by its caster, and I'm Amalie incarnate. No one on this planet is going to be strong enough to break my own magic besides myself. Even if the Warden knows there's an illusion down there, he wouldn't be able to get anyone besides me to end the spell."

Kallie gasped, like all the pieces finally made sense. "If Amalie used all her magical energy to portal the ship inland, and create the illusions to hide and protect it, she wouldn't have had any magic reserved for herself. It's no wonder she and Dante got caught. She didn't have the energy to fight back or portal them away once they were on land."

"So we can sensibly assume that *The Assassin's Destiny* is in the lake, and so is the merfolk key!" Ava proclaimed.

"And you want to go after it?" Marcus asked in disbelief. "Ava, we could leave *right now*."

"Without my brother? What about Opal, Chancey, and Alistair?" Ava challenged. "This is a quick, easy job. We need to gather our things, get the merfolk key, then we can make a run for it. The Warden doesn't know Kallie can make a portal with your art. We can leave at any time."

"So let's *go*, before he finds out!" Marcus insisted. "We don't know for sure that *The Assassin's Destiny* is in the siren lake."

"We don't know that it isn't," Ava shot back. "Marcus, we're so close, and we need to act *fast*. We can get this done tonight. Then, once we have the key, we can use this portal to get the hell out of here."

I stepped forward. "Ava's right. We can't afford to come back to Darke Island once we're off of it. It's too risky, and if we have a chance to obtain a key tonight, we need to take it. So here's what we're going to do. Ava and I will find Hemlock and Takahashi. They have to know about our change in plans, so they can alert the Demigod Guardians and arrange a place for us to meet up with them. We need a place to hide once we leave the island. We'll run back to our room and gather some essentials, and get Sprigs. Marcus and Kallie will go get Alette and Kallie's grimoire."

"What do I need to do?" Ivy asked. "Because you damn well know I'm not gonna stay in this joint while the rest of you book it outta here."

"You go gather the others and tell them what's going on," I said.

"The four of us will meet up at the lake and get the key, while the rest of you wait for us in the Lair, so we can escape through the portal together."

"Finally, a decent plan," Ivy said. "You know, big shot, this just might work."

"Hold on a second," Ava said. "We should take the keys that we already have. If we're breaking out, we need to have them on us at all times, so if something happens and we can't come back to the Lair, we don't leave them behind."

"Right. Marcus can always paint us another door that I can shift into a portal if we get stuck somewhere," Kallie said.

Ava went to the magical chest Kallie had created with her illusion magic, the one that only *we* could unlock. Ava withdrew the four keys we already had in our possession— the keys for elementals, witches, fae, and angels— and put them into her pocket. My heart was pounding wildly. We were making so much progress... all we had to do was not screw it up.

Kallie closed the portal, and we hurried back inside the prison. The halls were eerily quiet as we went our separate ways. Ava and I rushed to Hemlock's classroom, but didn't find her there, so we continued down the hall to Takahashi's office in the counseling tower. Ava waited at the bottom of the stairs as Oberi and I took several flights up, but we found that room was empty as well.

Fear gripped my chest, though I forced myself to stay calm. Where were they?

Did you find them? Ava asked telepathically when we returned to her side. She was worried about speaking out loud, which was a genuine concern, with how silent these halls were.

No. They're not around, which is weird, because they told us one of them would always be in their office if we needed them, I added.

Something's wrong, Oberi panted.

Yeah. It's too quiet, I mused. *Where are all the guards?*

What if the Warden found out Takahashi and Hemlock were working with us after Esther reported our potion? Ava thought frantically.

I didn't get a chance to respond before we heard shouting down the hall. "Hey! You kids aren't supposed to be down here!"

Heavy hands landed on us, and Oberi barked.

"Mandatory assembly! All students are to report to the Hall of Mirrors immediately," the guards growled.

I went to yank my arm away, but thought better of it. Ava had the keys on her, and if I fought back, they'd search us. It was best to go along with them right now.

Something's going down, Ava said, and her thoughts tightened with worry.

Don't let them find the keys, I warned.

I won't.

The guards didn't give us any choice. One of them pushed Ava's wheelchair— without asking, I might add— and the others held my wrists tightly as they escorted us to the Hall of Mirrors.

The room was in chaos when the guards shoved us inside. Judging by the noise, every inmate in the school had to be packed into this room. Confused chatter filled the area, like nobody quite knew what any of us were doing there. Our friends must've seen us, because they hurried to our side. They were all here, gathered in a tight group in the back corner of the room.

"What's going on?" Ez asked us. "Ivy said—"

"I said *nothing,*" Ivy interrupted, warning Ez not to say anything out in the open.

"The Warden's searching our rooms," Kallie said in a panic. "The guards picked up Marcus and me in the fae cell block. We saw them confiscating my things, including my grimoire. They shoved Alette into a cage and took her away!"

I gritted my teeth. "That means they've got Sprigs, too."

Alistair cracked his knuckles. "Where'd they take them? I'll get 'em back."

"Let's not go in guns blazing until we know what's happening," Chancey told Alistair.

"Does anyone know *why* we're here?" Opal asked.

"No idea, but it can't be good," I said. "We couldn't find Hemlock or Takahashi."

"Which means something's wrong." Ava's voice was dark. She was certain the Warden was planning something big.

The sound of voices rang out overhead, playing a chord in harmony. A choir stood on the balcony, filling the room with their tune, and the crowd around us quieted. The harmonious chord should've sounded beautiful, but the music grated on my nerves.

This is quite the spectacle, Oberi said snidely.

The music cut off. It became so quiet that a single pair of footsteps echoed off the walls.

Ancestors, what is the Warden wearing? Oberi asked rhetorically.

He's got on a white robe, and he's glowing with angel magic, Ava told me. *Esther's standing beside him in a gold dress.*

It sounded a bit *too* angelic, if you asked me. What was the Warden up to?

It looks like... Ava paused, like it made her sick to say. *Like the Warden's portraying himself as a god.*

I was going to barf.

"Thank you all for joining us today," the Warden said— as if we'd had a choice. "The time has come for me to bring you a message. Until now, we have concealed the God of The Mission. Today, we are bringing that new god into the light."

The Mission kids clapped, and the Warden waited for the applause to die down. He was really drinking this up.

"This new god is a more fair god than all the gods who have come before," the Warden announced. "This god believes that together, The Mission will unite to bring down the evil and unjust deities we previously put upon the throne of the afterlife, who watch and observe as we suffer on this planet, and do nothing to intercede in that suffering. Today, I proclaim that we will worship these vile deities no more. Your new god is a moral being who will rule fairly, providing mercy to the suffering, a god who will deal punishment to villainous souls. I say to you now that this god of truth and wisdom... is I."

The sound of shuffling bodies met my ears, and I realized people were *bowing* to him. Panic filled my chest. The Warden was no longer concealing his true motives, but working out in the open. And people were *worshiping* him for it. It made him more dangerous than ever.

The Warden spoke louder, like he couldn't contain his pleasure. "As there can only be one true god, there can only be one true chosen one. My dear niece, Esther Taurus, is my chosen daughter, the one I have hand-picked for the crop of The Mission, to absolve you of your sins and lead you into the light."

Esther's voice boomed over the crowd. "I have a special magic, to see the pain inside of all of you. As a Mission member, I vow to use my powers for good. I choose to take on the pain of every Mission member, and be the sacrificial offering in order to pursue my lord's work! Come to me and tell me your troubles, and your lord will forgive you of your sins and crimes!"

"Rise up against your captors and join me in this battle against the gods of old," the Warden continued. "Together, we will make this world a better place for all those who inhabit it. I vow to you now that I will end the war between our supernatural communities, and unite them all under my banner, so that there will evermore be peace in this world. Cast away your sorrows, and help me create this new world where this is no pain, no sorrow, no suffering. For in my world, we will no longer experience death! Once we overthrow the gods of the afterlife, I will abolish suffering and dying. Join our holy army, and put upon the armor of The Mission's word, to combat those lost souls who continue to worship false gods. In doing so, you will receive a spot in eternal paradise. Defy us, and you will be cast into darkness!"

"May the lord's eyes be upon you!" Esther called brightly.

"For he is always watching," a collective voice replied.

It caught me off guard, and I took a step back, though the wall was right behind me. The Mission kids must've been learning that prayer for months in their training. It was creepy as hell.

"In order to achieve the goal of The Mission, we need to unite, and that starts with uniting our family here at the Institute," the Warden said. "Many of our brothers and sisters are lost, but they will find their way back to us."

Ancestors, I couldn't believe anyone was buying the shit he was selling. The Warden wasn't a savior. He was a tyrant, and these people needed to see that, before it was too late! He was trying to start a holy war with heaven itself, and I knew he'd use the dark gods he'd made deals with to raise hell against them.

My spirit became heavy as I realized the Warden actually had a chance at implementing, and succeeding, in his insane plan. He had dark gods on his side, and the army of The Mission behind him. He'd use the chaos going on between the supernatural communities to his advantage, and grow his cause. Desperate people who'd been displaced and hurt by the war would look for an answer to their suffering, and the Warden would offer them one. Hell, he was promising an end to the war, to *all* wars, forever, and that's all some people wanted. Others outside the Institute would join him. And he'd make his followers so radical that they'd eliminate anyone who dared to stand up to him.

We were so fucked.

"Changes are coming to the Institute," the Warden announced. "Curfew is now waived for all members of The Mission, and those who join us will be given free reign of the Institute grounds. Students who have yet to join The Mission will now be considered a threat unto themselves and put on lockdown, until they are lost no more."

Someone booed loudly, but the guards quickly stepped in and silenced them. I heard an *oof*, then the sound of feet dragging as the guards pulled them out of the room. My friends and I kept our mouths shut.

"The Mission is an essential component to running this school," the Warden said. "All professors, staff, and students will be properly educated on the goals of The Mission. Those who oppose The Mission will be detained and will undergo a training seminar. These seminars have a high success rate. All will be healed and join us."

Of course it had a high success rate. I bet he tortured people until they agreed to bow at his feet and call him *lord*.

A wave of nausea passed through me as I realized that's what he was doing to Hemlock and Takahashi at this very moment. They'd been captured, and he intended to brainwash them by any means necessary. It chilled me to think of what methods he might use.

"The time to unite our family is now," the Warden concluded. "Our lost brothers and sisters will be escorted by the guards to their new holding cells, where they will await their training seminar. And remember... the lord is always watching."

Thundering applause erupted toward the front of the room. The Mission kids were *celebrating*, while the rest of us remained dead quiet. This was a death sentence for anyone who didn't join The Mission.

The crowd started to move, though I didn't think it was on their own accord. We were crammed closer into the corner.

"Seminary kids, let's get moving!" a guard barked.

The guards are on the move, Oberi said.

"They're going to lock us up!" Opal panicked.

"We have to make a break for it," I stated in a low whisper.

"We can't leave Hemlock and Takahashi behind," Ava argued. "The Warden must have them detained somewhere."

"We may not have a chance to save them," I told her quickly. "The last time we tried to save people, we went to the Underground, and we didn't all make it out alive. We can't risk that again."

"We may have already lost our chance to escape," Marcus whimpered. "Kallie can't portal from anywhere in the Institute— she needs my art to do it, and I don't have time to paint another door. We have to use the one in the Lair."

Ava hesitated. It really fucking sucked to talk about leaving people behind, but at this point, we had no time to lose. We couldn't go through a repeat of what happened in the Underground. If we didn't make it, it wasn't just our lives on the line; it was the fate of the world. Ava and I still had a prophecy to fulfill, and we couldn't do it under the Warden's torture. We had our chance to leave...

And I feared we might've already missed our window.

Ava's thoughts slipped through our bond, and I knew she was warring with herself. She didn't want to leave anyone behind, but we'd run out of time. We had to get out of here, and nothing could slow us down.

Takahashi and Hemlock would want us to run, I told her through our thoughts. *They'd tell us to go.*

Mentally, I felt her reserve crack and break. It was such an odd feeling, to experience Ava give in, that it made me ill. I *never* wanted Ava to give up, to break her spirit. But we'd run out of options.

"There's no choice," Ava finally said. "We get the key, and then we run."

"The guards are coming," Ivy warned.

"Ez, take the keys," Ava whispered. They clinked lightly as she handed the magical keys to her brother. "The Warden will be watching me. He can't find these keys on us."

"I'll keep them safe," Ez promised.

The guards' footsteps came even closer. I knew I needed to give orders now, before they overheard us.

"No matter what happens, we all have to find a way out *tonight*," I said to the others quickly. "Break out anyway that you can. We'll meet in the Lair."

"You got it, boss," Alistair replied, then he was smart enough to shut up— we all were.

There were screams around us as inmates were cuffed and taken away. The Mission kids cheered, like they were *happy* we were getting dragged off to ancestors only knew where and forced into The Mission's indoctrination.

They thought they were saving our souls. They didn't realize we were all being played.

"Get your fucking hands off me," I heard Chancey say, and he shoved at a guard. He tried to fight back, but I heard his voice carry off as a mess of guards yanked him away.

Marcus and Kallie stuck with Ava and me, but I heard the rest of our friends being forced in different directions, and taken to opposite holding cells.

I knew this was it. We either broke out of this prison tonight, or we'd be dead by morning. I refused to let myself be a pawn for the Warden and brainwashed into his mad crusade for power. If I had a choice to join him or perish, that decision would be death.

I knew the Warden would make good on that promise.

TWENTY-TWO

This was bad. No, it was *worse* than bad. We were in some deep shit, and if we didn't figure it the fuck out, it was all over from this point.

The guards took the four of us, along with about fifty other inmates, to some sort of storage room that they were using as a holding cell. Bunk beds were packed inside, but that was the only furniture in the blank space. The walls smelled like they'd just been painted, a morbid color of gray. There were a couple of empty wooden boxes in the corner, and a glass wall at the far end of the room that was on our level, but that was all I saw. Worried conversation and a few suppressed sobs filled the room as the doors slammed shut behind us.

I still had my bag, so they didn't take our stuff, just put us in a place where we were confined. The moment we entered, I immediately felt sick. There was inferichite inside the walls of the room, and wards alongside it, coupled with noxite... and inferichite. My powers felt heavily suppressed.

"Listen up! None of you kids are getting out of here unless you convert to The Mission!" the guard boomed. "The rest of you are stuck here until you comply, or you'll be sent to conversion therapy first thing in the morning. Might as well get comfortable!"

A couple of students called out swear words and weak threats, but nobody dared to attack the guards. A small group hurried toward the guards and agreed to join The Mission, and they got to leave, but the rest of us stayed back. I heard the doors to the room lock, sealing us in.

"We can't let them take us to conversion therapy. They'll separate us, and who knows what they'll put us through to get us to convert," I whispered to the others.

"But how are we supposed to get out of here?" Kallie asked. "You guys can feel it. There's inferichite all around this place!"

"Where are the guards?" Charlie asked.

"Two are guarding the door. The rest are on the other side of a glass wall," I said glumly. "It's some type of observation room. They can see us, but we can't get into it."

"There are a set of keys hanging on the wall in the observation room, over a desk, which probably opens the door out of here," Marcus added. "But there's no way we can get inside. There isn't even an entrance to the area from this room."

"I can't pick these locks open, even if the guards got out of the way," Kallie said. "I can sense that they're locked down with magic. Maybe I could overpower it, but it would take time, and we'd be caught by the time I broke it or Ava melted the locks."

"Can you reverse time?" Marcus asked Kallie.

Kallie pulled at her hair. "I can, but I don't want to unless it's a last resort. There are too many potential consequences, especially around inferichite. We can't afford to go back and fix anything if we mess up. We need to get out cleanly on the first try, and that's just too difficult with time travel."

"Can you paint a door if Kallie conjures some paint, Marcus?" Charlie asked.

"No. The guards are going to notice. I can't do it in secret, it would take too long, and it's too dark in here to paint well. I have to make the painting as realistic as possible for us to use it as a portal," Marcus replied.

"Then we're going to have to find another way," Charlie said. "Perhaps we can use the darkness to our advantage. We can create a distraction."

"No," I said firmly. "If one of us causes a distraction, then that person would have to be left behind, and we're not leaving the Institute unless it's together."

"We also can't be detected," Kallie added. "Otherwise, they'll follow us to the lake."

"There's too much inferichite in here. Magic isn't going to get us out," Marcus said. "The only thing that's going to get us out of here is the real thing— the key hanging in the observation room. But without magic, we can't get to it."

A snarl across the room broke off our discussion. "What right do you have to keep us here?" a shifter boy demanded. He was facing off with the guards at the door, backed up by a couple of his big friends. "Let us out, before things get ugly!"

"I'll only give you one warning to stay back," a guard said as they raised their weapon.

"I'm going to call my parents and tell them *exactly* what's going on here," the shifter snarled. "And you're not going to stop me!"

The shifter started forward with his fists raised. There were a couple of loud shots— *actual* gunshots, not just the whooshing sounds of noxite darts. My breath caught in my throat as I watched blood spray as the shifter went down. Screams filled the room, and the faces of his friends went white. A pool of red flooded the floor, before the shifter took a gasping breath and died.

Holy shit. I felt my body shake as I processed what had happened. Terrible things went on at the Institute all the time, but the guards never actually *killed* someone out in the open like that.

"Take the body out," the guard ordered, and the shifter was dragged away, leaving a blood trail. The guard rolled his shoulders and added, "Anyone else got some funny ideas?"

Nobody said a damn word. My blood became frozen at the same time my mouth went completely dry. These guards weren't playing around anymore.

"We can't get caught," Kallie hushed. "They'll shoot us, too."

Rishi meowed and pawed at Marcus' leg. Oberi tilted his head and said, *I believe the cat has an idea.*

"I'm not sure what he wants," Marcus said. "But just act natural."

Marcus took a seat on one of the bunk beds by the wall, while Kallie leaned against the railing. Charlie stood next to me, always on the alert to take action in case another crisis went down.

I tried to keep my hands steady, but they were shaking. I'd seen people die in front of me before, but I hadn't been expecting the guards to do that. There was no preparation time— he was here one minute, gone the next, just like Monica.

A long time ago, Charlie had said he was a damn good con man, but he couldn't outtalk a bullet. That's exactly where we were at right now. There wouldn't be any more negotiating with these people. They'd kill us the second we stepped out of line. It was dangerous to leave, but at this point, staying was even more dangerous. We had to get out of here *now*.

I tried to focus my attention on what Rishi was doing, while at the same time, keeping my eyes down so I didn't draw any attention. Out of the corner of my gaze, I watched as Rishi pawed at a vent at the bottom of the wall, which was partially hidden by the bunk bed. It was a tiny vent— only big enough for a cat to get through. Rishi managed to get the vent cracked open enough so he could slip through into the air ducts, and he vanished.

The guards shut off the lights, only leaving one singular red bulb glowing in the middle of the room. People started going to bed. We made a show of lying down, but I knew Rishi was crawling in the air ducts around the storage room. The lights remained on in the observation room, so the guards could watch us as we slept. Creepy bastards.

When the room fell quiet, the guards behind the glass pane started bullshitting with each other, making dumb jokes and loudly complaining about their lives. I barely heard their muffled voices through the pane on the other side.

After a while, I heard a couple of snores. Most of the inmates around us had gone to sleep, and those that hadn't had silenced the sounds of their crying. The eerie quiet that filled the space put me on edge.

"Come on, Rishi," Marcus whispered, and I heard Kallie shudder in the bunk above him.

A couple long moments passed that felt like the equivalent of an eternity in hell. I heard a soft, scratching sound, and Rishi slipped out of the vent, holding a set of keys in his mouth. Rishi had gotten the keys from the observation room undetected. The guards had been too busy talking to notice him slip in and out. Marcus reached out and took the keys from Rishi to tuck them slowly into his pocket.

We had a key. Now we just had to get the guards away from the door.

Rishi darted off into the dark. Across the room, I heard a collection of the wooden boxes that I'd seen earlier crash to the floor. The noise was profoundly loud. A couple of students awoke blearily, complaining to keep the noise down.

"Who's crawling around out there?" a guard demanded. "Nobody should be out of bed!"

Another crate smashed loudly against the tile, and the guards protecting the door started forward. "Anyone sneaking around after lights-out is gonna get it!"

"Let's go." Marcus was already on his feet, and Kallie jumped down from the top bunk. Charlie silently helped me back into my wheelchair, and we proceeded toward the entrance. The fact that it was almost completely dark in the room concealed our movements, but we'd only have seconds to open the door and slip out before the guards returned.

Marcus fumbled with the keys and almost dropped them. Kallie cringed, while I hissed. If he got us killed, I'd kill him *again* later, because we couldn't afford to fuck up this time.

He finally got the right key and fit it into the lock. Marcus opened the door, and I thanked the ancestors it didn't creak. We slipped out into the dark hall, and Rishi sprinted through the open crack just before Marcus shut the door behind us.

I wanted to breathe a sigh of relief, but we were far from out yet. These hallways were crawling with guards, and we had to get outside if there was a chance of us reaching the lake.

"Do you think they'll notice we're missing?" Kallie whispered.

"It's so dark in there they won't realize we're not in bed until they turn the lights back on. Let's hope they don't do that," Marcus worried.

"Quiet. Before someone hears," Charlie demanded.

When we came to a corner, I dared to peek my head around it. Guards were wandering up and down the hallway with flashlights, patrolling the area. Along the floor were open and empty cardboard boxes from the factory— boxes that had previously held the brand-new, shining rifles that the guards carried now.

Charlie waited at the head of the group. The darkness didn't slow him up like it did the rest of us, so he was able to hear where the guards were, and told Rishi when to move. We had to create a distraction to get past them, because we couldn't leave a trail of bodies behind, or they'd find us.

Rishi swished his tail, then raced forward. A guard swept his flashlight, but Rishi jumped in one of the cardboard boxes, concealing himself from view. Once the light shone down the opposite end of the hallway, Rishi leapt out of the box and continued running. He darted from box to box, shielding himself from the glow of the flashlights until he'd gotten to the end of the long hallway, and into the cafeteria. From far off, we heard an assortment of pots and pans clatter to the floor in the kitchen.

The guards hurried off that way, leaving the hallway empty. We hustled through it. Kallie went to put her hands on the door that led outside, but Marcus grabbed her wrists.

"I can feel a ward here," Marcus said. "The Warden's armed the doors to the exit with alarms. We'll have to crawl through a window."

"That would be fine if my chair could fit though," I grumbled.

"You can ride on Oberi's back once we're outside. Marcus can subconjure it for later," Charlie said.

We changed directions and headed into a classroom, looking for a window that was big enough to crawl through. We found one at the back, near the teacher's desk. All of the windows were fitted with bars, but I used my Fire magic to melt them off. Marcus put a silencing ward on the room, and Charlie gritted his teeth as he broke the window. The sound of shattering glass caused me to bristle, but we waited for a minute and didn't hear any guards.

Marcus carefully climbed through the broken window first. I heard an *oof* as he fell on the ground. Oberi jumped through, landing cleanly on his feet before transforming into a unicorn. The illusion saddle appeared on her back, at the ready. Marcus reached his arms up for me, and Charlie picked me up, passing me through the broken window. Charlie got a cut on the back of his hand, but he didn't flinch, just proceeded like he didn't feel the pain. Marcus helped me onto Oberi as Kallie and Charlie climbed through the window after us. I healed Charlie's hand. He couldn't be leaving blood droplets for the guards to follow.

"Where's Rishi?" I asked, but as I did so, the cat came slipping out through one of the drains at the base of the building, squeezing through the bars. He must've found the drain in the kitchen and followed it out here. The tip of Rishi's tail twitched as he looked onward with huge eyes, observing the gaping expanse of the prison yard.

There weren't any guards patrolling the grounds, but they were up in the towers, using searchlights to scan the yard. The round spotlights seemed so pervasive and all-seeing. How were we going to get past them without being spotted?

"There are spotlights everywhere. Stick to the wall," Kallie rasped.

My leg skimmed the side of the stone wall as Oberi cautiously crept forward. The sound her hooves made as they clacked against the asphalt surrounding the school made me wince. The others followed behind me, but I felt terror explode inside my chest as I realized one of the spotlights was coming right toward us. My heart leapt into my throat, and Oberi came to a rough halt as I watched the spotlight span the stone wall ahead. The spotlight edged up the tip of Oberi's hoof, seconds away from revealing our location.

Rishi darted through the middle of the spotlight and in the other direction. The guards shouted as they saw movement, and the spotlight followed Rishi as he sprinted across the prison yard.

I heard the cocking of a rifle, and shots were fired. My eyes watched Rishi as he zig-zagged across the prison grounds, the spotlight trailing his every move.

There was another round of shots, and the spotlight halted in place. A chill swept through Oberi and across our bond, into me. Marcus gave a choked gasp as shots from the rifle echoed through the prison yard. From this point, we were too far away to see Rishi. We held our breath as the distant voices of the guards in the tower above us spoke.

"Did you shoot it?" a guard asked as he leaned over the tower's edge.

"I think so," the other guard said slowly. "Whatever it was, it stopped moving. It's just an animal."

"A shifter?"

"Nah, it was small. Probably a fox or something,"

"Is it a rabbit? No use wasting good meat. I'd love some stew."

"The Warden said no one leaves their post. Just keep an eye out."

"I don't see why," the guard complained. "None of these kids are stupid enough to be out here."

Marcus shook below me. "Rishi."

"They didn't get him," I promised, praying to the ancestors I wasn't lying. Marcus gave a soft whimper.

Once the spotlights had swept in another direction, we moved toward the sanctuary of the woods that surrounded the lake. I didn't dare to take another breath until we were in the trees within the prison grounds and out of the reach of the spotlights. Charlie bent over his knees, looking like he was going to throw up, while Kallie took a few ragged pants.

Marcus stood at the edge of the tree line, almost at a point where it was risky. His head looked from this way to that, waiting for Rishi to appear.

My heart dropped. "Marcus..."

"Where is he?" Marcus demanded, and he dared to poke out of the foliage. "He has to be here!"

An icy coldness climbed along my insides. We couldn't wait for Rishi. If the guard's aim had been true, he was already gone. We needed to keep moving.

I opened my mouth, trying to find the words. But the fear squeezing my lungs immediately ceased when I heard a soft *mew* below me.

"Aw, nice kitty," Kallie said as Rishi wound himself around her legs. Marcus scrambled to pick him up.

"Rishi, you good boy!" Marcus said as he squeezed Rishi tight, and the cat's eyes bugged out as everyone gathered around them. Marcus kissed his head and added, "I thought you were a goner!"

"You're such a smart demigod cat," I praised, and he purred as I reached down from Oberi to stroke Rishi's ears.

"We wouldn't have made it out without him, that's for sure," Charlie said as he scratched Rishi's chin.

"You can have all the catnip you want once we get out of here," Marcus promised.

"Let's get moving," Charlie said. "So we can grab that key and leave."

The lake's shore was dark when we reached it, but even so, I feared that guards could be lurking anywhere around its edge.

We heard movement in the trees beside us, and we summoned magic immediately to take down whoever it was. The fireball in my hand burned bright, threatening to eliminate whatever walked through those trees.

"It's us!" I heard Opal call, and I gave a sigh of relief. We allowed our magic to ebb away as she, my brother, and Alistair stumbled out of the trees. The three of them were covered in cuts and bruises, and were bleeding from several places, but nobody appeared seriously hurt. Tahoma had blood dripping from his antlers, like he'd torn apart someone who'd tried to hurt Ez, but otherwise, I didn't see a scratch on the elk. Pig's fur was ruffled, and she was bleeding from a few spots on her pelt.

"You guys all right?" Kallie asked.

"A little banged up, but we managed," Alistair replied.

"How'd you escape?" Charlie asked.

"We got lucky. A huge fight broke out between the students and the guards in our containment room," Ez said. "A bunch of people got shot, but Chancey and Ivy overpowered one of the guards and stole their keys so we could leave. They were in the same holding room we were. There was a lot of chaos going on in that room, so I don't think anybody noticed us escaping."

"Where are they? Did they get out?" I asked.

"I don't know. We lost them in the fight," Ez said. "We decided to come to the lake first, to see if you guys needed any help locating the key. It won't be long before the guards figure out we're gone."

"I'm coming with you," Opal said, already stripping off her sweater.

"Opal, you don't have to do this," I insisted. "If we get caught, they won't let you see your daughter—"

Opal's eyes became misty, but she said in a strong voice, "Marina is well-taken care of. The Warden's already got it out for me for associating with all of you. He'll never let me see my daughter again, anyway, because if we don't break out, I'll never get out of this place. And you guys need me."

I couldn't be more grateful for the depth of the sacrifice she was making. Oberi carried me to the water and laid down on the shore.

"Take my journal, and my compass," I said, digging them out of my bag and handing them to Marcus. "We can't afford to lose my aunt's prophecy now."

Marcus subconjured it into his stash. Kallie stopped at the lake's edge, kneeling to put her hand in the water. "I have to break the illusion hiding the ship first."

There was a great *thudding* noise, and a geyser of water shot up out of the lake, blasting twenty feet upward before crashing back down. I cringed at the loud noise it made. Kallie stood, shaking off water droplets from her fingers.

"Did you break it?" I asked.

"I broke the illusion hiding the ship. You should be able to see it now," Kallie said. "Though I couldn't break the illusion of the giant squid. It's too strong. If it doesn't let us pass to get the key, we're going to have to fight it to break the magic."

Kallie's magic had caught the attention of the sirens in the lake. I saw the splash of a couple fishtails before Arsinoe's head popped out of the water. The siren we'd made our former deal with hovered at the surface, appearing frightened.

"What are you doing out here?" Arsinoe hissed. "The Warden's locked everything down!"

"We have to search the lake again," I begged. "It's an emergency!"

"If he finds you out here with us, we're all dead. You need to leave!" Arsinoe demanded.

"I promise that we wouldn't be here unless we absolutely had to be. But if we don't get in that lake, what the Warden is going to do will be even worse than him finding us here. You have to trust me," I pleaded.

Arsinoe's eyes narrowed. "If it's that important and you won't go away, fine. But payment is required to enter unharmed."

"We don't have another body!" Kallie protested.

"We'll kill the giant squid," I offered quickly. "It won't be able to hurt you anymore."

We had to get past the squid anyway to get the key. Might as well do the sirens a favor and stop it from killing anyone else.

Arsinoe raised an eyebrow and said, "It'll kill you if you try, but if you must, go ahead. Either the squid will be dead, or we'll feast on your corpses. A good trade no matter what happens. We just don't want to get caught with you in our waters."

"We'll be in and out, I swear."

Arsinoe swam away. She didn't want to be around if the guards found us, because she knew she'd get in trouble. I saw the fins of the other sirens flash as they sped away to the other side of the lake to hide. At least they'd give us a wide berth. The minute she was gone, Opal waded into the lake, taking on her fishtail and swimming into the lake's middle.

Marcus gave me a witch light to hold so I could see clearer underwater. Opal said she didn't need one— her merfolk powers enabled her to see far underwater, even in the dark. Charlie helped me into the lake, and my Toaqua powers sustained me in the water as I propelled myself backward to join Opal.

Once I got in the water, the sound of a deranged, loud screech resonated from below the surface. My whole body shivered as the sound became closer, a wail from a monster emerging within the deep.

"Shit. The squid knows I broke the illusion disguising the ship. It's coming for us!" Kallie yelled.

A massive wave splashed against the surface. Opal swam with it, and I used my magic to keep my head above water as the powerful wave washed me across the lake.

I looked up to see the kraken had surfaced, and it looked *pissed*. Its massive, bulging eyes pivoted in every direction as it raised several terrifying tentacles out of the water. The tentacles were as big as some of the Institute hallways, and the kraken smashed them onto the shore, causing miniature earthquakes.

Alistair was grabbed by a huge tentacle and tossed into the woods. I heard him give a cry of pain as he hit something, probably a tree. Pig hissed, and Ez ran off to help him, Tahoma racing after. Kallie conjured a sword and began hacking at the squid's tentacles with the blade, while Marcus shot battle orbs at the squid's eyes. Charlie summoned both his Earth and Air magic at once, attempting to pin the squid's tentacles to the ground with rocks as each limb came crashing down, whipping up a windstorm around the squid's massive mantle to disorient it.

Their attempts to bring the squid down were like child's play. I gasped and got a mouthful of water as one of the tentacles hit Marcus, sending him flying. Another tentacle wrapped Kallie up in its grasp, squeezing her tight, but she transformed into a wolf and bit the tentacle roughly, ripping out chunks. The tentacle dropped her, only to start grabbing the boulders Charlie was piling on top of another arm. The squid tossed the boulders back at Charlie, who exploded them into dust before they hit. Still, a couple of them got too close, and he had to duck behind a set of trees to avoid being crushed. Oberi ran along the shore, shooting fireballs out of her horn at the monster.

"Ava, go! We can handle this!" Charlie yelled over the sound of the kraken's screams.

I froze, unsure of what to do. The noise the squid was making was *definitely* going to attract the attention of the guards. We had minutes to find the key and leave the lake before they showed up.

"Ava, come on!" Opal yelped, and she dove underwater. I took a deep inhale, then submerged to follow her. The three of them could handle the giant squid. I had to take the opportunity they were handing me so I could get that key. Oberi dodged a flying tentacle, shifting into a narwhal mid-air and diving in an arc so she could swim after me.

The thrashing of the giant squid made shockwaves resonate through the water. I had to force my powers to keep me in a straight line as Opal, Oberi and I swam around the whipping tentacles still submerged. Even after we'd gotten a safe distance away from the squid, I could hear it raging from the depths of the lake.

The deeper we got into the lake, the darker it got. I was grateful for Marcus' witch light, because it created a beam that I could follow here in the pitch black of the lake's bottom. Opal flicked her tailfin ahead of me, and I took it as a sign to follow her.

Underneath Opal was a spectacular sight. An Elven galleon appeared, resting at the bottom of the lake. A multi-deck ship with four different masts, *The Assassin's Destiny* was a wooden testament to the beauty of Elvish craftsmanship. The ship was huge, one of the biggest and finest that I'd ever seen. It resembled some of the ships that had washed onshore in Kinpago many years ago. There was a nautical figurehead of an Elvish woman carved into the front of the ship, and decorative wooden designs running up the sides.

Two of the masts were broken in half, and there was a massive hole in the side of the ship that the storm had caused. It was why the ship had sunk.

We approached the ship cautiously, though nothing emerged to fight us. Amalie— correctly— had assumed the giant squid would be strong enough to defend it. The three of us swam around the ship. Opal searched the galley, while I swam through the hole in the side of the ship to begin my search there. I found a variety of broken and rotting furniture, along with sunken supplies like dishes and other cargo. Oberi overturned boxes, while I rummaged through drawers and wardrobes, but we found nothing resembling a key. My powers rocketed me upward to follow Oberi, scanning the ship's deck for any sign of a clue.

In here! Oberi pointed her horn to a door on the ship, what I could only assume were the Captain's quarters. I raised my hand, and a blast of Water funneled through the lake and burst the door open. Oberi swam inside, and I trailed her. Lying against the wall of the ship was a desk and chair that had been tossed when the ship had sunk. In the middle of the floor was a wooden chest, lying on its side.

There was a thin resonance inside of me, and I heard a faint buzzing sound. My heartbeat picked up as my demigod magic surged against my chest. The key had to be near.

I overturned the chest, and Oberi picked the lock with her horn. It broke off, rusted from years of being submerged underwater. I slowly opened the trunk. There, at the bottom, was the merfolk key.

Being underwater for over a hundred years hadn't rusted or damaged its surface in any way. The key was gold and teal in color. It had the image of a shell on the bow, with the illustration of a mermaid swimming across it. A depiction of coral and seaweed wrapped up the blade, while the tip was fashioned in the appearance of a mermaid fin.

I grabbed it, and a burst of power flooded through me once I had the merfolk key in my grasp. My demigod powers rejoiced, as if reuniting with an old friend. The two contrasts of magic danced inside my core brighter than even my Fire magic blazed. I clenched on to the key tightly, thanking my ancestors and all who had brought us here.

Thank you, Amalie. Thank you, Dante. Thank you, Erasmus. We wouldn't have found it, if it wasn't for you.

It's brilliant, Oberi said as she gazed at it in my palm. *Two more keys to find, then all shall be united once more.*

A tightness clenched in my throat. I was losing air. We'd been down here almost ten minutes, and I couldn't hold my breath longer than that. I had to surface.

I pointed upward, and Oberi understood. We left the Captain's quarters and began our journey up.

"Did you find it?" Opal asked. She could speak underwater. I opened my hand to show her, and the glisten of the merfolk key shone against the witch light. Opal ran her fingertips over it like she was enchanted, mystified by the history of her people.

Oberi nudged me, and I again felt the desperate need for air. My Water magic rocketed me upward, until I reached the surface. I slowed down, breaking the water gently so as to not cause a disturbance. I took a fresh gulp of air and turned in place.

The giant squid was floating on the top of the lake, a massive smoking hole in its head. One of my friends had ended it. I felt sad for the mystical creature, because even though it'd been an illusion, it must've had some sort of consciousness, some sense of life after Amalie had created it. The creature deserved better than this, but attaining the merfolk key had to come at any cost.

I searched for my friends onshore, but didn't see anyone. I turned in place, feeling a slight pinch of fear begin to grow in my chest. That fear exploded into a panic, and I didn't understand why I felt that way...

Until I realized that frantic emotion was coming from Charlie, and almost as soon as it landed upon me, it left. Our connection had suddenly been cut off.

Oberi swam up beside me. She turned in the water frantically as she gasped, *Charlie's in trouble—*

Her words were cut off as a mass of rope fell over top of us. The witch light went out, leaving us under nothing but the illumination of the moon. The object fell heavily over top of me, and with absolute horror, I realized that Oberi and I were caught up in a net.

I flailed helplessly as Oberi got her fin tied up in the net. The net was tight around me, so I couldn't use my powers to jet away, though my Water magic rocked me from side to side in a desperate attempt to break free. I attempted to light the net aflame with my Fire magic, but though the embers caught and sparked, the net was damp from the lake, so it didn't light.

The net began tugging me toward shore. I screamed, and got water in my mouth as Oberi and I were pulled to land against our will. The more I struggled, the tighter the rope became. My legs hung uselessly, unable to help me get loose.

I saw a flash of mermaid scales within the water. I took a breath, and submerged my head. Opal was tugging at the net, trying to rip it free.

This was a magical net. Her merfolk strength wouldn't be enough to get me out of this. Desperately, I had the wild thought that the Warden *could not* catch me with the merfolk key.

I slipped my hand through one of the holes in the net and dropped the key. Opal floundered to catch it, then gave me a terrified look as she clutched it in her hands.

"Ava..." she whispered.

I shook my head, knowing she'd get the message. *He can't find it.*

Opal floated for a moment, before she bit her lip and turned away. Her tail flicked upward as she dove to the bottom, swimming to the other side of the lake and taking the merfolk key far away.

A great splash came as I was hauled ashore with Oberi. I sputtered as I choked up water. Guards had their hands all over me as they yanked the net off. Before I could so much as summon a fireball, they'd locked two inferichite bracelets on my wrist— one on each arm.

Oberi yelped as he changed back into a husky, but the guards fitted an inferichite muzzle over his snout before shoving him into a tiny cage.

I can't change, Oberi whimpered. *I can do nothing.*

I couldn't either. These inferichite bracelets were heavy, weighed down with massive crystals that were at least five times bigger than the crystals in the cuffs we'd been fitted with before. With so much inferichite running through my system, I wasn't able to summon any magic at all, not even the powers that weren't connected to my demigod blood.

Footsteps approached through the sand. I sneered as I slowly raised my head to meet the eyes of the Warden.

He didn't appear to be gloating, as I figured he would. Rather, he almost looked worried. And even in the worst of moments, that gave me a sly satisfaction I didn't bother to deny myself.

Behind him were a host of guards. Kallie, Charlie, and Marcus were already cuffed, wearing bracelets that were identical to mine, and stronger than the ones we'd been fitted with at the start of the semester. We'd been right. The Warden had been replenishing his supply of inferichite, and had saved it up all semester for us.

I didn't see Ez or Alistair. Ancestors, I hoped they got away.

The Warden's chest heaved. "Where is it?" he hissed. "Where is the merfolk key?"

"I don't have it, dickhead," I spat. "Clearly, we didn't find it."

"You're *lying!*" The Warden bellowed. "Guards, search them! Search all of them!"

A *clang* sounded as my wheelchair fell out of Marcus' stash. Warlock guards used a powerful spell to force Marcus to reveal his belongings. Rugged hands fell upon me again, and my wet clothes tore as the guards roughly searched me for the key. I cringed away from their touch, absolutely hating this. I wanted to curl up in a ball of humiliation. The only thing that kept me from doing so was the rage that continued to mount in the Warden's eyes as the guards searched.

"This seems important, Warden," a guard said. My heart fell as he handed over my journal, along with the compass. The Warden rifled through the pages before a wicked smile crossed his face.

"Excellent," he said as he pocketed the journal inside of his suit jacket, then tossed the compass aside to a guard. "This will be of use to me."

"You aren't going to understand shit about that journal," I spat.

"I'm sure I'll gain something useful from the information inside," he replied snidely.

"The rest of them are clean, Warden," the guard stated. "No keys here."

I couldn't help but let out a twisted giggle. *Take that, you sick fuck.*

"Wipe that smirk off your face!" the Warden barked at me. "There's no reason to smile, not where you're going!"

"Go fuck yourself. We beat you again. We *always* beat you," I hissed. "You still haven't learned that I never lose."

"You think this is a game?" the Warden seethed.

"I do. This is a game we play, you and I, and I'm tired of pretending it's not," I replied. "So what's your next move, Ophio? Because I'm already getting bored."

"Fine. It's a game, but I assure you, it's not a very funny one, at least not for you," the Warden threatened. "Let's see how long you'll be laughing."

The Warden grabbed me by my hair, then shoved me down into the sand. I landed face-first, but didn't cry out in pain. I refused. Instead, I let out another insane snicker. The Warden didn't realize that after the fear came the fun. I excelled in this kind of environment, where my back was against the wall and I had nothing to lose. Try and scare me now.

One of the guards yanked me upright by the back of my shirt. My partial hilarity became obscured as I watched Chancey and Ivy be hauled out of the woods beside Marcus, bound in handcuffs. Both of them were bleeding and bruised, like they'd put up a fight but had failed to get free.

"Running an illegal nightclub on school grounds is an instant termination of graduation rights," the Warden told Chancey and Ivy.

"You always knew about The Devil's Playground," I seethed. With a jolt of clarity, I realized the holding cell they'd taken us to earlier had *been* The Devil's Playground. The Warden had destroyed the stage, turning it into the observation room, and renovated the place in order to keep students in there for his ridiculous conversion practices.

"Yes, well, it was a good little hub for information, but I've found its usefulness has run out. Yours, however, is still boundless to me." The Warden turned upon me, and I swear, it felt like the wrath of the devil himself. "I followed your degenerate friends to your little clubhouse. I have more than enough evidence now to do whatever I like to you, and not the Union, nor your pathetic parents, have any authority to get in my way."

Though I was trying to put on a good front, I felt the color from my face drain away. They'd found the Lair. They'd found everything.

The Warden turned his back to me. "I am going to bleed you of every bit of power you dare to have. Guards, take them— all of them— down to Cellblock 9."

That was it. Cellblock 9 was the one place none of us wanted to go, but we were heading there. There wasn't any way out of this.

We *had* to break these inferichite bracelets. We'd done it before; we could do it again. But the crystals in these cuffs were much larger, and so heavy. I felt like I might die with each passing second that the stones touched my skin. I attempted to force magic into the cuffs, explode them like I had in the Underground, because I was that desperate, but I couldn't even summon a spark right now. Two guards hooked me under the arms and began dragging me after the others, who were kicked and slapped as they were marched to Cellblock 9. Oberi whimpered as the guards picked up the cage that held him and carried him in another direction.

"*Oberi!*" I started crying. Out of everything that had happened, watching the guards take him away was the worst. Oberi pawed at the cage door, but couldn't break free. It wasn't long before he was out of my sight. With the inferichite bracelets on me, I couldn't feel him or Charlie across our bond, or speak to them telepathically.

As the guards hauled me off, I caught sight of two faces in the bushes. My brother and Alistair— they appeared completely horrified. Ez went to take a step forward to intercede, and Tahoma shook his antlers beside him, ready to fight.

Don't. I couldn't say anything, but I could plead with my eyes. Ez and Opal had the rest of the keys. It was all we had left.

Ez paused, and he put an arm to Tahoma's front to hold him back. Tears welled in his eyes and ran down his face, but he gave me a quick nod before backing away into the dark, secluded trees. Alistair and Tahoma followed, along with Pig.

A tiny sense of relief rushed through me, mixed amongst the impending doom. At least the Warden wouldn't find the keys... not yet.

And that was my only comfort. Because where we were going, I knew we wouldn't find any. I promised myself going down there that we'd survive, and we'd get out. *All* of us. I swore upon my soul that no matter what torture the Warden put us through, we'd be the first people to break out of Cellblock 9.

Even if there wasn't much left to save once we came out of those doors.

Let the Warden do his worst. I'd faced the afterlife and come back even stronger. I wasn't afraid.

After all, what more could he do to me?

I'd already died.

charlie

TWENTY-THREE

My pulse pounded in my ears, and time seemed to slow as the Warden ordered the guards to take us to Cellblock 9. We'd been ambushed and bound by inferichite cuffs before we knew what was happening, and we hadn't been able to fight back.

These weren't the measly little inferichite cuffs we'd broken earlier this semester. They were thick and solid, bigger than the crystals Jaymin had tried to use on Ava in the Underground. I tried to shake the earth, to brew up a windstorm— *anything*— but my magic didn't respond. There was so much inferichite in these cuffs that they didn't just block our demigod powers. They rendered us completely powerless. It didn't matter that we'd resisted inferichite before or that we were immune to noxite. Our powers were locked down tight under the weight of these crystals.

My perception became skewed as pure rage ignited throughout my body. I heard the sound of a cage clang shut as they locked Oberi inside. Rishi howled as he too was thrown in a carrier. The distant sound of the Warden's threats to Ava met my ears. I struggled against the guards and kicked my feet out, but I didn't have the strength to break free— not with the inferichite bracelets binding my magic. The crystals were more than we'd ever resisted before.

A guard smashed a fist into my gut, and I nearly spewed my guts right there. The inferichite was so strong, it was enough to make me gag, and the beating didn't help.

The guards hauled us inside. The air grew damp as they forced us down a flight of stairs. Several locks clanged loudly and echoed off the stone as we were ushered inside the high-security cell block.

Ava gave a bitter laugh. She was utterly pissed. I didn't have to feel our bond to know it.

"You think you can lock *us* up?" Ava spat. "I'm going to tear this place to pieces before I get out of here— just like I did to your precious Underground."

"Go ahead and try, sweetheart," one of the guards replied. "It already cost you your legs. I'd like to see it cost you your life."

It was cold down here, and the air felt stale. Water dripped from the ceiling and landed on my head. My feet splashed in small puddles throughout the hall. Something scurried across the top of my foot, and chills of disgust traveled up and down my spine. It reminded me a bit *too* much of the Infernal Underground, except it was *loud*.

We hadn't reached the cells yet, but inmates' voices echoed down the hall as they shouted obscenities and insults at one another. These weren't the petty jibes you heard around the Institute, either. These were honest-to-god death threats... and other things I didn't care to repeat. To think of what the inmates did to each other down here churned my stomach. Guards barked back at the inmates. Metal clanged loudly, and my best guess was the guards were threatening inmates by banging on their cell bars with batons.

We must've reached a crossroads, because the guards stopped. They all went silent as heavy footsteps landed against the concrete.

"Well, well, well..." a deep voice drawled. "Would you look who it is."

My guts clenched. I knew that voice. It was Captain, the ex-military vampire who ran the underground fight ring. He was head of security around here, and I guess that meant he ran Cellblock 9, too.

I gritted my teeth and forced down the lump in my throat. The last thing I wanted was to show weakness in front of this man.

"Forget everything you know about prison life up there on the surface," Captain barked, before leaning so close to me I could feel his breath on the side of my face. "The Institute belongs to the Union. Here, you belong to *us*."

It was a threat. Captain got his kicks watching inmates beat the shit out of each other, but something told me the fight club was child's play compared to what went on down here. Captain's message was clear. In fight club, there were rules. Here, anything goes. Cellblock 9 was a lawless land where the guards could do whatever they wanted and pit the inmates against each other. The people here had nothing to lose.

Problem was, I wasn't one of those guys. My friends were still alive, and until each and every one of them was executed, I still had something to fight for. I had to play along, or risk losing them all.

"Girls to the left, guys to the right," one of the guards growled, before the others dragged us in our respective directions.

"Where does this one belong?" a guard holding Ivy asked, sounding disgusted.

"Hmph," Captain said as he came forward.

"Get your slimy hands off—" Chancey started, but he gave a heavy *oof* as a guard punched him in the stomach.

"Leave him alone!" Ivy protested.

"Send him with the boys," Captain said.

The guards already had me halfway down the hall when I heard the chilling voice of the Warden. "Don't send this one to her cell just yet. She deserves... a *special suite*."

My stomach dropped from my abdomen. Panic overcame me, because I knew exactly who he was referring to. I could only imagine what the Warden had in store for Ava, and none of it was good.

"Oh, yeah, you wanna start with me, first? Let's fucking go!" Ava screamed back. "Go ahead and try to break me, you sick motherfucker. You haven't done it yet!"

She let out another insane laugh, and the Warden responded dryly, "The point isn't to break you; it's to take what you have. Escort her away."

"Ava? AVA!!!" I screamed, struggling against the guards. Ava gave a wicked screech in reply that I swear shook the walls. I thought I heard Kallie and Marcus screaming for each other as they were pulled in different directions, but I couldn't be sure what they were saying over my panicked cries for my wife.

I never heard her reply, because someone smashed the end of a weapon into the back of my skull. "Shut the fuck up!" a guard sneered as I fell to the ground.

I caught myself with my hands. My left hand landed in a puddle of water, while my right landed on something soft and warm. Something squealed, and it wiggled out from beneath my hand. Fucking rats!

A shoe landed on my fingers, and Marcus cursed as he tripped over me.

"Get up!" the guards growled as they hauled us both to our feet.

"I can't see a thing down here!" Marcus protested.

"Get used to it," Captain snapped as he followed us down the hall. "It ain't all sunshine where you're going."

My head spun from the blow, and I stumbled a few times as I tried to find my bearings. I tried listening for Ava, but I heard nothing. We were far away from the girls by now.

My heart hammered as the guards dragged us into a room far away from the sounds of inmates. A heavy door clanged shut behind us, and I could no longer hear the inmates shouting in the distance. We must've been in some sort of boiler room, because I could hear the whirring of equipment. Several inches of water covered the entire floor, deep enough that it seeped through my shoes.

"Strip down," Captain ordered.

"For what, you sick pervert— ow!" Chancey started, but one of the guards shoved him to the ground. Water splashed around our feet when he landed, and Ivy whimpered from beside him.

"Do as you're told, Chance," Ivy whispered.

"You best listen to your girlfriend," Captain taunted. "Strip down and stand against the wall!"

The four of us follow orders, because what the hell else were we supposed to do? My hands shook as I removed my clothes. The last thing I wanted was to give the Warden reason to hurt Ava any more than he already planned to. It was naive of me to think my good behavior would change his mind, but I knew he'd use her against me if I stepped out of line. I frantically searched our bond for any signs of Ava and Oberi, but these damn inferichite cuffs had completely cut off our connection. I didn't know what dangers either of them were in, and that terrified me to the very bone.

Apparently, we weren't moving fast enough, because the guards barked orders, then began tearing our clothes off our bodies. Fabric ripped, and clothes splashed in the water as the guards tossed them aside.

"Against the wall! Now!" Captain barked.

My feet stung as I walked through the ice-cold water. We were forced to press our bodies against the cold stone wall.

Captain laughed, like he was enjoying the show, the sick fucker. "Give 'em the hose!"

The hose—?

My thoughts were cut off as a powerful jet of water slammed into my back. I opened my mouth to scream, but the wind was knocked out of me and I was pinned to the wall by the stream of water. The jet was so powerful that it was similar to my skin being cut away from my muscles. This was a fire hose, if anything. I received a moment of reprieve as the guards swept the hose the other way, but my friends' pained screams followed. The jet hit me again, but it was aimed lower this time, and I was knocked off my feet. My feet flipped over my head as I tumbled across the room. My skull cracked against the floor, and the guards' heavy laughter filled the room.

I turned inward, because it was the only way to ignore the pain. But that wasn't much better, because all I could think about was what the Warden might do to Ava. We'd found torture devices in the Infernal Underground, and I had no doubt he had a collection of them here. He'd do whatever he had to in order to carve her demigod powers out of her, and when he was done, he'd come for the rest of us. The least I could do was pray she'd be alive by the end of it.

The thought of Ava in pain was worse than any physical torture I could ever bear, so I let myself take on the stinging jet of water. It made me forget for just for a moment that Ava and I were separated.

The guards continued spraying us until it felt like the water had removed layers of skin.

"They should be all cleaned up now," Captain said, sounding amused. "On your feet!"

We were ushered into another room. The floor was dry here, but the air made me shiver. Guards shoved clothes into our hands and forced us to dress. Whatever they gave us was some kind of rough material.

"You boys look cute in orange," Captain said with a laugh.

We put on our jumpsuits, which were really itchy and didn't fit quite right. We were provided a pair of shoes each, but they had a putrid scent that was both a mix of sweat— from a previous inmate, I was sure— and rat urine.

We looked like real criminals now in our orange jumpsuits. Everyone called the Darke Institute a prison because we were confined within a fence, but the real prison was down here in Cellblock 9.

The guards escorted us down the hall, until we came to a long row of cells. The hall was narrow, and the ceiling couldn't be more than a few feet above my head. I nearly gagged at the smell of sewage.

As we walked, I could feel the heat coming off lightbulbs, but they were few and far between. Marcus wasn't lying when he said there wasn't much light down here. Good thing I didn't need it.

Inmates shouted and reached through the bars of their cells to grab us as we passed. I yanked my arm out of several sweaty grasps. The guards yelled as they banged on the cells, threatening the inmates to keep their hands inside.

Something warm touched my leg as I passed by a cell, and I realized in disgust it was a stream of piss. Someone had just *pissed on me.*

We kept walking. As we passed one of the cells, an inmate whooped loudly and shook their cell bars like a mad man. "The Bandit's come to play!"

I couldn't place the voice. There were too many of them, and I figured most of these people had been down here longer than I'd been at the Institute. My best guess was Cellblock 9 housed at least a hundred criminals.

Ivy gagged from behind me, like they couldn't stand the smell.

"Hold your breath," Marcus whispered.

"I can't hold it forever," Ivy told him. "I'm only half-vamp."

"Against the wall," Captain barked.

At first, I thought he was talking to us, until someone in a nearby cell groaned. "I've been on my best behavior."

"I don't give a shit. You're done with your cushy one-man cell. Meet your new roommates," Captain said, before grabbing me by the back of the collar and shoving me inside the cell.

I tripped and caught myself on a cold metal object. It smelled fucking awful, and as I felt around, my hands landed in cold water. I realized it was a toilet— filled to the brim and obviously clogged. I gagged and scrambled away from the stench.

I continued feeling around the cell, and I suddenly felt claustrophobic when I realized how small it was. The cell couldn't be more than four feet wide and seven feet long, if I was being generous. Unlike the door that was made of bars, the walls were solid metal, blocking us from the neighboring cells. There were two slabs of metal bolted to the wall that were supposed to be our bunks, but there weren't any mattresses on them. The "bunks" and toilet were the only things in the cell. We weren't even granted the courtesy of a barred window.

Chancey toppled into me as he was thrown into the cell. The cell door slammed shut, before the guards moved on to the adjacent cell and shoved Marcus and Ivy inside.

"Listen here," Captain demanded as he paced in front of our cells. "This ain't nothing like the Institute you attended before. There, you were students. Here, you're prisoners."

Chancey approached the bars. "When do we get to leave?" he asked sarcastically.

A baton clanged against the bars, and Chancey cursed.

"What do you think this is? A Girl Scout training camp?" Captain roared. "You ain't ever leaving here, and you best get used to it."

I hated Captain, but he was right. The only way out of here was if Marcus painted us a door so Kallie could portal us through it, but we'd been separated, so that plan was out the window.

"On the ground now!" Captain ordered.

"For what?" Chancey balked.

"Strike one, asking stupid questions. Strike two, questioning my authority. Want to go for strike three?" Captain came so close to the bars that spittle flew into our cell and sprayed our faces.

Chancey's voice was resentful. "No, sir." Reluctantly, Chancey lowered himself to the ground. There was barely enough room for one man to stretch out, and his elbow hit my leg as he was forced to do push-ups in the confined space.

Captain continued pacing. "These cages will be your home for the next infinity. You get one hour a day outside your cells for showers and recreation. Step out of line, and you will be severely punished. Behave yourself, and you'll be granted access to your magic."

Granted access— as if the guards owned our magic now. Hell, they did. They owned *us*. Magic was all these inmates had left, which made it the only thing the guards could control them with.

Captain patted something on his hip. "These tranquilizer guns ain't like the ones you've seen before. They aren't diluted to slow you down. The noxite in these guns will drop you on the spot."

He chuckled in amusement, and something clicked in his hand. "And the bullets in *these* guns will kill ya. Believe me, my guards don't miss."

With that, Captain turned on his heel. Chancey breathed a sigh of relief and started to get up, but a heavy clang reverberated off our bars.

"DID I SAY YOU WERE DONE!?" Captain bellowed. "You're not done until I say you're done. Back on the ground!"

"Y— yes, sir." Chancey scrambled to the ground again, doing push-ups faster than before.

Captain laughed as he marched back down the hall, followed by the guards. Nobody spoke until Captain was long gone.

Our cellmate was the first to break the silence. "You'll learn pretty quickly not to mess with Captain."

"Believe me, that man has a personal vendetta," Chancey said as he did another push-up. "He's still bitter that we dipped out of fight club."

"Ouch," our cellmate said. "Best thing to do is lie low. A place like this will really fuck with you."

"You've been down here what? Three months, Jeffrey?" Chancey asked.

I realized then who our cellmate was. *Jeffrey Johnson.* He'd disappeared after he insulted Esther when she arrived on campus. The Warden didn't take kindly to *that*. This kid was harmless.

I went to sit on the bottom bunk, but Jeffrey shoved me. I landed against the wall *hard*. "The bottom bunk's *mine*," he sneered. "You and Chancey can share the top bunk. I've earned my place here."

"What are you going to do? Fight me?" I demanded.

"Charlie's got a mean right-hook!" Marcus called from the cell beside us. His voice sounded strange, like he was right next to me instead of separated by a wall.

"Chance hasn't lost his last two fights," Ivy added.

"Thanks for that," Chancey grumbled from the floor. Yeah, it sure made him seem *tough*.

"I can take 'em," Jeffrey spat. "What you can do to me isn't worse than what they've already done here."

Cellblock 9 had really toughened this guy up. It wasn't worth fighting him, not when we had to conserve energy to figure out how to get the hell out of this place.

"Whatever," I said. "We'll take top bunk."

"You're lucky Charlie isn't fighting you," Marcus trash-talked, though he wasn't very good at it. "He'll fuck you up."

"Relax. I'm not fighting Jeffrey," I stated. "We're buddies, aren't we?"

Jeffrey hesitated, then clasped my outstretched hand. "Yeah. Buddies."

Ancestors knew we'd need allies down here. Might as well start with this kid. The last thing we needed was another enemy.

"It's not so bad down here. We're making friends already!" Marcus piped up. He still sounded weird.

"Marcus, what is up with your voice?" I demanded. "You're projecting it or something."

"No. I'm right here."

I followed the sound of his voice and felt around, until my fingers poked through a hole in the wall— and straight into his mouth.

Marcus sputtered and backed away. "Ew! Get your fingers out of here."

The hole couldn't be more than three inches across, and it was shaped like a triangle, like someone had purposely cut it there.

"I suggest you keep *everything* out of that hole," Jeffrey said as he lounged on the bottom bunk. "You know what that's used for, right?"

He didn't have to tell me. Marcus, however, wasn't that quick. "Passing messages?"

Ivy sighed and whispered something on the other side of the wall.

"Oh! Ewwww!" Marcus cried.

"Don't look at me," Jeffrey said. "It was here when I got here, and that cell's been empty until you arrived."

"I'm *sure* you never..." Chancey coughed as he struggled to continue his push-ups. "Thought of..." Another cough. "Using it. Fuck. How much longer do I have?"

"Until Captain decides you're done," Jeffrey said. "Could be hours."

"I'm not gonna last that long." Chancey's stomach rumbled. "I'm out of shape—"

He didn't get the words out before he gagged loudly and vomit splattered across the floor.

Great. Now I was covered in piss *and* vomit. Just what I'd ordered.

"Sorry," Chancey mumbled as he covered his mouth.

"Who said you could stop!?" a guard roared.

Chancey went back to his push-ups, but the guard taunted him with a click of his gun. "A little to the left."

Chancey hesitated, then moved over, until he was doing push-ups in his vomit. The guard laughed maniacally. Chancey strained and groaned, but didn't stop.

From the other side of the hall, inmates watched on and taunted Chancey. "Can't handle a few push-ups? What a pussy!" someone laughed.

"I like pussy," another cried gleefully like some sort of crazy person. "Let's get him out in the rec yard and—"

And *that's* where I stopped listening.

This place was disgusting. At least the Institute pretended to be a college. Cellblock 9 was more or less a glorified torture carnival where the guards were free to do whatever they wanted, and the inmates would do worse.

"You guys need to be careful. It's best to keep your head down and not draw any attention to yourself," Jeffrey said lowly.

In other words, keep your fucking mouth shut, or become a target. We all went quiet, though other inmates continued to yell at one another beyond our cell.

There wasn't much space to move, so I hopped up on the top bunk. It was barely as wide as my shoulders, and several inches too short. The ceiling was mere feet above my head, so I couldn't sit up. No way would Chancey and I actually fit on this thing together, which meant someone was sleeping on the cold, damp floor next to the vomit and the clogged toilet.

I rolled around, trying to get comfortable. Something sharp jabbed into my shoulder, and I jumped.

I felt around and realized the edge of the bed was rusted to a point. I tried to wiggle on it to see if I could get a piece off and use it as a weapon — ancestors knew we'd need one— but it didn't budge. If the guards or the inmates didn't kill us down here, infection would for certain. I didn't know how some of these guys had lasted this long.

As the first long hours in lock-up passed, I realized the worst thing about Cellblock 9 wasn't the damp floor or the clogged toilet. Hell, it wasn't even the threats from the guards and other inmates.

The worst part was *yourself.* There was nothing to do here to keep your mind occupied, other than to sink deep inside of it and forget you'd been locked up in the first place.

But I couldn't forget, because all I could think about was what the Warden might be doing to Ava right now. I thought of our friends— Ez, Opal, and Alistair, who'd hidden in the trees with the keys. The guards must've found them by now. There was nowhere to go— no way to escape. The Warden had all the keys... and all my friends.

We'd totally fucking lost.

Eventually, Captain returned and gave Chancey a lecture about how to never question him again. Chancey heaved heavy breaths as he tried to climb onto the top bunk.

"Move over," he rasped.

I tried to squeeze myself as close as I could to the wall, but there was hardly enough room between the bunk and the ceiling to turn sideways. Chancey pressed up against me.

"Ugh," I groaned. "We are *not* fucking cuddling."

I barely nudged him, and he nearly fell off the bunk before catching himself.

"Oh, but you know how long I've been wanting to get you into bed, Charlie," Chancey joked.

"I'm a married man, and you're not my type, anyway." I shoved a hand in his face, and Chancey toppled off the bunk.

I'd have let him stay— honest. But he collapsed onto the floor and fell asleep under Jeffrey's bunk. I didn't think he had the strength to pull himself up again.

I tossed and turned all night, and nearly fell out of the bunk more than once. I must've drifted off at some point, because I was woken by the sound of a loud buzzer echoing through the cell block. Our lock clicked, then the door slid open. The other cells opened all at once, causing a ruckus all throughout the cell block.

"On your feet!" Captain barked.

Ancestors, I barely felt like I'd gotten two hours of sleep.

"Hurry up," Jeffrey snapped. "They don't wait for anyone."

Chancey scrambled to his feet, and I jumped down from my bunk. I hurried to follow everyone, but before I could make it out of the cell, a guard shoved a mop and a bucket in my hand.

"Scrub fast!" he ordered.

I didn't have the luxury of questioning it. I quickly began mopping the vomit from our cell. He must've given Chancey a plunger, because Chancey gagged as the toilet made sloshing noises. We were barely given a minute to clean our whole cell before the guards determined we were done and yanked the mop out of my hand.

"Line up," they snapped.

Chancey and I were ushered into the hall, where I nearly tripped over a chain on the floor. Marcus caught me, but the guards quickly yanked us apart. They slapped cuffs on my wrists and ankles. The chain was attached to the other inmates, and they yanked harshly in both directions.

"Simmer down!" a guard ordered, and the inmates chained to me quickly settled.

"All right, Chain Gang!" Captain called. "Let's move it!"

The inmates began walking in unison down the hall, all chained together in groups of at least a dozen, probably more.

"This is so we *don't run*," Jeffrey whispered sarcastically.

I scoffed. "Run where?"

"Exactly," he said.

It was to humiliate us more than anything. We entered a room at the end of the cell block, and the door locked shut behind us before the guards came around to undo our cuffs. The room wasn't very large, but it managed to house all the guys with a bit more elbow room than the cells. Ivy breathed a sigh of relief once we were released.

"I thought you were into handcuffs," Chancey teased them lightly.

He was trying to lift the mood, which was fucking impossible down here.

"Not unless they're the pink fluffy kind," Ivy replied sourly.

"It's best to pretend they're the fun kind," Jeffrey said. "You'll have to get used to them. We get forty-five minutes in the Happy House, then fifteen minutes for showers. Then it's back in our cells with two meals per day. Rinse and repeat."

"What's the Happy House?" Marcus asked.

"It's the recreation room. The guards named it. They throw all the inmates together for free time, and whatever happens, happens," Jeffrey said dully.

"But why is it called the Happy House?" Marcus asked fearfully.

"You shouldn't have to ask, Marcus," I said.

A loud argument had already broken out across the room, and the guards next to us rushed to break it up. A few hung back, but I heard a *snap* as they unholstered their weapons.

"Isn't this... dangerous?" Marcus asked. "Throwing us all into a room together?"

"They keep the worst of the worst locked up during recreation time," Jeffrey explained. "Some of these guys have caused so much trouble that they have their own rec time. Can't be trusted around anyone else. Some guy got beheaded last month."

"That's the *last* thing I wanted to hear," Ivy said, squeezing closer between Chancey and me.

Jeffrey laughed. "It's far from the worst thing that's happened here. Personally, I think that's the way I'd want to go— being ripped apart by a vampire. Quick and fast, you know?"

"That can be arranged," a mocking voice came from behind us.

We all turned, and someone cracked their knuckles as the voice approached. Another pair of footsteps followed.

"It wasn't an invitation, Deuce," Chancey sneered.

Fuck no. I'd been hoping this asshole had died down here. Deuce was in Cellblock 9 because of me, after I'd blamed a murder on him a few months ago.

"But I'm *hungry*," Deuce shot back.

"Look, buddy," Jeffrey said. "You're not getting anywhere near this jugular. If you even *think* about it, my friends here will rip you apart."

"Please," Deuce scoffed. "I've already beaten them *both* in fight club."

His buddy punched his fist into his palm. "I think another fight's due. Bandit's the one who got us sent down here in the first place."

A chill traveled down my spine when I realized who it was. *Digger.* He was a warlock who was at the Institute because he'd killed his whole family. I planted nightshade in his cell after he threatened Ava, which had earned him a one-way ticket to Cellblock 9. I apparently had a habit of getting assholes sentenced.

Not like they didn't deserve to be here. Digger had a reputation for roofying people's drinks, and Deuce had threatened my friends more than once. I was still pissed at him for shoving Ava out of her wheel-chair. Maybe I'd get a fair shot at him down here in this madhouse.

The gang members took a step toward us, and my friends shied back.

I wasn't going to back down to these motherfuckers. I planted myself in front of my friends. "What are you going to do, knock my teeth out again? Fight club was child's play."

"You insulting me, Bandit?" Digger sneered.

I'd forgotten he was missing a few teeth. He was probably jealous I'd regrown mine. The potion I'd received from the infirmary was fucking awful, but my teeth were back to normal.

"If I can send you to Cellblock 9, I can send you straight to hell," I said. "Believe me, you don't know what I'm capable of."

"With those cuffs on? Not much, I bet." Digger laughed maniacally. "I've been on my best behavior, saving my magic just for you."

Everything happened so fast. Magic crackled in Digger's hand, the same time Jeffrey yelled, "Get down!"

The spell blasted in my direction, but I ducked the same moment a gun clicked. A noxite dart sped through the air, but I couldn't tell where it went. I didn't think it'd landed before a guard grabbed Jeffrey.

"Stealing a guard's gun is an offense punishable by death!" the guard roared.

"He was going to—" Jeffrey started, but he was immediately cut off as the guard hissed like a wild animal.

Warm liquid sprayed across my face, and people gasped as they backed away. Jeffrey tried to scream, but it came out as a gargle that twisted my guts. The gun clattered to the ground. Jeffrey had stolen the guard's gun from his hands, tried to shoot Digger in self-defense, and was being eaten alive by the vampire guard as a result.

"NO!" I screamed. Without thinking it through, I ran forward to grab Jeffrey's arm and yank him away from the guard. "He was only trying to protect us!"

I pulled Jeffrey free of the guard, but it was only a beat later that I realized the guard had *let him go*. Jeffrey's body slumped to the ground, and his arm was limp in my hand. The guard had already drained him.

The guard backed away, laughing like he enjoyed the sight of the dead body. The entire room had gone silent, and that cold, maniacal laughter was all anyone could hear. It echoed off the chamber, chilling me to the bone. I stood over Jeffrey's body, shaking as I tried to process how fast it all happened.

Then came the sound of heavy footsteps behind me. I knew the beat of those footsteps anywhere— the all-too-familiar cadence of Captain's disappointed gait. Everyone must've been watching as he bent down to pick up the gun. He circled me, and I forced down the lump forming in my throat. The last thing I wanted was to end up like Jeffrey, and it could happen in an instant as long as I wore these inferichite bracelets.

"You wanna play God down here, Bandit? Then tell me," Captain said, loud enough for everyone in the Happy House to hear. "Do you think Jeffrey Johnson got what he deserved?"

I steadied my tone. "He was trying to protect us, sir. Digger was going to—"

"You think I give a rat's ass what Digger was going to do to ya?" Captain bellowed. "Ain't *no excuse* to touch a guard's gun!"

Captain lunged at me. He grabbed me by the hair and yanked my head back, then shoved the barrel of the gun against my chin. My nostrils flared, but I did my best to steady my breath as he leaned toward me.

"You want this gun, Bandit?" He shoved it deeper into my skin for show. "Go get it."

He sounded disgusted as he tossed the gun across the floor. I remained rooted in place. I *didn't* want the gun. But apparently, that was the wrong answer.

"I said *go get it!*" he roared. Captain shoved me onto the ground, and I caught myself with my hands.

"I'm not supposed to touch the guards' guns," I stated coolly.

"You'll do as you're told," he snapped. "If you don't pick it up, I'll make sure there's a bullet in your head."

I began feeling around where I thought the gun had landed, but I felt nothing except the cold stone. Dirt and grime coated my hands. Captain began pacing around me, boxing me in. "Seems to me the newbies don't know the rules around here. Should be obvious that you don't approach a guard, and you don't touch his GODDAMN GUN!"

Captain laughed as I continued feeling around. My fingers grazed cold metal, but a heavy boot kicked it away.

The guards joined in on the laughter, followed by the inmates. Soon, everyone was laughing as I struggled to find what I was looking for. This whole exercise was designed for pure humiliation. I didn't know if the gun was two inches in front of me or if it wasn't there at all. Either way, the crowd was really getting a kick out of it.

It reminded me just what the world thought of me. Ever since I discovered I had magic, I'd felt a sense of *normal*. I fit into the magical world, because I could pull off incredible feats of power like everyone else.

But it didn't matter how many tools I obtained. Everyone was always going to see me as different— as *disabled*. Bitterness festered inside of me as I was overcome by complete shame.

"You think you're ever getting out of here, Bandit?" Captain mocked. "Hell, you can't even see what's staring you in the face. You're in my world now. You'll never navigate your way out of here."

He stopped pacing when he'd made a complete circle and ended up next to my friends. "What's your name, warlock?"

"M— Marcus," my best friend squeaked.

"You're Pipsqueak now," Captain said, before shoving Marcus toward me. "Help the Bandit find it."

Marcus hesitated, but he did as he was told and tiptoed around me. He knelt down, and I barely heard the sound of the gun rattle against the floor before a heavy boot landed. Marcus let out a sharp breath, and laughter filled the room again.

Marcus sucked air between his teeth. Judging by the sound of his pain, a guard was stepping on his hand. Another guard came forward, and Marcus cried out as they kicked him. A heavy *thud* sounded as his body landed on the ground.

Captain stopped beside me and leaned down. "I'm going to ask you one last time. Do you think Jeffrey Johnson got what he deserved?"

I didn't think Captain wanted me dead. I was a shiny new toy here in Cellblock 9, and he wasn't done playing with me yet. Didn't mean he wouldn't get bored sooner or later.

"Yes, sir," I answered.

Captain scoffed. "You're pathetic. And filthy."

Yeah, that's what crawling around on this disgusting floor will do to you, I thought sarcastically.

"Hit the showers," Captain demanded. "You, too, Pipsqueak. And *be quick about it!*"

I started to get to my feet, but Captain kicked my legs out from under me, and I landed flat on my back. People roared in laughter.

Marcus scrambled over to me. He helped me up, before the two of us took off to the showers.

The showers were in a room next to the Happy House, and the guards let us pass. I felt along the wall and found that the room was one big open area filled only with pipes. There weren't any stalls or anything. The floor was wet and slippery, and it wasn't properly graded for draining. I found a knob on the wall and twisted it to get the water warmed up. Ice-cold water splashed into my face, spraying at odd angles from the broken pipes.

I stripped off my shoes and jumpsuit, then rinsed my clothes under the water. They stunk of piss and vomit, and I figured a quick wash might help.

"See any soap?" I asked Marcus.

"None," he said as he stripped down.

It's like the guards *wanted* us to die of infection down here... and pneumonia, apparently, because the water wasn't getting warm.

I did the best I could to rinse out my jumpsuit, then squeezed the water out until it was damp. I hung them over a pipe, but I paused when I heard the sound of footsteps approaching.

"Bad news," Marcus whispered under his breath. "It's Digger, Deuce, and a whole gang of losers— six total."

Apparently Digger had dodged that noxite dart, because he was fully conscious and ready for a fight. I didn't know how they'd slipped past the guards stationed outside the showers.

On second thought, I bet Captain sent them in here after us. He always liked to pit students against each other. It was his kind of entertainment.

"Told you the Bandit wouldn't last a day down here," Digger said.

Deuce laughed in agreement, before he uttered, "Get 'em, boys."

I heard the crackle of a spell and ducked as it whizzed overhead, and I knew they were coming for me.

Fuck it. I'd survived the streets; I sure as hell could survive down here. I quickly reached for my jumpsuit and flipped it off the pipes toward a guy running at me. I spun around and wrapped it around his neck. He went to cry out, but only the first note of a sonic scream came out before I silenced him. I pulled the fabric as tight as I could, before dropping him and moving on to his friends.

Two guys jumped on me, while the others went for Marcus. I figured these guys were warlocks or elementals because I easily matched their strength. Didn't mean they weren't fucking good fighters, though. Without my magic, I felt completely disoriented, and it was hard to tell where the fists were coming from.

A fist landed against my gut, which quickly transformed into a battle spell that blasted me into the wall. The back of my head slammed into a pipe, and I felt blood spring from the wound. Deuce and Digger roared in laughter as they watched on. They'd rather see the show and let their cronies fuck us up until they could finish us off.

Fuck it. I'd finish *them* off.

I got to my feet and flung myself at one of the guys, tackling him. We landed hard on the ground, and I forced his face into a puddle. He sputtered, but the sound stopped almost immediately.

Water entered my nose, burning my sinuses. I realized he was Toaqua— a water elemental. He forced the water through my airways, then out my nose again. He formed the water in a ring around my body, pinning my arms to my sides as the water turned to ice. I strained, but the ice tightened around me until I felt the crack of ribs.

Fucking hell!

I bit back a curse and flexed my muscles as hard as I could. The ice broke to pieces and clattered to the floor.

Marcus, somehow, managed to hold his own. He must've kicked one of the other guys, because someone tripped and landed into the elemental asshole. I heard Marcus grunt as he fell to the ground, but it had to be intentional, because he slid past me and knocked over one of the other guys like a bowling pin. All the sparring and working out we'd been doing this semester was apparently paying off.

"You four are useless," Digger sneered. He threw himself at me. He landed a few blows to my broken ribs— which hurt like hell— but I got in a few good punches myself.

I didn't know what Digger's warlock powers were, but he couldn't have been too strong, because he was throwing more punches than he was battle magic. I'd seen Marcus perform incredible feats of magic as a warlock. Digger was acting like he'd barely seen a spell in his life. I threw a punch, and my fist landed against his jaw, but he only responded by punching me in the side. He could fight— I'd give him that. But so could I.

I stumbled back a few steps, wiped my bloody nose and taunted, "That's all you got? I thought you were saving your magic for me."

It hit me then. Digger *had* been saving his magic for me, but that one measly spell he'd blasted off in the Happy House was all he could manage. I'd never known Digger's warlock Cast, and I realized maybe he didn't *have* one. Marcus had told me he had to undergo a ceremony to unlock his powers, gifted by his goddess.

"Was that all you had?" I taunted. "You have no magic because you're not good enough for your coven?"

"You know nothing about me!" Digger sneered.

"Is that why you killed your family?" I asked. "Your goddess rejected you, so you went on a killing rampage in a fit of rage?"

"Shut the fuck up!" Digger roared.

I let out a maniacal laugh. I'd finally figured this bastard out. "That's why you roofie your victims," I continued. "Because drugs are the only power you actually have."

Digger screamed at the top of his lungs. He flung himself at me again, and my feet slipped out from under me. We both landed on the floor. He curled his hands around my neck, fully intending to kill me. One of his cronies stomped on my leg, and I gasped as the pain of tearing tendons shot through my knee. My leg had never healed quite right after I broke it in the Underground, and the assault only made it worse.

It fueled my anger— that was for sure. I got my good leg under Digger and kicked him off of me.

Deuce was obviously getting impatient, because he yelled from across the room, "This ends now!"

He appeared next to me in under a second, then grabbed me by the hair and yanked me to my feet. Deuce was stronger, because he was a vampire, and no amount of struggling would loosen his hold on me. He dragged me to the edge of the room and began bashing my head into the pipes. Pain shot through my nose and across my entire face. I could feel the bruises forming immediately, swelling my right eye closed. He smashed my mouth into the pipes, and my lip split open.

"Bleed, god fucking damn it!" Deuce spat. "I want to eat you alive. And when I'm done with you, I'm going for your no good crippled wife — only unlike you, I'll have my fun before I dispose of her."

That pissed me the fuck off. *No one* dared to threaten Ava, not while I was still living and breathing. If this fucker wanted to get to her, he was going to have to kill me first, and I'd come back from the dead before I'd ever let anyone touch her again.

With blind fucking rage, I managed to slip out from under his grip and shove him off. I grabbed Deuce by the back of the head and slammed his face so hard into the pipes that it knocked him out cold.

It took a fucking lot to knock out a vampire, but Deuce went down like a dead body. Hell, I would've thought I'd killed him if I didn't know he was immortal.

Marcus landed one final blow to one of the gang members, and I heard another body hit the ground. The ones left standing backed away, clearly horrified that I'd managed to knock out a vampire.

"Who's next?" I demanded.

Digger and his gang scrambled out of there as fast as they could. Now that I knew Digger's secret, I didn't think he'd be messing with us again.

I went over to Marcus and helped him to his feet. He was in rough shape. We both were. We limped around the room to gather our wet clothes, and had barely pulled them on when inmates began flooding through the doorway. It wouldn't be long before the guards found Deuce lying on the floor, and I didn't want to stick around when they did.

Marcus and I fled for the exit, back toward the Happy House. We must've looked rough. Pain pulsed through my nose, and blood trickled down my lip. My whole face was swollen, and my right eye wouldn't open. Not to mention the broken ribs. I couldn't walk without limping.

I clapped Marcus on the back and leaned into him, only to realize he was clutching his arm.

He inhaled a sharp breath through his teeth. "They broke my arm."

"Fuck, man," I growled. "You did well in there, though."

Marcus breathed a sigh of relief. "I'm surprised we made it out alive."

Hand landed on us, yanking us apart.

"You, with me!" one of the guards barked at Marcus, while the others held me still.

"Where are you taking him?" I demanded.

The guards chuckled, as if they were amused by my audacity to question it. "You'll find out soon enough. The Warden's saving the best for last."

Panic filled Marcus' voice. "The *best for last?* What does that mean? Charlie! Where are they taking me?!"

Nowhere good. My teeth ground together, but the guards holding me had to be vamps or angels, because I couldn't struggle out of their grip. For the first time since being thrown in these cuffs, I could feel my magic rattling around inside of me, begging to escape. I'd bring this whole place down on these motherfuckers if I could.

"Don't play his game, Marcus!" I called after him. "You don't give in!"

A heavy door clanged, and the sound of Marcus' panicked cries faded. My stomach dropped out of my abdomen, and I resisted the urge to drop to my knees and curse the gods for abandoning us down here. The Warden was picking off my friends one by one, like cattle set for slaughter.

I realized something even more terrible. The Warden had taken Marcus, which meant he was done with Ava-Marie. She could be dead right now for all I knew... but I *couldn't* know, not as long as these damn cuffs were blocking our bond.

Screw the fucking Warden! These games he wanted to play ended now. He could take my Familiar from me, he could take my friends, he could even take the love of my life away. He could rip everything I had to live for out of my grasp, but one thing would always keep me going.

My revenge. If I had no one left to live for, I'd certainly live long enough to murder the Warden, and make him pay for doing this to us.

The guards hauled me back to my cell and threw me inside. I winced as I lowered myself onto the bottom bunk. My head swam, and I didn't quite know which way was up or down. My stomach clenched, and I wanted to puke, but nothing came up.

Eventually, Chancey and Ivy returned with the chain gang.

"You look like shit, man," Chancey said when he saw me.

"Where's Marcus?" Ivy asked from the next cell.

"Taken," I rasped out as I held my pounding head. "By the Warden."

"What are they going to do to him?" Ivy squeaked.

"I wish I knew," I said, trying to steady my breath. "There's nothing we can do about it anyway."

Ivy got really quiet. We all knew I was right. We could worry about our friends, but it did them no good. No amount of worrying was going to save them.

"Fuck. This. *Shit!*" I roared as I punched the wall. The radiating pain in my knuckles almost made me forget about my pounding headache for a second. Then it was all back a moment later. Pain pulsed through my head, my torso, my leg... *everywhere.*

I'd been in some pretty dark places, but this had to be the worst. It wasn't the physical pain; I could handle that. Hell, I'd been on the edge of death more times than I could count. But until now, I'd never felt so powerless.

"Let me help," Chancey offered, before placing a hand on my head.

I winced. "You can't help me."

"I can try," he insisted. "Angels have healing magic. I've never done it before but... gotta try, right?"

His hand warmed on my skin, and I felt tendrils of magic enter my body. Angels had the power to heal, much like the Anichi tribe of Elementai culture. But it took a powerful angel to heal all the damage that had been done to my body. Chancey was average, at best, and I'd wager a bet he wasn't as powerful as he considered himself to be. Ava's healing magic would have knit my lip back together and fused my broken ribs in moments. All Chancey's magic did was take the edge off, which honestly was better than I anticipated, so there was that.

Chancey tried again, but I waved him off. "Don't strain yourself."

To be honest, I preferred the pain. It was easier to focus on that than on the horrifying thoughts flitting through my mind.

Ava was likely dead by now. Ez, Opal, and Alistair had surely been executed the second they were found with the keys. They were no use to the Warden, so he wouldn't bother keeping them around. Marcus wasn't far behind any of the others, and who knew if Kallie was still alive?

If he didn't kill Ivy and Chancey, they wouldn't last long down here, anyway.

Maybe it was better this way— to just get it all over with. The Ancestral Lands sounded nice...

Except we had to *make it there* first. With all the terrible things that me and my friends had done, I didn't know if they'd accept us into the Blessed Haven. If we became trapped here, and couldn't cross over into the afterlife, was it any worse than surviving in this prison? I didn't know what your soul being trapped looked like. I'd witnessed a glimpse watching Thaddeus go through it, and I was certain I didn't want his fate to be my eternity.

That thought sent me on another spiral, because it was *our* fault Thaddeus was trapped in the first place. All my friends could end up just like him, haunting the Institute forever, stuck in this hellhole that none of us could escape.

This was bigger than the war going on inside my own head. Death wasn't an end in the supernatural world, and if I gave up, I damned people like Thaddeus... like Ava. There was still a chance to save them.

I'd stick around as long as I possibly could to do just that. I would have my revenge on the Warden, but more than that, I would save the souls he'd trapped and tortured here at the Institute.

I wasn't giving up. I wouldn't play the Warden's sick games— or Captain's, for that matter. They knew the power of the mind, and how Cellblock 9 played on psychological turmoil. They knew as well as I did that the real prison was inside your head. They could lock you in these cells, torture and humiliate you, but we could not become their prisoners without consent. They *wanted* me to give up, but I wouldn't choose that option, no matter how much they pushed me.

Hours of agony passed. It was all too easy to see why an inmate would give up here. Going numb and succumbing to the madness was the only way to free yourself from it. Hanging on took conscious energy and effort. It was a hole you were trying to climb out of, only these assholes kept throwing dirt on your head. It'd be easy to just lie down and let yourself be buried alive.

But I was made of Earth, and I'd throw that dirt right back in these motherfuckers' faces.

I drifted in and out of consciousness, until I heard a tray being slipped under the door of our cell. Chancey helped me sit up to eat something. It was the first meal we'd had in over twenty-four hours, and we scarfed it down within minutes. There wasn't enough to satisfy me, but I was no stranger to hunger. All I could do was lie back down and wait for my next meal. That was the only thing worth looking forward to in here, no matter how nasty it tasted.

At some point, the exhaustion overtook me, and I drifted off to sleep.

I woke to the sound of guards yelling. Our cells hadn't been unlocked yet, but heavy footsteps passed by as guards ran down the hall. I sat up and listened carefully, but inmates had started to rouse. People talked so loudly that I couldn't figure out what was going on.

"Code red in the Happy House!" a guard shouted.

A door opened down the hall, and we could hear the distant sound of high-pitched screams. It had to be the girls' recreation time, because it sounded like the female inmates were fighting down the hall.

The door slammed shut again, echoing throughout the cell block. People shook the bars on their cells and demanded to know what had happened.

"Hands inside your cages!" a guard barked as he went around smacking people with his baton.

Whispers began to spread from cell to cell.

"Apparently, the guys in the cell at the end of the hall saw blood on the guards' uniforms," Ivy whispered through the wall. "The guards mentioned a few of the girls died."

"They're trying to scare us," Chancey insisted.

"Nah. I can smell the blood," Ivy said.

The truth became utterly apparent once we were led to the Happy House. We were escorted down the hall in chains, and my shoes squished through a sticky liquid that had to be blood.

"There are bodies up ahead," Chancey told me. "A bunch of girls, all piled up on one another."

"Keep it moving!" the guards demanded. "Nothing to see here."

We entered the Happy House and were unchained, but the room seemed quieter than usual.

I leaned over to Ivy. "What's going on?"

Ivy swallowed audibly, and I could feel them shaking. "There's blood everywhere— puddles of it."

"Looks like the other vamps in here want to drink it, judging by the red in their eyes," Chancey whispered.

Someone pushed past us— a vamp, judging by the strength. "Free breakfast!"

Slurping noises came from the ground, and I realized he was *drinking* it. I waited for the guards to come, to make a scene out of it. No way would they let the vamps find *pleasure* in this. If anything, I thought they left the blood there to torture them.

"Where are the guards?" I asked.

"Good question," Chancey mused. "There are a few, but not as many as yesterday."

"Come to think of it, I haven't heard Captain all morning," I realized. "This isn't right. Cellblock 9 should be overflowing with guards. The Warden must be up to something."

The vampire kept slurping, and Ivy nearly gagged. "That's absolutely disgusting."

The vamp on the ground must've heard him, because he leapt to his feet. "You think you're *better than me?*"

One second the two vampires were standing beside us. The next, the vamp's voice came from across the room. Ivy cried out, as if they were being pinned to the wall. Chancey and I raced over to them. I grabbed for the vamp, but he swung his arm out and hit me in the face. My lip, which had been healing, split open again, and pain radiated across the bruises. Chancey threw some punches, but he was flung backward into me.

"Oh, you're a darling," the vamp said as he held Ivy to the wall. "I didn't realize we were in the presence of a *lady*. How *rude* of me. Perhaps I should share."

The vamp grabbed Ivy and hauled them back over to the puddle. He was so fast that Chancey and I couldn't get to him.

"Drink!" the vamp demanded.

"Ives, you don't have to!" Chancey insisted.

"Let go of me!" Ivy screamed.

We reached the vamp, and I nearly tripped over Ivy's legs in the process. The vampire pinned Ivy down, holding their head into the pool of blood. We tried to pull him off our friend, but in the state I was in, I was no match for him. He elbowed me hard in the ribs, and I gasped for breath.

Hands landed on me and yanked me backward. Chancey shouted curses as he too was pulled off.

Digger laughed in my ear. "Settle down, Bandit. We want to watch the show!"

It wasn't guards that had dragged me away; it was inmates.

"Struggle all you want, pretty lady," the vamp sang. "We're finally going to see what's under that jumpsuit."

Blind rage overcame Chancey. He roared beside me and started beating the shit out of whoever was within reach, and you know what? I was with him.

I gritted my teeth. Forget my broken ribs and lack of magic. These motherfuckers weren't getting anywhere near Ivy.

Ivy let out a primal scream of rage. At the same time, I yanked my arms free and grabbed Digger. My hands tangled in the collar of his jumpsuit, and I slammed my fist into his face.

Blood spurted across my front, and he went completely limp in my hands. He was so heavy that I dropped him. I didn't know what had happened. I wasn't *that* strong.

All around me, bodies began to drop. People screamed and scattered, but they didn't make it far before they too fell to the ground.

Wind whipped through my hair, and I realized Ivy was dashing around the room at lightning speed. I knelt beside Digger and felt around, only to find that his throat had been slashed open and torn to bits. Blood spilled out of his lifeless form. Blood began to creep toward me from all angles, the warm liquid soaking into my jumpsuit.

Ivy had killed Digger, killed others... *dozens of them.*

Guards barked orders at one another, and noxite guns clicked. Ivy was moving so fast that they missed.

Until suddenly, everything stopped. Ivy came to a halt in the center of the room, giving gasping breaths.

"None of you bastards are ever going to *touch* me again," Ivy breathed. Their voice was thick, as if blood was pouring from their mouth, tone completely manic. "I'll die first."

A noxite gun clicked again. Ivy gasped once before slumping to the ground with a hard *thud.*

"Take him to solitary!" a guard commanded. "Along with his little boyfriend over there."

"Fuck you! *Fuck all of you!*" Chancey screamed. His voice got farther away, and I knew he and Ivy were being dragged off to solitary confinement.

"And *you,*" the guard sneered as he grabbed me and yanked me upright. "We've got a better idea for you, *boy.*"

Panic swelled within me. A guard slapped cuffs on my hands, binding my wrists together. They yanked on my arms, but I slipped in a puddle of blood, and my legs fell out from under me. The guards dragged me away so fast I couldn't find my footing.

"Dead man walking!" the inmates called out, but my pulse pounded in my ears so loud I could barely make it out. Their chants echoed in my mind, even long after their voices faded down the hall. It all happened so quickly that it didn't feel real.

Then I finally processed what they'd been saying. *Dead man walking...*

I was headed to Cellblock 9's death row.

"No!" I panicked. I tried to break free, but this was it. I was bound by inferichite cuffs and beaten to my utter limit. Right now, lying down in my grave felt like a pretty damn appealing option. I could go numb... dissociate, not feel a thing when they killed me.

Because they would. I was certain of it.

The guards dragged me into a room and hauled me onto a cold metal table. This was my last chance to make a run for it. I tried to struggle free, but it did no good. I searched for my magic deep inside of me. If I could break these cuffs, I could siphon these motherfuckers' power and tear this place down.

But I couldn't find my magic. There was nothing I could do.

The guards chained me to the table, then left the room.

My heart pounded like a heavy drum. I couldn't make sense of my surroundings through the panic. I tried to listen, but I heard nothing. I was in a void, where nothing but this table, these chains, and my frantic mind existed.

Then I heard footsteps. "Have you brought him to me?"

My blood chilled at the sound of the Warden's voice.

"Yes, sir. We have the Elf prince," a guard said.

"Good," the Warden praised. "You have served The Mission well. You are all dismissed."

The door opened. Absolute fury erupted in my chest as I heard those calculated footsteps lure closer.

"What did you do with her, you fucking psycho!?" I demanded. "Where's Ava-Marie? Where's my wife?"

The Warden let out a chilling laugh as he circled my table. He set something near my head, and I knew instantly by the twisting in my gut that it was inferichite. I could already feel it pulling on my energy.

"I assure you, your wife is suffering adequately," the Warden said in amusement. "She is a demigod no more, and neither will you be when I am finished with you. After all the experimenting we've done, our work has finally paid off. But I'm *done* experimenting now."

He slammed his palms against the table, making me jump. I kept my breath steady, to show him he couldn't get to me that easily.

"I was saving you for last, Elf prince. I will have all your power now. And once I do, I will finally be strong enough to become the god I was born to be."

TWENTY-FOUR

Two days earlier

I should've felt terrified. I was going down to Cellblock 9. I should've been absolutely losing my mind at the thought of what the Warden was going to do to me and my friends.

I didn't. All I felt was this all-encompassing fury that drove me into a mad rage as the guards dragged me down the darkened hallway and into a stainless-steel room. It looked like an operation center, with tall cabinets, bright medical lights affixed to the ceiling, and a rolling tray full of surgical instruments.

In the middle of the room was a broad table, fitted with clamps for the wrists and ankles. The guards slammed me onto the surgical table, and I arched my back as I screamed, not in protest, but in hatred for the Warden and all that he was doing to us, for all that he had done and would ever do.

"Stop screaming, Mrs. Wahkin. No one is going to hear you down here." The Warden entered the room. The guards fixed my wrists and ankles to the clamps, so I was even more helpless. I felt like a butterfly pinned to a board as the Warden scowled, looking down at me from overhead.

"What now, huh, Warden?" I rasped. "Show me the next step in this big plan of yours."

"My plan has never changed. It's only just now become possible," the Warden replied. "And since it has, I see no reason as to why I shouldn't start with you."

"Fuck you. You're no god," I sneered.

"That's something you don't understand. I *am* a god because I believe myself to be, and others will follow me without question. You don't need to prove power, Mrs. Wahkin; you just need to convince other people that you have the ability to save them. Once I've drained you of your demigod abilities, I will."

"Taking my magic isn't going to make everyone want to follow you. There will be others who will rise up," I hissed.

"That's the secret, my dear." He leaned down, so he could whisper in my ear. "I don't *need* your power to convince the other supernatural societies to follow me. I just want it because... well, why not? Why wouldn't I want to become a supreme being? If I am truly going to challenge the gods, as I fully well intend, I'm going to need all of your magic. And I'm going to leave you nothing for yourself."

I spat in his face, but the Warden sidestepped away and shook his head. "You'll never learn, will you? I've managed to break everyone that's come into this prison but you, and I have to say, I admire that about you. Perhaps there's something in that magic of yours that'll give me just as much courage."

"Go ahead and take it. I'm still going to stop you," I promised.

"By the time I get done with you, there will be nothing left to fight me with."

The Warden placed two inferichite crystals by the sides of my head. I gave a sputtering laugh. "This again? It didn't work the last time. What makes you think it'll work now?"

"Because after all these years, I've finally perfected the ceremony. I know exactly what I must do," the Warden replied. "I wish I could promise that this won't hurt... but, I'm sorry. I'm actually happy that it will."

My wrists yanked at the clamps as I gave another infuriated, carnal scream. The Warden hovered his hand over my temple, reciting the ceremony's incantation. "*Nunc hac potestate utar meo. Hanc nunc exhauriam victimam, ut sit deus, ac flos efficiar.*"

The words were still Latin, but different from when Jaymin Riske had used them in the Infernal Underground. *I now take this power to use it for my own. I now drain this victim, to become god, and become elite.*

A thick tendril of magic erupted from both inferichite crystals, smashing into the sides of my temple. This time, the ceremony was even more painful than the last. The power the inferichite held completely dominated my system, pinning me to the table so I couldn't move, couldn't writhe in pain. My mouth opened in a silent scream, my throat unable to produce words. I waited for the infinite agony to wash over me, for the endless torture to twist my body into an unimaginable state of suffering.

And the pain did come... but it was *so* different this time. Almost familiar, in a way. I felt the stabbing knives of the inferichite piercing my organs, my magic burning me up and drowning me all at once while my healing abilities tore my muscles in two, trying to end it all. My bones turned to blades to rip apart my skin, my lungs struggled to gasp for air amidst the holes in my chest, and yet...

This was absolutely nothing. I'd once thought the pain the inferichite gave me was the worst pain I'd ever experienced, but it couldn't hold a candle to the months I'd spent in the hospital recovering from my spinal injury, my surgery, and all that had come along with it. The ceremony was more intense, because it was all at once, but nobody understood that I'd been subjected to agonizing bouts of torment for months on end. After what I'd experienced, the inferichite couldn't touch me. I remembered the long days after I'd woken up from my coma, the hours I'd spent struggling through class when I wondered if I was going to pass out from the hurt, the night I'd begged Charlie to end it all. That was *real* pain. Compared to that, this might as well have been a vacation. It was almost *enjoyable.*

The Warden believed everything he'd put me through would end up crushing me, but all he'd done was create something stronger than he'd ever imagined. He'd made a superweapon that was practically invulnerable to pain, one that wouldn't rest until he was put down.

What. A. Dumbass.

Though the Warden kept the spell going, laughter began to bubble out of my throat, beginning as small giggles before becoming full-on, insane laughs. Was this *really* the best he could do?

Through my half-shut eyelids, I saw the guards in the room giving shifty expressions, appearing uncomfortable at my delirious laughter. "Uh... sir," one of them stated. "She doesn't appear to be reacting like the other patients."

"Her reaction means nothing," the Warden snarled. "Her power is mine."

Despite me struggling against it, I watched as the tendrils of magic that connected with my head funneled into the inferichite, before transferring into the Warden. The tendrils snaked around his fingers and up his arm, winding downward until they connected with his chest.

Panic flooded through my body as I felt my magic being drained away. The embers of my Fire magic flickered and died as my Water magic went from a powerful wave inside of me, to mere droplets dissipating into the air. My healing magic flared, igniting like a firework before slowly fizzling out. I attempted to summon my powers, get something to respond, but nothing caught a spark, because it was all going to the Warden. His body began to glow with a hideous dark energy as the inferichite channeled my powers into him. The room shook, and the lights flickered overhead. The table beneath me rattled, and my laughter changed into gasping breaths as I did my best to hold my magic back, and failed. I felt a last wisp of magic leave my body and enter the Warden's as the ceremony was complete. My body sagged onto the table, completely spent.

He did it. The Warden overpowered me. He took a deep breath, as if inhaling all the magic from me that he'd just taken, enjoying the resonating effect it gave him.

"It's so... unique. All this power," the Warden muttered. "How do you go about your life and not notice it racing through your bones, demanding to be released?"

I went to reply, but all that came out was a whimper. I didn't even have a voice. I was so weak. The only thing that seemed welcoming now was impending darkness.

The Warden's voice was a thick quiver as he spoke quietly to himself. "It took me over a hundred years... but now, *finally*, I have what I've been searching for."

There was nothing left inside of me but the wasted feeling lingering in my blood, and the infinite power emanating from the Warden as he turned upon me. "Which means there's no more use for you."

My chest rose and fell. I felt my eyelids fluttering closed as I fought to stay conscious.

A guard stepped forward. "What do you mean to do with her, Warden?"

"Throw her in a cell and let her rot. She needs to spend her dying hours pondering how she's lost the game she chose to play with me."

He wanted to gloat that he'd won. Killing me wasn't enough. He had to be completely satisfied by making me suffer.

As if I was nothing more than garbage he'd used and discarded, the Warden turned his back on me. He held his head high as he practically drifted out of the room, all the elegance of a deity encompassing his form.

He was a demigod now, too. And it was all thanks to the magic he'd taken from me. Now that he'd proven he could do it, he'd move on to the others.

The distant thought of my friends... of *Charlie*... forced me to stay awake long enough to become aware that the guards had uncuffed me from the table and were hauling me in a different direction. In my ears rattled the screams of women, and we passed row after row.

A creaking sound filled my ears. They were opening a door. The sensation of falling through the air passed over me, and I realized the guards had tossed me inside a cell. My legs failed to support me, and I fell forward. I put my hands out as I collapsed onto the floor and smacked my head against the concrete. A cut formed over my eye, oozing blood into my failing vision.

I pushed my hands against the floor, but my arms shook, and I fell forward again. I no longer resisted the darkness as it swept over me, shrouding me into an empty void of no escape.

I WAS ASTONISHED when I woke up, because I didn't believe that I would. I was certain when I blacked out that my life was over, and I was going back to the Ancestral Lands, because I didn't think I'd be able to recover from the inferichite taking my magic.

Awaken I did. My eyelids were heavy, almost as heavy as the weight that was bearing down on my body from all sides, though there was nothing there to hold me. The exhaustion I felt, mingled with the dull throbbing of my middle, told me to stay down... to give up the fight.

I didn't give up. That wasn't me. Groaning, I used what strength I had to push myself up and drag my body backward so my back was propped up against the wall. There was nothing in this tiny cell, not even a bunk. Just three concrete walls and a barred door preventing my escape. I couldn't see anything except the cell across from me, which was barely lit by a small lightbulb in the hallway. That cell was devoid of life and completely empty. I must've been tossed in a hall that was isolated and didn't have any people in it.

Yet I still heard the screams. This row had to be connected to the female cell block, because girls all over Cellblock 9 were shouting, both insults and pleas for mercy. They mixed together, a variety of threats and begging, with echoing cries of sorrow mixed in.

I had to be in the female section of Cellblock 9. I didn't want to know what they were doing to those women here.

My stomach growled loudly, and I realized my mouth was pitifully dry. I was weak, not only from dehydration, but lack of sustenance.

"Somebody please get me out of this," I whispered, and I wiped at my forehead, where the cut on my head had accumulated a mass of dried blood.

From the corner of my cell, something materialized. What I thought must be a ghost turned into something more solid, a spirit glowing with colors and light. Red and blue lines mixed together as Coyote Spirit appeared in the corner of the cell, blinking at me as he cocked his furry head.

You have been asleep for nearly two days, Coyote told me. *It is evening.*

"Ugh, gross." No wonder I felt like shit. I hadn't had my pain meds in a while.

I shook my head blearily. "I should've woken up sooner."

Your body takes longer to recover than the others, as it has been through much.

"Well, we didn't have time for me to take a nap." I rubbed my wrists and winced. They had developed a red rash from the inferichite bracelets, which were still on me. "Why haven't I been taken out of this cell?"

Coyote flicked his tail. *The Warden plans to leave you here to starve.*

How thoughtful of him. "What happened to Kallie and Marcus?"

The Mistress of Time has already been drained. I am unsure about the Lord of Death.

"And Charlie?"

They will take his power soon.

"Dammit." I cringed and propped my body up further along the wall. "Can you get me out of here?"

Coyote bared his teeth. *Unfortunately, that is beyond my power.*

"Why are gods so useless?" I felt frustration well up inside of me, not just at Coyote Spirit, but at all the gods in their domain. The Warden was plotting to overthrow them all, and they were content to sit on their thrones and watch him do it. Were they going to aimlessly sit by until he came marching through their gates?

The power is not in us, but in you. Coyote strolled toward me and nudged my face with his wet nose.

"Gods are *supposed* to be all powerful. We're taught that your magic is infinite and that no one can stand up to you, but the way I see it, you're completely worthless," I spat. "If you can't help me, then why are you here?"

Because you need me.

"I don't need anyone. I can take care of myself."

Ava, love. You need to get out.

"Do something!" I screamed, and my voice echoed down the desolated hallway. "Rescue me, rescue my friends, give me my magic back, at least!"

You don't need me for any of those things.

My lip wobbled with how impossible all this was. "I'm in pain... I haven't had any of my prescriptions, water, or food in days. I can't walk, and I don't have any magic. How am I supposed to do this on my own?"

You must find a way. Coyote reached out and placed his paw on my knee. *You don't understand what is happening in the Ancestral Lands, what is happening for all of the Blessed Haven. I have attempted to send you messages in dreams, but my ability to reach out to you becomes weaker every day.*

I vaguely recalled the dream I had before my trial— the vision of a gate closing, and thousands of people swarming in panic as the light was cut off and the gate shut. "The spirits of the dead are trapped, aren't they? The gateway to the Blessed Haven has been shut."

Yes, my love. The connection between this world and the spiritual realm is closing, and thus, the ability of the gods to influence things here has been lost, Coyote informed me. *I have put myself at great risk by coming to Earth, yet in doing so, I give you hope.*

It became very clear why Monica hadn't crossed over to speak with me in person when she'd had the chance. She didn't want to risk leaving the Ancestral Lands, because there was a possibility she might get shut out. Marcus sensed something was wrong months ago when he tried summoning Thaddeus, but he'd misattributed the problem to the wards around the prison. This had been happening for longer than we realized.

No wonder Thaddeus hadn't been able to find his way into the afterlife on his own. I wasn't even sure if Marcus could've helped him cross over before he became a poltergeist. "What's happening to all those lost souls?" I asked softly.

They are stuck in a sort of in-between place, as the Elves foretold, Coyote replied grimly.

Ava, love, you are the only one who can stop this, because you are the only one who may rescue Charlie and help him to open the Elven gate. If the Elf prince does not fulfill his prophecy and lead his people into the Blessed Haven, the afterlife will be inaccessible for all souls who seek to enter it until the end of time, at which they will no longer exist, and by the Great Spirit himself this cannot be allowed to happen. Somehow, you must get out of this cell and save the others, for if you don't, your doom will signal the doom of all gods and souls that exist now, and will ever be.

My heartbeat was ramming up against my ribcage so hard I thought one of them might crack. I'd be freaking out, but I really didn't have time to lose my shit right now. "The Warden's going to find out about this."

Indeed. Now that he has a demigod's power, he will utilize it to open hell wide, and set the dark gods free so they can challenge those that remain in the Blessed Haven. It will take time for him and the gods of darkness to cross the broken boundary that has been created between Earth and the spiritual realm, but with the power he has, he will do it, Ava. With the followers he will gather in the meantime, I am unsure if we in heaven will be able to withstand his forces once he arrives. If he takes over, he will have control of that divide, and it is true that he will be the one to decide who finds salvation within the paradise the Blessed Haven offers, and who he will enslave within hell's gates.

"What do you want me to do about it? He took my magic from me." My voice cracked, and I struggled to swallow down the lump that had formed in my throat.

You are a demigod, and thus, your magic will regenerate, because you have the ability to create energy from nothing. But to do so, those inferichite cuffs have to be off of you, Coyote replied. *Once you get out of this cell, there will be a hallway on your left you will need to take. At the end of that hallway will be a door, and if you can enter it, you will find what you need.*

Coyote's form wavered, and the colors in his fur began to vanish. *I am weak, Ava. I must return to the Ancestral Lands, before it is too late. We will do what we can to help you from the other side. I wish I could say you are not on your own.*

Coyote cringed and gasped out, *But you are. I wish you luck. We are all depending on you.*

He vanished, and the cell became darker than ever before. The loneliness that overwhelmed me once Coyote was gone almost inspired me to give up. I might be able to do this on my own, as long as I had him around to at least cheer me on. But now that I knew the entire afterlife was depending on me, it wasn't like I had a choice.

"Thanks for putting on the pressure," I grumbled. I thought about the huge task in front of me, and nearly decided not to do it. How did Coyote expect me to break out of Cellblock 9, a place that had never been broken out of, without magic and without the ability to walk? He was asking for the impossible.

I remembered the Warden's cruel expression as he'd taken what he'd wanted from me, then told the guards to throw me away. Absolute hatred ignited in me and blazed up an inferno inside of my spirit that my Fire magic had never come close to touching.

The Warden thought I was no longer a threat? Big mistake, buddy. He was going to regret not killing me when he had the chance.

I took a deep breath, assessing my options. First, I had to get out of this cell. Then, transportation. If I didn't get access to a wheelchair of some sort, I wasn't going anywhere fast.

"Gotta do everything by my damn self," I grunted. "Here comes Ava to save the day!"

Someone owed me a massage after this. I slid onto my belly and pulled myself around the cell, looking for some sort of object I could use. I located nothing. I shook the rusty bars, but the door was firmly locked.

I examined the lock on the door. Kallie had taught me how to pick locks, and how the ones at the Institute worked. From what I could see, the lock on this cell was similar to the ones we had on our rooms on the main level. It had an automatic deadlocking system where once the door was shut, it latched on its own, and deadlocked by itself. It appeared to have two bolts; a lock bolt that was spring loaded to extend into a strike plate so the door remained closed, and a deadlock bolt, which prevented the latch bolt from being moved without a key.

If I could wedge something into the latch bolt, I might be able to pry the door open. Time had done part of my job for me, as the cell lock was worn from use and attempted tampering by other inmates.

I wiggled the door again, and I noticed that it was slightly loose, though still locked. Kallie had told me some of the latch bolts at the Institute were so old they failed to fully engage, so they could potentially be slipped open with things like soap, floss, or even pieces of paper. I needed something to slip into the lock, so I could get it around the latch bolt and pop it off.

Whatever I could use needed to be on me, because there was nothing in here. I looked down, then reached for my shoe, quickly untying the lace from my sneaker. Once it was undone, I did my best to jam the shoelace through the lock, threading it around the latch bolt so I could do what I could to pry it free.

It took *forever*. The work was tedious, moving the shoelace back and forth intricately to slip it underneath the latch bolt. The door squeaked as I worked, and I cringed, hoping none of the guards would hear me messing with the door and come running.

I'd been working on the door for almost an hour, and was nearly ready to try something else, when finally— in such a way that I didn't expect it— I heard a *click,* and the door slightly opened. My jaw dropped open in complete shock as I slightly swung the door back and forth. It worked!

I wound the shoelace around my hand and pulled myself through the cell, then shut it quietly. If the guards came down here and the door was closed, it was so dark that they might not even notice I was gone.

This was the part that was going to suck— crawling around on this dirty ass floor. I wrinkled my nose and tried not to pay attention to how soaked and filthy my clothes got, dragging my legs through puddles that ancestors only knew what was in them. I tried telling myself I was crawling around in a cave, on an archaeological dig with my grandfather, and not slithering around a high-security cell block on a last-ditch effort to save my life, and it helped... kind of.

I got to the end of the hallway, though my arms were burning from dragging my body all the way down it. *Coyote said turn to the left,* I thought. I poked my head around, though my stomach bottomed out when I saw two guards. They were standing around a pile of bodies, looking down.

"What a mess. I can't believe I got stuck doing this," a younger guard complained. He looked like a warlock. Probably wasn't much older than me. The other guard was middle-aged, and probably a merman.

"These bodies aren't gonna take care of themselves. Dump them out back, rookie, before we report you again for slacking off," the older guard said. "Captain's not gonna be happy if these corpses aren't moved to the yard pronto. It's already caused some trouble, so you'd better have it cleaned up by the time we get back."

The warlock grumbled as his supervisor headed down the opposite hallway, but he bent down to pick up a body. With a closer look, I realized with horror that the bodies lying on the floor were all female inmates.

At the same time, my devious mind began to figure how I could use this to my advantage. Coyote said I needed to get to the door at the end of the hallway, but maybe if the guard carried me out to the prison yard, I could find help.

Once the guard left while carrying another corpse, I did my best to crawl down the hallway and to the bodies of the other girls. I hated doing this, but these girls might have something on them that would help me escape. I began searching bodies. I cringed as I touched the ice-cold corpses, hoping I'd discover something in one of the jumpsuit pockets.

My fingers curled around something small and sharp. It was a shiv, made up of a razor blade taped up to the end of a toothbrush. It was the only weapon this girl had down here, and it had probably taken her months to scrounge up the materials. She'd died before she had a chance to use it.

"I'm sorry," I whispered. I grasped the shiv in my hand, concealing it from view. I forced myself to lay face-down amongst the bodies, praying the guards would buy the ruse.

It was absolutely gruesome, posing still amongst the corpses of the other young girls and pretending to be dead. I shut my eyes, ignoring the vacant, wide-eyed stare of the girl next to me, whose soul had left her form hours ago. She, and the other girls here, were probably stuck in the in-between place before the Blessed Haven, wondering why they couldn't get in.

I was doing this to get out of Cellblock 9, but I wanted to make things right, too. I couldn't help the girls that had died in Cellblock 9, but I could help Charlie get their souls to the right place, so nobody was going to stop me from getting out of here. I forced my limbs to remain still, although they wanted to quiver in fear, as I heard footsteps return from down the hall.

"How's it going, rookie?" The merman had come back to check on his progress. "Hell, are you slow. This is going to take all night."

I felt the warlock's boot nudge my thigh. "Hey, is this one supposed to be here? She doesn't have a jumpsuit."

"How should I know? One of the boys probably stole her from upstairs and snuck her past intake to have some fun with her in the Happy House. It's happened before."

My insides curled in disgust, but I refused to allow myself to move, because if I even *breathed* and these guys saw it, I was dead.

"Take your pick of the bodies," the rookie guard joked. "They aren't going to fight back."

"Back to your old ways, huh. That already got you in trouble the last time."

The rookie guard was quiet. "If she's from upstairs, we should probably get rid of her first, before Captain finds out... unless this is some sort of trick."

"What do you think's going to happen? She'll jump up and dance like a zombie? Double-check, if you're so scared she's not dead."

I heard the withdrawal of some sort of blade— probably a military knife. My heart stopped, and I held in a frantic breath as I realized what the guard was about to do. I didn't know if I needed to move, to defend myself, or stay still.

I wasn't able to make a decision in time, and I heard the blade *whoosh* through the air. I gritted my teeth, expecting it to land in the back of my chest and pierce through my heart.

I heard the knife sink into flesh, and felt a pool of warm blood ooze out underneath my thighs, but there was no pain. I realized the guard had stabbed his knife into my calf, where I didn't have any feeling.

Ha. Losers.

"She's dead, all right. Nobody alive would be able to take that with a straight face," the warlock replied as he withdrew the knife.

"Then quit standing around talking about it. It's best if this girl disappears. We don't want her parents, if the poor bitch has got any, poking around down here," the merman demanded.

"Yes, sir." The guard reached out to lift me into his arms. I did a good show of playing dead as he began to carry me down the hallway, and his supervisor returned to the base of the Happy House.

We were almost at the end of the hallway, and I thought I was getting out of here, when I heard the warlock catch his breath as he looked down. "Hey, wait a minute—"

Fuck! He'd felt the warm blood coming out of my leg. I felt the guard go to drop me. I swung one arm up, wrapping it around his shoulders so I could support myself, then did what I had to do as I took the shiv and stabbed it into the warlock's neck. I used as much force as I possibly could, aiming for the area Charlie had told me to— the impression where the artery was located. I drove the razor blade in, cutting into the neck before I stabbed the area where I knew his vocal cords had to be.

The warlock fell to the floor, and I dropped with him. He tried to let out a scream, but blood was spilling from his throat, and he couldn't speak. I watched him grasp his neck, attempting to fumble to hold in the blood while the other hand reached for me. It wrapped around my throat, squeezing tight, and I immediately felt my air supply cut off. I saw stars, and my chest tightened in pain as I struggled to receive air. I tried to push him off, but he was far stronger than I was, and I couldn't break his grip on me.

Go for the eyes, I heard Charlie say, so that's what I did. I stabbed the shiv into the warlock's left eye, then the right. I stuck the shiv so far into that one that I wasn't able to pull it back out. He immediately let go of me, clawing at his face as I took in a desperate amount of air.

The warlock's body slumped to the side, into a pool of his own blood. He'd finally bled out. His body twitched, throat rasping for a moment or two.

A distant chill writhed down the top of my spine. I'd killed people before... but with my magic. Not like this. Violence always seemed something distant, not up close and personal.

My father had done terrible things during the Hawkei Civil War— I was sure he did. He'd never told me about them, but there'd been rumors of things he was forced to do during battle. My mother had also committed terrible things while fighting for her people. I was of their blood. If they could do things like this to protect the ones they loved, I wouldn't hesitate, either. It was my life, or theirs, and I damn well wasn't going to die down here.

Charlie would do it. I'd *seen* him do it. He'd taken lives with his bare hands right in front of me and hadn't even flinched. If he could murder so carelessly, I would, too. I had to be like him, because I knew he was still down here somewhere, surviving. It's what he knew how to do best. I'd taught him how to live, and he'd taught me how to survive. Taking on my twin flame's mentality was the only way I was getting myself out of Cellblock 9.

The warlock rasped again, but I thought of Charlie again... he could turn his emotions off. So that's what I did, too. I just... turned them off. Because I knew they weren't going to serve me down here.

I didn't stick around to watch the guard die. While he was breathing his last breath, I rifled through his pockets for anything of use, and I found a security keycard.

I tried to get the shiv back out of his eye, but it was stuck in there, so I decided to leave it behind. Now covered in blood, I left a trail of red dragging behind me as I pulled myself down the rest of the hallway and to the door Coyote had mentioned. Above me was a box that acted as an entry system, one that was only accessible to a guard with a pass.

Ancestors, I hope nobody comes down this way. If one of the guards found a body, I was so fucked, because I'd left a trail that would lead them right to me.

I reached up to press the keycard against the entry system to the door. It unlocked, and I dragged myself inside. Hope stuttered within me as I realized that this was the room where they kept the things guards had taken off inmates. My wheelchair was in a corner of the room, along with my compass, but my journal wasn't here. The Warden must've kept it for himself. I hefted myself into my wheelchair with shaking arms, and grasped the compass in my hand as I searched for other things here I could use.

There wasn't much— a lot of drugs, mostly. I didn't find any weapons, just a bunch of junk that would be useless down here. I held my compass in my hands, watching the needle spin. The compass would guide me to what I needed the most, and right now, I needed my friends more than anyone.

"Please," I begged. "I need you guys. If you can reach me through the broken boundary, you have to tell me where my friends are."

I wasn't sure if Lindsey or Miranda would have the ability to reach the compass from the Ancestral Lands now that the divide was formed, but the needle suddenly stopped spinning. It pointed toward the door, and I held my breath as I rolled toward it.

I had to squeeze my chair against the wall to get past the body of the guard. My wheels rolled through the blood puddle, leaving a path behind me. Shit, I was so fucked if anyone came down this way. I placed the compass in my lap and kept glancing down at it to guide my move-ments through the tight hallways. The needle tilted slowly, giving small motions this way and that.

I got to the end of the corridor, and stopped before I turned the corner. Fear crawled up my flesh when I heard a conversation between two guards standing watch in the middle of the hallway.

"The Warden's been moving everyone out all day. The last of us leave tonight. We need to be ready when we're given the order to move out."

"Did he inform Captain where we're headed?"

"He hasn't told anyone. The Warden's not giving any details until the Institute's been cleared."

A knot formed in my throat. What the hell were they talking about?

"Almost feel sorry for all these poor bastards."

"They had their chance to join The Mission. Anyone left behind is a lost cause, at this rate, and in my opinion these kids deserve to die."

I glanced down at the compass again. I wanted to go a different way, but the compass needle stubbornly pointed in their direction.

I felt a bead of sweat form at my hairline. I couldn't take on two guards at once. But I had to pass them, and there was nowhere for me to hide if they came down this way, which, eventually, they would. They'd see me in mere moments, which meant I needed to come up with a plan to take them down.

Ancestors, I hoped this worked. Silently, I got down from my chair and hid around the corner. I grabbed the sides of my chair, then pushed it as hard as I could around the opposite corner and down the hallway, away from the guards.

"What was that?" I heard footsteps as both guards turned around. They began walking in the direction of my wheelchair to investigate the sound. My body tensed as they grew closer, and I knew I'd only get one shot at this.

"Go check that out," a guard ordered, and both of them hurried toward the wheelchair. Just as they walked past, I reached out and grabbed his ankles, yanking backward so that he was tripped off his feet. The guard stumbled into his companion, and both of them went down. I crawled on top of the first guard the second he went flat, then immediately went for the pistol holstered to his side.

His mouth dropped open, but I pointed the pistol and pulled the trigger before he had time to give another reaction. Blood splattered against my face, and I heard the thick crunch of bone shattering. The other guard reached for his gun, but I fired a second shot, and it was so close range that my aim didn't miss.

My hands shook as I lowered the pistol. I reached for the other guard's gun, taking out the bullets so I had some remaining ammo. I didn't know how to load a gun, but because I had to, I'd learn. I didn't pay attention to the brain matter streaked across the floor, or the cracked skulls. I just did what I had to do and hefted myself back into my chair so I could continue onward.

I laid the pistol beside the compass in my lap and forced my quivering fingers to push me faster. I had to get out of the area. Someone might've heard the gun go off, and if they did, the time I had to find my friends was even more limited. *Please, let them be close.*

The guards I'd shot looked like they were shifters. I guess it was lucky I'd run into them, and not others, because a bullet wouldn't take down an angel or a vampire.

But something was off. Where were all the vampire and angel guards? I'd run into other races down here, but the Warden's favorite lackeys were nowhere to be found, and I figured they'd be crawling around Cellblock 9. This was the highest security area in the prison, and yet, the entire cell block seemed to be empty.

My mind ventured to the conversation I'd overheard moments ago. The guards had said the Warden was moving everyone out... but by everyone, I was certain it only meant the people who had agreed to do whatever he said without question— teacher, student or otherwise. The Warden's favorite guards weren't here because something big was happening. Now that he had our demigod magic, the Warden was concocting another plan, and he was going to set it in motion... tonight.

I needed to get myself and my friends out of here before whatever he was constructing went down, because it was happening *right now*, and by the sound of it, the Warden didn't plan for anyone to get off Institute grounds who wasn't following his orders.

I took a look at the compass again, and it stubbornly pointed forward, to a thick metal door over a hundred feet away that only had a small window. I guessed that was where they kept the inmates in solitary.

I wondered why the Warden hadn't placed me down here, until I realized he'd ordered me tossed me into one of the cells they didn't use anymore, because in the hallway I'd been in, no one would notice me starve, not even if I cried for help. There was no chance of anyone rescuing me but myself, and the Warden thought that would be impossible.

He really needed to learn nothing was impossible for Ava-Marie Wahkin.

When I got closer to the metal door, I was able to work out more details. There was an entry box on the handle, but when I pressed the keycard to it, it denied me access. Must not have enough credentials to go in.

I couldn't lift myself high enough out of my chair to look through the window, so I had to take a gamble. I took a shaky grip on the pistol, then banged on the door as loudly as I could, acting like I was knocking. I lifted the keycard and pressed it against the window.

"Godsdammit, Barry, I told you before! You can't come back here until the Warden—"

The door opened— *Bang*. The gun went off again, then a second time. I gave a quiet yelp and nearly dropped the gun as the body of the guard sank to the floor, crumpling beside a desk.

A couple of tears shakily made their way down my cheeks, but I reminded myself that I wasn't supposed to feel anything, so I shoved my emotions down and moved on. I pretended like the body of the guard wasn't there... didn't exist... as I maneuvered my chair around it and surveyed the room.

It was some sort of security holding that had access to all the cells in solitary. There was a circuit board inside that had buttons to open the doors to each individual cell in solitary confinement. Right now, only four of the cells were full. I checked the names in the logbook beside the guard's desk, and nearly gave a cry of relief. I pressed every single one, then pushed open another door to venture down solitary's hall.

It was just like any other cell block, except the doors here were actual doors, and not barred gates, ones that were made of metal and reached from the floor to the ceiling. The doors creaked open, and three figures stumbled out, wincing at the brightness of the lightbulb suspended from the ceiling.

"Oh, precious, thank Atlantis." Ivy's sobbing voice cut me to the core. "I thought for sure you were dead."

"Ivy..." My stomach churned as I gazed over their battered appearance. Their clothes were torn, and they had two black eyes, along with an allotment of bruises up and down their form.

Somebody had hurt them badly. Worse than that, they were covered in dried blood. Their clothes were strained red, skin bloody up to their elbows. Around Ivy's mouth and running down their face and neck was the worst of it. It looked like they'd used their fangs to tear a whole room apart.

"I've been through worse, precious. Don't worry about me," Ivy choked out. "I'm just glad you came."

"Ava, how'd you make it?" Marcus winced and held his arm as he stumbled closer. He, too, appeared absolutely shaken and completely mistreated. More than a few people had gotten some good hits on him down in Cellblock 9. By the way he was holding his arm, I figured it was broken.

"I managed," I whispered. Chancey stood beside him, and although the angel sported fewer injuries than the other two, the place had definitely made him worse for wear. He kept glancing around, jumping at every drop of moisture that slid from the ceiling onto the floor.

"You don't know what it's like in there, man," Chancey said, and he gave a shiver. "No light, complete silence... hell would be better than that."

A groan came from an open cell door, and Marcus ducked in. I heard a hissing sound, like a brand being pressed to skin, and the sharp scream of a woman as Marcus carried someone out of it with one arm.

It was Kallie. Her skin was covered in what looked like fresh burns that'd been carved into it. Her fae blood had made crossing through the iron door incredibly painful.

I peeked into the solitary cells, and saw that they were empty rooms devoid of all windows, sealed off with a silencing spell so no light or sound could enter.

I couldn't imagine what it'd been like for them, sitting there in complete silence and darkness for hours, nothing but the sound of their own breathing to remind them that they were still alive.

They were braver than I was. I would've lost my mind.

"The doors here are made of pure iron," Kallie gasped. "I couldn't cross it, but they threw me in anyway. It burned me, and made me so weak. I thought I was going to die."

"It's all right. I got you out," Marcus said, and he embraced her with his good arm. She returned his hug with a quiet shiver.

As I took each of them in, I felt relieved, and terrified. They were here. They were all here... but one. My heart leapt and dropped at the same time.

"Ava, why do you have a gun?" Marcus asked, his voice cracking.

I wouldn't answer him. "Where's Charlie? Does anyone know?"

"The Warden probably took him to drain his powers," Chancey rasped.

I absolutely wanted to panic— to open my mouth and scream as loudly as I could, right then and there.

"Charlie's a fighter. He's gotta be out there," Ivy insisted, grasping my shoulder. "We just have to get to him."

Marcus took a short breath. "They must've taken him to a containment room to be tortured. It'd be the same room I was in. I..."

He cringed and held his broken arm tighter as he continued. "I remained conscious after they drained me. I memorized the route, just in case."

"Then take us to it. Does anyone have any magic?" I asked desperately.

"The Warden drained us, just like you," Kallie said glumly.

"We got noxite in our system," Chancey mumbled, gesturing to himself and Ivy. "Our magic is as useless as yours is."

"Great. Fucking perfect." As if things could get any worse.

"Give me the pistol," Ivy said. "I know how to use it."

I handed it off without question. I didn't want to touch it anymore. Ivy loaded the spare bullets, and Kallie said, "We should get moving. Charlie's in danger."

I looked up at Chancey, and he got my signal that I was too tired to move on my own. He grabbed the handles of my wheelchair as he pushed me after the others, while Marcus led the way. Marcus groaned as he cradled his broken arm, and Kallie hissed as her jumpsuit brushed up against the burns on her skin. I really wanted to heal them... all of them... but I couldn't until I got my magic back, and getting these cuffs off wasn't as important as finding my husband.

"Gods, Ava..." Kallie whispered as we passed the body of the guard I'd shot, but she didn't say anything else. Nor did the rest of them. We remained quiet and stuck to the wall, until Marcus held a hand up to stop us.

A group of guards rushed past, two hallways down. I counted up to twenty of them before they disappeared entirely. They looked like they were in a hurry.

"Who lit a fire under their ass?" Chancey mumbled.

"The Warden's moving the guards and The Mission off-campus. I overheard some of them talking about it," I whispered. "From what I heard, they're planning on leaving some of the inmates behind."

"For what?" Kallie asked.

"I ain't sticking around to find out, sorry to say," Chancey replied.

We were too hasty, and we ended up running into two guards on our way to confinement. I had the thought we were caught, but Ivy slammed the pistol against the temple of one of the guards, before they wrapped their arm around the head of another and swiftly broke his neck. My hand flashed to my throat as both guards went down. Beside me, Kallie gave a sigh of relief.

"Fucking hell, Ivy." I shuddered.

"Done this before," Ivy said, far too casually. "Stealth missions are kind of my thing."

"It's not a mission, it's a breakout," Marcus hissed. "Now we have two more bodies to lead them right to us!"

"Not if we get our asses moving. Let's go!" Chancey shoved Marcus forward, and he stumbled over the motionless guards. I kept my eyes focused forward, trying to block it all out as we ventured onward.

"It's going to be okay, Ava," Kallie whispered, but I didn't know if it would be. I was a villain... but this wasn't the kind of villain I wanted to be.

We passed a set of metal pipes in the wall, ones that had previously been used for plumbing but now looked all but completely useless. I knew we were nearing the confinement rooms long before we got there, because I recognized the sound of Charlie's screams. I let out a little whimper and nearly cried in relief, because he was *alive*, before realizing that if he was screaming in such a terrible way, they had to be doing something awful to him. I put my hands on the wheels of my chair and tried to go faster, but Chancey held the chair back firmly.

"No, Ava. We gotta do this the right way," he hissed.

Charlie gave another tormented wail, and I began to cry.

"There's gotta be vampires in there," Ivy muttered. "I can smell the blood from here. They're making him bleed before they end it, cause they get off on it."

"We can't kill *vampire guards*! All we have is a gun, and that's basically useless!" Kallie snapped.

"Three ways to kill a vampire. Beheading, fire, and a sharp object through the heart," Ivy replied, glancing at the pipes beside them.

Chancey began ripping metal pipes off the walls. It made a loud sound, but Charlie's screams of pain were louder, so no one heard it. He bent them until they snapped, creating jagged edges. He distributed the makeshift stakes amongst the group. "Don't fucking miss."

I clutched the rusty pipe he gave me. If this was all I had to fight a vampire, it was more than enough, because I'd do anything to stop them from hurting Charlie further.

Chancey stopped me outside the door to the confinement room, then leaned against it. He nodded, telling us to get ready.

We all poised, waiting to go on the attack. Chancey rammed his shoulder into the door, and it flew open as the lock broke under his weight. He ducked as Ivy came charging in, firing the gun into the room.

There were three vampires each, and they all looked up at the sound of gunshots. A bullet hit each of their foreheads and sunk in, but didn't appear to do any damage. Their fangs flashed as they hissed at us, and their forms became blurs across the room as they raced in our direction.

I thought I was ready, but you really couldn't prepare for how quickly vampires moved. I felt my chair fall backwards, and the wind was knocked out of me as I slammed against the floor. The pipe flew out of my hands with the force of the tackle, rattling up against the wall. The vampire guard let out a screech, his hot venom dripping onto my skin as he displayed the full length of his red fangs.

Awesome, I was going to have my throat ripped open by a fucking psychopath. The vampire bent down to tear through my jugular, but the hiss he made became a strangling sound as I watched a metal pipe erupt through his chest. Ivy stood over him, gritting their own fangs as they shoved the metal pipe through the vampire's back and clear through to his heart.

The vampire's body fell forward, but Ivy tossed him off of me. Ivy righted my chair back up, helping me get readjusted as they brushed back my hair. "Precious, you good?"

I gave a frantic nod. Kallie had staked a separate vampire guard through the heart, who was dying as I watched, and Chancey had already taken care of the other. Their bodies became discarded casualties as my eyes locked on the person imprisoned on the metal table. "Ancestors, *Charlie*."

He lay in a pool of his own blood, which was dripping off the table. Surgical instruments stuck out of him at every which angle. The vampires had spent who knew how long *bloodletting him*.

I rolled up to the table as quickly as I could and started pulling the instruments out of his body. They weren't in too deep. It wouldn't kill him, just hurt, so I had to get these things out of him. Charlie gasped with every object I yanked out, giving a few mottled coughs. Blood sputtered past his teeth and over his lips.

"I'm sorry, I'm sorry!" More tears snaked down my cheeks, until I could barely see straight. Kallie and Marcus busied themselves with getting the cuffs off that held Charlie to the table. Once he was free, Chancey lowered Charlie to the ground. He was strong enough that he was able to prop himself up, though the breaths from his lungs sounded rattled and thick.

This was worse than the Infernal Underground. It was so much worse.

"I can't believe you guys found me," Charlie rasped.

My lip wobbled as he spoke. He didn't even *sound* like himself.

"You should be thanking Ava. She rescued us," Ivy proudly informed him.

"Pidge, how'd you manage that by yourself?" Charlie's head lolled. I shook him, to keep him awake.

"It doesn't matter." I slid out of my chair so I could be at his level. I tried to wipe the blood away from his lips, and failed. "I just have to get these inferichite bracelets off, so I can heal you!"

"We're not getting them off, pidge. There's no magic left." Charlie pushed back his hair to hold his temple, and a fresh stripe of blood streaked across his forehead.

"We've done it before, we'll do it again," I said firmly. "We've gotten this far. Now our next step is to get our magic back."

"How do we do that?" Charlie asked tiredly. Kallie sat beside us, with Marcus taking the other side. I knew they were too exhausted to stand.

"We use simultension, just like we did before," I insisted. "Combine your powers with mine."

"There's no magic left in any of us. The Warden took it all," Marcus objected.

"I don't believe that. I *never* will," I swore. "We're stronger than he could ever imagine."

"Ava's right. We just gotta dig deep, deeper than we ever have before," Kallie said. "I believe that there's still something there. Our demigod powers wouldn't have the ability to regenerate if we didn't have *some* kind of access. Let's use it to fuse our magic together and break inferichite's hold on us for good."

"Combining three different kinds of supernatural magic?" Marcus asked. "I guess we don't know if it's possible, but we should try anyway."

"I know we can do anything, so long as we think we can. My mother taught me that," Kallie said firmly. "Guys, we have to *try*."

Kallie reached out to take Marcus' hand, before she grasped Charlie's. I reached out to hold Marcus' other hand, then entwined my fingers with my husband. I ordered my magic to connect, and felt my intention entwining with the abilities of those who surrounded me. Kallie's fae magic felt light, and full of endless possibilities as her illusion power opened doors for me to new worlds I had never envisioned before. Fae magic was full of mischief, adventure, and ideas that had never been conceived until the moment they were born by their creator.

By contrast, Marcus' magic was dark, full of musing contemplation and quiet innovation. I marveled at its ability to take the smallest things and tamper with them to create outcomes of his own design. I felt different vibrations, some of them smooth, others chaotic, and I marveled at his ability to control all the different spells he cast.

Charlie's magic was as familiar as my own, masculine, secure, and grounding. It was a simple power that was similar to taking in a breath, or running your fingers through grass. But that power also had the ability to create a maelstrom, or command a mountain to move, and it would do so just by him asking. His Elven magic resonated with a spirituality that I'd only found, and missed, in the Ancestral Lands, a conception that was able to ignite the desires of the gods themselves, and make dreams real.

My Water magic desired to soothe. My Fire magic needed to rage. But over both of them, my Spirit magic longed to heal. I felt the power of my feminine Spirit magic entwining the other abilities of my companions, bringing them in, sewing them into a thick cord that had thousands of strands and was just as endless as the beginning of time.

The inferichite binding our powers attempted to hold us back, but together, it was similar to the effect of a singular being attempting to withstand a tidal wave. We couldn't break the inferichite crystals alone, but with each new ability that we added to the spell as demigods, I felt the dark crystals weaken. It wasn't enough to have two or three— we needed *all* of us to render the inferichite's power obsolete, and I felt our intentions combine into the thoughts of one being as we drove our complicated spell into the inferichite. At that moment in time, there weren't four of us, but one, as if we were a united soul.

All of the inferichite crystals binding our powers shattered into pieces, and the bracelets completely broke in two, falling uselessly off our wrists. The tracking cuffs we'd been fitted with earlier this semester fell off, too. A surge of powerful energy came rushing back into me, and it felt like the kiss of life. Renewed power amplified through my body and echoed outward. I was born again as my demigod abilities came beaming back to life, and with it, my magic.

Each one of us took a simultaneous breath in unison. I watched as their expressions brightened, hope surging back into the features of my friends. I didn't waste any time, and got to work. I healed Charlie first, surging my Anichi energy into his body to heal his cuts and bruises, leaving him completely well before I moved on to mend Marcus' broken arm, then Kallie's burns. I didn't even think— I merely touched them, and all their injuries went away at my thoughts, melting away at my fingertips as if I'd commanded them to go away merely by my will, leaving them perfect. It took no time at all, unlike normal healing magic did, and left me feeling energized instead of spent. It was *effortless*.

"I feel amazing," Kallie said, and I watched her transform, shaking her wolfish pelt and giving a growl. Marcus conjured a battle orb to test out his magic, smiling as he tilted his hand to observe it.

"Pidge, you're so wonderful." Charlie bent down to hug me, then lifted me into my chair. "You never give up, do you?"

"I can't believe we really pulled that off!" Marcus yelped. "Guess all we needed was to stick together, huh?"

I healed Chancey and Ivy, and used my Anichi powers to dissolve the noxite in their system. Chancey didn't waste any time on moving forward.

"Awesome, the power of friendship saves the day. So can we *fucking leave*?!" Chancey asked.

I ignited a fireball in my hand, and it flared all the way up to the ceiling. "Oh, *hell yeah*."

"Hold on," Kallie said. She opened cabinet drawers and started rifling through them. "There are files here in Cellblock 9. We should take everything we can find."

She yanked out stacks of files from every drawer in the room, then handed them to Marcus to subconjure. "We gotta find Rishi and Oberi," Marcus said hastily.

"Ava and I can feel him," Charlie noted. "They have to be nearby."

Charlie and I followed the mental trail leading us to our Familiar. The moment we stepped outside the door of the room we'd been in, there was a host of guards waiting for us in the hallway. They raised their pistols, taking aim.

They had no idea who they were dealing with. My sights fell on three guards, and before our eyes they spontaneously combusted into ash, their forms becoming a pile of embers without a singular flame. Charlie's Air magic blasted them backward, sending three guards sailing down the hall with so much force that their bodies were crushed when they finally hit the concrete wall at the end. Kallie conjured swords with her illusion magic, which hovered in the air before they spun into the hearts of four other guards, slicing them from shoulder to belly. As their entrails collapsed from their middles, Marcus used telekinesis to lift the guards off the floor, smashing them into the ceiling before wrenching their bodies back down to the floor.

"All right, now we're talking!" Ivy shouted as we moved forward. They gave a wicked cackle and racked the pistol.

Oberi's panicky urges through our bond made us move quickly. I attempted to speak to him, but I don't think he heard me, because he didn't respond. I felt his terror resonating in a room about fifty feet down the hall. There was a guard protecting the door ahead, and he raised his pistol to shoot, but Charlie lifted his hand, and the guard put both hands to his neck as he immediately lost the ability to breathe. He rasped as his lungs were crushed, attempting to uselessly conjure a fireball before it fizzled out. Charlie grabbed him by the shoulders and tossed him out of the way as Chancey opened the door.

My stomach clenched painfully as we entered the room, and I observed the area. It was some sort of pound for Familiars and animal companions of those in Cellblock 9. The walls were lined with cages, rows of them stacked one right on top of the other. The room appeared empty, all cages vacant. I worried we'd found the wrong place, or that they'd been moved.

A low whimpering in the corner of the room caught my attention. Charlie and I pivoted toward it at the same time, drawn to the call. We rushed forward, and my heart was wrenched out of my chest as I saw Oberi shivering in a little cage, which was on eye level with us. He still had the muzzle on, and looked completely terrified. When he saw us, he gave a low whine and wagged his tail slowly. He appeared absolutely pitiful, and I wanted to cry. No dog, especially not Oberi, belonged in a pound.

"Rishi!" Marcus stood on his tiptoes, looking into a cage above us. "He's here!"

I heard Rishi give a low yowl from up high. Charlie grabbed the cage holding Oberi and shook its door, before he drew back with a hiss. "The bars have inferichite in them."

"Let's break it together." Kallie grasped the door, and the three of us copied her movement. Simultension formed our powers together in one blast, and the inferichite stood no chance against it. Our magic ripped apart the inferichite lock keeping the cage door closed like it was nothing but a piece of paper caught in a hurricane, and the lock blew into pieces.

We combined our powers to let Rishi loose, before Charlie ripped open the cage door that led to Oberi. He wrenched the muzzle off of Oberi's mouth and tossed it to the floor, then took Oberi into his arms and cuddled him to his chest. "Oh, Oberi."

Our Familiar shook as he licked Charlie's face. *You found me, you found me!*

"Of course we did," Charlie said, and he buried his face in Oberi's shoulder fur while I patted his head and kissed his nose. Oberi gave me an affectionate lick before Charlie set him down, and the husky began hopping furiously around on his paws.

Gods. I'm pissed, I'm SO pissed, Oberi fumed. *How dare they put me in a tiny cage! I am not one for tiny cages!*

Rishi gave a surly meow from Marcus' arms. His eyes were half shut, lip curled as his nose shriveled up in distaste. He was certainly *not happy.*

I glanced quickly around the pound. "I don't see Tahoma or Pig. Maybe they never found Ez or Alistair. What if they got out with the keys?"

"Let's hope so. What's our next move?" Chancey asked.

"I can paint a door," Marcus offered.

"We need to find Sprigs and Alette first. The Warden's also got my grimoire," Kallie said breathlessly.

"My journal, too," I added. "He can't be allowed to have it. He'll figure out my aunt's clues and use them against us."

"I'll bet anything they're in his office," Marcus said shortly. "It'll be faster for us to walk there than it will be for me to paint a life-sized door."

"Good plan. Come on." Charlie grabbed my wheelchair handles and pushed me out of the pound, which I was grateful for, because I didn't want to be in there for one more second.

I asked my compass to direct us toward the exit. The needle spun, and we followed its instructions until it led us to a set of staircases that went upward. There was a slight beam of light resonating from the top of them, and it appeared to be the light of salvation.

My arms shook. Ancestors, we were almost free.

Until... my attention was stolen away as we passed a door by the base of the stairs. "What's that?" I asked, grabbing my wheels so Charlie knew to stop.

"It's the control room. Who cares?" Chancey asked.

"Wait," I said, and Chancey gave a groan. "Hold on a minute."

I used a fireball to melt the lock on the door, and Ivy propped it open for me. I wheeled inside and observed the control panel inside the room, which was very similar to the one in solitary except for one thing.

"What's this big red button do?" I asked as I stared at it. I was itching to press it, mainly because the warning inscribed by the button told me not to.

"It's an emergency release. It overrides all the locks and instantly opens every cell in the block. I learned about them while Marcus and I were investigating death row," Kallie informed me, looking down at it.

All was quiet for a second, before I brought my hand slamming down onto the button. The minute I touched it, an alarm siren blared. Spinning red lights lit up in the control room and down the hallway, signaling an escape.

"Ava, what are you doing?" Charlie asked. The red light flashed across his face as the sirens around us sang.

"I'm letting everyone out of Cellblock 9," I said. "The good, the bad, all of them. Everyone deserves a chance to get out of here."

Charlie nodded shortly. "Then you gave them their chance. We can't offer them anything else."

"Are you *crazy*?! Now the Warden's gonna know we're coming!" Chancey yelled.

"Who gives a fuck?" Marcus snarled. "He's not stopping us now."

I completely agreed. The inferichite had been the only thing containing us inside the Institute, and with the four of us together, we'd learned how to break it easily. There wasn't a prison on this planet that could hold us anymore. Go ahead and let the Warden try.

We left the control room, and the others began sprinting up the stairs. Even from here, I could hear shouts, screams, and the sounds of battle as the inmates were set free within Cellblock 9. Guards fired their pistols to stop them, but soon, the inmates weren't the only ones screaming as the room dissolved into pandemonium.

Oberi transformed into a Fire unicorn, and the illusion saddle instantly appeared on her back. *Time to leave.*

"Up you go, pidge," Charlie said, and he boosted me onto Oberi, attaching my legs to the straps quickly. "You've gotta be able to move fast."

Marcus subconjured my wheelchair, and Oberi carried me briskly up the stairs. I expected everything to be dark and quiet as we burst through the doors that made the entrance to Cellblock 9, but instead of silence, I received chaos.

Students and guards flooded the hallways, heading in every direction. There was a lot of noise and shouting, spells flying overhead while the sounds of bullets ricocheted off the walls. The hallway was crowded with hundreds of students, and an equal amount of guards. It was absolute madness.

"The other kids locked up by The Mission must've escaped!" I yelled over the noise. I yanked Charlie out of the way as a battle orb went sailing by, and Kallie pressed herself against the wall before a stunning spell knocked her off her feet.

The crowd became a stampede as inmates pressed together, attempting to escape the rampaging guards. Oberi pushed people out of the way, shoving them aside from Charlie and me, but in the chaos of the crowd, we began to get separated. Ivy was dragged in one direction, while Marcus and Kallie were pulled in another. They began shooting off spells, and were more or less able to stay in one place, but Ivy panicked. I heard the pistol go off twice as Ivy shot it, and several people in the hall screamed, but it didn't do any good as the crowd began to carry Ivy away like a wave.

"Help!" Ivy cried. Panic erupted inside of me as I watched Ivy's head vanish underneath a crowd of inmates as they were carried to the other side of the room by the velocity of the mob, which was beyond anyone's control.

"Ives!" Chancey didn't think twice. He went after Ivy, pushing people over to get back to his love. Eventually, he too dissolved into the crowd.

"Guys, wait!" I screamed.

I was on Oberi's back, so I had a good vantage point over the mob. I was able to keep an eye on them, until the sound of shattering stone arose from the Institute's ceiling. Stones began falling one by one, creating a barricade as Nivita guards caused them to tumble overhead. It sliced the crowd in two so half of the inmates had nowhere to go. The stones piled up, blocking our way to Ivy and Chancey as the guards cornered us against a huge pile of rubble. I reached out my arm for Charlie, and he took it, swinging himself onto Oberi's back behind me as the guards advanced inward. Kallie and Marcus fell beside us as dozens of students attempted to climb the rock wall to get away.

The crackling sound of the intercom broke out over the noise. The guards stopped marching, and the screams halted. Nobody dared to utter a syllable as the Warden's smooth voice echoed through the Institute halls.

"Good evening, students. And welcome to our cleansing," the Warden began. *"You all had your chance to seek my guidance into the new world, but failed to take my hand. Now you will pay the price. By my command, only the strongest will survive this test by faith. I've ordered the guards to kill all of you. Those of you who are capable enough to defeat them shall perish in the flames of my judgment. If, by some miracle, you outlast my trial by fire, I will consider you worthy of joining The Mission. You're all participating in the Games, now. Stay vigilant. Stay alive."*

The sick motto of the Darke Games blared through the loudspeakers, before the Warden gave an unhinged laugh and the announcement was sharply cut off. The screams started up again, louder than before, and the guards began shooting. People fell to the ground at Oberi's hooves, and that was the moment Marcus completely snapped.

"You wanna throw us back in the Games!?" Marcus erupted, facing the guards. "The Warden wants to act like this is some twisted joke? Well, he doesn't know who the *fuck* he's playing with!"

The guards turned their rifles on Marcus, but he maneuvered his hands in a circle before thrusting them outward. The souls of the guards he was facing erupted out of their bodies, and their corpses collapsed to the ground as Marcus took control of the ghosts he'd just created. The wayward souls had no chance to understand what had happened to them as Marcus used his Death magic to take control. The room filled with Marcus' demented laughter as he forced the ghosts to turn on the other guards. The ghosts gave unearthly howls, ones that matched the cries of terror their victims gave as they were torn open.

Kallie growled, and she changed into a wolf. She used her illusion magic to duplicate herself a dozen times, then attacked a full battalion of guards all on her own. The guards shot at her duplicates, and when a bullet landed, the duplicate went down, but all it did was simply vanish. They had to hit the real Kallie in order to kill her and stop the duplicates from attacking, but they didn't know which one to aim for, because each wolf looked the same. The wolves ran throughout the hallway, slaughtering guards and taking them down beside the ghosts Marcus had created.

"Charlie, I need your help. Let's make a storm!" I shouted.

I grabbed his hand, and my Water magic combined with his Air power as a rumble broke out overhead amongst the collapsed ceiling. Lightning flashed, and rain poured down from the sky in buckets as the wind strengthened. Charlie created a miniature tornado in the middle of the room, and I fueled it with my Fire, guiding it along until it was a spinning vortex of death and flame that completely enveloped each guard it met. The guards were pinned down by our wind and unable to see through our rain, held in place as the Fire tornado incinerated their pathetic forms.

As we were fighting off the guards, I realized the inmates behind were *cheering* for us. Rebellion grew inside me and exploded at their praise. These guards had mistreated us, humiliated us, and abused us for years. Let's see how *they* liked it.

For a brief moment, I felt like a hero. I think we all did. But really, we weren't heroes. We weren't doing this to protect people. We just wanted to give these guards a taste of their own medicine, but if revenge was our motive, and it defended the people who'd been mistreated by these monsters... well, that was just a bonus.

When the area was cleared of guards, Charlie and I withdrew our storm. Kallie faded away her duplicates, and Marcus lifted his control of the ghosts, who hovered in the room for a moment before vanishing entirely. Wherever their souls were going, it was probably to hell, because they worked for the Warden. They could continue their service to him in the afterlife. I hoped each of them remembered it was us who'd sent them there.

Inmates began running in every direction, crying out thanks as they left. At least we gave them a chance to get away. Charlie used his Earth magic to tear apart the stones that had fallen from the ceiling, but once we got a clear way through to the other side, my heart dropped. The hall was already empty. The mob had left, carrying Chancey and Ivy to a place we didn't know.

"They're not here," I informed Charlie, dropping my head.

"We have to keep going. They'll meet us at the Lair," Charlie said.

If they were still alive. "Which way to the Warden's office?" Kallie asked.

"I know the way. Follow me," I said.

I pulled on Oberi's mane, and she turned to the left. Kallie changed into a wolf, and faced Marcus as she said, "*Hop on.*"

Marcus gave a snicker, then stroked her pointed ears. "Such a pretty girl, aren't you? You're *my* pretty girl."

Rishi gave a surly growl, and Kallie stumbled backward, like she didn't know what to think. Marcus had the biggest shit-eating grin on his face as he pulled himself onto Kallie's back, then buried his face in her fur.

"I think he's lost his marbles," Charlie mumbled. "*Awesome* timing."

"Well, he's been through a lot today. We all have. I don't blame him for not being able to keep it together," I replied. I urged Oberi into a canter, and she surged down the hallway as the rest followed.

The Warden's office wasn't far from Cellblock 9, so I figured we'd be there in less than a few minutes. But as we rounded one corner into another, I realized that instead of the lane that led to the office, we were in the corridor that was by Commissary.

"What the hell? This isn't where we were two seconds ago!" I shouted.

"Then where are we?" Charlie asked. Marcus slid off Kallie's back, and she transformed again, wandering around to observe where we were.

"We started near Cellblock 9, which is only a block away from the Warden's office, but now we're near the cafeteria, which is clear on the other side of campus!" I complained. "How the hell did we get here?"

Kallie walked backward, then ran her fingers over what appeared to be thin air. A shimmering veil formed before her, a piece of nearly translucent fabric fluttering in the wind. "He made fae guards change some of the hallways into traps," Kallie said. "So students will go through them trying to escape, and it'll put them in different parts of the prison than when they came. It's meant to confuse, and to test who's smart enough to figure out they're being misled."

"He wants us to be like rats in a cage," Charlie growled.

A laugh bubbled out from Marcus' throat. "Tricky, tricky. He makes games, we break them."

"Can you break the traps?" I asked Kallie.

"Absolutely. Give me a second." Kallie placed her hand flat against a wall, and there was a high-pitched sound, one that sharply rose, then lowered, in pitch. The shimmering veil vaporized into mist, and Kallie brushed off her hands on her jeans. "There. That should've broken all of them, wherever they are around the prison."

"We still have to go all the way back, and now we know the Warden is setting traps," I grumbled. "Who knows what we'll find on the way there."

"Maybe we can take a shortcut," Kallie offered. I turned Oberi down the hallway, and we trotted up to the cafeteria. Kallie went to take a step down another path. "Should we go this way, or—"

Our debate was solved when, without warning, Marcus kicked down the cafeteria doors. "DING DONG, MOTHERFUCKERS!"

The cafeteria was an absolute beehive for guards. Hundreds of them swarmed around the area, waiting on the Warden's orders.

Marcus stood in the doorway. Dark power swirled around his form, and it made the entire room go dim. Wisps of purple and blue magic traveled up his legs and down his arms as his curls fell into one eye. He gave a twisted smile.

"Hello, boys. Let's play a game." Marcus hissed. He conjured a battle orb, hovering it in his palm as he took a ragged step toward the guards.

"Oh, look, shiny!" Marcus proclaimed as he bounced the battle orb in his hand. "You wanna know what happens when I make this go *boom?*"

The guards raised their rifles, but Marcus tossed the battle orb with a yell, and it sailed to the middle of the room. Tables and benches went flying as an explosion erupted. Kallie threw up a shield to protect us, and I watched as bodies were tossed against it in the blast.

A massive crater was left in the center of the cafeteria. The guards who'd survived were lying on the floor, staring up at Marcus in a mixture of terror and respect.

"What the hell are you?" a guard asked in fear.

"I'm what happens when you allow a theater kid to survive!" Marcus conjured more battle orbs and tossed them around the room in quick succession. Guards put up shields and responded with magic of their

own, throwing spells around the room that blew chunks off of concrete pillars and made holes in the wall.

The explosion had caught the attention of other guards, who swarmed in from different entrances. Kallie raced forward to join Marcus. She grasped his hand, and a dark stream of magic wrapped around them tightly as they joined their powers with simultension.

The two of them didn't even have to *speak*. It was marvelous. I watched as their combined powers shot out at a dozen guards. The spell squeezed their torsos, and the guards' screams of pain morphed into withered old cries of desperation. I observed as the strong bodies of the guards lost their muscular form, becoming aged and bent-over. Lines showed on their once-clear faces, changing their features from young to elderly. Kallie's time magic had merged with Marcus' death abilities, and they'd used it to physically age the guards in moments. Years of their life passed by in seconds, until the wrinkled faces of the guards dissolved as they turned into skeletons, then poofed into nothing but dust.

A couple of bullets grazed by our heads. Oberi turned and began shooting fireballs out of her horn. Charlie wrapped his arms around me and squeezed as our powers united once more. Like Kallie and Marcus, we didn't have to think about what to create. Our magic worked for us, and the cafeteria shook with a massive earthquake as the ground completely split open, leaving a cavern in the ground miles deep. From the depths, my Fire magic and Charlie's Earth magic intertwined to summon magma, and it sizzled as it bubbled up from the mantle. The magma grew, forming into itself as it became a massive lava monster, one that groaned and moved of its own accord.

The guards shot bullets at the lava monster, which did nothing to stop it. The massive beast swept its flaming hand out at a pile of guards and made contact. The magma left burns on their skin, and the force of the lava monster's blows killed most of the guards on the first hit. The lava monster continued its fiery rampage, chucking guards across the room and destroying whatever it came in contact with.

One of the guards noticed that we were controlling the lava monster. He raised his hand, and a battle orb exploded out of his palm. It missed me, but hit Charlie directly in the chest, sending him flying off of Oberi. The lava monster dissipated with the blow, the magma sinking back into the crevice we'd made in the earth as Charlie hit the ground almost fifty feet away.

"Charlie!" I yelled. He struggled to get up. That battle orb must've hit him hard.

I instantly incinerated the guard that had hurt him, but a whole battalion of guards had noticed Charlie was down and were running across the room to advance on him. They raised their hands and their guns, to throw an assault of bullets and spells that would surely take him down.

Oberi tossed her head and stomped her hooves against the floor as she let out a bray. *No one shall harm what is mine!*

Oberi's form turned warm underneath my body and took on a white glow that obscured all of her features. My legs moved as her middle expanded, and I realized Oberi was *growing*. The illusion saddle shifted and changed to fit as Oberi's body morphed into something larger. Through our bond, I felt her body shift from feminine to masculine. I clung to Oberi's neck, which became long and scaly underneath my hands. Horns formed at the top of his head, and his feet became massive, clawed, and reptilian. A long tail grew behind him, one with a poisonous, pointed barb at the end. Poisonous spines ran along his back, and leathery wings folded over my legs to protect them. His jagged scales were an arrayed mottled color of brown and black, with sharp points at the end. From this point on his back, I was more than twenty feet up. The cafeteria could barely contain him.

I couldn't be more elated. Oberi had changed into a very large, very angry, and very male wyvern.

HA HA HA HA! Oberi bellowed. *PUT ME IN A TINY CAGE NOW, YOU INSOLENT FOOLS!*

Oberi began spitting venom at the guards who'd surrounded Charlie. The venom was purple, and once it landed on the guards, it began eating away at their bodies like acid. The venom consumed skin and flesh, until bones poked through and holes were made in the guard's bodies. They perished horribly, letting out cries of agony as they suffered horrifying deaths.

Oberi bent down and picked up Charlie with his long fangs. Charlie yelped as Oberi deposited him behind me, before the wyvern continued his perilous rampage.

I SHALL TAKE YOUR LIVES ON A WHIM! Oberi screamed. He lifted his giant feet and began crushing guards underneath them, roaring as he did so. Oberi lifted his tail, and used the curved pointer to stab guards in the chest. Their bodies filled with venom, and the purple substance pooled out of cavities in their chests as the guards collapsed on the floor. They gave a few convulsing movements before they choked on the foam that was gushing from between their lips.

"What'd he turn into?" Charlie asked in astonishment, doing his best to hang on as Oberi rocked us back and forth.

"A wyvern," I replied, just as Oberi gave an earth-quaking roar that split the cavern in the room even farther in two.

"What's that?!"

"Uh, basically a dragon hybrid, poisonous tail, spits venom," I replied nonchalantly. "This form definitely comes from you. Air type."

With the appearance of Oberi's wyvern form, the guards finally gave up. Those that still remained alive ran screaming from the cafeteria, preferring to face the Warden's wrath rather than continue to fight us. Once the room was empty, Oberi's sides were left heaving, his wings shuddering as he attempted to contain his lust for revenge.

Marcus giggled. "Blood, blood, blood everywhere!" He splashed in the red puddles like a little kid. Rishi meowed loudly, batting at his shoes.

Holy hell, he was actually *enjoying* all of this. Kallie was completely bewildered as she stared at him, then turned back to us. "I don't know if this is hot, or disturbing."

"You can think about that later," I said. "Either way, nobody's getting in our way now."

I now have all five of my forms. I am complete and unified. I feel as if I am a god! Oberi extended his wings. They slammed up against the cafeteria walls, which nearly buckled under his weight.

"Take it easy, big guy." Kallie patted Oberi's scaly paw. "We still gotta get out of here."

That we did, and with Marcus going around purposefully starting fights and causing a ruckus, it was taking us way longer than I wanted it to. "We still need to get to the Warden's office. You're gonna have to shrink down if we want to get through these hallways."

Aw. But I like being big and ferocious, Oberi complained.

"You can eat all the guards you want later, but for right now, you're gonna have to wait," Charlie said. "You're too big to fit through the door, let alone the rest of the building."

Oberi grumbled, but shrank back down to unicorn size. We went back into the hallway, but as we did so, I noticed the temperature in the building had definitely elevated. A thin trail of smoke hovered throughout the hall and my Fire magic tingled inside of me, telling me something was wrong.

We turned down another corridor, and that's when I noticed it. Flames were licking up the walls of the building, spreading over the ceiling and the classrooms at large. They were monstrous, large flames that could only be cast with magic, ones that ignited everything they touched, even the stone. The flames were spreading quickly across the prison, and screams echoed through the hallways as inmates and guards both struggled to escape the inferno.

My journal... the fire. Another one of my aunt's visions had come true.

Perish in the flames of my judgment. The Warden's speech echoed through my mind, and I gripped Oberi's mane tightly.

"The Warden did this," I said. "He set the Institute on fire. It's a part of this test he's making everyone go through."

"So call off the flames," Charlie suggested. "You're strong enough to put the whole thing out at once."

I thought about it, taking my time as I mused over the possibility. Then I shook my head slowly as I replied, "No."

"*No?* Our friends are out there! Your *brother* is out there!" Kallie protested.

"I know. But we have to let it burn anyway."

"Ava, what are you talking about?" Charlie asked gently.

I didn't know if they'd understand. But I had to tell them... show them. "The Institute is a horrible place. It's tortured, maimed, and killed people for centuries. Even before the Warden took over, it was used to hurt everyone who passed through its doors. It can't continue to stand. It doesn't matter if the Warden abandons it. Someone else, maybe someone even more terrible than he is, will come here and use it to destroy and experiment. We need to fulfill these prophecies, and we can't do that if the Institute is continually used to manipulate and exploit people. It needs to burn at any cost. Even if we end up losing the ones we love because of it."

"This is a villain's choice. The Warden is the villain, not you," Charlie protested.

"I'm a villain, too. Just a different kind," I replied. "And I became the villain because the world didn't allow me to live my life the way I wanted to live it... the way that I knew was necessary for me to survive. I was different. All of us were. And we didn't get the resources, or the help, or the understanding we needed to cope. Then we came here, and it got even worse. Not just for us, but for all these broken, troubled kids. They tried to fix us instead of understand us. When they couldn't fix us, they used us for their own gain. We have to let the Institute burn, so no one else can be taken advantage of. There won't be another Infernal Underground, or Cellblock 9, at least not here on Darke Island. If that's all I can do for the good of the world, well... it's worth the sacrifice. Because I don't think any of us want another person to go through what we all did."

Everyone was quiet. Charlie wrapped his arms around my middle as he asked, "Are you sure?"

"I am. I just wanted to live in peace, but the world wouldn't let me. It'll *never* let people who are different be who they are. So now it has to suffer the consequences."

"Then we let it burn." Charlie placed a kiss on my neck.

No one objected, and I knew they understood. Most people wouldn't. I'd be seen as a terrible person for allowing this to happen when I could do something to stop it.

But it wasn't my fault. I hadn't done all these terrible things; they'd happened *to me.* And I was tired of being at the mercy of powerful persecutors who were willing to *make me suffer* because I had something they wanted. I wasn't the only one who'd experienced that here. That cycle had to end, even if it required sacrifice to do it.

I never really believed in sacrifice. I didn't think it was necessary, that it was an excuse tyrants used to justify their evil actions. But now that I had a choice to rescue the kids who were still inside the Institute, most of whom were already gone, or prevent countless others from ever entering this building in the first place, it was almost an easy decision.

Almost.

I patted Oberi's side. "Let's go home."

Where is... home? Oberi asked.

"Wherever we decide," I responded. "We're not accepted anywhere, so we'll make it for ourselves."

The Institute wasn't home anymore. Maybe it never really had been. It'd just been a place we'd made into home, because we weren't allowed to choose anything else. And I didn't believe I could move on to a new life until this place was lying in desolation behind us. The past was over and done. I was finally free.

We all were. Now was the time to embrace that freedom. What we did from this point on was, finally, up to us. Whether we used it for good, or bad, didn't matter.

All that mattered was that it was ours.

charlie

TWENTY-FIVE

I'd never been closer to death than when I was lying on that operating table, being stabbed with scalpels and tortured for the pure enjoyment of complete psychopaths. The Warden had completely drained me of my magic, then left me there for his guards to kill, instructing them to drag it out in the worst possible way. Killing me wasn't enough. He wanted me to suffer beyond comprehension before I died, and he'd definitely found the right monsters to do it.

For the briefest of moments, I let myself believe the Warden had won. I went numb, so I didn't have to feel it when I died. Soon, I'd be with my love.

Then I heard her voice. The sound of my name had never sounded so good. Ava was *alive*. Hell, *I* was still alive. It didn't seem possible.

We had a habit of defying the impossible.

Then we shattered those inferichite cuffs, and the magic the Warden had tried to take from us came back even stronger than before. Our magic was uncontainable, and that was a dangerous weapon in the hands of delirious, unhinged inmates with their sights set on revenge.

The Warden had no idea what kind of enemies he'd created in his search for power. He should've killed us quickly, instead of trying to humiliate us before our demise.

Because now? We were unstoppable. We didn't have any reason to stay here anymore, any motivation to act nice and behave. Our magic could finally be free. And all of us were begging to set it loose against the first sick fuck who crossed our paths. I was *pissed off*. We all were. And we were *done* playing around. This prison was ours.

The temperature rose as we raced through the halls of the Institute, leaving the dilapidated cafeteria and dead bodies far behind us. The fire was gaining, eating up the building as the sound of flames roared in my ears.

"How far to the Warden's office?" I asked above the clatter of Oberi's hooves. I rode on her back, holding Ava close to me as our Familiar ran.

"It's just up here!" Kallie said as we rounded a corner.

Oberi skidded to a halt, and Ava's gut sank so quickly that I felt it through the bond. Their thoughts were so clear that they didn't need words. There were guards up ahead, blocking our path.

"Let's move it!" one of them shouted. "We've got three minutes to get everything out of here!"

They must've been sent by the Warden to clear out his office before everything went up in flames. I heard the sound of a heavy door slamming shut, then the shouts of the guards when they spotted us.

"It's them!" someone screamed.

Barely a second had passed before Ava flung her hands outward. Blazing heat hit my face, and a massive wall of fire *whooshed* as it swept down the hall, assaulting the guards before they could reach for their guns.

I expected the bodies to drop, or the guards to scream as they were incinerated by her powers. Instead, they hissed like wild animals.

Fire-proof suits! Ava thought.

Of fucking course, because the Warden had sent them back into this burning building.

The guards jumped out of the flames so quickly that I couldn't track them. Marcus and Kallie shot defensive spells, but the guards dodged them as they closed the long distance between us in a second. I swept my hands out in a desperate attempt to save my friends. A guard touched my foot, but he was blasted backward by my Air magic before he could grab me. There had to be twenty guards swept up in my spell. Heavy *thuds* sounded as their bodies hit the floor down the hallway.

"Ava!" I screamed. "Stop their hearts!"

She was strong enough to use her Water magic to manipulate their blood and kill them in moments. I had no doubt she could take them all at once.

"I can't!" she cried. "They're all vampires."

Fucking hell. Vampires were some of the hardest supernaturals to kill, and we were up against twenty of them. We couldn't use our elements to stop their hearts or suffocate them, so our powers were practically useless. Elementai were no match against a horde of vampires...

Let's see what they thought about an Elf.

I jumped off Oberi's back and planted myself in front of my friends. The vampires raced toward us so fast that to Oberi and Ava, they looked like mere blurs. I could sense through our bond when exactly to reach my hand out and grab the first vamp around the neck. He stopped dead as I lifted him by the throat and dangled him several inches above the ground. Elven magic surged through my body, and in a single beat, I siphoned the vampire's super strength and speed.

Holding him tight by the throat, I spun around and used the momentum to toss him down the hall. He landed against the nearest vampires and knocked them over. It happened so fast that the other vamps never had a chance to touch my friends.

A solid sword formed in my hand, conjured by my Elven magic.

To your left! Ava communicated telepathically.

I flung myself at the vampires, slicing my sword through the air and severing their heads from their bodies.

Right! Oberi instructed.

The vampires' necks were like stone, shattering as my sword sliced clean through them. Heads fell from shoulders and smacked on the ground like hunks of concrete dropped from six feet up. Thick, viscous blood splattered across my face and clothes. When the vampires died, they became stone-like, their bodies falling to the floor like broken statues as I eliminated their lives from this Earth. I moved in a blur like they did, thanks to the powers I'd stolen. I was only aware of how fast I was moving by Ava and Oberi's thoughts, guiding me left and right to sever the heads of my opponents.

In less than two seconds, I was standing in a pile of broken bodies, as if they were nothing more than bricks that had tumbled from the ceiling. I panted heavily and waited for more instructions, but it never came. All

I felt was a sense of pride rushing through the bond. Oberi was *impressed*.

"Charlie," Kallie said gently. "It's over. You got them all."

She sounded shocked, and I suppose it *was* a bit unexpected. I'd never moved like that before. My sword clattered to the ground as I came back to reality. I realized that I was covered in the thick, lead-like blood of the vampires I'd slain. Above me, Ava let out a swooning noise, and I felt a blush creep over her cheeks across our bond.

"Babe, that was *so sexy*!" Ava gushed. "Please do it again. I am like, barely staying on this unicorn right now."

Marcus gave an inane giggle. "She thinks murder is attractive. Little pieces of vampires, all around my shoes."

Marcus kicked a vampire head, and the stone bit skittered to the end of the hall. Rishi's paws thudded by me as he went chasing after it like a toy.

"We don't have long," I said. "Let's get moving."

I could feel the heat of the fire in the walls, and I didn't think we had more than a few minutes before this section of the Institute would be completely engulfed in flames. I approached the door and reached for the handle, but it didn't budge.

Marcus pushed me aside and started banging on the door with his fists. "Let me in! *Let me in*, you motherfucking asshole rotten piece of shit limp dick cock of a man!"

"Out of the way," I said. I slammed my shoulder against the door, trying to ram it open. Rishi yowled loudly, as if he too was cursing out the Warden.

Magic swelled, and I was blasted backward. I landed against the opposite wall, gasping for breath that had been knocked out of me.

"Charlie!" Ava cried.

"I'm all right," I gasped as I got to my feet. "The wards are still active."

"Marcus should be able to break it—" Kallie started, but Marcus didn't seem to hear her.

He was already approaching the door again, muttering lowly to himself. "Ha! The Warden put up a cute little ward. He thinks that will stop us? So funny, so funny."

Marcus gave a snicker that caused my skin to crawl. My Elven magic sensed power surge through the hallway, raising the hairs on the back of my neck. It grew bigger and bigger, tingling all up and down my body until—

Crack!

A massive sound like shattering glass echoed through the hall, and the magic dissipated all at once.

I didn't know what Marcus had done, but I'd never witnessed anything like it. Every time he'd broken a ward before, he had to transform the spell into something new, because energy couldn't be created or destroyed. But we were demigods, and we *could* create something out of nothing— which meant we could destroy it, too, and Marcus was definitely at the height of his abilities right now.

Even if he'd had to go completely psychotic to access them.

"I broke his ward, like snapping twigs," Marcus said gleefully. "Maybe I'll break his neck, next."

"Marcus, calm down," Kallie demanded. "You're going to hurt yourself."

Marcus laughed maniacally. Kallie must've been shaking him, because his laughter sounded garbled as his head swung back and forth.

"Marcus, cut it out!" Kallie ordered. When he didn't stop, the crisp sound of a bitch slap filled the hall.

Marcus went dead silent for a moment, but his laughter returned a moment later, like he hadn't felt a thing.

"Whew!" he cried. "Do that again!"

"Leave him alone," I said. "We'll get him help when we get out of here."

Marcus was fucking insane right now, but he was functioning, and it actually seemed to be working in our favor. We didn't have time to bring him back to Earth at the moment.

We wound up the tall tower that led to the Warden's office. I levitated Ava up the stairs with my Air magic, and Oberi shifted into a husky so he could fit through the narrow stairwell. Kallie jumped back as she approached the door, nearly knocking into me. "It's iron. I can't get through."

I lifted my hands. My Earth magic twisted around the iron and crushed it at a simple thought. I tossed it aside with my Air magic like it was nothing more than a crumpled piece of paper. It skidded across the room, the scraping sound echoing around us.

Well, that's one way to do it, Oberi said.

"Let's hurry up," Ava insisted. "The fire's almost here."

"The door won't hurt you, my pretty, yes," Marcus cooed as we walked through. I figured he was stroking Kallie's hair.

"Oh my gods," Kallie grumbled.

We hurried inside, and Ava instructed me to place her in a chair... but not just *any* chair. The big, imposing one that sat behind the Warden's mahogany desk.

"Let's see what the Warden's been hiding," Ava snarled, and she began ripping open desk drawers, rifling through the contents.

I immediately followed the sound of rattling. I found a small bird cage sitting on a wardrobe, and my Air magic felt Alette's wings fluttering happily inside. She was thrilled we'd come to rescue her. Sprigs reached through the bars, and his tiny little leaves brushed against my skin. I opened the cage and put Sprigs in my chest pocket, while Alette fluttered over to Kallie.

"I've got the grimoire and my journal," Ava said, and she yanked out a desk drawer so hard that it fell onto the floor. She didn't bother to put it back.

"Guys... I've got some stuff you might want to see," Kallie said as she shuffled through papers. "It's our criminal files. They were scattered all over his desk, like he was studying them."

"Take them," I decided. "We can look them over once we're somewhere safe. It'll help us learn what he knows about us."

"It's a lot," Kallie said apprehensively. "He's got everything in here—dear gods."

Kallie drew a sharp breath, giving the rest of us pause.

"What did you find?" Ava asked carefully.

Kallie's breath wavered. She paused, like she wasn't sure if she should answer, before she said, "It's... medical records from your surgery. The Warden hired angel surgeons to work on you."

"We know that," I said. "The Warden wouldn't trust anyone else."

"It's not just that..." Kallie sounded concerned. "The Warden has pages of notes detailing their observations. It's like they were looking for something. Listen to this; *Doctors performed a living autopsy on the subject in order to find the source of her demigod powers, and observed the subject's Anichi magic working to repair her spine in real-time. No abnormalities were found during the living autopsy to indicate a physical connection to demigod abilities."*

Kallie paused for a beat as she looked over the notes. I could feel the horror of what she'd found permeate the room before she said anything.

Her voice sounded hollow. "They made incisions to Ava's spine while it was mending, because Ava was unconsciously healing herself too fast for them to make their observations. Her Anichi powers were trying to put her body back together, but the surgeons kept undoing what her magic was trying to fix, hoping to bring her demigod powers out."

Kallie went on. "Eventually... what damage the surgeons did became irreversible, because Ava's Anichi magic fused her spine back together improperly. That's why Ava can't heal her spine... that's why no magic can. Ava's magic was trying to save her, but now that the injury is fixed in place, there's no undoing the damage."

"That fucking bastard!" I yelled. The ground rocked beneath us as I filled with rage. I was starting to lose a grip on my magic.

"This is all his fault. I could've..." Ava's voice tightened, and she managed to choke out, "I could've healed myself. I could've *walked* again. But the Warden had to poke around inside of me and undo all the progress my healing magic made. Now I'm never going to heal properly... ever... all because of him."

If there was ever a shred of hope that Ava could walk again, it was completely obliterated. Ava's spine had healed incorrectly due to what the Warden's surgeons had done to her. Nothing— not even magic— could reverse it. This wasn't like when Ava had healed Ez when he had sepsis, because in this circumstance, her magic had been manipulated against her, and she couldn't undo what her own power had done.

Devastation permeated our bond. We all knew the chances of Ava walking again were slim to none, but we didn't understand the gravity of the situation until now.

I knelt in front of her. "Pidge..." What did I say to her, in a time like this? I was absolutely gutted; I couldn't imagine how *she* felt.

Ava didn't speak. Not at first. Then she took a quivering breath and stated, "This changes nothing. The Warden has done everything he can to crush us, but I am fucking done playing his games. He doesn't realize who he chose to fuck with. If this is my fate, then I have to accept it, because I'm *not* giving up. I swear to you now, I'm going to become the biggest supernatural criminal mastermind in history. And after that, we're going to make the Warden pay."

A few silent beats passed as we all absorbed her words. Ava didn't want to give up— not for anything. This news was devastating, but even Kallie's time powers couldn't take us back in to stop it. We'd already tried.

I reached up to take Ava's hand. "Then that's exactly what we'll do. Kallie, get Marcus to subconjure those files. Grab anything that looks important. We're going to give the Warden hell."

Kallie rushed to gather as many papers as she could. I walked over to the nearest bookcase and felt around. It was filled with all kinds of potions, books, and files— whatever the Warden thought was useful in his mission to become god.

He wasn't getting any of it back.

There was a loud, smashing sound. Something splashed across my shoes, and I heard Marcus let out an aggravated noise as he threw a potion on the ground.

"He broke Ava," Marcus said. "Let's break his things. Before we break him."

There was a beat of silence. Then I heard an angry noise as Kallie tossed something across the room, and it crashed through the glass ceiling.

Marcus had never had a better idea in his life. I conjured a baseball bat in my hand, gripped it in two hands over my shoulder... and started swinging. Potion vials shattered, and the spines of the books burst as papers scattered all around the room. I brought my baseball bat down on the bookcase, and it blasted through five shelves at once, spilling the rest of the contents onto the floor.

The Warden thought he could take my wife's legs away? The broken contents of this room would be the last of his worries once I got done with him.

Ava cheered as I went absolutely crazy tearing the room apart. Marcus laughed like a mad man as he tipped over the wardrobe, and

Oberi growled as he began ripping things off of shelves, tearing them to pieces with his teeth.

"Charlie snapped, oh how fun! I think I'd like to join." Marcus said the words like he was reciting a nursery rhyme, and Rishi yowled.

I handed him my baseball bat and conjured another for myself. "Go wild, kid."

Kallie conjured a bat of her own, and we went full-on vandals as we tore the room apart. Oberi changed back into a unicorn; she neighed loudly and stomped on the Warden's desk with her front hooves. It cracked under her weight. Ava must've grabbed some papers off the desk, because a tearing sound filled the room.

Bang! Crack! Tear!

The satisfying sound of absolute destruction filled the space as we obliterated all the Warden's belongings and trashed his office. I swung my bat toward the window, and it shattered to bits. A heavy gust of cold air swept through the room, sending a shiver down my spine. I hadn't realized how warm it'd gotten in here. It was like a sauna, which meant the room would soon be engulfed in flames.

Good. Let the Warden's prison fucking burn—

My thoughts halted as a huge explosion rocked the building. I swayed on my feet, and my ears rang.

"We got what we came for. Time to go." I said. "Kallie, let's portal the hell out of here."

"We've got to get to the Lair," she insisted.

"We're more powerful than ever before," I said. "Marcus can break the ward on the Institute, and you can portal us anywhere."

"In the state he's in?" Kallie demanded. "He can't write his name, let alone paint a door."

Marcus was still laughing maniacally, swinging his bat at pieces of furniture.

He looks like he's in a sword fight with the toppled wardrobe, Oberi said. *He's barely functioning.*

"The Institute's ward is stronger than the one on the Warden's office," Kallie said. "Marcus and I have been trying to break the ward since we left Cellblock 9, but it's over a hundred years old and self-sustaining, generating its own power. It'll take time we don't have. The fastest way out of here is to get to the Lair, where I can make portals through Marcus' art, because it's already there."

"Then let's get moving," I said quickly.

We fled the Warden's office and back down the stairs. I hefted Ava up onto Oberi's back, and climbed on behind her before we went running down the hall. By now, the flames engulfed the walls, but Ava ordered the fire aside so we could get through. I shot my magic outward, and a hole blasted through the side of the building.

We made it out into the prison yard, where the sounds of screams were deafening. Fire crackled and burned from behind us, and the intense heat followed us as we ran across the grass. Inside the building, we could hear the dying screams of inmates as they were burned alive. Those who had survived seemed to be crowded near an area of the fence, their voices so distant I couldn't make out what they were fighting about. They were on the opposite side of the prison yard, and we were almost to the trees beside the lake.

"They're trying to jump the fence," Ava told me. "People are climbing on each other to get out, but they can't get past the noxite or the barbed wire."

She wasn't concerned, but rather narrating out of habit, to help me understand what was happening. It was strange how cold and uncaring her voice had become, but I felt the void within me as well. We should be asking how we could save them— hell, *if* we could save them.

But we were done trying. The only people we could save now were ourselves.

The screams weren't the only sound. Sirens blared above our heads, and a guard barked orders into speakers mounted on the guard towers. "Back away from the fence!"

As if the inmates would actually listen. Gunshots rang out over the prison yard, and inmates cried out in pain as they were killed on the spot.

The sound of a diesel engine revved, then came the noise of spinning tires before a vehicle took off across the prison yard, gaining speed as bullets clinked off the metal frame. The screams turned to cheers as I heard the sound of tearing metal.

"Holy shit, someone's stolen the submarine bus!" Ava told me.

Metal clanged as the bus plowed into the fence, blasting straight through it, judging by the sound of twisting and groaning. The bus continued driving, the sound fading into the distance. The crowd roared in excitement as they shouted cries of freedom.

Good for them. I hoped the poor bastards on that bus got the hell off Darke Island, never to be seen by the Warden again.

"We're free!" Marcus changed directions and raced toward the hole in the fence.

"Marcus, no!" Kallie cried. "The Lair's closer. We're almost out."

"I'm faster than bullets. Faster than lightning!" Marcus laughed.

"The spotlights—" Kallie started, but it was too late. The guards had already spotted him, and gunshots sounded. Marcus cried out, and Rishi howled.

Not good.

I leapt off Oberi's back while she was still running, and rolled against the ground to take the fall. Marcus was on his knees, and I grabbed him under the arm to haul him to his feet. Blood gushed out of a wound on his arm and coated my hand.

"Huh. Looks like I've been shot," Marcus said, like he hadn't felt a thing.

"Move, or you'll be shot again!" I demanded.

Gunshots sounded in the air, and I fully expected one of them to hit me. I flinched, but all I felt was the lightest touch as my skin rippled against something.

I skimmed it with my fingers. It was a small bullet hanging in the air, as if someone had hit pause on a remote a split second before it was meant to penetrate my skin.

"Let's *go!*" Kallie demanded. "I can only buy us a few seconds. Time magic is too volatile, and if I mess it up, we aren't getting out of here!"

She hadn't slowed down time completely, because I could still hear the sirens blaring above us. But she had slowed time around *the bullets* so they wouldn't hit us.

I would marvel at her magic if I had the time, but I didn't, so I tossed the bullet aside and grabbed Marcus. But he resisted, pushing me away. He wasn't done just yet.

"You think a measly little bullet is going to stop *me!?*" Marcus shouted. He reached an arm back, and I felt a spell sizzle in his hand. "Rishi, *kill them all.*"

Rishi gave a primal hiss as he jumped on my shoulder and used me as a springboard to jump toward Marcus. Rishi melded into the spell until they became one, transforming into something akin to my Air, but much more dark and sinister.

Judging by Ava's thoughts, Rishi had transformed into a black cloud of death. I could sense the foreboding nature of the cloud, even though I couldn't see it. A low, angry growl emitted from the cloud, then Rishi attacked.

That's my boy! A spirit of death, Oberi praised.

The guards must've been scared shitless, because they unloaded their guns into Rishi's spirit form. It didn't do any good. Rishi swept around the prison yard, darting between guards and ripping the life from their bodies one by one. He was so fast that by the time one guard dropped to the ground, two others were already dead.

It bought us time to make it to the tree line. By the time we reached cover, only a few guards were left shooting. Men screamed and begged for mercy, but Rishi silenced them with his Death magic. The last of the gunshots died, followed by a scream that seemed to be falling through the air. Something *crunched*, and I realized a guard had jumped from one of the towers to escape Rishi's wrath. The last of the guards inside the tower screamed as they fled.

Rishi growled lowly as he circled the guard tower, then a powerful battle spell erupted out of him. It was so strong I could feel the magic from here. A massive *boom* sounded over the yard, and the tower exploded so forcefully that tiny bits of rubble rained down on us. The ground shook as the tower toppled over and crashed to the ground.

"Gods, Rishi!" Kallie cried in a panic. The cloud of death had disappeared, and I could no longer feel his magic. We didn't know where he'd gone, or if he'd been crushed by the tower.

Then we heard a tiny mew, and Rishi came running out of the rubble and into the trees.

Kallie practically sobbed in relief, then bent to pick up Rishi. "Good boy."

We stood there for a moment to catch our breath. The entire Institute was engulfed in flames by now. Even from the tree line, we could feel the heat. The screams were distant, mostly coming from inmates who had escaped. The guards had been obliterated.

"My aunt's vision came true," Ava said quietly, and I felt an evil note of fulfillment at her words. The Institute would burn, and we would take pride in knowing this place was gone for good. It was satisfying, really. The Warden had our powers now, but his precious Institute was no more.

I turned to lead my friends to the Lair, but as I did so, my Earth magic through my feet. I paused, and panic filled my chest.

"Charlie, what's wrong?" Ava asked, her voice raising a pitch. She could feel my fear through our bond.

"Something isn't right," I said.

The ground began to shake violently. Overhead, thunder cracked. Oberi neighed, and her hooves stomped upon the dirt as she tried to stay upright. I had to steady myself against a tree to keep from falling over. Wind whipped around us as a wicked storm began brewing.

"Charlie, what's happening?" Kallie yelled over the roaring wind.

I could feel something deep within the earth, welling up inside of it with power I'd never felt before. I tried to calm the storm with my Air magic, but it resisted me.

"I don't know!" I called back. "Whatever it is, it's just as strong as we are!"

A deafening *crack* sounded, and I was tossed upward before landing flat on my face. My friends screamed as they fell over. The earth continued to rumble, but we were thrown sideways every time we tried to stand upright. The sound of the storm and earthquake combined was deafening.

A crater opened up in the prison yard! Ava told me.

She didn't have to tell me in words. I could read the concepts in her mind as she witnessed what was going on. A huge tunnel of red light beamed up from the ground, shining into the swirling clouds above us.

Over the quaking of the earth came the sounds of monsters— roars and tortured screams of demons escaping from their hellish prison. I felt Ava's fear sink through my gut as she observed animalistic monsters clawing their way out of the depths of the earth. There were all different kinds— some appearing as dark spirits, others as monstrous animals with sharp teeth and razor-like claws.

In the middle of it all was the Warden, his arms held to the skies as he manipulated his new power to his will— bringing hell upon Earth.

"You cannot escape me!" the Warden's voice rang above the storm. He didn't need a loudspeaker to project his voice across the entire island. He was a demigod now, and was more powerful than ever. "My monsters will hunt you down, until every last one of you has suffered for turning your back on the one true god!"

Cries echoed in the distance as the monsters caught up with the students who had escaped. Animalistic roars filled the air.

"What do we do?" Kallie demanded.

Ava and I didn't answer. I should've felt the desire to stop this. To kill these monsters, and end the Warden's rampage...

But I didn't.

"Ava! Charlie!" Kallie yelled. "We're unstoppable now. We can bring down the Warden. We already let the school burn. Are we going to let him get away with this, too?"

"He already has," I said as more and more screams reached our ears. "The Warden took our magic, so he has our powers now. He's as unstoppable as we are."

"We can take him, and his monsters! We're strong enough!" Kallie protested.

"Not without risking our lives, and we don't need to die tonight!" Ava cried.

"What about our friends?" Kallie asked.

"It doesn't matter now," Ava shouted back. "*None* of this matters until we get the remaining keys!"

"What do you mean?" Kallie yelled.

"We don't know whether our friends are dead or alive, and we can't risk our lives trying to find out," Ava insisted. "If the Warden got to them, they're already dead, and he took the keys we found. There are two more keys to find, and at least one of them is off the island. Marcus' locator spell showed us that. Our priority now is getting those last two keys before the Warden does, because if he gets all seven keys, it's over. Our friends will suffer a fate far worse than death."

"What are you talking about?" Kallie demanded.

"I'm *talking* about the afterlife," Ava said harshly. "When I was in Cellblock 9, Coyote came to me and told me the afterlife is closed to new souls. If our friends are dead, they're stuck in the in-between, and they're not moving on. The Blessed Haven is shut down, which makes our mission more crucial than ever. If we want to save everyone from this hell the Warden's created, save all the souls that ever were, we have to go *now*."

It was worse than we could ever imagine. I didn't have to think before I made a decision. "If that's the case, nothing is more important than getting those keys. Even if we stop the Warden tonight, it's useless if we don't open the Elven gate. Ava's right. We can't put our lives at risk fighting him when there's a prophecy we have to fulfill. We can't stay here any longer."

We turned from the tree line. As we did, I felt a horrible sinking in my gut, and the hairs on the back of my neck rose. I could feel someone's eyes on me.

I realized they *were*. I was feeling Ava through the bond, perceiving what she saw. The Warden had spotted us at the tree line and locked eyes with her. The whole earth stopped shaking for a second as his magic faltered in disbelief. An angry roar erupted around us from all angles as the Warden screamed in frustration.

"After them!" the Warden ordered. Roars echoed, and a stampede of monsters started running in our direction.

"Time to go!" Marcus exclaimed.

We took off running. An explosion sounded behind us, and I felt the earth snap once more. I quickly ordered my magic to seal the crack forming. The Warden surely intended to trap us in it. His magic warred against mine, and the monsters' footsteps came closer.

"We're almost there!" Kallie shouted.

Her voice became muffled as she slipped inside the Lair, followed by Marcus. I rushed to lift Ava off Oberi's back, so that he could change into a husky and fit through the opening.

A monster growled, and a claw sliced my jumpsuit a moment before I slipped through the rock. The monster must've been huge, because he reached his arm inside the door and scratched at the floor. I used my Earth magic to seal the entrance off, and his arm snapped as it severed in two.

The earth continued to shake, and monsters roared from outside as they tried to claw their way into the Lair. My Earth magic felt the rocks breaking as long claws chipped away at the rock.

Oberi barked, and I felt his horror through the bond.

"The Warden's defiled Marcus' painting!" Ava cried, and my stomach hollowed as I read her thoughts. Marcus' beautiful paintings had been scratched to pieces. The door he'd painted that Kallie had used to make a portal barely looked like a door anymore. Remnants of the painting remained, but so much of the painting had been destroyed that Kallie couldn't combine her magic with Marcus' art.

"He's going to have to paint another one," I demanded.

Rock crumbled above us. I concentrated my thoughts on keeping the stone above us in place, to buy us more time.

Kallie ran to where Marcus had stashed his paints. "Marcus, paint a door."

Marcus scoffed, like he had no idea what was going on around us. "A door, my pretty? Why not something more interesting?"

Bits of rock fell from the ceiling, and air whooshed into the room as the monsters punctured a hole in the roof.

"I can't hold them off forever!" I told Kallie.

"Marcus, for the love of the gods!" Kallie screamed. "Repair this godsdamn painting before we die! *The Warden is coming.*"

Marcus wasn't quite himself, but he obeyed. Paint cans rattled, then hissed as he sprayed designs over the rock.

Monsters used their powers to break the rock even more. Hell, this was like the Darke Games all over again, but about a million times worse. Ava blasted spells at them through the openings in the stone, but as soon as she knocked one out of the way, another came to take its place. Ava tried to incinerate the nearest monster, but he must have been made of fire, because it didn't even faze the creature.

These monsters were unlike the creatures we'd fought before. Their skin was impenetrable and magical, and they resisted our spells like they were nothing.

"Faster!" I screamed.

"Almost there!" Kallie shouted.

Rock crumbled all around us as the monsters found their way inside. One of them landed in front of me, and I felt its sickly breath on my face as it roared, blowing my hair back.

Oberi barked loudly and shoved his head into my legs. I stumbled backward and flinched, expecting to slam straight into the wall...

Instead, the scene transformed around us. The temperature

dropped, and the air became damp. The earth stopped rumbling, and the sound of monsters ceased. My jumpsuit tore as Ava and I fell to the ground. She rolled out of my arms as I collapsed flat on my face.

Oberi sagged beside me in relief, and Kallie and Marcus groaned from nearby. Rishi meowed loudly. Sprigs wiggled out from beneath me, and Alette fluttered overhead. Ava crawled over to me, taking my hand in hers.

"Charlie, are you okay?" she asked.

I struggled to catch my breath. "Yeah, pidge. Is it over?"

"We made it," she assured me. Ava's hair tickled my arm as she swung her head from side to side. "Where *are* we?"

Kallie got to her feet and dusted herself off. "I portaled us to a forest in France— a nature preserve. My dad and I used to go hunting here. It's the most isolated place I could think of, and far away from Darke Island. There shouldn't be anyone around for a hundred miles."

Marcus groaned as he rolled over. Rishi made gross slurping noises, like he was licking Marcus' face.

"Whew!" Marcus sighed as he sat upright. "Almost lost my cool back there."

"Almost lost your—" I nearly choked on my words. "Ancestors, Marcus. You were like a crazy person!"

"How'd we get here?" Marcus asked blankly. His tone had changed, from maniacal and aggressive, to the passive and gentle voice he usually spoke with.

Kallie knelt beside him. "You don't remember anything?"

"I remember we were in Cellblock 9, then..." he trailed off. "I don't recall anything that happened from then to now. I must've blacked out from stress."

"You've got to be kidding me," Kallie growled under her breath as she helped Marcus up.

"I bet I was useless out there, just cowering behind you guys. Sorry," Marcus apologized. "I'm sure I held the team up, what with you having to drag me around."

"That's one way of putting it," Kallie said, disgruntled.

He'd had some sort of psychotic break, that was for sure. I didn't blame him, either. Tonight had been intense.

After we'd caught our breath, Oberi shifted into a unicorn, and I hoisted Ava onto her back again. The forest around us was silent, and the vastness of the nature preserve encompassed me. I realized, with breathtaking beauty, that no one on Earth knew where we were but us.

It was a brilliant feeling.

"Charlie... what do we do now?" Ava asked.

It was an impossible question. We were out from behind bars for the first time in two years. We could go anywhere. We could do anything. We were finally free.

But being free didn't mean avoiding responsibility. To know where we were going, we had to know where we were, and we didn't. We didn't know for sure if the Warden had the Divinity Keys, or where to find the next two. We didn't know if our friends had survived, and if they did, where to find them. We'd escaped the Warden, but we'd been running away, and now we had to figure out where to run *to*.

There was no place safe for us, especially not during a time of war. Everyone had family, but if we went to them, we put them at risk. Our societies wouldn't be safe if we returned to any of the supernatural cities, and now that the Warden knew we were still alive, he'd be looking for us.

Everyone turned in my direction, looking for an answer. The decision was up to me. Whatever I told them to do, they'd follow.

It should've felt like a huge weight on my shoulders, to take control of what we did next, and to be responsible for these people. But it didn't. These guys were my family, and I took care of my family.

I shrugged. "Whatever the hell we want. We're giving the orders now."

"Is that your plan? To set us loose on society?" Marcus asked.

"Why not? Who's stopping us?" I asked.

"I don't mind being the bad guy," Ava said, and she snickered. "We tore the Institute down. Why not the rest of the world?"

"We have to find those keys at any cost," I said. "We've already sacrificed so much to get the keys we had, and they were taken away from us. As far as I'm concerned, nothing's off limits when it comes to getting them back."

Oberi gave a huff from beside me. *If this is your decision, I will stand behind you. I will join you in your quest to burn this realm to the ground. But this is no small task, and I hope you are prepared to follow through with the monumental choice you are about to make. Turning away will no longer be an option, and the pain it will bring to finish the job may be more than you know.*

My response was cold. "The world's already turned their back on us, Oberi. It's time we turned our back on the world."

"Villains to the end," Kallie agreed.

Marcus cleared his throat. "I'm tired of trying to convince the world that I'm a good person. I started this journey as a villain, and I'm going to end it like one."

Rishi meowed in agreement.

At least the demon cat is with us, Oberi noted.

"When I was in the Institute, I was the Warden's puppet," Ava said. "Now I can be the real me. And she's more dangerous than he could've ever predicted. I wasn't born to fit into society's cage. Now, I'm free."

"Freedom isn't enough. As long as the cage exists, someone out there will always be a prisoner," I stated lowly. "We're not here to break out of the cage. We're here to *destroy it.*"

Oberi's hooves spun in the dirt as Ava turned her around. "Let's go have some fun, Charlie."

We didn't have a plan. Really, our only plan was to go out there and fuck some shit up. And that's exactly what we were going to do. They called us thieves, murderers, and degenerates, until that's all we knew how to be. We'd transformed into the villains they'd always said we were, after spending years trying to be accepted in a world that would never accept us. They promised us if we followed the rules, we'd be safe, but society would never provide sanctuary for people like us. We were done waiting for it. We'd create it ourselves.

So be it. If they thought we were villains, they hadn't seen the worst of us yet.

END OF BOOK FOUR

Continue on to read a special excerpt from Book Five: *The Devil's City.*

HIDDEN LEGENDS

Read more from the Hidden Legends universe! Each Hidden Legends series takes place within the same world, but in separate and unique societies. Every series stands on its own, and they can be read in any order.

ELEMENTALS, DRAGONS, & MORE

Academy of Magical Creatures by Megan Linski & Alicia Rades

SHIFTERS, FAE, & SORCERESSES

University of Sorcery by Megan Linski

WITCHES, DEMONS, & REAPERS

College of Witchcraft by Alicia Rades

Never miss a new release! Join our newsletter at
hiddenlegendsbooks.com/fanclub/

THE DEVIL'S CITY
CHAPTER ONE

Charlie

Freedom had never been a privilege afforded to a guy like me. All my life, I'd been scraping by with the bare minimum, taking only what I needed to get by. I'd been really fucking good at it, too, but that life was over.

Now, the entire world was mine for the taking. Anything I desired, I could have.

And why not? I was a freaking demigod, and no one was going to stop me— not even the Warden. We'd escaped his prison, and we were finally free.

I held tight to my Familiar's scales as the wyvern flew high above the French nature reserve, where my friends and I had been hiding for the past two weeks since our escape from the Darke Institute. The wind whipped through my hair, and my Air magic buzzed throughout my body in exhilaration.

This was true freedom. There wasn't a soul around for miles, and I was completely surrounded by my elements. Earth and Air magic pulsed through my veins, and the setting sun touched my skin.

Hold on tight, Charlie, Oberi stated through our telekinetic bond.

He should know me better by now. I spread my arms out wide and let out a gleeful laugh as air rushed by me. Oberi dove downward, and my stomach leapt into my throat.

"Wahoo!" I cried as I plummeted toward the ground. I relished in the high. I'd never felt anything quite like it.

Oberi shifted his weight, and we leveled out over the treetops. He pumped his wings, pulling us higher into the air. I squeezed my legs against his form and held tight to the spines on his back. Oberi flipped through the air, and I laughed as my stomach flopped in my abdomen.

"Again!" I shouted over the roar of the wind.

As you wish, Oberi said. He was having just as much fun as I was.

Oberi reared his head upward and tilted his wings. We flipped over backward... and I loosened my grip. I slipped off his back, and although my heart hammered as I fell through the air, I'd never been more at peace.

I tumbled through the open air, my arms spread out wide as I took in the thrilling sensation. I couldn't see the incoming treetops, but I felt them with my magic. I intended to catch myself with my magic, but instead, a loud cry came from above me, and Oberi plucked me out of the sky with his talons. He tossed me upward, and I landed on his back again.

I'd never gotten to be a kid, or felt that careless sense of freedom other children had growing up. For the first time, no one was going to hurt me for letting my guard down, so I was going to enjoy it as long as possible.

I couldn't stop laughing as I clutched one of his spines and righted myself again. "That was incredible!"

You were about to become shish-kabobbed, Oberi said.

"Relax," I told him, patting his scales. "I'm a big boy. I can catch myself."

Playtime is over, Oberi said. *We're supposed to be scouting.*

"Well, what do you see?" I asked. Oberi was our eyes up here in the sky, but I could sense supernaturals with my Elf magic. I didn't feel a soul anywhere.

Nothing but trees and mountains, Oberi said. *No signs of life.*

"Perfect," I replied. If I could live in the wilderness with my friends the rest of my life and no one bothered us, I'd be golden.

We can't stay here forever, Oberi stated, catching my thoughts. *Eventually, we have to get back to fighting the war.*

Out here in the nature preserve, it was easy to forget the supernatural communities were bombing each other. It had only been two weeks since we escaped the Warden, but already it felt like the man had only been a figment of my imagination— a specter I'd conjured up while being locked up in the Darke Institute for Supernatural Offenders. Of course I *knew* he was still out there, but some days it was easy to forget a whole world existed outside of this little slice of heaven my friends and I had created.

I spot a white wolf, Oberi reported.

"Let's see what she found," I said.

Oberi swooped out of the sky, and we landed in a small clearing. I beamed, still riding the high of the flight. I slid off his back, and he transformed into a husky beside me.

The white wolf approached. *"Did Oberi see anything?"* she asked.

"Nothing," I said. "What's your report, Kallie?"

My friend's heavy footsteps became light as she transformed back into her sorceress form. "I didn't pick up anything for miles— not so much as a scent."

"So we're still safe," I stated.

"For now," Kallie agreed as we started back toward our camp. "But we're going to have to get moving soon, Charlie."

"Why?" I asked. "If the Warden was able to find us, he would have by now."

"That's only because we have strong wards keeping him from tracking us," Kallie said. "But we can't survive out here without resources. Eventually, someone is going to notice us. We can't keep going into town."

Our first night here, we'd portaled to the nearest town to steal food. Ava was feeling reckless and wanted to shoplift, and Marcus was too chicken to stay in the woods by himself. Kallie and I were both strong illusionists, and our illusions were enough to give us shelter and clothing, but illusion food had no substance, and we'd starve without real food.

My illusions were getting better. The clothes I created were solid, and they'd stay that way forever, unlike Kallie's illusions that vanished when she got too far away from them. I'd even learned how to apply color to my illusions, which was significant progress. But any food I tried to create had no nutrition. It really fucking sucked, because I was all too familiar with the ache of hunger, and it seemed like the one thing I couldn't provide my family with at will.

My days of thieving and conning had come in handy, because at least if I couldn't conjure real food, I could steal it.

And maybe that was the problem. I'd grown up fighting for scraps, and my relationship with food was far from the best. I never once believed that food could be permanent, and so it was impossible to create it.

At least if I couldn't create food, I could steal it. I knew how to get resources one way or another, but unlike before, I was no longer starving. I could take whatever I wanted, and not a damn soul on this Earth was going to prevent me from doing that.

I'd never had so much fun stealing things than when I did it with my friends. I used to be scared that I'd get caught, but now, I was unstoppable. Ava didn't care one way or another if we stole shit or not, and I had to admit, her encouraging me to misbehave only made me want to commit more crimes. The Institute hadn't changed that part of me at all. If anything, it'd only made me a better thief, and my wife was more than willing to be my partner in crime.

Up ahead, I heard a door shut, then the sound of my wife's wheelchair on a ramp as she came out of the cabin. Our camp was nestled in a tiny clearing, just big enough for a cottage, a campfire, and a picnic table. Kallie had created a nice little cabin with her illusion magic that we'd been staying in, and it was spacious and comfortable. We had a roof over our heads, and really, that was all I could ask for.

"How's the temperature?" Ava asked in the distance. She must be approaching the campfire, where Marcus was brewing our potion.

"It could be hotter," Marcus replied. "I need the potion at a rolling boil."

"Here, let me help," Ava offered.

I heard the crackle of a fire, then the snap of bubbles.

"Perfect," Marcus said, though his voice sounded strained.

"Are you hungry?" Ava asked, sounding concerned. "We have a few extra rations."

"No," Marcus answered, almost too quickly. "Save it for the others. Charlie and Kallie will be hungry when they get back."

"You haven't eaten all day," Ava pressed. "There's enough for—"

"I *said* I'm not hungry!" Marcus snapped.

"All right," Ava huffed, and I knew she had to be rolling her eyes. I heard the rustle of a bag, then a gasp.

A twinge of agony rippled up my back, and I knew instantly it had come through our bond. The pain ebbed slightly, but Ava had failed to hide it from me. She was powering through and using her healing magic to help with the pain of dealing with her spinal injury, but it wasn't always enough.

Kallie grabbed my arm, and I stopped in my tracks. She pulled me behind a big tree and lowered her voice. "Charlie, they're getting worse. We need to make a decision."

"You're talking about leaving," I stated flatly.

"We have to do *something*," Kallie pressed.

It felt like an impossible ask. I'd never felt safer than I did in this forest, shielded from the world by these trees and encompassed by my element. Here, my wife had a warm bed to sleep in every night, and my Familiar could roam free. The last thing I wanted to do was leave. No one would bother us here. Everything would stay perfect.

"Charlie," Kallie prodded when I didn't say anything. "We can't keep hanging around. Marcus is on the edge of losing it because he doesn't have his antidepressants. If he's not brewing that potion, he's in bed, and it's only getting worse. Ava's off her bipolar meds, not to mention she's out of painkillers. That's dangerous for both of them, because Ava quitting her lithium and Marcus stopping his SSRI's abruptly could really hurt them. Ava's healing magic is only enough to prevent the worst side effects, but if she doesn't get back on something soon, she'll start having withdrawals or she'll go completely manic, not to mention Marcus is already showing signs of a depression relapse. None of us want him to get suicidal again. We need to go find some medication for both of them. And if you and Ava want to keep getting it on like you do, you're going to need a new dose of birth control."

I groaned and rubbed my face. "Okay, fuck. I don't need a lecture on safe sex."

"You *do* need it if it's going to get you to move," Kallie insisted. "I know you were on birth control at the Institute, and that it was specially brewed using magic. I know where we can get our hands on more."

"If we run, we can't ward ourselves from the Warden," I argued. "Wards don't work that way. They're stationery, so our wards are the only thing keeping him from finding us right now. Besides, we don't know where the next key is, so why are we talking about leaving when we don't know where we're going next?"

"We've been here too long. We need to move to another isolated location," Kallie argued. "Wards or not, the Warden will eventually track us down."

"Okay, so let's do that forever, so we can't be found," I said, completely serious.

"You can't keep living your life only looking ahead for the next couple of days."

"Why not? It's worked before."

"Look, you can sit around and convince yourself that running is the only way to survive, but we all know what will happen if we don't find those keys," Kallie said. "What happens when you die and you're trapped in the in-between forever, just like all the other souls, because you never opened the Elven Gate? We can't do nothing while the Warden is taking over the world. I know you like it here, Charlie. But you have to decide once and for all if you're going to lie down and take it, or if you're going to go after the keys."

I rubbed my face. "We can't go anywhere, anyway. Moving is risky without the anti-tracking potion, and Marcus hasn't finished it."

"I know we should wait, but I don't think we can any longer," Kallie insisted. "Not when it comes to their meds, at least. These two need some happy pills."

I hated to even consider Kallie's argument, because all I wanted to do was keep my friends safe behind our wards, never to face the Warden again. But they weren't safe, if they weren't getting the medical care they needed. I turned my attention back to my wife. In the distance, I could hear her rifling through papers. She'd barely taken her eyes off the files we'd stolen from the Institute since we got here. We'd been studying what the Warden knew, so we could accurately predict where he was going and how to face him. It was a long, arduous task that I could tell was weighing on Ava-Marie. Even from here, I could hear the quiet moans of discomfort as she shifted in her chair.

A ripple of pain slipped through our bond, and it felt like someone had lit my spine aflame. I grabbed the trunk of the tree to keep from falling over. Ava usually shielded her injury from me, but the fact that she couldn't anymore was telling. She was in far more discomfort than I could fathom, and the only reason she was getting by was because she was so used to being in pain.

"All right," I agreed. "We need to come up with a plan."

"Let's go talk to the others," Kallie suggested.

We approached the camp. Ava immediately slammed our bond shut when she heard us approaching. She hadn't realized we'd been in the trees, or that I'd felt her pain only moments before. It wasn't that she was trying to hide it from me. Rather, she didn't want me suffering alongside her, because no matter how much of her pain I felt through our bond, I couldn't take it away from her.

"How was the flight?" Ava asked, keeping her voice even.

"It was nice," I stated, but the high I'd felt had vanished. Now I was more worried than anything. To steady my hands, I approached Rishi, who was lounging on the picnic table atop the files Ava was studying. I stroked the cat's fur, and he purred under my touch. Alette fluttered by and landed in my hand. Sprigs quickly joined her, tickling my fingers with his spindly legs. The sentient twig climbed atop the moth, and he gave a tiny cry before she took off, fluttering him around the campsite.

"The perimeter is clear," Kallie reported. "How's the research going?"

Ava shuffled papers around. "I found a file detailing the Warden's experiments. He's somewhat cryptic with his notes, almost like he was intentionally hiding details in case anyone came across them. But from what I can gather, stealing our powers and becoming a demigod himself is only the first step in his master plan. With enough power and inferichite, he should be able to make demigods out of anyone."

"So he's building a demigod army?" I asked roughly.

"In theory, he *could*," Ava said. "He's limited by inferichite, though, because it takes so long to grow."

"He's got plenty," I stated. "Now that the Institute is destroyed and we escaped, he has no reason to leave the inferichite perimeter around the property. He could've dug up all those crystals to reuse."

"Yes, but now they're *his* weakness, too, since he's a demigod like us," Ava pointed out. "Just being around inferichite is going to slow him down."

"Slowed down or not, he's still got to be going through with the ceremonies," Kallie said thoughtfully. "We already know he's had demigods working for him for a while, though I think we can reason that Esther and Mad Dog are both natural-born demigods. How many more do you think he's created by now?"

"And *who?*" I added.

Ava flipped through a few more papers. "I'm not sure. From what I can tell, the ceremony won't work on just *anyone*. The subject has to be strong enough to withstand a demigod's power. He killed a lot of people running his experiments, and he's surely killing again. But whoever he's recruiting, they surely have to be as loyal and crazy as Esther and Mad Dog—"

A sizzling sound cut her off, and we all whirled toward the fire.

"No!" Marcus exploded. "No, no, no, no, no!"

His voice grew with intensity with each passing word. It sounded like his potion had boiled over. No one had quite forgotten how he'd gone psychotic the night we broke out of the Institute. We'd all been a bit on edge, hoping it wouldn't happen again.

Kallie was right— he really needed his meds.

"Marcus, calm down," Ava insisted. "I've got this."

The temperature around us dropped, and the sizzling stopped. Ava had used her Fire magic to kill the campfire and stop the boiling.

Marcus began pacing back and forth. "This is all wrong. It's not working!"

"What's the problem?" Kallie asked. "Maybe I can help."

"You can't come along and fix this with your false realities and illusions!" Marcus raged. "We need better ingredients— *real* ingredients."

Marcus wasn't acting like himself. He didn't usually yell at her about things like this. He was losing his patience with Kallie, and that was telling of how low he felt. He definitely was getting depressed.

"Hey, I'm good for more than just my illusions," Kallie snapped. "Get me a list. I'll get whatever you need."

Marcus scoffed. "From where? I need *magical plants*, Kallie. In case you haven't noticed, they aren't exactly bountiful in this stupid forest."

Kallie walked over to Marcus, and his footsteps came to a halt as she shook him. "Marcus, I need you to pull yourself together and get me that list. I know a fae apothecary not far from here. Charlie and I will go. I'll portal us there, and we'll get everything you need."

"You're not going to find what I need at any random apothecary," Marcus insisted.

"I'll find it at this one," she promised.

The message was loud and clear. This wasn't just any fae apothecary, bound by the rules of Malovian law. She knew about black market dealers, and she was willing to walk us into danger to get what we needed. It was either that, or eventually let the Warden find us. We really needed this potion if we wanted to move about without being tracked.

"What if someone recognizes you?" Marcus demanded.

"I can disguise us with glamour," Kallie said. "It's a simple illusion that will conceal our features. See?"

Magic tingled over my skin and across my nose. I had no idea what I looked like, but judging by the way Marcus gasped, I must've looked like a completely different person.

"What if the Warden's tracking you?" Ava asked nervously. "You'll be leaving our ward."

"We'll be quick about it, before his spells can find us," Kallie said. "We have to take the risk to get the ingredients."

"All right. Give me a minute." Marcus came over to the picnic table. He must've conjured a paper and a pen, because he began scribbling something down. The paper rustled as he handed it to Kallie. "I hope this place really has the stuff, because if it doesn't, we're fucked."

"We'll get it," Kallie promised again, though I heard uncertainty in her tone. "Charlie and Oberi are with me."

Magic bloomed in front of us, and Kallie took my hand and led me through the portal. The temperature dropped, and my feet hit solid pavement. Voices came from somewhere nearby, echoing off walls around us. It seemed we were in some sort of alleyway.

"Get down," Kallie hissed.

The three of us ducked, and I leaned against the cold metal of a dumpster. I knew that feeling all too well, after spending many nights on the streets. I missed the forest already.

"We're in the alleyway behind the pharmacy," Kallie said. "They're closed for the night, but there are cameras on both sides of the alley. I should be able to scramble the images with my magic."

"The pharmacy?" I asked. "I thought we were headed to a black-market dealer?"

"Two birds with one stone, Charlie," Kallie said. "The pharmacy is a front for the magical dealings that happen behind the counter. We're getting Marcus and Ava their meds *and* the ingredients for the potion. These places are usually warded against magic, so we'll have to get in the old-fashioned way."

We could try bartering first, Oberi suggested.

"With what?" I questioned. "They'll spot an illusion from a mile away."

"Come on," Kallie hissed. "We don't have much time. Oberi, keep watch."

On it, sister, Oberi said.

Kallie dragged me forward. She pulled something out of her hair and shook out the strands, nearly smacking me in the face. Kallie knelt beside the building, and the lock wiggled as she stuck her bobby pin inside it.

"Once I get this open, an alarm will go off," Kallie said. "We'll have to disable the alarm system immediately."

I smirked. Working with Kallie was better than any thief I'd teamed up with in the past. "I'm guessing you know how to do that."

"You learn security systems really quickly when you're a vigilante assassin," Kallie said proudly. The lock clicked, and the door swung open. "We're in."

We hurried inside, and Oberi slipped through the door behind us. A keypad beeped as Kallie hacked it to disable the alarm system before it could notify the owners.

"Done," she announced. "Come on. The pharmacy is this way."

Kallie led me down the hall, and the air expanded to a huge room, like the grocery stores back home. She picked another lock and disabled the alarm system again. I entered some sort of storage area. I reached out and felt shelves, all lined with bottles.

"You and Oberi find the meds," Kallie said. "I'll cover the apothecary and get the ingredients on Marcus' list, and get you your birth control. We'll meet back at the exit in three minutes."

"Got it," I agreed.

Kallie fled the room, and I heard her footsteps racing down the hall. Oberi was already sniffing around, searching the shelves for the medications we needed. In husky form, he was particularly sensitive to smell, and he didn't need to read the labels to know which meds Ava and Marcus usually took.

Here's the lithium, Oberi said, nudging his nose at a bottle on the shelf. I felt for it and gathered several in my arms. He hurried down the aisle and found the antidepressants, along with painkillers.

The bottles were big, at least a quart each. I wanted to take as many as possible, so we didn't run out. Whatever we didn't need, I could sell for real cash, so I could make sure my family had whatever they needed. I'd given up drug dealing a long time ago, but I'd do it again if I had to.

That should be it, Oberi said. *Let's go.*

I left the storage room, but two bottles slipped out of my arms. I knelt to pick them up, and another one slipped.

Screw this. I went to create a backpack so I could carry them that way.

An alarm squealed overhead, and my heart lurched. Everything happened so fast I couldn't quite process it. The magic concealing my features disappeared. Oberi barked once, then came the sound of her phoenix cry.

Something's wrong! Oberi screamed in my mind.

I felt her shift again, and Fire blazed across the bond as she became a Fire unicorn. Shelves knocked over as her form grew, and the smoothness of Water magic filled the bond. Her horn poked me, and I jumped out of the way before I could be impaled by her narwhal horn.

"Oberi, what's happening!?" I screamed.

I can't control it! she cried.

The bond shifted again, becoming masculine. I heard the unfurl of leather wings as he shifted. Oberi grew so large that his wyvern scales squashed me against the wall. The ceiling shook overhead, and dust rained down on me. Shelves crushed under his weight. Oberi barely fit inside the store.

The alarm came to a sudden stop. Although the room had gone silent, I could still hear the heavy pulse of my panicked heartbeat in my ears. Oberi shifted again, shrinking to the size of a husky.

"What the hell happened?" I demanded.

Some sort of magic, Oberi said.

"Yeah, I figured that," I growled. I slung the backpack over my shoulder, the medications rattling around inside of it. "Let's go, before it happens again."

I started for the hall to find Kallie, but the sound of a male voice stopped me.

"You're not going anywhere," he sneered. He spoke in a Malovian accent, so he had to be some kind of shifter. "Hands in the air, or your girlfriend dies!"

Kallie let out a pained cry, as if the shifter had her by the hair.

I went to cast a battle spell, but Oberi barked. *He's got a dagger to her neck!*

"Charlie!" Kallie cried, causing me to hesitate. She knew all too well what I'd do to this guy if given the chance. "If we kill him, we'll attract attention from the whole supernatural community!"

"The glamour's gone," I seethed. "Better to leave no witnesses."

"Kill me, and she dies with me," the shifter threatened.

Kallie could kill him in heartbeat, but she was right. If we left a trail of bodies, other supernaturals would come after us. We had to get out of this clean, and without anyone on our tail.

"You think you can steal from *me?*" the shifter said with a laugh. "Some thieves you are, casting magic in my shop. My spells have revealed you for what you are."

I realized that I'd fucked up. Kallie had said we couldn't cast magic to get through the wards. I didn't realize a simple illusion spell would set things off, as it wasn't an outright attack. I mentally kicked myself for the stupid decision. The spell had stripped us of our glamour and forced Oberi to reveal all five forms, all for a dumb backpack.

I had to find a way to get through to this guy, because we weren't leaving here without our stuff. I didn't care if Kallie thought we couldn't leave bodies behind. I would if I had to.

"Please, sir," I said sadly, throwing in a voice crack for show. When you wanted to run a con, you had to play to what was important to the person you were trying to fool. Hopefully this guy had a shred of empathy. "We don't mean anyone any harm. My wife is in a wheelchair, and in a lot of pain. We have nothing left, and we just want to help her. Don't you have a family? Wouldn't you do anything for them?"

He didn't seem to care. Instead, he scoffed and said, "You think I'd believe a sob story like that? I should be turning you into the authorities right now!"

"So why aren't you?" Kallie asked.

"Because I've seen what you can offer," he practically sang. "I'm willing to forgive you for trespassing and sell you whatever you want, in exchange for one of those wyvern scales."

"What do you want me to do? Just pluck one off his back?" I sneered.

"If you don't want me turning you into the authorities, you will!" he demanded.

"That's a rip-off," Kallie spat. "One wyvern scale is worth a hundred times what we're here for!"

"You destroyed my entire pharmacy!" the shifter roared. "I think it's a fair trade."

"Or I could just kill you and walk out of here," I said with a shrug. Screw conning the man. I was ready to get this over with.

"Kill me, and other fae will be here in moments to hunt you down," the shifter said. "Now that I've stripped your glamour, I've got you on camera, and the recording has already been sent to an off-site server. Give me a wyvern scale, and I'll wipe any traces of you ever being here."

"Charlie, do it," Kallie insisted. The last thing we wanted was to be followed.

I gritted my teeth. I didn't like being pushed around by some sleazy black-market dealer, but no one could find out where we were. It was the one weakness we had, and this guy knew how to play it.

If it gets us out of here without a trace, I'll give him one of my scales, Oberi told me.

"Fine," I growled. I turned to Oberi, and he shifted. He didn't make the full shift, or he'd take up the whole room. It was just enough that I could feel his scales. I pinched a scale around his neck and ripped it out. Oberi winced.

I held up the scale to show the shifter, but I didn't hand it over right away. "Let my friend go."

"Give me the scale first," he demanded.

"I said—" I started, but Kallie cut me off.

"Charlie, just give it to him so we can get out of here."

I placed the scale in the shifter's outstretched hand, the same time I grabbed Kallie and yanked her away from him.

"Now get out of here!" he yelled. "I don't want to see either of you back here ever again."

We scrambled down the hallway.

"Did you get it all?" Kallie asked.

"Yes, you?"

"Everything. Including your anti-baby meds. Let's get out of here." Kallie created a portal in front of us, and we leapt through. We landed on soft ground, and the scent of the forest filled my nose.

Oberi shook out his fur. *I can't believe I gave a scale up to that stinky old dude! That guy was suspicious.*

"Of course he was," I said. "What else did you expect from a black-market dealer? Do you think he recognized you, Kallie?"

Kallie hadn't been seen around these parts in over two years, but the fae wouldn't soon forget the face of the young princess who'd been sentenced to prison for an assassination attempt on the king.

"I don't think so," she said. "If he had, he would've asked for a lot more. That wyvern scale should keep anyone from coming after us. It's worth a lot of money."

She seemed so certain, but I couldn't help but keep my attention on the forest, listening for footsteps or any other signs of life. I heard nothing.

We returned to camp, and Marcus and Ava were gathered around the fire. The sun had set by now, and the air grew colder.

Marcus scrambled to his feet when he heard us coming. "How'd it go?"

"We got it all," Kallie said, dropping to her knees beside the fire. Vials rattled, and bags rustled as she laid the contents of her haul out in the dirt. "How long will it take to brew the anti-tracking potion?"

Marcus mumbled under his breath as he looked everything over. "It'll have to simmer overnight. We should be able to leave in the morning. Once we take the potion, the Warden can't track us anywhere."

"Then let's pack up so we're ready to go as soon as possible," Kallie said. "We got something else, too."

I slipped the backpack off my shoulder and pulled the medicine out. Oberi sniffed the bottles, then took one in his mouth and walked over to Ava.

"Medication?" Ava asked.

"You both needed it," I said, handing a bottle to Marcus.

He hesitated, but took it anyway. "Thanks."

Ava didn't say much, but I felt her relief slip through our bond. She hadn't wanted to ask us to obtain her medication, but she was grateful it was there. At the very least, it would give her some relief from her pain, and we'd stolen enough meds to last quite a while.

"What happened to you out there?" Ava asked as we all sat around the fire. She must've noticed my agitation.

We told them about our run-in with the black-market dealer. Ava seemed nervous when we finished telling her what happened.

"Are you absolutely *sure* you weren't followed?" she asked.

"Certain," I said. "He got the better end of the deal, so he's not going to follow us."

"He sounds sketchy, no matter what you gave him," Ava replied.

"We portaled out of there, so I don't know how he'd find us, even if he wanted to," I said. "We didn't leave a trail behind."

Ava didn't say anything more, but I knew she was still concerned. She'd been paranoid since we'd left the Institute, worried the Warden was going to find us sooner or later.

Hell, let him. I'd kick his ass all over this forest.

Marcus mixed his ingredients together, and the potion bubbled lightly. Finally, he said, "The potion should be done in a few hours. We should all get some sleep."

We gathered our records spread over the picnic table, and Marcus subconjured them, along with the medication bottles. I helped Ava to bed, then gave Marcus her chair so he could keep it in his stash. That way we could leave as soon as possible.

Oberi curled up at Ava's feet, but I sensed he wasn't sleeping. The hair on the back of my neck stood, and I paid close attention to the sounds of the forest, but I heard nothing except the wind rustling the trees.

I tried to tell myself we were safe here. The Warden couldn't track us behind our wards, and the guy at the pharmacy didn't know where we'd gone. Still, I couldn't shake the odd sensation crawling up my back as I climbed into bed beside my wife. I didn't bother changing into pajamas, because I wanted to be ready to get the hell out of here as soon as the potion was ready.

I loved it here. I never wanted to leave. But now that we'd been spotted, I didn't think we could stay any longer. The fae apothecary hadn't been far from here, and even if our cabin was secluded, they knew where to start looking.

It was time to start moving and find the rest of the Divinity Keys before the Warden did.

I lay awake for a long time, unable to sleep, but eventually, I drifted off.

Bang!

I startled awake as the front door of the cabin burst open. I immediately reached over for my wife, and she grabbed on to me. Oberi barked loudly, and my heart hammered.

Ava's panic flooded through the bond. "Charlie, what's—?"

A deafening noise came from above us, and dust rained down on our heads. Wind came rushing into the room as debris flew everywhere. It was like someone had ripped the roof of the cabin off. I threw myself over Ava to shield her, wondering what the hell had happened now.

"Come out, come out, wherever you are!" a deep voice rang from outside.

Holy shit. That sounded like Mad Dog.

I didn't have a second to process it before the bed vanished from beneath me. Ava and I fell to the forest floor as the illusion broke, and the cabin around us vanished. Ava let out a pained cry, and Oberi shifted into a wyvern, spreading out his wings to shield us. I felt Sprigs jump into my pocket, and a whizzing sound as Alette hid beside him.

We're under attack! Oberi cried.

I didn't care if Mad Dog was here or who he brought. We were demigods; we could take on anyone.

Oberi's venom sizzled as he shot it at our attackers, but it made a *splatting* sound, like it hit a pane of glass before disintegrating.

I can't get past their shields, Oberi panicked.

"Hold them off, Kallie!" Marcus screamed. The firepit hissed, like he'd spilled some of the anti-tracking potion into it.

Everything that we'd made with illusion magic was gone. The only things that remained were our real belongings, like Marcus' cauldron and the vials we stole from the apothecary. Marcus sounded like he was rescuing the potion, while Kallie fought off the attackers in the open clearing.

My whole body shook as I rushed to cradle Ava in my arms, but she was already blasting off magic. I felt Water and Fire converge through our bond as she used simultension on herself, creating that deadly blue Fire she'd made in the Darke Games. Ava shot it off, but I heard it fizzle out before it made its target.

"What the hell?" she growled.

She shot off another spell, but it ricocheted back in our direction, and the Fire seared the ends of my hair as I flinched away.

Someone cackled loudly. "You think your Fire is a match for us? We're demigods now, and we're stronger than you'll ever be. All the other Mission kids who wanted to become demigods died, but *we* were strong enough. Your spells can't touch us."

There was only one person who would brag that much during a fight. It had to be Deuce, the vampire who got sent to Cellblock 9 after I framed him for murder. Last I saw him, he was lying unconscious in Cellblock 9. The fact that he was strong enough to withstand demigod power was impressive, considering I'd knocked him out more than once.

Oberi threw himself in front of us again, letting out a loud, threatening cry.

Ava clung to me. "It's The Mission! Esther, Naya, Mad Dog, and Deuce. Charlie, they're stronger than I've ever seen them. I don't know how, but they're shooting my Fire back at me!"

I wasn't sure how they'd gotten here so quickly. The bastard at the pharmacy must've ratted us out!

"Stay low," I warned Ava. "I won't let them hurt you."

It killed me to leave my wife's side, but these fuckers would die before they touched her. I leapt onto Oberi's back and conjured a spear, which became solid in my hand. It was the easiest illusion that came to mind, and appeared almost without thought.

To the right! Oberi told me. Through the bond, I could sense the exact spot I needed to aim, and I thrust my spear forward.

Something shattered, and I realized my illusion spear had been broken. I blasted off battle spells, but each one fizzled out. Below me, Marcus and Kallie threw spells, but I heard their magic wither away before they could do any damage. I heard the shattering of glass, as if their shields had been broken.

"Stop playing this game, and submit to the lord!" a woman's voice came from above me. Feathery wings flapped, which meant it *had* to be Esther. Only she would try preaching about her god while actively trying to kill us.

"I think they're better off dead," a woman laughed. Her leathery wings flapped nearby. It was definitely Naya. We'd had far too many run-ins with this succubus for me to ever forget her voice.

Gathering all the magic I could, I thrust a heavy gust of air above me, and Esther went spinning downward. She knocked into Naya, and they both spiraled into the ground. A tree cracked and groaned, but Naya only laughed. The succubus was as hard as rock. I doubt I left so much as a scratch. Oberi lifted his head and spat venom at Esther.

Esther screamed. I expected the venom to encompass her and kill her like it did the guards the night we escaped, but she flapped her wings again, flying high above us.

"The lord has foreseen your deaths!" Esther shouted. "It is his will that you perish!"

She sounded perfectly fucking healthy to me. Damn angel healing magic.

Mad Dog laughed maniacally, like our magic was nothing short of amusing to him. "Your wyvern is weak, just like the rest of you," he sneered.

Something shifted in the bond, and I didn't know what it was at first, until I realized Oberi was *shrinking* beneath me. He shifted so fast that I fell out of the air and landed hard on the ground. Oberi roared loudly, but it morphed into a bark as he became a husky.

I can't shift! Oberi panicked. *It's some sort of compulsion!*

Mad Dog had used vampire compulsion to kill Thaddeus, but back then, he'd used blood magic to do it. It seemed that his demigod powers were growing, and he could compel anyone, blood magic or not. I barely had a second to take it in before Ava screamed my name.

"Charlie!" Her panicked cry cut through the forest.

I felt the rush of air swirling through the clearing as Mad Dog raced toward her at super speed. I moved so fast that I crossed the impossible distance in less than a second. I threw my hands upward and caught him around the throat before he could go in for the kill. Magic swelled through me as I siphoned his super strength and held him back. The magic felt familiar, and it occurred to me that I moved so fast because I'd siphoned his super strength at a distance, before I consciously decided to. They didn't know who the hell they were messing with.

Mad Dog hissed as his fangs protruded, pressing into the skin on my neck. He never got the chance to break the skin, because I used his super strength against him. I lifted him by the neck, then slammed him into the ground so hard that it left an impression. I forced the earth open beneath him, and it swallowed him whole as I buried him alive. It wouldn't kill a vampire, but it'd hold him off for a bit.

Esther's feathery wings continued to flap above us. She'd turned her sights on Kallie and Marcus as they shot spells in her direction. A clap of thunder rang out around us, and the air sizzled as we narrowly missed being struck by lightning. An explosion blasted off near Kallie and Marcus, and the whole earth rocked back and forth.

Fucking hell. Esther was one strong angel. She'd learned to manipulate energy to create electromagnetic blasts and bombs!

Kallie and Marcus were able to defend themselves— but barely. Deuce was killing their spells every chance he got and shattering their shields the moment they cast them. Esther aimed energy at them again, and they got out of the way just in time, their screams echoing through the trees. Dirt flew into the air and rained down on us.

Ava was casting whatever was in her arsenal— Fire, Water, Spirit magic— yet none of it had any effect. We were practically sitting ducks. There was a whine of agony, and I felt a slicing sensation across our bond as I felt Oberi be cut open by one of Esther's spells.

"Kallie, get us out of here!" I screamed.

I heard the snap of her fingers... then the strangest sensation surrounded me. The sounds of the forest vanished. The rustling of the trees was gone, and the dirt falling from above halted mid-air. I could still feel pebbles of dirt on my skin, and I knew Kallie had stopped time.

So why did I still hear the sound of beating wings above us?

"Charlie, duck!" Ava screamed.

A wave of Fire blasted past me as she went to defend me, but Esther got to me first. The angel hit me so hard I nearly blacked out. Angels were fucking strong— I knew, because I'd fought them in the ring. But Esther was one hell of an angel. We'd severely underestimated her power.

I went flying across the clearing and landed against a tree. I felt something snap, and at first I thought it was my back, until I sensed the tree waver above me. The sounds of the forest returned, and time began moving forward again. The tree groaned as it began to fall, but I levitated it with my Earth magic and threw it at Esther. She let out a heavy *oof* as it hit her and she toppled out of the sky.

"Ooh, what's this?" Naya practically sang, sounding amused. "The fae princess can stop time?"

Fuck. Kallie had been learning how to stop time without influencing other demigods, but we were in too close proximity. She couldn't pick and choose to take us and leave them behind. Now they knew what she was capable of, and we'd revealed one of our greatest assets.

"It changes nothing!" Esther roared. She was obviously getting impatient. "Our lord wanted them dead, and so they shall be!"

All at once, my friends let out a collective scream. Oberi yelped like he was in pain, and Rishi hissed. I didn't know what had happened.

She's blinding us with her light magic! Oberi cried.

Did this bitch forget that I was blind? I was unaffected, and I went in for the kill. I had Mad Dog's super strength and speed, so I crossed the distance to Esther in a moment. I pummeled my fist into her face, and blood spurted over my shirt. Damn it all if that wasn't satisfying.

Esther got a hold of my wrist. She wrapped her legs around my middle, then curled her wings around my entire body as she dragged me to the ground. "Submit to his will," she demanded.

A familiar pain overcame my body, and my muscles seized up. I remembered it all too well. The Warden had used this power on me in

Forevermore. It was a type of life-force manipulation angels had, a way to suck the life energy out of you by sheer will.

Back then, I couldn't defend myself from it. But I was stronger now.

My magic warred against her, siphoning my energy back into me. I tugged even harder, trying to take her power for my own, but I couldn't muster anything beyond her super strength. Her demigod powers were a match for mine, and I couldn't take anything more than her weakest asset. She was powerful— I'd give her that. All her healing abilities and energy manipulation powers were beyond my reach.

I threw a punch, but she dodged it, and my fist met nothing but air. I went to sink the other fist into her gut, but she drew her knee upward and blocked the attack. It was like she knew what I was going to do before I did it.

That was her demigod power, I remembered. She always had a way of reading our weaknesses, and now she knew how to read us better than ever. She knew every attack we were going to throw at her before we even thought of it ourselves.

This bitch may have been at the Institute voluntarily, but she was the worst inmate they'd ever let in that place. There were only so many ways to kill an angel. Let's see how well she functioned without a head.

I conjured a sword, and it pierced her wing. Esther screamed in pain as I yanked the sword downward, slicing through her wing. Esther leapt backward, and I jumped to my feet. I wasted no time aiming the sword at her head, but before it could make contact, it disappeared in my hands.

Shock must've crossed my features, because Deuce stood by the tree line, laughing maniacally.

Of fucking course; because he always needed someone else to fight his battles.

Before I could conjure another spell, the dirt beneath me shifted. I hadn't realized I was standing right where I'd buried Mad Dog, and he was making the climb out of his grave. A hand curled around my ankle and yanked me to the ground. I aimed a blast of battle magic at him, but panicked when the magic never came.

I felt Mad Dog's compulsion locking my powers down tightly, forcing me to hide my own magic from access. I wondered why he didn't just puppet us around and make us kill ourselves like he'd done to Thaddeus, but I realized we were too strong for that. He could compel our magic against us, but he couldn't overcome our consciousness.

Mad Dog let out an angry roar— almost animalistic.

"A little help!" I screamed.

"Let him go, you soulless bastard!" Marcus sneered.

I thought it was just an empty insult, because vampires still had a soul, until I realized what Marcus was doing. Mad Dog's scream came to an abrupt halt the same time an image formed at my feet. An ethereal picture of a furious vampire appeared, his spirit hand curled around my ankle.

If I could see him, that only meant one thing. Marcus had *ripped* Mad Dog's spirit out of his body.

"What have you *done*!?" Esther screamed.

I heard her footsteps racing forward, then felt her body land on top of Mad Dog. For the briefest of moments, his grip on me loosened. Then his spirit vanished and he clutched me even tighter, as if Esther had shoved his soul back into his body.

Obviously she did, because she could manipulate a person's life force. That had to have some effect on the soul. Even if Marcus could take someone's soul out of their body, Esther could just put it right back. I kicked Mad Dog hard in the face, and he dropped my ankle.

"Rishi, attack!" Marcus screamed.

Marcus cast a spell, and Rishi transformed into a deadly spirit. He dove toward Mad Dog and Esther, and his form swept through me for a moment. I saw the ethereal shape of a cat's face as he dove toward our attackers. As soon as he passed me, the image vanished.

Rishi hissed as he went in for the kill, but he never made it to Esther and Mad Dog. Instead, he shifted course, and turned straight toward Marcus and Kallie.

"Rishi, no!" Marcus screamed. Rishi lashed out, and I heard the tearing of fabric as he swiped his claws out at Marcus.

"Stop!" Marcus ordered. The spell broke, and Rishi landed on the ground.

Naya laughed, and I knew whatever happened had been her doing. She had some way of turning our powers against us.

This was *bad*. If Naya could turn our spells back on us, Deuce could break them, and Mad Dog could cut off all our magical access, we were fucking screwed. There was *no way* we could fight these people, no matter how much power we had, because their special demigod abilities prevented us from fighting back.

Our only option was to run.

I raced to Ava and scooped her up in my arms. Marcus and Kallie sprinted to our side.

"Kallie, a portal!" I screamed.

"I *can't!*" she yelled back.

Mad Dog must've been blocking her power. We had to get far enough away so his compulsion wouldn't affect us.

"You aren't going anywhere," Esther sneered. Her wings flapped again, which meant she'd healed already. A spell crackled, and Oberi barked loudly, warning us of the incoming blast.

Ava threw up her hands. Protection magic bloomed out of her so strong it seemed to rock the very earth we stood on. The explosion sounded all around us, but never touched our forms.

"Holy shit! Ava can make shields!" Kallie cried.

Magic smashed against Ava's shield, never touching us. Curiously, I reached out my hand, and my fingers connected with something solid. An image formed in my mind, because the shield was made with Ava's Spirit magic. I saw what appeared to be a big glass dome encompassing my friends and me, pulsing with spiritual power, thin beads of energy moving throughout. I'd heard Anichi could create shields, but I didn't know it was possible for Ava. I felt her strong emotions bleeding through the shield, created out of Ava's love for us and her fierce instinct to protect us.

"Get them!" Esther barked.

"Deuce can't break it," Marcus realized.

"Then let's go!" I demanded. "We need a portal now, Kallie."

"We have to get further away!" she insisted.

"I can't hold this for much longer," Ava whimpered. Her whole body quivered in my grasp as I felt the shield drain her magical energy.

We ran into the trees. The earth shook beneath us as Ava's shield grew stronger. A deafening *snap* sounded, and the earth split in two at the strength of Ava's Spirit magic. Trees groaned and toppled over once they hit Ava's expanding shield, and I heard Naya scream.

Good. I hope she'd been pinned under one of them.

A shattering sound filled the air, and Ava went slack in my arms as she passed out. Her shield broke and faded away, leaving us completely vulnerable. Esther's wings beat from overhead, and the others followed.

"We have to keep going! Mad Dog's cutting off my power," Kallie yelled.

"Submit to the lord's will, for he is always watching!" Esther screamed in the distance. She was coming for us quickly. We had mere moments before she caught up.

Then the air shifted around us. I felt familiar sparks as I heard a portal bloom in front of us.

"Thank the goddesses your ward finally fell," a voice came from the other side of the portal. "We've been trying to track you all for weeks!"

"Quickly, everyone drink the potion, so they can't follow us," Marcus insisted. He shoved vials into our hands. The vials were wet, as if he'd spilled a lot of the potion while he'd been trying to bottle it up. We downed the anti-tracking potion without question, and I tipped a bottle past Ava's lips. She coughed as she drank, but didn't wake up.

"Come with me," the strange voice said.

I didn't know who this guy was, but something told me we could trust him. Anywhere was better than here, at least.

Esther let out a primal scream as she dove for us. We jumped through the portal, and it slammed shut. Feathers drifted over me, but I realized they must've been cut off from Esther's wings as the portal shut, because she hadn't made it through.

I dropped to my knees and set Ava in the grass beside me. I pulled her into my lap and pushed her hair out of her face. "Pidge, are you okay? Wake up."

She took a rattling gasp, and breathed, "Charlie."

"Are you hurt? That was a pretty big spell," I worried.

"I'm fine," she said warily. "Just a little shaken up."

I held her for several long moments, then sagged onto my back, trying to catch my breath. Alette fluttered away, and Sprigs hopped onto my shoulder.

We made it! Oberi cried.

"Barely." I breathed a sigh of relief. We'd been training with our demigod powers for months, but we'd never had to go up against other demigods before. They'd caught us off guard, and we weren't prepared to fight them. I would *never* let that happen again.

I got to my feet. I didn't know where we were, but I turned to the individual who'd portaled us to safety. I reached out a hand out to shake his. "Thank you for coming to our rescue. We wouldn't have gotten out of there if it weren't for you."

He didn't shake my hand, though. Instead, he dragged me into a tight hug. He was taller than me, and I recognized his scent.

Holy shit. It couldn't be—

"Master! I'm *so glad* I finally found you!" my guard squeaked.

This couldn't be real. I felt the world tilt on its axis as I asked in complete disbelief, "Eddie?"

Continue The Devil's City and follow Ava and Charlie on their quest to become the darkest supernatural crime lords in history!

BONUS OFFERS

Find coloring pages, games, quizzes, and bonus content at hiddenlegends-books.com

Join *Orenda Academy: Hidden Legends Fan Group* on Facebook for all things Hidden Legends!

Check out the *Prison for Supernatural Offenders Official Playlist* on Spotify!

Never miss a new release! Join our newsletter at hiddenlegendsbooks.com/fanclub/

ABOUT THE AUTHORS

Megan Linski (left) and Alicia Rades (right) are best friends and the authors of the Hidden Legends universe. Both are USA Today bestselling authors of young adult and new adult fiction. Megan Linski is a coffee connoisseur who enjoys ice skating, horseback riding, and shopping. Her stories feature themes of community and friendship while advocating for the rights of the disabled. Alicia Rades is a mother who loves baking cookies, reading tarot, and binge-watching Netflix. She has a passion for personal development and strives to incorporate emotional-empowerment themes into her books. Both girls love nature, animals, sexy romances, and eating cheese.